DARKE MISSION

A JJ DARKE THRILLER

DARKE
MISSION

SCOTT
CALADON

Matador
9 Priory Business Park,
Wistow Road, Kibworth Beauchamp,
Leicestershire. LE8 0RX
Tel: (+44) 116 279 2299
Fax: (+44) 116 279 2277
Email: books@troubador.co.uk
Web: www.troubador.co.uk/matador

ISBN 978-1784620-509

British Library Cataloguing in Publication Data.
A catalogue record for this book is available from the British Library.

Printed and bound in the UK by TJ International, Padstow, Cornwall
Typeset in 11pt Aldine by Troubador Publishing Ltd, Leicester, UK

Matador is an imprint of Troubador Publishing Ltd

For Those Who Love Me.
They know who they are.

CONTENTS

PROLOGUE

THE SCIENTIST

"Are you satisfied Farzaneh Tehrani?" asked the middle aged woman's political superior and deputy chief of Department 101. Farzaneh stared at the photograph, absorbing every detail, committing it to memory in order that she could recall the image at will, or at least until the next time. It was painful to look at, but joyous to behold.

"I am," she replied, truthfully in this instant, but lying outright in the bigger picture.

"Good," responded Ramin Mehregan, a few years Farzaneh's senior, shorter and heavier. "Now you can get back to work. We need those precision detonators. How long before they are complete?"

"Maybe one month, two at most," Farzaneh replied.

"You are head of our, let us say, private nuclear research programme, Dr Tehrani. This is an outstanding and unique achievement for an Iranian woman. You have done excellent work for many years. Now is not the time for tardiness. Make it one month," ordered Mehregan.

"I will do my best," she replied.

"Yes. You will. I am sure of this," said Mehregan with an even tone.

She knew what he meant, the threat was implicit. Farzaneh left the government building in Tehran escorted, as she had been every month for eight years, by two officers, nay, personal minders of the IRGC's Intelligence Office. She sat in the back seat of an Iran Khodro Samand white saloon car. The drive to Isfahan would take four and a half hours, due south. It was tiring but she needed to make the journey only once every month. She would have done it willingly, enthusiastically even, every day if there was a new photograph to see, but there was not.

Farzaneh adjusted her rusari, placing it a little further forward, to hide her hair, undid the buttons of her rupush and closed her eyes. Iran may be the world's eighteenth largest car manufacturer but this old jalopy she was bouncing around in did not have air conditioning or even properly functioning side windows. It was oppressively hot and the mordant niff of double man sweat did not improve her mood. Farzaneh kept the photograph sharp in her mind's eye for as long as she could. She replayed in her head the meeting with Mehregan. She had indeed done excellent work for years even to the point that her deliberate delays had gone undetected.

Now the end game was upon her. Her invention of breakthrough precision hi-tech detonators for nuclear warheads was about to transform the efficacy and reliability of Iran's new Shahab-7 missiles. Once they were ready, the missiles could be launched and exploded at will. Mehregan had given her one month. She could not delay any longer for fear of the most heinous, heart-breaking reprisal. Mehregan, the purgemeister of the Intelligence Ministry, had no moral code. Farzaneh Tehrani was weeping silently, trembling imperceptibly. Ramin Mehregan had congratulated her on being the head of Iran's secret nuclear research. Just great, she thought to herself in red-raw anger. Several of her peers had been blown up or murdered in their sleep; the suspected handiwork of Mossad or the CIA. She had inherited dead men's shoes.

Her Persian name meant 'wise one from Tehran'. She was

wise alright, too fuckin' wise for her own good and she bitterly regretted it. Her PhD thesis on *Nuclear Fission and Advanced Weaponisation* had attracted the good, the bad, and the pathologically insane. Now she worked for the pick of the pile in the latter looney group.

'A unique achievement for an Iranian woman' that loathsome slug Mehregan had said. Well, she wasn't from Tehran, she wasn't even Iranian and she wasn't a Shi'a, Sunni or Sufi. Farzaneh Tehrani needed to get out, needed to reclaim her life, get her own name back. Above all, she needed to return to her family. The only problem was that she did not know how to do it.

1

FATHEAD

"It's a meta-game, Fathead."

"What the holy baloney is a meta-game JJ?"

JJ Darke had no idea why Toby's nickname was Fathead. He had more like a pinhead than a fat head. Maybe it developed from the same school of thought as Little John in Robin Hood stories. He wasn't little; he was big, about 7ft tall according to the early ballads. Historians suggest that the giant merry man's real name was John Little, but what the heck maybe irony was alive and well in the 12th century.

In any event, Fathead was pouring over a mass of data on a spreadsheet and a gaggle of graphs on his fancy dan computer screen.

"A meta-game is a branch of game theory, Toby. The Greeks cannot pay their debts, The European Union, the IMF and the Greeks all know this. To prevent default and ensuing market meltdown they need to conjure up a deal that seems credible. So what you need to do is map out the different scenarios, policy options, points of conflict and finally, a pay-off matrix. If you need some help I'll be free in my office in about an hour," said JJ.

"Thanks JJ," said Toby none the much wiser. The only game theoretic example he'd ever heard of, or remembered, was The Prisoner's Dilemma and that was fairly simple and one-dimensional. Meta-games, jings, how analysis had changed since he started working life as a foreign exchange and commodities trader.

"Hey JJ," called Toby as JJ was moving away. "Are you going to have the FX quiz and limerick this year?"

"Yes, I'm just doing it now, so the winner can get his or her prize before Christmas," replied JJ.

"What's the question and opening lines?" asked Toby.

"The question is: Which currency would a Scottish dwarf open a door with backwards? The opening two lines of the limerick are:

There was a young man from Ireland
Who liked to eat often at Pieland…" said JJ.

"I'll do the limerick JJ, but I can never work out the currency question and I'm a bleedin' currency expert. You've a warped mind chief."

JJ headed off to his office with the hint of a smile on his face. Of course he had a warped mind; he was head of portfolio strategy and investment at one of Europe's most successful asset management firms. His first degree was in Economics and Mathematics from the University of Glasgow, the home of Adam Smith. Not bad for a skinny Scottish lad whose dad was a welder. He then got his Master's degree in International Politics and Finance at Warwick University. After a few other jobs, one or two of which were outside his academic field of expertise, he was headhunted for his current position three years ago.

Momentum Asset Management or MAM was based in London's 'hedge town' i.e. anywhere within a half mile radius of Piccadilly Circus in London, in MAM's case just off St. James's Square. MAM had around $75 billion under management and a total staff of less than 200. The offices were modern on the inside, all flashing lights, wide screen televisions, open plan offices, but the outside fascia was traditional. It was a nice mix. JJ's office was on the fourth floor of five; it wasn't open plan but it was spacious, with a large desk, two pedestal-mounted computer screens, a Bloomberg keyboard, the latest high tech tablet, and a few phones, landline and mobile. He had his own wall art, mainly photos of cars, football and Roy Lichtenstein prints. In addition to collectable watches, that just about summed up his out of work interests. On the wall facing his desk, he had a huge widescreen flat television which was nigh permanently switched on to *CNBC* or *Sky News*, except when the World Cup or Wimbledon was on live.

To be honest it was a cushy number. He was paid to think, and though he thought well, and there was occasional mental stress, it wasn't a real job. JJ had funded his way through university by taking summer jobs as a street sweeper, a grave digger and a skivvy in a sugar refinery who had to take samples every day from a cockroach infested container. If the gathered masses ever saw the critters you get in a sugar refinery they'd cut it from their diets pronto. JJ's uncles had been shipyard workers, bus drivers, labourers. Real workers and here he was reclining, stretching out his 6ft plus frame in his designer leather chair, feet on desk. Thinking, daydreaming, musing, it was hardly life-threatening and a far cry from his old job. Just as JJ was about to reminisce, Fathead came knocking on the open door.

"JJ, have you got a minute, these numbers are shit scary…" Despite his pin head Toby was a bit on the chunky side, he was looking dishevelled, shirt barely tucked into his pants, tie skew-whiff, glasses wonky.

"C'mon in Toby, sit down and let's get all Greek about it." The Greek situation was long in the making and short in the unravelling. By mid-2012 total Greek debt was over $400 billion, not too far short of 200% of GDP or $35,000 for every man, woman and child in the Hellenic Republic. Billions of euros in aid from the European Union and the IMF were doled out to Greece to prevent and/or delay a catastrophic default by Athens. In return, Greece enacted a series of fiscal austerity measures, including tax hikes and deep public spending cuts. The Greek economy collapsed, unemployment soared to over 30% of the labour force and protests against the government mounted. The ruling New Democracy party, led by Antonis Samaras, pleaded with the EU and IMF to give Greece a two year breathing space before fully enacting some of the more draconian public sector cuts. This was granted, but now time was running out.

In the midst of all this Greek tragedy JJ had authorised a significant Greek bond buying programme for MAM. The fund had missed the peak yield of over 48% in March 2012, but entered the trade in the summer of that year and had held a substantial part of the bond portfolio into the spring of 2013, when yields fell to around 10%. The capital gain to MAM was massive and enhanced JJ's standing both as a risk-taker and as a manager. The two year breathing space was nearly over. Financial markets are both forward looking and myopic at the same time. The goodwill shown to Greek and other Eurozone assets may well not persist for much longer unless either Greece fully enacts the austerity programme forced on it by supra-national powers and/or a renewed and credible deal forthcoming.

"The key to this game," started JJ, "is credibility, a ranking of the various outcomes and the ability to bluff convincingly. Ranking the feasible outcomes, Greece would favour a new bailout first, austerity second and, we assume, default third. The main lenders, i.e. the IMF and the EU, would prefer the first two scenarios in reverse order, but still rank default third, due to the catastrophic contagion into the likes of Italy, Spain and possibly even France and the UK if Greece defaulted."

Fathead nodded as JJ looked at him enquiringly, trying to

ascertain whether, so far, the game's procedures were going into his head, fat or pin.

"The other key player is the markets. It's tough to know their collective ranking of feasible outcomes but they're not altruistic. So, we assume that the markets prefer default first – more volatility, more profit – austerity second and bailout third. From our point of view, at MAM, we want austerity and bailout to continue as the two most likely outcomes as they will keep rates down and lock in our profit on the Greek 10 year bonds. But you don't always get what you want, whether you really really want it or not. So we have to outline a game tree of feasible outcomes and then attempt attaching subjective probabilities to these outcomes. This is the payoff. If the subjective odds in our favour ever drop below 65% we are out, sharpish. Got it?" asked JJ.

"I've got it JJ, but I'm not the one who can map out the game tree nor attach the probabilities. I only trade the junk!"

"I know Toby, and you trade it very well. Get that French quant geek we just hired from Imperial College to give it a shot and then I'll look it over."

"Yves-Jacques?"

"Yes, him. He's supposed to be a maths wizard and his master's thesis is in game theory if I remember right. Give him a deadline, close of business tomorrow."

Toby sauntered out of JJ's office to seek out the French analyst and give him his orders.

The rest of JJ's day wasn't expected to be eventful. He was scheduled to have a conference call with the head of the New York office, a 2,000sq ft floor of a bright modern office in a Park Avenue skyscraper with a staff of around forty-five, and a meeting with H.R. to discuss leaving terms for one of the junior analysts. He had to follow the markets continuously though. JJ's Bloomberg Launchpad page was permanently up on one of his computer screens, on his tablet and his BlackBerry. On one page he could see the prices of the key exchange rates, interest rates, soft and hard commodities, government bonds, and major equity market indices. These prices were real time, flashing green if they were going up and red if they were going down. He also had Bloomberg instant messenger whereby he could contact dealers and brokers immediately without having to speak to them. He didn't like speaking to humans he didn't know. With *CNBC* or *Sky News* babbling away on his TVs and Bloomberg news on his Launchpad page, JJ was never out of touch with the prices of all MAM's investments or the breaking news which may affect them. He was conscientious. Whether in the gym or at home playing Wii games with his son, his BlackBerry was on, flashing, beeping, transmitting information and emails, useful and useless.

In the great financial crisis of 2008 market commentators and academics appeared bewildered that such chaos could happen. After all we were in the age of instant information, sound-bites, transparency. Everybody knew everything more or less at the same time. The Efficient Markets Hypothesis told us that the markets would disseminate all their information efficiently and lead asset prices to a fair value or equilibrium level. In turn, this would help lead to an efficient allocation of resources among consumers and producers etc. Bubbles and chaos were things of the past.

What a heap of elephant dung, thought JJ. This theory was thought up by closeted academics that either had nothing better to do or had been mesmerised by mathematical beauty over real world human behaviour. People may well receive the same information at more or less the same time but their response to it won't necessarily be the same. If at 4.52pm on the last Sunday of the Premier League season, Arsenal have qualified for the Champions League and Tottenham have not, then Gooners and Lillywhites fans will get the information at more or less the same time, but their reaction to the same information will be markedly different. Reaction functions, animal spirits, the ability to make the information work for you. That's what distinguishes the financial leaders from the followers. Have a read through *Extraordinary Popular Delusions and the Madness of Crowds* by Charles Mackay. Efficient markets, my left butt.

While he was conscientious, JJ also had a conscience. For many years past he had given away most of his annual bonus, once he had set up his own family with a degree of security. He donated substantial sums to charity; children's charities in Scotland and England were the primary beneficiaries, followed by several providing health and well-being for children in Africa. As a youngster, he was so impressed by Bob Geldof's verbal meltdown on live TV and Freddie Mercury's unparalleled Wembley performance at *Live Aid* in the 1980s that he just had to contribute. When he had little money his donations were a pittance but when he became 'over-rich', as his mum called it, they were often into six figures at a time. In those days, he had never given much thought towards other charities, but his young son was so affected by the plight of the snow leopard that many of his recent donations were channelled to the animal kingdom.

JJ hadn't left himself short. He liked the material things that many successful men of his generation appreciated, fast cars, cool watches and stylish but not trendy suits, shirts and shoes. He lived in a five storey Regency terraced house just off the King's Road in Chelsea. If he drove to work, parked his car, got his breakfast as soon as the EAT or Pret shops opened at 6.45/7am, and sat in his very comfortable chair in the office, then his door-to-door record commute was seventeen minutes. He hadn't been on a bus or a tube for over fifteen years. Not for any snobbish or arrogant reason but because (a) driving his own car was quicker and (b) once on GMTV an elderly Scottish university professor got yanked off the screen because he said that the most dangerous transmission mechanism of transferable disease in the UK was public transport. Oops! The truth will out but you can't go around propagating that one.

Now in his early forties, JJ had calmed down about cars. He owned only two, a Porsche Carrera 4S Tiptronic for his short, daily commute and a prized 1967 AC Cobra 427 garaged at his mum's house in Scotland.

The one material item JJ hadn't calmed down on was watches. Indeed, he was a bit *American Psycho* passionate about them. His collection amounted to around twelve examples. His philosophy on watches was based on the premise that a man should have at least three wristwatches. These didn't need to be expensive but should fall into three categories. The first was for work, if that work entailed wearing a suit or at least a shirt with long sleeves. The second category was casual wear, which encompassed normal weekend attire or beachside cool. For the majority of men of the modern age over thirty years old, categories one and two cover most activities but for a select few there is also category three. Category three is for dangerous living types. For instance, mountain climbing would be one as well as being a member of the armed forces. In this line of work, particularly the latter, you have to assess the need for tools in a fight or a tight spot. In addition to being sturdy, waterproof and visible a watch can be a dangerous weapon, an aid to survival, an instrument to pinpoint your location. In this category a man might have a Breitling Emergency, an MTM Cobra or even an Invicta Subaqua Noma IV Chronograph. The first two could help you out of a difficult situation either by transmitting signals to rescue services if you were stuck up a mountain (the Breitling) or if you needed the aid of a compass or slide rule (the Cobra). The Invicta could not do any of that but if you flicked the quick release deployment bracelet and dropped the watch to cover your fist then you would have one of the most effective knuckle-dusters around. One blow to the head would result in man down, with a few indentations where indentations are not meant to be.

Just as JJ was studying the sweeping second hand on his IWC Top Gun Miramar ceramic pilot's watch on his left wrist, almost mesmerised by its metronome movement, a gaunt fellow stepped gingerly into his office.

"Mr Darke, may I come in?"

"You can call me JJ, Yves-Jacques, most folk do. I thought you had until tomorrow night to work on the game theoretic Greek problem, or is this a different matter?"

"No Sir. I've spent most of the morning on the Greek game tree and thought my observations were about ready for you," said Yves-Jacques. "Fathead, I mean Toby, told me it was important."

He seemed confident enough, thought JJ. Only twenty-four years old, thick dark hair, about 5ft 9in tall, slim and dressed in that Eurotrash manner that tends to irk American investment bankers. Yves-Jacques's English was excellent even though his French accent came barrelling through. He looked a bit like a thin version of Henri Leconte, the legendary French tennis player.

"Tell me Yves-Jacques, have you ever heard of the Norman Tebbit test?" asked JJ stoically.

"No."

"OK," said JJ not offering any explanation. "Let's say we're at Murrayfield and Scotland are playing France in a match that matters in the Six Nations Championship. You and I are sitting together and you're surrounded by patriotic Scots, singing 'Flower of Scotland' and generally abusing the French, albeit in the friendliest possible way. France scores a match winning try. Do you leap off your seat like a demented Breton screaming 'vive la France', or, mindful of your surroundings, do you clap politely and commiserate with the downfallen Scots – which in case you had forgotten includes your boss seated next to you who determines your bonus, even your continued employment?"

The young French man studied JJ's face for clues as to how he should answer. JJ was impassive, neither his eyes nor his facial expressions gave anything away. He had no tells, as poker professionals would call it, the Scotsman's early training took care of all that.

Devoid of hints, Yves-Jacques blurted out, "I would leap off my seat like a demented Breton, though strictly speaking I'm from Paris, so I guess I would leap like a demented Parisien."

JJ waited for a few seconds before responding, making Yves-Jacques a little edgy but not for so long as to make him too uncomfortable. Finally "Good," said JJ. "You and I are going to get on fine. Now let's go through the game tree and see if we need to change the firm's portfolio or not."

With that, JJ and Yves-Jacques moved to the round, wooden meeting table in JJ's office and both men put their minds to the probabilities and improbabilities of the Greek drama. For the next two hours this modern Auld Alliance between the Scot and Frenchman worked away together, calculations, dynamic model simulations, brainstorming and finally a decision tree that they both thought was the most probable outturn for Greece. There was to be a vote in the Greek Parliament in two weeks covering further austerity cuts, the bailout terms and the need for more time to meet the financial targets set out by the EU and the IMF. On the lenders side the main protagonist was Chancellor Merkel of Germany. In the midst of the Greek unravelling in 2012, Greek protesters often hoisted flags with either a Swastika or Merkel's face with a Hitlerian moustache on it. She wasn't popular down Athens way. The Greeks needed tough love and none of the indigenous politicians were fully up for it. JJ and Yves-Jacques concluded, with a subjective 70% probability, that the Greek government could not afford to deviate from the fiscal hair shirt path set out by the EU, i.e. Germany, and the IMF. The decision was to hold the Greek bonds for now.

After that, JJ had had enough for the day. There was nothing much else going on in the markets, at least as far as MAM was concerned. He could do the New York call from home and H.R. had postponed the meeting regarding the leaver till tomorrow. Feeling tired after all that thinking, he decided to leave his car at the office and take a taxi home. His son, Cyrus, didn't have any after school clubs as it was school holidays, so maybe they could have a *Mario Kart* challenge. Once Cyrus had passed the age of six, JJ rarely let him win easily at games, electronic, athletic or otherwise. He wasn't cruel about it but Cyrus was a sensitive boy and JJ knew that the real world could be a harsh place for sensitive kids so he wanted to ease his son into understanding that he couldn't win at everything he tried. As it happens *Mario Kart* was now just about the only Wii game that JJ still had any chance of beating Cyrus at. From the age of nine, the kid would toast him at all the other games, *Super Smash Bros. Brawl, Wii Sports Resort, Skylanders Swap Force*, you name it and Cyrus would win at it. He often taunted his dad with 'Loser, Loser' while making the L letter with his forefinger and thumb and sticking it in front of his forehead. That made JJ smile. The boy's computer skills had grown and grown.

Cyrus's fourteenth birthday was coming up in a few months and gadgets and games were top of his wish list. JJ had promised him a smartphone, feeling totally amazed that he'd managed to fend off that request for as long as he had. While he was still thinking about his son, JJ spotted a traditional black cab on St. James's Street and hailed it. He preferred these cabs to the newer multi-person vehicle ones. In those ones you'd rattle around like a gob-stopper in a tin can if you were on your own. While it took JJ under fifteen minutes to get from the King's Road to St. James's Square early in the morning, it was normally five to ten minutes longer on the way back. The back end of Buckingham Palace Road was like a building site and once you were in Victoria there were always buses galore nose to tail and often traversing several lanes. The King's Road never stopped. People walked onto the zebra crossings, fell onto them, ran across them, cycled over them. There were too many people and that was that.

The cab pulled up outside JJ's house in Markham Square. Although all modernised inside, the shell of most of the larger houses on the Square were built in the mid-1830s. Strictly speaking it's a Regency terrace rather than a square because the fourth side of 'the square' is the King's Road itself with only a set of wrought iron railings on it.

Markham Square has an interesting history. It was built on a field which was part of Box Farm in 1836. The farm was owned by a Pulham Markham Evans, hence the name of the square, and the nearby street and place. For the more eclectic, it is the square where barrister Mark Saunders was shot dead by police a few years ago after the lawyer decided to fire bullets across the square willy-nilly into neighbours' houses. A former supermodel of Wonderbra fame has a house on the east side and some folk believe Ian Fleming had it as the location of James Bond's flat in London. Those folk were wrong; 007's flat was meant to be in Wellington Square.

JJ's five storey creamy white exterior house was on the east side. In the basement he had it set out as a personal gym near the front of the house and an open space training area for martial arts towards the paved garden at the rear. Though not with the intensity that he used to, JJ still trained with one-on-one instructors for both Krav Maga and Jeet Kune Do, twice per week. The ground floor had a modern kitchen and dining area with a small sitting room near the Square end. While meals were being prepared, cooked or heated he and Cyrus could sit together, have a chat or watch TV. It was hard to get that intersecting Venn diagram moment when he and Cyrus could watch an equally enjoyable programme on TV. Tennis would do the trick, as would some music channels but football or motor racing wasn't really to Cyrus's liking. Perhaps oddly for a boy who was so tech savvy, Cyrus was an avid fan of the *Antiques Roadshow* or indeed any show about antiques wheeling and dealing especially involving auctions. When he was six JJ took him to an antiques fair in Chelsea's Old Town Hall to get a present for his mum. He spotted Mark Tracy, well known TV antiques personality, the minute he walked in. Mark was very nice to him and he was impressed, or convincingly pretended to be, that Cyrus had negotiated down the price of a 1940s porcelain fawn figure from £35 to £25. That was the last present Cyrus was able to give his mum before her fatal accident.

The top two floors of the house were bedrooms. Cyrus's was on the top level. His room was full of the paraphernalia that young teenage boys have, mainly books, games, irreverent wall posters, manky clothes all over the floor and the like. He could play the flute, which was a very difficult wind instrument to master, all about the shape of the lips rather than how hard you could blow. JJ had hoped Cyrus would take to the flute playing of Ian Anderson of Jethro Tull à la 'Living with the Past' but the boy preferred the music of Jeanne Baxtresser. He said it calmed him down if he had a bad day at school or if he lost to one of his pals at some computer game or other. Cyrus was competitive, but selectively so.

JJ's bedroom and sizeable en-suite bathroom was below Cyrus's. This had the strategic advantage to check out any nocturnal movement of the boy. Cyrus had never snuck out of the house at night. He may have wanted to but he had become ever closer to his dad and knew JJ, as the sole parent, would freak out if he didn't know where his son was. JJ wasn't over protective given the situation he found himself in but he was above average security conscious and virtually on permanent high alert as far as Cyrus's safety and well-being was concerned. From JJ's viewpoint there were too many committed and opportunistic assholes around in any big city or even small town in the world for any caring parent not to try to know where their kids were. In *About a Boy* starring Hugh Grant, the kid Marcus, played by Nicholas Hoult, realised that both parent and child needed backup. Cyrus knew he had his dad as number one backup, then Gilian his nanny. The rest of his family was in Scotland which was too far away for instantaneous response if needed. Cyrus knew that JJ had no backup. His dad was an only child and he had very few friends as far as he could tell. In a few years' time Cyrus would be his backup. He loved his dad very much.

JJ's bedroom was much the same as he and Eloise had designed it. Loads of built in wardrobe space, theoretically meant to be allocated half and half but turned out to be four fifths, one fifth in favour of his wife. A super king size bed, wall mounted TV, loads of photos of them and Cyrus and modern furniture. While Eloise's clothes and shoes were no longer there, it was nearly eight years since she had died; JJ hadn't the heart to change anything around much. The room wasn't effeminate, but it had memories, the vast majority of which were good.

JJ came in through the heavy duty wooden front door. When they had bought the house Cyrus asked if the door could be painted Chelsea blue. His mum and dad said fine, but asked why since he wasn't a Chelsea supporter or even any kind of football fan. Cyrus said that when Chelsea were playing at home loads of Blues supporters were often milling around, mainly at the Pizza Express or Starbucks on the King's Road, but some would occasionally be seen wandering up and down the Square, either killing time before the match or being a bit worse for wear after a few beers when the match had ended. Cyrus reckoned that if his door was Chelsea blue it was much less likely to have anything thrown at it or graffitied on it. When asked what about the away team's supporters Cyrus said that they tend to come in coaches directly to Stamford Bridge or the nearest tube station to the match at Fulham Broadway. The probability of a wandering Gooner or Tooner was very low. The boy may not know diddley-squat about football but he sure had a clear view of the logistics of supporters' travelling habits. Anyway, Cyrus's favourite colour was blue so it was a no brainer, the door was Chelsea blue, and in the many years of living there, no graffiti, no rotten eggs and no one peeing down the outside stairs.

"Cyrus, are you in?"

"Yes, Dad, I'm in the living room," Cyrus called back.

"OK, I'll be up in a minute. Do you want a drink or a snack?"

"Thanks Dad, a juice and a packet of curlies would be good," came the reply.

JJ took an orange juice from the fridge in the kitchen and a packet of organic tomato and cheese puffs from the snack shelf – curlies to the cool dude teenager – and made his way up the narrow, steep but well carpeted stairs.

"Here you go," said JJ as he placed the juice and curlies on the desk where Cyrus was staring at his computer screen like only teenagers can do, his wavy locks flopping over his forehead and ears. "What are you up to, zombie boy?" quipped JJ.

"I'm researching some stuff for a science project at school," Cyrus replied but didn't avert his eyes from the screen to acknowledge his dad, his juice or even his favourite snack.

"Good job I know you love me," said JJ, wishing he would have been granted one of Cyrus's engagingly warm smiles.

"Of course I love you Dad. I'll be done in a few minutes. Do you fancy a game on the Wii or has all that high-falutin' financial stuff shrunk your game brain even further?" asked Cyrus.

"I'll take you on kiddo and it doesn't even have to be *Mario Kart*. I'm in the zone tonight, I can tell."

"Yeah, the twilight zone, big daddy. We can play something you've got a fighting chance at. How about virtual tennis or ten pin bowling, you've won at those on the odd occasion."

It was mid-December, so JJ thought he'd keep it real, or as real as a virtual game can get, by opting for ten pin bowling. "I'm just going to check my BlackBerry for emails and prices, Cyrus, but give me a shout when you're ready and be prepared for a strike and spare tsunami young man. By the way, where's Gil?" enquired JJ.

"She said she had to go out for some messages, but would be back in about twenty minutes to cook us dinner."

Although Cyrus was not born in Scotland he had picked up quite a few Scotticisms as he grew up. The word *messages* was a case in point. When JJ first arrived in London, he shared a house in Southfields with four other guys who all worked for the same company as him. They were English to a man and he was the only one who had not gone to Oxford or Cambridge University. It was a low cost rental and they had to look after themselves. Every evening after work, JJ would casually mention to his fellow housemates that he was popping out for a few messages. After about a week of this one of the guys, Tim, a portly but pleasant fellow from Peterborough, said, "JJ, every bleedin' night you go out for messages, you can't have people wanting to contact you every single night, what's the scoop?"

JJ laughed a moderate decibel laugh and regarded this as yet another example of how the Scots and English are separated by more than a border. "Tim," said JJ, "in the west of Scotland, the 'messages' means the shopping; things like milk, bread, eggs etc.

It stems from the time when it was safe enough for mums to send their kids to the local shops to get supplies. As the kids tended often to be as young as five or six, the mum would write out a list of things to get and then wrap it around a bunch of coins to pay for it. The kid then gave this to the shop keeper, he'd check 'the messages' and send the kid back with the goods."

"Fucking Jock," said Tim appearing somewhat annoyed. "I've spent a whole week thinking you were getting instructions that the rest of us weren't getting."

"Ignorant Sassenach," responded JJ. "It would behove your current employment Tim if you had noticed that I had come back every evening with a bag of groceries. Observation is part of your job, young padawan."

So Gil was out getting some groceries for their dinner. Gil was American. She was more than ten years younger than JJ and they met when he first went to the USA on a work secondment from London. Gil was forced to retire through injury from the job she had in the States and JJ, who was effectively her specialist British mentor, offered her employment, mainly with the family but also occasionally with work issues. As far as HMRC was concerned, she listed her job as professional nanny. Now that Cyrus was a teenager he could hardly tell anyone that Gil was his nanny. He was too old for a nanny. There had to be another word. In the same way that that period in a human's life when you're more than a baby but less than a toddler, you're obviously a 'boddler', there needed to be a worthy non-parental title for someone who looked after you, cared about you, helped with your school work wherever possible, and just generally made your life easier than it would otherwise have been. Cyrus was close to Gil and though he never regarded her as a mum substitute, he surely clung a wee bit more to her because his mum was no longer around.

When Cyrus was with his friends and Gil ever turned up, he would tell them she was his bodyguard. His friends rarely batted an eye lid at this since many of them had gone to the same Chelsea school and that school had also been the alma mater of the children of Russian oligarchs and several celebrities whose kids had chauffeurs, bodyguards and other folk who drove traffic wardens mental as they parked their reinforced Chelsea tractors outside the school's front gate, blocking oncoming traffic and generally annoying the somewhat pampered residents of SW3. Gil quite liked being called Cyrus's bodyguard. It reminded her of what she once was capable of. She used the gym in the basement and sometimes even sparred with JJ. She too was skilled in Jeet Kune Do and though her injury prevented her from launching a devastating roundhouse kick to the head, she could break your leg with one well planted foot, make you gasp for breath with a straight finger jab to the throat or do you severe visual damage with a targeted strike to the eyes. Cyrus did not know that Gil had these skills. He knew she sometimes trained with Dad and that they had known each other for ages. Cyrus simply knew that Gil was wicked back-up. It was cool in a weird way, having a bodyguard thought Cyrus. Just how cool, the curly topped youngster would soon discover.

★ ★ ★

Toby Naismith was lolling back on a black leather sofa chair, downing his third Sonic Screwdriver of the night in Nobu's bar and restaurant in Berkeley Street. It was nearly 10pm and a good sprinkling of hedge fund types, bankers, beautiful people, wannabes and, possibly, hookers were in that night. The bar was heaving, the noise was cacophonic. Deals were being done in one dark corner or the other, hopeful bankers were hitting on their hot secretaries, it was all going on. Toby was there with a couple of broker-dealer mates that he did most of his currency and commodity trades with, one from Credit Suisse and the other from JP Morgan.

Toby lived in a bachelor pad in Islington, he was a London boy, born and bred. He could have afforded somewhere more expensive as his bonus for the past few years had been substantial but he enjoyed the bohemian buzz of N5. He did a great job at MAM and he was happy to report to JJ. The warped-minded Scot had shown belief in him from the start and increased the risk capital he had control over after only twelve months of monitoring his trades. He liked JJ. His boss had never asked him awkward personal questions, never stitched him up, never nailed him about his somewhat dishevelled appearance much of the time and, most importantly, trusted his judgement when it came to pricing in the FX and commodity markets.

"Hey Jay," called Toby as he was trying to get the attention of his pal. "Will we order some food for the table, the Wagyu beef with those hot sauces and the Hamachi and jalapeno starter?"

Jay nodded and then continued his deep conversation with Kai whom he had known for years, way back to when they were students at Birkbeck.

OK, thought Toby. I guess I'll be the dynamic motherfucker who goes to all the bother of trying to attract the all too good looking waiters or waitresses to take an order, despite the fact that it's my credit card that's behind the till racking up the bill. At least I'll know I've ordered what I want. These two neer-do-wells can like it or lump it.

Toby liked Jay and Kai. When the three of them were together he called them J-K, partly because it saved a millisecond of time compared to saying both their names in full and partly because it conjured up visions of that Jay Kay singer bloke with Jamiroquai.

The songs were rubbish thought Toby but the crazy frontman had a passion for supercars so he couldn't be totally useless.

Toby looked like a man who liked his beef. He was slim once, maybe even twice, but years of sitting in a chair, looking at a screen had taken its toll. He was thirty-nine years old but looked well older than JJ who was three or four years his senior. He didn't go to the gym, he didn't swim, he didn't cycle. He didn't have kids to keep him on his toes either. Indeed, Toby was a bit of a sloth, but he had his hair, his own teeth and no STDs to tell of, despite a few risqué encounters and, relevant to his continued employment, his trading brain was as sharp as a great white's teeth.

Toby tracked down Fernando, the waiter. He had no idea whether or not he was called Fernando, but he had that dark, Hispanic look about him, like Antonio Banderas or that tennis geezer Verdasco. Or it could just be Nobu's lighting and he was like Casper the friendly ghost in daylight. Toby placed an order and went back to J-K. They were out of their deep conversation, and K beckoned Toby a bit closer.

"Tobester my man. What do you think about gold? You've got a great track record on it and we're seeing a lot of activity in the hedgie space." To Kai everything was a –ster. The Queenster, the Boltster, even the wifester and the kidster, if he had any. But he was a smart kid i.e. under thirty, and the guys at JP Morgan held him in high regard.

"Ah, the barbarous relic," replied Toby, recalling what John Maynard Keynes, probably England's best ever economist, had called the shiny metal. "Gold is unique. It was once the centre of the international monetary system. No other commodity has ever been that. Central Banks hold it in reserve by the tonne. Indians love it (dot, not feather), rappers stick it in their teeth, Californians used to kill for it and children are told they're 'good as gold', not platinum, or titanium or any other –um. So the first thing to realise about gold – is that it's special."

When it came to business, Toby was always serious. There was no sign of any effect of his now four Sonic Screwdrivers as he continued to present the potted history of gold to J-K, whether they wanted it or not. He was one of only a handful of financial types who could speak while eating and not simultaneously spray half munched bits of food over his attentive audience. Toby had skills. During another mouthful of delicious Wagyu beef, Toby now turned his attention to the current position of gold.

"Gold yields no income, it's not a bond, it's not an equity and it's not a currency deposit. When global interest rates are high, holding gold in your portfolio has a substantial opportunity cost. If the price doesn't go up then you're left with a big bar of metal doorstopper. Today global interest rates are not high. Therefore, you can be patient holding gold, as it's not costing you much to do it. There are two other non supply and demand characteristics of gold; one is as a financial safe haven and the other is as a geopolitical safe haven. In the 1970s, the gold price rocketed from $200 per ounce to $800 per ounce. Mainly this was because inflation was high, thus devaluing the real purchasing power of fiat currencies like the British Pound, the US Dollar, the Deutschmark etc. Inflation is low these days, so that form of purchasing power erosion is not in play. Geopolitical issues are influential because when there's a coup here, a government collapse there, investors do not want to be exposed to the currencies, bonds or equities of those countries that are having or could have a coup. Gold is attractive under these circumstances."

J-K were clearly awaiting the punch line. Toby had a long sip of his Screwdriver and then followed it up with the last forkful of his beef. Nobu's portions were a bit on the meagre side for a beefmeister like Toby.

"Gold is $1,500 per ounce, today," informed Toby. "My view is that it will be $2,000 per ounce by the middle of next year and maybe over $3,000 per ounce before we next get a Labour government! Whichever it is, my friends, I'll be trading the holy crap out of it. Kerching!" Toby ended with a flourish and a spot of Sonic Screwdriver on his shirt as he raised his glass.

With that done Toby relaxed back into the soft sofa and gestured that he wished the attention of Fernando. While the three traders were busy chatting away they hadn't noticed that Toby's Blackberry was slithering around on the table top. It was on vibrate but it wouldn't have mattered if it was ringing as Nobu noise was the dominant aural force. Finally, when the device eventually cosied up to Toby's tall cocktail glass he noticed it and picked it up.

"Toby, is that you?" said one of those Antipodean accents that should come with subtitles.

"Yeah, yeah. Who's that?"

"It's Marcus from Wellington. It's five in the morning here but we need to talk *now*. We're going to get royally shafted by those Greek numpties if we're not a bit Usain Bolt, my friend. I'll tell you what's up and then you need to get JJ."

Marcus Whyte was MAM's researcher, based in Wellington, New Zealand. He was virtually a one-man office, had been around for a long time and had worked with Toby for six years. He knew JJ for about three. Most of the time, he didn't have a lot to do but Wellington, then Sydney were the first FX markets to open up in any given day so it seemed wise to MAM's Board that they should have someone there, just in case.

The only other time Marcus was notably useful was the weekend in July 2003 when the British scientist and expert on biological warfare, Dr. David Kelly, was found dead. It was a few days after he was cited as a source questioning the authenticity of the dossier on weapons of mass destruction that Tony Blair, British Prime Minister, seemed to use as his catalyst for war on Iraq. This news came after the European, UK and US markets had closed on the evening of Friday the 19th. It was likely to be a robust blow to Blair's government and his own standing in the Labour Party. Markets love conspiracy theories and this one had a weekend to brew. Market traders, like Toby, knew they could do nothing about it at the weekend. The pound would surely get mullahed on the Monday morning. If you were short sterling then great, windfall profit coming your way but if you were long then wallop; half a year's bonus could be down the tube in an instant. Foreign exchange liquidity on a Monday morning in Wellington would be poor. Normally, it would take trades of several hundred million pounds at a time to move sterling's price significantly during European and American hours. In early New Zealand time, however, small trades of five or ten million would be impactful. In addition, often traders would leave stop-loss orders with their counterparts in Wellington or Sydney just in case an unexpected event flared up over a weekend. These orders set a pre-determined price whereby either electronically or manually a trader was taken out of a position if the price was hit. The difficulty from the aspect of currency management was that these stop-losses tended to be stacked. If, for example, a trader had bought 100 million of pounds versus the dollar at 1.5420, 'cable in a Spaniard' in FX lingo, but placed a stop-loss at 1.5390, the loss if hit would be under £200,000, not great but manageable. Problems tended to arise when there was a thin market (low liquidity) with stop orders placed close to each other. In this circumstance, the stop could be activated several big figures below where it should be. If the trader was taken out at 1.4900 instead of 1.5390, the loss would be £3,500,000 not £200,000. In the early hours of the

Monday following Dr. Kelly's death, Marcus Whyte had given Toby the heads up about early price action and volume in cable, saving MAM several million pounds.

The standing order was when Marcus Whyte called you listened. Toby wasn't just listening, he was on the move, jacket in one hand, mobile phone in the other as Marcus outlined the problem to him. Now he was standing in Berkeley Street, hailing a cab with his jacket hand and kind of tumbling in a non-Olympic way into the back seats. His phone was still glued to his left ear. "Markham Square," Toby responded when the cabbie asked him their destination. A few minutes later Toby and Marcus ended their chat and Toby sent a text message to JJ. He knew he'd still be up though it was 11pm and he wanted to give him a little bit of notice that he was on his way. Toby was glad that he'd had his Wagyu beef at Nobu. This was going to be a long night and JJ usually only had relatively healthy fayre in situ or those lightweight snacks that Cyrus liked. Toby was only five minutes away now from JJ's house. He would try to compose himself, pop a tic-tac or six in his mouth and do his best to recount all the key elements of Marcus's news. Friggin' Popadopadopolases Toby thought, not the best pleased with the way the night was developing. 'Beware of Greeks bearing gifts' the old saying goes. Well for him, JJ and the rest of MAM it was beware of Greek interest bearing bonds. Friggin' Popadopadopolases.

JJ was waiting at the front door for Toby.

"Sorry for the text and the late hour JJ but we're in a bind."

"No problem, Toby, come on in." JJ was in his night time casual gear, polo shirt, cargo pants, no socks, and comfy leather slippers that could have passed for casual loafers. Toby's shirt still only had a nodding acquaintance with his pants. JJ wondered if he slept in it.

24

"Hey Toby," called Cyrus. He had heard his dad's colleague come in and JJ had told his son that game night was over and that he'd be up for a while. Cyrus didn't mind, he was already pulverising his dad at virtual ten pin bowling.

"Hi Cyrus. How's it going? Still playing that tin whistle?" responded Toby.

"It's a flute, plank!" Cyrus retorted. He and Toby often had a sharp exchange of banter. Both of them enjoyed it.

"Given that you're here at 11.30pm at night Toby, does this mean you've done serious damage to my piggy bank?" Cyrus asked. He wasn't that bothered about money but he was mature enough to realise that that opinion was held predominantly by people who had plenty of it.

"Well, I haven't but there's a bunch of Greek fucks who might want to rob you and then sell you back your little bank of pig empty." Toby was immediately embarrassed about dropping the F-bomb and looked at JJ, hoping for not too much disapproval.

"Don't worry, Toby, Dad's from Glasgow. The F-word is not so much an expletive there as an everyday adjective."

JJ reluctantly recognised that Cyrus was right. In Glasgow it wasn't a very sunny day, it was a fuckin' beezer day. JJ had tried ever so hard to eradicate his casual use of the F-word, and the B-word and the C-word etc. but the boy knew his dad. There was no way Toby was in trouble. Well, at least not for his language.

"OK, you two. Verbal fencing time over," said JJ. "Cyrus, I'll see you tomorrow. Have a good sleep. Don't feel too bad about losing at bowling. Love you." JJ was amused at his attempt at stealing the bowling crown.

"In your dreams, big daddy. Love you more." With that Cyrus headed up to his room for some peace and quiet or 'piece of quiet' as he used to say as a kid.

JJ and Toby headed into the living room. Toby sat in one of

the cosy, huge, armchairs. "Do you want a drink, Toby, or are we going to have to have the clearest heads possible?" asked JJ.

"We're going to need the clearest heads possible chief, but I'll have one of those eighteen year Macallans, straight, if you still have it."

For a Scot, JJ didn't drink much. He didn't like beer at all and when he was at university he did have one term in his final year when he thought it would be seriously manly to drink Guinness. That whole term was a blur. The only good thing to come out of it was that he sat his final maths paper more or less drunk as a skunk and he was so relaxed, he just rattled through the exam and got a first. If Guinness TV adverts weren't so good, he'd have offered his story as a sales pitch. JJ did like the occasional Macallans or even the peatier Languvallen. He used to drink it straight, never with ice, but now he diluted it with a splash of Canada Dry. He got Toby his and one for himself.

"OK, Toby, what's up that couldn't wait till tomorrow?" enquired JJ as he settled down on the sofa opposite Toby. Toby took a sip or two, actually it was a glug or two, and began.

"So the short and long of it is that, according to Marcus, that bailout vote in the Greek Parliament scheduled for a fortnight's time might be tomorrow evening instead. Marcus has a pal, Theo Spiridakos, who is high up in Syriza, the official Greek opposition party. According to Theo, several of the PASOK party, the junior party that makes up the government along with New Democracy, are fed up to the back teeth with Prime Minister Samaras and, more importantly for us, no longer want to support New Democracy's commitment to the bailout package. If you take the number of MPs that Syriza has and add it to the smaller opposition parties MPs then you would have 145 votes if they all voted in unison. ND has 127 seats and PASOK 28, making 155 in total. Marcus says his information is that 6 PASOK members are ready to switch their voting allegiance. That would give the opposition 151 votes and the government 149. Marcus said that, in Theo's view, Alexis Tsipras, Syriza's leader will offer the opposition minnows more or less anything to vote with him against the government. Tsipras's plan is to win that vote, then call for a vote of no confidence in the government, win that, tell Merkel, the EU, the IMF and anybody else who cares to listen, to shove their bailout plan, default on their debts à la Argentina at the turn of the Millennium, come out of the single currency, whatever the legal ramifications, go back to their own currency, devalue by 40% vis-à-vis the implied current price for the drachma versus the euro, call it the New Drachma and, fucking hey presto, Greek exports will boom, imports will fall, unemployment will decline and all will be happy in the Hellenic Republic." Toby felt the need for a few more glugs of Macallans at this point.

JJ had listened to Toby's tale without interruption. As each snippet of information came out, JJ's brain was assessing, analysing, calculating. If the information was accurate then, at best, they only had till Friday, tomorrow, lunchtime to ditch one big bucket load of Greek bonds.

"Toby, given that the entire crux of this depends on how worthy this Spiridakos fellow's information is, what makes Marcus think that it isn't some desperate spin doctor's wishful thinking. The bloke's in the opposition party, perhaps he wants a bit of market chaos to put pressure on the government ahead of the vote. In fact, would Marcus's pal, who he may not have seen for ages, really tell him this kind of stuff?"

"Well," said Toby deliberately, "Theo Spiridakos is not so much Marcus's pal, as his brother-in-law. Marcus believes the information is 100% reliable."

Now it was JJ's turn to have a gulp of malt whisky. "Jesus

Christ, Toby," said JJ after a pause. "There is no fucking way we can unload our Greek bonds by tomorrow lunchtime, even if we have till tomorrow lunchtime, without causing serious, or even fatal, damage to our unrealised profit on those suckers. The market won't wait till they find out if Tsipras's plan works. They'll just beat the holy shit out of the bonds, the euro, equities and whatever else is directly linked to them, the bloody second they smell that any of those PASOKs are going to jump ship. It's the fucking financial equivalent of shoot first, ask questions later. And if they shoot, we're dead."

"I know," said Toby, feeling a bit worse for wear by now. "That's why I'm here on your armchair. It can't wait till tomorrow and I don't know what to do."

JJ stood up, walked over to his drinks cabinet and poured himself another whisky and Canada Dry, gesturing to Toby asking if he wanted another one. Toby was flagging at this point and declined. Toby was expecting JJ to say something and sensing this JJ said softly, "I'm thinking, give me a few moments," and sat back down.

While the Scot's internal computer was whirring away, Toby was contemplating his potential financial demise. If these Greek bonds went belly up, he'd be getting no bonus and if JJ got the chop because of any debacle then he'd certainly be out as well. In hedge fund world you're really only as good as your last trade. Reputation takes time to build but a nanosecond to lose. Who'd want to hire a trader whose CV read 'butt-fucked by a bunch of Greek wankers'. Nobody was the answer.

JJ was contemplating. All that time it took to research the Greek trade, the work with Yves-Jacques on the game tree, the apparently misplaced confidence that there was a 70% probability, at least, that the unrealised massive profit in the bonds was intact. It was all about to go down the toilet because a few Greek politicians couldn't take the pain of the hair shirt that their own prior mistakes determined that they should don. There was no point greetin' too much over that now, thought JJ. It's in the past. If Marcus's brother-in-law was straight up then by tomorrow afternoon there was going to be a shit-fest of red on all Bloomberg screens. Ironically, as it would be the first Friday of the month, US non-farm payrolls data, the pivotal data statistic of any month, would be released at 1.30pm GMT prompt. These were expected to be good, around 300,000 new jobs created in November if market consensus expectations and Wednesday's ADP job figures were anything to go by. NFPs were often regarded as the key market data release from the US depicting the health of the economy. From a proper economist's perspective they had no predictive value. After all, they were out of date and more accurately reflected what the economy was like three to six months ago, but the markets had taken them to be predictive and that was that. In any event, it didn't matter a monkey's butt what the US jobs numbers were tomorrow. Greek news, if there was Greek news, would dominate and any asset price linked to a bullish, optimistic view of the world, would in an inkling turn crimson red.

"Toby, are you still awake?" JJ eventually piped up.

"Yes, chief. Do we have a plan?"

"Kind of. Can you make sure that Yves-Jacques gets out of his pit now, or whoever's pit he's in, and gets himself into the office. I'm assuming he's got a twenty-four hour pass?"

"I'll send him a message right now and if I don't get a reply in five minutes I'll hound his Gallic ass till I do," responded Toby, now feeling somewhat more upbeat as JJ might have a plan, kind of.

"Tell him we'll meet there in half an hour. The Asian markets are already open but equities are up so far in China and the Nikkei is having a good start, something to do with the weaker yen and plans for more infrastructure public spending by the Abe government. That means there's been no whisper of Greek drama as yet."

Both men finished up their Macallans and JJ texted Gil to see if she could come over and just be there when Cyrus awoke. She was on her way. He popped upstairs and quickly got changed into his work gear; a dark Zegna suit and shirt, black socks and a pair of shiny black leather size ten brogues were the order of the day. No time for a shower, so a quick squirt of Knize Ten. If things went well he might try to pop over to the RAC club in Pall Mall where he was a decade-long member and have a shower later. Same watch as yesterday, the IWC Top Gun Miramar pilot's watch. Time would be of the essence tomorrow, actually today, but whatever watch he wore wasn't going to make any difference. Nevertheless it was big and bold and that's exactly what JJ and his team needed to be for the next few hours. JJ picked up his leather back pack and he was ready. By the time he came back downstairs, Toby had contacted Yves-Jacques and had a response in return. The young Frenchman was in his own bed with his own girlfriend so that worked out well. Toby had Hailo-ed a cab which was now ticking over outside JJ's house. Yves-Jacques would be at MAM's offices before them, computer fired up and hot to trot. Game on.

On arrival at the office, JJ and Toby went straight to the third floor where Yves-Jacques's open plan desk was situated. The night security guard on reception didn't really recognise any of them, why would he, none of the band of three had ever before been to the office shortly after midnight. They all had their swipe ID passes with photographs so there was no delay.

"Hi Yves-Jacques," called JJ as he and Toby marched towards the Frenchman's dark mop of hair. He didn't look in too bad a way given that he'd been summoned out of his REM time without as much as a by your leave. His shirt wasn't fully tucked into his pants, not quite Fathead style but close enough for JJ to hope that this particular style virus wasn't contagious. JJ's thought processes often wandered off into the irrelevant when he was under pressure, but he swiftly realised that the time for daydreaming was not now, get back to the point he told himself.

"Thanks for coming in, in the middle of the night, Yves-Jacques," said JJ. "We're in a mega bind and over the next few hours the three of us had better prove our worth or we'll all likely be seeking new employment," he continued.

"No problem, Mr Darke… I mean JJ. Hi Toby." The French analyst tried his best to appear normal but inwardly he was startled by JJ's reference to potential unemployment. He'd only just been employed! He loved it at MAM and he sure didn't want to be seeking a new job, especially as it was nearly Christmas. No joyeux Noel for him if he was in the dole queue.

JJ and Toby briefly filled in Yves-Jacques about the problem, Toby refrained from too many 'fuckin' Popadopadopolases' insults and JJ didn't drop the F-bomb once.

"Right," said JJ in a manner that meant his two colleagues needed to pay attention now. "Here's the plan. It's plan A and it's the entire alphabet plan. We have neither the time nor the luxury of a plan B so we're going with this one for better or worse. Toby, the face value of our entire holding of Greek bonds is, what, approximately €400 million?" enquired JJ. Toby had a spreadsheet open on his laptop.

"€420 million JJ."

"How much could we reasonably unload between 8am and 12 noon this morning without markedly moving the price against us and assuming there is no breaking Greek news to our detriment?" continued JJ.

"Well, if I get the guys on the trading desk to help…"

JJ interrupted, "Forget it Toby. It's just down to us. If you get the guys on the desk to help, they'll blab whether they know they're blabbing or not. It'll be on their BBMs and within twenty minutes it'll be all over everybody's BBMs that MAM are dumping Greek bonds. That'll cause the dealers and brokers to smell a rat and they'll start digging. Loose lips don't just sink ships, they torpedo hedge funds as well."

Toby knew JJ was right. The time between one Bloomberg instant message and then getting the initial message back to you from some random dealer was often no more than twenty minutes.

"OK," reassessed Toby. "Spread evenly over three or four hours with multiple dealers, I can probably sell around 120 million of the 420 million without triggering chitty-chatty price anxiety amongst the community."

"Fine," responded JJ. "Toby, that's your target and your job. Spend the next half hour or so preparing your call list. Once you've done that get a nap on the sofa in my office. You're going to need to be as sharp as a tack from the off," instructed JJ. Toby stayed where he was and browsed through his laptop to begin the process of listing the victims he'd try to sell his bonds to.

JJ continued. "We've still got €300 million of toxic Greek junk even if the first part of the plan works. If Greek yields go from 10% to 20%, which they surely will immediately on the first hint of a parliamentary showdown, we'll lose €75 to €100 million, potentially more if our information turns out to be right. We can't do anything about that; we have to hold them, not least of which because liquidity will dry up until the picture is clearer. So Yves-Jacques, here's your task. This is a multi-faceted game. You need to run your correlation and variance-covariance matrix model programs. We need to have a target of liquid macro assets that are inversely correlated to the price of Greek 10 year bonds. These asset markets need to be open from the first thing this morning till at least the release of US NFPs at 1.30pm our time. We need to have more than one asset available for selection because, again, we don't want to tip-off the market vultures that there's something afoot. As you know, every asset has different volatility characteristics. 100 contracts of gold futures are not the same as 100 contracts of silver futures. Once you've got the target list, run it through my portfolio optimisation program and that will spew out how much of each asset we need to buy to match the expected loss on the Greek bonds. Got it?" enquired JJ of Yves-Jacques.

"Yes I can do this. It'll take me an hour or two to run these programs in their entirety," said the French man awaiting confirmation from JJ that the time needed was alright.

"That's fine," said JJ. "It's 3am now. If all hell breaks loose before our target markets are open then we're stuffed anyway. We may as well try to do it right. As a starter, Yves-Jacques, make sure you include S&P 500 futures, gold, the yen and one other liquid equity market that we can short. Don't include any bonds. While there may be a flow into Euro Bunds or US Treasuries out of Greek bonds, the markets will worry about the break-up of the euro, and if the US jobs numbers are good, Treasuries will drop. We should be set up to short the S&P 500 and buy gold and the yen. Once you've got the bare numbers let me see them. Toby, you'll have a bit more to do then, though at least with the target list programme you can involve one or two of the guys on the trading desk."

So that was the plan. It wasn't perfect. You can never match the profit/loss on trying to hedge one asset against a selection of other assets. In the financial crash of 2008, risk management tools like VAR (value at risk) and optimisation programs just blew up, they were worthless, as Lehman Brothers discovered. The key to success of JJ's plan was stealth. The less chatter generated by their selling and buying programmes, the more chance the calculated hedges would hold up, the more chance the targeted assets would remain liquid and, critically, the more chance that Greek bonds wouldn't go prematurely terminal. The structure of JJ's plan needed to be robust, Yves-Jacques financial programs needed to be efficient and accurate and Toby's trading skills needed to be honed to perfection. Black Friday or Golden Friday – who knew? Well, the world would in a few hours one way or the other.

It was 8am, on Friday, 13th December. The first floor of MAM's offices was buzzing. This was the trading floor. If you weren't at your desk by 8am you weren't important in the scheme of things. The first floor accommodated around a hundred people, about fifty traders, twenty-five or so quants and the balance made up of support staff. It was open plan, with a gazillion screens, moderately less desks, all wooden beige with metallic legs, and lumbar supporting modern chairs. Off in the far corner, Thomas Meltzer, MAM's chief economist, was giving an early morning interview for CNBC Europe. US jobs data was the main topic. Meltzer was German, about 5ft 11in, with straight blond hair and vivid blue eyes, only partially hidden by his gold rimmed specs. His English was so good he could tell jokes in it.

JJ nodded to Thomas as he sauntered by. He liked the German, his work was more thoughtful than most and he had manfully resisted the modern day temptation to have a view on everything and a 'sound-bite' for everybody. JJ was glad Thomas was pontificating on the upcoming US non-farm payroll numbers because that meant that there was no Greek news of note. JJ had already had a brief chat with David Sutherland, the head and founder of MAM. He was well into his sixties now but was still very sharp. His skill was in delegating, a skill never underestimated by

Ronald Reagan, in JJ's view America's second most effective President of the post World War II era. Sutherland was a little shorter than JJ, less hair, more body mass, but better teeth and clothes. He was old Etonian and Oxford with good political contacts. JJ liked him mainly because he just let him get on with his job. They had little in common apart from a desire to grow MAM from strength to strength. Sutherland was concerned by JJ's news on Greece but a lot calmer when the Scot had outlined his plan. Now JJ had to discover whether his plan was up and running or not.

Toby's desk was at the far end of the trading floor, near the quants. He liked it there mainly because he had a good view over St. James's Square from the floor to ceiling windows, one of the few non-original aspects of the building's fascia. JJ walked slowly towards him, hoping to create an atmosphere of casual intent rather than alarm if he had rushed up to the head FX and commodities trader.

"How's it going, Fathead?" asked JJ. He thought it would further add to the casualness if he called Toby by his nickname.

Toby looked up. He wasn't surprised to see JJ there. He was on the phone to one of the dealers so put up his arm with one finger raised, not the middle one of course, to signal that he'd be with JJ in a moment. Phone call over. "It's going well," said Toby in a voice low enough that neighbours could not hear any detail above the office hubbub. JJ had a small smile as he sipped on his take-away Starbucks double espresso macchiato.

"I've sold more than two-thirds of the €120 million bonds, but I need to pause for a bit. A couple of the more alert dealers asked me if anything was up. I just said we were doing a bit of portfolio rebalancing before year end but that we were maintaining our core holding." The truth in fact but not spirit thought JJ. "There is one thing, though," Toby said. "I haven't seen Yves-Jacques or his list of assets to buy. Have you got it?"

JJ's smile was a tad smaller now. He had seen Yves-Jacques about an hour ago and they had agreed the target buy list. Toby should have had it by now. "Give him a ring, Toby, and ask him to hotfoot it down here no matter what he's doing. It's 8.30am and the clock's ticking. We'd better be too."

Within two or three minutes, Yves-Jacques could be seen scuttling across the trading floor heading for JJ and Toby. Without being obvious about it JJ signalled to the young Frenchman to slow down. Stealth was still the order of the day.

"Yves-Jacques, where's our list, Toby needs to get cracking?" asked JJ without too much urgency in case it freaked out the young analyst.

"I've got it here," he replied, clutching a few pages of hand written instructions. "I was delayed because I decided to re-run your optimisation model program JJ as it might not have been properly set up for relative value trades."

JJ nodded, he was a good mathematician and econometrician but it's possible that analytics had progressed since he designed MAM's portfolio optimisation program three short years ago. "Go on," said JJ.

"Well, last night or early this morning you mentioned that we should include one other liquid equity market to short as well as the S&P 500. If we had done that in the size we needed to do it, it would have breached the fund's internal risk rules."

JJ realised they didn't have time to get down to the nitty gritty of the program's details now so it was whether or not he trusted Yves-Jacques and whether or not he had a solution to this glitch. "I take it from the fact that you've not disintegrated into a greasy spot Yves-Jacques that you're confident you're right and that you have a recommendation to keep us on track," said JJ.

"Yes, JJ, I do," replied Yves-Jacques, confidently, seemingly comfortable enough with no more 'Mr Darke' as he addressed JJ.

"If we put on a relative value equity trade, in particular we go long the SMI (Swiss Market Index) and short the MIB (Milano Italia Borsa) we reduce our overall risk, break no rules and we can do it in the same size as before."

JJ contemplated this recommendation for a few seconds. Switzerland wasn't in the EU or the euro. As such its equities tended to fare a lot better when Eurozone troubles popped up. Italy, by contrast, was in the euro, albeit crying a lot about being in it now and the shares on their stock market, the MIB, would get hammered if the Greek drama unfolded the way Marcus Whyte had warned.

"OK Yves-Jacques, sounds good," said JJ. "Give your list to Toby. Toby you get cracking with your guys and let me know how it's going. No emails or BBMs. Use your personal mobiles or come and see me if anything significant is happening different to our plan."

Toby nodded and turned back to his screens and headset. Time to give J-K a call he thought. Those two boys better not have stayed at Nobu too long.

"Yves-Jacques," said JJ. "You come with me. Let's look at my flawed optimisation model." Yves-Jacques smiled. He knew he was right and he knew JJ wouldn't mind if he was. After all, he had passed the augmented Norman Tebbit test.

The rest of the day went well for JJ and his colleagues. J-K had come through for Toby, Jay had sold over 10,000 contracts of S&P 500 futures before the US jobs data was released. He also managed to put on Yves-Jacques's relative value trade in size and that was working a treat. Kai bought 4,000 gold contracts for Toby and went short a yard and a half of USD/JPY which ended up having a 2.5% move on the day. Toby had shifted all €120 million worth of Greek bonds by 10.30am. US jobs data came out on the dot of 1.30pm, with non-farm payrolls up by 315,000, moderately above the consensus expectation.

The news on the Greek bailout vote started hitting the tape by 2.30pm GMT. Marcus Whyte's brother-in-law's information was spot on. There was going to be an extraordinary parliamentary vote that night, some of PASOK's MPs indicated that they no longer supported the majority party's policy on the bailout and that they would support the main opposition party. Greek bonds went terminal. Having started the day yielding 10.3% their closing yield was 22.6%. Holders of Greek bonds had experienced a catastrophic loss on the day, and probably worse when markets re-opened the following Monday. MAM had suffered a microscopic loss on the day but JJ's plan had worked. The loss was a few million, no more than it would have been on a normal, quiet not so great day. He was well satisfied. Toby and Yves-Jacques had been brilliant and David Sutherland had congratulated them personally on a job well done. It was 4.30pm. JJ reclined on his ergonomic leather chair, feet on desk and drinking cool water from his evian bottle. He tended to be all patriotic about his water consumption and more often than not he'd have Highland Spring bottles in his office fridge. He was partial to the French today, however, so he thought he would go with evian.

JJ was looking forward to the weekend. He hoped Cyrus wanted to play some real, as opposed to virtual, tennis on Saturday. He would still get beaten as Cyrus was good at proper tennis too but at least they would get some exercise. It may be early winter but the hard surface at Burton Court was all year round playable. Before he set off for the day JJ thought he'd take a quick look at his email inbox. The activities of the past eighteen hours or so had meant that he hardly had any time to look at his Outlook page. As he scrolled through his dozen or so unread mails, two stood out. One was from his G.P. Probably just an invoice with an inflated bill simply for telling him he was in good shape for a forty-three year old. He liked his G.P. Dr Guy Marshall, he was about sixty years old and had a straightforward and pleasant manner. As a patient, JJ wasn't a lot of trouble to Dr Marshall, the only time he had needed any treatment in the past year was to get some wax syringed from his right ear. Apparently, that meant you slept most of the time on your right side.

JJ opened Dr Marshall's mail.

> *Dear Mr Darke,*
>
> *I thought I'd drop you this email so that you can come and see me next week. The blood tests we took last week were broadly fine. Your cholesterol is low and liver, kidney and all bodily functions seem to be in good order. The tests did, however, throw up a PSA score of 23. The normal range is 0-2, so this is high. It may be a mistake, PSA scores are notoriously unreliable but arrange for an appointment please and I'll check it out. Have a good weekend.*
>
> *Regards,*
> *Guy.*

JJ had no idea what a PSA score was. He was old school Glaswegian when it came to health. If it wasn't broke he had no intention of trying to fix it. He felt good, trained hard and, most of the time, ate well. He'd check it out on Sunday, if he could be bothered.

The second unopened email was from Neil Robson, which was much more intriguing. Neil was the Financial Secretary to the Treasury. He reported directly to the Chancellor, Jeffrey Walker and was regarded by many in Whitehall as the sharpest tool in the box when it came to Britain's financial matters. More pertinent from JJ's perspective was that he hadn't heard from Neil since their time together in MI5.

2

DEFENCE OF THE REPUBLIC

"It is," said Carolyn.

"No, it isn't," said Dannielle.

Carolyn Reynolds peered closer to her screen. To random passing people, not that there were any of those types at this facility in Springfield, the screen looked like a black and white jigsaw made of spaghetti with lots of pieces missing.

"It's a Borei, Dannielle, I tell you," insisted Carolyn.

"It's definitely not a Borei," retorted Dannielle with even greater emphasis. "Look, Boreis are 560ft long. That yard has never handled anything more than 135ft long. They don't have the facilities and they don't have a Borei. Even if they did it would be on the east coast, in one of the larger, more technologically advanced bases."

Carolyn looked again. She had known Dannielle for nearly two years and she was very, very good at her job. When it came to image analysis she was second to none. Well, thought Carolyn, maybe second to one.

"OK, let's take it to Henry for a third opinion," said Carolyn.

"Fine," said Dannielle moderately peeved that her colleague and friend wouldn't take her word for it. "The big Maasai will agree with me," pronounced Dannielle with a mischievous smile on her face.

"If the big Maasai agrees with you, Danni, it'll only be because he thinks you're cute," replied Carolyn. She figured that would discomfort Dannielle a little since she knew that Henry Michieta liked her, but as she was a total professional, that particular liking wasn't going anywhere outside of the big Maasai's head.

"Low blow Cally," muttered Dannielle in jest. "I'm so right honey, that I'm prepared to bet you a steak dinner with all the trimmins," she said with a mock Southern drawl, carved straight from the shanty hovels of *Deliverance*.

Later that night, as Carolyn was filling her somewhat small mouth with a special order Chateaubriand, well done, with fries and shitake mushrooms at Marty's Steakhouse on Old Keene Mill Road, she looked up at Dannielle, with a superior smirk. "Told ya," she managed to splutter out.

"Henry didn't say it was definitely a Borei," replied Dannielle looking moderately crestfallen at the thought of the $80 plus bill she was going to be landed with in an hour or so. "He said that the image was consistent with a Borei but could be several Sang-O's nose to tail."

"Fore to aft is probably what you're looking for Danni-girl when it comes to boats," interrupted Carolyn, still smug and still eating.

"Whatever," said Dannielle spikily. "In any event all he said was to do more research and analysis and, I might add, *and* he agreed with me that in the possible event that it was a Borei it should be parked on the east coast."

"Berthed," interjected Carolyn.

"What?" said Dannielle, loudly.

"If it's a boat it's berthed, not parked," said Carolyn, fully realising that her annoyance factor was growing pari passu with the bill.

"Good thing I like you Ms Reynolds," replied Dannielle

"because you're one annoying bitch." With that, they both laughed heartily, knowing that the next few days would yield the truth about that spaghetti image on Carolyn Reynolds' computer.

The Borei class submarine is a nuclear-powered ballistic missile submarine, made in Russia for the Russian Navy. They were first developed in 1996 and built at the Northern Machine-Building Enterprise (Sevmash) in Severodvinsk. The Russian authorities intended that this class of submarine was to be the cornerstone of their fleet until at least 2040. There are different configurations, but the three already built out of a planned ten, were approximately 170 metres long with a beam of 13.5 metres. It carries about 100 crew, has a submerged speed of over 30 miles per hour, and has unlimited range, only constrained by food stores. The sub has a desalination plant on board so it doesn't need to surface to get essential fresh water.

The submarines were re-designed under Project 955 to accommodate Bulava submarine-launched ballistic missiles (SLBM). The range of these missiles is 5,000 to 10,000 miles, depending on the variant on board. The Bulava's advanced technology meant that it could carry up to 10 hypersonic, individually guided manoeuvrable warheads. It has mega evasion capabilities making it highly resistant to most missile defence systems. The Bulava has programs of evasive manoeuvring, mid-course countermeasures and decoys. Each of the 10 warheads has a yield of 100 – 150 kilotons. That was firepower. It had taken only one 12.5 kiloton nuclear weapon to destroy Hiroshima in Japan in World War II. The distance between Vladivostok, where the Boreis are based, and Washington DC is 6,500 miles, a fact not lost on Carolyn Reynolds. These facts and figures were well known to the US military, their intelligence forces and security services. The basic information was not difficult to find and through satellite tracking and imaging the whereabouts of these warrior submarines were well observable under most circumstances. What was preying on Carolyn Reynolds' mind though, was not that she had probably identified a Borei class submarine, but that she had identified it on the west coast of North Korea, not the east coast of Russia.

The National Geospatial-Intelligence Agency (NGA) is based in Springfield, Virginia and also has other facilities in St. Louis, Missouri. The NGA employs professionals from a wide variety of specialisations including aeronautics, navigation, topography, imagery and geopolitical analysis. The NGA team's most treasured result to date was their crucial involvement in Operation Neptune Spear, which culminated in the killing of Osama bin Laden at a fortified compound in Abbottabad, Pakistan on 2nd May 2011. The NGA works with the US Department of Defense, Homeland Security and, predominantly, the CIA.

Henry Michieta was studying the report of officers Reynolds and Eagles. He was sitting upright at his desk in his office on the third floor. Henry's office was voluminous, as befitted a section chief. The NGA building wasn't limited in space, with all of its 2.3 million square feet and an atrium significantly taller than the Statue of Liberty. He was as black as the ace of spades. Born in Alabama, forty-five years old, and hugely proud of his African heritage, which showed without doubt that he was descended from the Maasai tribes on the west coast of Kenya. At 6ft 4in and athletically built he knew his lineage was unlikely to be disputed by anyone. He shaved his head and had an almost imperceptibly small, clear diamond earring in his right pierced ear, both signs that the Maasai ways were still in his blood. He was born in Mobile and attended the University of Alabama in Tuscaloosa where he studied Aeronautical Engineering, then a Masters in Communication and Information Sciences. He was bright and he was powerful, and had been a member of both Alpha Lambda Delta and his college football team.

It wasn't Henry's unit that had been directly involved in pinpointing bin Laden's Pakistani hideout. As a proud and loyal American he didn't much care who took bin Laden out, he was just glad that somebody did. As section chief in the geopolitical and imagery division of the NGA he was, nevertheless, a bit deflated that it was one of his colleagues who scored on that one. Directly from university Henry joined the CIA's junior officer training program. Most of his training was at The Point as the facility at Harvey Point, North Carolina is known. His basic course lasted a year. He excelled in surveillance and cryptography but, for a large man, struggled with paramilitary training and the physical demands of other tradecraft. His senior evaluators at The Point had been quick and accurate in their assessment of the young Maasai and had earmarked him for the NGA, while he was still in his mid-twenties. Now, twenty years later, he was in charge of about fifty officers who were assigned to a plethora of surveillance and interpretive roles. He loved his job and he felt lucky to have it, but deep down in his Maasai warrior heart he wanted to be on the NGA's roll of honour.

Today, though, indeed in about ten minutes, he was going to have a meeting with officers Reynolds and Eagles. Cute as they were, especially Dannielle Eagles, that was an event that would likely require him to have a nuclear strength coffee right now.

Carolyn and Dannielle were both twenty-five years old, both from the east coast of the United States and both slim and pretty. Dannielle at 5ft 8in was taller by a couple of inches, with darker, straight hair, but Carolyn wore bigger heels to compensate and had somewhat fairer hair. Carolyn had her dad's grey-green eyes which seemed to go vibrant bright green when she was angry while Dannielle's were sultry dark brown. They had trained together at The Farm, the CIA's other training facility at Camp Peary, Virginia and their skillsets definitely complemented each other. On her training course, Dannielle stood out in analytical tradecraft, interrogation and surveillance. She was also a regular star in any honey trap role play, which much amused her colleagues who knew to keep their distance in the real world. Carolyn's standout skills on the training course were her ability to maintain cover under duress, amazing for a slightly built girl, and steganography, essentially obscure code writing that only the sender and intended recipient can understand, even if seen by the unintended. Both could shoot to kill and physically disable an assailant without requiring any weapon. They were, Henry thought, a tour de force, if only they didn't speak! Henry was trying not to be sexist but he often got ear-ache from their machine gun rat-a-tat-tat delivery. Carolyn was worst, or best depending on your viewpoint. She could talk seemingly forever, without a single breath. Had she been a man Reynolds could have been a star in the Navy SEALs underwater demolition squad, mused Henry, just as the two in question came barrelling into his open door office.

"Sit down ladies," welcomed Henry.

Carolyn's rear had just about made contact with the chair when she blurted out, "Henry, I'm more convinced than ever that this is a Borei. I've had the satellite imagery checked by the forensic image guys and they confirm that it seems to be one continuous vessel of around 560ft in length. That's exactly the length of a Borei class submarine. The beam width is greater than that of the Sang-O II class sub that is, or maybe was, the best the Korean People's Army Naval Force have or had. So, although Dannielle thought that it might be three or four Sang-O's forward to aft," Carolyn glanced cheekily at Dannielle at this point, "it isn't."

"What do you think Dannielle?" asked Henry.

"Carolyn's probably right that it's not a bunch of smaller subs in a line, on further inspection, but we seem to have reliable information that Russia has built only three Boreis so far, out of their planned ten, and they're all accounted for. Two are in dock at the Vladivostok complex and the third one is on manoeuvres in the Sea of Japan. I conclude," noted Dannielle, glancing back at Carolyn in a fashion that said I'm about to go one up, "that barring further information this isn't a Borei."

"At the risk of being simple," interjected Henry, "can't we just commission one of those drones to fly over and take a look?"

"No, we can't," responded Carolyn. "North Korean defence systems around naval bases are well capable of downing one of those drones before it gets a chance to take a decent photograph. In any event, there's some kind of floating shed or roof over the sub to render that route pretty useless since the drone's imaging capability, if obscured, is less than the satellite picture we already have."

Henry looked suitably chastised but, with Reynolds, he knew that it wouldn't end there.

"I've been in touch with one of my pals at Langley," continued Carolyn. "He works in the Middle East section, specialising in crude oil movements. He says they regularly take satellite images of land based oil fields e.g. in Saudi Arabia, to gauge the depth of oil in any given fields and wells, just in case the Saudis try to pull any fast ones re oil quotas. It didn't take me long to convince him to divert the CIA satellite for a quick tour over North Korea's west coast. Here's the image." Carolyn handed it to Henry.

"It's very colourful, Reynolds, but what does it mean? It looks like one of my daughter's colouring in books." Henry didn't have the nerve, at this point, to ask how Carolyn managed to get a CIA satellite diverted.

"As you know, Henry," said Carolyn giving her boss the

benefit of the doubt, "satellite imagery is different from taking a photograph. A photo can only record what our eyes see. A satellite image can record infrared and ultraviolet light which we can't see, as well as the visible spectrum. Our computers then assign colours to the invisible spectrum to produce a near photograph. Petroleum geologists sometimes use this type of analysis to see how much oil is in a well, something that can't be seen from the surface. Sometimes, if the geologists really want to get the detail of what's going on under the surface without digging, they use this imagery and computer models to build a 3-D seismic cube. This can then be pictorially sliced vertically or horizontally to measure exactly what's going on underground. This is such an image taken from Langley's satellite positioned over Haeju, south of Pyongyang."

Dannielle and Henry looked at the colourful picture intently.

"And this tells us what?" asked Henry.

Dannielle realised that this was the further information she needed. She interjected in an attempt to recover some standing on the matter. "It tells us, Henry, that there's a Borei class nuclear submarine parked, I mean berthed, off the west coast of the Democratic People's Republic of Korea."

Needless to say the conclusion of that meeting triggered significant activity among the intelligence agencies and the US military. Henry wasted no time in sharing Reynolds' and Eagles' report with his boss at the NGA who, in turn, got in touch with his counterparts in the CIA and Department of Defense. A mere two days later a high level meeting was scheduled at CIA HQ in Langley, Virginia, a few miles west of Washington.

At 10am on 9th March 2014 the scheduled meeting began in a secure room on the ground floor. There were only six attendees. Officer Reynolds and Eagles were both there. That may have seemed like overkill, one of them would have been enough, but they were the joint authors of the report and the CIA's Associate Director for Military Support, John Adams, asked that they both attend. In addition to Adams, a short chunky man in his early fifties with cropped silver hair, all salt and no pepper, there was Timothy Thornton from the Special Activities Division of the NCS and George McAllister representing the US Pacific Fleet's interests in the Department of Defense. The final attendee was a well-defined but slim young man of about twenty-five, short cropped fair hair, 5ft 10in and wearing the uniform of a commander in the Navy SEALs. His name was Mark O'Neill. The meeting was chaired by John Adams and after brief introductions, he began.

"Thank you all for coming here today. You've read the report produced by the NGA officers, who are here to elucidate and answer any questions. What I want to know is, is it real? If it is, what do we do about it?"

Lieutenant McAllister was based in Honolulu and he was regarded as the Pacific Fleet's expert on submarines. He was in his mid-forties with longish, dark hair and an educated east coast accent. "Look," he began. "The report is detailed, thorough and on the face of it accurate. However, we have been monitoring Russian subs for countless years. Not only do we know where they are, we've virtually got the names and addresses of all their crew."

This opening little anecdote generated a modicum of mirth among half the attendees; Reynolds, Eagles and O'Neill being the abstainers.

McAllister continued. "The satellite images aren't perfectly clear and the fact that there may be a covering over whatever vessel is there makes it more difficult to be sure what's underneath. Also, the Haeju naval yard on the west coast is equipped for primarily the servicing and repair of merchant vessels; this could easily be a cargo ship undergoing repairs." With that Lieutenant McAllister paused for a sip of water. Associate Director Adams turned to the NGA team and motioned with his eyes that a response may be in order.

Carolyn Reynolds piped up. "With all due respect Sir," she started. Dannielle Eagles grimaced because she knew what was coming next, maybe not in content, but in attitude. All due respect wasn't a trio of words that was regular in her friend's vocabulary. "The satellite images, which have been checked and rechecked by many of our colleagues at the NGA show a vessel that is over 550ft long. Yes, that could be consistent with a small merchant or cargo ship, but the beam is around 44ft. That's about one quarter the length of an average container ship's beam or one third of any merchant vessel that's ever been at the Haeju naval yard," stated Carolyn with authority. "It's not a ship, gentlemen. It's a sub and its dimensions are virtually identical as far as we can tell to a Borei class Russian Navy submarine." Now it was Carolyn's turn to drink some water. She was enjoying hers a lot more than McAllister was enjoying his.

Tim Thornton was a serious looking man in his mid-thirties. He had a thin face, light brown hair, a full beard with a hint of ginger in it and a kind of perma-tan which made him look healthy, albeit a little orange. "As far as you can tell Officer Reynolds, is the submarine carrying weapons?" Thornton knew enough about satellite imagery to know that shots taken from space could not give enough detail to determine whether there were missiles or torpedoes on board. He fully expected a don't know response and that would be the first hint of indecisiveness from the NGA officers.

"No, it's not weaponised as of the date of our satellite image, three days ago," responded Carolyn.

"How can you tell?" asked Thornton. "Satellite images—"

"Can't go that deep," finished Carolyn. "No they can't Mr Thornton, but after the initial image we dug a little deeper and modelled a 3-D seismic cube, as petroleum geologists do when investigating the dimensions of oil wells. The unladen, un-crewed displacement of a Borei class sub is just over 14,700 long tons if surfaced. Our analysis was consistent with that with a +/- 1% margin of error. If the sub was weaponised it would have at least five Bulava RSM-56 ballistic missiles on board. That would have taken the estimated displacement of the submarine outside of our estimated +/- 1% margin of error with a 98% probability. No Sir," Carolyn concluded, "this Borei is not weaponised... at the moment."

After that, there were no more questions regarding the content or accuracy of Reynolds' and Eagles' report. They had delivered well, answered any questions that had been forthcoming with precision and authority. The general agreement now in the meeting room was that North Korea had a nuclear powered Borei submarine at its Haeju naval base on the west coast of the mainland. Unanswered questions like how it got there, how was it paid for, what was Russia's involvement, could wait for a later date. The only questions that mattered right this minute were what were Pyongyang's intentions and what was the United States going to do about them?

From the perspective of the American government and its people, in fact, the same perspective for much of the civilised world, North Korea was a secretive society with a crazy man as leader. It was easy enough to dismiss Kim Jong-un, North Korea's supreme leader, as no more than a sabre rattler extraordinaire but, in the first half of 2013 his sabre rattling was extremely loud and clear. The People's Democratic Republic withdrew from a non-aggression agreement with their southern neighbours, the North Korean army moved its Musudan missiles to their east coast, where they could threaten Japan and America's Pacific military bases. Vast military rallies were ever more frequent and the thirty-one year old glorious leader himself was photographed brandishing guns and stirring up his troops to a frenzy. Who knew what was coming next?

What was a known known as opposed to a known unknown, was that if North Korea's recently acquired nuclear submarine became weaponised, the missiles did have the range and destructive capability to take out much of America's eastern seaboard, with millions of lives lost and a degree of contamination that might not dissipate for twenty years.

The remainder of the meeting that morning principally involved brainstorming as to military options for destroying the Borei. An air attack was entirely possible, but that would be highly visible and could trigger a North Korean response to attack the South, Japan or most likely the Pacific Coast of the United States.

There was some discussion, mainly between McAllister and Thornton about undertaking a Navy SEALs operation. SEALs Teams 1, 5 and 7 had worldwide capabilities and were all headquartered in Coronado, California. Commander O'Neill kept his peace bar to confirm that these teams were indeed HQ'd in California. This discussion went on for about twenty minutes. Reynolds and Eagles didn't have much to offer. While they had been trained in paramilitary skills and hand to hand combat they certainly didn't have the need to put these skills to the test at the NGA, and they had no knowledge of the ins and outs of first strike options.

Lieutenant McAllister, clearly keen to make an impact on the meeting after his initial feeble effort at suggesting the sub may be some type of skinny merchant vessel, broke up the side chats by announcing, "We could destroy the sub. Our SEALs teams have the capability."

Associate Director Adams scanned the room for further comment. Thornton nodded his approval, Reynolds and Eagles shrugged and Commander O'Neill sat there as inscrutably as he had done from the start. John Adams, though, wasn't going to let him get away with this oriental ploy any longer.

"Commander O'Neill, do you have a view?" enquired Adams.

"Sir," began Mark O'Neill. "The SEALs certainly do have the expertise, the capability and the commitment to carry out such a mission. Without having yet studied the layout of the geography near Haeju, a squad of five to ten could evade the North Korean radar systems, be dropped off a couple of miles off the coast in a rubber raiding craft, attach timed explosives to the hull of the sub and then get out," he detailed. As Mark O'Neill paused, McAllister and Thornton were all ears and clearly relishing the prospect. Associate Director Adams had a neutral expression but his ears were still alert.

"There are at least two problems though," resumed O'Neill.

"They are?" interjected McAllister.

"Well, one of the arguments against destroying the sub is that it is highly visible. Everyone would know it was us. Friends would applaud us, foes berate us and, as you discussed, said action could trigger a devastating response from the North Koreans. When President Reagan ordered the air strike on Libya in 1986, or even when we eliminated bin Laden, we didn't care if the world knew; hell we wanted them to know. Mess with the United States and pay the penalty. However, Libya was in no shape to mount any significant retaliatory actions and a leaderless al-Qaeda would take years to even begin to pose the same widespread threat again."

McAllister's face revealed that he was in the process of racking up zero for two. Tim Thornton was less expressive, but ever so slightly shifted his chair an inch or so away from the Lieutenant.

"The second problem," continued O'Neill, "is time. The satellite images before us are now three days old. Who is to say in that time the Borei hasn't been weaponised? After this meeting any conclusions or recommendations will find their way up the hierarchical tree, eventually to the President himself. At best, that journey and any final decision by the President will take another four or five days. Who's to say that the sub won't be packing ballistic missiles by then? My point is, even if we are successful in destroying the sub, we'll set off a nuclear explosion and an even more powerful one if it has SBLMs on board. This will cause devastation to their west coast. While we may not lose any sleep over that, the Pyongyang government would have time at least to launch their land based missiles at Seoul, Tokyo and maybe even us."

John Adams was getting that sinking feeling. He had to report the findings of this meeting to Fred Goss, the Director of Central Intelligence and he, in turn, to Garrison Putnam, the Director of National Intelligence, before it reached the National Security Council and the President. John Adams was so not coming out of this meeting with a feisty, colourful report, but one devoid of feasible recommendations. After a few seconds, which seemed like hours in brain time, Adams asked, "Well Commander O'Neill, you've been successful, I feel, in dismantling the appeal of our strike options. Do you have any brilliant ideas as to what to do with this submarine?"

O'Neill looked Adams straight in the eye and without a hint of hesitation responded. "We could always steal it, Sir."

★ ★ ★

Haeju is one of the Korean People's Navy's (KPN) largest bases on the west coast of Kim Jong-un's empire. The city is located in the South Hwanghae Province and is 100km south of the capital Pyongyang. The overall population is close to 400,000, around one-eighth of whom either work directly in the naval base or in factories which support its daily activities. The average high temperatures at this time of year are 15 – 20 degrees Celsius with 2 – 3 inches of rain. The city is only 60km north of the Demarcation line with South Korea. It is not very mountainous, with the largest one, Mountain Suyang topping out at just under 950 metres. Ben Nevis, in Scotland, is the UK's highest mountain at 1,345 metres.

Commodore Woo-Jin Park has had the responsibility of managing the Haeju naval base for four years. The KPN was widely regarded as a green water navy, indicating that its tasks were mainly that of coastal defence rather than anything more adventurous. The KPN fleet is split into east and west coast squadrons but sheer geography and the limited range of most of the navy's fleet meant that were there to be a sea battle with the South, the two squadrons could not support each other. As a young man, Woo-Jin Park served aboard one of the navy's frigates and more recently a Romeo class submarine. He was promoted from Captain to Commodore in the early 2000s and in 2010 made officer in charge of the Haeju base.

Park was a man of short stature, thick black hair of medium length for a serving officer and wore metallic framed spectacles, silver in colour and round in shape. He took his job seriously, even to the extent that his marriage had broken down as a result of his total commitment to the cause. His marriage had been more or less arranged anyway, so, deep down, he wasn't that bothered. He had no children of his own, and though he was a decent uncle to his sister's children, his babies were right here at the Haeju naval base.

Today he was a proud man. Vice Admiral Goh, his

commanding officer, had explained to him that a new submarine was to be docked at Haeju. Goh made it clear that this was of the utmost importance. He told Woo-Jin Park that Haeju had been selected for its excellent repair and servicing facilities. In part this was true but it had also been selected because it was less obvious as a submarine dock than several of the east coast bases. Goh also told Park that a specific repair and enhancement programme was to be carried out on the submarine. Goh omitted to tell Park that it was also to be weaponised. That piece of information was on a need to know basis and Park didn't need to know just yet.

Woo-Jin Park looked out of his office window down at the submarine. He knew exactly what it was. He had been a competent submariner and he kept up his interest in these submersibles as the years went by. The one he was looking at, well not exactly looking at since there was a rubberised roof covering its length and obstructing his view, was a Russian Borei class nuclear submarine. The KPN's pride and joy, to that point, had been several Sang-O II class subs but this was altogether a different kettle of fish. This was a great white. This was king of the ocean. This was the submarine of superpowers, well one superpower anyway. Commodore Park was not a stupid man. He knew that if this submarine needed to be repaired or serviced then, if it belonged to the Russian Navy, it would be having all that seen to in a Russian naval shipyard. By dint of logic it must now be a vessel of the Korean People's Navy.

True, the great leader's missives were all about waging war with the South and striking at the heart of the evil empire, the United States of America. Any strike, however, on these two, pre-emptive or reactive, would surely be from land based missiles. The KPN was a coastal defence operation and would have little to do other than that. No, unless this Borei class submarine was weaponised, and to his knowledge and inspection it was not, this submarine must just be berthed here as a favour to the Russians, as a pit stop on its way somewhere else. Just as that thought crystallised in Commodore Park's mind, three long and modified KAMAZ 5460 trucks pulled into the yard.

* * *

Two days had passed since the meeting at Langley. Commander Mark O'Neill was back at his headquarters in Coronado, San Diego, California. Associate Director Adams had been true to his word and had fast tracked the Borei report and recommendations through the CIA hierarchy and the Department of Defense's chain of command. The President had initially baulked at the idea but came to understand that O'Neill's recommendation was the best one; or at least the one with least potential loss of human lives and political downside, both factors high up on the President's priority list. It was clear that an air strike was too risky as the ensuing chain of events could put the United States and North Korea, or what was left of them, at war. This was especially true if the submarine at the heart of the matter was weaponised, a known unknown currently being investigated by the two NGA officers whose report started this particular scramble.

Any other form of destruction of the submarine would also likely leave fingerprints as to the perpetrators. Although the US naval and other military forces could perhaps disguise the make and type of the explosives used, there would almost certainly be giveaways as to their manufacture and source. If any US military personnel were killed or captured they would not necessarily be easy to identify or extract information from. In the end, though, they probably would give up what they knew and the trail of blame would lead directly to Washington. So, for the Commander in Chief, destroying the North Korean's recently acquired nuclear submarine was not an option. Leaving it in peace was not an option either. On the scale of clear and present danger, a nuclear submarine that could fire deadly ballistic missiles at the USA in the hands of America's craziest and most unpredictable enemy, was highly visible and catastrophically dangerous.

A mission to steal the submarine had merits. First, if it failed then the loss of human life was probably contained to the SEAL team undertaking the mission and a few hapless North Koreans. While regrettable, that was manageable as far as the White House was concerned. Media coverage would be more of a pain, and the North Korean propaganda and sabre-rattling machine would have a field day or even week. The probability of a nuclear missile launch by Pyongyang would be under 20%, however, according to the war games statisticians at the DoD. Stealing an enemy's submarine may not be optimal but in the real world, proliferated by second best solutions, this seemed to be the one to go for.

Secondly, stealing the sub at least gave the US the opportunity of plausible deniability. While the North Koreans would clearly initially suspect the South, America or Japan, in that order, they did seem to be a bit careless with their submarines. In early April 2013, two North Korean submarines went missing off the coast near Hwanghae Province. Admittedly, they were small submersibles of 130 tons and a ten man crew, and admittedly they may just have been winding up the South Koreans. The White House, however, thought that this episode was evidence enough of careless submarine management to allow the US at least a feasible 'it wasn't us' story that would fly on American TV channels, the nation's websites and among the global twitterati community.

So there it was. Operation Philidor Defence was a go. Mark O'Neill preferred Operation North Wind as the mission's title. Boreas meant North Wind in Russian and that was why the Borei class submarines were so named. However the military's mission computer had randomly selected Philidor Defence. His task now was to put together his team for the mission.

Mark O'Neill was quite young to be a commander, twenty-seven years old and looking a little younger. He had joined the Marines at eighteen after high school but had requested a transfer after the accidental death of one of his best friends at Marine training camp. He knew the SEALs training programme would be even tougher but he just had to get out of the atmosphere surrounding his friend's death. SEAL training is rigorous and punishing. The drop-out rate is over 90% and, in total, training can take up to five years, no less than two, before a Navy SEAL is ready for his first deployment. Mark O'Neill took two and a half years to complete his training. He was truly physically and mentally exhausted after that but now he was the lean, mean fighting machine that his country needed.

Commander O'Neill was part of the west coast SEALs team, the Naval Special Warfare Group 1. The decision had been made that two five man teams would be the operational minimum to steal and operate a Borei class submarine. A larger operational group may have been desirable but for SEALs the more the merrier didn't really apply. The key for O'Neill was the composition of the teams. A Borei class submarine would normally have a crew of a hundred or so, maybe nearly half of which were officers. If you stripped out the cooks, the medics, the scientists and the politicos then you were down to around forty. A further ten or so could be lost if you excluded first time submariners, effectively trainees, and a further ten if you took out sailors who were essentially back-up for key positions, e.g. missile launch. That would leave around twenty as the bare essentials for manning and driving the submarine. After much discussion with his colleagues at the Naval Amphibious Base in Coronado,

O'Neill concluded that around ten suitably skilled SEALs could do the job of twenty Russian submariners. He also concluded that he would select his guys from SEAL Teams 5 and 7, both teams had six platoons, a worldwide mandate, were based in Coronado and had the diversity of talent needed for this operation.

Considering the task ahead, Mark O'Neill was quite relaxed in his quarters at the base. He was checking files, backgrounds, assessments and skill sets of the available for selection SEAL team members. He knew many of them first hand. One of them, Billy Smith – he got a lot of stick for his name even though he couldn't act and wasn't black. His ears did stick out a wee bit though. He was with O'Neill when they killed the pirates who hijacked the Maersk Alabama in April 2009. From a floating submersible off the coast of Somalia, Billy had taken out one of the three pirates with a single sniper shot to the head. Though this wasn't meant to be a shooting mission, Billy was in the team. O'Neill, who was no mean sniper himself, probably could not have hit such a small target while bobbing about on the ocean.

As he was mulling over all the other potential team members, he was sifting through his brain cells for what was really needed on this mission. O'Neill had not gone to university, but he was no dummy, having an IQ of over 140 and scoring in the nation's top five percentile in his SATs. His family were relatively low income for those living in California, his father had a career-ending accident being involved in a car crash, and his mother did a wonderful job bringing up him and his sister. Back on point, O'Neill concluded that after the usual suspects, i.e. submariners, radar operators, skilled shooters, one medic, and an explosives expert it would be necessary to have someone who could speak either Russian or Korean. Preferably both, however unlikely that was.

As he was mentally juggling with the permutations, his tablet beeped, indicating that he had received a secure email. Commander O'Neill opened his mail, it was from the NGA.

Commander O'Neill,

Request that officers Reynolds and Eagles are included in your team for Operation Philidor Defence. If you wish to discuss this please contact me directly.

Regards,
Henry Michieta
Section Chief
Geospatial Analysis

Mark O'Neill read the short email again. Now those two ladies were smart and they were feisty, especially Reynolds if he recalled accurately, but no fucking way Jose was his initial thought. By law, women could not join the Navy SEALs so the mere thought of having those two cuties, albeit CIA trained, splashing about in the Sea of Japan, with ten testosterone filled SEALs, was a total non-starter. What was Michieta thinking, the moron. In any event what could they do? They were analytical officers not field operatives. There would be no need for analysis of satellite images as, hopefully, they'd be underwater and steering the sub to a destination as yet undecided. Jesus. Preparing for this mission was tough enough without that kind of distraction. Commander O'Neill was contemplating not even replying to Michieta, when his tablet beeped again.

Sorry Commander, I was interrupted before I could complete my mail.
Reynolds can speak and read Korean and Eagles emigrated to the

United States, aged 10, from Russia and remains fluent in her native tongue. They want to be included, as to how is entirely up to you.

Mark O'Neill put his head in his hands. There was no one in SEALs Team 5 or 7 who could speak or read Korean and the only two fluent Russian linguists were already on a mission in Eastern Europe and could not be recalled. Either or both languages may be essential to interpret any operating instructions, especially since the SEALs would only be a skeleton crew. This wasn't happening, no way, the two NGA officers looked about the same age as his little sister for god's sake. They were talented alright and they were pretty, he thought, especially Carolyn Reynolds. These aesthetic visions needed ejecting pronto from his head. It was *not* happening. What if they were killed or captured? He'd need to tell their families, their photos would be all over the media. It had disaster written all over it. No, no, no, no, quadruple fucking no, he concluded. No girls on tour.

★ ★ ★

Commodore Woo-Jin Park hurried down the stairs from his office to the yard below. The three KAMAZ 5460 trucks now parked in the reserved area of his naval base were each with full trailers. A dark red jeep was stationary next to them and two plain-clothes men emerged from the car, an imitation of the real thing, produced by the Sungri Motor Plant in Tokchon.

"Commodore Park," began the taller of the two men. "I am Gok Han-Jik and this is Sunwoo Chung."

Commodore Park shook Gok's hand and acknowledged Sunwoo who was standing a little further away.

"I am a lieutenant commander in our glorious navy,

Commodore Park, I report directly to Vice Admiral Goh. I am out of uniform today to attract less attention. Here are my papers."

Woo-Jin Park accepted Gok's papers, at the same time thinking that in a naval base being out of uniform was more likely to attract attention than being in it. After inspecting his papers and gesturing to have a look at the speechless Sunwoo's, Commodore Park was satisfied that they were who they said. Gok then handed Park further paperwork which turned out to be from Vice Admiral Goh explaining the contents of the trailers on the Russian built long haul trucks and Park's role in supervising and managing their installation. Park knew he had to get a move on as Goh wanted to have the submarine fully prepared, sea-worthy and ready for action in less than two weeks. It was a tall order but Haeju had the manpower and Park had the dedication. As he was walking with his two uninvited guests towards the berthed Borei he was glad Vice Admiral Goh had trusted him with the knowledge of what the trucks were carrying. He was also glad that the still mute Sunwoo was apparently the man who knew what to do with the odd pieces of angular metal shapes that took up virtually all of one truck's available space, because he sure didn't.

Sunwoo didn't stay mute forever. By twilight he was barking orders at several of the Haeju yard's painters and a different set of orders at their welders. He was a short man, 5ft 5in tall, rotund like a fat rodent with wisps of fading hair clinging to his head. He definitely wasn't going to be on the cover of GQ in any of its guises. This didn't bother Sunwoo anymore. He was in his late forties, never married, no children. He had an unhealthy interest in soft child pornography but never acted on his most base desires. When the sexual urge overcame him a quick call or visit to Pyongyang's red light district did the trick. Compensating for his personal weakness and foibles, or so he told himself, was that he was a fine scientist. Not any run of the mill scientist but an engineering based scientist who was second in command of the KPN's scientific division. His speciality was submarines and his jewel in the crown was disguising their presence. Stealth technology, the west called it; he was more used to the term low observable (LO) technology. His task now was to be as LO as you could go. Vice Admiral Goh wanted this submarine to be invisible.

Sunwoo's undergraduate studies had been at the People's Friendship University of Russia, in Moscow. There he learned all of the basics of mechanical, electrical and aeronautical engineering, eventually earning a Bachelor's degree, First Class, in Automation and Control of Technical Systems. He followed this up with a post graduate Doctorate in Aeronautics and Astronautics at MIT in Massachusetts, USA. Oh, how easy it was to get into America, a forged South Korean passport, letters of recommendation and he was in. Sunwoo loved his studies, all the information he gleaned from the Materials Science and Engineering optional course was sure coming in to play now. He hated the American people. They were loud, they were superficial, all *American Idol* and *X-Factor* reality shows, celebrity watchers. *I mean*, he thought, *does anybody really care what Kim Kardashian wore last night or that Justin Bieber changed his hairstyle yet again?* Nearly everyone he came across in Boston looked down on him, both literally and metaphorically, but his revenge on these slights was now underway.

The Haeju painters were coating a section of the metal plates with radar-absorbing materials. This worked by absorbing the radiated energy from a ground based or air based radar station; the heat is trapped in the material and not reflected back to the prying radar station. This form of stealth is not 100% efficient and in a submarine is only useful when it is surfaced. It would, nevertheless, certainly delay significantly enemy tracking of its location. A submarine's degree of surface invisibility can also be enhanced by the shape of the craft needing camouflage. The Borei submarine they were working on was the archetypical submarine shape, mainly curves and bends. The most efficient way to reflect radar waves is to use orthogonal metal plates. The idea was to make a corner deflector comprising two or three plates, then experimenting with different angles such as in the American F-117 aircraft. Under Sunwoo's instruction a series of these dihedral and trihedral plates were being assembled to be welded on to the submarine at the critical points and at a specific angle. Sunwoo's metal construction was as aerodynamic (maybe aquadynamic was more appropriate) as practicable but the sub would lose a couple of knots of surface speed once they were attached.

Much of the time, though, submarines are submerged, not surfaced, especially when they are in attack mode. This was not lost on Sunwoo. Enemy detection of a submerged submarine would be primarily through the activation of passive sonar arrays. It may seem like an afterthought but extensive rubber mountings on the inside and outside of the vessel's frame had produced good test results in dampening the acoustics over and above what was already in place. The whole process seemed a bit Home Depot. It would have been ideal if our Russian friends had loaned us one of their new 5G stealth submarines, thought Sunwoo. These subs were being built from scratch using advanced special materials for the hull and building in deflector mechanisms and acoustic dampeners. Beggars can't be choosers, rationalised Sunwoo. In any event by the time he was finished applying his knowledge, this particular submarine was going to be seriously difficult to detect by friend or foe.

★ ★ ★

"C'mon Henry," pressed Carolyn Reynolds. "We really want to go. What about my fluency in Korean and Dannielle's Russian? We were made for this and, in case you've forgotten, we were the ones who spotted the damned Borei!" Carolyn was visibly heated. She was standing, leaning on the back of a chair in Henry's office, next to the seated Dannielle. "What did O'Neill say Henry?" demanded Carolyn.

"You don't want to know what he said, I assure you, but it boiled down to no, a big no," replied Henry.

"What did he say Henry?" added Dannielle, seated quietly and giving the big Maasai the look that said you know you're going to tell me eventually so you may as well blab now.

"Alright, he said no girls on tour," blurted out and instantly regretted by the section chief.

"What!" exclaimed Carolyn. "That fucking sexist jarhead." She blamed her dad for the language but at this moment it was firmly aimed at Commander Mark O'Neill.

"I think you'll find, Cally, that fucking jarhead is a derogatory nickname for a marine not a Navy SEAL," corrected Dannielle, pleased that she had prompted Henry Michieta to spill.

"So what's a SEAL's nickname pray tell?" asked Carolyn in an unexpectedly calm tone.

"I think frogmen or green faces was the norm in their early days," offered up Henry.

"OK," said Carolyn. "Fucking Kermit features has no right to say no, let alone a big no with sexist remarks attached." Officer Reynolds was back on the attack.

"Dial it back Carolyn. He does have the right," countered Henry softly. "He's in charge of this mission and he gets to pick his team. You may not like it and you may need to lump it but there it is. You both did a great job spotting the Borei, bringing it to my attention and then briefing Associate Director Adams and colleagues on it. Be satisfied with that."

The stern look on Carolyn Reynolds' face indicated that she was not satisfied. "Were there any non-SEAL combatants with Team 6 when they killed bin Laden?" asked Carolyn calmly enough.

"No," replied Henry firmly.

"What about that woman CIA officer who spent half her career tracking down the son of a bitch?" responded Carolyn.

"She wasn't on the Geronimo mission, Cally," interjected Dannielle. "As far as I know, she was close, following proceedings from their base in Afghanistan."

"Good," stated Carolyn. "Henry, please tell Kermit that we'd like to be close, so that we can follow proceedings, maybe use our language skills, maybe keep the Neanderthal amphibian and his froglets out of trouble, maybe be fucking involved."

Henry Michieta knew that it was in his best interests for a life of peace and quiet that he send Commander O'Neill another email.

★ ★ ★

Mark O'Neill had more or less settled on his team. In addition to Billy Smith, he had selected three others from Team 5. One underwater demolition expert, a definite veteran of thirty-six years old, Joe Franks. One lead driver/navigator, Tommy Fairclough, and one whose expertise was in maritime engineering, Barry Minchkin. As well as being lead on this mission, O'Neill was the leader of Team 5. SEAL Team 7 was headed by Lieutenant Evan Harris. In consultation with Harris, O'Neill had selected the three remaining members from Team 7, making nine in total. All SEAL team members were trained to a high level in the skills that could be needed on any clandestine mission they were asked to undertake. Team 7 had two very interesting and appropriate characters for Operation Philidor Defense, David McCoy and Yang Dingbang or Ding as he was called.

McCoy was thirty years old, 6ft tall with short, wavy dark brown hair. He was a fitness freak and well known in the SEALs community as the best submarine pilot of his era. Much younger, he saw active submarine service in the Iraq war. Piloting the last of the Skate class mini subs he helped rescue nearly forty of his SEAL colleagues who had come under constant heavy fire from 300 embedded Iraqi soldiers with armoured vehicles near the Al Basrah oil platforms. The remainder of the SEALs squadron were relieved by 42 Commando of the British Royal Marines but McCoy's skill under fire undoubtedly saved countless American lives. He was awarded the Medal of Honor.

Yang Dingbang was a fourth generation American whose family had originally emigrated to New York from what was then Peking. Ding was around 5ft 9in, short black cropped hair and scored highly in nearly all his training courses. His forte was radar, having been clearly the best operator in his year. His other speciality was mixed martial arts and had he not made it as a SEAL his plan B was to enter the Ultimate Fighting Championship, middle weight class. Ding was a committed and loyal American and he thanked his country for the protection and standard of living that it had given his family, present and past.

Commander O'Neill was satisfied with his team. He personally knew more than half of them and in Evan Harris he had a second in command whom he had the highest respect for. Team selected, now it was time for the mission brief. Gathered in meeting room two of the SEALs HQ, Mark O'Neill outlined the mission. There was initially a certain degree of bravado among the team. These were predominantly young men. Their civilian contemporaries spent much of their time chasing girls, drinking beer and watching football. These SEALs thought it great that they were going to steal a North Korean-based Russian submarine. Franks and McCoy, being a bit older and wiser, dampened down the heist bombast.

"Where exactly is this sub, Commander?" asked Joe Franks.

"It's Mark, no ranks needed here Joe," started O'Neill, keen to keep the meeting relaxed, if a little less boisterous. "Our information is that it's a Borei class Russian nuclear submarine, berthed at the Haeju naval base on the west coast of North Korea, about 100km south of Pyongyang."

"What's the terrain like there and how is it protected?" asked McCoy.

"The terrain is mainly plains, with a couple of mountains, nothing dramatic," said O'Neill. "We've decided to come in from the sea, as there is less likelihood of meeting a sizeable military presence."

"Surely the submarine itself will be heavily protected?" McCoy responded.

"It will be protected for sure," agreed Evan Harris. "From our information though the North Koreans have no idea that we know the sub is there. Normally, any of their larger submarines would be berthed, serviced or repaired on the east coast at one of the more advanced bases like Wonsan. The satellite images provided by the NGA officers who initially spotted the Borei, indicate some type of covering over the sub, like a floating aircraft hangar. As far as the North Koreans are concerned, we haven't a clue."

"As such, we are assuming that the military security around or even on the sub is light," continued O'Neill. "For this same reason we are not deploying drones. You've been told why we are not going to destroy the sub and we also do not want to risk alerting the North Koreans by having a drone hum overhead taking photographs. The NGA and CIA are going to direct their satellite over for one more image before we head out, to give us the most up to date interpretation of the sub's status."

"Commander O'Neill," said Barry Minchkin deciding not to be informal. "How are we getting there and when are we going?"

"We're heading out in two days' time, so anything personal you need to do or anything required for your successful participation in this mission, now's the time to do it," responded O'Neill. "As to how we're getting there, we are privileged to be the first operational SEALs team to piggy-back a ride on the USS Zumwalt, our flagship stealth destroyer," announced O'Neill. Smiles all round at that piece of information.

The commander continued. "North Korea operates a 50km exclusion zone around its perimeter so the Zumwalt will drop us off as near to that in the Gulf of West Korea without risk of detection. The two teams will then take to the augmented rubber raiding crafts we know and love."

Yang Dingbang was a thoughtful soul and to this point he had taken everything in but said little. "Commander O'Neill," he piped up, deciding not to call him Mark as they didn't really know each other and because he regarded Evan Harris as his team leader.

"Yes, Ding," said O'Neill.

"Do we know where we are delivering the submarine, Sir?"

"No," replied O'Neill. "We do not know and we will not be told until we have successfully secured our target and have exited the exclusion zone."

"On that point…" responded Ding. "It's a Russian sub in a North Korean naval base. There is bound to be information regarding the sub's security in Korean and, I'd be almost certain, the operating system for the radar will be in Russian."

Unfortunately, thought Mark O'Neill, as his body tensed and his throat dried up, he knew where this was going.

"None of us speak or read either language. We'll be a bunch

of dead in the water fuckbrains if we're sitting in the sub, wondering how to get it started and/or how to drive it," continued Ding. "What's the scoop, Sir?"

"It's funny you should bring that up, Ding."

★ ★ ★

Carolyn Reynolds liked her apartment in Key Towers, Alexandria, not far from Springfield. It was modern with all the gizmos a young woman could want. She was on the fifth floor, had decent views from her bedroom and living room and the lift always worked. Her two bedroomed flat was decorated in mainly light colours, creams and pastels for the most part and her Queen sized bed was big and fluffy. When she was little her dad called her Princess, surely like a lot of dads to their baby daughters, but it felt special to her. As a princess she thought she needed a princess bed so from then on her bed was the most important piece of furniture. She still recalled vividly her mum or dad sitting on the chair reading her bedtime stories. Her mum preferred to read Dr Suess books to her, which were great, her favourite being *Horton Hears a Who!* Her dad preferred to read fables and tales of adventure like *Sinbad, Ali Baba,* and more modern stuff along those lines. Maybe it was her dad's entertaining delivery of the derring-do books that led her to the CIA, then the NGA. She loved her work at the NGA and felt lucky to have a friend and colleague like Dannielle, and a boss like Henry Michieta, even though the big Maasai preferred Danni, she smiled to herself. Anyway, tonight she was meeting up with Danni in downtown Alexandria. They were going to The Lounge Restaurant for some good food and drink. Well, a decent burger and a Bud for starters.

Dannielle lived in Springfield itself. It was only about ten miles away, so under twenty minutes for her to drive to Cally's.

She was looking forward to having a night out with her friend. Neither of them had boyfriends, their jobs at the NGA took up nearly all their awake time, and they had been so absorbed by the whole Borei story that they hadn't had any free time for what seemed like weeks.

Dannielle's original surname was Kulikova. She was born in a Moscow suburb to a doctor dad and a housewife mum. Her father had felt that the Putin regime was becoming unfriendly and more claustrophobic for even middleclass families. He opted to revitalise the family's life in the USA. Dannielle had a younger brother, Arkady, and they all packed up and went to New York. Dad got a job in the New York Presbyterian Hospital, Mum looked after everybody and in late 1999 Dannielle and Arkady enrolled in the Abraham Lincoln High School. That was about fourteen or fifteen years ago, and her life had been at full pelt ever since. The family name was changed to Eagles, she went to university, became a US citizen, then the CIA, and now the NGA. Given her Russian origins, the CIA checks were particularly extensive but no worries, her entire family were clean and un-indoctrinated. Like Carolyn, she loved her job at the NGA and she had become closer to her friend the longer they worked together.

"Hi Cally," said Dannielle as she strode into The Lounge looking very tall with her killer heels on.

"Hi Dannielle," Carolyn replied. "I've been here less than five minutes and I'm starving so I've ordered a Bud Light and a double cheeseburger. Will I order you something?" she asked, clearly pleased to see her friend.

"I'll have a Bud Light too, and some ribs, medium-rare," Dannielle said to the waitress as she sat down opposite Carolyn.

"I don't know how you stay so slim, Cally, given that your eating habits are those of a pig," jested Dannielle.

"It's the Celtic genes, Ruski," Carolyn spiked back. "Or maybe the two hours in the gym or out running I do every morning or the fact that big meals are few and far between in our jobs. Anyway, you're no heffalump yourself and you're more or less having the same as me!"

"Must be the Russian training camps," said Dannielle. "I was just checking the mood you were in. Heard anything from Henry?"

"No," said Carolyn slightly less bubbly. "At the last count Kermit still said no. Henry sent him another email but the SEAL knucklehead was adamant. No girls on tour. Jeez how that winds me up."

"Never mind Cally, tuck into your burger and fries and let the comfort food do its work!"

They clinked their Bud glasses and Dannielle was now also tucking in. Their conversation was continuous, their laughter loud and the music lively. The two attractive women were hit on by a couple of the locals and it was difficult to judge which of them had the better fixed stare which said 'on your bike'.

It was 10.20pm now, not late for two twenty-five year old civilians, but getting on for NGA officers who likely had a full day ahead. As Dannielle was sorting out her black leather clutch bag she noticed her smartphone was vibrating and flashing away.

"Dannielle, is that you? Is Reynolds with you?" It was Henry Michieta.

"Yes, it's me and yes she is," said Dannielle.

"I've been ringing for ages. Where the hell are you? It sounds like a karaoke club on full blast, I can barely hear you," moaned Henry.

"I'll step out for a second," Dannielle indicated to Carolyn that she was just going outside of the restaurant to take the call. Carolyn nodded.

"OK Henry, is that better, what's up?"

"Do you want the good news or the bad news?" asked Henry, who often, mistakenly, thought he was funny.

"Always the bad news first," replied Dannielle.

"Well the bad news is that you and Reynolds are not going to North Korea."

"That's not news, Henry," shouted Dannielle into her phone. "We knew that already. You'd better have some bloody decent good news after that."

"The good news is you're both on for Operation Philidor Defence. Commander O'Neill wants you based in the South, where it's safe, but close enough to hear what's going on and to be of assistance on any language issues or last minute information from satellite sweeps." Henry was feeling like the bearer of good tidings. "You and Reynolds are booked on a flight to Seoul, where you will be met by the local CIA senior officer and he will help you set up a listening post. Your flight leaves in thirty-six hours, so sober up, get some sleep and be in my office at 7.30 tomorrow morning for the rest of the briefing."

"Thanks Henry, we'll see you in the morning." Dannielle hung up, strictly speaking finger slid across the smartphone, and walked back into The Lounge.

Carolyn was waiting for her, munching on a few cold fries and draining the last dregs of her Bud Light. Dannielle sat down.

"Now Cally, do you want the good news or the bad news?"

* * *

Commodore Woo-Jin Park, Lieutenant Commander Gok Han-Jik and Sunwoo Chung were standing on the longest dock of the Haeju naval base. They were admiring their work. Actually, they were admiring the work of the painters, welders and engineers of the base and Sunwoo Chung's metier. The Borei submarine looked totally different now compared to when it arrived ten days ago. The corner deflector metal plates were in position fore and aft and Sunwoo's special recipe radar deflection paint had actually changed the colour of the submarine to an even darker grey. Along with advanced rubber mountings, designed by Sunwoo, to reduce hydroacoustics and thus, any sonar ability to detect the sub's underwater location, these measures were all that Sunwoo could do. Commodore Park was delighted that this camouflage work had been completed three days ahead of Vice Admiral Goh's deadline. The Vice Admiral, himself, was delighted too and informed Park that the hundred or so submariners who would make up the Borei's crew would arrive at the Haeju base in a few days. Woo-Jin Park didn't really know what was to happen after that, but Gok Han-Jik did.

Both Park and Sunwoo knew that the lieutenant commander reported directly to Goh, what they didn't know was that he was also Kim Jong-un's cousin. The supreme leader liked to keep things in the family especially when it came to military matters. It was Gok Han-Jik who had persuaded his younger cousin that trading some of the DPRK's haul of gold reserves for a Russian nuclear sub was a good idea. The Russians didn't really need the gold, their oil wealth was staggering with light crude at over $100 per barrel. However, geopolitically, they wanted to stay friendly with Kim Jong-un. Even considering the huge cost of over $1 billion for each sub, that represented but a few weeks of oil sales for the Russian government. Russia was to receive quite a few more bars of gold in payment and their military strength was not really affected. A slam dunk trade if ever there was one. Or 'hy ho' as they'd say down at the CSKA multisport arena in Moscow.

Gok turned to Park and asked how long, once the crew arrived, before the submarine would be ready to put out to sea?

"About twenty-four hours," he replied, "maybe slightly less. Once we get the food and medical supplies on board, any other last minute equipment and brief the crew on its mission, then we're good to go."

Gok was content. He would contact his cousin that night. While he did not know the precise intentions of Kim Jong-un regarding the submarine he did know that Kim wanted the vessel to leave the 50km exclusion zone and be in a position to fire on the DPRK's enemies. Enemies was quite a broad set when juxtaposed with the DPRK. Gok reckoned that it would not be the South. Despite all of his sabre rattling, and even if the United States did not retaliate on South Korea's behalf, their hated southern neighbours were a bit close for comfort when it came to nuclear contamination. So, either Japan or the USA were the likely targets concluded Gok. Sunwoo Chung knew which of the two he'd vote for.

***

Several contemporaneous travel events began that US morning of 19th March 2014. The stealth destroyer *USS Zumwalt* set sail from San Diego, destined for the Gulf of West Korea. If it got a shifty on it would take about six days before it could unload its only cargo, Mark O'Neill's hand-picked SEAL team. Officers Reynolds and Eagles of the NGA were on Korean Air flight KE94 from Washington Dulles to Seoul Incheon International. They would take just over fourteen hours to get to their destination. Around 110 submariners, officers, medics and the rest left several KPN bases on the east coast of North Korea, mainly Wonsan and Rason, preparing to head by land to Haeju. As the crow flies it was only 150km. The terrain to be traversed, the secrecy and the logistics of finding, informing and re-assigning all the selected crew members meant that the full complement of KPN submariners intended for Haeju would not arrive at the naval yard until the afternoon of 24th March.

The *USS Zumwalt* had made good progress on its journey. Three days had passed since leaving San Diego. The South Atlantic Ocean had not thrown up any severe weather issues and the forecast for the Indian Ocean, which they would be approaching soon, was fair. If the weather luck continued and if there were no change to orders the *Zumwalt* would reach its target drop off zone in just under three days' time.

The *USS Zumwalt*, named after Admiral Elmo Zumwalt, was one fine piece of engineering. Nearly every major defence contractor in the United States was involved in its construction, with Northrop Grumman and General Dynamics, at their Bath Iron Works, being the lead contractors for the hull, mechanical and nautical designs. All in, the cost of the *Zumwalt* exceeded $7 billion. Even Carlos Slim would need to think twice about having one. Total crew on board, excluding the SEALs, was in the region of 140. The ship was armed to the teeth with a total of eighty launch cells, including Sea Sparrow and Tomahawk missiles. On board were one MH-60R helicopter and three MQ-8 Fire Scout VT-UAVs. These Northrop Grumman Fire Scouts were unmanned and primarily intended for reconnaissance and precision targeting support for ground, air and sea attack forces.

Commander O'Neill sincerely hoped that none of the aircraft or indeed missiles on board would come into play on this mission. If they did then it meant that the greatest naval heist in maritime history would be a dud, a damp squib, a fucking huge embarrassment. Worse than that, the *USS Zumwalt* was the pride and joy of the navy and even with the stealth technology, attack and defence armoury on board, one SBLM direct hit from a Bulava missile launched from the target Borei submarine would disintegrate the *Zumwalt* and probably kill the entire crew. There was a lot at stake. O'Neill was mulling this over as he joined Rear Admiral Lower Half, Eugene Kaplinski, on the bridge. Given the nomenclature of the ship, O'Neill thought, in a moment of self-amusement, that the destroyer's pilot definitely had a name of equal worth.

"Commander O'Neill," said Kaplinski in a genuine and welcoming tone. "How are your men, they seem to be relaxed enough?"

"They are well, Sir, mostly preparing for the task ahead, though one or two are becoming slightly anxious. They want to get going and get it done," replied O'Neill.

Both officers knew that only one of them had been briefed on the details of Operation Philidor Defence. Rear Admiral Kaplinski did not mind. He was delighted to be selected as the ship's commanding officer for its first operational foray, even if it was as the world's most expensive ferry.

"We should be off the Gulf of West Korea in under three days, Commander, so your team doesn't have too much longer to be kicking their heels," said Kaplinski reassuringly.

Below deck, the evidence seemed to support O'Neill's assessment of his team. Smith, Franks, Minchkin and Harris whiled away the hours reading, playing various card games or writing letters to loved ones back home. Use of electronic devices had been banned until the mission was complete so no phone apps or tablet based games were allowed. Billy Smith spent a lot of his time assembling, re-assembling, cleaning and checking his M14 rifle. It wasn't the newest available to the SEALs but it was the one he never missed with. While he knew that this was a mission on which his primary skill was not likely to be deployed, you never know, and in truth he wouldn't mind taking out a few gooks. Billy Smith was a good man, but he was old school, unreconstructed, non-PC.

Yang Dingbang was also checking over his weapons. His standard issue M4A1 Carbine was fine he felt, and he had a SIG Sauer P228 handgun as back-up. Most of his team mates carried a MK23 USSOCOM pistol as back-up but he preferred the feel of the SIG Sauer. Ding's equivalent to Billy Smith's affection for his sniper rifle, if such equivalent affection existed, was his knife. He packed an Ontario MK III with a rubberised indented grip and a six inch blackened blade. Ding was not really expecting to be up close and personal with any North Koreans but he was anticipating that the Borei sub was not going to be unmanned and a gun battle would be a right pig's ear of a mess.

O'Neill and Harris had already ensured that their and their team's weaponry was both adequate and efficient for the job. From handguns, rifles, knives and grenades this team was about as armed as the *Zumwalt*. After his chat with Rear Admiral Kaplinski, O'Neill headed below deck to seek out Evan Harris. The Commander was satisfied that his team were mentally and physically prepared, well-armed and ready. He needed to talk to his number two, however, about logistics and getting from the *Zumwalt* to the Borei.

It had been decided early enough in the mission's planning stage that entering Haeju naval yard by land was a non-starter. This was the correct decision thought O'Neill, too many opportunities to be spotted if they parachuted in, and too many Korean military on the ground. An approach from the sea was the only feasible option. The problem there was the DPRK's 50km exclusion zone. For sure, the *USS Zumwalt* could not gaily sail into that, it would need to be at least 100km off the coastline to avoid arousing any interest from the North Koreans. The SEALs team's normal nocturnal approach craft was the F470 Combat Rubber Raiding Craft. Realistically, two of these could carry the nine man team but conditions that far out and the limited range of this small, weaponless dinghy was a major obstacle. O'Neill and Harris had anticipated this before leaving San Diego but the approach plan needed more fleshing out.

"So, Evan," began O'Neill. "What do ya think?"

"I think it's a bloody good job we hoisted that Mark V on board before we embarked," replied Harris. The Mark V Special Operations Craft was the size of a patrol boat but could carry up to sixteen sailors. It was armed with heavy machine guns and grenade launchers and had a range of 500 miles. Just as important for this mission was that its angular design and low silhouette reduced its radar signature making it harder to detect and locate.

"It is, Evan, and at least we've got the new improved version," added O'Neill. "The original MAKO could generate 20 g-force while ploughing through the waves. We'd need A&E even before we got to Haeju."

"We still have a problem though," Harris pointed out. "The MAKO makes a noise and though it's kind of mini-stealth it's not invisible. We can't get close to the Borei in that, in fact, we can't cross the exclusion zone perimeter in it."

Mark O'Neill nodded.

"We're going to have to use the dinghies," said Harris, using the popular term for the F470s.

"Most of it works," commented O'Neill. "The two we have on the ship can easily carry the nine of us. They're compact when stowed, easily inflated in under two minutes and can handle high seas. It doesn't have any weapons but we'll all be armed anyway so that's OK. Its maximum payload is 1,250kg, so four/five in each, indeed maybe even all nine of us in one works," elaborated the Commander. "The problem is the speed of the dinghy and the distance we need to travel. If the *Zumwalt* drops us 100km off the west coast then we may be able to go another 40 km or so closer in the MAKO. The *Zumwalt* has the lockout chamber needed to put us silently in the sea. That still leaves us 60km offshore, or about 37 miles. If the sea's calm enough and with our calculated payload, the F470s can manage a surface speed of around 18 knots or 21 mph. It'll need to be at night time, so possibly somewhat less."

"That means we'd be in those little rubbery fuckers for about two hours," highlighted Evan Harris, proud of his sharp calculation, but concerned for his 5ft 11in, 85kg frame.

"It does indeed," said O'Neill having mentally checked the arithmetic, "but we don't have any other choice, buddy."

★ ★ ★

Commodore Woo-Jin Park and Commander Kun-Woo Moon of the Korean People's Navy had different logistics on their minds. The Commodore knew that around 110 of the KPN's finest were going to descend on Haeju in a couple of days. The naval base did have accommodation quarters but only to a decent maximum of around forty. Commodore Park had already commissioned the building of temporary accommodation but as these had to be assembled in a hurry they were of the pre-fabricated Portakabin variety. This would be acceptable for one or two nights for the bulk of enlisted men, but the officers would need to be housed in Haeju City. In total, this would be around thirty personnel except for Commander Moon whom Park had invited to stay at his house. Suitably spread across the Haeju hotel and local guest houses this number of naval officers would not arouse any special interest among the local population. They were so used to naval comings and goings in the city that not an eyebrow would be raised. In North Korean society anyway, eyebrow raising and ear-pricking were not recommended, if you valued your freedom, limited as it was.

Commander Kun-Woo Moon was based in Rason, a major naval operating and training centre on the East Coast. He was around thirty-eight years old, 5ft 10in and well known to Vice Admiral Goh. He was ambitious and he was also competent and had no black marks on his record. Moon had served aboard several of the KPN's submarine fleet including the Sang-O class and the midget Yono class. He was Goh's selection to oversee the logistics of crew assembly for the Borei submarine. This was no simple task. The crew had been carefully selected by the Vice Admiral and Lieutenant Commander Gok Han-Jik. Moon had not been party to the details of the mission at hand, Goh and Gok gave very little away. However, pure deduction from the sheer numbers and some of the specialities requested of the crew led Moon to believe that an important submarine mission was underway. Further, deduced Moon, the crew he had been asked to assemble and transport to Haeju was way in excess of that needed for the KPN's flagship Sang-O II class sub. Something was afoot. He didn't ask questions of Goh and Gok, but he would find out, he told himself.

His immediate orders, however, were to get the requested submariners to Haeju. He had located the whereabouts of all of his targets and their collection and transportation were both in hand. Commodore Park of the Haeju Naval Yard had been most helpful regarding accommodation, especially his kind offer to house him in the Commodore's private quarters. Yes, thought Moon, I'll have everybody there by my 24th March deadline. Then I'll find out what all the fuss is about.

★ ★ ★

NGA Officers Reynolds and Eagles had settled in quickly to their embedded positions at the CIA's premises in downtown Seoul.

This was one buzzing city with a population of over 11 million or 26 million if you include the entire metropolitan area. They were located in the Gangnam district, made globally famous by the singer Psy's 'Gangnam Style', a year or so back. Stylish it was, with its cool shops, heaving clubs, healthy food restaurants and expensive schools. If they had been normal single twenty-five year old women they'd be having a whale of a time. They weren't. They were NGA officers on a top secret mission and guests of the local CIA Chief, or Korean Liaison Officer to give Jim Bradbury his official title. The external façade of the offices fitted in perfectly with the district, all big windows, mood lighting, vibrant décor. Nominally, a tailored travel agent for the privileged, PAU Travel it was called, Personal And Unique. They were located not far from Gangnam station, did a reasonably healthy business in travel arrangements for the locals and generally did not attract unwanted visitors.

Jim Bradbury had been the KLO for over three years. He was a career CIA officer, spoke Korean fluently and so far had no reason to use his specialist CIA combat training or wet work skills. He had been instructed by no less than Fred Goss, the Director of Central Intelligence, to give Reynolds and Eagles every assistance. Bradbury did not know the details of why the NGA ladies were there but they were set up in a secure room near the back of the PAU shop, and had a fully kitted out listening post and high level computer systems in with them. He was smart enough to know they'd be listening to North Korean electronically transmitted traffic but it had to be more than that as that task was down to his team already in situ.

Jim Bradbury was pleasant enough. Nearly 6ft tall, forty years old, thinning blond hair with an unfortunate widow's peak. He hailed from Phoenix, Arizona and had not lost much of the local drawl.

"Good morning," he greeted politely, if not warmly, Reynolds and Eagles.

"Hi Jim," they responded. They'd acclimatised to the somewhat humid weather and had the night before eaten Korean at a swish restaurant close to the Bongea Temple. Eagles was quite impressed by Reynolds' ability to order in Korean, though some rustiness must have set in, as they got cold peas, not warm cauliflower, with their dinner. After the pleasantries, Eagles and Reynolds got hunkered down in their room. It may have looked like the officers had a big slice of the National Security Agency's $40 million a year electricity bill solely for eavesdropping, but in truth, they had a lot less. The room was set up to intercept emails, phone calls, internet messaging, and any relevant communication along the electromagnetic spectrum. In addition, the NGA officers had been given specially augmented laptops that could download and manipulate satellite images from the CIA's KH-12 satellite in the sky.

The KH-12's predecessor, the KH-11, was the first reconnaissance satellite which had a resolution of 800 x 800 pixels. It was a K-11 image, so clear, that it allowed ultimate precision bombing of the Zhawar Kili compound in Afghanistan. This camp hosted Taliban and al-Qaeda personnel. The picture was impressively detailed. It allowed Richard Beck, a geologist at the University of Connecticut, to inform the US Department of Defense that he could identify the rocks in the background of a bin Laden propaganda tape in 2001. The images over North Korea being studied by Reynolds and Eagles were even clearer. The satellite images, although real time, were not continuous. The K-11 and K-12 satellites are in sun synchronous orbits, on two planes. Shadows help define ground features so western plane satellites photograph the ground in the morning hours and eastern planes observe the ground in afternoon hours. The images of North Korea presently being studied by Eagles and Reynolds were from the morning of 22nd March. They knew that Commander O'Neill and his team on *USS Zumwalt* were still a couple of days away from the Gulf of West Korea, but the point of no return for Operation Philidor Defence was looming and they needed to be on their mettle.

"What do you think, Danni?" asked Carolyn studying the area around the KPN's east coast fleet near Wonsan.

Dannielle Eagles looked closer and then looked again. "There seems to be more largish vehicles in this image than the one we looked at yesterday, especially around the naval complex, just here," pointed out Dannielle.

"Yeah, I see it," said Carolyn chewing on some Double Red gum that she'd picked up from a local supermarket. "Do you think they're crewing up for the Borei? We know they couldn't possibly man it solely with the seamen on the west coast, not enough of them with the required skill set."

"Could be," said Dannielle. "The images shot around Haeju at the same time did not reveal much more activity than the previous day. There are three big trucks with trailers in the yard, but no significant increase in daily traffic. There's some construction going on, but that's it."

"The trucks are probably carrying the Bulava SLBMs, Danni, so we will need to let Kermit know that by the time he gets there the Borei will likely be fully weaponised."

Dannielle nodded and set about sending Commander O'Neill a high level encrypted message with that information.

"Do you know what bothers me, though, when I look at today's image of the Haeju base?" said Carolyn with a suitably quizzical look on her face.

"What?" asked Dannielle.

"These images are as sharp as a rapier's point. I mean

pixilation of 1,000 x 1,000 are the bee's knees, the dog's bollocks, and the—"

"I get the picture," interrupted Dannielle, keen to hear what was troubling her friend.

"Well, the outline of the Borei is less sharp now than when we first spotted it in Springfield, and it's less sharp than the first image we received when we set up here. We know it's there and we know it hasn't been eaten by Formosan termites…"

Carolyn looked up at Danni and, in unison, they blurted out: "Stealth!"

Just as the two NGA officers were preparing another encoded message for Mark O'Neill, there was a knock on the door of their operations room. Carolyn's gaze was focused on her screen. Dannielle opened the door but the man standing in the doorway looked right past her and fixed his grey-green eyes on Carolyn.

"Hi Princess," he said.

As she turned around Carolyn's quizzical look had in an instant transformed into a jaw dropping pose that could only be captured by the very best Manga cartoon artists. "Dad!" she eventually exclaimed. "What the hell are you doing here?"

"I'm a man with a plan, Cally," said JJ Darke.

3

MEET JOE FORD

Three weeks before arriving in Seoul, JJ had been seated in the waiting area with his A6 notepad and black rollerball pen. He was sketching a diagram. It was entitled 'The Non-Linearity of Bladder Fullness'. Along the horizontal axis there were three key points of time, zero, R and P. The vertical axis represented fullness of bladder in millilitres. In the guts of the graph there was a 45 degree straight line drawn from the axis which represented the hypothetical optimal path of bladder fullness. The second line was more parabolic after a linear start, and was labelled actual path of bladder fullness. At time zero JJ drinks 250ml of still water. At time R, radiotherapy is scheduled. JJ is ready for it. At point B, bladder is optimally full. At time P, roughly twenty minutes after time R, radiotherapy is well late and bladder is supra-optimally full and ready to burst. The shaded area between times R and P, where the actual path of bladder fullness deviates exponentially from the hypothetically optimal path, needs to be avoided. Today it has not been avoided. JJ hands his diagram to the manager of the radiotherapy department, tells him in a mumbling incomprehensible fashion, to shove his treatment for the day and then heads rapidly to the nearest toilet for a pee of some force and length.

It's absolute crap being diagnosed with prostate cancer, thought JJ, but there it was. Warren Buffett has it and Sir Michael Parkinson was diagnosed with it in July 2013, but these two members of the great and good fraternity were in their seventies and eighties. JJ was forty-three. *WTF!* kept going through his mind. He soon found out what a PSA score of 23 meant after visiting his G.P. It meant, literally, get your arse down to a specialist for a biopsy, then an MRI scan and get it seen to. So, off he went down to a private consultancy on the King's Road. The specialist, Mr Mark Wright, was meant to be a leading light on men's cancers and had invented some futuristic robotic cutting implement that meant you were less likely to die if they wheeled out your prostate. Leading light or not, getting snippy snippy up your butt, bleeding away from it, and then having to take antibiotics of such a size and strength that they'd kill a Clydesdale horse, is no fun. You needed the antibiotics just in case the biopsy procedure gave you blood poisoning. "If that happens," said Mr Wright, "then just call 999 and get an ambulance to take you to A&E immediately." Great, thought JJ, at that point still feeling somewhat sorry for himself. Not only was there a bunch of murderous evil cancer cells trying to kill him, there was a chance that the procedure for finding out exactly how murderous might fuck you up anyway.

The good news didn't end there. A PSA score can be whatever it wants to be, but it's only a marker. It tells you that probably something's up if it's over 2, but it doesn't tell you for sure and it doesn't tell you how far up the something's up may be. In JJ's case it was well up. His Gleason score was 8 to 9 in four cores of the prostate. That was bad. Assuming you had to have prostate cancer, you'd want your Gleason score to be under 4. Essentially, JJ's prostate was being devoured by cancer. Mr Wright said surgery, even by his state-of-the-art robot arm, was out. Although the prostate is about the size of a walnut, the surgeon specialist said to think of it as a small orange. If all the wee cancer bleeders were inside the orange peel then surgery may be the answer: cut it out and wave sayonara to the scunners. If the cancer had munched through the outer peel and was either sitting on top of it or had gone metastatic into other parts of your system then surgery was out. It was out because the procedure itself may accelerate the spread of the cancer.

After the biopsy, the MRI scan and then another scan called a Choline PET scan, where you had to drink some radioactive tracer stuff and not hug small children for twenty-four hours, the multi-disciplinary team (MDT) at the Royal Marsden Hospital on the Fulham Road concluded that JJ's cancer was 'locally advanced'. This meant that the cancer cells were sitting on top of the orange peel, getting ready for even more action. Dr Paul Van den Berk, the head of the MDT and now JJ's Consultant Oncologist, said that hormone treatment combined with radiotherapy was more or less the only option. The good doctor wasn't certain that a random, cheeky, cancer cell or three had gone to JJ's lymph nodes near the pelvis but they may have, so Dr Van den Berk said he was going to blast these nodes with radiotherapy too. He had helped develop a new, fast, painless radiotherapy procedure. The patient turned up for a few days, got zapped, left, kept calm and carried on.

"Not for you, Mr Darke," said the white South African who was a little bit older than JJ. "Your cancer is too advanced for that procedure. However, the Choline PET scan showed up where the hot spots of cancer were and it has not gone metastatic. We need to get a move on, to treat you, before it does."

JJ, never one for volunteering for anything medical that wasn't absolutely necessary, asked him how long he'd live if he did nothing. JJ had been reading up on prostate cancer and there were plenty of stories about men not knowing they had the cancer, or having it but dying from old age or a heart attack or something else.

"Four to five years," said Dr Van den Berk. There weren't any add-ons by the straight talking doctor. No 'maybe longer'. So there it was. JJ was down for three years of hormone treatment to kill off his testosterone and radiotherapy every day for two months, barring weekends and bank holidays. This approach to treating prostate cancer is the starve and burn option. The injection of hormones into your lower abdomen every three months is meant to starve the cancer cells and the radiotherapy is meant to burn them while they're starving. JJ was still in his emotional down phase about the whole issue but the mental picture of ugly black cancer cells, screaming in agony, writhing in torment, vaporising out of his system did make him feel that justice was being carried out on these criminal body invaders who had clearly entered without permission.

JJ decided not to tell Cyrus or anyone at MAM about his condition or treatment. Although Cyrus was probably old enough to handle it, he had lost his mum at a young age. He was getting on well at school and JJ didn't see any advantage in letting him worry that he might be an orphan soon. If all went royally pear-shaped then, ignoring normal actuarial probabilities of death, JJ still had four to five years, by which time Cyrus would be nearly twenty and set on his life path, whatever that would be. JJ did tell Gilian. He knew she would keep stum about it and that she would be alert for any material information lying around that might give away this secret. In the same way as you can have white lies and black lies, this was a white secret, not a black one. Keeping MAM out of the loop was a decision arrived at via a different thought process. There appeared to be no reason why JJ could not continue working. His routine normally involved his getting in around 7am and leaving at 4 or 5pm. As he took his work home with him at least as far as monitoring the markets and MAM's investments were concerned, nobody bothered when he left.

JJ had scheduled his radiotherapy appointments for 4.30pm every weekday. The process itself took about thirty minutes, with less than a quarter of that lying on the radiotherapy table, shirt up, pants down and flaccid willie out and about for all the world to see. He could walk from the Royal Marsden to his house in Markham Square in seven or eight minutes, so he'd still be in before 5.30pm. Cyrus wouldn't notice anything unusual and his work responsibilities would not be undermined.

By the time JJ had the presence of mind to deliver his non-linearity of bladder fullness diagram to the radiotherapy department's manager, his course of radiation treatment was about half way through. He had settled into the routine. In the radiotherapy department, which was a floor below the department of nuclear medicine – Jings, thought JJ, what the heck goes on there – the three linear accelerator machines more or less in constant use were named Carlyle, LA3 and Joe Ford. For the vast majority of his sessions JJ was scheduled for Joe Ford, named after a pioneering and much loved Consultant in radiotherapy at the Royal Marsden and St. George's Hospital. The treatment room itself was all Blake's 7 spacious, bright, with a big whirring, round, flying saucer thingy above the narrow table bed you lay on. The type of radiotherapy delivered by Joe Ford was called RapidArc. The whizz kid radiotherapists use computer imaging to dial in the angle of the beam, the dose rate, and the leaf speed, all intended to target the cancerous cells supremely accurately and leave alone the healthy tissue surrounding them. The program is specific for each patient and uses 3-D volume imaging to get it down to pin-point precision. The only potential flaw in this truly amazing procedure is that the efficacy of the laser hits also depends on the patient's bladder being nearly full (comfortably full in the hospital staff's lingo), and being in the same state of fullness every session and as it was at the imaging practice run undertaken a couple of weeks before treatment began.

JJ took all this precision seriously. Each day, exactly forty-five minutes before his scheduled treatment, he'd drink precisely the same amount of still water, ensuring he had emptied his bladder beforehand. The taxi from MAM's offices to the Royal Marsden was normally around fifteen minutes. JJ was always on time for his appointment. There were several young radiotherapists organising the patients for the various machines. They did a great job. Sometimes patients would emerge looking a bit wappit but JJ seemed to be lucky. He wasn't meant to feel a thing as he was being radiated and he didn't. At the beginning it was a bit embarrassing given the state of half undress he was in, but he got used to it. When he first went to the Joe Ford room, the elevator music playing was Phil Collins; god it was awful. He provided 'The Killers' and 'Queen' CDs to the radiotherapists and the eight minutes or so he was lying on the table were now at least musically credible.

The day of the diagram though had gone a bit awry. He had had a tough day at work, just managed to get a cab and was sitting in the waiting area, about five minutes before his 4.30pm due time. One of the radiographers, a fairly pleasant Welsh girl called Bronwyn, popped her head out of the wooden double doors leading to the treatment rooms and said, "Mr Darke, are you ready?" She did this every day she was on duty at that time. Of course he was bleedin' ready. He was born ready, drank ready and his entire daily schedule had been shaped to have him ready for this moment of radiation joy. On diagram day though, Joe Ford wasn't ready. About fifteen minutes had elapsed since Bronwyn had asked her question. JJ's willie was throbbing by now, his bladder was bulbous, and a pee was imminent. Of course, if he pee'd then the game was up, no RapidArc radiotherapy for him. He'd need to hang about for another forty-five minutes to an hour post pee and drink more water to allow his bladder to get to its equilibrium fullness state again. Even then, he couldn't be sure he would be seen. The treatment rooms were busier than Heathrow Terminal 5 on an August weekend. There would be holding, stacking, circling delays. Who's to say he wouldn't need to pee again! It was too much for him, the diagram needed to be drawn and the radiotherapy manager needed to be given it. JJ left that day without treatment. Luckily for him, the doctors thought it was OK and they'd just add a day to his schedule. Great.

The next day when he went to the Marsden, his diagram was the talk of the department. One of the radiotherapists, Richard, a tall olive skinned Liverpudlian, who always defended putting Luis Suarez in his Fantasy Football team, despite the wee Uruguayan's vampiric tendencies, asked if JJ could turn his graphical presentation into a mathematical formula. Apparently Richard was studying for an advanced radiotherapy qualification and his thesis was to be on the behaviour of the bladder over the period of a linear accelerator radiation course. JJ said sure, and wondered how he could inveigle Yves-Jacques into this task without giving the game away. JJ was also a bit sheepish because he was all girded up for a verbal battle with the staff about his diagram and somewhat twee moaning given the time pressure they were under. Instead, they all thought it was either funny or informative. These guys were high quality and doing a real job. JJ behaved himself after that and fully appreciated that these young radiographers were doing the best for him that they could.

While all this radiation and white secrecy was going on, JJ had tried to be as committed to his son and his work responsibilities as best he could. He sincerely believed that Cyrus had not noticed the difference in either their relationship or their pastimes. That was good. He also seemed not to have tweaked the curiosity of any of his work colleagues which in such a den of gossip, innuendo and blatant untruths, was quite some feat. JJ had also been a bit lucky on the markets front, as they were on the quiet side and certainly displayed no repetition as yet of the Greek chaos.

The one area where a few rumblings and mumblings had occurred was in his initial meeting with Neil Robson, Financial Secretary to the UK Treasury. JJ had tried to put Neil off after replying to his email on that fateful Friday, but Neil was a northern lad and not easily put off. He was born in Middlesborough and was the MP for the Conservatives key constituency in that town. He had wide responsibilities in the British government, including financial stability, bank lending, the regulatory Financial Conduct Authority and the EU budget. His remit also included supporting the Chancellor of the Exchequer, Jeffrey Walker, on many issues including international finance. JJ always thought it amusing that not too long after President Barak Obama had called the coalition's first Chancellor 'Geoffrey' at a G8 meeting in Northern Ireland instead of his name which was 'George' the Prime Minister had dumped George for Jeffrey, albeit spelt differently.

JJ and Neil Robson had joined MI5 at the same time, more or less straight from University. While JJ had studied at Glasgow and Warwick, Neil had gone to Cambridge and then to the London School of Economics. Neil's educational path was more well-trodden as far as spies and spooks were concerned but even the security services had to have the odd provincial every now and then. Neil and JJ were virtually the same age. JJ was taller, more athletic and, in his arrogant moments, probably thought smarter as well. Neil had a devious, dark side that may have helped him accelerate through the ranks of MI5 a little bit quicker than JJ. They were both recruited as intelligence officers. JJ had been on only four field missions by the time he left MI5 but Neil had at least a dozen before he resigned. JJ and Neil were never the best of friends. JJ thought Neil was a bit sleekit, never apparently helping his colleagues and often rumoured to have stabbed a few of them in the back, metaphorically speaking. Neil liked politics, journalists, cricket, and any sleazy activity going. None of these were on JJ's radar so, outside work, there was little to talk about. JJ sensed there was a grudging mutual respect though. He assumed Neil was very proficient on his field missions. For a start, he came back from them, and he kept getting selected for more. Neil seemed to appreciate JJ's research and analysis, they kept him out of some tight spots. Still, they were like a couple of cage fighters who didn't relish being the one to engage first, for fear of letting their guard down. That was all history. Neil Robson was now in his dated but comfy surroundings in HM Treasury on Horse Guards Road and, JJ assumed, not out in the field topping random bad guys.

JJ didn't want to meet up with Neil. Partly because he couldn't be bothered, he knew they had little in common, and partly because his mind was full of radiation thoughts, hormone injections, survival and all that jazz. Neil had promised that the meeting would be very short, just intended to establish whether JJ was in a position or not to help the government, and then JJ could be on his merry way.

Robson was true to his word. They met for an early afternoon glass of wine at a wine bar just around the corner from his offices at the Treasury in Westminster. JJ could easily walk there and back to MAM's building in twenty minutes. Though the medical advice was not to drink alcohol while undergoing hormone treatment, apparently the occasional glass was OK. In any event, JJ took the view that a glass of red wine was meant to be good for the heart and that he may as well attempt to keep that organ going for as long as possible given the other health issues dominating his mind and body.

The meeting was indeed short, twenty minutes or so exclusive of the time it took to order, but it was seriously weird. Neil started by asking JJ if MAM had any investments in South Korea. JJ was unlikely to blurt out where any of MAM's investments were to anyone, let alone a slimy weasel like Robson. JJ replied that MAM had been known to invest in South Korean equities and sometimes traded the won on the foreign exchanges but that he wasn't sure if they had any right now. Of course, in truth, JJ knew exactly MAM's position in South Korean assets but he clearly wasn't letting on. This was a white lie, it clearly being for the greater good. Then the Financial Secretary to the Treasury asked if MAM traded gold on a regular basis. That was more of a general enquiry, thought JJ so no white lies necessary. He explained to Neil that MAM often traded in gold, in size, and that in Toby Naismith they had one of the best gold traders in London, if not the entire global financial community. That may have been bigging up Fathead a bit too much but JJ thought it might balance out the paucity of information he'd given Neil regarding MAM's investments. On receipt of the gold information Neil took a sip of his house Chianti Classico and gave a little nod of approval, or so JJ thought.

The meeting ended friendly enough; they shook hands and both went in the respective directions of their offices. Neil said he'd be in touch, JJ hoped he wouldn't but at that moment he had peeing on his mind so he didn't think twice about Neil's comment. In fact, he was so distracted he didn't even bother to ask Neil why the questions!

As JJ walked briskly towards his offices he felt something vibrate in his pocket. He knew it wasn't his willie, the first dose of Zoladex hormones had seen to that; it was his BlackBerry.

"Hey JJ, it's Toby," said a familiar voice.

"Hi Toby, I'm just on my way back from the Treasury. What's up?"

"Well, you know the FCA, the Financial Conduct Authority, one of those twin peaks regulators that try, on occasion, to prevent us earning a living, or at least a fast buck."

"Yes, Toby, I know of them. We haven't done anything to get in their bad books, have we?"

"I'm not sure. Compliance gave me a ring and said that one of the FCA's officers had been looking at a selection of hedge fund trades that were done on Friday, 13th December last year. Remember that?"

How could he forget thought JJ. A day that had gone so magnificently for MAM but had ended with an email that was a precursor to a life changing event. "Yes, I remember, Toby," said JJ, attempting to be nonchalant. "How come we've lit up their radar screen?"

"Compliance wouldn't say but the inference was that we had done a whole lot better that day than virtually any other London based macro fund and the FCA just wanted to check that it was all above board."

"Have they set a meeting time?" asked JJ.

"Yes, they want to come in on Thursday, around 11am, to see me as the head trader and you as the head of portfolio strategy," replied Toby.

"OK, that's three days away. I'll be back in ten minutes, we can have a brief chat, but then I need to head off. See you soon."

With that JJ ended the call, almost not waiting for Toby to say cheerio. Even in his radiated and hormoned body, JJ knew what was afoot. MAM had stolen a march on all the other hedge funds that day, partly because they had a researcher in Wellington, partly because that researcher had a brother-in-law in a Greek political party whose single audience information release was spot on and partly because the three MAM amigos' plan had worked like a Patek Philippe tourbillon. Some overzealous regulator eejit may want to try to make an insider trading case out of this, reasoned JJ but he was determined to ensure that that particular chunk of cow muck was going nowhere near MAM.

JJ's main attribute as a fund manager was his commitment to deep research and analysis. If you read it in *The Financial Times*, then it's too late. JJ distinguished between economic commentators and economists. The former could write well, maybe even knew superficially what they were writing about, could meet deadlines and appear to the man in the street as quite knowledgeable. Proper economists, however, could take on issues and dig deep, eke out robust theoretical underpinnings, undertake detailed analysis and then solid statistical and/or econometric testing. JJ had been mulling over this opinion as he lay on the radiotherapy table that day. While 'Human' and 'Spaceman' were playing on Joe Ford's music system he decided he wasn't totally satisfied. He had absolutely no doubt that by the slide rule of traditional medicine, he was getting state of the art treatment. The Royal Marsden was the leading cancer hospital in the UK, maybe even further afield. Dr Van den Berk was justifiably regarded highly by all his colleagues and staff and Joe Ford's RapidArc transmission mechanisms would have made it on to *Tomorrow's World*. After further contemplation, JJ firmly believed that as far as mainstream medicine was concerned he was getting the best treatment around.

The nagging doubt in his head though was triggered by a memory of his first analytical job for MI5. The security services were concerned that OPEC's massive wealth was, advertently or inadvertently, funding some pockets of terrorism aimed at the UK. For every $1/barrel the price of crude oil rose how much of that went to nefarious groups and deadly organisations? JJ was asked to investigate and report back. He was fresh out of university, so his technical analytical brain was fully engaged.

Within a few weeks, he had completed a detailed study of the impact of oil on consumer prices, output and employment of the G7 economies plus Russia. For good measure he even built a small econometric model, using vector autoregressive analysis and dynamic optimisation programs which spewed out a ranking of the G7 currencies for any given oil shock. He was pleased with his work and gave it to his boss. She had a brief look at it and asked, 'What does OPEC do with the money?' JJ nearly collapsed in a mental heap. He was so taken by his efforts at estimating the direct economic impact of an oil price hike on the major economies that he had forgotten completely that OPEC had received a windfall gain and that they had to do something with this gain.

JJ scuttled off back to his desk and worked day and night for two weeks on this question. Different OPEC countries were in different stages of economic development. Many would need to spend their relatively new found wealth on infrastructure like roads, hospitals, schools etc. The more economically advanced, like Saudi Arabia, may have peaked on infrastructure building so their excess cash tended to go into financial assets. US Treasuries were a favourite as nobody thought the US government would ever default, as were some hard commodities like gold, silver, platinum and copper. However there was other stuff. It was impossible to account for every last dollar that OPEC countries received in oil revenue. Saudi Arabia was probably America's closest ally in the Middle East, but Osama bin Laden was a Saudi and fifteen of the nineteen suicide bombers who flew into the World Trade Center and the Pentagon in September 2001 were Saudis. That operation, heinous as it was, took money, planning, secrecy, and albeit from the coldness of a black ops perspective, expensive skill. By the time JJ had completed his research he gave his superiors an incredibly detailed breakdown of what the key

OPEC countries did with their oil wealth. The estimated gap between the revenues and the resulting outflow of cash into real and financial assets, reserves, overseas aid, military purchases etc. was called the 'funding gap' by JJ. His boss had decided to term it PTF, potential terrorist funds. It was a large enough gap to be well scary.

By the time Brandon Flowers had blasted out the 'Spaceman' track, JJ had decided he needed to do a bit more research into prostate cancer. The iffy nature of his particular position i.e. locally advanced and not far from metastatic meant that his treatment program had been put together in a bit of a rush. With the nature of that news, the Greek plan, the peculiar Robson meeting and worrying about Cyrus, JJ hadn't properly delved into the wider and deeper issues on the cancer.

Well, it's just as well that he decided to. After Cyrus had gone to bed that night, JJ opened up his computer tablet and got going on research. He usually had his tablet with him and it was not synchronised with any of his work computers so he was reasonably confident that planned or opportunistic prying eyes would not get any information reward. JJ wanted more answers on several scores. First, the side effects of his treatment and was there anything that could be done about that. Secondly, was there any alternative to mainstream medicine as it related to cancer cures.

JJ ploughed through a skyscraper's worth of information. The side effects of both radiotherapy and hormone treatment were not pleasant. The lightweight side effects of hormone treatment that were most common included excessive tiredness, hot flushes like a menopausal woman, weight gain and body hair loss. The more heavyweight side effects included the possibility of liver and kidney toxicity and immune system dysfunction. You were well up the Swanee if the latter three took hold.

After about an hour of not too informative browsing, JJ came across a 2010 article by Heba Barakat of the Department of Biochemistry and Nutrition in Ain Shams University in Cairo. Dr Barakat had conducted an extensive experiment involving forty healthy adult albino rats. To cut a long story and a lot of research short these rats were randomly assigned to different groups with one of the groups given regular doses of Cyproterone acetate, essentially the generic name for the hormone that JJ's abdomen was implanted with. The data from the experiment suggested that the rats who were given nothing but Cyproterone suffered diminished liver function and hepatic oxidative stress. The rats who had been given green tea extract as well both before and during the experiment's procedure, were fine and dandy, both in their liver function and their immune system. The results and statistical analysis attached to this piece of work were impressive by scientific and probability benchmarks. JJ quite liked green tea. Now, he was going to love it.

Over the next few evenings JJ continued to investigate. The side effects of radiation weren't good either. Several bodies of work, JJ hadn't yet decided whether it was good and relevant work or not, said outright that the radiotherapy was as likely to kill you as the cancer. The general opinion from the alternative medicine school of thought was that the radiation stays in your body for a long time and slowly but surely closes down your organs and your immune system. These researchers and commentators agreed that the statistics showing that patients who had undergone the radiotherapy and hormone combo for non-metastatic prostate cancer had a survival rate of 80% plus were misleading. These alternative medicine types claimed, as it turns out correctly, that mainstream cancer statistics counted you as having survived if you lived for five years after your initial diagnosis and treatment. Prostate cancer, however, was more often than not a slow to develop cancer. Even in JJ's locally advanced case, Dr Van den Berk had said he'd probably live for four to five years even if he had no treatment at all. 'Lies, damned lies, and statistics', recalled JJ. This was not good. Apart from concluding that he had to eat even more healthily, take a targeted selection of vitamins over and above the usual suspects, fill up on antioxidants and keep up his gym and martial arts training even if knackered, JJ realised that it was time to supplement Joe Ford's laser assault on his cancer.

After a few more hours of research, JJ came across one seriously interesting human being. One Dr Mirko Beljanski, deceased. Dr Beljanski was a French-Serbian molecular biologist, who died in 1998, seventy-five years old. In the same way that there are proper economists and the rest, there are proper molecular biologists and the rest. Dr Beljanski was a proper molecular biologist. Among his published 133 scientific papers, he produced research which seemed to indicate that an extract from the Amazonian rain forest tree Pao Pereira suppressed prostate cancer cells. This was published in the *Journal of Integrative Oncology* and was widely revered as a major breakthrough on the subject. Even more intriguing though was the link between Beljanski and President Francois Mitterrand of France. In September 1992, it was announced that the President had prostate cancer. The seventy-five year old vowed to stay in power, some were happy about that, many others were not. A year later, Mitterrand was seriously ill with the cancer and it was believed it had gone metastatic. The doctors gave Mitterrand three months to live and towards the end of 1994, in great pain, he succumbed to radiation treatment. Eventually Mitterrand was persuaded to take some of Mirko Beljanski's formulations. Mitterrand's health started to improve, he ate better, felt better and looked better after about eight weeks of consuming Beljanski's products. His political enemies were not happy bunnies. President Mitterrand completed his second term and stayed alive for about another year after that.

While Mitterrand was alive, the powerful but ultimately dark forces of his political enemies and the pharmaceutical industry left Beljanski and his research team alone. It did not last. At 6am on the morning of October 6th, 1996 the GIGN (National Gendarmerie Intervention Group), trained to deal with violence, riots and terrorism, descended on the Beljanski laboratories. Involved in the operation were eighty anti-terrorist soldiers, a helicopter, police dogs, machine guns, flak jackets and all the hardware reminiscent of a siege scene from *Braquo*. Dr Beljanski, now seventy-three years old, was rudely awakened from his sleep, placed in handcuffs and forced to do the 'perp walk' so popular with US police officers. Dr Beljanski's laboratory was closed down. This was a true story and it didn't get any better. Dr Beljanski was set to be put on trial. Tragically, he died while awaiting the opportunity to state his case. In May 2002, four years after his death, the European Court of Human Rights ruled that Mirko Beljanski had been denied a fair trial and the opportunity to defend his research. The French authorities were truly fucked up, thought JJ and he was glad that these days they were more or less a lapdog of the Bundestag. JJ decided not to share that opinion with Yves-Jacques.

Fortunately, for JJ, and probably a host of other cancer patients, Dr Beljanski had a loving, clever and committed daughter, Sylvie. She went to New York and arrived with much of her father's research that she had salvaged from the outrageous intrusion by the GIGN and set up an institute in her father's name with the intention of helping those with cancer worldwide.

While sifting through other research articles by this truly amazing molecular biologist, JJ came across another one of direct relevance to him. Apparently, and obviously before he was hounded to his death by French bureaucracy and vested interests, Dr Beljanski had won a contract from the French army to study the effects of wartime radiation on their soldiers and try to discover ways to alleviate it. The talented scientist beavered away and eventually showed that the golden leaf extract from the Ginkgo Biloba plant had beneficial effects on the immune system, protecting it against the negative impact of radiation. The golden leaf extract has a totally different biochemical composition from the more commonly seen green leaf.

JJ was so impressed by Mirko Beljanski's work, his story, his daughter, his brain, that he blasted off an email to the Beljanski Foundation in New York and, via their supplier, ordered their Pao-V and Ginkgo-V products. Protecting the body from radiation effects and suppressing prostate cancer cells were just what the doctor ordered, so to speak. With a wry smile on his face, JJ was now looking forward to his next appointment with Dr Van den Berk. He fully intended to tell his consultant that he was going alternative.

JJ was emotionally feeling a bit more relaxed about his cancer fight. He now believed his attack arsenal against the cancer enemy had just muscled up. He was on the traditional medicine path, and he was committed to it, but JJ believed he had augmented his weaponry with select supplements like, taurine, selenium, magnesium citrate, saw palmetto, lycopene, turmeric and green tea extract. The Beljanski products, he hoped, would further raise the attack and defence capability of his cancer weapons of mass destruction.

Finally, after even more hours of research, browsing, rejecting and accepting linked articles on his tablet, he added one final alternative medicine regime: the Budwig Protocol. This approach to killing cancer was developed by Dr Johanna Budwig and essentially involved digesting a diet of cottage cheese and flaxseed oil thoroughly mixed. Nigh every nutritionist's advice on dairy was to avoid it and on the face of it cottage cheese should be in the trash. However, Dr Budwig had shown that the dairy properties of the cottage cheese were eliminated when combined with the flaxseed oil in very specific proportions. The resultant mixture, or gruel as JJ was to call it in the future, was meant to revive stagnant electrons in the body, which in turn dissolved the cancerous tumours, wherever in the body they may be. Solely based on his research, and a somewhat cursory perusal of Budwig supporters and Budwig detractors, JJ concluded that while not as apparently impressive as Mirko Beljanski's contribution to his armoury, the Budwig Protocol had enough going for it to give it a try. After all, in the grand scheme of things, how much damage could an odd tasting yogurt-like concoction really do, and you never know, it might do some good.

JJ was now set on his strategy and tactics to battle prostate cancer. The strategy was to burn the cancer cells and starve them by traditional means. Then he'd strengthen his part of the battlefield with vitamins, minerals, antioxidants and products which protected his immune system from radiation and the gooey side effects of hormone treatment. Just in case those black-hearted, soulless, carnivorous cancer cells were hanging on for dear life, he'd also hit them with a few Beljanski Pao Pereira pills and a daily dollop of Budwig gruel. If the little shits were still going after all that, thought JJ, then he was truly in deep doo.

While JJ was feeling somewhat pleased with himself regarding his research findings and his augmented plan, Cyrus was in his room, playing *Sonic Racing* on the latest version of Nintendo 3DS. He hadn't really played that game for some time, but the graphics and the circuits had become ever more visually captivating. He was tired anyway after tennis club and wanted to wind down playing something non-athletic that was easy for him even when the game was on its hard setting. Occasionally Cyrus felt a bit lonely, he wished he'd had a sister, big or wee, but that didn't seem on the cards now.

Cyrus knew something was up with his dad. In many ways it all seemed fine, JJ would still come home at a normal time, they'd chat about the usual stuff, his day at school, his pals, any girlfriends and the like. They'd play a Wii game or two sometimes and Cyrus occasionally could talk his dad into playing *Yu-Gi-Oh* which was a card based non-electronic game involving spells, traps and monsters. Cyrus had liked that game for a long time and now that JJ had at least partially assimilated the rules, the game could be quite interesting. It made Cyrus chuckle though when his dad launched a big monster attack with an elemental hero, just knowing that he was going to drain Cyrus's remaining life points and win the game, to be told by his son 'Not so fast. I play the trap cards Mirror Force and Cemetery Bomb'. The first one negated his dad's attack and the second one cost him 100 life points for every card in his dad's graveyard. Cyrus had already mentally counted the cards in JJ's graveyard, a bit like an autistic savant, so he knew his dad's life points would shrink to zero and he would be down and out. When this happened JJ would fall on his back and let out a child-like *Aaaaarghh!* Cyrus thought this was funny. JJ was a great dad and a good pal.

In recent weeks though Cyrus had noticed that when his dad stayed up late he could no longer hear the distant hum of the television or the occasional tyre screeching and fender bending racket that usually meant JJ was watching, for the umpteenth time, one of the *Fast and Furious* films. Number 5 was his dad's favourite mainly due to the participation of 'The Rock' and the selection of muscle cars, street racers and warrior trucks involved. This franchise of movies had now matched the number of *Rocky* films there were but Vin Diesel was chubbing up a lot and the tragic death of Paul Walker meant the onscreen chemistry was never likely to be the same.

These days it seemed a bit quiet in the living room. Cyrus had once half snuck down the stairs like a ninja to see what his dad was up to, but he seemed simply to be staring at his computer tablet, taking notes, and not doing much else. The angle of the dangle of Cyrus's viewpoint didn't allow him to see exactly what his dad was looking at. God, he hoped it wasn't porn and that his dad was not in the beginning of a mid-life crisis. That would be sad. Maybe understandable since as far as Cyrus knew, JJ hadn't had any female encounters of the sexual kind since Mum died, but sad anyway. He'd talk Gil into finding out. There were bound to be some legit dating websites thought Cyrus, even though in his heart of hearts he wasn't sure he could easily handle the prospect of his dad with another woman.

Cyrus finished up his game of *Sonic All Star Racing*, read a couple of chapters of *The Hunger Games* and slowly dozed off. As he was drifting off he was thinking about Lucy. Lucy was in his class and they'd known each other since they were two years old, having met at a local nursery. They weren't girlfriend/boyfriend in any touchy feely way but they were close and both sets of parents always thought it would be super cute if they ended up getting married. A few years back, when Cyrus was a novice computer literate outside game world, he sent Lucy an email from his recently enabled school email account. Cyrus was nine. The email was innocent enough simply saying 'Hi Lucy. I like you very much. I hope you like me too'. Now, in Lucy and Cyrus's case that was almost a rhetorical question. They both liked each other, they both knew it and everyone at school knew it too. Both Lucy and Cyrus were in year 5 at the time. However, the internet gremlins clearly had it in for young Master Darke that day. His email went to another Lucy, this one in year 6. The format of email address at the school was your first name in full and then the first letter of your surname. Lucy's surname was Hamilton but there was a Lucy Hemmingway in year 6 and by gremlin or by seniority Cyrus's email found its way to Miss Hemmingway. Cyrus learned several lessons from this experience. First, check you've got the right email address before you plop yourself in a hole. Second, once in a hole with your life long girl friend looking down on you, stop digging, go mea culpa or plead insanity and make it up to her.

The Lucies didn't make Cyrus suffer too much. The year 6 Lucy just made him cringe with the occasional 'Hi Cyrus' in that teasing, drawn out, *High School Musical* insincere way that can only mean trouble. The real Lucy let him off the hook after a few ice creams, a cinema visit, help with her homework, some bag carrying and a small present. JJ thought this episode was hilarious and mused that nine year old girls in his Glasgow school in the day weren't as sharp. They didn't have school email accounts either. Cyrus didn't think it was hilarious but he made very few computer mistakes thereafter and was most relieved that Lucy Hamilton had remained to this day his best girl friend.

★ ★ ★

Zhang Bai Ling was American, twenty-nine years old and about 5ft 7in, quite tall for a girl of Chinese descent. She was slim, long dark hair and deep brown eyes. More importantly, she was a mathematical child prodigy and at the age of fourteen used to wind down trying to solve Yang-Mills existence and glueball mass gap. At age twenty-one she was recruited to the NSA and a year later was working for them in a non-dangerous undercover role at LINEAR, the Lincoln Near Earth Asteroid Research program based in Socorro, New Mexico. LINEAR was sponsored by MIT, arguably the best university in the world, the United States Air Force, and NASA. The American authorities were obsessed with their enemies in inner and outer space and somebody elevated in the Department of Defense's hierarchy thought that all those asteroid belts and meteors that were peppering outlying districts of Russia in 2011 and 2012 were too much and too often to be sheer coincidence. If they could pepper the Russian badlands then they could shower the homeland so somebody better get inside LINEAR and keep a watchful security eye on events. That somebody was Bai Ling.

The main task of LINEAR was to apply the most sophisticated technology to the problem of detecting and cataloguing Near Earth Asteroids (NEAs) that threatened our planet. These were also known as Near Earth Objects (NEOs). The LINEAR team used ground based deep space surveillance telescopes. The data were collated and then sent to the main Lincoln laboratory facility in Lexington, Massachusetts. Once the data were compiled and checked they were forwarded to the MPC, i.e. the Minor Planet Center, not the UK's Monetary Policy Committee. The MPC then assigned designations to LINEAR's new discoveries of NEOs, comets, unusual objects and main belt asteroids. By the middle of 2013, LINEAR had sent a total of over 50 million observations to the MPC. Of these, around 5,000 were NEO discoveries and about 800 comet discoveries. The data content that had triggered the interest of the NSA was that, in the past year or so, the number of NEO events had deviated sharply upwards from their annual average of the previous few years. Something was going on and the NSA wanted to hear about it. Bai Ling was sent there to listen, observe and report back.

The NSA has more numerous and sophisticated electronic eyes and ears than any other secret agency in the world. It plugs into emails, phone calls, internet usage of many, many Americans, and people of interest on and off American soil. It may be legal and it may not be but after 9/11 America's clandestine agencies didn't much give a monkey's toss. Their job was to ferret out mega bad guys, in particular any who might even be thinking about a terrorist attack on US citizens and properties. Yet even armed with all that hardware and software a determined terrorist cell or lone wolf activist could not be caught if all of their communications were verbal, face to face, eschewing all modern and electronic means of conversing. So good guy human plants were still necessary.

Bai Ling was a proficient martial artist, came second in her training class on firearm skills and long distance target shooting i.e. sniping. She yearned for a more front line anti-terrorist role than the one she had been allocated. Whatever some crazy Star Wars fed Dr Strangelove type in the Defense Department might think, Bai Ling seriously doubted that there was a Death Star annihilation beam aimed at the United States, or anywhere else in the world for that matter. In fact, she was getting more than a little bored with her job at LINEAR. None of the chitty-chatty of her normal, daily work routine contained anything suspicious at all. The scientists and mathematicians that she came in contact with were either pure workaholics or workaholics that wanted to grope her. They got short shrift but she resisted injuring them severely, which she could have done very easily.

Bai Ling's main task today was a case in point. She had been sent to the Lincoln Lab in Lexington and asked to help select the honor students and teachers who would get a minor planet named after them. This was part of the Ceres Connection, a program designed to teach students about how a planet was located and to discover more about them. All planets named in the Ceres Connection were discovered by LINEAR. For a child prodigy whose mathematical ability put her in the top 1% of American mathematicians, this was a mind numbing exercise. She thought she would spice it up by having some anagram fun with student names. Just as she spotted something mildly amusing her cell phone rang.

"Zhang. You're up," said the familiar Kentucky voice of her boss Kevin Morgan.

"Hi Kevin, what do you mean?"

Kevin began, sounding both urgent and upset. "There's been a terrorist attack, we think, at the Boston Marathon. Two explosions for sure. There are definitely several people dead including children and a whole lot more injured."

Bai Ling took in the headline news, but didn't know what to say.

"The facts are sketchy just now but I've been in touch with Ricky Deslauners, the FBI's special agent in charge of the Boston office. He says the bombs contained BB-like pellets and nails. One of the bombs was hidden in a small pressure cooker in a backpack, the other was in some form of metal container too. Ricky said he's not sure but it might not be Al-Qaeda or any of those other towel-head mother fuckers. He said the bombs seemed to be a bit amateurish, not really the power or timing to do maximum damage, but they were lethal enough. Apart from the dead, it's been reported that many of the injured lost limbs or parts of limbs from their lower body. It's a fucking mess and we're in the frame for answers along with all the other agencies." Kevin paused for breath.

"What can I do?" asked Bai Ling. "I'm no bomb expert and I'd have thought the Feds and the CIA would be all over this like a rash?"

"They are, as are Homeland Security, the Boston Police and anybody else who thinks their ass is on the line." Kevin continued, a little calmer now. "Our guys in Boston are reviewing all the phone calls, emails, texts, instant messages, internet communications, anything that they've intercepted in recent weeks. They're already plugged into all the operating CCTV cameras in the area of the attack and they're working round the clock. They're short staffed and they have a billion truckloads of data to search. You're the closest NSA Intelligence Officer to Boston. They want you there. A fresh pair of eyes and ears. Also, since they hadn't picked up one damn inkling of intel before the attack, it may be that the bastards have used some coded communications that the Boston guys missed. Time to get that big brain of yours into gear."

Kevin was right about the geography, Bai Ling knew that Lexington was only twenty miles from Boston. She had her car with her in the LINEAR car park, and always had an overnight bag in the trunk, though it sounded like she may well be there for more than one night.

"I can be there in less than an hour, Kevin. What will I tell my boss here at LINEAR?" asked Bai Ling.

"Don't worry about that. Concoct a story of family bereavement and that they shouldn't expect you back for a couple of weeks. When you get to the Boston office ask for Jane Hayden, she'll brief you. Call me later with an update. Good luck."

"Sure, bye Kevin."

Bai Ling's head was whizzing round and round or so it felt. A bomb attack in Boston. My god! Who could have done it? Why hadn't the NSA or the other security agencies picked anything up? She had wanted more front line exposure and now this bloody tragedy had given her that opportunity, not the way she wanted it but she'd need to deal with that emotion before getting down to hard analysis and acute observation. As she gathered her things, phone, bag and the pair of silvery white trainers under her desk, she could not have known that she would not be returning to LINEAR, that this was going to be her first and only field mission for the NSA and that she would never see Kevin Morgan again. She glanced back at her computer and just as she was shutting it down she felt the faintest of smiles grow on her face. Her selection for honoured Ceres Connection student 2013 was Gilian Baz Haning, a young woman of similar age to Bai Ling with a Spanish mother and Swiss father. Great name, thought Bai Ling.

* * *

JJ had prepared well for the FCA meeting. This relatively new regulator of the UK's financial system, along with the PRA, Prudential Regulation Authority, had emerged like a phoenix from the ashes of the FSA in 2013. JJ thought that, in reality, the FSA had been hard done by. He knew the FSA's boss, Hector Sants, he was as honest as the days were long, a good leader, articulate and motivated. The several years after the 2008 financial crash had left the British government with what seemed like a carte blanche mandate to allocate blame for that disaster, as long as all fingers were pointing away from Westminster. There was nothing the FSA could have done any differently that would have lessened the economic impact of the crash but the entire jigsaw puzzle involving Lehman Brothers, Bernie Madoff's fraudulent activities, the LIBOR scandal, to name but a few, meant that someone or other had to be sacrificed to the baying pack of media hyenas and men in the street. Hector and the FSA got chomped.

The night before, JJ had organised an offsite with Toby and Yves-Jacques. Not so much a lavish 1980s style offsite where you could slope off to some fancy country house or other for a few days to discuss the most irrelevant of stuff. This was the 'hair-shirt teenies' so a cheap drink in a wine bar was your lot. JJ and his colleagues were going over the sequence of events that led up to their extraordinary 'good luck' last December. The only electronic communications there had been before the action began were Marcus Whyte's initial call to Toby's mobile phone, Toby's text message to JJ, and his text to Yves-Jacques to get himself into the office sharpish, then Toby's chaser call to Yves-Jacques on his work landline to get a move on with the target buy list. The latter communication contained no potential regulatory haz chem material. A head trader urging a young analyst to get a move on was normal daily chatter. Thank god the other three communications were mobile to mobile.

At the first meeting the FCA bods probably wouldn't ask for mobile phone records. They would already be armed with any emails that day sent or received by the relevant MAM employees and a print out of any Bloomberg instant messages or chat room exchanges with brokers. MAM's Compliance department, a bunch of barely living no-marks as far as Toby was concerned, were actually very good at their jobs. John Cougar Mellencamp's line about life continuing even if living was no fun any longer surely must have been aimed at Compliance personnel, whether or not they were called Jack or Diane. Living or not the Compliance geeks would already have handed over all the relevant electronic communications of that day. JJ had made this all crystal clear to Toby and Yves-Jacques at their offsite. There was no point denying what was in black and white, especially since most of it would have been typed by one of the three amigos. The key to a successful FCA meeting today was to be light heartedly content with how lucky MAM was in its timing of the trades, to have a credible, watertight explanation when the FCA fellow or fellowette enquired why trade so large that day and to ensure they left satisfied with no need or desire to requisition personal mobile phone records.

JJ wasn't even sure that it would pass muster as an insider trading issue. Marcus Whyte was a paid employee of MAM and he was paid to do research. He'd have been in regular contact with PASOK Theo, his brother in law, anyway. Theo may or may not have known MAM had a bucket load of Greek quasi junk bonds when he blurted out his bailout vote news to Marcus. JJ had already asked Marcus, by a circuitous non-traceable route, i.e. first class air mail letter, since destroyed, whether or not he had given Theo a backhander for his info. Marcus said no. JJ had other issues with the insider trading nomenclature and regulation. Many economists thought information not in the public domain was fine, that if acted upon it simply meant a reallocation of capital, but with no overall negative effect on world utility. Usually, this group was populated by the same bunch of dismal scientists that thought all drugs, Class A and otherwise should be made legal. The argument was that if they were legal and readily available then the price would drop relative to demand. Drug cartels, dealers and couriers would go out of business and those folk who just did things because they were illegal cool would need to find something else to be dope about. Convincing as JJ felt his thought processes were he didn't think that this morning's meeting with the regulatory boys and girls was the optimum arena to air them. Those FCA hounds would probably believe that if it wasn't on a Sky News, CNBC and CNN loop then it wasn't in the public domain. No, JJ would be needing to answer some potentially barbed questions. The thorniest of them all would probably be why the three MAM employees were in the office in the middle of the night.

"Hi. I'm Tom Watts," said a slim English fellow of about 5ft 10in, thirty years old, short blond hair, trendy rimless glasses and a difficult to place regional accent. "This is Rachel Woodhouse, and Gareth Jones." Tom Watts was clearly the lead FCA officer, backed up by some moderately stylish eye candy and a Welshman, just in case a sing-song was on the agenda, thought JJ, irreverently.

"I'm JJ Darke, head of portfolio strategy and investment. This is Toby Naismith, our chief FX and commodities trader, and Yves-Jacques Durand, an analyst in the Research department. Please sit down."

They all exchanged business cards, not meant to be a contact sport but often was when there were six or more at a table, three a side. They were in one of MAM's larger meeting rooms on the fifth floor with a nice view, albeit a bit bleak that day. They sat in very comfortable black leather chairs which surrounded a two tone long leaf shaped walnut burr table. Still and sparkling water and glasses were already on the table. JJ suggested to his FCA guests to help themselves to the water.

"If anyone wants tea or coffee let me know," said JJ, presently the perfect host. Yves-Jacques was about to ask for a coffee, but Toby gave him a painless dunt in the ribs with his elbow. All the FCA-ers had declined and Toby knew JJ wouldn't want the meeting either held up or interrupted by the junior analyst satisfying his Gallic desire for yet another strong morning coffee.

The meeting began like all these meetings do, on a slow burn. Tom Watts thanked JJ for taking the meeting, knowing full well that had he not there would have followed a summons to FCA headquarters. Eye candy asked some questions that she and her colleagues already knew the answer to and the Tom Jones wannabe just took notes. Then, 'ding'. Round One.

"Your Compliance department's records show that you all came into this building in the early hours of the 13th of December," stated Tom Watts. "Mr Durand, you entered first at 1.55am and Mr Darke and Mr Naismith, you both entered a few minutes later at 2.04am. Why was this?" Watts continued, adding that surely that wasn't a normal or regular time for them to be working. Eye candy looked smug and young Gareth looked up from his notepad.

"Yves-Jacques, you go first," instructed JJ.

"A couple of weeks prior to the 13th December," began Yves-Jacques, "Toby, I mean Mr Naismith, told me that Mr Darke wanted me involved in developing a game tree and a pay-off matrix regarding various probability outcomes for our portfolio of Greek bonds."

"And you just wanted to do that at two o'clock in the morning on 13th December?" interrupted Tom Watts.

"No Sir," responded Yves-Jacques with a decent measure of deference in his voice. "I had been getting behind in the deadline for my work to be completed. I knew the weekend was coming up and I'd promised my girlfriend a couple of nights in Paris. That would have made me even further behind. I couldn't sleep properly so I just got up and came in."

"Did you finish the task?" Bejesus thought JJ. Eye candy was paying attention.

"Yes I did. It's all on my computer, it can be easily checked," said Yves-Jacques calmly. JJ thought the young chap was playing a blinder so far.

"Mr Darke, you and Mr Naismith's nocturnal work ethic, was that coincidence too?" interjected Watts.

"No," said JJ swiftly, then pausing.

"Care to enlighten us?" continued Watts.

"Toby had been out celebrating a few good trades with a couple of his broker dealer friends at Nobu. He gave me a ring, a bit worse for wear, and asked if he could come over to partake in a decent malt Scotch. Cocktail bars, even in the heart of London, don't always have the best malts." JJ was dragging out the description of this social scene. "I said fine. I'd been playing a Wii game with my son, he's fourteen soon, he toasted me as usual,

116

and I would have stayed up a while longer anyway after he went to bed. I'm a widower so seeing a work colleague who is also a friend for a few whiskies seemed like a good idea. As it turned out it was a very good idea," finished JJ. Lone parent, sympathy vote, JJ was laying it on thick.

"How so?" asked Watts.

"Well, after a couple of eighteen year Macallans when we had passed the peak of bonhomie and were on the slowing down phase we started talking about work. Naturally enough our Greek bond position came up. It was our largest exposure in both the bond portfolio and our emerging market debt programme so it was the one to talk about," elaborated JJ.

Gareth was taking a few notes again and eye candy didn't look quite so smug. The tale of two guys, drinking spirits and talking about Greeks was not fully engaging her mind any longer.

"By about 1, 1.30am or thereabouts, we realised that neither of us was going to get any sleep that night, so we more or less mutually agreed to go into the office and sort out our Greek portfolio once and for all, before year end and before market liquidity dried up as everybody headed for their Christmas break. Toby Hailo-ed a cab, I sent my son's nanny a text asking her to be in the house before Cyrus awoke and we headed off. On arrival, we knew Yves-Jacques was already there, the night security guard on the desk mentioned it. That was a bonus. If we needed any top mathematics on hand, then we had it."

Tom Watts couldn't tell whether this was a load of old tosh, or one of those occasions when a major hedge fund got itself a lucky break. He had checked all the FSA and FCA files on MAM's three employees before today's meeting. The French dude was a bit too new to have much of a file and both Darke and Naismith's records were clean, spotless, whiter than white. Watts' FSA and FCA record at nailing financial miscreants was second to none. He was partly responsible for digging out some Madoff connections in London when he was in his twenties and he helped bring two of the LIBOR fixers to light. Jail terms and substantial fines ensued. He knew that if this MAM incident was an insider trading case and he proved it then his regulatory star would burn even brighter in the night sky.

After a minute's pondering, Tom Watts said, "I've one final question, Mr Darke." Watts had racked his brain and forensically studied every communication that MAM's Compliance department had given him. Their file was comprehensive, detailed with no time gaps or omissions. Any content, Bloomberg, BlackBerry, landline or email communication that December day was in his sticky mitts and those mitts were not yielding any wrongdoing. He could ask for their personal mobile phone records and he might still do that. At this juncture, however, he did not have the size of a gnat's eyelids piece of dirt on these guys. He had one more shot.

"Do you Mr Darke or your colleagues have any Greek family or friends?" asked Watts.

JJ looked at Toby then Yves-Jacques straight in the eye. "Well, I don't," said JJ. "How about you guys?" Toby said he hadn't and Yves-Jacques shook his head. Good job he wasn't Bulgarian.

Tom Watts looked a little deflated, eye candy was already off her seat, ready to leave and the note taker had closed his pad and tucked his pen away in his man bag. JJ and Tom Watts both knew that Round One had gone to MAM. One of them hoped it was a one round contest and while the other did not, Watts' sad little chopper expression suggested that he wasn't thinking there was going to be a Round Two. JJ was also moderately amused that their answer to Tom Watts' hopeful silver bullet question was totally truthful. Neither he, nor Toby, nor Yves-Jacques did have any Greek family or friends. Marcus Whyte did, but Marcus hadn't been asked to the meeting, Marcus Whyte didn't do any of the trades and, from an FCA perspective, Marcus Whyte was a ghost.

After the FCA contingent left, Toby and Yves-Jacques were all full of the joys of life. JJ was a little more reserved. He knew that the FCA could return with more questions if they felt the need. The only real part of their story that seemed less than titanium robust was the apparent spontaneity of Toby and him just deciding to go to the office at two in the morning, all Macallaned up. If the FCA came back for mobile phone records then the gig was up. JJ could still argue that there were no net losers from their actions that night. The gainers were MAM and its employees, outside investors who were already short Greek bonds and equities and short USD/JPY. The losers were holders of Greek bonds, equities and those long USD/JPY. He had almost convinced himself it was a zero sum game, no overall winners or losers, just a redistribution of capital.

JJ left for the Marsden and then home that night reasonably content with his day's work. The only thing that bugged him was the phrase, in the public domain. Zero sum game or not, if the phone calls from Marcus Whyte or Toby ever saw the light of day then it was that requirement that would send them all to buggery in a handbasket.

* * *

Bai Ling was lying nearly flat out in her gadget full seat in the new Boeing 787 Dreamliner plane, first class, aisle seat, starboard side, heading from Boston's Logan airport to Heathrow. As a child she had preferred the window seat on a plane, in fact she still preferred the window seat if truth be told. Her left knee, however, hurt like hell even though it had been a few weeks since Boston.

She needed the aisle seat for ease of access, but it was still awkward and incredibly annoying. The bullet hadn't smashed her kneecap to smithereens, but the knee is a very complex mechanism, made up of muscle, ligaments, cartilages and bone. The 9mm projectile had more or less destroyed her medial collateral ligament, one of the four major ligaments of the knee. Normally, certain skiing injuries and contact sports like American football – helmet to knee action – can severely damage this ligament but, hey, a stray bullet can do the trick too. The medical profession grades this type of ligament injury from one to three, with three being the most severe. Bai Ling's was about one and a half. She still had a small limp but the doctors had said that with regular physio and then light exercise that may go away. It hadn't yet. She wouldn't be running the 100 metres in Olympic qualifying time though and, more distressing for Bai Ling was that she would not be capable of any roundhouse kicks to the head on anybody taller than an oompa loompa.

Psychologically Bai Ling was still coming to terms with her career ending injury. She had gone to the NSA's offices in Boston as ordered by Kevin Morgan, got in touch with Jane Hayden and joined the listening post team, dialling into chatter, email surveillance and all the recent communications from millions of people in and around the Boston area. By that time, the death toll had amounted to three people, including a kid, with 176 injured, some severely. The suspects emerged as two brothers of Chechen descent but who had been in the United States for several years. The call came in that one of the suspects had been shot dead by the Boston Police in the Watertown area, where the MIT campus was situated. An MIT police officer had been shot and later died in hospital. A manhunt was underway for the second brother, nineteen years old and the younger of the two Tsarnaevs as it turned out. Normally, a primarily office based surveillance team would not be sent out to a conflict zone. However, the security agencies were still smarting because they had had no warnings about the Boston bombs and, frankly, very little information about the whos, whys and wherefores of this attack. The whos were becoming clearer but the other critical information was still lacking.

'Zhang, you need to go with the team.' Bai Ling could still recall Jane Hayden telling her that although she had just arrived, she was to join her new found colleagues, Tim Peterson and Jerzy Kowalski in their technology bursting silver GMC SUV and get as near to the MIT campus as possible. Their job was to listen to all communications that were near at hand, and any inter-agency talk. Neither Jane Hayden nor Kevin Morgan wanted to be seen as doing little in the midst of what might have been the most devastating attack on American soil since 9/11.

"Are you packing?" Tim asked Bai Ling as they parked up their truck.

"No, I didn't have time to go to my apartment and pick anything up. I came straight here after I got Morgan's call," said Bai Ling.

"I thought as much," said Tim. "Here," and with that he handed Bai Ling a 357 SIG Sauer handgun, holstered. The CIA and FBI tended to equip their agents with Glocks but for some reason the listening agency often preferred semi-automatic SIG Sauers. The variant handed to Bai Ling was non-reflective black, weighed just over 30 ounces, 7 ½ inches long with a 4 ½ inch barrel. This one had 12 rounds in it though the 357 could take up to a 15 round magazine. She was comfortable enough with her borrowed firearm as she strapped it on but did not feel that there was much chance that she'd use it.

The Boston Police, FBI and Homeland Security had locked down the Watertown area near Boston. Agents and officers were conducting house to house searches, there were roadblocks everywhere and surveillance helicopters black dotted the skies. If Dzhokhar Tsarnaev got out of this one, then Houdini was surely a Chechen. Bai Ling and her two colleagues parked up on Franklin Street. There was a lot of activity in the night, most of it official but the occasional local pea brain who felt the need to accost the authorities for one protest reason or the other did make the odd appearance.

After about forty-five minutes of listening and surveying nothing very illuminating, Bai Ling said she was going to step outside for some air. Tim and Jerzy were fully in the zone of their work and Bai Ling was feeling a bit claustrophobic. She was leaning against the back of the silver SUV checking her own emails on her smartphone when suddenly there was chaos. An African American man, dressed like a rapper with no style was running amok, firing a gun at a couple of uniformed police officers and bellowing about his human rights. Bai Ling felt an agonising sharp jolt in her left leg and crumpled to the ground. Jerzy heard the commotion and Bai Ling's screams and came hurtling out of the back of the van. Bai Ling was clutching her leg, which was now in excruciating pain, there was blood all over her trousers and spilt on the road. Jerzy comforted her, called the paramedics immediately and got Tim to call the office.

The styleless rapper dude was shot by an FBI agent but not fatally. He was a known drug dealer who lived and dealt in the area, who was out that night doing his evil work, pissed as a newt and high as a kite. As he was publically relieving himself he came across a pistol that had been chucked in some bushes. Whatever lunacy triggered that part of his brain that he should go on a shooting spree, most likely consumption of his own product, triggered it was and bang, bang he went. To add insult to severely painful injury, Bai Ling discovered that the pistol was a Ruger

9mm semi-automatic that Tsarnaev the younger had lobbed before he was captured that very same night, hiding in a boat in a backyard. Bai Ling wasn't prone to swearing but 'for fuck's sake' did emit from her small oriental mouth more than once that night and in the following few days.

Under normal circumstances, once Bai Ling had recovered sufficiently from her wounds and her mental and physical rehabilitation was on track, she would have gone back to her NSA job. More than unfortunately, however, the hunt for the Tsarnaevs was one high profile, real time media fest. No sloping about in some Pakistani shit hole looking for the American people's most wanted. Oh no, grumbled Bai Ling, every media channel on the continent was in Boston, hoping to catch a televised glimpse of the tousle topped teenager, who looked way too much like a young Bob Dylan to be a murderous bastard. Well, they got their glimpse or six, but bad news bears for Bai Ling, they also got more than a glimpse of the injured NSA agent. Her strained visage was all over *Sky News*, *Channel 5*, any media outlet you could think of. The reporters and journos dug and dug over coming days. They worked out that she was not a long-standing LINEAR employee. Anyway, what would a LINEAR employee be doing with a holstered firearm – that annoyed the crap out of Bai Ling too, she never even got a shot off at the idiot druggy dude – lying on the ground, bleeding, crying in a Boston suburb in the middle of a manhunt. It didn't take too long for the truth to out that she was an NSA agent.

Well, that was the end of that. Spooks can be many things and they can come from all sorts of backgrounds, with all sorts of personal baggage. One thing they had to be, really really had to be was – anonymous. Bai Ling was so anonymous now that she even had to turn down an interview with Oprah. As she lay in Boston's Brigham and Women's Hospital, she got a phone call from Kevin Morgan and flowers and a visit from Jane Hayden.

Bai Ling's parents and younger brother lived and worked in the Hong Kong retail business. She used to send part of her NSA monthly salary back there regularly, and they promised to visit her soon. They were extremely relieved that their beloved daughter and sister was alive and recovering. It was during Jane Hayden's visit that Bai Ling fully realised that she could not return to the NSA. Ms Hayden was a forty-five year old NSA veteran, who looked a lot like the American actress Elizabeth Mitchell.

"How are you holding up, Bai Ling?" asked Jane.

"The doctors think I'll get much of the use of my knee back in about ten weeks," Bai Ling replied but with no positive emotion involved in her response. "It hurts a lot, I'm bored rigid lying here and I'm gutted about the whole incident. If I'd just stayed in the SUV…"

"You can't beat yourself up about that," interrupted Ms Hayden. "It was a natural thing to do, step outside the hot tin can and get air. You were just extremely unlucky. As Lauren Oliver said in *Before I Fall*: 'Chance. Stupid, dumb, blind chance. Just a part of the strange mechanism of the world, with its fits and coughs and starts and random collisions'. Your knee collided with the last of the eight rounds in that Ruger. It's changed your life and it was a shit dose of bad luck."

"Whatever," retorted Bai Ling. She was in no mood for fancy quotes or a dollop of official sympathy that would be forgotten by the weekend. "What happens next?"

Jane Hayden wasn't too far into her explanation of what happened next before Bai Ling started to feel progressively worse. As expected, while her injury would not have prevented her returning to the NSA, even to her undercover role at LINEAR, the media attention had transformed her into a B-list celebrity. There was more or less no option but to retire her. The financial package wasn't bad. Under the Federal Employees Retirement System (FERS) Bai Ling, as a permanent employee, would qualify for their three tier compensation package which covered basic benefits depending on age, length of service and average high salary over her most recent three year employment. On top of the basic benefits and disability benefits, agent Zhang also qualified for some monetary release from the Social Security Fund and a Thrift Savings Plan. In total, Bai Ling was in line for a decent stipend for life. Good enough for a twenty-nine year old, but not exactly what she had planned. Jane Hayden unloaded the rest of her information, including reminding Bai Ling of her continued commitment to The Espionage Act of 1917, a US law with similar components to the UK's Official Secrets Act.

Bai Ling couldn't really get to sleep properly on the plane. Her seat was great, turned into a nearly bed easily. It wasn't too constraining for a slim woman and the new mood lighting in the cabin was genuinely soporific. Her knee hurt though. The flight was about half way across the pond now and though it wasn't quite the classic 'red-eye' she knew she was going to be drained when she arrived at Terminal 4. Bai Ling readjusted her gammy leg and positioning in the seat. She thought she'd try to get some brief shut-eye before all the cabin's lights went on blazing and the stewardess shoogled awake anyone daring to sleep close to landing time.

As she was dozing off she was evaluating her decision to leave the USA for the UK. There didn't seem much for her career-wise in America, especially since she was still sometimes recognised when she was out and about. She had spent long enough bemoaning her lot and thought that a change of scenery and a less eventful job may do her convalescence of mind and body some good. Kevin Morgan had approved a change of identity. Though she wasn't a witness protection-like candidate who often needed whole new lives, her name and image were fresh enough in the minds of media ferrets on both sides of the Atlantic that she wanted to go for disguise-lite. Bai Ling had her hair cut and coloured a bit lighter which was sufficient to change her appearance quite a lot. She changed her name to Gilian Haning, after that CERES Connection honor student, since that was the last time she remembered having a smile on her face. Brits tended not to either have or use their middle initials with the passionate frequency that Americans do, so in her fake passport produced by Jane Hayden she left out the Baz middle name of the student. It also meant that her new name wasn't either the description of a small planet or a direct anagram of her real name and, thus, less likely to be uncovered by intrusive paparazzi.

Now all she had to worry about was her new life in London, working for her old mentor and finding out more about somebody called Joe Ford. JJ Darke, she thought, ready or not, here I come.

4

THE WOOLWICH FEDS

"We need a spook with a brain," said Chancellor Jeffrey Walker, with confidence and intent, as befitted an Eton and Cambridge man.

"We do indeed Chancellor," replied Neil Robson, not batting an eyelid as to their needs, mainly because it was he who had sown the seed of this outrageous idea in Jeffrey Walker's consciousness a few hours ago. "I have just the one in mind."

Britain's finances were in an unholy mess. The much vaunted recovery of 2013 seemed to have fizzled out. 'Green shoots', the government's catchphrase of that and previous summers, had not developed into luscious green plants or even real grass. *The Guardian* had headlined the latest public sector borrowing figures and what they meant for the economy as a damp squib. Given that it was *The Grauniad*, as the typo prone broadsheet was known, at least they hadn't called it a damp squid, that being perfectly reasonable in the daily life of the fast moving cephalopod.

The UK's overall public sector net debt was around 80% of Gross Domestic Product (GDP). That seemed like a lot, and indeed it was a lot, being well over £1 trillion. It was not out of line with some other countries being a little more than America's net debt as a % of GDP and a lot less than Italy's. Chancellor Walker would stand up at the dispatch box in the House of Commons later in the day, defend the numbers articulately and make verbal mincemeat of the Shadow Chancellor, Arthur

Molloy as he laid into the hapless Labourite. That wasn't the problem. The problem was deeper and multi-facetted. The first issue, as many households in the UK and elsewhere discovered after 2008, is that there is a difference between your stock of outstanding debt and your cash flow's ability to pay the interest on that debt. Mortgage payments, credit cards, and personal loans can add up to a very tidy sum, but if your cash flow can handle the monthly payments then bobby bailiff will not darken your doorstep. Jeffrey Walker's bind was partly because the government's cash flow was drying up.

The annual budget deficit had risen to 10% of GDP or around £150 billion. The cost of interest payments on years of accumulated debt had risen very sharply in the past two years, were already over £50 billion per annum and rising exponentially. The budget deficit had been funded by selling UK government bonds, aka gilts, to the private sector, the Bank of England and overseas investors, the latter accounting for about one third of the funding. Normally, there would be no real problem with funding the budget deficit. Walker had hosted several private meetings in recent weeks with leaders of banks, building societies, and pension funds both home and abroad. Unfotunately, they indicated that their bond holdings were completely full on a prudential risk measurement. The Governor of the Bank of England also indicated that they would not voluntarily increase their bond buying program or quantitative easing as it had become well known. That only left fickle foreigners, thought Walker, and not enough of them at that, certainly not with the required readies.

Jeffrey Walker had witnessed the demise of Greece, Cyprus and Portugal. Their economies were dud, their government finances virtually non-existent or totally supported by the International Monetary Fund (IMF) and European Union (EU).

There were prolonged catastrophic riots in their streets. With unemployment over 30% what else was there to do? Spain was on the brink and even France looked to be in trouble. The Chancellor had been confident that this would not occur in Britain. The English didn't riot much he thought, unless it was too hot, the Scots were too involved with their independence, the Irish too tired of fighting and the Welsh too oblivious to most things. That thought, unfortunately, did not seem to have much of a half-life as he sat today in his office in number 11 Downing Street with his Financial Secretary to the Treasury.

"Remind me Neil…" enquired Walker "… what's the annual budget for the cost of the police force?"

"Taking everything into account, and estimating the cost savings for this financial year, around £14 billion," replied Neil smartly.

"The armed forces?" continued Walker.

"About £10 billion excluding equipment," said Robson.

"And the public sector's wage bill?" asked Walker once more as his silvery haired head sank deeper into his pudgy white hands.

"That would be in the region of £15 billion this year," said Robson. The Chancellor wished, on occasion, that Neil Robson didn't have all these facts and figures to hand, but he did.

"When are we going to be unable to pay the police and most of the NHS, Neil?"

"We're basically £3 billion short, Sir. With income tax, VAT, and other tax structures that we have in place we'll be out of cash in around six months."

There was to be a general election in just over a year's time. Walker knew that there was absolutely no chance of legislating a tax hike on the population before then. The Prime Minister, John McDonald, had no idea the country's finances were as dire as they were, mainly because his Chancellor had deliberately concealed from the PM what had been staring him in the face for several months. Even if he had known, the Coalition's majority did not look robust enough to withstand the probable number of seats lost as a direct result of any tax increase.

The UK had run out of borrowing options too. The EU would not lend any money to the UK without extracting commitments that were unrealistic and unacceptable. They would split the Coalition government and turn the voting public against both parties. That route was an election loser if ever there was one. The IMF, in times gone by, would have been an option even though the last time Britain went there cap in hand, the media made it seem like the end of the world as we knew it. No, any money from the IMF would trigger the same electoral result as begging from the EU. In any event the Fund didn't have any money. The financial drain of Greece, Portugal, Cyprus, Spain, Eastern Europeans and Africans to name but a few meant that the UK was firmly last in the queue, begging bowl out but nothing to put in it.

So there it was, the UK could not sell the necessary amount of gilts to raise the funds to plug its financing gap, it couldn't raise taxes so close to an election and it couldn't borrow from abroad. If this perfect storm intensified and rendered the government unable to pay the police, NHS staff and the army, then widespread rioting would no longer be off the agenda. A Coalition victory at the next election, by contrast, surely would. Bereft of a single workable idea in his Chancellor head, Walker turned to Robson, with desperation written all over his face.

"Does anybody owe us any money?" he asked.

"Well…" began Robson who had been doing his research. 'Well' wasn't 'no', Walker registered instantly, his head and his ears now perked up somewhat from their slumped position.

Robson continued. "In 1984 North Korea defaulted on their

government bonds, the main overseas holders being ourselves, West Germany and Switzerland. In nominal face value the DPRK bonds held by us amounted to around £460 million."

"That's a lot of money Neil," interjected Walker. "But it's way short of the £3 billion pounds we bloody well need." Chancellors of the Exchequer rarely used the F-bomb, unless they were from the west of Scotland, so 'bloody' was an accurate gauge of Walker's grievous angst.

"The power of compound interest Sir," resumed Robson.

"What?" said the Chancellor impatiently.

"The DPRK bonds had a yield of just over 6% per annum. That was quite high by international comparison but clearly included a risk premium, which was justified, on the possibility of a North Korean fiscal meltdown, or as it turned out, default. Now, £460 million of nominal bonds yielding 6% per annum over 30 years amounts to—"

Walker interrupted. "Tell me it's close to £3 billion Neil, please tell me that," the Chancellor pleaded.

"It is indeed Sir," confirmed Robson. "£3.6 billion to be exact."

Chancellor Walker felt instant gratification but was also puzzled. "Why haven't we pursued this before, Neil? It must have surfaced in a previous government's tenure?" asked Walker, not allowing himself to believe that there was such an easy way out of his financial straightjacket.

"The Germans and Swiss kind of let it go…" responded Robson "… and we followed suit. There were some negotiations regarding payment in the early 1990s but then the Argentinian debt mess and default of 1999 – 2002 and the emerging markets balance of payments crisis of 1998 were regarded by North Korea as some kind of precedent. So they told all and sundry to bugger off, so to speak, and we haven't really tried to bugger back in since."

The Chancellor motioned to ask another question of his Financial Secretary but Robson indicated he had more information to divulge.

"I've enquired discretely of our international lawyers and our embassy in Pyongyang," continued Robson. "The lawyers confirm we are, under international law, still owed the money in the amount I indicated. Freddie Wycliffe, our man in Pyongyang, disappointingly said that the initial discussions with his counterpart in the DPRK were unfruitful."

"Unfruitful!" exclaimed the Chancellor. "What does that mean?"

"Freddie says the official North Korean position is that if we want our money, then come and get it, I believe was the literal translation."

"A lot of bloody good that is," said Walker, visibly infuriated again. "We can't just gaily waltz into Pyongyang and demand £3 billion or whatever the won equivalent is."

"No we can't," confirmed Robson. "North Korea have not paid one paltry bean of the debt they owe to any government who holds their defaulted bonds. They're not going to start now. Under Kim Jong-un, they're militarily stronger and even less inclined to be accommodative than ever before to any friend of the United States. We are not going to get what we need through normal political channels, Sir," continued Robson. "Freddie Wycliffe says he is 100% certain that the DPRK government will not entertain any further discussion on the matter. In any event, even if we could go that route, the Prime Minister would then know, the Opposition would know and the media and voting public would know. Too much information I fear in too many hands. If it got out that we went begging to North Korea, we'd lose the election anyway and maybe any support we still have from the USA. We could emphasise that the money was rightfully ours and that we weren't begging. That might work but then the media, financial journalists and City economists would dig and dig into the government's finances until they uncovered the time bomb we have kept quiet. Again, we'd be dead in the water."

Chancellor Walker knew all this but he had switched off a few of Neil Robson's sentences ago. "Neil," said the Chancellor, indicating that he wanted to ask a question. "You said we were not going to get what we needed through *normal* political channels. Does that mean that you have some abnormal channels in your mind that will get us a result?"

"Yes Jeffrey…" replied Robson with a smirk on his face that had illegality written all over it.

★ ★ ★

JJ Darke had no real idea why he had been summoned to Neil Robson's office in HM Treasury. Sure they had had a drink a week or two ago and Robson had said he'd be in touch, but the email he had received yesterday from his old MI5 colleague seemed a bit more formal and had urgently requested today's meeting. JJ was in a decent mood. Cyrus had come top of his class in computing and JJ had the results of his first post-radiotherapy PSA blood test. The score was good, down to 0.8, a far cry from the 23 that had triggered his whole cancer fighting protocol.

JJ was met at the security desk on the ground floor by Neil Robson's PA, a 5ft 7in, twenty something, unnatural blonde called Becky. She was agreeable enough, both in manner and appearance. Becky seemed somewhat uncomfortable though in her figure hugging hot pink top, high heels and tight black skirt. Indeed, the young lady was a little bright all round for the dingy interior of the Treasury. Maybe she was appealing to Robson's basic instincts in the hope of swift social climbing, or even some other sort of climbing. They went up the stairs to Robson's office on the second floor, engaging in the usual small talk as they went.

"Come in JJ," said Neil Robson, his expression in neutral. "Sit down, some tea or coffee?"

"No thanks, Neil, I've just had breakfast and I've a full day ahead. What's the urgency?" asked JJ, anxious to get this unappealing start to the business day over with.

Neil Robson sat in his dimpled green leather chair and pulled a file from the right hand drawer of his antique and large leather topped desk. "This," began Robson, as he held aloft an enclosed document in a blue cardboard folder, "is a file which does not cast you in a good light, my friend."

JJ's decent mood had instantly evaporated. Even before knowing what was in the file, the mere fact that Robson had called him friend meant he was in trouble. They weren't friends and they both knew it. JJ was expressionless and said nothing. Robson looked as if he couldn't contain himself.

"I have a report from the FCA, specifically from Tom Watts and Rachel Woodhouse of the FCA," continued Robson. JJ's face remained unperturbed but his innards and his brain were already in the formative stages of turmoil. "Seems you have been a naughty boy, JJ," said Robson, smug and condescending. "Greek bonds, dodgy phone calls, in the office in the middle of the night to unravel toxic positions. It's got insider trading written all over it," Robson blurted out, with some glee.

"I had a meeting with the FCA team, Neil, I think they were satisfied with my explanation of that night's events," said JJ, hoping beyond hope that Robson's mention of dodgy phone calls was just one generic element from a gallimaufric collection of possibilities that could be involved in an insider trading event.

"They were JJ, they were," commented Robson, clearly dragging it out and in no hurry to ease JJ's concern. "But you should never underestimate the forensic powers of an ambitious woman, JJ. Apparently, young Ms Woodhouse, who reports to Tom Watts who, in turn, reports directly to me…" Robson ploughed on "… simply could not accept what seemed to be a too good to be true tale. She obtained the authority to requisition your mobile phone records, without your permission, and those of Toby Naismith and Yves-Jacques Durand." Robson paused for a sip of tea provided a few minutes earlier by the candescent Becky. "Tut-tut, JJ. I'm fairly certain that those phone calls add up to a robust insider trading breach, involving you, your colleagues and your firm."

As he was taking this all in JJ's brain was whirling around like a banshee. Dear god, he thought, eye candy had stitched them up and she hadn't even looked that interested during the meeting at MAM's offices. Robson was still babbling on about sizeable fines, suspensions, even legal proceedings but JJ had moved off that train of thought. That was all a given if the insider trading allegation was proven. What JJ was wondering was why he had been summoned to Neil Robson's office in the Treasury to be confronted with this. Normally, such an accusation would have been made in a formal letter from the Financial Conduct Authority or, at least, in a high level meeting at the FCA. He knew for sure that neither Fathead nor Yves-Jacques had received any FCA communication about this issue. Yet, here he was, sitting opposite the Financial Secretary to the Treasury, slimy toad that he was, over a cup of tea for one and having a little chit-chat. JJ decided to play along for the moment.

"It's debateable whether it's insider trading Neil," said JJ, very composed. "We got the information from a paid employee of MAM in Wellington and we acted on that with all due haste. We didn't have time to check whether or not it was in the public domain, perhaps it was, and perhaps it wasn't. There were no backhanders, no bung. We, at MAM, were not the sole beneficiaries of the Greek news. It was a zero sum game, with winners and losers cancelling each other out. Hardly the classic insider trade," concluded JJ.

Robson was pensive for a moment then resumed the attack. "JJ, you must think I'm a fucking idiot. You may think you're smarter than me, but you're not. You may think you can outmanoeuvre me, but you can't. Do you want to know why?"

"Why?"

"Because I represent the fucking British government. You represent that festering bunch of hedgies that no one, but no one, outside of Mayfair cares a flying rat's arse about. I was elected by the people, you fucked the people or so they have been led to believe by the unbalanced media of this country. I don't drive a new Porsche and live in a £6 million house off the fashionable but morally decrepit King's Road. Are you getting the picture, smart boy?" ended Robson in a much less friendly tone.

"I get the picture, Neil," responded JJ calmly. "But why am I being shown the picture here and not at the FCA? Why do my accused colleagues not know anything about it? Why does my boss at MAM not know anything about it?"

"Because my friend…" said Robson back to his calm but superior tone, "I alone can offer you a way out of your predicament."

The following two hours unfolded into two of the most incredulous hours of JJ Darke's professional life. Robson outlined how it was well within his powers to damage not only JJ himself but Toby, Yves-Jacques, and the whole of MAM. He made it abundantly clear that he would leak the story to the *Financial Times*, thereby making it seem weighty and true. JJ may be able to withstand the financial maelstrom that would follow once he had paid substantial fines but Toby Naismith might not and Yves-Jacques Durand would be finished in the financial world even before he had properly started. Investors would redeem millions and millions of pounds, dollars and euros from MAM. The fund's profitability would shrink and there would be many lay-offs. Neil Robson also made it clear that he would press the legal system to push for the maximum penalties for JJ and his two amigos. The legal bills would finish off Naismith and Durand he emphasised and while they might not finish off JJ, a term at her majesty's pleasure would ensure that there would be no future financial career opportunities. Robson had thought this through well. He continued with painting the bleak picture for JJ. Even if some investment house was imbecile enough to offer JJ a job, Robson explained that he would ensure that JJ's registration with the FCA as an 'approved person' was locked away in a drawer never again to see the light of day.

JJ was analysing all this vitriol as it entered his head. He told Robson that he would take the fall, if a fall was coming, but to leave Toby and Yves-Jacques out of it, as they were simply following his instructions. Robson was having none of it. He made it clear that if JJ refused the opportunity, as Robson had called it, then no matter the veracity and commitment of JJ admitting it was his responsibility alone, the Treasury, i.e. the government, would pursue JJ's two colleagues and David Sutherland, the head of MAM, with the full force of the law and beyond. JJ knew Robson had him by the short and curlies, a most depressing thought on any level. He knew that Robson was a vengeful, vindictive bastard from their time in MI5. He knew the Financial Secretary to the Treasury would not rest at fines, suspensions, sackings, even jail time. By dint of his murky past and hint of his venomous mouth Robson made it clear that JJ was caught between the biggest rock and the most solid hard place. He was damned if he took the fall for alleged insider trading and he was damned if he tried to fight it. Whichever form of damnation he opted for, his friends, his colleagues and, above all, his son would suffer distress for years to come.

In the best traditions of carrot and stick Robson gave JJ his 'solemn word' that if he carried out the plan then the file in his hand would disappear without trace. There were no copies, he swore, hard or electronic, and both Watts and detective Ms Woodhouse would be made to understand that it was in the country's interests that no regulatory or legal action should be taken against the three MAM employees. Like magic it would all dissipate into the ether and JJ's life could continue as before. JJ was no fool. He realised he was in Robson's dirty vice like grip. JJ had been prepared to accept the results of any insider trading enquiry by the FCA and any consequent penalties, however harsh. Robson clearly did not want that, indeed he would not allow it. If JJ did not comply then pain and suffering would be heaped upon anyone who happened to be in JJ's circle of family and friends whether or not they had anything to do with Greek bonds. JJ tried to squeeze every last brain cell in his head to produce a way out, but there was no way out, he was stuffed and he was toasted.

"OK, Neil," said JJ. "What's your plan?" Before his capitulation JJ knew he could not trust Robson. The slimy toad's 'solemn word' had no credible content. JJ knew that he'd need to deal with that problem later, even though he hadn't a blind clue, at this juncture, how to deal with it.

JJ listened to Robson's plan. It so wasn't a plan, thought JJ. It was a wild, fantasmagoriacal notion that not even Ethan Hunt in *Mission Impossible* with all the stuntmen and CGI characters could pull off. The guts of Robson's notion was for JJ and a select team to stroll into North Korea and steal their gold.

"What the fuck, Neil!" exploded JJ. "Are you out of your tiny wetwork mangled fucking mind? That's not a plan, it's a whimsical improvisation of a desperate man, indeed a desperate government." JJ caught a glimpse of Robson's face, it wasn't happy. JJ thought he'd better calm down fast. "Fine, I get why you're on this particular path, but is there nothing else? Maybe something with a remote chance of success?"

Robson's facial expression had become more neutral again. "Look, JJ. You're in no position to be mouthing off and while I'm not going to divulge the details of the government's finances to a spiv hedgie like you, let me assure you there is no other way. I've told you where the gold is and I can tell you how much of it we need. I can also tell you the budget for the mission and how to access the funds you will need. The rest is up to you. You need to select your team, the smaller the better, and I need to vet and OK all of them. You need to turn my, what did you call it, 'whimsical improvisation', cheeky fucker, into an operational plan."

Robson was calm and confident, reflecting his total belief that he was the man on top. "Once you've got the gold…" he continued, "… and get it you'd better had for your and your friends' sake, you need to sell it somehow, deliver the proceeds to me and I will then quietly disburse the monies to various areas of government. Simples, as Vasily the meerkat would say." Robson was clearly pleased with himself and his little quip. "Take this mobile phone; it has my details in it. Contact me using this phone only."

That was more or less the end of the meeting. JJ was reeling. Even bright Becky didn't register in his mind's eye as she escorted him to the front doors of the Treasury. He didn't really know where to start. Robson wanted this theft to be undertaken by the end of March which was only two or three weeks away. His initial thought was to go to the media himself, expose Neil Robson for the crook he was. That however was not a quality first thought. Robson would still have the opportunity to reveal the FCA file and JJ, Toby and Yves-Jacques would still be in the pungent doo-doo. JJ had no proof of the content of the meeting with Robson. It was face to face, no electronic communication of any sort. Robson had him for sure so JJ's second thought was that he had better get a move on.

* * *

JJ's initial research was not yielding happy answers. North Korea was believed to have extensive mineral deposits, including gold and silver. However, limited domestic technology and the isolationist government's policies of no business contact with perceived enemies meant that the DPRK did not have the necessary mechanical and electronic engineering equipment to mine for these minerals efficiently. Their extraction was slow and laborious so maybe only two tonnes of gold were mined each year. If he was to acquire the full amount then JJ needed way more of the shiny yellow metal than that. In any event, even if the North Korean mining industry was the world's finest, JJ and his team could not just hang about looking suspicious at the top of a gold mine shaft and ask the miners to pop a few tonnes of gold into their waiting trucks, thank you very much. They would need to get their target supply of gold from somewhere else, already above ground, refined and in storage.

The first port of call would be the central bank of the DPRK in Pyongyang. Central banks always had gold bullion in their vaults. The Bank of England has around £160 billion in the gold vaults well beneath Threadneedle Street. Under the 'Old Lady's' skirts were piles of 28lb (12.5kg), 24 carat gold bars. A fraction of that would do JJ just fine. Immediately, though, this threw up two obstacles. First, JJ had no idea how much gold was stored in the vaults of the DPRK's central bank or whether or not the gold bars in Pyongyang were of the same size and weight. Bullion bars come in all shapes and sizes, as small as 1kg or as large as the majority in the Bank of England's vaults at 12.5kg. The second immediate difficulty was weight. Even if the DPRK's central bank had the required amount of pure gold Neil Robson was demanding, how were they going to transport it out of Pyongyang over the border to South Korea and then on to good old Blighty. That didn't even take into account how JJ and his team were going to break into the central bank or the length of time it would take to load the gold onto whatever transport they had. All of this was supposed to happen without being rumbled by North Korean military or secret service forces. It was impossible.

Still, JJ's mum had always said that when there were a list of obstacles to overcome or questions to answer start at the beginning and tick them off one by one. Mum was talking about sports and school tests right enough, not an outrageous and audacious idiot plot to steal a bucket load, actually maybe thousands of bucket loads, of gold from a loony despot.

Another fact that JJ discovered in his research is that it is notoriously difficult to gauge how much gold is in any central bank's vaults, even in those countries who lodge data with the World Gold Council and the IMF. It is widely regarded that the USA has the most, well over 8,000 tonnes, with Germany and the IMF next in line though far behind the USA, with 2,000 – 3,000 tonnes each. China is in the top ten gold holders, as you might expect, but below that though still in the top twenty are, perhaps, unexpected names like Lebanon and Taiwan. South Korea was estimated to have around 110 tonnes. The North would surely have less than that even with the hoarding tendencies that mushroom in a secret society. Further research by JJ discovered that in July 2013, North Korea had exported two tonnes of gold to China, raising US $100 million in cash. Industry experts reckoned that these two tonnes came directly from the central bank gold vaults in Pyongyang and were replenished later that year. More interestingly though, were reports that a mysterious agency known as Room 39 managed the gold sales on behalf of Kim Jong-un, the DPRK's supreme leader. Fuck me with a barge pole thought JJ, the wee scunner is siphoning off gold and cash into his personal account!

The North Korean leadership's fascination with gold appeared not to be recent, it went as far back as Kim Il-sung, the current leader's grandfather. The mines in North and South Pyongan Province are estimated to have between 1,000 and 2,000 tonnes of gold deposits. Extracted and purified with their limited technology, maybe two tonnes per year for thirty years, yielding a maximum of sixty tonnes of gold held in storage. A 'gift' or two from Russia and China over this time frame could bring that up to, perhaps, eighty tonnes. This mission had hit a wee glitch right at the outset. JJ needed to acquire the whole caboodle to make up £3 billion at today's price of gold. At best, it would seem that North Korea held around £3.5 billion equivalent. It was tight, it had better all be in the central bank's vaults and the price of gold had better not drop.

It didn't take JJ long to work out that two articulated lorries, or American semi-trucks, each carrying forty tonnes could carry the load. Caterpiller, Volvo, Ford all made appropriate tractors and trailers but these makes would stick out like a sore thumb in the streets of Pyongyang. FAW semi-trucks were all over China so that would be a possibility. More worrisome than finding an appropriate truck was the transport plan itself. It didn't really make sense. While the border with South Korea was only 60km away, there would be various military checkpoints along the route and heavily fortified ones near the demarcation line. Two trucks, of whatever make, with two to three foreigners in each of the cabs would arouse more than a passing interest. A quick glance at the load and all hell would break loose. Bars of gold just didn't migrate from North to South in the dead of night. Even DPRK citizens couldn't do that in the middle of the day. The transportation plan needed to be better, a whole lot better.

JJ had done enough thinking about this for the day. He was exhausted and had taken the day off work to concentrate on it. He thought he'd better give Toby a call. In fact, he needed to fill Toby in because Fathead's skills were going to be essential later on and JJ needed a credible cover story for his upcoming 'vacation'.

"Hi Toby, it's JJ."

"Boss man!" exclaimed Toby, happy to hear from his leader and mentor. "How are you, how's your day off? Did you get up to no good?" asked Fathead, clearly in a buoyant mood.

"How are the markets today, Toby?" asked JJ, more or less ignoring all of Toby's questions.

"They're good for us, JJ," replied Toby. "Gold and crude were up, bonds were down and stocks have been treading water. We're in good shape."

"Do you fancy coming over for a couple of those rare Macallans that I keep hidden? I need to run a few things by you," asked JJ.

"Sure JJ, you know me, never say no to a rare malt. What time?"

"Around 8.30pm if that suits. Cyrus will have done all of his project and school work by then and Gil's going for an evening gym session."

Toby knew JJ well enough to tell that his tone was not full of the joys of spring. "Is there anything up JJ? You don't sound like a happy bunny."

"I've been concentrating all day Toby on stuff that I don't

want to be concentrating on so I'm a bit brain-tired. I'll give you the scoop when you come over. See you at 8.30."

Toby said his cheerios and hung up. He always liked having a good malt with JJ, maybe even some banter with Cyrus and the opportunity of an ogle at the hot Oriental Gil. It was 6pm. He'd pack up now and grab a bite at Franco's in Jermyn Street. JJ never had enough food supplies in as far as Toby was concerned and if he tried to raid the fridge Gil would just look at him as if enquiring if he still wanted to live. No, Franco's was the better, the tastier and the safer option.

Toby arrived at JJ's house in Markham Square at 8.30pm prompt. He knew the Scot didn't like being late for anyone nor anyone being late for him. In fact, Toby mused to himself as he rang the bell, JJ was so time conscious that he knew when he was going to pee next. I'm going to the loo in about twenty minutes he'd say, and he would. Who *does* that?

JJ met Toby at the door, took him inside to the living room and settled him down with a large glass of twenty-five year old Macallans single malt whisky. JJ had one too.

"Toby," began JJ. "I'm going to tell you stuff that you'll believe and I'm going to tell you stuff that you won't believe, but on my honour it will all be true. It'll take some time so feel free to help yourself to a top up whenever you want." Toby knew immediately that something wasn't right. JJ never said help yourself to him as far as whisky was concerned. Sensible enough.

JJ began his tale of woe with the meeting with Neil Robson. Toby was well slumped and uncomfortable in JJ's large, cosy armchair at the thought of an insider trading case. He'd be bankrupt with little hope of re-employment in the financial sector and no hope of a boss as good as JJ. He'd need to go abroad. He didn't want to do that as he didn't like foreigners much. He'd only just taken a liking to Yves-Jacques and even then only because he was one of the three amigos. Three amigos who were facing jail time if the worst came to the worst according to JJ's tale. Toby was on his second Macallans before he had the nerve to interrupt JJ and ask any questions but his Dutch courage was mounting.

"I haven't even heard a whisper about this JJ," said Toby. "Am I, are we, going to receive formal letters from the FCA soon?"

"No Toby, we're not."

"How come?"

"I used to work with Neil Robson. He has a plan, well let's call it a tadpole of a plan when you need a Goliath frog one, to keep us all in the careers we're in now," said JJ.

Toby began to cheer up a bit. *That's cool* he thought. *Trust JJ to be buddies with the Financial Secretary to the Treasury.* "That's all good then, JJ. Wow, you had me going for a while. I thought I was going to be destitute or holed up in some mud hut in a rainforest."

"It's not all good, Toby," replied JJ somberly and uncharacteristically omitting to nail Toby's comment as a rainforest would be the last place you'd want to be holed up in a mud hut. Toby was visibly coming back down to the real world of pain and unhappiness.

"How so JJ?" asked Toby with concern. "You're buddies with Robson, right? You worked with him, right? He has the power to make this go away, right?"

"Well, you've got two out of three right and one of them is a curse not a blessing," said JJ. "I'm not friends with Robson. I think he's a slimy toad, mainly out for himself and a touch power mad—" JJ was going to continue but Toby butted in.

"You said he was prepared to make this insider trading thing go away. Why would he do that if he wasn't your friend?" asked Toby, reasonably enough he thought.

"Because he wants me to do something for him in return,

something outrageous but something if it works that may leave our normal daily lives intact."

The next hour or so was taken up mainly by JJ informing Toby that he used to be an MI5 intelligence officer, the outline of Robson's either audacious or stupid plan, JJ's role in it and Toby's late stage appearance if the plan actually got that far. There was not enough malt whisky in JJ's cabinet, maybe even in all the whisky cabinets in Chelsea and Knightsbridge combined that could relieve the aching pain in Fathead's pinhead. He heard what JJ was saying, and he believed it, because JJ had never lied to him about anything, but he couldn't really take it in. It was too much, too crazy, too outwith the realms of his life to date. Strangely, though, after about three or four double whiskies, Toby was beginning to sober up. Bleary eyed but sharper of mind, he simply asked, "Tell me again, JJ, how much physical gold am I going to have to sell?"

★ ★ ★

Police Officer Ethel Rogers was following her normal daily routine. She was in the women's changing locker at West End Central Police Station in Saville Row putting on her uniform and tools of the trade, baton, speedcuffs, CS spray, pistol and taser. Her normal routine had been disturbed a couple of years ago when she had to appear before the Independent Police Complaints Commission, but that went well for her and her two colleagues who appeared with her. She had been promoted as well to senior Authorised Firearms Officer (AFO), not bad for an early forty-something woman in an occupation dominated by men. Rogers was pleasant looking but no stunner. She was around 5ft 6in in height, slim and toned with thick mousy brown shoulder length hair.

Ethel's normal routine was to be disturbed again today. Her boss told her she had to take a meeting in the station in a few minutes and that the as yet unnamed visitor had requested her specifically. Rogers grabbed a disgusting cappuccino from the rickety tin vending machine outside the locker and headed into the meeting room on the first floor of the station. As she entered the sparsely furnished room she recognised the man in the well-cut dark suit, but no tie, sitting down at the plain wooden table. She could not immediately put a name to his weathered but attractive face.

"Hi Ginger," he said.

Now that immediately set her memory banks into overdrive. Only her close friends and a few special colleagues addressed her by her somewhat obvious nickname. This guy was none of those. Fortunately, he had the good grace to introduce himself before that awkward moment when you just can't remember somebody's name turns into a major embarrassment.

"JJ Darke," he said extending his hand.

Ethel Rogers shook JJ's hand and her memory now had a slightly clearer picture of how they knew each other. "It's been quite a while JJ, and I believe you've changed occupation since I last saw you."

"Well, I have and I haven't Ethel," replied JJ, not exactly sounding at ease with his reply.

As they engaged in a few more minutes of small talk and catch-up, Ethel's memory banks were putting the pieces into place of the jigsaw that connected them. She had been the youngest police officer to be accepted into the ranks of CO19, Scotland Yard's specialist firearms unit. In total CO19, now SCO19 due to a police merger, has around 700 members, including training staff, specialist firearm officers (SFOs) and armed response vehicles (ARVs) operators. Their specific mandate was to tackle any armed incidents in London. The SFOs were the proactive wing of SCO19. These days this comprised of around 120 officers in six teams, stationed around different areas of London or driving around in ARVs. A small group of SFOs were also earmarked for training duties. Primarily this was to show all British Police Officers authorised to carry weapons how to use them. Very rarely they would also be asked to undertake some weapons training of the UK's Security Forces, MI5 and MI6. Now it was all becoming HD in Ethel's mind. She had helped train MI5 Officer JJ Darke.

"So, JJ do you still prefer the Glock 17 that I trained you to use or have you advanced to those fancy SIG Sauers?" Ethel smiled, partly because she recalled that JJ was top-notch accurate with a Glock and partly because she remembered him at all.

"Well, Ginger, in recent times I haven't really had much need of a Glock 17, but I still have my original one, tucked up and locked away," he said, pleased that Ethel remembered something of their connection. "How about you?"

"I still prefer the Glock, JJ, and a cut down MP5. The bad guys are getting badder and better armed, so the good girls need to be too."

"So how come you tasered that Adebolajo arsehole in Woolwich last year instead of taking him out?" asked JJ getting down to business.

Ethel was taken aback by the abruptness of the question. One minute they were chitty chatting about old times and the next a guy she hadn't seen for ten years turns up and asks her one of the same questions that the IPCC had asked her. Ethel Rogers was a well-balanced, mentally robust woman. Her boss had told her to give JJ all the help he needed but she was not used to being questioned by folk outside of the police system and she sure wasn't going to spill before she knew what the hell was going on.

"I might answer that question JJ but you're going to have to give me a whole lot more info before I do. Why are you here? What do you want? Why me?" she said. "And it better be good because, as interesting as you are, I've got better things to do than small talk away an hour or so with a former trainee of mine."

JJ was glad that Ginger had not lost any of the spark that he remembered. He told Ethel about the mission at hand, leaving out the blackmail by Robson and the concomitant insider trading issue. As far as Officer Rogers was concerned, he had been called out of MI5 retirement to extract from North Korea monies owed to the British government and people but which North Korea adamantly refused to pay. It was a last resort but one that had been sanctioned by the Chancellor of the Exchequer himself. The Metropolitan Police Commissioner had rubber stamped JJ's approach to Officer Rogers but it was ultimately down to her whether or not she wanted to volunteer for this off-piste mission.

Ethel thought that JJ's outline was one wild plan. It seemed to have the moral high ground and the fact that the head of the police force had authorised her personal involvement added to its credibility. She wasn't scared of the dangers involved. Whether it was a North Korean soldier running at her in Pyongyang or an armed lone wolf terrorist in Woolwich, didn't really matter. They were going down.

JJ could see that Ethel was taking his story in, but he too was on a timeline. "So, Ginger, why didn't you shoot to kill in Woolwich?"

"You need to understand a little about that day, JJ," she began. "I was in a small ARV with two colleagues and driver, parked just off Lewisham High Street. We got the call that there was an armed attack near Woolwich Barracks. We were the closest 19 unit, so we responded. We were there in under ten minutes. Given London traffic at that time of day, it was quick. When we got there it was mayhem. Locals were milling around on the street, unarmed police officers from the nearby station were keeping small crowds of people back. A couple of armed youths, standing in the middle of the road were shouting and bawling some stuff you couldn't understand. One of them was hovering over a prostate body, Lee Rigby, as we later found out." Ethel paused for a sip of the now cold disgusting coffee. "Our driver stayed in the ARV. One of us took up position at the rear of the car. Peter Blackwood and I hunkered down at the front. We had the doors open for protection. The two armed guys made no attempt to run or hide. They could have been out of their minds on drink or drugs. Pete called out for them to drop their weapons and get on the ground. Instead, they rushed at us, the lead one with a meat cleaver and a gun. Pete shot low and stopped the second suspect. In the instant that you need to make a decision, I decided to taser the lead suspect, rather than shoot. It would have been easy for me to say I don't know why I tasered rather than shot. The IPCC asked me the same question and I just replied 'instinct'. Looking back, my decision was more complex than that even though all the complexities had to be weighed up in a split second."

"Are you going to share, Ethel?"

Ethel looked straight at his welcoming grey-green eyes and continued. "It boiled down to this. The guy rushing at me was not heavily armed, clearly not a professional. He was waving his weapons around for god's sake. There were plenty of civilians in the vicinity. I didn't feel life threatened but I did feel in danger, so I tasered him and he went down. If he'd got up and moved closer I'd have popped a 9mm in his lower body. My Glock was on the ground beside me, ready. I'd have had no hesitation in taking him out, but I didn't need to in order to contain the threat," Ethel finished, emitting a very low decibel sigh.

"Has anyone beaten your target shooting score at firearms

training yet?" asked JJ attempting to lighten the atmosphere a little.

"No," replied Ethel, swiftly, softly and with the hint of a smile.

JJ had found out what he wanted to. Ginger was as balanced as he had always remembered, the best shot in CO19 and this, perhaps, coupled with the best judgement in a tight spot. JJ's team for the North Korean operation needed to be small, definitely no more than six. At least half to two-thirds of them needed to be able to shoot but also know when not to shoot. JJ was confident enough that he had these skills and confident enough that Ginger had them too. JJ also wanted to keep his team as close knit as possible. People he knew, had known, or that his friends knew. He could have tapped a couple of old pals in MI5 but Neil Robson had blocked that in case any of them knew or remembered the now Financial Secretary to the Treasury.

"So Ginger, are you in?" JJ asked.

Ethel Rogers hesitated before replying, there was a lot she still needed to know. If truth be told, however, the action of the 'Woolwich Feds' as popular local culture had since named them, was the last action she had been involved in. While she was no warmonger and did not believe in violence for the sake of violence, it was quite an adrenalin rush. At forty-two years old she was unlikely to continue in 19 for that much longer. Indeed, she may even want to leave the police force altogether and start a family with her architect husband. It wasn't too late in the modern world, though babies were expensive she was led to believe by her civilian friends. The police pension plan was OK, but with one government official after the other on *Sky News* every day telling folk to belt-tighten, there was no guarantee that her pension would not come under threat. JJ's promised bonus, on mission completion, amounted to nearly eight years salary for a police officer of her rank and service. A baby could be well cosy on that.

"I'm in JJ," she said thoughtfully. "I've one more question for today, though," she continued.

"Sure," said JJ. "What is it?"

"Can I select my weapons please?"

"Yes, Ginger, you sure can."

JJ and Ginger parted company like old friends, with a hug and appropriate cheek kiss. The limitations set by Neil Robson on team selection were an obstacle for JJ but so far his two picks were his first choices. Admittedly, Fathead would not set foot on North Korean soil but his eventual role was critical as the ability to sell such a hefty amount of gold efficiently, at a good price, and without generating market speculation would be no mean feat. JJ and Toby agreed to leave Yves-Jacques out of the loop. The third amigo was a fine, intelligent analyst but he was young and inexperienced. If he got wind of an insider trading case against him he'd probably have brain freeze at best, or at worst, leap off the top of the *Coq d'Argent* restaurant near Bank tube station. That may be particularly appealing to Yves-Jacques given the French connection; it certainly appeared to be an attractive prospect for the four or five business types who had made the suicidal leap in recent years. No, thought JJ, the young Frenchman could stay in the dark till all was clear or even darker.

JJ had been thinking hard and fast about the task ahead. He had not solved the transport issue of how to get the gold from Pyongyang in the North, through the demarcation line to the South, nor how to get it back to the UK. The latter in theory, was easier as a big enough plane could carry the load. He also knew that he would need at least two Koreans in the team, two who would know the layout of the land, speak the lingo and understand the local customs. Blending in and around Pyongyang would not be simple.

Neil Robson had explicitly banned JJ from using any MI5 sources or assets. This was a bind, but in the particular case of the hunt for two helpful Koreans it did not matter. Neither MI5 nor MI6 had embedded offices in South Korea. The CIA did. It was fortunate for JJ that he had kept in touch with Jim Bradbury, his best friend and contact in the US security services and now the agency's Korean Liaison Officer (KLO) aka head of the CIA's operation in Seoul. Neil Robson had to pull a few strings, which he mumbled, grumbled and swore a lot about, but at least he opened up the right channels and got the approval for the Seoul CIA office to help JJ. The cover story was that JJ was on an exfil mission to spring a key asset out of a compromised position in the North. Jim Bradbury was happy to assist and he had the two helpful Koreans in his team, ready to go.

At most he needed two more to complete the team. One would need to be an explosives expert, specifically a quiet explosives expert capable of opening any unopened doors or vaults in the DPRK's central bank. That was going to be a tough slot to fill. JJ knew a few guys who could blow things up, but noisily. He'd delegated that discovery task to Ginger on the basis that her inside knowledge of illegal activities may help. The other operational omission at this point was HGV drivers. All the team so far could drive but none had any experience of or licence for heavy goods vehicles. If they had to proceed at pace from Pyongyang with trucks of gold they'd need to have drivers skilled in handling such large vehicles without spilling the swag all over the roads of Hwangae Province. As JJ was mulling this over, his phone rang, it was Toby.

"JJ, we're in schtook," began Fathead.

"How come?"

"Yves-Jacques knows," blurted Toby.

"Knows what Fathead?" asked JJ becoming more anxious.

"Knows that there's an insider trading case hanging over us and that we're concocting some plan to get us out of it," replied Toby, shakily, fearing the worst.

"Well, how the holy hell did he find that out, Toby?" bellowed JJ.

"It was my fault, JJ, I was trying to be nice to him, taking him under my wing, that sort of thing…" explained Toby already sounding remorseful. "So I took him to Nobu, we got drunk, well I got drunk, and blabbed."

"For fuck's sake Toby, this isn't a game; we're far enough up shit creek that a paddle or two won't help," replied JJ clearly annoyed. "How is he, what did he say? Can you see him – he's not gone to *Coq d'Argent* has he?" JJ asked, clearly becoming more rattled.

"He's fine, I think…" responded Toby wondering what the Coq whatever had to do with anything. "He says he wants to help," added Toby.

JJ was glad Yves-Jacques hadn't either topped himself or ran about MAM's building screaming about a roast beef conspiracy. That was at least something. "How can he help Toby? This isn't a mathematical problem or a game theoretic one. It's not about portfolio optimisation or stock selection. It's about staying out of jail, having a career. Goddammit staying alive!" shouted JJ into his smartphone.

"I don't know, I was a bit worse for wear as the evening wore on. He said something about skunkworks in a Paris suburb that were doing innovative research on materials and minerals," said Toby, beginning to hope that he was contributing something positive to a difficult phone call.

"Fine," said JJ. "I'll be in the office in half an hour. Get a meeting room. Book it for two hours. Me, you and Yves-Jacques." With that JJ hung up. He jumped in a cab and was heading straight for Mayfair.

In the cab, JJ's mind was on two parallel trains of thought. The first was easy enough. Fathead was a drunken dope and he was about to be banned from alcohol for the duration. The second was more intriguing, why would a young French mathematician know anything about skunkworks, let alone where one was. This should be interesting he thought as his cab raced along The Mall.

★ ★ ★

The following morning, JJ and Yves-Jacques were on the first Eurostar train from St Pancras International to Gare du Nord in Paris. From there they would take a taxi to Montparnasse in the 14th arondissement, drive to the Foundation Henri Cartier-Bresson and be met by one of Yves-Jacques old university chums. As JJ settled back for the two hour or so train journey he was thinking about the hidden depths of the young Frenchman. He knew well enough about Yves-Jacques' mathematical capabilities but he hadn't really focussed on that part of his CV which had detailed his additional qualification in physics. He was second in his year at the École Polytechnique Paris Tech (EPPT), one of the top fifty universities in the world. He worked in a team under eminent scientists like Luca Perfetti, completed a two year course and was outscored only by his friend Vincent Barakat, who they were soon to meet.

While this was all good and interesting stuff that JJ had found out at yesterday's meeting at MAM with Toby and Yves-Jacques it didn't really seem that relevant to on-going events of a Korean nature. Yves-Jacques had handled the full story from JJ well, well it wasn't full but it was a story and it was Yves-Jacques' turn to explain why he could help. Once young Durand had babbled on enough about his smarts, the interesting content emerged.

Apparently, one of the science professors at the EPPT, Henri

De Brugne, didn't like teaching much. He did it for the money. What he did like was exciting and innovative research. He had convinced the Board of the EPPT to allocate him some funds to do offsite research with a few select students in their own time. His hope was to stay at the cutting edge of discoveries, mainly in physics and chemistry, to tap the best of new, young brains around and, if really lucky, to discover a process which was sellable to the corporate or industrial world. Yves-Jacques was one of the students selected, as was Vincent Barakat, whose specialty lay in the study of materials and chemical engineering. So, under the auspices of this leading French scholar they set up a skunkworks and called it PLP, after Pepé Le Pew, arguably the most famous fictional skunk in the world and star of many a Looney Tunes cartoon. Very appropriate thought JJ.

In modern terminology a skunkworks project was one where a small group of like-minded people set about to do research and development in a particular field with the aim of radical innovation or discovery. The origin of the term was much older, dating back to Lockheed's Skunk Works project in World War II. Apparently, Lockheed set up an incubator for the design of the P80-Shooting Star jet fighter in a circus tent near a plastics factory in Burbank, California. The pungent smells wafting into the tent from the factory made the Lockheed design team think of the Skonk Works factory in Al Capp's *L'il Abner* comic strip, the job no one wanted. Voila skunkworks!

The skunkworks projects at PLP in the 14th arondissement, this fine spring day, were of a different nature. The one that captivated the attention of JJ Darke was the chemical engineering experiments of Vincent Barakat. Specifically his experiments on the melting and liquefying of precious metals. As they climbed the stairs of the Foundation Henri Cartier-Bresson building, Yves-Jacques spotted his friend straight away.

"Vincent!" he called out, waving his right arm vigorously. Vincent waved back and as they collided softly, they gave each other two of those Gallic kisses that only French guys can get away with. After the pleasantries, Yves-Jacques introduced Vincent to JJ. The Scot extended his hand swiftly, none of that man-kissing malarkey was ever on offer in Glasgow and he sure wasn't becoming an instant Euro fag just because he was in Paris and desperate.

Yves-Jacques had given Vincent the heads up on the visit, the untrue version that is. Mr Darke was head of portfolio strategy at Yves-Jacques' firm. They had acquired legally in the course of business a sizeable amount of physical gold which was stored in vaults of various European banks. Mr Darke wanted all this gold in London and was concerned that the usual modes of transportation, truck, van or plane were too open to a hijacking, especially as their purchase of the gold bars was well known in some financial circles both legit and shady. Yves-Jacques had mentioned Vincent's experiments to his boss and he felt it interesting enough to make a day trip to Paris. Yves-Jacques had indicated that his boss would gift €10,000 to PLP just for one day of Vincent's time and substantially more if any of his work was capable of being used in the transport of the gold. Vincent knew that was a great deal. €10,000 would fund better some existing projects for PLP and if it were indeed to develop into substantially more maybe they could start on some new ones.

Vincent Barakat was about the same height and build as JJ, 6ft. He had a shock of dark, curly hair, swarthy skin, deep blue eyes. He had an engaging smile and appeared to be around the same age as his countryman, in his early to mid-twenties. He took JJ's extended arm, shook his hand firmly and, thankfully, made no attempt to plop a soppy one on the Scot's cheek.

"Good morning, Mr Darke," said Vincent, warmly enough and in very crisp English.

"Good morning, Vincent," said JJ in return, ensuring to pronounce Vincent as Vansaan. "Your English is very good. Thank you for seeing us at such short notice."

"My nanny was English when I was young so I picked it up fairly quickly," he informed JJ.

"Here's a banker's draft for the €10,000 as promised," said JJ, handing it to Vincent, enclosed in a plain white envelope. "Just to get it out of the way so that there is no awkwardness later in the day," he added.

"Thank you. I hope I can show you something which makes you want to give us an even bigger one!" Vincent replied, laughing out loud.

JJ smiled and the three of them headed off. PLP's laboratory was only a few minutes walk from the famous photographer's foundation. Vincent and Yves-Jacques led the way, chatting away in their native tongue. JJ kept a few paces behind.

It was a very nice day in Paris, thought JJ, fresh, but comfortably warm and a cloudless sky. He wondered, as he strolled, whether he'd get the opportunity to enjoy any more such days or would he soon be lying lifeless in some Pyongyang street gutter, or banged up in some manky British gaol. His wondering ended as Vincent announced they had arrived. Great, thought JJ, and not a nostril's whiff of stinking, burning plastic to tarnish the moment.

The PLP laboratory was housed in a stand-alone structure behind a large retail outlet in Boulevard Arago. Externally, it resembled a garage or a large storage facility. It was on one floor. The building was far enough away from shoppers and other pedestrians to attract no attention. Perhaps even more importantly it was far enough away from any other building that occasional scientific pops, bangs, wallops and smells from PLP would not be noticed. Inside, the décor was bright and industrial. Concrete floor, whitewashed brick walls, overhead fluorescent tube lighting which covered the length of the ceiling. There were about a dozen or so laboratory style tables packed with equipment for the lab's experiments. About half of the tables had at least one or two PLP staff at them. At the near end to the door there were two makeshift offices, packed to the gunnels, with desktop computers, laptops, tablets and all the electric paraphernalia you could imagine. Each office had a small unladen table and a couple of cheap, maybe even IKEA wooden chairs. These scientists really didn't have much desire for meetings. One of the offices was Vincent Barakat's and that's where they headed.

"So, Mr Darke," began Vincent as they all sat down. No tea or coffee on offer but at least a small bottle of evian each to keep hydrated. "Yves-Jacques has told me that you are interested in the transportation of gold bars but that you are concerned with their security?" asked Vincent.

"That's right, Vincent," responded JJ. "Specifically, so as not to waste your time, I was wondering whether or not the properties of the transported gold could be changed such that it retained its full purity, and hence value, but did not appear to be what it was," said JJ anxious to get to the nub of the matter.

Vincent nodded, had a quick look at Yves-Jacques who nodded back. These two friends trusted each other so Vincent was now operating on the basis that JJ Darke was trustworthy too. He seemed OK, he thought, and he'd paid up front. All good.

"Clearly, Mr Darke," resumed Vincent, "I know nothing about security of gold transportation. What I do know about is gold itself. Without going into the whole chemical history of gold, the two main methods of refining gold after its initial production are the Wohlwill process and the Miller process. The former uses electrolysis and the latter chlorination. The Wohlwill way results in a higher purity of the refined gold, nearly 100%, but it is a complex and time consuming process. The Miller way involves blowing a stream of pure chlorine gas over and through a crucible filled with molten but impure gold. All the elements in the gold that are not pure form chlorides before gold does, essentially leaving behind what is more or less pure gold. Normally, this process is performed on an industrial scale and is extremely messy. It is, however, quick by comparison with the Wohlwill route," Vincent paused for a long drink of his evian.

JJ was listening intently. Vincent was on the ball but he was skirting the issue as far as the mission at hand was concerned. However backward the North Korean gold extraction and refining process was, JJ felt that the gold bullion in the vaults of the DPRK's central bank would be pure enough. If the DPRK had a gold guru he certainly would not be volunteering to tell Kim Jong-un that his gold was only 90% pure. The supreme leader and his forebears dealt only in fine gold. On top of that, thought JJ, North Korea's gold gifts from Russia and China were sure to be top quality. JJ thought now was the time to slightly redirect Vincent's train of thought.

"Vincent, thank you. In our particular case, though, the gold is already of maximum purity. Being very straight about it, my interest is in disguising the gold. Yves-Jacques told me that your speciality was on the melting of precious metals. Is there anything you have discovered in that research that may help?"

Vincent Barakat put his evian back on the rickety table. "Gold melts at 1064 degrees Celsius, Mr Darke. Traditional methods of melting gold tend to be messy, sometimes losing part of the gold content. Also, the reverberatory furnace, or cupolas required are large, stationary and demand constant monitoring. With the price of gold at nearly US $1,500/oz, and households all over the world sending in their scrap jewellery, old watches and gold coins for cash, the melting and purifying of gold has attracted the attention of gold refineries around the globe. The specific interest you have, Mr Darke, is also the specific interest of the EuroGet Group, France's largest gold refiner. They gave PLP €50,000, half in advance, to discover an efficient method of melting gold, on a smaller, more versatile scale."

"How are you progressing with that, Vincent?" enquired JJ.

"Very well," he responded. "Would you like to see?"

JJ replied in the affirmative. The three of them left Vincent's office, made their way through the PLP lab and ended up at the far end of the building. Vincent unlocked the metal door of a spacious room which had a sign on it:

Empêcher d'entrer. Expérimenter en cours.
Keep out. Experiment in progress.

When JJ entered, it was hot but not unbearably so. He was looking at two machines which resembled elongated horizontal sunbeds with perforations on their top cover.

Vincent began. "The cleanest way to melt gold, Mr Darke, or almost any other precious metal, is through induction. Essentially, you build a super-efficient electromagnet and pass through it a high frequency alternating current. The AC frequency used depends on several factors including object size, material type and penetration depth. For gold bullion bars the frequency would need to be in the range of 5-10 kilohertz. Some specialist refineries already have in production induction furnaces to this end, but again these tend to be large, immoveable constructs. Our innovation here is two-fold. First, we have built these two mini furnaces if you like, to see whether the induction process can be undertaken efficiently on a significantly smaller scale. Secondly, we have improved substantially the conductivity of the water cooled copper rings inside the furnaces, which are necessary to complete the induction process."

Now we're talking, thought JJ, his analytical brain zooming through everything that Vincent was telling him and projecting ahead.

"Vincent, this is most impressive. I have several questions. Is this process totally reliable right now? How much do these mini furnaces weigh? What weight of gold does each sunbed, for want of a better word, process? How long does the gold stay molten? Any problems with your process?" JJ was sounding keen, perhaps too keen, but Vincent was impressed enough with himself that he just took it for professional admiration.

Vincent resumed. "Each of these 'sunbeds' as you called them, are around five and a half metres long, and weigh 300kg or a lot more when fully loaded. Due to the materials we have used and the ergonomic design, each sunbed can take up to twenty tonnes of gold. Obviously, we have not been able to experiment with that amount of gold but I think it is a reasonable extrapolation. The gold stays molten for as long as the electromagnet is in use. From a cold start it would take forty-five minutes to an hour to melt the twenty tonnes. That's very fast by comparison with other methods." Vincent looked at his friend who had also been listening intently. Yves-Jacques gave him the thumbs up.

"Any problems with the process or the machinery, Vincent?"

"Not really, Mr Darke, apart from one…"

JJ raised his eyebrows and gave Vincent a little nod, it was time for the young scientist to reveal the glitch.

"The perforations at the top of the mini furnace provide a degree of cooling," began Vincent, "as do the overhead fans, but we are having problems with the sunbeds' stability when the internal temperature is over 1,000 degrees Celsius for more than fifteen minutes. We're concerned that the sunbeds themselves will melt."

JJ was pensive. After a few more moments he asked, "What are these mini furnaces made of, Vincent?"

"Mainly alumina, silicon and magnesium mixed with small insertions of fire clays. We need high refractory materials and these were the ones we could both get supplies of and afford."

"What about Kevlar or carbon fibre?" asked JJ.

"Apart from the fact that we could not afford those materials, Kevlar is out," began Vincent. "Kevlar loses its tensile strength nearly exponentially as the temperature rises. At just over 250 degrees Celsius, Kevlar's strength is reduced by 50% in about two to three days. If the temperature was over 1,000 degrees then any Kevlar structure would start to buckle, after twelve to fifteen hours at best."

"What about carbon fibre?"

Vincent thought for a moment. "Yes, in theory," he said. "There are many carbon fibres and carbon fibre composites. The ones which retain their tensile strength at super high temperatures are used by NASA in their space programmes. I believe they are a composite material involving a glass-ceramic matrix combined with specialised heat-resistant carbon fibres."

JJ now knew what he had to do. He thanked Vincent for his time and information, it had been very helpful. He promised to wire PLP a further €20,000 in good faith so that JJ could contact Vincent if and when necessary over the next few days. He would add a further €20,000 if, for the next two weeks, Vincent and his team put JJ's interests and requests above those of all other clients, including EuroGet. He didn't need or demand permanent exclusivity, just a head start, a window of exclusivity. Vincent agreed. Short term cash flow can often be the key financial bugbear for a small skunkworks outfit.

JJ and Yves-Jacques made it back to the Gare du Nord in time for their 4pm Eurostar departure. They chatted about the day. JJ thanked the young Frenchman for his forethought and the introduction to Vincent Barakat. It had turned out to be a fruitful day trip. Though JJ and Fathead had agreed to leave Yves-Jacques out of the North Korean loop, Toby's alcohol induced loose lips and Yves-Jacques' stellar contribution meant that he was well and truly in the loop now.

As the train was whizzing along, JJ checked his emails and texts on his smartphone. One unread text was from Ginger. It simply stated: *I've found us a safe cracker.* That was good news. Ethel was well aware that the safe cracker for this trip better know how to get into a serious mega-vault. No cat burglar or opportunistic gonk that wanted to drop a safe on its head and hope it burst open. This was the real deal. JJ replied thanking Ginger and suggesting they meet up tomorrow to discuss.

There was an email from the slime Robson. He wanted to know how things were going as the clock was ticking. JJ sent a one word reply saying: *Fine.* He realised Neal Robson was not going to be satisfied with that but he needed to check out a couple of things on his tablet before formulating a proper reply.

"Yves-Jacques," said JJ, getting the attention of his young colleague sitting opposite. "How long do you think it takes Renault to build an average family car?"

Yves-Jacques pondered the question. Clearly Renault family cars were not hand built and clearly they were chugging along the production line at pace. "From scratch?" asked Yves-Jacques.

"From scratch," confirmed JJ.

"Maybe a day?" ventured the French man.

"Actually, depending on the specifications it would be two to four days from scratch. High spec sports cars or rally cars would take longer. Renault aren't any better or worse than other major car manufacturers. I just wanted to be local about it," JJ smiled and Yves-Jacques went back to his laptop game.

JJ returned to his smartphone and texted an old friend of his, based in Surrey, Harold McFarlane. He hadn't spoken to Harold for a few years but the Surrey born and bred Englishman had been instrumental, nay essential, to JJ's fun a few years ago. Harold had hit upon hard times, not through ill health or job loss, but his extended family were not as productive in their daily lives and had become quite a financial burden. He loved his two daughters enormously and they were bright, lively girls. Harold could not afford to send them both to university at more or less the same time and it was this issue that weighed on his mind more than any other. JJ gave him £10,000 to allow both daughters to get their desired higher education. Harold did not want to accept the money, and only agreed when JJ had said to treat it as a loan. In their hearts they both knew it was a gift. Harold in all likelihood would not be in a position to repay £10,000 and JJ had no intention of trying to recoup it. The last he heard, one of Harold's daughters was an accountant and the other one ran a small, but successful internet-based business.

JJ's phone vibrated. It was a reply from Harold.

No, we're not overloaded right now. The team has gone to Oz and we're not expecting them back for 3 weeks at least. It's great to hear from you. I hope everything is OK. Regards, Harold.

It was all fitting into place now. After a few more moments thought JJ decided it was time to bring Gil into the picture. He sent another email.

Gil,
I'll explain more tonight but for the moment I need you to organise the following:
Acquire two tractor units fitted with empty fuel tanks on

their trailers. Both trucks need to be of the dimensions and style of a Chinese FAW Jie Fang truck capable of carrying a Shaanxi 6x4 20cbm fuel tanker. Once you've acquired the trucks, deliver them to Harold McFarlane at the McLaren Technology Centre, Chertsey Road, Woking. He's expecting them in a couple of days.

JJ.

JJ knew that Gil would be on the case in a flash. She was a great friend, nanny and bodyguard to Cyrus. Now some of her other skills may need to come to the fore.

It may take Renault and other car manufacturers a few days to build a car, but a top notch Formula 1 team can build a race car from scratch overnight. JJ leant back in his Eurostar seat and closed his eyes. This had been a good day. He was silently humming in his head Ray Parker's *Ghostbusters* theme.

Harold McFarlane was the answer to your question, Ray.

5

THE WAY OF THE FIST

"C'mon Cyrus," yelled Gil Haning. "Shift your skinny butt and turn your computer off. Time to exercise your body not just your mind."

Gil, aka Zhang Bai Ling, had already been training herself for about thirty minutes in JJ Darke's gym at his house in Markham Square. Her solo training sessions were akin to a religious ceremony. She always wore a black short-cropped sleeveless top with sports bra, specialist lightweight black and grey three-quarter length pants, and her favourite silvery white trainers.

Tonight the starting point, after warming up, was a session with the heavy bag. She recalled the first time she had put on boxing wraps. It was a nightmare of dexterity. Now with her Fairtex wraps, she was like a machine weaving the material in and out of her slim fingers, ensuring the knuckles were fully protected, that the wraps were tight and secure, and that the loop at the end was firmly in place. Then she'd slip on her mid-weight Immortal black boxing gloves. They felt good. On her toes, but not moving like a gazelle given her limp left leg, she circled the heavy bag, securely hanging from the basement's ceiling. Left jab, right jab, a few slow shots to the bag, just to get the range. Left hook, two straight right jabs, upper cut, right cross. She continued on her routine. Once she was confident enough with the timing and power of her punches, she gradually introduced elbows and knees. Elbow shots were her favourite attack blows. However, unlike the hands and knuckles, they were unprotected. Badly-timed elbow shots meant grazing, bleeding and annoying though moderate pain. Some nights after training, she'd be bleeding from both elbows. She regarded it as a badge of honour, but in fact it meant that her timing was out. On a heavy bag or a training pad a well-timed elbow shot made the sound of a dull thud, a badly-timed hit led to a scraping one. Tonight she was all dull thud. Knee shots currently meant left knee shots. To retain balance and be in the correct posture for a powerful knee attack to the groin or stomach meant that your standing leg had to be firmly planted on the ground, supple but stable. Gil's left leg was still hobbly-wobbly so right knee attacks tended to be weak, limp, poorly timed. Similarly, her roundhouse kicks tended to be with the left leg. The limb was still powerful enough to do damage, indeed Gil's skills were sufficient to break any attacker's leg with one blow.

Hooks, jabs, crosses, knees and elbows were the potential weapons of the human body. They were developed into a system of attack and defence moves by Bruce Lee and called Jeet Kune Do, the way of the intercepting fist. Essentially, Lee had become unenthused about traditional Chinese martial arts, he wanted to discard the flowery, purely aesthetic and rigidly systematic moves for a process that was more useful in the real world, a system that was not a system, but flowed like water. To the casual observer, JKD combined Western boxing techniques with Eastern kicking ones, and an elbow and knee from mixed martial arts. Along with Krav Maga, it was perhaps the most street wise of the martial arts.

Having previously trained in martial arts, Gil had stood out when JJ ran a 12 week course for a select few in the US security services, back in 2010. JKD students from the CIA, FBI and the NSA came to JJ's classes and several of them, including Gil, continued training on their own or with personal instructors thereafter. JJ was somewhat JKD old school, had a 2nd ranking and had one of the meanest spinning elbow shots Gil had ever seen. When they sparred now, with protective helmets on, JJ was a tad slower than he used to be but this was balanced by Gil's limp. They were nearly evenly matched but the Scot still had the greater power.

"Cyrus!" bellowed Gil yet again. "For goodness sake, c'mon, you need to release some of those endorphins dormant in your nerdy body."

"OK, OK, I'm coming," groaned Cyrus, loping unenthusiastically down the stairs to the basement. He looked like the guy from *Napoleon Dynamite*, all gawky and uncoordinated, regular T-shirt on, baggy white shorts and a pair of black and green trainers. "Do we have to do this Gil? I'm tired and I could happily flop," said the kid.

"Yes, we have to do it Cyrus," Gil replied. "I know you play tennis and do a bit of gym training, but what happens if you get bullied at school? Are you going to run to the teacher blubbering?"

"I've never been bullied at school," Cyrus responded quick as a flash and mistakenly thinking that the exit door was opening.

"What if somebody tried to harm your girlfriend, what's her name, Lucy?" Gil countered.

"She's a girl friend, Gil, not a girlfriend," emphasised Cyrus, a little embarrassed.

"Doesn't matter," said Gil. "One day or night she may be in your company and some knucklehead wants to move in on her, pulling and pushing her a little. You ask him to stop but he doesn't. Do you take the pose of a curly-topped pipe cleaner or do you do something about it?"

Although at this precise moment, Cyrus was finding Gil very very annoying, he did indeed like her and liked having her around.

She was right. Cyrus was no fighter, he wasn't even that tough. He kind of ghosted his way through school having only a couple of close friends and, as yet, not crossing the path of any enemies or bullies. He did like Lucy and while he'd never admit it under parental or 'bodyguard' questioning, he did want to be her boyfriend. The black scenario painted by Gil that Lucy was in trouble, did indeed disturb Cyrus. What would he do in that position? Calling for help would take too long and there'd be no guarantee help would come. Trying to talk the knucklehead down was a possibility but, unfortunately, one of the characteristics of knuckleheads was that talking and listening were often too much of a strenuous task.

"Fine," Cyrus said eventually. "What are we practising tonight?"

"Well, young man…" beamed Gil who really liked Cyrus. "You're going to start with a ten minute warm-up on the treadmill, then we're going to give those peas you call muscles a bit of a going over with biceps curls and triceps extensions. Remember arm pain is good pain. No pain, no gain. We are going to build those arms so that the Muscles from Brussels would be happy to have a beer with you."

"I don't drink beer," said Cyrus cheekily and feeling somewhat ancient that he actually knew who the Muscles from Brussels was.

Gil gave him a look. Cyrus plodded on to the treadmill, started with a two minute slightly inclined walk to check hamstrings and the like and then picked up the pace.

"Once that curly top of yours starts to reveal the glistening signs of sweat, we'll move to the weights. Then we're going to practise the art of accurate and timely fist strikes. Got it?" said Gil, now clearly getting her own way.

"Got it, uber-fuhrer Haning," replied Cyrus and off he went, however reluctantly, on his exercise regime.

Gil was looking at Cyrus like a big sister to a wee brother. He was a good-looking boy, clearly smart and the apple of JJ's eye. He was tall and slim but he was going to need to develop his stamina and strength. This was a far cry from her NSA work at LINEAR and an even farther cry from that fateful night in Boston, mused Gil, as she was studying Cyrus's running style. She was very grateful to JJ for the opportunity to come to London to rest and recuperate. She found out that it was Jayne Hayden, the NSA's chief officer in Boston, who had made the call to JJ. They had known each other from their CIA and MI5 days respectively and had kept in social, if not operational, touch. Jane knew that Cyrus's mother had died and that JJ was attempting to raise Cyrus on his own. She asked JJ if he remembered Zhang Bai Ling, and he had as she was one of his best JKD students.

Jane Hayden proposed that Bai Ling could do with a non-operational role outside the USA for a while, maybe even a very long while, and JJ felt that an interesting young woman may make a good companion, nanny or even 'bodyguard' as Cyrus called her. Gil had said yes to the job offer and much of it was enjoyable. She was well paid by JJ. On top of her Federal pension that she received as part of her forced retirement from the NSA, that was a welcome income. She lived in a cool part of London courtesy of the NSA, and still had enough spare cash to send regular amounts to her family in Hong Kong. JJ was a good boss and a fine friend. He never bothered her in the way that forty-something men can sometimes bother younger women. He appeared to care for her well-being and he trusted her implicitly with Cyrus.

It was good but it was not all good. She loved being with JJ and Cyrus. She was determined to teach the younger Darke some skills that he might need whenever he left the uniquely closeted atmosphere of private schools in Chelsea and into the darkness that was the real world. She was a maths genius and one of the youngest NSA officers to see action. She missed both. Her left knee may be dud but she did not want her brain or skills to atrophy as well.

As Cyrus was wilting under the pressure of his third set of fifteen bicep curl repetitions with two 10kg weights, Gil's smartphone beeped from the bench opposite her. It was an email from JJ. He wanted to acquire two trucks that were of comparable dimensions to Chinese FAW Jie Fang trucks with Shaanxi tankers attached. He'd explain why later. Once acquired, she was to have them delivered to Harold McFarlane at the McLaren Technology Centre in Woking, Surrey. In the next day or two would be fine.

Oooooh, thought Gil. That wasn't pick up some groceries that Ocado didn't deliver, or make sure Cyrus didn't stay up all night on his computer. That request had a hint of action about it. Trucks that looked like Chinese trucks, tankers attached, top-notch Formula One team. I wonder what's afoot, she thought. Gil replied to JJ's email straight away. She was on it, well she would be on it once she finished training and exhausting Cyrus. Tomorrow she'd quiz JJ. Things were looking up, maybe.

"Right Cyrus," said Gil somewhat more bouncily than earlier in the evening. "Get your wraps and gloves on. You're going to do some damage to this here heavy punch bag and then we'll spar for a few minutes. I'll show you how to do your wraps again if you've forgotten. C'mon, chop-chop, get a shifty on, no time for lolly gagging. Time to turn you into a lean, mean pipe-cleaning machine," encouraged Gil, laughing slightly as she said it.

Cyrus struggled to his feet, popped his Century full-face protective helmet on and wearily tried to do his own wraps. *That Gil's due some payback*, he thought, in the nicest possible way.

★ ★ ★

McLaren's Technology Centre was a piece of art. Indeed, it was shortlisted for the 2005 Stirling Prize, only to be beaten by the Scottish Parliament building. JJ liked that. However, neither Scotland's Parliament building in Edinburgh nor its in-house parliamentarians were going to be of much use to JJ today. No, today was all about design, technology and speed. In total, the MTC was around half a million square metres, all artificial lakes and glass fronted buildings. It had cost around £300 million to build and was completed in 2004. It was the brainchild of Ron Dennis, CEO and joint owner of the McLaren group. He wanted to consolidate all McLaren's activities on one site as opposed to the eighteen previous operations scattered around southern England. Much of McLaren's activities on this site spearheaded the advancement of the Formula One team and the sports car division. It had a state of the art 145m long circuit shaped wind tunnel for the aerodynamic testing of the F1 cars.

As JJ and Gil drove along the A3 in JJ's Porsche the wind tunnel building would not be on their itinerary. They were headed for a different building at the far end of the complex. While the majority of McLaren's work force, over 1,000 strong, were involved in the design, assembly and testing of F1 and super car vehicles some fifty or so excluding drivers were involved with McLaren's massive trucks. These both transported the F1 cars and housed much of the on circuit technology to assess their performance, the weather, the tyres and the like. It was here that JJ and Gil hoped to discover some good news.

It had been two days since JJ had emailed Gil her instructions. True to her word she was on it in a flash and had found two Volvo FMX trucks with tankers attached ready for sale and collection. These were as close as she could get to the dimensions and silhouette of the Chinese FAW trucks that JJ had detailed and they should be at McLaren this morning. As befitted their partnership,

McLaren used primarily Mercedes trucks to transport their F1 cars across the world but occasionally these were all tied up and extracurricular manufacturers were called upon. With the Formula One team and full entourage in Australia for the opening race of the FIA Championship it would not have been unusual for those in Woking to see a Volvo truck or two drive into the MTC.

After JJ had returned from his Paris day trip with Yves-Jacques, he had informed Gil of the reason for the trucks and, indeed, filled her in on the whole story, blackmail and insider trading included. Gil had wanted to take Neil Robson out, after all she was a first-class sniper, and could drill the conniving sludgeball from over 3,000 metres away. JJ smiled at that prospect but pointed out to Gil that the file would still exist even if Neil Robson didn't and that FCA officers Watts and Woodhouse would sense an even smellier rat.

"How do you know this McFarlane dude we're going to see?" Gil asked JJ as they sped past the Esher exit on the A3, on their way to Woking. JJ was keeping more or less to the 70mph speed limit. This wasn't that easy in a Porsche Carrera 4S that almost by instinct wanted to exceed whatever speed limit was applicable but JJ could do without any more hassle. A fine or a driving disqualification was not on the agenda for today.

"He worked for me indirectly when I used to do some GT racing," he replied. "For a season I ran a McLaren F1 GTR in club and FIA GT races, culminating in a Le Mans entry, then I ran a Porsche team in the Porsche Super Cup. This was about fifteen years ago, before Cyrus was born. Harold made the cars work, fixed their broken parts and ensured that my cars were on track, on time and in good shape. He was on a bit of a financial downer, could not afford to send his two daughters to university, so I helped him out."

"And you think that's enough for him to do this truck-enhancing task for you?" pressed Gil, unconvinced.

"Harold's team are subcontractors to McLaren. They're allowed to do other jobs, as long as they don't clash with McLaren's F1 activities. Provided they're fully funded Harold and his boys can utilise McLaren's facilities except the wind tunnel and any engineering machinery earmarked solely for the F1 team. While we may need to drive these trucks fast from Pyongyang to Seoul I doubt that wind tunnel testing is needed. Nearly all the key McLaren technicians are with the F1 team in Australia. That's a lucky break for us because Harold and his mechanics, electricians, engineers etc. can work on our trucks unencumbered and legitimately," concluded JJ.

"Does Harold know why we want the trucks changed, enhanced and disguised?"

"No," responded JJ. "He trusts me and he knows he and his team are to be paid well enough not to ask. The disguising of the Volvo trucks to look like Chinese FAW trucks may raise the odd eyebrow and if and when Vincent Barakat has his sunbeds ready to install that will raise a few questions. We'll cross those bridges when they appear. In the meantime, Harold will probably go along with the plan or the abridged version as he knows it."

JJ parked up at the back end of the McLaren Technology Centre. He could see the Volvo trucks and tankers in the far distance and in the near distance a smiling Harold McFarlane was striding his way.

"Hi Harold," said JJ extending his hand. Harold McFarlane was in his mid to late fifties, about 5 foot 9 inches, stockily built with short almost snow white hair.

"JJ!" he exclaimed clearly happy to see his old buddy, to the extent that he gave the Scot a big man hug, not the usual mode of man to man greeting of his generation. "How are you, you crazy

Jock?" asked Harold. "Done any motor racing or are you just a desk bound old fart now?" Harold's sense of wicked humour had clearly not dissipated with age.

"I'm fine Harold. It's really good to see you too. No more racing for me I'm afraid but I've been dragged away from my old fart desk job for a bit."

JJ enquired about Harold's two daughters. They were well and thriving so all was good in the McFarlane household.

"Harold, this is Gil Haning," said JJ introducing the Oriental lady at his side. "She's my PA, even aide-de-camp on this exercise, totally trustworthy and sharp as a tack." Gil quite liked her job description; at least it was better than nanny to my teenage son.

"Nice to meet you Harold," said Gil.

"You too Gil," replied Harold. "Let's go over to my garage." Garage was what he euphemistically called the super high tech structure they were all now headed for. "I've got a few of my guys in there. We've nothing much to do at the moment so your job is very welcome. I wasn't too sure about what you wanted apart from some enhancement to these Volvo trucks, so let's grab a coffee, have a chat and take it from there."

"Great," said JJ. "Just the ticket."

As Harold and JJ imbibed some decent cappuccinos from the McLaren coffee bar and Gil had a fruit juice, JJ unveiled his cover story. It was not vastly adrift of the version told to Vincent Barakat but with a few geographical tweaks here and there. As far as Harold and his team were concerned JJ's company needed to transport some precious cargo from the capital of North Korea to the South. Volvo trucks normally decaled would attract a little too much attention in the DPRK but Chinese trucks were all over the place. JJ told Harold he was concerned about hijacking or even being ripped off by North Korean border officials and that an inspection of the lorries' load would be less automatic if the carriers had the logo and paintwork of often seen Chinese trucks. Harold nodded away at this story. He was no geopolitical aficionado but he knew that North Korea was some kind of secretive society and their leader something of a nut job.

"That's fine JJ," said Harold. "You sent through the dimensions of the Chinese trucks and photographs of their paintwork, logos and decals. We can do the disguise on the Volvo trucks fairly easily. The Volvo cabs are a little squarer than the FAW ones but nobody is going to really notice. I guess the North Korean security forces won't have a first class degree in tractor shapes!"

Harold laughed out loud and Gil and JJ followed suit, albeit a little quieter. Harold was probably right but who the hell knew what the North Korean military knew and didn't know. It was an unknown unknown.

"From your email, JJ, I got the impression there was something else?" said Harold enquiringly.

"Yes," replied JJ, reaching into his slim leather briefcase. "There's these." He handed Harold a very detailed set of schematics. Harold had a brief glance.

"What are they?" he asked, never having seen the like before. "They look a bit like… like long sunbeds," Harold ventured.

"You wouldn't be the first to say that my friend," said JJ, meaning friend not the opposite. "For the moment, let's call them super sunbeds but we need them installed in the tankers of the trucks in a very specific way made from very specific materials. The raw parts will be with you in the next thirty-six to forty-eight hours along with detailed instructions on how to assemble them. Once assembled, they need to be attached, permanently, two sunbeds in each tanker to the ceiling of the tankers. On the roof of the tankers we need sizeable and numerous perforations to allow cooling but they need to be less than fully visible."

"OK," said Harold not knowing just at that moment whether it was a 100% OK or one of those OKs you utter just because you don't want to hear anything else. "Anything else?" Harold asked with reticence.

"Yes Harold," said Gil. "If anyone was to, let's say want to look inside the tankers from the outside we'd like them to think they were looking at crude oil or some kind of fuel. This means that any peepholes, for want of a better word, would need to be camouflaged so that the appearance of the liquid inside was dark, like crude oil. Furthermore, the liquid that will be inside the tankers has no odour. We need it to smell like crude oil. Sour crude oil has an abundance of sulphur in it and stinks like rotten eggs. Sweet crude oil has much lower levels of sulphur and a much more pleasant smell. We need something inside the tankers but not in the liquid itself that smells like sweet crude oil."

"What," asked Harold, "like those pongy air fresheners that hoons like to hang from their muscle car mirrors?"

"Yes," Gil and JJ said in unison.

Harold took a few moments to look at the diagrams of the sunbeds. Then he looked at Gil and JJ then back to the diagrams. "You say we'd be working with carbon fibre and other refractory materials?"

JJ and Gil both nodded. Harold had another look at the diagrams, stroked his imaginary beard, and looked up again at Gil and JJ then said, "We'd need to test the strength and durability of the tankers and these sunbed thingies would need to be attached to the floor of the tankers as well as the ceiling otherwise their stability at speeds of over 20mph would be compromised."

JJ indicated his approval. Harold piped up again. "We can paint and augment the tractors, build these sunbeds, attach them to the tankers securely, disguise the appearance of what the true liquids are in the tankers and make them smell nice," he said feeling all pleased with himself. "When do you need this task completed by JJ?"

"ASAP Harold, and definitely no later than one week from today," said JJ.

Harold pondered. The F1 team would be away for the next full week and Harold and his team were not opposed to hard work and overtime. It was possible. "It will cost you JJ," said Harold hopefully.

"£60,000 now for you and your team over and above materials costs, for you to distribute as you see fit. A further £60,000 on our return to the UK," said JJ swiftly.

Harold didn't need to have a calculator app on his phone to realise that amongst six of them that would be £20,000 each for a week's work. That was a big chunk of money and would be most welcome.

"You were never as stingy as your nationality was made out to be JJ," said Harold happily. "You're on."

JJ and Harold then Harold and Gil shook hands and they all stood up to leave. JJ would contact Vincent Barakat forthwith re the status of the mini furnaces. By the time the Volvo cabs were repainted, re-decaled and made to look like the Jie Fang FAW trucks the sunbeds materials would hopefully be at McLaren ready for assembly and installation. As JJ, Gil and Harold were walking through the car park towards JJ's Carrera 4S, the former getting some light hearted abuse for turning up at McLaren in a Porsche, Harold stopped walking.

"JJ," he said. "One final thing. The liquid you're going to have in the tankers it's going to be a bit hot isn't it, given that your super sunbeds are in fact induction furnaces?"

"Yes Harold," replied JJ. "Maybe more than a bit hot."

"How hot?" asked Harold, for the first time looking anxious.

"About 1,000 degrees Celsius," replied JJ.

"Woking, we have a problem," responded a worried Harold McFarlane.

★ ★ ★

While they were driving back down the A3 to London, Gil at the wheel, JJ was on the phone to Vincent Barakat. The young French scientific researcher and his team had been working flat out on JJ's project. The mini furnace parts would be ready that night and they would be on transporters the next morning. JJ told Vincent where the transporters should go and all was well.

Harold's envisaged problem was that at 1,000 degrees Celsius inside the tankers, the metal of the tanker shell would be extremely hot, including to the touch. There was no concern regarding the melting of the tankers. The ones attached to the Volvo trucks were made of steel. Steel's melting point, at 1,370 degrees Celsius, was higher than gold's, but if any inquisitive DPRK security guard leant against it or had too close a look he'd start to fry.

"Vincent, thank you for your hard work and ingenuity. I will ensure that you and PLP are rewarded as promised."

"Merci Mr Darke," said Vincent. "Please keep in touch with the progress of your task."

JJ knew that was polite French for please remember that you promised PLP further research funds if the mini-furnaces helped in the clandestine transportation of the gold. JJ didn't mind the reminder. Vincent Barakat's work was crucial to JJ's transport plan and he had been on point since they met.

"No problem, Vincent, I definitely will," replied JJ. "Vincent, if you have a minute, there is one hitch in our plan that I need to run by you. Is that OK?"

"Oui, bien sûr, Monsieur Darke," responded Vincent defaulting to his native tongue.

"The mini-furnaces are to be placed inside a sizeable steel container as they are to be transported. As you will know, the melting point of steel is higher than that of gold but the external shell of the container will be roasting hot when the furnaces are up and running. Is there any way we can reduce the heat?" asked JJ.

Vincent thought for a second or two, it didn't take him much longer. He was on top of his game.

"Yes, Mr Darke, there is," he responded. "Carbon fibre is very malleable and can be produced in very thin strips or panels. If you lined the inside of the steel containers with the correct thickness heat resistant formulation then the outside of the container would not feel hot."

That boy's a fucking genius thought JJ. "Great, Vincent. Assuming each of the mini-furnaces was running at full blast for, say, up to one hour, can you calculate the optimum thickness the carbon fibre lining needs to be to keep the external surface of the steel container cool?"

"Yes," said Vincent with no hint of doubt. "I'll get on it straight away and I'll have an answer for you by tonight. Do you need me to order in more carbon fibre, we will have used all of our stock in preparation for the sunbeds?"

JJ told Vincent that would not be necessary, thanked him again and hung up. If Vincent ordered the carbon fibre it would take another couple of days to get it, a couple of days they could ill afford. Once Vincent had calculated the optimum thickness of the carbon fibre and the amount needed, after JJ emailed him the dimensions of the containers, JJ would turn to Harold McFarlane. If you can't get a sizeable lump of carbon fibre at, arguably, the world's most advanced F1 technical centre then you couldn't get it anywhere.

JJ and Gil were now only five minutes away from their house.

Harold confirmed that they could access immediately sizeable stores of the carbon fibre used in the F1 cars. Once he had the desired thickness they could prepare and install the lining in the tankers. As Gil was parking up, JJ was running through the transport plan in his mind. Harold and his team would finish their work on time, JJ was confident of this. He would then organise the transportation of the disguised trucks to Seoul. Organising flight itineraries for large trucks was bread and butter for Harold. He'd done it a hundred times at least. There had been GPs in South Korea, at the Korean International Circuit in South Cholla Province, so no one would think anything extraordinary was underway. Admittedly the F1 race would normally be in the British autumn and the circuit was 250 miles south of Seoul, but F1 teams may have wanted to test there early. In any event, the trucks would not be going south to the circuit.

JJ was confident that Vincent Barakat's sunbeds would work, if they actually got that far in this audacious heist. He was also sure Jim Bradbury would provide the two helpful Koreans necessary for the operation and he was sure that Ethel Rogers was the right choice as his number two on the operation. There were still gaps in the plan though.

Ginger had said that she'd found a safe cracker and that a meeting had been set. That still left some known unknowns. Two HGV drivers were necessary, but they'd need to come from either the security forces or underworld. If the latter then there'd be all sorts of risks of reliability, hijack potential, squealing. That problem needed sorted fast. What else needed sorting fast was how were they going to get the gold out of the DPRK's central bank vaults, even assuming they'd got into the vault in the first place. They could not manually load the gold, each bar was quite heavy at over 12kg. They needed maybe 6,000 bars. Even if it took only five minutes, for six people carrying two bars each, to get from vault to truck, that would take over four hours. JJ and his team could not afford to be in the DPRK central bank for that long. Still troubled by these obstacles, JJ opened the door of his house and he and Gil entered.

"Hey, Cyrus are you home?" JJ called out. "It's me and Gil."

From the underneath that was the basement Cyrus called back. "Hi Dad, Gil. I'm down in the gym on the treadmill so that Gil doesn't give me grief for having no stamina," came the teenager's haughty reply. A small light bulb went on in JJ's head and he smiled. *That Vincent Barakat may be one big fucking brain, but my son can have his moments.* "A treadmill," he mumbled to himself.

★ ★ ★

Commander Kun-Woo Moon had completed his assignment. All 110 of the KPN's personnel he had been asked to deliver to the Haeju naval base were well and truly delivered. Commodore Park had done an outstanding job in organising the erection of prefabricated housing for the enlisted sailors. Each portakabin had ample room for around twenty submariners, in sturdy bunk beds. They had wash and eating facilities, though the latrines were outside. The Commodore had also helped organise accommodation for the majority of the officers in Haeju City. Though they were unlikely to be staying there for more than two or three nights maximum, the guest houses and small hotels offered reasonable comfort and cleanliness to their guests.

Commander Moon was staying with Commodore Park at his quarters within the naval yard's perimeter. He was looking forward to dinner that night with Park, mainly because he really did want to know what was happening. It wasn't every day you were ordered to select and transport the crew necessary for a very large submarine. Commodore Park had informed Moon that there would be two additional guests for dinner, Lieutenant Commander Gok Han-Jik and Sunwoo Chung, a leading light in the KPN's scientific division.

Commodore Park had two of the naval yard's cooks prepare a good sized and omnivorous plate for his guests. As they took their seats around the square, wooden table in the dining room, these guests marvelled at how comfortable the Commodore's premises appeared to be and how lucky they were to be about to enjoy a veritable feast. Commodore Park opened two bottles of wine, Desoju, normally imbibed on New Year's Day and Podoju, an alcoholic rice and fruit wine. He poured each guest and himself a glass of both and they all stood to toast their supreme leader, Kim Jong-un and the Korean People's Navy.

Re-seated, they all looked at the food on offer, which included kim-bahp, d'okk, sashimi and whole fried fish. Park gestured for his guests to help themselves. The rotund Sunwoo was on the kim-bahps like a fly on shit. He loved these little rolls of rice with fresh meat inside; they looked like sushi rolls but were different as the meat was cooked and the rice was plain not vinegared. The non-scientific personnel around the table were more polite in their food acquisition. The d'okk selection, a Korean pastry, was filled with either meat or fish and they proved popular with both Gok and Moon.

"This is excellent Commodore," said Commander Moon. "Thank you for your hospitality." Gok and Sunwoo raised their glasses and nodded in the direction of their host, signalling their agreement with Commander Moon. After several more mouthfuls of kim-bahp and a few helpings of sashimi, Sunwoo Chung had clearly had enough of pleasantries and small talk.

"Commander Moon," Sunwoo began, to attract the attention of the naval officer sitting opposite. "Are your men in good shape and fully briefed on their mission?" Sunwoo was knowingly chancing his arm as no one seemed to know what the mission was.

"Well…" started Commander Moon, just washing down a piece of fish with a gulp of Podoju, "my men are in the state of physical and mental fitness you would expect from elite submariners in the KPN." He replied confidently but disguising the fact that he had no idea what shape they were in, he'd only been asked to transport them, not give them a full medical. "As to the mission, I have no information," he added. "Indeed, I was hoping to glean some here, this evening." Moon, glanced in the direction of his host.

"I am somewhat in the dark too, Commander," interjected Commodore Park. "My orders from Vice Admiral Goh were to berth and protect the Borei class submarine and to supervise the enhancements provided by our fellow diner, Sunwoo Chung." Park acknowledged the scientist with a nod. Gok Han-Jik had been fairly quiet during the evening's proceedings so far, concentrating more on ensuring he had his fill of this most appetising fayre that lay before him. Clearly feeling satisfied he finally spoke up.

"I have Vice Admiral Goh's orders here," Gok said, tapping the outside of his blue naval jacket, but clearly meaning in the left-hand pocket inside. The one thing about a mission, Gok was absolutely aware of, was that the people on it needed to know what they were doing. Up to this point, Commodore Park, Commander Moon and Sunwoo Chung had all done their jobs. They seemed loyal and trustworthy. The mission was to be underway in less than forty-eight hours, they needed to know on a need to know basis and that need was now.

Commodore Park was wondering why he was not the one to receive the direct orders from Goh, but his experience and common sense led him to gauge that this was not the moment to ask that question.

Gok continued. "The men will be briefed tomorrow morning

at 10am. By the following morning, at the latest, the Borei will be ready, weaponised, seaworthy and on standby for sailing later that day. I will be in command of the submarine and its crew." Gok paused for another drink of wine, maybe his last for quite some time, and to allow his comrades to ask questions.

Sunwoo Chung was first in. He felt he had done everything in his skillset to make the submarine as invisible as possible. He wanted to know what the application of all that knowledge was for. "What are you going to do with the sub, Lieutenant Commander Gok?" Sunwoo could have been less formal and addressed him as Han-Jik, after all they'd been on a road trip together to the yard. However, the dinner seemed formal and Gok had his uniform on. Gok knew he could keep the other three diners in the dark, but what was the point? They all wanted the greatest glory for the DPRK, they all were completely loyal to the supreme leader, his cousin, and they all had done their jobs precisely as ordered. Perhaps it was a little too much Podoju or perhaps it was because he had been given command of a nuclear, fully weaponised sub that he was bursting with pride and wanted to let it all out. Gok remained calm but was prepared to spill.

"My orders are to leave the 50km exclusion zone around our shores. Once safely away and in deep water we will submerge. Once it is clear that we are undetectable," a simple nod to Sunwoo at this juncture, "we will then launch three of the SLBMs."

Sunwoo was listening intently, Commander Moon still enjoying his dinner and Commodore Park becoming concerned; the tone in which Gok was delivering his information did not seem like the missile launch was to be a test, even though missile tests seemed to irk their enemies quite a lot.

"Do the proposed missile launches have targets?" the Commodore asked firmly. Gok may have been the submarine's commander but Park was the ranking officer around this table.

"They do," replied Gok. "Two of the Bulava's will target the Pacific Coast of the United States of America, one will target Tokyo. If there are any signs of retaliation we will fire all remaining missiles at Washington D.C. and Seoul." Gok delivered his information in such a matter of fact way that he could have been ordering a Chinese takeaway by rote. He displayed no emotion whatsoever.

Sunwoo Chung looked happy, though he'd have preferred if at least one of the missiles was headed for Boston. Commander Moon stopped eating before Gok had finished. He didn't know what to think, other than he didn't want to be near the naval yard or Pyongyang when it all kicked off. Commodore Park was phlegmatic. He had served the KPN with honour and had been fiercely loyal to all the Kims who had been his country's leader in his time on this planet. This action was way more aggressive than he had ever imagined likely, however, and it would be naïve to the power of n, where n was a very large number, to believe that the DPRK's enemies would not retaliate with massive destructive force. Millions and millions of lives would be lost immediately on first strike, and millions more, agonisingly, later as contamination took hold. Commodore Park was over fifty years old, so at least he had had a life. But his sister's children had not really, nor had the children of ordinary Korean families nor even those of his perceived enemies. As soon as Gok gave the order to launch the first of the SBLMs, their lives were over. As Commodore Park was contemplating this horror and his supreme inability to do anything about it, he recalled Edmund Burke's famous quote: *All that is necessary for evil to triumph is for good men to do nothing.* Park knew deep down that the Irish philosopher's comment was correct, but he had been brainwashed and indoctrinated enough to think that while Gok was soon to unleash evil, it was primarily evil aimed at the corrupt and colonial predators that formed the nub of the

USA. Maybe it was a price that he, his family and the children of the DPRK just had to pay.

The Commodore was holding that thought, and the rest of the dinner table was engaged in deep discussion as to the whys and wherefores of the upcoming attack on America and Japan. Tea was about to be served and one of the enlisted sailors entered the room holding aloft a decorative mahogany tray, with four floral china cups and saucers, biscuits and two teapots, one brewing ginseng tea and one a local herbal tisane. The tea never arrived at the table. Well actually it did, but more in the fashion of a tsunami fountain of hot beverage rain, rather than a delicate teapot pouring operation. For down in the yard, there was a loud commotion, there was nocturnal motion and there were at least two unexpected explosions.

★ ★ ★

"That was fucking great Billy," yelled Joe Franks to his teammate amid the mayhem. "Now we've got their attention that we didn't want," Franks continued as he was setting explosive charges to the base of one of the watchtowers at Haeju dock.

"It's not my fault, Joe," replied Billy Smith, taking cover, part kneeling, behind some old wooden crates lying on the dock, next to the watchtower. "I didn't know that the stupid gook was hiding among a bunch of petrol drums. The shot must have gone through his skinny gook body and into the drum behind."

SEALs teams 5 and 7 had arrived at Haeju naval base. The Borei class sub was berthed and tied to the dock but it was not heavily guarded, just as hoped for by Commander Mark O'Neill and his team. Lieutenant Evan Harris, leader of SEAL team 7, and O'Neill's number two for this mission was already on board the sub as were most of the rest of 5 and 7 including Tommy

Fairclough the lead driver. Unfortunately, as they were boarding they caught a glimpse of two KPN armed sailors on guard at the top of the submarine. Yang Dingbang and O'Neill had moved like veritable ninjas and silently slit the throats of the two sailors before they could raise the alarm. One of them was a bit chubby and as his lifeless body belly-flopped into the dark water it caused such a splash that a passing sailor on the dock noticed it. Now he was barrelling off at pace to warn the rest of the KPN sailors housed near the submarine. Billy Smith just had to shoot. He needed to rush but took aim with his trusty M14 and pop, one in the running gook's arse. The hapless and now injured in his left butt sailor crawled off and hid behind some petrol drums, unbeknown to Billy Smith. The M14 was silenced with a Vortex Flash suppressor attached so the first shot did not trigger any KPN activity but, as he correctly surmised, the second one went straight through the sailor's right eye, its socket, his brain and skull and embedded itself in the petrol drum. Flash, bang, wallop, up it went.

Joe Franks, a lanky Texan, with ginger hair and freckles, had been pals with Billy Smith for years. He had seen the petrol drum incident unfold and came to Billy's aid. Now there were dozens of sailors running around with pistols and rifles, yelling away in Korean and trying to pin point the source of the attack. There were no officers in the yard. They were in Haeju City. There was no military order. Franks was in his mid-thirties but could still move like a twenty year old. He was the team's explosives expert and he concluded that diversion was the way forward. He planted the small devices at the foot of the watchtowers on dockside and on a pillar structure that appeared to be supporting some kind of living quarters.

"C'mon Billy," yelled Franks to his pal after setting the explosives. "These little firecrackers are going off in thirty seconds, the sub's going to leave and we need to get the fuck out of here and on there," he continued, pointing to the sub.

Billy Smith fancied unloading a few more rounds into the sailors on the dock, but the more he fired the more his position would be revealed, even with the flash suppressor on his rifle. He jumped up and headed off at pace. "Last one on board's a chicken," he shouted to Franks. He too was up and running.

As they got to the sub, Yang Dingbang and O'Neill were letting loose the last of the berthing ropes. There were sirens going off, spotlights searching and rapid but random gunfire all over the dock. "Get aboard you two," shouted O'Neill to his sprinting men. "Tommy's got it fired up, we're leaving now."

Just as the last of the four of them disappeared down the hatch and into the sub, Joe Frank's explosions went off, one boom, two booms, three booms. It was boom number one which caused the tea fountain in Commodore Park's dining room. As a child, Sunwoo Chung liked fountains, but he didn't much like the one that had just drenched him. He had been scalded down the right side of his face and was screaming in agony. Eventually, the racket would subside, but the ugly scars remaining after all the burnt flesh had frizzled up and peeled off, would not. He held a cloth to his burned face but that wouldn't help, for as soon as he took it away he'd take away some of his face too. His head was hurting as well. What had happened? Commander Moon was unconscious on the floor; he had banged his head on one of the square dining table's corners as it shifted following the explosion.

Commodore Park was also looking a bit queasy, crawling on his hands and knees among the furniture rubble that used to be his dining room. He had, fortunately, escaped both the tea fountain and the table's corners, but his premises were a mess and sloping at a 30 degree angle. Once his senses had returned, though, he'd probably feel a lot less fortunate.

Lieutenant Commander Gok Han-Jik was physically unscathed after the explosion but his mind was both scathed and numb. From the dining room's half collapsed window frame that only a few minutes earlier had had a window in it, he looked out at the dockside. Beyond the chaotic and random running of many KPN submariners, he could just make out the pattern of distinctive ripples in the water that revealed that a vessel had just left. Not any old vessel, he realised, but a Borei class Russian nuclear submarine, armed with ten Bulava missiles. His mind raced through all the expected questions following such an event. Who did it? Why did they do it? Why wasn't the submarine guarded better? The question that made his brain ache with the most excruciating pain ever was how will he tell his cousin, North Korea's supreme leader Kim Jong-un?

★ ★ ★

JJ and Cyrus were cosying up on their expansive dark blue leather sofa. JJ was trying to sketch something but in truth he did not even have the skill to draw stick men well. Cyrus had his feet up, legs outstretched on the sofa, taking up all the space apart from the small section that he allowed his dad, mainly so that JJ could act as the boy's headrest. Cyrus had downloaded some classic tunes and was listening through large, white, round headphones as he read the last few pages of *The Hunger Games*. Classic for Cyrus meant the Kinks, the Beatles, T-Rex, Human League or Heaven 17.

JJ was getting a bit frustrated with his lack of artistic ability, so he gave Cyrus a gentle dunt to get his attention. Cyrus removed his headphones. "Are you concentrating, Cyrus, or can I get your help on something?" asked JJ remembering that not only had Cyrus won a school Design and Technology bursary in his day, he had also had a painting of his exhibited at The Royal College of Art when he was six. Admittedly, it was abstract but it must have taken some ability to have been selected from the hundreds and hundreds of school kid hopefuls. JJ never forgot the day that he and Eloise went along to see their son's painting, proud parents given that neither had any artistic acumen. In advance, they had asked Cyrus what he had painted so that they could find it among the various categories on the RCA's display walls. The boy had said he'd done a *Power Rangers Ninja Storm* morpher. JJ had to sit through enough episodes of *Power Rangers* on TV to know that there was more than one type of morpher, depending on which incarnation of *Power Rangers* was on. At the end of the day, though, the morphers were similar, they kind of all did the same thing, you flipped them open, hit a few buttons, they beeped and, hey presto, either you suited up into Rangers, other Rangers came to your aid or they ordered the formation of huge and powerful zords. JJ and Eloise knew what they were looking for. After about twenty minutes scanning walls with paintings on display they could not see anything that looked like a morpher. Cyrus was with them, so JJ asked him if he could spot his own painting. A minute or two later, he bounced up with pleasure and said, "Here it is!" pointing at a multi coloured painting. JJ and Eloise looked at it closely, but to them it seemed more like a house than a morpher. It was definitely striking and it was definitely well done, but it so wasn't a *Power Rangers* morpher.

"Cyrus, this is brilliant, but it doesn't look like a morpher," said JJ.

"I did the morpher last year, Dad, this is our house and garden, can't you tell?" replied the six year old. JJ noted his son's skill for disinformation, it could come in useful one day he laughed to himself.

"I'm not concentrating, Dad, just chillin' to 'Waterloo Sunset' and worrying about the fate of Katniss Everdeen," replied Cyrus.

He knew his dad was well acquainted with both so he didn't need to elaborate much. JJ preferred the Kinks to either the Beatles or the Rolling Stones and it was he who first introduced Cyrus to *The Hunger Games*.

"Great. Thanks Cyrus, so here's the scoop. In the course of business, MAM has acquired quite a chunk of physical gold. It's in the form of bullion bars, each weighs about 12.5kg, so they're a bit heavier than the weights Gil has been torturing you with. We need to find an efficient way of loading these bars from vaults, which may be under street level, and onto secure trucks. I'm trying to devise some kind of treadmill or travelator machine to do this but I can't sketch a stick man, as you know."

Cyrus knew his dad was rubbish at drawing. He also knew that his dad didn't often ask for his help in relation to his work, so this was quite cool, the teenager thought. "I get it, Dad, you need a conveyor belt system to transport the gold and it needs to be capable of going uphill with quite a heavy load on it."

Smart boy, thought JJ, *he was on it straight away.* "Yes, that's it, Cy. You don't need to worry about weight or dimensions etc. I have a manufacturer in mind, but a decent sketch or drawing of what it might look like would be handy."

"When do you need it, Dad, and do I get a financial incentive for my work?" asked Cyrus, cheekily and with a broad capitalist smile.

"Tonight would be good, young man, and yes you can have a decent bonus if it's up to scratch," replied JJ, ruffling Cyrus's curly locks and giving him a wee hug.

Cyrus worked on his sketches for a few hours. They were good and clear. He even included a collapsible version where the conveyor belt could be made smaller and then extended when necessary. This was likely to be a very useful variant.

Overnight JJ worked on the loads that the conveyor belt

would need to carry and support. The next morning he contacted Harold McFarlane at McLaren to find out whether they had anything comparable in stock, surely McLaren would need such a gizmo at some point, or at least know of one. Harold said that they did not. However, a while back, he recalled Ron Dennis had asked him something similar regarding baggage handling for his private jet. Harold had gone to Herbert Systems in Cambridgeshire, and they constructed a small mobile conveyor system for them. Harold suggested that JJ scan the diagrams he had and email them to him, sharpish. He'd get on the phone to Herbert's and see if they could do a rush job. JJ thanked Harold, scanned and e-delivered the diagrams and hoped for the best.

The timeline and deadlines for this mission were seriously constraining. So far, luck had been on his side, meeting Vincent Barakat, his old pal Harold, the availability and skillset of Ginger, his US buddy Jim Bradbury being in Seoul and his offer of two helpful Koreans. Ginger had earmarked a safe cracker, whom he was going to meet later today, his son could draw and Toby was doing a good alcohol-free job of covering for JJ at work. The non-existent law of averages suggested that this could not last, but, hey, let's ride that lucky train for as long as it's chugging along.

JJ still had not solved the thorny issue of the HGV drivers. Sure it was easy enough to get such drivers with the requisite skills and licence but the vast majority of these would be legitimate, no knowledge of the criminal world or the security services, and no desire to get involved in a life-threatening heist. If Ginger's safe cracker was up to scratch then JJ would turn his mind to finding the final piece of the pre-match jigsaw. Maybe Harold could help. He must know a gazillion HGV drivers, but it was how to approach it. In any event, they all needed to be on a flight to Seoul in three days' time, no matter what.

★ ★ ★

"I think my fucking leg's broken," wailed Joe Franks as he peeled Billy Smith off the top of him. The two of them plus Mark O'Neill and Yang Dingbang had literally dived into the sub through the surface hatch. There was no time for climbing down the integral ladder or following protocol. They were under fire and down they went like apples from a barrel. Joe Franks drew the short straw and both Ding and Billy landed on him as they hit the sub's unwieldy floor.

As Joe Franks stayed down, clutching his right leg, O'Neill was up and shouting, "Medic!" The approved medic on this operation was Garrison Whitton, one of Evan Harris's team. He had been a SEAL for only two years, hailed from Washington State, but was widely regarded as one of the best patch up guys in the Navy. So far, he had had little to do on this mission and while he would have preferred that Franks didn't have a broken leg, at least he didn't feel like a spare part anymore. Whitton headed straight for Joe Franks with his medical bag. The rest of the team could not afford to hang about however much they cared for their buddy. There was an enemy nuclear sub to drive to safety and there were only an effective eight of them to do it.

"How are we doing, Tommy?" Commander O'Neill asked of Tommy Fairclough, the main driver, backed up by David McCoy.

"Fine, Sir," he replied. "We're under way and we'll soon be underwater. Those NGA girls did a good job with the crib sheets they sent through. The main instructions for this sub and all the labelling on the instruments are in Russian. I think there's a Korean translation in this drawer, but I've not had time to look at it. Not that it would do any good. If we get stuck on translation can we contact them?"

"Not yet. We need to be sure we're undetectable first. You're right about the NGA girls. Not only have they sent us a workable translation of the key operating instructions they let us know that the submarine was supposed to be all stealthed up. We'll find out soon enough if that's accurate," said O'Neill, clapping Fairclough on the back and then checking the status of the rest of the men.

Evan Harris joined O'Neill on the conn. While all aboard were Navy SEALs they could afford to dispense with much of the usual submarine specific language. There was no need for a Chief of Boat (COB) as the discipline and good order of the crew would not be an issue. O'Neill was the Commanding Officer (CO) and Harris the Executive Officer (XO). It needed both Fairclough and McCoy to drive the sub efficiently, one to control the tail action and one the sail. Normally, there would be another submariner behind them issuing instructions but this skeleton crew did not have that luxury. Barry Minchkin was the Chief Engineer, essentially the only engineer. He was critical to the supervision of the nuclear reactor on board, and any tweaking that was necessary to keep it operating safely. Barry was also doubling up as the Communications Officer. Ding had been put in charge of weapons, not that they were likely to use them but they needed checking anyway. It would have been Joe Franks' job but his injury prevented him from moving around efficiently to inspect the various weapons positions. There was no Supply Officer, indeed there seemed to be no sign of supplies on board at all. O'Neill hoped that would not become an issue later on.

"Preparing to dive, Sir," announced Tommy Fairclough.

McCoy repeated the announcement though he didn't really need to as O'Neill and Harris were both well within earshot. McCoy opened the valves at the top of the ballast tanks and as the air escaped and seawater came in, they headed lower.

This Borei could submerge lower than 1,000 feet but

Tommy Fairclough had set the stable depth to be 400 feet. He was taking no chances with either the sea bed or his crib sheet instructions. Evan Harris had undertaken emergency specialist sonar training when he knew about Operation Philidor Defence. On this operation he would only be deploying passive sonar to detect where other subs or ships were without revealing the Borei's location. So far, so good, there was nothing within detection distance, and that detection distance was more than 1,000 nautical miles. The Borei class subs had a sonar processing power of around 2,000 laptop computers.

The KPN were not giving chase. As the submarine settled at a depth of 400ft, Commander O'Neill relaxed a little. They'd acquired their target, only one non-life threatening injury to the team, and now they were deep underwater and very difficult if not impossible to detect. The submarine was moving along at close to 25 knots or just under 30mph, and could go a little faster if necessary. As O'Neill was contemplating the next phase, Garrison Whitton came into the room. Whitton was in his mid-twenties, slight of build, dark brown straight hair, not cut short enough in O'Neill's view, with blue eyes and an upright posture.

"Sir," he said, attracting O'Neill's attention. Normally, he would have addressed his usual team leader, Evan Harris, first but he was embroiled in sonar work and Whitton judged it best to leave him alone.

"Yes, Gary, what is it?" asked O'Neill.

Whitton was pleased that the mission's team leader knew who he was and that he felt comfortable enough to address him by his shortened first name.

"Two things, Commander," began Whitton. "Joe Franks has two fractures of his right leg, the major one is a clean break of the tibia and I think at least three of his proximal long bones in his foot are also broken. I've put a makeshift splint on his leg and wrapped his right foot as best I can. He's effectively immobile just now but may be able to hobble about in a day or so. I'll have a ferret around the ship to see if I can make a temporary set of crutches."

Mark O'Neill did not think that Whitton's report was the end of the world. He'd kind of assumed that Joe would be out of action given the wailing noise he'd made when hitting the deck. "And the second thing?" asked the Commander.

"Once I'd patched Joe up, Sir, I thought I'd have a look for food stores. I know we don't have a Supply Officer so I thought I'd double up. I can cook a bit, but there's nothing to cook. In fact, there's nothing to eat at all. They had not provisioned the sub, Sir, as of tonight."

"Is there anything to drink?" responded the Commander.

"Yes, Sir, there's plenty of water, the desalination plant on board means we have as much fresh-ish water as we need." Gary Whitton was glad he had at least one positive to tell O'Neill.

"Thanks, Gary," said ONeill, not wanting to show any emotion to the medic. "Good job on Joe. Now go and check that the rest of the men are hydrated and do not need any medical attention." Even though he showed no sign of it, he was a little worried.

As every SEALs team would do on a mission they had packed emergency food supplies, unappetising as they all were. For this mission they had only two full days' supplies in tow. As this was sinking in, Barry Minchkin came up to him.

"Mark, you've received an encrypted message from John Adams." Barry Minchkin handed Mark O'Neill his tablet. Modern sub technology meant that you could get a signal and receive electronic communications even 400ft below sea level.

Mark O'Neill remembered CIA Associate Director for Military Support Adams from the Langley meeting that had kicked all this off. He seemed solid and sharp. Once decoded the communication stated: *Well done on target acquisition. Proceed with due haste to latitude 56° 04' 12"N, longitude 04° 45' 49"W. Good luck.* The message wasn't long but O'Neill was still looking at it. He was familiar with latitude and longitude coordinates but did not recognise this exact location. "Barry, where's latitude 56° 04' 12" North, longitude 04° 45' 49" West?"

Barry tapped the coordinates into his tablet. "Scotland, Sir, specifically Faslane on the River Clyde."

They both looked at each other. Why the holy moly would they be taking the sub to Scotland? Of more immediate concern to Mark O'Neill was the distance. Scotland had to be over 5,000 miles away. The Borei could travel at 25 knots all day and night long without a break if the system was operating efficiently. That still meant a near seven day journey.

"Jesus believe us!" O'Neill muttered under his breath, thinking about the food supplies. *We'll all be auditioning for the Broadway version of Bridge on the River Kwai by the time we reach bonnie old Scotland.*

* * *

Harold and Herbert Systems had come up trumps. With the offer of double time for their engineers and a bonus on completion they had built in record time the conveyor system sketched by Cyrus. There were six individual conveyor systems in total, each one looked like a big 'Toblerone' with embedded wheels and rubber treads attached. They could be used individually or, thanks to an ingenious design by one of Herbert's engineers, interlocked in up to a six times larger configuration.

JJ had asked Gil to go to McLaren Technology Centre to check them out and to ensure that the installation of the 'sunbeds' into the Volvo/FAW trucks was proceeding on track. The clock was ticking and JJ needed to delegate even though he really did want to eyeball the finished trucks before they were flown to South Korea. Harold had assured JJ, who had in turn been assured by the Managing Director of Herbert's that the 'Toblerone' conveyors would leave Wisbech that morning and be in Woking by lunchtime.

JJ had lent Gil his Porsche for the trip. He wouldn't normally do that, he was a bit particular as to who drove his car, but she hadn't crashed or dinged it at their last foray up the A3 so he was OK with it. In addition, he needed to be very nice and sensitive towards Gil. JJ had told her that she was not going on the field trip to Korea. Initially, she was livid and made the case for her inclusion with aplomb. JJ had eventually convinced her that he needed someone trustworthy here in London, someone he could rely upon to protect Cyrus. If they both went to Korea and it ended badly, Cyrus would have no one within 400 miles to take care of him. JJ couldn't have that and worrying about Cyrus would prove a distraction on a mission where distractions would be punished harshly. Gil understood. Once she was convinced that her exclusion was not because of her gammy leg, she realised JJ was right. In any case, she enjoyed being with Cyrus and she vowed to whip him into shape in his dad's absence. If Cyrus had been aware of this oath, he'd surely have gone into deep cover hiding.

As JJ was musing over Gil and Cyrus, his cab pulled up outside the police station in Saville Row. Ginger had organised a meeting with the safe cracker but as he was presently a guest of HM Prison Belmarsh in Greenwich, the meeting had to take place under police supervision. Belmarsh was a Category A prison and some folk, overly concerned with the human rights of total wasters, said it was Britain's equivalent to Guantanamo Bay. Its infamous collection of inmates ranged from Abu Hamza the terrorist loving so called cleric to Ronnie Biggs, one of the Great Train Robbers. As JJ entered the same meeting room that he last saw Ginger in, he was hoping that the safe cracker was more of the latter's mind set than the former's. JJ greeted Ethel Rogers with a hug and they both sat down opposite a very young looking man.

"JJ Darke, meet Victor Pagari," said Ethel. It was kind of difficult to greet the young man in the traditional way as he was handcuffed. JJ gestured to Ethel and she undid the cuffs. If Ethel and JJ couldn't handle the kid, they shouldn't be doing what they were about to do.

"Thank you, Officer," Victor said very politely to Ethel, with the definite hint of an Italian accent. Victor was around 5ft 10in, slim and wiry, with a somewhat pointed but not unpleasant face. His nose was quite long but slim, le nez aquilin it would have been termed in France. He had short dark hair, no doubt cut by the prison barber who was no Nicky Clarke, thick eyebrows and deep brown eyes.

"Victor," began JJ. "Do you know why you are here for this meeting?"

"I have some knowledge, but not full information," he said as he took a sip of water. At least he had the good sense not to ask for a coffee. "Officer Rogers tells me that you have an offer that I should not refuse," said Victor calmly. "I have found previously that these types of offers I really should have refused," he added with a degree of humour. Obviously prison had not beaten him down too much.

Ethel interjected. "Look, we're on a meter here Victor. Why don't I fill Mr Darke in and you interrupt me if I get anything wrong. OK?"

"OK," said Victor.

"Victor is the grandson of Albert Spaggiari, he changed his surname slightly so as not to be labelled immediately by police forces all over the continent." Victor smiled and JJ was, as yet, none the wiser as to who the young man's grandfather was. Ethel resumed. "Albert Spaggiari was a career French criminal and one with a sharp brain. He is credited with one of the most audacious bank robberies in French history. He formed a gang and, in 1976, robbed the Société Générale bank in Nice, relieving them of over 60 million French Francs worth of cash, securities and other valuables. He did eventually stand trial, but duped the judge and leapt out of the courtroom window onto a waiting motorcycle. Albert was never caught, nor was the swag from the heist. He died from throat cancer, aged fifty-two. When the French gendarmerie investigated the robbed bank vault it had a message on one of the walls, *sans armes, ni maine, ni violence.* This translates as *no arms, nor hatred, nor violence.*"

JJ thought this was a fine story, but not sure what it had to do with Victor. He was already 1-0 down to his granddad, as he was caught, and was a Belmarsh HSU inmate.

"Fine, but has Victor here inherited his grandfather's skillset or what?" JJ asked impatiently, keen to get to the punch line if ever there was going to be one.

Ethel responded. "Despite his youth, he's only nineteen, Victor is the best undercover CI that this police force has ever had. He's presently doing time in Belmarsh as part of that cover. Do you remember the London Silver Vaults robbery last year?"

"Yes, it was all over the news. The gang had broken into the vaults but were caught on their way out. They nearly got away with £100 million worth of silver and jewellery."

"Nearly £300 million," corrected Victor.

"Well," continued Ethel, "Victor was the safe cracker on that job. He's a friggin' computer genius. Disabled the outer locks with a very small explosive and used a smartphone and two laptops to break the security codes of the back-up doors. Don't ask me for the technical details. He told me once but it may as well have been in Ancient Egyptian. Once all the gang were inside the vaults Victor sent a signal and that's how they were caught. The real crooks had no idea that he sent it, his computer magic was such that those Neanderthals had no clue about what was happening. We had to lock him up for a while to keep his cover intact."

JJ took this all in. He remembered the silver vaults robbery. The vaults there were meant to be in the top ten of impenetrable vaults in the world. If he recalled correctly, the same type of vault was used as part of a 1957 US nuclear test in Nevada. The 30-odd kiloton nuke tore away the vault's steel reinforcements and some trim, but the core of the vault remained intact. Here they were with a 19 year old kid who undid it with a phone and a couple of laptops. JJ was warming to Victor.

"How come you've got an Italian accent?" asked JJ directly.

"My maternal grandmother was Italian and I stayed with her for a lot of my early life."

JJ didn't really have anything additional to ask Victor. His credentials were his results and Ethel's recommendation. Ethel had recruited Victor as her lead CI on financial crime and he had never let her down.

JJ proceeded to outline the North Korean mission to Victor. He was free to choose whether to participate or not, but if it was not then he'd need to spend the next few weeks in solitary, just in case. If he said yes then Ethel would provide a cover story for Belmarsh, officials and selected inmates alike. Victor listened intently to JJ's tale of adventure. For indeed, it was a tale of adventure to him. He was nineteen and full of the vim and vigour normally found in a French/Italian teenager. He understood why he had to be incarcerated in Belmarsh, but it was rubbish. He felt claustrophobic and surrounded all the time by seriously odd and dangerous scumbags. He was to be paid handsomely for his participation in North Korea and Ethel promised he'd be given a new identity on return and would not need to see the inside of Belmarsh ever again. Of course he was in.

The meeting ended with three happy participants. JJ added a few more essential details and he shook Victor's hand with enthusiasm.

"Mr Darke," said Victor. "One final thing. Do you know what type of vaults are in the DPRK's central bank?"

"No, Victor, I haven't a Scooby-Doo. That's a piece of research you could get cracking on, if you'll forgive the pun," said JJ jovially. The three of them laughed. Victor was especially happy that he could ditch his prison issue maroon jogging bottoms and faded anonymous T-shirt. Not the threads that a cool dude safe cracker should be seen in. Bring on the adventure.

★ ★ ★

JJ, Ethel and Victor were all on the morning BA flight from Heathrow to Seoul. It was an eleven hour flight so plenty of time for them to contemplate the universe. There would be no chatter regarding the mission. Walls have ears and so do planes. The disguised Volvo trucks were also en route via a DHL cargo plane, courtesy of Harold McFarlane and his team. Harold had also loaned JJ two HGV drivers, at a price, to ensure that the trucks got safely off the plane and out of Seoul Incheon International airport. There was no thought or discussion regarding any further participation by these drivers. The 'Toblerone' conveyors were with the trucks, housed in a dark blue Mercedes Sprinter van, significantly tweaked and enhanced by Harold's engineers and described as 'the fastest van in the West' by his friend. The Mercedes logos and badges had been removed. Harold may not have known exactly what JJ was up to, but he was wily enough to realise that disguise and anonymity were the order of the day.

As JJ was dozing in between half watching movies he had already seen, the three things he was worrying about were Cyrus, the precise details of the heist and the needed truck drivers, in that order. He thought Cyrus and Gil would be fine. He had told Cyrus he was on a business trip and that he would be home within a week. Cyrus was OK with that. JJ just hoped that it turned out as advertised. The drivers were still an issue. He hoped that Jim Bradbury, the KLO and his American friend, would have an idea or two. It would not be easy keeping Jim out of the loop. The ex-fill cover story was adequate but if he asked Jim about truck drivers and, given that the two helpful Koreans from his office would at least see them, he was going to need to feed Jim a few more information morsels.

The night before, JJ, Ethel and Victor had been discussing the break in. JJ had already acquired diagrams and detailed schematics of the DPRK central bank in Pyongyang. He had a good idea of the layout now. He and Ethel would scope out the visible security the day before the heist and hope it was not markedly different at night. Victor had done his research and discovered that the secure room leading to central bank's gold hoard was most likely protected by a UL Class II vault. This was meant to be the second most difficult vault to penetrate, taking at least sixty minutes, according to the performance standards set by Underwriters Laboratories, the major underwriter and overseer of the world's best bank vaults.

Victor had obtained images of vaults likely to be similar to that in the target central bank. It probably would be a dual custody lock which protected it rather than a time lock he concluded.

That would be relatively good news, but it would still require two people to dial the different combinations at exactly the same time. Victor was still working on the details. JJ was hoping that one of those details was how to reduce the breach time well below sixty minutes.

There was very little else that JJ could think about just now. He'd more or less shoved to the back of his mind that he was in this position because of Neil Robson's blackmail and desperate need for government monies. He knew he could not trust him but he also knew that there was little he could do about that right now. Right now, he'd better put together a significantly more comprehensive plan than the one that was currently on offer. His own life, that of Ethel, Victor, Jim and the two, as yet unmet, Koreans were at stake. If they were caught in the act they'd be executed or dumped in a North Korean prison camp that would make Belmarsh seem like Butlins. He would never see Cyrus again. That was JJ's prize. No matter the obstacles, curve balls, negative random surprises that this mission threw up, being a dad to Cyrus, his mentor, his friend, was his true incentive to overcome everything that North Korea and cancer could throw at him. He needed to stay alive. With that thought, JJ slowly fell into a deep slumber.

★ ★ ★

JJ had hired an E-class titanium hued Mercedes AMG at Seoul airport. He was driving, Ethel was in the front passenger seat and Victor, all hooked up with his laptop and smartphones lolling about in the back. They had just passed Gangnam Station and were on the lookout for PAU Travel, the CIA's cover for their embedded office in the South Korean capital. The FAW-style trucks and tankers had been parked up a few minutes away in a vast multi-storey car park that was full of trucks, buses and other large vehicles. The Mercedes Sprinter van was parked there too. The car park, really it was a truck park, had twenty-four hour security so JJ felt comfortable. Being out of sight in plain sight was often the best way.

JJ parked on the street just outside of PAU Travel. Before he could even ring the bell, the door opened and there was Jim Bradbury.

"Saw you coming, JJ, you must be slipping in your old age," said the man from Arizona, giving JJ a full strength man-hug.

JJ was happy to see Jim. "You don't sound very Korean for a KLO, Jim."

"I can turn on the Korean when I want, as you know," retorted Bradbury.

JJ introduced Ethel and Victor. Jim didn't ask them or JJ anything about his companions, their backgrounds or their skillset. They were here with JJ, his old pal, and that was good enough.

"Come on in and sit down and let's grab a decent coffee," Bradbury said as he motioned his three guests into a meeting room just beyond the front desk of the apparent travel agency. "Let me get a couple of the guys," said Bradbury, clearly referring to the two helpful Koreans that he had mentioned before.

Ethel and JJ were enjoying their decent coffees, Victor stuck to water, he was still footering about on his tablet. Jim Bradbury returned with two Koreans, both apparently in their early thirties, though it was difficult to tell with an untrained eye. One was about 5ft 10in, slim and athletic looking, the other about three inches shorter, more stocky and with muscles bulging through his upper shirt sleeves. Both had dark brown hair, cut short.

"This is Kim Min-Jun," said Jim Bradbury, pointing to the muscly shorter one, "and this is Kim Chun-So," he added introducing the taller one. "We call them Lily and the Iceman."

JJ wanted to know why those nicknames but he would find that out later. For the moment, he was just interested in what these two Korean CIA officers could do. Both Kims had trained at 'The Point' in North Carolina and had gone to university in the same state. They had become the best of friends and had requested their current assignments in South Korea. They had been briefed by Jim Bradbury that an ex-MI5 Officer and his team had been ordered to carry out a delicate ex-fill operation in the North and that the CIA was to assist. Beyond that they knew little. This first meeting was unlikely to enlighten them any further.

As JJ and Jim Bradbury stepped out of the meeting room, the two Kims, Ethel and Victor got to know each other a little. The discussion was primarily small talk, background, training etc. It was relatively straightforward for Ethel, she explained CO19 and her role in it and said that she'd been selected for the mission primarily for her shooting prowess and that she had known JJ for a long time. Broadly speaking that was true. Victor piped up and said that he was 'the knowledge' as far as any type of electronic communication and surveillance was concerned. This was broadly true as well. However, had his moral code been guided by the Roman Catholic catechism whereby actual sin is 'every sin which we ourselves commit, by thought, word, deed or omission' then he'd have been branded a liar on the last count. No mention of safecracking or Belmarsh was on the table today.

As the four teammates continued their chat, Jim and JJ were standing outside, leaning against the water cooler. JJ was particularly happy to get rehydrated. He didn't drink as much water as he should have on the plane, either on the grounds of general well-being or more importantly given his particular health concern. It wasn't for a good reason either, simply because when he was down and comfy in the plane's seat, he never felt like getting up to pee every five minutes, or queue to pee, or get knocked out by the stench of pee in the plane's loos after a multi-hour flight. Some guys' aims are a disgrace.

"JJ, it's really really great to see you and you know I'll give you every assistance that I can. After that time in Bosnia when you saved my skin, I've always owed you, even if you didn't feel owed," said Jim.

"I know you will, and it's no sweat, you'd have done the same for me," replied JJ.

"I like to think I would have, but, in the heat of the moment, under heavy fire, you never know," Bradbury said, realistically. "Look, JJ, I know there's more going on than an ex-fill operation. However important the ex-fill is, British Intelligence would have sent a regular MI6 team, not a retired MI5 Officer. Ethel might pass for an intelligence officer, but the kid, Victor, he seems more like a student on dope than an agent. I don't expect you to tell me everything, and I'll help you no matter what, but things around here have become a bit unusually active and I'm dedicating two of my men to your team. I need some kind of heads up."

JJ contemplated Jim Bradbury's comments. He knew he was right. The man from Arizona was no dimwit and JJ was on his patch. Lying to him would be wrong and unprofessional. He was going to need to give Jim more information but not full information, just yet.

"Fine, Jim. Let's get some privacy and I'll fill you in."

"Thanks, JJ. Much appreciated."

As JJ left the support of the water cooler, preparing to have a one on one with his friend, Jim Bradbury put his hand on JJ's shoulder.

"Before we go into all that, JJ, there's someone in our secure communications room I think you'll want to meet."

6

LILY AND THE ICEMAN

"How's your mum, Cally?"

JJ and his daughter were having dinner at Omoya, a Japanese Izakaya, not far from Gangnam station. JJ remembered that as a child Carolyn loved roast chicken and she still did, her second favourite dinner meal after Châteaubriand. The katsu sauce at Omoya was outstanding, robust and tangy. Carolyn was tucking in heartily.

"She's fine, met an American guy who works at *The Wall Street Journal* in New York, so they chat about news stories all day long."

Father and daughter dinners can be very rewarding or they can be awkward. This was a little awkward to begin with tonight, not really through the fault of either Darke.

"Jim Bradbury tells me you're going by your mother's maiden name?" JJ mentioned but he didn't want to push the issue too much.

Though it was Carolyn's mum who left him when he was in his early twenties and the baby only five years old, JJ hadn't been an overly attentive father. He was a student when he met Rebecca Reynolds. He was at Glasgow and she was an exchange student from the University of California at Berkeley. They met at a boisterous disco in the Adam Smith building at Glasgow University, had a torrid love affair and, whazam, nine months later out popped Carolyn. The three of them lived together in a student flat just off the Byers Road in Glasgow, then moved to London after they both had graduated and JJ had been recruited by MI5.

Rebecca struggled to settle in London. All her family were from San Francisco and she missed them. JJ worked long hours and, on occasion, would disappear for weeks on either a training course or, on a dangerous field mission. Rebecca, who had suspended her promising career as a news reporter to care for Carolyn, did not feel that JJ's paternal support for their daughter was up to scratch. So, with JJ's extremely reluctant blessing, Rebecca and Carolyn went back to the United States.

JJ missed his daughter with an agonising ache that had no words to describe it. Deep down he knew he chose work over family life, however important he had felt that work to be. He helped support Carolyn and Rebecca financially until the latter told him she was more than self-sufficient many years later. He kept in long-distance touch with his daughter and knew that she had joined the CIA. As the years went by however, the calls were a little more sporadic and the topics of discussion narrower and narrower.

"Once I'd joined the CIA, I thought it best to use mum's name. Darke is a memorable surname and you were still known to several of the CIA veterans," Carolyn explained, saying veterans with cheeky intent.

JJ looked at Carolyn and, for the first time in a long time, he had tears in his eyes. His beautiful baby daughter was all grown up and had developed into a gorgeous young lady. He had more or less missed all of her teenage years and early career, the kind of times that having a good father around can be very useful.

He felt as emotionally rough as he could remember feeling, and for the first time in weeks the mission was not at the forefront of his mind. He knew he had to get back on focus so he looked lovingly at Carolyn for only a few seconds longer.

"So, Cally, what are you doing here in Seoul, at PAU Travel?" he asked.

Carolyn knew her dad would not expect her to spill her guts. Though she had successfully suppressed it for years, she remembered playing with him as a child. He was fun, loving and caring. She hadn't really understood back then why her mum had taken her to America. It seemed to boil down to a conclusion that several uncles, aunts and grandparents added up to more support than one, often absent, dad. Carolyn wasn't sure that was the right conclusion. But it was what it was, and she too needed to get back on point.

"I'm on a job for the agency," she replied very matter of fact. "What are *you* doing here?"

"I'm on a job too," JJ replied with equal stoicism.

"You're not MI5 anymore, are you?"

"No, I'm not, but I've been hauled out of retirement for one last job and that job is here."

Carolyn knew that jobs for the British security services were not likely to be wholly fulfilling here in Seoul. "Are you going across the border?" she asked a little more penetratingly.

JJ knew his daughter was no dummy, so there was no point in lying. In any case, the PAU Travel office would be all abuzz with the recent activity of visiting personnel. Two NGA women locked up in the secure communications room and now an ex-MI5 officer and his entourage decide to visit. Something was afoot.

"I am, Cally," JJ replied a little somberly. "In the next day or so. I can't say I'm really looking forward to it but it needs to be done. How about you?"

"No. My job here, with Dannielle, is a listening, translating, observation and reporting assignment, no wetworks or black ops," she replied, sounding a little disappointed.

JJ was still getting used to his daughter being all grown up, having a career, let alone having a blind notion what wetworks and black ops were! *God, this was hard* he thought. "Is Jim looking after you and Dannielle?"

"Yes, he's great, very pleasant. He doesn't bother us, just makes sure we have the equipment we need and any local knowledge to help us. You two know each other don't you?"

"We do, we were on an op together many years ago. We didn't start out on the op together, Jim being CIA and me MI5, but force of circumstance threw us together. Luckily for us, it also threw us back out again in one piece!" He didn't feel like bringing up the fact that he had saved Jim Bradbury's life.

The atmospherics between father and daughter continued to improve as the evening progressed. They started chatting about their colleagues at PAU Travel. Carolyn told her dad that, like many more regular professions, the people were fixated by nicknames.

"Yes, I gathered that," said JJ.

"Jim introduced me to two of the locals who have effectively been seconded to me for a while, Lily and the Iceman."

"Have you worked out those names yet?" asked his daughter.

"Well, I think I've got the Iceman. I'm assuming that Kim Chun-So was hired before Kim Min-Jun?" ventured JJ.

"Correct," said Carolyn.

"And so he may have been called Kim 1, which looks like Kimi," continued JJ. Carolyn was smiling. At least her dad still seemed to have a brain.

"Kimi would have been associated with Kimi Raikkonen, F1 driver and former world champion," elaborated JJ. "They're all motor racing mad down here, and Kimi Raikkonen's nickname is the Iceman," concluded JJ.

"Spot on," said Carolyn. "What about Lily?"

"I haven't a clue, Cally, enlighten me."

"It's not as good as the Iceman, but as Kim Min-Jun is

noticeably shorter than the Iceman, and was assigned to PAU Travel a few months later, apparently, he was clearly Kim 2 and nicknamed after Lil' Kim the American rapper."

"How about Jim Bradbury, anybody brave enough to give him a nickname?"

"Road Runner," replied Carolyn. "Partly because he's from Arizona and partly because he goes for a run along the streets of Gangnam every single morning before coming to the office."

"And you and Dannielle?"

"They call Dannielle, Olga, after the actress in the *Hitman* movies. She was Russian as is Dannielle's family."

"And you?"

"Well, I didn't have a nickname until you waltzed into the communications room. Now they all call me Princess," said Carolyn with a very sweet smile that might have been a grimace.

JJ recalled that he had nearly always called Carolyn, Princess, when she was little. He didn't mind that the Korean outpost of the CIA called her that too.

The rest of the meal went well. A renewed bond between father and daughter had emerged. This was the last stressless evening that either of them would have for quite some time and they both seemed to be enjoying it very much. After JJ kissed and hugged his daughter goodnight, dropping her off at her apartment in Gangnam, Carolyn turned and waved.

"By the way Dad, your nickname is Braveheart."

That was one to live up to, thought JJ.

The following morning, in the front meeting room at PAU Travel, JJ, Ethel and the Kims were engrossed in a map of the Korean Demilitarised Zone. If ever there was a misnomer, the DMZ was it. The DMZ is a piece of land that acts as a buffer zone between North and South Korea. It is 250km long, 4km wide, and runs

214

across the 38° parallel. It is the most heavily fortified border crossing on planet earth.

JJ explained that on this mission the border needed to be crossed four times. The first time was to get to Pyongyang to stakeout and survey the central bank and the visible security, then return. The third time was to get the disguised trucks across the border and then return. The probability of doing that illegally four times without capture was unhealthily low. The anticipated fourth crossing was, in all likelihood, the one where they would most need the option of a fast, illegal incursion across the border, from North to South. The four in the meeting room thought it best therefore to try to cross legally, or apparently legally, the first three times.

Lily spoke up first. "The best legal crossing from South to North is at Panmunjom," he said, pointing to the village which was the site that the Korean War ended. "The Kaesŏng rail and road crossing was re-opened in 2009. The railway line is used primarily to transport South Korean workers and materials to the Kaesŏng Industrial Group up in the North. It would be relatively easy for the Iceman and me to get the necessary papers, disguise ourselves as workers and get across. We can arrange for a car to be left for us, just on the outskirts of the region. The drive to Pyongyang would be just over an hour from there. If we left tomorrow morning, we could be back by tomorrow night."

JJ was considering this. Ideally, he wanted to check out the central bank himself. But a foreign visage would attract much more attention and have their papers checked much more thoroughly by the North Korean border guards. He also had to consider that he, Ethel and Victor would all need to cross with the Volvo/FAW trucks and the Sprinter van the following day and their story at that crossing would need to be very convincing.

"OK," said JJ eventually. "What about the next day when we all need to get across?"

"Straightforward enough for the Iceman and me," began Lily. "As we are supposed to be workers, they'd expect to see our faces every working day. For you guys it's more problematic. The road at Panmunjom, or Highway One, as we call it has very strict border controls. There is a bridge there that needs to be crossed and the North Koreans sometimes make you cross on foot, then pick up your vehicles at the other side. You will be body searched and your papers will need to be accompanied by some official letter or order authorising you to enter the DPRK. The vehicles will be inspected too, so we can't have anything dodgy poking out of them, like weapons or explosives."

JJ and Ethel looked at each other and nodded. There was no perfect way to cross the border from North to South Korea and vice versa. There were huge risks at every checkpoint, but time was pressing and they had to get on with it.

"Fine," said JJ. "Lily, you and the Iceman get going with acquiring or even making the right papers, initially for you both. I'll have a think about our cover story. If you're ready by tomorrow morning then get across the border and stakeout the central bank. If you're up for it, we'll have another briefing tomorrow night, if not then the following morning first thing."

With that Lily and the Iceman got up and left the meeting room. JJ told Ethel that he'd need to get a hold of Jim Bradbury to keep him in the loop. While he was doing that, she should get a hold of Victor, find out how he's getting on with his research on the vault. They'd meet up again in about one hour.

★ ★ ★

"For fuck's sake, JJ," said Jim Bradbury. "That's a suicide mission. Four border crossings between North and South in a matter of days, break into their central bank, steal Kim Jong-un's gold haul. Jesus Christ, why don't you save yourself the bother and just shoot yourself in the head!" The KLO clearly wasn't that enamoured with the plan.

"I don't have much choice Jim," said JJ who had now given his friend the guts of the operation. "My government thinks it's a legitimate mission," JJ continued, having left out the blackmail and insider trading elements. "They're desperate. The North Koreans refuse point blank to pay their debts and my country is nearly bankrupt," added JJ trying to put the gloss of legitimacy on his task.

"Why you and not an MI6 black ops squad?" asked Jim.

"Well, in addition to the issue of deniability, it would look a bit odd if the Bank of England suddenly had several thousand additional gold bullion bars one night with official assay stamps on them. As well as steal them, I'm supposed to disguise them, then organise their sale on the physical gold market, then give the monies to my government."

"And you have the skill to do all that?" enquired the Road Runner.

"I'm supposed to have, Jim," replied JJ. "I run a large hedge fund portfolio in London and I and my team there know how to buy and sell gold. We do it nearly every week," he said wistfully, thinking how nice and safe it would be back in London.

"It's still mega-fucking hair-brained," said Bradbury. "I know I said I'd help, and I will, but this mission is nuts. On the other hand…" Jim Bradbury said with a grin and after a short pause. "It may be the most action we've had around here for quite some time and I, for one, am getting bored out of my pants reading intercepted emails and the like. Bring it on, what can I do?"

Needless to say JJ was absolutely delighted that he could fully rely on his old friend. Jim Bradbury had skills, not least of which was, he knew how to drive heavy trucks. Apparently, in his student days in Arizona, the only summer job he could get to pay him enough to get through the expensive university system in America, was driving semi-trucks for a friend of his dad's road haulage company, based just outside Phoenix. After that particularly helpful revelation, JJ and Jim decided that they would not try to recruit an external HGV driver. Jim would drive one of the Volvo/FAW trucks, the Iceman the other. The Iceman did not have an HGV license, nor had he ever driven a truck so large, but Jim Bradbury knew he was the wheelman on several of PAU Travel's surveillance operations and that involved reasonably large vans, packed with equipment. He was sure he would be fine.

Thank god for that, thought JJ, at least the driver issue was now solved. Assuming Lily and the Iceman came through tomorrow's surveillance op in one piece, the next day would see six of them attempt to get into North Korea in two large trucks and a Sprinter van.

"JJ," said Jim. "While the two Kims are getting their papers sorted for the border crossing tomorrow, the rest of us need to scope out two things. First, we need to look at the photographs, diagrams and schematics you have for the DPRK central bank. When Lily and the Iceman return tomorrow, we need to check out how their visuals match our diagrams. Information about the North can be sketchy and even those intrusive fuckers at Google maps can be out of date."

JJ thought it somewhat amusing that Jim felt Google maps were intrusive given the multiple intrusions that his friend had authorised or carried out in his career.

"Secondly," Jim continued, "we need really good covers for us taking two big trucks and a van into the North. They're as twitchy as a guy with Tourette's on speed," referring to the DPRK border guards. "If we muck it up on that crossing there'll be no gold for your bankrupt country and a muddy grave for all of us."

* * *

JJ, Jim and Victor were back in the meeting room, perusing overhead shots of the new DPRK central bank building. The CIA satellite had taken a decent image of the large, impressive structure in the tree-lined boulevard, close to Taedong River. The shot was from only two nights ago and it was clear that the tallest part of the building complex was complete but that one of the two smaller structures on either side was not. The central bank had previously been located near what is now The People's Theatre in the Changjon street area. This was torn down a few years ago and the new building was much more of a statement.

"This new building is good news and bad news," said Victor. "The good news is that the construction may not be fully completed from what we can see. This means that the security guards will be used to building workers, electricians, painters, etc. milling around. They would all need to be authorised and probably subject to spot checks but at least it would not be unusual to see them on the premises. Further good news is that there are parking zones across the street, under the trees. See here," highlighted Victor, pointing at the photograph. "Lily and the Iceman may be able to park up there and observe."

"And the bad news?" asked Jim Bradbury.

"Well," said Victor. "The building is new, so it is likely to have state of the art security installed. As it is only the main tower which is finished, it is probable that the vault rooms are in that building, more likely underneath it."

JJ and Jim were not overly fazed by the bad news. They had assumed that the central bank would have state of the art security. They also knew that a tunnelling operation was out of the question, it would take too long, and probably be too noisy. In any event, it looked like the central bank structure was stand alone with no adjacent shops, theatres, cafés or other establishments. No, they thought, this breach would need to be quietly through the front door or something very similar.

"Is there a car park?" asked JJ.

"Yes," said Victor. "Here behind the main building, facing away from the river, towards the centre of Pyongyang."

JJ and Jim Bradbury considered the information so far. Assuming all had gone well up to that point, the secret service friends concluded that it would be feasible to park their Mercedes Sprinter van in the central bank's car park. There would probably be CCTV there but Victor intimated that he could freeze the camera's picture frame or send it on a continuous loop. The heist would be after business hours so any security officer looking at a picture of no action in the car park would just assume that that was what should be going on in the central bank's car park in the dead of night – nothing.

"We still have a problem," said JJ, "the van's got the 'Toblerone' conveyor system in it. Assuming we've opened the vault without setting an alarm off, loaded the gold onto the 'Toblerones', and then loaded the gold bars into the van, we're not going to have the space to re-load the conveyor system into the van. We can't leave them there. While there are no markings or manufacturers stamp on the 'Toblerones', we need them again to load the tankers with the gold. It's the same problem as getting the gold from the vaults to the van. We can't spend sixty hours doing it. Even sixty minutes could be too long."

"Can't we drive the tankers to the DPRK car park and load the gold straight on to them?" asked Victor, reasonable enough he thought.

"No," JJ snapped back not unfriendly, but with purpose. "We can check when the Kims return, but I'd bet anything that there will be no trucks or tankers in the car park. It's a central bank, not a supermarket or petrol station. There will be saloon cars, executive cars, maybe the occasional sports car but the largest vehicles in that car park will probably be vans like our Sprinter, carrying supplies for the central bank's daily operations and its workers. Two disguised Volvo trucks with tankers attached, however decaled, would stick out like the proverbial."

Jim Bradbury didn't have a lot to offer at this point, but Victor did not seem defeated by his earlier no good idea.

"We could always hot-wire one of the vans in the car park," he ventured. "I'll have the cameras on a loop so they won't notice a thing."

JJ thought immediately that was a workable option. "Good," he said. "Well done Victor. We'll check with Lily and the Iceman. If there're a few vans dotted around the car park that'll be good news."

Jim Bradbury still appeared thoughtful. "What about the tankers, JJ?" he asked. "Where are they going to be?"

"When I was looking at the maps and satellite image coordinates with the Kims, I noticed there is a substantial petrol station, south of the river across the bridge, right here," said JJ stabbing the map with his right forefinger. "During the daytime, Lily told me, it is quite busy given that there are not many petrol stations in Pyongyang. Apparently this one was built recently by Pyeonghwa Motors, has four to five rows of pumps and, more relevantly from our point of view, a trailer park where trucks and fuel tankers can park up before either unloading or loading their goods or petrol. Often, according to Lily, there can be several tankers there overnight. At night the petrol station is much less busy. This is the ideal location to park our trucks and to do the gold transfer."

Victor, Jim Bradbury and JJ thought that they had accomplished as much as they could on the transport plan for the moment. They'd await the scouting report from the Kims if and when they got back from their surveillance op, before making any adjustments. In the meantime, they'd find Ethel and start to work on their stories for the border crossing.

★ ★ ★

While the boys had been figuring out the transport plan, Ethel and two of the junior PAU Travellers had been working on the Volvo/FAW trucks. Their main task was to decal the tankers with the logos and paintwork of PetroChina, one of China's largest oil and gas companies. The main decal looked like a fully-open flower with serrated edges, mustardy-yellow on top and solid, rust coloured red on the bottom. It was distinctive and it was all over North Korea.

Ethel's phone beeped. It was a message from JJ asking her ETA back at PAU. Ethel replied ten minutes. They'd finished up on the trucks and a fine job they had done, she thought. Now, back to the grungy part of the mission.

"We've got the trucks set up as Chinese FAW tractors delivering petrol from PetroChina in Shaanxi tankers," began JJ. "That part has been relatively straight-forward. We'll aim for a border crossing just after breaking dawn on Thursday. That way the border guards may be a bit sleepy and less inclined to go through with a thorough inspection. The issue for this meeting is our collective covers."

Ethel, Victor, the two Kims and Jim Bradbury were listening attentively. This is where the pre-match heist would succeed or fail. Lily and the Iceman felt comfortable enough with their plan for the surveillance operation on the DPRK central bank tomorrow, Ethel felt that the trucks would pass muster and Victor seemed content with his research and all the equipment he had in tow.

"The starting point should be that we are delivering new petrol tankers to Pyeongwha Motors in Pyongyang from PetroChina in Beijing. Lily and the Iceman can be the drivers just for the border crossing itself. Don't panic Lily, you'll be approaching the border guards at, maybe, 10mph; you'll need to get out and speak to them to allow you to cross. One of the guards may even get in the cab with you, but that's no sweat. Once crossed, Jim will take over truck driving," said JJ. "You two stars," he continued, pointing to the Kims, "need to be the first contact. You look local, you sound local, in fact are local so the initial response will be that you are not a threat. You'll be dressed in PetroChina overalls, so the first impression as to how you look and talk will seem OK. The rest of us will be dressed in suits. Jim and I will appear to be PetroChina executives. Foreigners but seconded from Beijing to Seoul, primarily to ensure the safe delivery of these new fancy dan tankers. Ethel will be our corporate PA and Victor a petrochemical engineer, specifically requested by Pyeonghwa Motors.

"Those of us who cannot speak Korean will say as little as possible. Victor, you need to seem like some babbling egghead so be prepared to drop stuff, generally be clumsy and geeky, etc. Ethel you need to get a pair of specs, look a bit like a PA and hang on every word that Jim and I utter," said JJ smiling.

Ethel gave him a look which said in your dreams, bub.

"Any questions?" asked the Scot, hoping that there would not be, but knowing that there would.

Jim was first to jump in. "OK, we can get the right overalls, suits, the look, and the necessary forged Korean papers but what about our authorisation, won't that need to come from PetroChina and Pyeonghwa Motors?"

"Victor has already downloaded the corporate logos and headed paper for both companies. We know who their senior personnel are, which department they're responsible for and who would authorise such a delivery. Jim, Ethel and I will also have authentic looking PetroChina business cards. Young Pagari, here, hasn't been wasting his time."

"OK," said Jim Bradbury. "Let's say we all look the part and have papers to prove we are the part. Why don't the border guards just phone up Pyeonghwa Motors and ask if the delivery of two trucks is legit?"

"When Lily and the Iceman hand over all our papers and authorisation to the border guards it will feel like a volume of the Encyclopedia Brittanica landed on them. If they persist, we will have given them letters of authority from Pyeonghwa Motors with contact numbers on them. Of course we'd be happy for them to call, but it'll be around 6.30 in the morning. They won't be able to get through till 8.30 at the earliest. In the meantime, we'll have two fat trucks and a van blocking up their bridge, with the workers for the Kaesŏng Industrial Estate about to pour over from 7am. The odds are they'd just want rid of us," concluded JJ, hoping that the early morning North Korean border guards didn't want major hassle before breakfast.

There were nods and approval mumblings around the table, it was a plan which may have merits.

"What about our weapons, Victor's equipment and the 'Toblerones'?" Ethel asked.

"The 'Toblerones' look fairly innocuous, so they do not need to be disguised," said JJ. "If the guards really insist then we can say they're for rotating the empty petrol tanks once off the trailers. They have no markings, no tells, they're fine. Once we've bagged up our weapons, and any breach specific equipment of Victor's, we'll be placing them in Gore-Tex bags and submerging them in the sunbeds in the tankers which will be temporarily filled with water. A friend of ours in Woking, Surrey had them made up. The bags are good down to 300m even under high pressure," said JJ, simultaneously thinking that Harold surely did know a lot of stuff.

He glanced at Jim. His Arizona friend smiled back and gave him one of those two fingered salutes from the side of the forehead, so often used by military types to signal A-OK. The two Kims were nodding and babbling away in Korean, clearly believing that this mission could be pulled off. Ethel had moved a little closer to Victor and they both seemed convinced by the plan so far. Without shifting her attention from Victor, Ethel gave JJ the thumbs up from behind her back.

JJ was satisfied with the progress. It had been a hell of a rush, just getting to this point. It seemed like an age since he had been admiring Cyrus's 'Toblerone' sketches and a veritable eon ago that he had first come across Vincent Barakat and PLP. Yet it was only days. The prelims were over, the tests were due to begin the very next morning. JJ and his international clan of clandestine chums better be on their marks.

★ ★ ★

Kim Chun-So and Kim Min-Jun had definitely been on their marks. They had no trouble whatsoever getting across the border at 7am. Hordes of workers joined them as they trudged across the footbridge at Panmunjom on their way to the Kaesŏng Industrial Region. Their overalls, caps and work bags looked authentic. The DPRK border guards, probably still short on breakfast, only stopped, searched and checked every fifth or sixth worker. They had done these checks a thousand times. Nothing ever turned up, the workers were too scared that they would not be able to return to the South, ever, if they were caught with the smallest suspicious item or any minor incorrect detail in their papers. The guards were bored, this was a monotonous job and, to a man, they wished some fool would make a break for it so they could have some target practice or at least beat him up a bit under harsh interrogation.

Lily and the Iceman could not risk carrying any weapons or equipment across the bridge. They would lose any firefight with the guards and, if captured alive, they would never see their families or friends again. The plan was to pick up a car near the industrial estate and drive to Pyongyang. The car would be left there by one of only two deep cover CIA officers in the whole of North Korea. Kwon Min-Ho had been posing as an official tourist guide for over two years and, so far, he had not been rumbled.

As the two Kims reached the outskirts of the Kaesŏng Industrial Region they could see the dark blue car parked in one of the region's remote car spaces. This model of car and its successor was the second best seller in North Korea, produced by Pyeonghwa Motors, one of only two car manufacturers in the country, along with Pyongsang Auto Works. It was in reality a re-badged and re-tweeked Fiat but it passed for a local car. In so far as any car on North Korea's roads was anonymous, this was it.

Cars were few and far between, even in the capital, Pyongyang. Pyeonghwa Motors apparently had facilities to produce up to 10,000 cars per year, but in 2012, had only made 600. Most North Koreans did not have cars either because they were too expensive or because they had nowhere to go. Still, this four-door saloon car would fit in on the roads of the capital and that was what the Kims were counting on. Lily and the Iceman got into the car and out of their workers overalls. Kwon Min-Ho had left them more city appropriate attire underneath the back seat. There was also an array of surveillance equipment in a canvas holdall in a secret compartment. Deep cover Kwon had done a fine job.

The drive North to Pyongyang would take around an hour and a half. The first half of the journey ought to be fairly straightforward, there were no major villages or towns. As they got closer to the capital, they would hit places like Hwangu, Songnim and Chollima. They would probably be stopped at least at one of the checkpoints and questioned but they believed their cover was solid. That belief was well founded. The two Kims had entered the capital without incident and were parked up on the main tree lined boulevard, almost directly opposite the central bank, with a view of the Taedong River to their right. At least another ten cars were parked on the same stretch of road and some of them were made by PMW, three of which were Hwiparams II or III. The Kims' car did not look out of place.

Although tourists can visit Pyongyang, there aren't many of them and they are accompanied by official tourist guides, many of whom are agents of the DPRK's secret police. One thing you can't do is take photographs willy-nilly. The guides tell you what you are allowed to take photos of and then they check your camera at the end of the day. Kwon and the Kims were well aware of this, so they would not be hanging out of their car's windows like happy snappers. Kwon had left them a skinny tube camera that was barely visible from the outside as it poked out of the front offside headlamp. Lily was manipulating it from the driver's seat and he now had its sightline focused on the front of the central bank.

"Nice building Iceman," he said to his friend and colleague.

"Hadn't really noticed yet, Lily," the Iceman replied. "I'm still checking what goodies Kwon has given us."

"Anything useful?"

"Well, we've got the basics, notepad, pencils, medical supplies, mini camera stuff, though God knows when we'll get a chance to use the camera. In high-tech world we've also got a directional zoom microphone with recorder, Sunagor mega-zoom binoculars and, wait a minute, the jewel in the crown, a mini-tablet with encoded note attached," said the Iceman.

"What does the note say?" asked Lily.

"Hold your horses, I'm still reading," muttered the Iceman.

Kwon had truly surpassed himself. He had left the Kims a mini-tablet with Xaver 600 technology. Apparently, for distances up to several hundred yards, this software enables the tablet to see through walls and seek out heat signatures from body movement. It is notoriously difficult, if not impossible, to get internet access in North Korea but Kwon had enhanced the software algorithm to tap into any passing satellite. It could only be activated for a few minutes, safely, to avoid detection. The enhanced tablet used high frequency radio signals to capture an image akin to a baby foetus in a mother's womb, then the computer software processes the signals and converts them into a 3D image of people or objects concealed by solid barriers.

"Wow," said the Iceman.

"What?" asked Lily anxious to know the scoop while still processing the images form the tube camera.

"Kwon's gone *Star Trek* high-tech, Lily," said the Iceman.

"We're going to be able to peek inside the central bank without even getting out of this car," he continued, with a broad grin on his face.

The two Kims spent the rest of the morning observing, listening, surveying activity inside and outside of the central bank. They drove around the block a couple of times before re-parking on the same street but in a different position. Even in a city with a population of over 3 million, there was never any issue about parking. Lots of spaces, not lots of cars. Kim Min-Jun was the first to need a pee, and it was nearly lunchtime.

"Iceman, I'm going for a jimmy riddle and I'll get us something to eat too," said Lily, showing off his command of rhyming slang which he had picked up on a vacation to London.

"Make sure you wash your hands before getting the lunch," instructed the Iceman. "I don't want any commy bugs in this dump giving me the skitters."

Lily nodded and off he went. About forty-five minutes later he returned.

"Where have you been, I'm starving," announced the Iceman.

"I went over to Juche Tower, near the Diplo. There's a decent fast food and noodle shop near the club, Kwon told me about it a while ago. Then I wandered along the street at the back of the central bank. You can see the car park through some hedges and railings. There are cars parked there as well as some delivery vans. That's good news for us. Anything going on here?" Lily enquired as he handed the Iceman a roll, a couple of basic noodle rice trays and a bottle of water.

"Not really," he replied, munching rapidly into his lunch. "There's a few suits coming in and going out of the place, nothing unusual. There's still some work being done on the left hand smaller building, but the workers have security guards with them all the time. There's definitely a basement level because some of the 3-D bodies that get in the main elevator kind of disappear when most of the ones that go up are clearly visible. I guess Braveheart was right, the vaults are likely to be below ground level. There's one potentially interesting development though," said the Iceman.

"What's that?" asked Lily, feeling much more lively after relieving himself and getting something to eat.

"Well, there's one security guard, stationed just outside the front door, who's got a right bitch on. Here, listen to this," said the Iceman, handing Lily the recordings from the zoom microphone. Lily plugged in and listened up.

People don't really moan much in the DPRK. If you were foreign and you were caught complaining about something, the food, the transport, the ever present official guides then you'd be deported. If your complaint was extended to the regime, its leadership, or even the supreme leader himself then it was bye-bye to life as you knew it. If you a were DPRK citizen and you were caught moaning much, you were likely to meet with an accident or simply vanish. Vanish in this context meant dumped to rot in one of the republic's many unsavoury prison camps.

The particular security guard that Lily was now listening to was called Ji-hun, and he was moaning to his security buddy about all sorts. He wasn't happy about being transferred to front door duty. He had been happy as part of the security detail supervising the vaults, nothing much happened there and, at least, he could sit down. He wasn't happy that his holiday request, which he had put in last January had only been approved this week and was due to begin tomorrow. He wasn't happy that he had no plans to go anywhere. He wasn't happy that he didn't have a girlfriend and that he lived in a sparse, cardboard box of an apartment next door to a family with three young and boisterous kids. If there was ever a certainty that needed no interpretation it was that Ji-hun was not happy.

His security buddy kept saying 'shut up Ji-Hun, we'll get into trouble' but Ji-hun was in full groaning flow. Lily took off his headphones and handed them and the zoom microphone's recorder back to the Iceman.

"Are you thinking what I'm thinking Iceman?"

"Depends what you're thinking."

"I'm thinking the moaner Ji-hun could be helpful to our quest," said Lily.

"Exactly what I was thinking," agreed the Iceman.

Kwon Min-Ho had informed the two Kims that the normal closing time for the central bank was around 6pm, though a few executives could still be working there as late as 9pm. The front door security guards normally clocked off at 6.30pm. At this time of year, sunset would be around 7pm in Pyongyang and twilight about half an hour later.

"If we grab him, Lily, we're going to need to do it between 6.30 and 7pm. Later would be better because there will still be a hint of daylight at 7pm, but the last crossing from the industrial region back to the South is at 9.30pm. We can't miss it or we're stuffed."

"OK. Although we can't take the moaner with us back to Seoul, and god knows what Braveheart and the Road Runner will say when we tell them we've snatched a security guard," he cautioned.

"Look Lily. We were both in the meeting run by Darke. We don't know for sure where the vaults are, we don't know what kind of vault the bullion bars are in and we don't know the extent of security protecting them. This Ji-hun guy will know at least some of that. We've got to get him."

Ji-hun finished his shift at precisely 6.30pm. He changed out of his uniform in the guards' locker room, put on his civilian gear and hot footed it out of the central bank. He had no wish to be there a minute longer and, at least, tomorrow began seven days of rest and recuperation, or so he thought. He headed out of the front door, turned right along the main boulevard and had every intention of walking the twenty minutes or so it would take him to get to his ground floor box in a high rise tower block.

It was 6.45pm. As Ji-hun took a side turning into a nearly deserted street, he noticed that a dark blue saloon car had just passed him and parked. As he bent his head a little lower to peer into the driver's side, Lily had popped out round the back of the car. Silently, he grabbed Ji-hun around the neck and stuck a ketamine filled syringe into one of the moaner's veins. Lily held him as his sedated body crumpled. Ketamine may not be the anaesthetic of choice for the world's best equipped intelligence services but Kwon Min-Ho couldn't be high-tech on everything. He had included the drug under medical supplies, presumably in case a bullet had to be removed from one of his colleagues in the field. Lily manhandled Ji-hun into the back seat of the car, returned to the front passenger seat and they drove off.

"How long will he be out for?" the Iceman asked his friend.

"Hard to tell. I put a full dose in the syringe. Probably keep him quiet for a couple of hours. We need to figure out what to do with him now we've got him. We don't have time to interrogate him. It's 7.15pm now. By the time we get back to Kaesŏng and park up we'll just about make the 9.30pm crossing."

"I know. Do we have any other supplies from Kwon that could be of use?" asked the Iceman.

Lily got Kwon's bag and had a rummage through the remainder of its contents. There was a small drill, speedcuffs, some duct tape, two ropes and a small plastic bottle with a label on it.

"Iceman, what's propofol?" Lily asked.

"Propofol is just what the doctor ordered," replied the Iceman, concentrating on the road out of Pyongyang but formulating a plan as he did so.

It was nearly 8pm. Lily and the Iceman had soon passed through Chollima and Songnim but the checkpoint they had previously been stopped at, on their way to Pyongyang, was about ten minutes' drive away at Hwangu. The Iceman stopped the car and then pulled over to a totally unlit part of the road. The two Kims transferred the moaner Ji-hun, who was of course not moaning at present, to the car's trunk.

The hapless security guard now had some additional accessories on, in the form of speedcuffs and duct tape. The two Kims and their acquisition passed the Hwangu checkpoint without incident. The guards just waved them through, noting that they had recorded their registration number earlier on the way to Pyongyang. The Iceman drove with purpose, but within the speed limit, to the same spot near the Kaesŏng Industrial Region that they had picked up the car in the early morning. It was 8.45 pm. They had time but they needed to do something with Ji-hun and they needed to let Kwon know what was going on.

"What's our plan Iceman?" asked Lily.

"First, let's make sure Ji-hun's still breathing." He was, confirmed the Iceman after checking his pulse.

"Secondly, I'll administer the propofol," added the Iceman. "You drill a few air holes in the trunk's lid. Try not to make them too obvious."

Propofol was sometimes referred to as the milk of amnesia. It looked milky as the Iceman filled the plastic tube with needle attached. It is a widely used anaesthetic and approved in over fifty countries. It leaves the sedated one less fucked up of mind and speech once they recover compared to most other sedatives. As the Iceman was preparing to inject Ji-hun he marvelled at how useful deep cover Kwon was. He was low-tech, high-tech, whatever tech you needed. No wonder he had gone undetected in the DPRK for so long.

Kim Chun-So was no doctor. Thankfully, Kwon had left instructions. If you want to knock the 'patient' out for eight to ten hours then start by injecting 10ml and then hook up the enclosed tube so that the entire contents of the small bottle can drip into him intravenously over time. The Iceman did the first injection, hooked the tube over and around one of the hinges on the inside of the trunk lid, held the contraption in place with some duct tape and checked that the milky liquid was flowing through. It was. Game on.

Lily had completed drilling half a dozen or so holes near the front of the trunk lid. They would not be noticed by passers-by, not that there were many of those right here, right now nor would there be till business hours tomorrow. The two Kims changed back into their workers clothes. It was 9pm.

"Right, let's get to the crossing pronto, Lily," said the Iceman. "The moaner here is alive and breathing, he should be out for the count till about 6am tomorrow, maybe a little longer since you drugged him up earlier. He'll be able to breathe OK now you've drilled some holes. In any case, he looks young and fit. If he wakes up early I've left him half a bottle of water with a message wrapped around it."

"What does the message say?" asked Lily as he and the Iceman were picking up the pace.

"I'll tell you later," said the Iceman, concentrating on brisk walking, but not so brisk as to alert any nosey security types.

"What about Kwon, isn't he coming to get the car tonight?" asked Lily, hoping that his friend had a better answer to that one than his previous question.

"I don't think he's coming for the car tonight Lily, we're cutting it fine to get out of the industrial estate with the other workers and across the border. There's no sign of Kwon. In a few minutes time it would seem highly unusual for a car to be driving out of the region and headed north. It's late and all the workers will have left in a few minutes. He probably had the intention of letting it stay here for the night. We'll take that chance. I left an encoded message for him under the front seat, with the keys, just in case. When we get back to PAU we'll send him another secure message." Lily was satisfied with that answer.

JJ and Ethel were in their hired Mercedes, far enough away from the border crossing to attract no military attention, but close enough so that Kim Chun-So and Kim Min-Jun could spot them once they were through. It would need to be that way round. The caucaesan pair had a hard enough time telling one Korean from another in multi fashion Gangnam without having to contend with the same dark green fabric workers boiler suits pouring across the border. Fortunately, Lily and the Iceman headed straight for the Merc.

"Hi guys," said JJ. "Good to see you. We were getting worried. That's the last crossing for tonight, isn't it?"

"Yes," said Lily. "We cut it a bit fine, but we needed to make a small detour."

"Not a shooting or car chase detour I hope?" said Ethel in a moderately concerned tone.

"No," replied the Iceman. "More of an acquisition detour."

As they drove off on the forty minutes or so journey to Seoul, the Iceman and Lily brought JJ and Ethel up to speed. JJ nearly drove off the road when the Iceman announced that they had kidnapped one of the central bank's security guards. A few Glaswegian expletive deletives filled the night air to boot. As the kidnap story unfolded though, JJ warmed to the acquisition detour. Provided the guy was still alive in the morning, he could be persuaded to divulge some very useful information. The Iceman was right, they didn't know enough about the bank's vaults, their whereabouts or mechanisms, the security guards attached, the timing of the watch. It could be a winner, thought JJ.

"What did you knock the moaner out with?" asked JJ, never one not to use a decent newfound nickname.

"First, ketamine, to subdue him," said Lily.

"Then propofol to keep him KO'd but with a functioning brain and understandable speech pattern when he woke up," added the Iceman.

"Wasn't it propofol that killed Michael Jackson?"

Before the two Kims could get worried, Ethel chipped in.

"Yes, but he was given it for sixty nights in a row by that odd doctor, I've forgotten his name."

"That's OK then," said JJ, not really certain that it was.

The remainder of the journey back to Seoul was accomplished in good spirits. Lily and the Iceman were in one piece and they had done a great job, notably and crucially assisted by the invisible Kwon Min-Ho. The two Kims had decided to nickname Kwon, The Doctor, for the sheer ingenuity and usefulness of his medical supplies. JJ thought that this was good. There had never been an Asian *Dr. Who*, though there had been three Scottish ones. Deep cover Kwon had earned his nickname.

It was 10.30pm. Although it was late, the four teammates drove straight to PAU Travel. Jim Bradbury and Victor would be waiting, anxious for a de-brief and hopeful that the Kims had gathered some useful intel. As they entered the covert CIA office, Lily turned to his friend and asked, "So what was the message you left for the moaner Ji-hun?"

"I told him that I'd wired the trunk lid to explode if he tried to open it from the inside. It would also explode if anyone, other than me, tried to open it from the outside. I told him to drink the water to get hydrated and that we'd bring him breakfast in the morning."

"That was considerate of you, Iceman," said Lily, very content at this juncture.

"I thought so too," replied the Iceman, yet another contented Kim that evening in Seoul. With his left arm over the shoulders of his shorter compatriot, the Iceman led Lily into PAU Travel. It had been quite some day.

* * *

"How's your dad?" Dannielle Eagles asked of Carolyn Reynolds.

The two friends and NGA officers were taking a morning break from the secure communications room at PAU Travel. They had decided to go in search of a good coffee shop that would also have quality pastries. Carolyn, in particular, had something of a sweet tooth. Jim Bradbury, the previous day, had pointed them in the direction of the Sinseong Building in the Yeoksom-Dong part of Gangnam. Jim said there were at least half a dozen coffee shops between Gangnam Station and the Sinseong so they should find something to their taste. He should know, thought Dannielle, because he ran part of that route every morning on his way to PAU. Jim's directions and advice were good. The two NGA women had counted eight cafés before they could see the Sinseong building close up. They backtracked about a block because café no. 7 called Septem, looked to be the one with the best pastries.

"It was really good seeing him. I had kind of blocked out his absence when I was a kid, and convinced myself that Mum knew best. JJ seems relatively cool for a dad, we've got a lot in common personality wise, so it was fun," she said, sipping on her double shot, extra dry cappuccino.

"Did he tell you why he was here, in Seoul?"

"It was a bit odd, actually, Danni. I can't remember if I mentioned it or not, but my dad used to be an MI5 officer. When he left the service he joined the financial community in London and ended up running some big portfolio for a hedge fund in Mayfair," explained Carolyn now munching into a giant slab of carrot cake. Dannielle contemplated this response for a few seconds, taking the opportunity to have a wee bite of her freshly baked ham and cheese croissant, and a sip of her latte.

"So is he on some sales trip or capital raising exercise?" asked Dannielle, fully aware that JJ Darke had been ensconced in several meetings within PAU and was accompanied by a fierce looking woman and a modern hippy.

Carolyn had known Dannielle for a few years and trusted her totally, but even with that, she was not quite certain that her dad would want her blabbing to her friend.

"Since we had only just hooked up after quite a few years, Danni, I didn't feel like quizzing him too much, especially since that may have opened the door for him to start quizzing me back." Carolyn hoped that was a good enough response to satisfy her friend's curiosity and lead to a change of subject, preferably shopping. She was wrong.

Dannielle persisted. "Well he's turned up at PAU with a woman and a hippy kid in tow and clearly knows Jim Bradbury. He must be up to something more than trying to sell his hedge fund or raise assets from investors."

Carolyn could not remember Dannielle ever annoying her very often but her tone was beginning, just beginning, to wrankle a little with this line of conversation.

"I don't really know, Danni," said Carolyn with a hint of sharpness in her voice. "I'll ask him when I next see him," she continued unsure of whether that would be the case or not.

Dannielle Eagles was very proficient at disconnecting her internal feelings from her external expression. Carolyn was a trained CIA and NGA officer, however, and she spotted the slight widening of her friend's eyes and tightening of her lips. Danni wanted to know more and wasn't over the moon at not getting what she wanted. There was a brief silence between the two which stopped short of being awkward.

"Have you heard anything from Henry?" asked Dannielle, more intent on keeping the conversation flowing than caring about the answer.

"Not really," replied Carolyn, pleased that the subject matter had moved away from her dad. "I sent him an encrypted email last night, asking whether he had any updates on Operation Philidor Defence but the big Maasai said that he had heard nothing."

"Do you think O'Neill's got the Borei yet?" asked Dannielle.

"Well, we sent them the information about the Borei's weaponisation and the cheat sheet of Korean and Russian key submarine words two days ago. Given where they ought to be in the Bay of Korea or the Yellow Sea, I would estimate that they would try for it tonight or tomorrow night."

"We know it wasn't last night anyway," said Dannielle. "The latest satellite image we got still showed the faint outline of the Borei nestled at Haeju dock."

Carolyn nodded and had some more coffee and cake. She couldn't explain it properly but the instinct inside her made her feel a little uncomfortable with Danni this morning, at least as far as discussing the mission or her dad's presence in Seoul was concerned. It was probably because she was tired or still a bit jet lagged. The strong coffee should perk her up. She liked Danni so it was time for her to get that relationship back on track.

"Hey Danni," said Carolyn catching her friend in mid croissant mouthful. "When we're finished here, will we go shopping? There's a billion super cool stores here in Gangnam, some labels we know, some we don't. I could do with a new suit, a pair of shoes and a better watch," she added, looking at her cheap digital no name plastic timepiece and recalling the frivolous abuse that her dad launched on it at dinner. He was a horological snob, thought Carolyn, but basically correct.

"Sure," said Danni, trying her professional best to seem interested. "I could do with a better, cooler handbag, shoes too, and we're not expected back at PAU till lunchtime. Let's go!"

With that the two friends got up, paid the bill and headed

into the mid-morning sunshine that swathed cosmopolitan Gangnam.

★ ★ ★

A couple of hours earlier, as he was trying to wake, the moaner Ji-hun did not find himself swathed in sunshine. He was still disorientated, had a headache, but was composed enough to realise he was bound, had tape of a sticky variety over his mouth and was in some kind of container. He struggled a bit, actually as much as the trunk of a small saloon car would allow and tried a muffled yell for help. As he was wriggling and muffling, he knocked over a small plastic bottle of water with a piece of paper wrapped around it and held on by an elastic band.

Ji-hun was twenty-four years old, very slim, probably weighing no more than 70kg, about 5ft 8 in tall. His middleweight division frame had more to do with his genes and the unappetising food he was faced with nearly every day of his life rather than visits to the gym. He was flexible enough though to turn fully around in the car's trunk. He was now facing the back seat of the car, hands tied behind his back and unravelling the piece of paper from the bottle. Ji-hun then rolled over again. The message on the bottle was a bit coiled now as the piece of paper had been in situ for some time. Desperate to read what was written on the paper he managed skilfully to hold one end down with the bottle and the other with his right knee. It was dark inside the trunk but there were several shafts of skinny light peeping through and just enough for Ji-hun to read it, a few words at a time.

Ji-hun had no real expectation as to what he was going to read, but he had worked out that he was in the trunk of a car and that some fucking asshole as he described it to himself, had rigged the trunk's lid with explosives! He couldn't see any wires or attachments, but then again, he did not have a clear 360° view of his surroundings. After a few more minutes of wriggling and shifting the bottle and his knee, he had assimilated the rest of the Iceman's message. Not only was his kidnapper a fucking asshole, he was also a fucking imbecile. *Drink the water to stay hydrated* the message read. *Yeah right*, the moaner thought, *how am I meant to hold the stupid bottle with my hands cuffed behind my back and how am I supposed to drink it with duct tape all over my mouth*. This was definitely one of those occasions where it wasn't the thought that counted.

Ji-hun was, if anything, less happy than he was yesterday. Here he was stuck in a ready to explode car trunk, sore head, tied up, gagged, thirsty and hungry. *Bring you breakfast in the morning* said the asshole imbecile's message. Sure. It was morning now, he could tell by the lightshafts from Lily's drilled air holes. So where's my fucking breakfast he wondered. Probably just another of the kidnapper messenger's thoughts that didn't count. Just as Ji-hun was ruminating further on his sorry plight, the trunk lid began to lift.

"Good morning Ji-hun," said the Iceman.

★ ★ ★

The border crossing that morning had worked like a dream. The border guards checked the two Kims' papers thoroughly. There was very little chance that the guards would recognise either Lily or the Iceman. For starters, at least four of the six guards on duty this morning were from a different detail than yesterday. Then, when the two Kims had crossed yesterday, they were wearing the same green fabric overalls and caps of many of the workers going to the Kaesŏng Industrial Region. Today, they were in the predominantly rust-red garb of PetroChina tanker drivers, wearing no caps. The border guards tensed up a little when they set eyes on the four white faces of the Kims' companions. However, as anticipated by JJ, the avalanche of paperwork that they gave the authorities, combined with the early hour of the day, rendered the border guards more complicit than normal. With Jim Bradbury babbling on in Korean about the importance attached to these new tankers by Pyeonghwa Motors, and the essential matter of maintaining good business links with China, Victor mumbling away in geek as he fumbled with his research papers and Ethel smiling all girly at them, they just wanted rid of this mini convoy. JJ hadn't needed to do anything but just sit quietly in the cab of one of the trucks. This was as smooth as a baby's bum, he thought, a little self-satisfied.

* * *

As the Iceman was untaping and uncuffing Ji-hun, giving him his belated water and shoving a baguette filled with ham and salad in his left hand, the others were parking up the tankers and the Sprinter van, just out of sight of any watchtowers on the Kaesŏng Industrial Estate.

JJ and the Iceman had removed Ji-hun from the trunk, and the three of them were sitting in the back seat of the four-door saloon, the moaner in the middle. Ji-hun could speak very little English so the Iceman was to lead the interrogation. Kim Chun-So explained to him the notion of good cop, demented cop. The Iceman was the good cop, he said, prepared to reward Ji-hun for his cooperation. Pointing to JJ, the Iceman said he was one vicious mother fucker waeguk-sarem. Ji-hun glanced at JJ. The Scot, revelling in his role as the bad foreigner, let the moaner catch a glimpse of his Glock 17 pistol and decorative cigarette lighter, a present from Eloise, though he didn't smoke. Ji-hun got the idea.

"Look, Ji-hun," said the Iceman. "We need to ask you a few questions about security at the central bank. If you answer them truthfully, and I assure you, we will know if you are lying, then you will be free to go and you will be financially rewarded beyond your dreams." The Iceman wasn't sure what Ji-hun's financial dreams may be and he omitted to be specific as to exactly when Ji-hun would be set free. He gauged that the moaner groaner was not a happy bunny, and the nine million won (about £5,500) that he had in an envelope in his breast pocket must be one big chunk of cash for a young DPRK security guard.

"How much?" spluttered out Ji-hun still kind of enjoying his promised breakfast.

"Given that you're not in the world's strongest negotiating position, young man, this envelope here," replied the Iceman showing Ji-hun the cash, "contains nine million won. It's yours for full co-operation."

Ji-hun was a moaner but he wasn't an idiot. Nine million won was slightly more than his entire annual income from his security guard job. It was indeed a small fortune, but what the hell would he do with it in Pyongyang or indeed any part of the DPRK. There wasn't a lot to spend it on, and he did not have anyone to spend it with. He could buy a car and some upmarket clothes. That would raise the suspicions of the snoopers, the secret police, the government informers. He may be nine million won the richer but he'd be 90% probable the deader or the imprisoned.

"Is it South Korean or North Korean won?" he asked.

"South," replied the Iceman. That was better thought Ji-hun, hard currency, acceptable all over the world. His captor's answer, though, further solidified an embryonic thought in his head, slightly less sore now than it was earlier.

"South Korean won isn't much use to me in Pyongyang. I'd need to convert it, annoyingly enough at my place of work, and all kinds of alarm bells would go off," he pointed out. JJ and the Iceman exchanged glances with one another. The moaner was right, and as much as they had no intrinsic feelings for Ji-hun they didn't really want to be the direct cause of his death or prison camp enrolment.

"What do you want then?" asked the Iceman. "Be quick about it, we're on a clock and my foreign friend here is itching for it to be his turn."

Ji-hun felt that the Iceman wasn't joking.

"I want the nine million won, safe passage to the South, new papers and identity so that I can stay in Seoul or surrounding areas, and a South Korean passport. If you give me that I will tell you everything I know about the central bank and its security," he said, thinking clearly and hoping for the best.

"Tell him we'll get him all that if we believe he is truthful and that his information is useful," stressed JJ, after the Iceman translated. The Iceman relayed the message to Ji-hun. The young North Korean was pensive.

"Can I trust you?" he asked meekly.

"I brought you breakfast as promised, didn't I?" replied the Iceman. While a token baguette for breakfast was no guarantee of a new life and nine million won, Ji-hun gauged that it was the best offer he was likely to get in the foreseeable future. As he was now officially on holiday, and had no friends or family expecting to see him, he would not be missed for at least a week. That was sufficient time, he thought, to either be rotting away with a bullet in his head in the trunk of a car or, alternatively, enough time to be getting used to Gangnam life. In either case, it was a no brainer.

"OK," said Ji-hun. "I accept." With that he shook the Iceman's hand, supporting his right forearm with his left hand, in the traditional and respectful Korean way. He exchanged nods of agreement with JJ, and the Scot re-holstered his Glock and put away his lighter.

For the next twenty minutes Sun Ji-hun sang like a bird. The central bank's vaults were indeed one level below ground level, as JJ and Victor had thought. They could be accessed by the main elevator, a service lift or down some stairs. The security detail on this level was primarily based in a bullet proof, glass fronted lockable office, normally with one or two guards inside. They had monitors and video surveillance equipment trained on the main vault where precious metals, cash and many safe deposit boxes were kept. Ji-hun wasn't certain but he thought that the vault had a dual combination lock because the only times he had seen it being opened, it required two executives to do it. Ji-hun added that the vault door also had a digital clock embedded in it, with a key pad underneath. Ji-hun continued to unload his information. JJ was taking notes, while the Iceman translated and kept eye contact with the moaner, making him feel appreciated.

It was nearly 8am and, in the distance, they could see the industrial region's workers make their way through the main gates of the estate. Perhaps Ji-hun could have made a break for it, or yelled his head off, but he knew that the bad motherfucker foreigner would kill him. In any case, he was warming to his new found job as an informant and allowed himself a brief happy thought about his forthcoming life.

Ji-hun's information was helpful and his final useful contribution was to tell JJ and the Iceman about the timing of the security guards shifts in the vaults, in the main hall and on the front door of the DPRK's central bank.

JJ and the Iceman stepped outside, intimating to Ji-hun not to move, and keeping low behind the car's body shell.

"That was useful?" said the Iceman to JJ, part statement and part question.

"Yes, it was," replied JJ. "We can get working on the time of the guards' shifts to gauge precisely when they're at their most lean and I'll give the vault information to Victor."

"Are we going to waste Ji-hun?" asked the Iceman, somewhat coldly thought JJ.

"No, we're not Iceman," came JJ's firm reply. "We're going to stick to our word, so that we don't wake up in a cold sweat every night with a troubled conscience!"

"What are we going to do with him then? We can't leave him here, we can't take him across the border right now and we can't go waltzing into the central bank with him," pointing out the somewhat obvious to JJ.

"I'm working on it," replied JJ. "For the moment, let's stick him in the back of the Sprinter van with the 'Toblerones'. When we're on the move you get in touch with deep cover Kwon, his unique skills may be required again."

The Iceman nodded and the pair of them escorted Sun Ji-hun to the back of the Sprinter van. Ethel and Victor were a little taken aback to see the young North Korean, looking pale and tired, scramble between six triangular conveyor systems. He seemed docile enough though and bowed politely to them.

"Ji-hun," said JJ, introducing their captive. "He's here to help."

★ ★ ★

Kwon Min-ho had been undercover in Pyongyang for two years. He was twenty-eight years old, about 5ft 10in, well built, but not fat. His black, straight hair was cut short in keeping with the standard look of many of the DPRK's official tourist guides. His eyes were dark brown and there was nothing spectacular about him, at least to the eye. This was good news for a deep cover operative. Most of the time Kwon was assigned to the Konyo hotel in Pyongyang, one of the three major hotels in the city designed specifically to cater for foreigners. He reported to the assistant manager of the Konyo, who also happened to be the senior state secret police officer on site.

In his two years there, Kwon had shopped a couple of foreigners to his boss. This needed to be done to maintain cover and the two people he had shopped were very unpleasant, one Russian and one American, who had only committed minor misdemeanours. The American wouldn't do what he was told regarding photography and the Russian was always complaining about the food, both inside and outside the hotel. They were deported, but apart from a bit of a rough man handling, both men returned to their respective countries in one piece.

Kwon was not a CIA officer and had not been trained at either of the two main CIA training sites in the United States. By quirk of fate, he was born in Israel to South Korean parents. His father had been seconded to the University of Tel Aviv from Seoul's Hankuk University of Foreign Studies and his mother came along for the ride. Dad enjoyed it so much he stayed. His mother, tragically, had been killed by a Hamas suicide bomber in the centre of a Tel Aviv market in 1996. From that day Min-ho had vowed to fight terrorism in any way he could.

He was a bright boy, attended his dad's university, studying medicine and political history. It was an odd academic combination and he had to get special permission from the university's board to do it, but his dad was head of the History department so that helped. From the university, Min-ho moved to the Centre for Political Research, the intelligence branch of the Israeli Ministry of Foreign Affairs and then on to Shin Bet. Most folk were familiar with Mossad as the main Israeli intelligence service. Mossad was concerned primarily with overseas intelligence work. After Min-ho's mother's death, however, he wanted to contribute to the internal security of his adopted country and that was the responsibility of Shin Bet.

Min-ho's tenure at Shin Bet was productive. After failing, in 1995, to prevent the assassination of the Israeli Prime Minister Yitzhak Rabin by a right wing Israeli radical, the domestic intelligence service was overhauled completely. Foreigners, or those who looked foreign but were Israeli, like Min-ho, were fast-tracked through the service. The new bosses took the view that to target and recognise domestic terror threats, the intelligence operatives needed to appear as multi-cultural as the likely perpetrators. North Korea had links with Syria and they, in turn, with Hamas. It was a soldier in Hamas' military wing, the Izz ad-Din al-Qassam Brigade, who had murdered Min-ho's mother.

The Shin Bet leadership and that of Mossad, the CIA and the FBI occasionally held joint consultations. They agreed on many intelligence issues and disagreed on some. One item they agreed upon was that deep undercover operatives needed to blend in better with their surroundings like a bottle of Coke in a Manhattan café. The US and Israeli intelligence services were urged to cooperate even more closely, as many of their enemies were common. From a memorandum that followed one of these joint consultations, Min-ho found himself seconded to the CIA, Seoul branch, under the auspices of Jim Bradbury.

Of the CIA officers in Seoul, only Jim knew his real name. Today, though, Kwon had a rare day off. It was around 8am but he was still lolling about in his pyjamas, eating some juk and plain toast and drinking a mug of green tea. He hadn't quite decided what to do today. He might make his way to the

Kaesŏng industrial estate and pick up the car he had left for his two Seoul colleagues that he had never met, or he may wait till Saturday when the road from Pyongyang to Kaesŏng would be busier with weekend drivers. Alternatively, it was a pleasant spring morning in the capital, sunny and not humid. It may be a day for a stroll along the banks of the Taedong River, relax, have a coffee, chill.

As he was mulling over his options, Kwon's pyjama pants began to vibrate. It was his cell phone, the secure one used only by his CIA colleagues. Once answered, the itinerary for his day would be set. It may involve the Taedong river, but it wasn't going to involve chilling. It was a text message.

Kwon, meet us at Songnim, close to the river port. We'll be parked up in a dark blue van near a couple of PetroChina fuel tankers. ASAP. Iceman.

While Kwon had never met Kim Chun-so, he knew his nickname was the Iceman, and it was also his communication call sign. As Kwon was getting dressed for his day out after replying to the Iceman, he was churning over in his mind as to why the Iceman and team were in the North two days running. That was unusual, if not unheard of. He said 'we' in his message so he wasn't solo. Still, yesterday must have gone OK, Kwon thought, since the Iceman is clearly still alive.

Kwon made his way to Songnim by railway. It was easier and he had not received any instructions to the contrary about being mobile. As he was strolling through the river port, he spotted the blue van and the PetroChina tankers. They didn't look that out of place. This was a relatively busy seaport, with many loadings, unloadings, tankers, containers, vans and lorries. There weren't any petrol or gas facilities though, but many long distance drivers parked there, like a lay-bye, to have a snooze or a snack or both.

Jim Bradbury saw Kwon coming. He donned a plain, dark

baseball cap and stepped out of one of the tankers' cabs. He still had his suit on, so he looked a bit fashion stupid but better stupid than having his foreign face stand out.

"Min-ho," said Jim, giving Kwon a firm handshake. "It's really great to see you," he continued, meaning it wholeheartedly. It was not easy being deep cover and seeing Kwon alive and well made Bradbury feel good inside.

"Hi Jim," replied Kwon, also happy to see his boss. "Guess you guys aren't here on a tourist package," he joked, nodding in the direction of the tankers and van.

"Guess not, my friend," replied Jim. "C'mon you need to meet some folks."

Kwon, the Iceman and Lily stood at the side of one of the tankers, out of plain sight, and gave each other a warm Korean handshake, with a few backslaps thrown in.

"Hey Kwon, your new nickname is 'the Doctor'," said Lily with mirth. "Because the stuff you left us yesterday was spot on."

"I like that," replied Kwon. "I do have a medical qualification and my mum was a big fan of the sci-fi TV show."

Under different circumstances JJ would have been content for the bonhomie to continue but time was flying and they were dawdling in a North Korean seaport. There was sure to be a military presence there. JJ stepped out of his tanker's cab, committing the same fashion faux pas as Jim Bradbury.

"Hi Kwon," he greeted the Doctor with a warm handshake. "I'm JJ Darke. I'm an ex-MI5 officer, good friends with Jim Bradbury and, for better or worse, the team leader for this mission. Great job yesterday, thank you, your work is much appreciated."

Kwon returned the greeting. He knew that standing on the Songnim dockside was not the place for the many questions he had for JJ Darke. Before departing Songnim for Pyongyang, JJ, Jim and Kwon sat in the cab of one of the tankers. JJ and Jim gave Kwon much of the information he needed to know and answers to most of the questions he asked.

It appeared that Kwon's immediate responsibility was to babysit the moaner Ji-hun. JJ wanted Kwon to keep Ji-hun with him that night, but to stay in contact in case he was required. If all went well then the next morning Kwon was to deliver Ji-hun across the border to awaiting PAU operatives, with his nine million won intact. The CIA team at PAU would then organise Ji-hun the correct papers, a new identity and a South Korean passport, as promised. Kwon thought that it was a lot of effort for one day's worth of snitching but he was professional and would do his best. He also admired the fact that this JJ Darke wanted to keep a promise in a profession where promises were often worth ziltch.

It was 9.30am and it was time to leave. Ethel, Victor and Ji-hun were in the Sprinter van, Jim Bradbury, Kwon and Lily in one tanker, and JJ with the Iceman in the other. The road from Songnim to Pyongyang was straight and should take about thirty-five minutes to get to the targeted petrol station to park the tankers. There was only one checkpoint on the remaining part of the road, near Chollima. Hopefully it would be as simple as the crossing at Kaesŏng. It wasn't.

The road was quite busy, insofar as any roads in North Korea could be termed busy. It certainly was not the M25 car park but there was a short tail-back at the checkpoint. One of the military guards had recently been promoted and, that morning, he was clearly hell-bent on thoroughness.

The Iceman was driving the lead truck and the guard asked him to step out of the cab. He checked his papers completely. They seemed fine but then he spotted JJ. With his rifle pointing at JJ he made the Scot get out of the cab and started barking orders at him. Of course, JJ hadn't a clue what he was saying but the Iceman translated. Do not move and give me your papers was the gist of the barking. JJ handed them over. Jim Bradbury saw the mini commotion, got out of his cab and walked, slowly and unthreateningly towards JJ. While the guard was inspecting JJ's papers, Jim politely interrupted. He explained in Korean to the guard why they were on the road. Delivering new petrol tankers from PetroChina to Pyeonghwa Motors in Pyongyang. He handed the guard the letters of authorisation from Pyeonghwa Motors along with all the other necessary paperwork. Your average military guard at these checkpoints would probably just look at the papers, maybe peek into the trucks and, if all seemed in order, then that would be that. Not this soldier on this morning. He signalled to his buddy to stand guard over these foreigners and their indigenous companions while he went to call Lee Gun-woo, Assistant Vice President for Logistics at Pyeonghwa Motors.

Lee was real enough, Victor had discovered correctly who the man in charge of transport vehicle logistics at Pyeonghwa was, but he hadn't ordered any new petrol tankers from PetroChina. The rest of the Darke mission team realised that something wasn't going smoothly. They had a vast array of weaponry with them, and they would have liked to be getting prepared if there was to be a shootout. Their vast array of weapons, however, was still snug as a bug in a rug in the Gore-Tex waterproof bags in the tankers. They were, de facto, totally unarmed.

"Hello, Kim Min-su speaking, personal assistant to AVP Lee," said the pleasant voice at the end of the telephone.

"This is Lieutenant Muk Woo-jin from the Chollima checkpoint, may I speak to Lee Gun-woo?"

"AVP Lee is on one day's vacation, Lieutenant, can I be of any assistance?" replied Min-su.

Muk thought for a moment. He could try and get Lee's PA to track him down, but that would probably take a while and the tail-back at the checkpoint was building up. While he wanted to be thorough, Muk didn't want to cause a traffic jam. One of the ruling party's politicians or army generals may be in the queue and he didn't want a bollicking for being overzealous. Lee Gun-woo existed alright and the letter of authorisation seemed real enough. It was probably OK, he thought, but I'll ask one more question anyway.

"Ms. Kim, are you aware of AVP Lee authorising the delivery of two PetroChina tankers to your company?"

Kim Min-su tried to open up her work email account on her antiquated computer. Everything electronic was going slow this morning and she wanted to catch a tea break with her friend. When the cat's away, the mouse will have a tea break she thought. This lieutenant fellow could be on the phone all day if I don't get rid of him.

"I do not recall, Lieutenant, but we often take delivery of cars and trucks from China. If the driver has a letter of authority from AVP Lee I am sure it is in order."

"Thank you," said Muk, and hung up. Lieutenant Muk Woo-jin waved the Darke mission convoy through.

There were silent sighs of relief all round in the PetroChina tankers and the Sprinter van. This mission was moving rapidly towards the business end of matters and with it the concomitant risk of discovery, imprisonment and death.

★ ★ ★

Dannielle Eagles phoned in sick that morning. She told her friend

Carolyn that she had eaten some bad fish and was chucking up all over the place. Carolyn wished her a speedy recovery and said that she'd pop round to see her later in the day.

In truth, Danniellle wasn't feeling that great, but it was more in the mind than in the stomach. She really wanted to know why JJ Darke was in town and she really wanted to know the status of Operation Philidor Defence. Carolyn hadn't been very forthcoming on the former though Dannielle did conclude that effective radio silence on the latter was to be expected. Yet, she still had a disturbing feeling in her gut, not the result of bad fish, but of nervous tension.

It was nearly midday in Seoul, so close to 7am in Moscow. Time to phone Mother Russia, Dannielle felt.

Dannielle's apartment in Gangnam was very pleasant. It was on a short term let, just for two weeks. She was on the fourth floor of a high-rise building, roughly equidistant from Gangnam station and the PAU Travel office. Carolyn was on the sixth floor. It made sense for them to be close, they worked with each other, got on well and went to the Gangnam office every day, bar today, together.

Today, though, Dannielle went into the keypad lockable safe in the wardrobe of her bedroom and extracted her iPhone. It wasn't any old iPhone but one with a Thuraya Satnav sleeve attached which turned it into a satellite phone. It weighed 3½ ounces and was a bit bulkier than a naked iPhone but the sleeve meant that you could make secure calls from more or less anywhere in the world, with a guaranteed signal and unobstructed transmission. It was not NGA issue. Dannielle only used this phone on special occasions. Today was one of those. Dannielle dialled, she was through.

"Kruglov," came the curt greeting.

Dannielle announced herself.

"Anyata Ivanovna!" responded the man, sounding delighted to hear from his caller, and using the familiar patronymic style of greeting to a Russian woman that he knew well.

"Igor," responded Dannielle, more formal but a friendly enough way to address the first Deputy Director of the SVR, the agency responsible for Russia's foreign counter-intelligence.

7

BOWSER'S CASTLE

"These numbers seem a bit suspicious," said Joel Gordon as he bounded into Neil Robson's office on the third floor of the Treasury.

Joel looked a little like Usain Bolt – not, maybe an inch shorter in height but outweighed by being several inches wider around his midriff. He was around the same age as the fastest man on the planet, came from a Jamaican background, and had indeed progressed up the two flights of stairs that separated his and Robson's office with a decent turn of speed. The similarities more or less ended there. Joel Gordon was a financial accountant and there was a lot less of the showman about him than in the Jamaican super sprinter. Joel Gordon was a top-notch number cruncher. He gained a BSc, first class, in Finance and Accounting from London's Brunel University, joined HM Treasury's finance department and gained a CIMA qualification, working at nights to complete the course. His grandparents had left Jamaica in the 1960s, determined to give their family a good education and better prospects. They settled in the east end of London, near Upton Park, and were a hardworking and honest family. Joel was the first of the UK-based Gordons to gain a place at University and he was determined to make the most of the opportunity that his grandparents had given him.

"Come in Joel," said Robson, a somewhat superfluous offer as the tall Joel was already inside Neil Robson's office. "Take a seat," the Financial Secretary to the Treasury continued. "Unload what's on your mind."

Joel shuffled about with his papers for a moment or two. Although his direct boss was Craig Wilson, the somewhat dull, pro-cycling Executive Secretary to the Treasury, everyone knew that if you had an issue that you wanted resolved then it was better to go to Robson. Even with that he would still have gone to Craig Wilson first, but he was on a cycling vacation in Belgium. *Good luck with that*, thought Joel.

"Well, Sir," began Gordon. "Mr Wilson asked me to check over our anticipated tax revenues for the current financial year and then compare them with our estimated government expenditures."

"That's a good thing, right?" said Robson, not yet even moderately fazed by the subject matter.

"It is, Sir, and I would have gone to Mr Wilson first, and not disturbed you."

"He's off pedal pushing in foreign parts I gather," interrupted Robson, who did not have much time for the MP for Kensington and Chelsea.

"Yes, he is," confirmed Gordon.

"And you felt that your number crunching could not wait till his return," interjected Robson again, not in an unfriendly tone, but pointed enough to hint to young Gordon that he had better have something worthwhile to say.

"Yes, Sir," replied Gordon. Robson stayed quiet but gave him a look which said get on with it. Joel Gordon recognised the look.

"The issue is, while I'm confident that the numbers we have anticipated for tax revenue in this financial year are attainable, and will stand up to scrutiny within and outwith the government, I'm less sure about the expenditure figures." Robson nodded and intimated that Gordon should continue. "In particular, the estimates we have for expenditures, including wages, of the NHS, the police and the armed forces seem unrealistically low."

"How low?" asked Robson now listening somewhat more attentively to the twenty-eight year old.

"I've checked and re-checked the figures, Sir," Gordon replied. "I've run them through several computer simulations with the government's budget constraint included. It looks like, well…"

"Spit it out, Gordon," spiked Robson.

"We're £3-4 billion adrift of where Mr Wilson, you, and indeed the Chancellor believe we are," concluded Gordon, closing his file of jumbled papers, little realising that, of the four of them, only the pedal-pusher was not in the know.

"Can there be no mistake?" asked Robson feigning concern.

"No Sir," replied Gordon. "I've re-done the arithmetic several times and I've no doubt that there is a £3-4bn hole in the accounts."

"Does anyone else know about this, Joel?"

"No, I brought my findings straight to you, Mr Robson. As you know I would have gone to Mr Wilson first, but I did not feel it appropriate to divulge this sensitive information in a phone call, email or any electronic transmission."

"You did the right thing, Joel," said Robson, significantly relieved. "Leave it with me, I'll take a look at your findings." Robson held his hand outstretched hoping to receive the file with the damning numbers in it. Joel Gordon hesitated ever so slightly before handing them over.

"Will you take it to the Chancellor?" Joel asked.

The Chancellor, Jeffrey Walker, already knew the UK government was in a big, black hole, £3bn plus deep, thought Robson, but he wasn't going to tell that to this overly inquisitive accountant.

"Yes, I will, Joel, thank you," answered Robson coolly enough. "In the meantime, I would be grateful if you would keep this to yourself. The general election is not too far away and any issues regarding government finances will be even more under the microscope than usual."

Joel Gordon nodded but didn't say anything. After a few moments pause, and urged on by the intrinsic gene of ambition in his body, he piped up.

"When you discuss it with the Chancellor, Sir, would you mention it was my work? I know it sounds pushy but the Deputy Head of the Finance department's job is up for grabs I believe and I would like to be considered for it."

Neil Robson thought that this was somewhat cheeky by the young fellow, but also recognised that he had to keep him on side and quiet. So far, in the government only he and the Chancellor knew about the £3bn black hole and the Financial Secretary's scarily audacious plan to plug it. Now, someone else knew, or thought they knew part of it. That increased the probability of a leak by 33.3% and that was too big a percentage to ignore.

"Sure, Joel," said Robson, trying to sound friendly. "When is Craig Wilson back from his vacation?"

"In eight days."

"Well, let's all meet up on his return," advocated Robson. "I'll have been in discussion with the Chancellor by then and I'll inform Craig what a sterling job you've done. Is that OK?" asked Robson, knowing, of course, that it would be.

"Yes, Sir, that would be excellent. Thank you," said the accountant. With that, they both stood up, shook hands, and Joel Gordon left Neil Robson's office and proceeded down the stairs to his, stepping jauntily on his way.

Neil Robson re-took his seat. He had no jaunty feeling right at this moment. On the one hand, he had that wise guy JJ Darke out on a thieving mission with very little communication from the recalcitrant Scot. Now, on the other, he had some excessively upwardly-mobile Treasury accountant being way too investigative on the plight of the government finances. Both of these issues needed sorting, thought Robson, as he scrunched up a piece of paper in his right hand largely oblivious to the fact that he was doing it.

Although Neil Robson was MP for Middlesbrough, as well as being Financial Secretary to the Treasury, he spent little time there and nearly always delegated his constituency duties to underlings. While he was born and bred in the area, he didn't give one jot about his constituents. He was one for the good life, which often, for Robson, meant the bad life. He lived outside of London, in St. George's Hill, Weybridge. Houses on that private estate tended to start at £3 million and proceed higher, maybe up to £8-9 million. Robson's house was in the middle of that range as well as, roughly, being in the middle of the estate. Many rich and famous people lived in St. George's Hill. Estate agents always described it as exclusive, which, of course, it wasn't. There were over 400 houses on the 964 acre estate. Admittedly, there was a golf course and a tennis club but if truth be told it was more like a compound than an exclusive estate. Once you stepped out of the barrier controlled gates you were essentially in no-man's land, all roads and cars but nothing much to do or see in the immediate vicinity. His ten year old nephew, whom he did not like nor he Robson, called this house Bowser's Castle and Uncle Neil was King of the Koopas as far as the kid was concerned. Still, if you wished to maintain a low profile amongst A, B and C list celebrities then this was the place to be. Sirs Elton John and Cliff Richard had residences there as did the Swedish criminal Stefan Eriksson. The famous and the infamous, St. George's Hill had them all. Unknown to most of his fellow residents, Neil Robson belonged to the latter group.

As he drove his black Bentley Continental into one of his integral garages, the prime thoughts on Robson's mind were to get in touch with JJ Darke for an update on the mission in North Korea, to figure out what to do with Joel Gordon and his discoveries, whether or not to have a quick snort of cocaine and whether or not to get changed and head to the Nicolas Casino, one of London's largest casinos and the one to which he gave much of his patronage. Patronage in this context simply meant Robson turning up and giving the casino his money. He was £2 million in debt to the casino, specifically its lugubrious Russian owner Vladimir Babikov. This may not be the kind of behaviour and pastimes that the Financial Secretary to HM Treasury should indulge in, but it was the life of Neil Robson. He left MI5 under a cloud and re-invented himself as a politician. He was good with numbers, articulate and an excellent public speaker. He could hold a crowd and he could convince the unsuspecting with his quick wit and superficial charm.

He rose swiftly through the backbench ranks of the Conservative party and came to the Chancellor's attention at a fund raising event in one of his rare visits to his native Middlesbrough. The party did not have much cash to put behind Robson's first attempt at election, but his oratory and local accent saw him trounce both the Labour and Lib Dem candidates in a by-election in the summer of 2009. Jeffrey Walker liked that a lot and soon Robson was ensconced in the Treasury, eventually reporting directly to the Chancellor himself.

Neil Robson was not content with the salary and life style of a quasi-mandarin. He wanted more. More money, more recognition, more most anything including casual sex and drugs. He was a man of action, for god's sake. He had killed two Provisional IRA gunsmiths in the mid-1990s and at least twice as many Iran sponsored terrorists in a MOIS cell, discovered in

Birmingham. He was an MI5 officer. That was what he was supposed to do. Well actually, he was supposed to capture and interrogate them but, what the heck; that took time and was hard work. Shooting the bastards was easier and quicker. He didn't like their stupid accents either. All that incomprehensible Irish brogue and abbydabbywallah girning of the towel heads. Even if they were giving up information after a beating, he wouldn't know what the fuck they were talking about. Maybe that was another reason he didn't like Darke. West of Scotland accents could be like Irish ones, all that Gaelic mumbo-jumbo at speed, it was a disgrace to the Queen's English.

Now he had to contend with another foreign accent, that friggin' Jamrock yardie accountant Joel Gordon. Neil Robson didn't like foreigners, he didn't like accents and he didn't like accountants. Trust that woose Wilson to promote the fuckwit who was digging way too deep for his own good and that of Robson. Wilson wouldn't be back for eight days so Joel Gordon needed to be dealt with by then. Tonight though was going to be casino night.

"Vladimir, it's Neil Robson. I was thinking of popping up to the Nicolas tonight. Any good action going on?"

Vladimir Babikov was old school Russian. He was around sixty-five years old, looked like Leonid Breznhev and smoked giant Havana cigars. He had a bodyguard squad made up of six ex-FSB thugs (actually, one of them, Vasily, was just a thug) and there were always at least two of them no further than ten yards away from his person. As he answered this phone call in his opulent office in the Nicolas Casino just off Leicester Square, he had a pair of 6ft plus 'comrades' at his side.

"Neil, my friend," Babikov replied, this time friend meaning not friend, not enemy, but someone who owes me money. "There is a high-roller blackjack game in a private room plus all the usual attractions," he continued. Neil Robson quite liked blackjack, he felt he had an advantage being exceptionally numerate and quick of thought. His £2 million debt tab to Babikov suggested otherwise.

"Great," said Robson. "I'll be up around 9pm."

"Sure, Neil. We'll have some vodka and a chat too. I may have a nice girl for you to meet."

Robson hoped that the vodka would be good. He wasn't so sure about the chat, and the 'nice girl' would be some high class hooker or Russian prostituka acquired by Babikov to keep his best clients amused – at a price to their wallet and potential reputation. The chat would be about the £2 million that Robson owed. There was no realistic way to dodge the debt. Babikov was rumoured to have ordered the death or mutilation of at least eight late payers. If you owed less than £1 million and were late you lost a few fingers, or an ear and then had 50% interest added to your bill. If you owed more than £1 million and were late you were tortured, mutilated and, after an agonisingly long while, killed. Babikov then went after your family for the debt. Nothing had ever been proven against the wily Russian but Robson had no doubt that the stories were true.

As Robson was driving into the Nicolas Casino's car park, at the top end of Leicester Square, he was mulling over his blackjack strategy for the evening, the problem of Joel Gordon and whether Babikov's nice girl was to be a blonde, redhead or brunette. At least two of these mulls were quickly resolved. Robson may be numerate but he was no *Rainman*. Before midnight, Robson's debt to Babikov had increased by a further £500,000. The nice girl was a lovely creature, skinny, great artificial tits and thick platinum bottle blonde hair with extensions. A quick shag in a side room was all he had time for before he was summoned to Babikov's office.

"Neil, come in, have a drink. Help yourself," welcomed Babikov, gesturing to an expansive burgundy leather chair on which Robson was to sit. On the dark mahogany side table next to him sat a bottle of Hangar One Vodka, with one crystal glass tumbler. Hangar One Vodka was interesting partly because it was distilled from viognier grapes and the process was done in an abandoned hangar, and partly because it was made in California. Babikov himself was downing a glass of Zyr vodka on the rocks; only pure Russian for him.

"I trust you have had a pleasant evening, Neil? Was Dina to your liking?"

"She was fine, Vladimir, thanks, short and sweet," replied Robson knowing that the pluses and minuses of his furtive fuck were not the main course on Babikov's likely menu of questions.

"Good, I am pleased," said Babikov. "We have this small matter of your debt to the casino, my friend. Do you have a plan?"

Under normal circumstances, Robson would not have a plan and would be fearful for his fingers, other appendages and his very life. The Englishman was a survivor, however, a sleekit beastie, but not at all timorous.

"I do Vladimir, I do," replied Robson. "It may be a bit more complex than you would like ideally but this is compensated for by the fact that you will get ten times what I owe you plus an additional fee if you can help me with a small problem I have at work."

Vladimir Babikov had been around on the planet long enough and had authorised the mutilation and murder of enough late payers to realise most debt repayment plans in this circumstance were a load of codswallop. Folk would say anything to save their limbs and their life and this was even more certain when they were staring at a pair of pliers or a canvas roll of shiny medical utensils brandished by evil looking Russians. Robson was different. For starters, he was a member of the British government and quite high ranking at that. At some point in the future that could be helpful. Secondly, he was an ex-MI5 operative. That made him tougher than most debtors, also more aware of the elements of darkness in the real world. He would surely not be stupid enough to try to fool this creditor. Thirdly, most debtors in this position struggle to have a credible plan just to pay back what they owe. Robson, however, was offering £25 million plus a fee paying job to offset a debt of £2.5 million. That was at least good enough economics to warrant listening to his proposal.

"Go ahead, Neil," resumed Babikov, filling his glass with some more Zyr. "Tell me your proposal."

Neil Robson gave Vladimir Babikov an outline of his plan. It omitted the state of the British government's finances, the outrageous nature of the gold acquisition plan and its dependence on a Scot that he neither liked nor trusted. Robson told the Russian that he was to receive a substantial sum of money in the next two weeks. That money would come from the sale of gold bullion that was to come into his possession. Robson thought it wise, on health and credibility grounds, to give some detail. He also thought that since Babikov must be heavily involved in the money laundering business, he may wish to hold gold bars instead of cash. The choice would be his.

"And you say you will have this money within two weeks?" asked Babikov, seeking additional confirmation of the timetable.

"Yes," replied Robson, knowing that a short, decisive affirmative was probably called for at this juncture. Babikov feigned pondering for a few moments. He felt this was a great deal on the face of it and he fancied having a few gold bars to look at. Even after the deal was done he would still have a bucket load of incriminating evidence on the Financial Secretary to HM

Treasury, ranging from excessive gambling and cocaine snorting to sexual indiscretions, so often the downfall of British politicians.

"OK," said Babikov eventually. "I agree. I am a generous man. I will give you four weeks from today. There will be no extensions, my friend. I am also a man of my word and should you decide to deceive me, you will be left with nothing much to extend on your body!"

With that pleasantry, Babikov roared with laughter and the two FSB thugs at his side allowed themselves a goony smirk or two. Robson wasn't roaring with laughter, but he was confident enough in his proposal to have another swig of Hangar One. He had always planned to siphon off a few hundred million from the North Korean gold haul, so £25 million or so to get this limb-chopping crazy Ruski off his back was neither here nor there. That fucking wanker Darke had better deliver he thought and he further thought that he had better get himself some additional leverage over the Scot.

As Babikov and Robson clinked their vodka tumblers to signal an agreed deal, the Russian asked, "Now Neil, about this small problem you have at the office?"

★ ★ ★

Joel Gordon was pleased with his day's work. He had been led to believe that Neil Robson was a bit of a dodgy character, but he had seemed pleasant enough to him today. He was glad that he had put in the extra hours on the expenditure figures even though it may mean something of a headache for Robson and Chancellor Walker. Still, one man's pain and all that. If it led him to being promoted to Deputy Head of the Treasury's finance department then great. Joel thought he would celebrate in advance by ringing his girlfriend Talisha to meet him at Pizza Express on Terrace Road, only about twelve minutes' walk from the Boleyn Ground, formerly Upton Park and a further ten minutes or so from where he lived. Normally, Joel preferred eating at the *Ronak Restaurant* in Romford Road because it had a wide selection of vegetarian dishes that he liked. Talisha liked pizza and every now and then so did Joel.

"Hi babe," said Talisha in that loudish way that is natural to Americans but still a bit noisy for the rest of us.

"Hi sweetie," replied Joel, standing up from the table and giving Talisha a warm squeeze. She was an African American by origin but had been transferred to London a few years ago, working for Arthur Anderson, the accountancy conglomerate. Talisha was curvy but slim, despite her liking of pizza, quite tall, with dark, thick brown hair and olive green eyes. Joel felt he was lucky to have such a looker as his girlfriend. They had been going out for about ten months, having met at a local wine bar, and were getting on famously.

"I've ordered your favourite, Margherita with extra pepperoni," beamed Joel, pleased with himself that he knew and remembered Talisha's favourites. "A Giardiniera for me."

"Thanks babe," replied Talisha. "You sounded happy on the phone, good day at work?"

"Yes, I won't bore you with all the details, but I did some good forensic work on the government's finances and I'm hoping that it will lead to a swift promotion."

"That's great, Joel!" exclaimed Talisha, genuinely happy for her boyfriend. He may not be the most handsome guy in the world, but they got on well, they both had good jobs and were ambitious. If they stuck together, she thought, they may soon be able to move from E13 and E6 to SW3 or SW1. They could still eat at Pizza Express, there was one on the King's Road she knew of but the other shops and their clientele were way more upmarket. Just where she wanted to be.

★ ★ ★

Around the same time as Talisha and Joel were tucking into their pizzas, Cyrus and Gil were tucking into theirs. Although the Pizza Express on the King's Road was literally an Olympic discus competitor's throw from their house in Markham Square, they had decided to order take away. Pizza Express didn't deliver so this meant Gil going to get them. She and Cyrus had best of three rock, paper, scissors to decide who should go and Cyrus had won 2-1. Gil claimed that, in fairness, she should, therefore get to choose the movie they would watch. Cyrus agreed but vetoed any out and out chick flick.

"Ok, so what are we watching, Gil?" asked Cyrus, having a hearty munch of his pizza.

"I'm trying to decide between *Skyfall* and *Casino Royale*. Even with the new Bond movie out, I think *Skyfall* may be the best Bond so far."

Cyrus quite liked the Bond movies. His dad had introduced him to them and, of course, being Scottish he had always claimed that Sean Connery was the best Bond. Even his dad, however, had recognised recently that maybe Daniel Craig was better, or at least more modern realistic with slightly less cheesy double entendres. Cyrus missed his dad and he hadn't had a phone call for a couple of days; he really hoped he was OK.

"I prefer *Casino Royale*," Cyrus piped up in between mouthfuls.

"You're only saying that because you fancy Eva Green," teased Gil.

"Were I to fancy any of the celluloid superstar girl actresses in the movie, Gil, it would be Caterina Murino, she's hot to trot, dark and sultry, more my type than the English rose," elaborated the young man.

"Eva Green is French," corrected Gil, pleased with her movie knowledge.

"Whatever," replied Cyrus, still the counter of choice for youngsters when they had lost a verbal joust. "My decision is based on the quality of the bad guy. While Javier Bardem is a great actor, I didn't like him in his role in the first three quarters of *Skyfall*. All that fake blond hair, touching up Daniel Craig on the island and pulling his own dentures out in the MI6 basement. It was gross. By contrast, Mads Mikklesen is all simmering danger, a financier of death, not someone to meet at night in a dark alley."

"What about his bleeding eye?" countered Gil. "Wasn't that gross?"

"It was, but not as gooey as Bardem's collapsed gob," conceded Cyrus, being especially Scottish at this particular moment.

"OK, OK," said Gil. "We'll watch *Casino Royale*… but the song from *Skyfall* is better."

"Agreed," said Cyrus pleased to have gotten his way in both movie choice and pizza delivery system.

★ ★ ★

While both sets of pizza eaters did not know each other, they were about to have more in common than they would have liked, courtesy of Neil Robson. The slimy debt-ridden politician had agreed to pay Vladimir Babikov £1 million each for two stakeout operations. Robson had had only a one word reply so far to his question to JJ Darke regarding the status of the DPRK operation. 'Fine' did not really quench the desire for information on the mission that Robson had burning within him, but that's all he had received so far. In case Darke was up to any shenanigans or even thought of double crossing his old MI5 colleague, Neil

Robson convinced Babikov to allocate him one of his ex-FSB bodyguards to shadow Cyrus Darke. This shouldn't be a difficult job, thought Robson. We're talking about a fourteen year old kid who was barely aware of his willie let alone the dangers that lurk around every big city corner. The kid went to school, sometimes had after school clubs, went home, went out and seemed to have a partially crippled Asian nanny to accompany him on occasion. Hardly a serious tester for Boris the thug, assessed Robson. Still, if Daddy Darke fucked up in any way, shape or form Robson needed to have instant leverage over and above the insider trading stick. The kid would be fine and dandy as long as his dad kept his end of the bargain.

Vasily the thug may have a more involved task to earn his boss the extra £1 million. Vasily's job was to shadow Joel Gordon. On the face of it, not that much more difficult than Boris's operation. Joel Gordon went to work, came back, sometimes went out with a girl, sometimes went to the gym. He was as easy to shadow as the Darke lad. Robson, however, was iterating towards the conclusion that Joel Gordon needed to have an accident. Neither he nor Chancellor Walker could afford to have any leaks sprung regarding the hole in the government's finances. It was a sure-fire election loser. Both the Chancellor and Robson would likely join the ranks of the unemployed and while Walker may earn a few bob with his soporific memoirs and some non-executive directorships, Robson at best, could look forward to a couple of high-paying after dinner speeches and then that would be that. If they were exposed before Darke came back with the gold then the Scot might feel that he and his colleagues were off the insider trading hook, and abandon the gold mission. No, no thought Robson, the young accountant had to be either talked out of it or taken out of it.

"Come in Joel," welcomed Neil Robson. "Thanks for agreeing to this meeting at short notice. Tea? Coffee?"

"A green tea would be nice if you have it," replied Joel Gordon. "A plain black one if you don't," he added. "No sugar."

He's a fucking dreamer, thought Robson. Green tea in HM Treasury. Give me a fucking break. He's lucky to get a proper cup, the dimwit. Robson poured Joel a cup of plain black tea and one for himself with milk and sugar included.

"Joel, I have news and I have a request. The news, and I hope you consider it to be good news, is that I've had a word with the Chancellor. He was very impressed with your detailed report. He instructed me to tell you that as soon as the election is won, you will get the Deputy Head of Finance position." Robson sounded convincing, as befitted his status as one of the government's better orators. In truth, he hadn't mentioned a word to Jeffrey Walker. The Chancellor was already having a queasy meltdown over the £3bn hole and the illegal plan to fill it. If he knew that Joel the financial Rottweiler had his teeth clamped on the issue, he'd probably throw in the towel.

Joel Gordon absorbed the news. Ideally, he had wanted the job before the election, but, hey, it was only a matter of months, he could wait.

"Thank you, Mr Robson, that's great news," said Joel.

"No need to thank me, Joel," Robson replied. "You've earned it through your work," he added insincerely.

"You said you also had a request, Sir?"

"Yes, Joel. The Chancellor and I believe strongly that we need to keep this information strictly between the three of us. Walls have ears and the Treasury has a lot of porous walls. We totally trust you but each additional person that knows, guesses, implies that the government has a £3-4bn black hole increases the probability of an external leak and one which would be fatal to the government's re-election prospects."

"What about Mr Wilson? He's my direct boss, the Exchequer

271

Secretary to the Treasury and he would need to know about my impending promotion," stressed Joel, being the consummate professional that he was.

"You can't tell Craig as yet," said Robson. His voice was not raised, but it was strong and deliberate. "Look, Joel, if you tell Craig then a sequence of dynamic events will unfold that we may eventually lose control of. First, if Craig knows you're leaving his office to be Deputy Head of Finance, then he will begin the search for your replacement. That will involve HR, maybe outside head hunters. They will ask questions and you may appear less than open if you do not tell all, which you cannot. Then your colleagues will ask about your rapid, nay meteoric promotion. That would involve more evasiveness on your part, of which you may not be skilled." Robson looked directly at Joel and he nodded, he sure was not skilled at evasion. The Financial Secretary to the Treasury spent a few more minutes detailing the potential pitfalls of Joel telling anyone about his findings or his upcoming promotion.

"Are we in agreement?" Robson asked.

"I guess so, Sir," said Joel, by now a little taken aback by the subterfuge surrounding the whole issue. Robson stood up to signal that the meeting was over. They shook hands.

As Joel was leaving Robson's office to return to his own, the Financial Secretary asked, "What time do you finish tonight, Joel?"

"Around 6pm, Sir, my usual time," he replied. It was 4pm now.

"Look, it's been a complex day for you, lots to think about. Why don't you leave a little early, say 5 o'clock, go home have a bit more relax time," Robson said cheerily.

"Thank you, Sir, I think I will," replied Gordon and with that he went back to his office. Neil Robson stayed in his till just before 6pm. He felt that he had been convincing and sincere enough in his delivery and content that Gordon would not mention his forensic accounting or upcoming promotion to anyone. Still, as he pondered further their conversation 'I guess so, Sir' did not really smack of full commitment and it was full commitment that Robson sorely needed at this point. MI5 officers are trained to leave as little as humanly possible to chance and he had not forgotten his training. Maybe he would just saunter down to Joel Gordon's desk.

"Becky, I'm going down to Joel Gordon's office. In a few minutes ring his extension and tell me his password for his work emails. Also, check with the switchboard to see if he made any external calls after 4.30pm today," asked Robson of his candescent PA. In truth, Becky was a little less luminous today, dressed mainly in monochrome.

"Sure," replied Becky. It was not unusual for senior Treasury and government officials to look at their junior colleagues' emails. Often the more senior officials worked longer hours or were abroad and may need access to information and projects at short notice or when the juniors were not there. The executive PAs, of which Becky was one, had a list of all the relevant passwords.

"Becky," acknowledged Robson as he picked up Joel Gordon's phone.

"Mr Gordon did not make any phone calls after 4.30pm today, Sir. His password for his private emails is *Talisha1*."

"Thanks," said Robson and then he hung up. Well at least that's encouraging thought Robson. No panic phone calls to anyone after their meeting. Maybe the ambitious Jamrock yardie was fully committed after all. Robson keyed in Gordon's email password and began to scroll through the list of mails. They looked fine until one sent email, timed at 4.45pm, stood out. Neil Robson's demeanour altered significantly. *Puerile peasant* thought

Robson as he looked at Joel Gordon's mail. It was to Craig Wilson. It read:

> Hi Craig,
>
> I hope your holiday has been good. When you return I need to talk to you urgently about a couple of crucial developments relating to government finances and my career.
>
> Regards,
>
> Joel

As Neil Robson leant back in Joel Gordon's chair, he closed his eyes and was silently lamenting that the young accountant's commitment to secrecy had barely lasted fifteen minutes. Maybe Vasily was going to earn Babikov that £1 million fee after all.

★ ★ ★

The next day Gil had decided to pick Cyrus up from school. Most days her ward didn't need or want to be picked up as he could easily walk from his Chelsea school to his Chelsea home. Today, however, the boys' tennis team from his school had a challenge match against the boys from the Harrodian, in Barnes near Richmond. They had been taken there by coach in mid-afternoon but Gil had already told Cyrus that she would collect him. She wanted to keep the boy as close as possible to her. Gil, too, hadn't heard from JJ in a couple of days and while that was to be expected given the nature of JJ's mission, Gil knew that she was solely responsible for Cyrus given his only living parent was in absentia. She also liked Cyrus's company; they were relaxed in each other's space and although the age difference was more than ten years they seemed to enjoy many similar things. Training in the gym wasn't one of them, however, but as last night was movie night, tonight was going to be gym night. Maybe a light session, thought Gil, since the boy would be tired after tennis though this would be somewhat balanced by the remarkable energy recovery capacity of the fourteen year old.

Cyrus jumped into the passenger side of his dad's Porsche and nonchalantly tossed all his tennis gear into the back bucket seats, designed for legless dwarves, but in the absence of wee folk, ideal for a tennis racket or two.

"Hi Gil," he said cheerily. "Thanks for picking me up."

"Hi Cyrus. By your happy expression I take it you played like the post-Lendl Andy Murray not the pre-Lendl version?"

"I won my match 7-6, 6-4. The team lost three matches to two, so I'm only partly happy. It was good fun, competitive but not overly aggressive," he added, as Gil pulled away from the school gates.

"Are you shattered?" Gil asked.

"No, I'm fine," replied Cyrus.

"Good," she responded. "Tonight is gym night young man. I don't want your father coming back accusing me of turning you into a teletubby," Gil said, laughing, as Cyrus was built like a rake.

"C'mon Gil! I've been playing tennis for nearly two hours, my shorts are falling off I'm so skinny. Give me a break."

"Let's have one of those widely recognised British compromises then," Gil retorted. "A soft warm up, no cardiovascular exercises but we train on the mat working on holds, how to get out of them and then evasive action dealing with knife attacks. No more than an hour tops."

"OK," said Cyrus, now reclining in his seat, eyes closed, earphones in, iPod music on. The twenty to thirty minutes it would take to drive from Barnes to Markham Square was enough for him to get a few tunes in and block out any further physical activities that Gil may be thinking of. As he was listening to his music he would also be going over in his mind's eye some of the moves involved in defence against common knife attacks. Oriental, ice pick, slash, he had dealt with them before but wanted to surprise Gil by remembering a good selection of the defensive countermoves she and dad had taught him previously. He didn't really mind the mat work either, at least you got to lie down and, as a bonus, you learned how to get out of choke holds, not that he'd ever need to, he mused. While Cyrus was listening to his tunes, Gil was keeping her eyes on the road. They were driving over Putney Bridge, soon to take a right into the New King's Road, which was a good example of a street name misnomer, as it looked more dilapidated than the King's Road itself.

One of the aspects of CIA, NSA and other intelligence services training, is that your neural network becomes differently wired to that of civilians. Normal good drivers keep two hands on the wheel, when not changing gear, look ahead to see what's happening and maybe, anticipate what might. Those who have done any type of circuit driving or race training tend to have more acute peripheral vision as well. Is that kid going to run into the road, is that cyclist going to ride onto the zebra crossing, is that mobile phone junkie going to notice that her dog is about to bolt across the street? That type of awareness. What even good civilian drivers don't really notice, unless lights are flashing or sirens wailing, is who is behind them. True, there is the frequent interior and exterior mirror glances, especially when changing lane or turning across traffic but, in truth, most drivers, on a twenty minute journey, could not tell you in any detail which cars were behind them for most of the trip. That is reasonable enough in the normal world. Who cares who's behind you? As long as they're not tail-gaiting or getting ready to cut you up, or travelling in a pre-arranged convoy, it doesn't really matter. It's different in the clandestine world. In that dark space, intelligence officers are taught to be aware of who or what's behind them. 'Cover your six' means protect your back, your most vulnerable part to enemy attack.

Gil Haning was no longer an employed intelligence officer. When she was, she was a good one and certain parts of her training had stayed with her, like riding a bike stays with you all your life. It was with this training, somewhere deep in her subconscious, undercover, mind that she kept glancing at one particular car, three or four vehicles behind JJ's Porsche. Cyrus was merrily unaware. Eyes closed, legs jiggling, curly mop bobbing from side to side. He was contentedly lost in his music.

Gil's biological neurons were also bopping away but in her case it was because her internal network was on alert. At this point it was a lot closer to DEFCON 5 than DEFCON 1, but on alert it was. The car in question was a black Mercedes E-class with tinted windows. Gil remembered seeing it near the Harrodian. It had not really registered, there was always a good sprinkling of high quality cars in south west London. However, the Harrodian was at the tail end of a residential road, leading eventually to Hammersmith Bridge. This car had been parked in the road, maybe a hundred yards from the school's gates. It was on its own. The other cars in the vicinity were parked either in the Harrodian's car park or the individual driveways of the houses, near the school.

It was there, and now it's here, three car lengths behind Gil and Cyrus, on Putney Bridge. Still not that unusual thought Gil. Lower Richmond Road, Putney Bridge, Fulham Road or King's Road, that would be a fairly normal route to get from the outskirts of Barnes, Roehampton or Richmond into central London. Let's see if the black Merc takes the Fulham Road route when we turn right into the New King's Road, thought Gil. It didn't. The traffic lights changed and Gil was on the New King's Road. The black

Merc was now two cars adrift as one of the other cars behind Gil and Cyrus had gone in the direction of Fulham Road. Gil still had not raised her DEFCON status. She couldn't work it out precisely in her head, but there had to be forty to fifty right hand and left hand turns a given car could take between the beginning of the New King's Road and Markham Square. The odds were that the black Merc would turn before they reached home. It didn't.

As Gil drove into Markham Square she could see in her rear mirror that the black Merc drove by on the main King's Road. The vast majority of the time that would be that. Maybe the Merc's driver lived a few streets further on, maybe he was on his way to central London, maybe he was going to have tea with the bleedin' Queen. While the sum of all those maybes added up to the most likely probability, it still left one maybe outside of that set. Maybe the driver of the Merc is a professional and he drove past to avoid arousing attention.

"Are we there yet?" asked Cyrus in a mock kiddie's voice and wondering why Gil had not fully parked the car in the Square.

"We're here Cyrus," Gil replied. "I was just dawdling a bit and thinking about the best parking spot. Don't want to kerb the wheels. Your dad would kill me!" she exclaimed. It made perfect sense too. While Markham Square was subject to resident parking permits, as was most of Chelsea, there always seemed to be more cars than houses. On top of that, certain parts of the Square had parking on both sides of the street so if two fat Chelsea tractors were directly opposite one another, then a third fat Chelsea tractor was going to struggle to navigate the Square without risking mirror bashing at best. Gil parked the car about two doors away from their house and tucked in the external mirrors.

"Cyrus, go into the house, stick the kettle on and let's have some green tea and a snack before we train in an hour or so. I just need to pop into Boots to get some woman's stuff," said Gil, with no hint of alarm in her voice.

"Sure," replied Cyrus, not wishing for any further detail. With that he extracted his tennis equipment from the back seats, closed his car door and skipped up the half a dozen or so stairs to his front door, all Chelsea blue and gleaming. Once inside, Cyrus dropped all of his kit just inside the front door. While he knew that Gil would return and yell 'Cyrus you're not six anymore, pick up your stuff slobboid', he'd await his admonishment before tidying up. Anyway, he felt like a brew of green tea and a biscuit or six before the hard work of reposing on a mat began.

Gil locked the Porsche and walked casually down the east side of Markham Square. A right onto the King's Road would take her to Boots the chemist in under one minute. She didn't take the right, partly because she had told Cyrus a wee white lie. She didn't need stuff from the chemist, woman's or otherwise. Her neurons were still a-bobbing and she just wanted to take a look up and down the main road, while always maintaining eye contact with their front door. About five yards before the junction of Markham Square and the King's Road, Gil stopped in her tracks. Directly opposite or, for the pedantic, almost opposite, was Smith Street.

There it was. Partially obscured by a few parked motorbikes and one of those electric cars; the black Merc. Gil turned tail and walked at her normal pace back up the Square. You didn't need to be a maths genius to work out that the probability the Merc driver lived in Smith Street, or had decided on a swift impromptu shop near that section of the King's Road, was very low indeed. The Merc had followed them all the way from Barnes. Turned left onto Putney Bridge when it was 50:50 to take a right or left turn at that point. Same again for the King's Road versus Fulham Road. Then the forty to fifty left side and right side potential exits off the King's Road before Markham Square, all with more or less equal probability. Already Gil's computer brain had calculated that there was a less than 1% chance that such a car on the same journey as she and Cyrus would arrive at Markham Square within five car lengths of each other. Now multiply that by the probability that in the whole of posh London, the Merc driver would live in Smith Street. Not a snowball's chance in the fiery furnace of hell, she concluded. She or Cyrus or both were under surveillance. In fact, a further moment's thought led Gil to conclude that it was Cyrus who was the Merc's person of interest. Gil had driven from Chelsea to the Harrodian with no tail. The Merc was already parked near the Harrodian when she arrived. It was Cyrus they were watching. She did not know who or why but logic deemed that it must have something to do with JJ. Time to get in touch with Daddio, Gil thought. Who knows whether or not surveillance was the end of the story.

Gil opened the front door, closed it behind her and double locked it. She turned round, tripped over Cyrus's tennis kit, kicked it, muttered the f-word under her breath but was thinking too hard to assail Cyrus with her usual banter of admonishment.

"Cyrus, is the tea brewed?" she asked on entering the kitchen.

"Just about," he replied noticing both that Gil had not chewed him out for his abandoned kit nor apparently had she returned with a Boots bag. "Unsuccessful chemist visit?"

"What?" said Gil, a wee bit more snappily than she would normally respond to Cyrus, but still distracted by the Merc.

"You went to Boots, but you've no bag with stuff in it," he pointed out.

"Sorry, Cyrus, I was in a world of my own there. No, I mean yes, it was unsuccessful. Didn't have what I wanted. No urgency. I can try tomorrow at a different chemist," replied Gil.

Cyrus handed Gil her mug of green tea with two chocolate

biscuits, took his mug with six non-chocolate biscuits and sat beside her on the sofa.

"What's the plan for tonight, Gil?" the boy asked, hoping slightly that she would have forgotten about knife training and the like.

Gil took a few sips of her tea and a bite out of one of her favourite biscuits.

"Tonight, Cyrus Darke, we're having our tea. Once fully digested we're heading for the gym. The focus will be on two things, deflecting knife attacks, and extracting yourself from choke holds, mainly from behind. Tomorrow night we're doing single strike training, aimed at disabling your attacker with one blow. We'll order in tonight. I can't be bothered cooking and I don't need to go out," listed Gil.

Cyrus was reluctantly content with tonight's plan, he already knew what Gil's training schedule was to be. He also fancied some Chinese food so ordering in was cool.

"We don't normally train two nights out of three, Gil."

"No we don't Cyrus, but you're getting older and more adventurous, and the world is getting rougher and tougher, more dark, more menacing. Your skills need to be honed. The longer you live, the more assholes you come across. They want what you've got and they mean to take it by fair means or foul. You're a good looking, smart, well-off boy. To the scum of this planet that's three strikes against you. They want to mess with your face, mess with your head, mess with your money. They have no morals, no limits to their evil, no respect. They are the dregs of the earth and they want you to fail and suffer. They will not succeed. You will be mentally and physically stronger than them, more skilful, more deadly. You will learn to trade low blows if you need to. You will drop to their level, gouge their evil eyes out, rip their lying throats and break their brittle necks. Then you will rise back to the level of decency that your mother and father have taught you. You are superior to the scum, you have high moral standards, you care, you work hard, you are a fine young man. You will not be soft, not be weak, not acquiesce to threat or intimidation however fierce. You will triumph because you are Cyrus Darke, son of Eloise and John Jarvis Darke. A good and loving boy," concluded Gil.

What the f is in this tea, thought Cyrus. He had never heard Gil like this before. She mentioned his dad's full name, nobody ever does that! She even sounded a bit like dad when he went on some rant or other about the state of the world. Wow.

Neither Cyrus nor Gil had any more tea and biscuits that evening. Cosy time was nearly over. They sat close together, contemplating, the symbiosis growing and developing. They were a team, a worthy team.

★ ★ ★

Unfortunately for Joel Gordon, he had neither the proven skills of Gil Haning nor the potential ones of Cyrus Darke. After sending his fateful email to Craig Wilson, Joel headed home. He got off the tube at Upton Park and casually strolled to his apartment, a three bedroom flat in Oberon Court, not far from Katherine Road, E6. It was a decent area, sometimes overcrowded with noisy football fans, but generally OK. His apartment was modern, all pastel shades and cream and beige furniture. It was a bright second floor apartment, exposed to the sun in the late afternoon which gave the lounge a very pleasant glow at this time of day, especially in the summer.

As he strolled along, he was mulling over his decision to let Craig Wilson know that he wanted to talk to him as soon as he returned from his cycling holiday. Joel felt it was the right decision. It would have been what his grandfather advocated. 'Tell the truth and be damned' the old fellow used to say, though it might have made more sense if the saying was tell the truth and be saved, thought Joel. Indeed, his grandfather, Simeon, never really seemed to be stressed about anything, he went with the flow, chilled with a thrill, relaxed with a passion. Telling the truth clearly had advantages, or at least peace of mind.

Content with himself, Joel entered his flat, left his work stuff on the sofa and flopped down next to it. He wasn't usually home this early so he was at a bit of a loss as to what to do. He decided to text Talisha, maybe she could leave work early as well and they could have a relaxing date night, watching a movie, or maybe be less relaxing with rampant sex on the floor. Wishful thinking rationalised Joel almost immediately. While Talisha was one great shag, she was somewhat partial as to where her bum lay. The floor, the kitchen table, pressed against a cold wall – these locations were off the map as far as sex was concerned. Talisha liked her bum to be comfy, all the time, and especially when she was being pounded by Joel's manhood. The bed or the sofa were her bum supports of choice. Joel texted his bum-sumptuous girlfriend.

Hi Talisha. I'm home early. Can you leave work soon? We could watch a movie or whatever you feel like. Love J xxx.

A few minutes elapsed and Joel's mobile rang. He had downloaded VS Schumacher's Crazy Frog ringtone to signal that he had received a text message. Hearing it for the first two hundred times was great he thought but maybe he had better change it soon to something more credible, possibly Bob Marley or John Newman. It was Talisha.

Hi babe. I can leave in ten. Be at yours by 6.30pm. Movie sounds good. No dick flicks. Something funny. Ben Stiller, Owen Wilson, Chris Rock that sort of thing. Love you xx.

Joel replied and set about scouring his DVD collection, box office and on demand on his widescreen, flat, television. *Zoolander* was an old favourite, as was *Meet the Parents*, even *Madagascar 3* was hilarious, if you were ten or had a ten year old's sense of humour. Talisha and Joel had seen them all before. They had been dating for only ten months, so he didn't want to reveal any lack of vision by suggesting they watch re-runs so early in their relationship. Eventually, he decided on *Tower Heist*. Neither Owen Wilson nor Chris Rock were in that but the reviews rated it highly and Ben Stiller was the lead. Joel knew that Talisha enjoyed this kind of light hearted caper and he was pretty sure that she had not seen it. Talisha lived about the same distance from Upton Park tube as Joel but in the opposite direction. Her flat was more expensive and luxurious than Joel's, as befitted her private sector job compared with Joel's government employment. However, Joel's living room was more spacious and he had better gadgets, TV, laptops, internet and broadband connections. She didn't mind spending some time there; relaxing with Joel and watching a movie appealed to her tonight.

As Talisha turned off Katherine Road towards Oberon Court, having walked from the tube station, she glanced at the Audi A6 parked about fifty yards from Oberon Court. Talisha wasn't really into cars but the black paintwork on this one was gleaming and it had matching black-detailed five spoke alloy wheels and tinted glass all around. It would hardly have merited a second look in Central London or the King's Road, but here in E6, it stood out a little. If she and Joel both got promoted soon, she might like to upgrade her car to an Audi, one like this would be nice, maybe a little smaller and absent the tinted glass.

Unbeknown to Talisha, Vasily Yugenov, comfortably

ensconced in the Audi driver's seat, was giving Talisha the visual once over. She was hot, thought the thug, though that J-Lo butt was a tad large for his normal Russian anorexic model taste. He watched Talisha go into Oberon Court, the same block of flats as his surveillance target, one Joel Gordon. Vasily wondered if they knew each other. After all, they were both black. Vasily was a more or less unreconstructed philistine. PC to him meant police constable or, at a stretch, personal computer. Politically correct didn't really appear on his mental or verbal radar screen. Babikov paid him well, let him wear decent clothes and drive a quality car. Every now and then he had to torture some idiot debtor, but that was kind of fun. He didn't like all the wailing, screaming, pleading and pant soiling that this often involved but once he'd broken a couple of fingers or pulled a few fingernails, the late payer usually pledged with sincerity that he'd promptly pay his debts.

Vasily was a 6ft 4in mountain of a man, weighing nearly 100kg, with cropped dark brown hair and muscles bulging from under his fitted, imitation designer suit. He was thirty-two years old and had arrived in London two years ago from Vladivostok. He didn't really enjoy life in his home town. It had been designated a fortress in 1889 and all times since had seen a military presence grow in this eastern outpost of Mother Russia. It was a bleak desolate place and was dominated by the military and crime lords. Vasily made his living through the latter. His progression through the timeline of crime was fairly straightforward. As a young teenager he began with opportunistic burglaries, then proceeded to more organised ones. Getting tired of climbing in and out of people's bedrooms, where often there was little of value to steal, he applied to be a bouncer at a local casino. He was proficient at chucking people out, stomping on their heads and generally doing wayward punters serious damage. One night in 2012, he went too far, breaking the neck of some poor unfortunate as he lay on the road. The unfortunate died on the spot. The casino's owner was Vladimir Babikov's cousin and between them they spirited the murderer out of Russia and into London. They supplied him with apparently legal immigrant papers, a job and a place to stay. Vasily was very grateful and he would not let Vladimir Babikov down.

His boss's instructions today were to tail this Joel Gordon abbyssyana and report back. Vasily visually picked him up coming out of Upton Park tube, no mean feat given the hordes of multi-coloured commuters pouring out of the place, but he had a detailed itinerary of Gordon's normal schedule, his address and several good quality photographs. He got a call to say Gordon would be early that day. So far, the job was a bit boring. The dude came out of the tube, walked home, was in his flat and now was probably being visited by a female abbyssyana. That wasn't much to report, but that was what he had.

Vasily was reasonably well prepared for the stakeout. He had brought sandwiches, water and a decorative hip flask of vodka. He had a long-range camera, binoculars, pen and notepad, his mobile phone, his gun and a fibre wire, wooden-handled garrotte. The weakest link in any one man stakeout is the obvious need to pee at some point if you were in situ long enough. Vasily had been in situ long enough. This was awkward he thought. There were no public toilets, shops, bars, cafés or restaurants on this road, it was totally residential. He didn't have a bottle or a can with him, and even if he did, pee stream accuracy from a sitting position behind the wheel of a car was notoriously random. He didn't want to wet his pants, whether or not his willie would get some fresh air or air conditioned air to be precise, and he sure didn't want to urinate on the Audi's leather seats. Babikov would go ballistic. There was no choice. He was going to have to get out the car and have an open air pee. He couldn't just do it in the street, there was the occasional passer-by and there were sure to be one or two curtain twitchers on this road. They might phone the cops. He could pop into someone's back garden but he might get caught there too and he might lose contact with his stakeout target. Vasily needed to decide soon. The waterworks were becoming voluminous, building to near pain level, trapped inside his circumcised knob, desperate to explode outwards. Needs must came to mind. Vasily leapt out of his car, power walked to one of the side walls of Oberon Court, yanked his zip down, his willie out and proceeded to urinate all over the nicely painted white wall. Relief beyond belief and who cared if his £90 leather shoes were having an unexpected shower. This was a necessity.

Vasily returned to the Audi, relieved and happier. No one had shouted at him so he and his pee had probably gone undetected and no one else had entered or exited the main doors of Oberon Court. Apart from the huge urine puddle on the side path of Oberon Court and the remaining droplets on his shoes, there was no evidence that Vasily had been anywhere but in his car. He made himself comfortable in his seat, turned on his radio at low volume, took a swig of vodka and was preparing to hunker down for the dreary long haul that was much of underworld surveillance.

His instructions from Babikov were that if there was no movement from Gordon by 11pm, Vasily could knock off for the evening and pick up his target again the following morning. It was about 7.30pm now, so he had a few hours to go. Vasily decided to take one swift scan of the exterior of Gordon's flat with his binoculars. The shades were drawn so he couldn't see much apart from the occasional flickering of what he assumed to be the light from Gordon's television screen. Vasily decided to make a timed entry into his notepad. He didn't want Babikov to think he had bunked off so even if there was nothing to report, he was going to report it. He didn't even know why Babikov wanted the black man tailed. Vasily did not recognise him as a casino regular and he definitely had not roughed him up at any point. Vasily had learned as a kid not to ask too many questions and he sure wasn't going to quiz Vladimir Babikov on the whys and wherefores of this particular task. Note completed, Vasily was now in that twilight zone where his eyes wanted to close for a mini snooze but his need to be alert kept jerking them open. The most recent jerk was augmented by the vibration of Vasily's mobile.

It was a message from Babikov. It was a short message, only two words.

End him.

★ ★ ★

Gil could not get hold of JJ. She knew enough about his mission to realise that this meant that he was likely to be in the field and could not answer his phone or communicate electronically, probably somewhere in North Korea. It may also mean that he was captured or dead but if that had happened in the recent past she hoped that some contact in the CIA would have been in touch. In any event, she did not feel in her bones that her boss and mentor was dead. The whole incident of the black Merc shadow had put Gil on alert. Her training session with Cyrus last night was reasonably hard core. The boy was exhausted and went straight to his room afterwards to chill, perchance to sleep. His self-defence skills were improving but he was still way short of being able to triumph in an unexpected street attack or having to face multiple assailants. He was only fourteen though, rationalised Gil, and he was probably in the top 1% of the earth's fourteen year olds as far as self-defence was concerned. That would mean he had about 1.5 million self-defence peers. Let's hope none of them were lurking near Markham Square.

Sometimes Gil had to mentally shake herself out of her mathematical train of thought. As a kid she was all about numbers, percentages, ratios. I mean, she thought, who else would bother to know how many fourteen year olds there were in the world at any given time? Back on point, Gil was up early today. She would prepare breakfast for herself and Cyrus. She had already told him that she would walk along the school route with him that morning, claiming she was on her way to check out a new gym but actually to check out the preponderance or not of black Mercs in the vicinity.

"Time to get up sleepy head!" Gil called up the stairs in the direction of Cyrus's bedroom.

"I'm up, I'm up, crazy woman!" Cyrus yelled back. "I'm going for a shower, I'll be down in fifteen minutes."

I'll hold him to that precise time thought Gil, working out when she had to start cooking the four egg plate of scrambled eggs for the boy, then the toasted and buttered bagel to go with it. An orange juice, some water and an apple would complete his breakfast fayre for today.

Cyrus came lolloping down the stairs, dumped his school kit in the hallway and sauntered into the kitchen, fully dressed, apart from his trainers, and curly mop all wet and floppy.

"Smells good," Cyrus said, feeling quite hungry after his major league physical exertion the previous night and his subsequent long sleep.

"Don't expect this treatment every morning, young man. You trained really well last night so now you have to feed those muscles. Any DOMS?"

"No DOMS," answered Cyrus, pleased with himself.

"Normally, I'd get some muscle soreness about twenty-four hours after training, so tonight may be a bit stiff."

The pair enjoyed their breakfast and then headed out. The route to Cyrus's school took him down Smith Street, towards Royal Hospital Road. There was no sign of the black Merc. Gil was relieved. Maybe yesterday was one of those one in a million coincidences. They do happen, otherwise they'd be none in a million.

"See ya later Gil," said Cyrus as he strolled through the school gates, fist bumping a couple of his friends.

"Bye, Cyrus, see you tonight," replied Gil, just dawdling long enough to ensure the boy was safely inside the fairly secure school grounds.

Gil walked straight on for a few yards, just in case Cyrus decided to have a look to see if she was going in the stated direction of the new gym. He wasn't looking. She turned around and re-passed the school gates. Seconds later Gil's body tensed sharply. At the edge of her peripheral vision she could see the offside exterior mirror of yesterday's black Merc sticking out from behind a narrower girthed car, in a side street opposite the school gates. Gil didn't need to see the whole car to know it was the shadow car. While the body of the Merc in question was all black, the exterior mirrors were silver in colour and she had noted that yesterday. There were many Mercedes cars in SW3, and a good sprinkling of them were black. E-class Mercs like this one, were quite popular too. E-class Mercs with tinted windows and silver exterior mirrors were not unknown but they didn't proliferate. Gil's NSA training and her prior state of alert kicked in. She did not turn her head fully to look at the Merc and she did not change her walking pace as she continued on her route back to Markham Square. Cyrus would be safe inside the school. One of the reasons JJ and Eloise had selected this school for Cyrus was that it seemed to be security conscious. You couldn't just stroll in even if you were a parent. There was an entry phone and you had to declare who you were to get in to the main building. Then you were met by a member of the non-teaching office staff. If your name was not already on their list of approved people or if you were not recognised you got no further, certainly not to any of the classrooms. Whatever this Merc driver was up to, snatching Cyrus, or interfering with him in any way was not going to be on the agenda, not at this school, not today, or any day, vowed Gil.

As Gil made her way back to Markham Square, intent on 'gearing up' in case things got ugly, Boris Akulov was sitting in his Merc fuming away. Not cigarette fuming but bad mood fuming. Boris was around 5ft 9in, thirty-four years old, slim, short blond wavy hair, pale complexion, uninteresting eyes and a long nose. His nose was so extensive, kids at his school in Moscow called him 'beaky'. After he had broken one of the other seven year old's noses, they kind of stopped calling him that, at least to his face. Beaky Akulov was in a foul mood because he didn't want this job, tailing a kid. He was an ex-FSB officer and, in Moscow, he had been used to forcibly entering people's homes catching them at all sorts, listening in to dodgy domestic Russian transmissions, generally doing stuff that helped maintain the internal security of Russia. Every now and then he had to manufacture evidence against some deluded dissident but, hey, that was fun, a bit like doing a creative writing story at school. Boris did not want to leave Russia and he certainly did not want to work for a scumbag like Vladimir Babikov. Beaky's Achilles heel though, as far as Russia was concerned, was that he was as gay as a parrot. In homophobic Russia that was not good. Gay folk were lobbed in jail, disappeared, beat up. It was illegal to be a gay man or lesbian woman in Russia and while national laws needed to be respected, all it did was force gay sexual desires underground, making them more dangerous and more disease prone.

His boss at the FSB had discovered his illegal peccadillo. It didn't take much intelligence work as he was caught red handed, or red knobbed to be accurate, shafting some poor FSB mail delivery boy in a dark and dingy corner of the mail room. Due to his prior sound record the FSB hierarchy gave him the choice of a couple of years in Butyrka prison or leaving Russia and seeking gainful employment elsewhere. Akulov's cousin worked as a croupier in one of Vladimir Babikov's gambling establishments in Moscow and he had recommended Beaky to his boss. It was an option with no other option. Moscow's Butyrka prison was horrendous, overcrowded, rat infested, absolutely disgusting and inhumane. As an ex-FSB agent he would not last a month in that snake pit. Babikov and London it was.

To begin with, working for Babikov wasn't all that bad. He had topped two of the worst debtors, one a pistol shot to the head and the other smothered by a pillow as he lay asleep. However, word was beginning to spread amongst the gambling community and the idiot punters were getting the pre-match message that being in debt to the scumbag Russian was not healthy. Topping targets had dried up and now here he was, Boris Akulov, ex-FSB officer and protector of Russian national security, tailing a curly topped kid who seemed to have an Asian cripple for a nanny. Still, thought Akulov, in one of his more optimistic moments, who knows where this job will take me. The kid's quite good looking with a pert skinny arse. Maybe I'll get a chance to explore that opening further, he smirked to himself.

★ ★ ★

Neil Robson did not know by name either Boris Akulov or Vasily

Yugenov. He would have recognised their faces as they were often at Vladimir Babikov's side in his office at the Nicolas Casino. Babikov rotated his six man bodyguard squad; he did not want any one or two of them getting too close and maybe learning more about his nefarious activities than he wanted. As Robson sat in his office in the Treasury, he poured himself a stiff scotch even though it was only 10.30 in the morning. He was confident that he had things in hand. He had asked Babikov for help and the grisly Russian assured him that both stakeout and surveillance operations were underway. The Gordon stakeout was likely to get a bit uglier soon, mused Robson but he could not, absolutely fucking could not, afford the Jamrock yardie accountant spilling his guts to Craig Wilson. If that limp-wristed woose of an MP got hold of the information on the government's finances he'd be all over it like a rash. As far as Robson and Chancellor Jeffery Walker were concerned that rash would develop into a terminal infection, costing both of them their jobs and probably entailing an unpleasant stay at Her Majesty's pleasure. If only the stupid dope Gordon hadn't emailed Wilson, then he may still have a career, even a life. Well, that's tough shit for him, thought Robson. In the decision tree of life choices that Jamaican had just crawled onto the last precarious branch.

Satisfied in himself that he had had no option but to order the silencing of Joel Gordon, the Financial Secretary to the Treasury turned his thought processes to the case of JJ Darke. He wasn't surprised or alarmed that he had not heard much from the miserable Scot. If the timetable was broadly intact then Darke would likely be in North Korea now and probably tooling up for the raid on the DPRK's central bank tonight or tomorrow night. It would not really be possible to have a cosy chat in those circumstances. Still, he did not trust Darke. The guy had an impeccable record at MI5 and even when confronted with this insider trading allegation he was all prepared to take the fall if his colleagues would be left untainted. The only reason he had agreed to this crazy plan, but potentially mega-profitable for HM Treasury and more importantly, Robson himself, was to protect his co-workers and, more crucially, his son. Indeed, realised Robson, young Cyrus Darke was the key piece in this particular game of clandestine chess. Whatever else was going on, JJ would strive to ensure that no harm came to the boy. If all went to plan, concluded Robson, no harm would come to him. A watchful eye on the young fellow was all that was needed for now. Anything more intrusive would be up to his dad.

★ ★ ★

Talisha had really enjoyed *Tower Heist*. Joel quite liked it too but hoped that the Ferrari 250 GT Lusso that got battered and gouged was not real. You didn't need to be a car lover to appreciate that many Ferraris of that vintage were indeed works of art. He needn't have worried on that score. As in *Ferris Bueller's Day Off* and the TV series *Miami Vice* the on-screen Ferraris used were not real. In the case of *Tower Heist* two replicas of the Lusso were built by an American coachworker, using the platform and selected parts of a Volvo 1800. Joel was feeling a bit horny now, not aroused by anything human in the movie but by Talisha's low-cut white top, which revealed way more than a glimpse of her wicked boobs. His luck wasn't in. Talisha had gone all 'not tonight Josephine' on him, a much quoted phrase incorrectly attributed to the most famous diminutive French general. She had had a tough day at work and while she was feeling loads better, she was becoming tired and simply wanted Joel to take her back to her apartment. It was only a brisk twenty minute walk away. Talisha would have stayed at Joel's but all her clothes were at hers and she needed to be more than presentable for an important meeting the next day. His ardour doused, Joel defaulted to his base position as the perfect gentleman.

"Sure, honey, I'd love to," said the now deflated Joel. "Let's freshen up, get our stuff and get going."

"Thanks babe," replied Talisha, Joel was a really nice guy she thought. The happy couple left Oberon Court hand in hand with the intention of cutting across Katherine Road, along Grangewood Street and then into Redclyffe Road where Talisha lived. Vasily Yugenov was alert in his car. After his murderous instruction from Babikov, Vasily had been contemplating awaiting the early hours of the morning, breaking into Gordon's flat and garrotting him. That plan was up the creek for now as he espied the two black people walking along the road away from the Audi. Talisha was tired and Joel was content that he had had a nice evening with her. Neither noticed the black Audi.

Vasily did not know whether the abbyssyanas were off for a late night walk or going to a bar, or a club, or whatever. He did decide though that he would be better following them on foot, as they did not appear to have transport or at least were not using it if they had. He did not take all of his surveillance paraphernalia with him, just his garrotte and pistol. The thug's pistol of choice was a MKIII Ruger .22 with threaded barrel. The type of barrel was important because the two Ruger models which had threads meant that they could accommodate suppressors. This did not make any shot completely silent but it was a whole lot quieter than a naked gun. The Ruger .22 was light, with polymer frame, steel barrel and weighing around thirty-two ounces, probably nearer forty with suppressor attached. Vasily's designer suit was too tight for him to wear a holster so he simply tucked the Ruger into his pants, safety catch engaged. In most close altercations, however, Vasily preferred his fibre-wire garrotte. He was a skilled killer with this weapon. Provided you approached the intended target with stealth, then once the garrotte was around the neck that was that. The target's windpipe was crushed, no sounds, no squeaks and no cries for help. Strangulation also did not involve blood spurting everywhere so liquid evidence, DNA samples and other incriminating elements were not left lying around.

The target and his tart were now in Grangewood Street. It was around 10pm and it was dark. Vasily was following behind, one hundred yards, or possibly eighty away. He could have been a lot closer as these two only had eyes for one another. He wore rubber soled shoes and was progressing along the rickety pavements of East London very quietly indeed. As he was tailing his target, Vasily concluded that he would need to take out the girl as well as his intended victim. He had no time to call Babikov to find out if that was OK and he wanted to show his boss that he could use his initiative. If he killed Joel first then the bitch would start screaming her head off, attracting attention; maybe getting help. By the look of her big tits, assessed Vasily, she could probably scream like a banshee. While appropriate in the circumstance a wailing black bean sith was not what was needed for Vasily to make a clean exit once Gordon was in his death throes. Vasily concluded that his most effective plan was to shoot Gordon first, from five or ten yards away, then immediately leap on the black bitch and garrotte her. She'd be history in under thirty seconds. Big tits maybe, but a scrawny neck and one that would crush easily and rapidly. Once she was silenced, Vasily would pop another 9mm round in Gordon's head, then walk calmly away and return to his car. Two down, none to go. Vasily liked his plan.

He was now about twenty-five yards behind Talisha and Joel. The couple were within minutes of turning into Redclyffe Road and they had not spotted the large man in a dark suit, blue and white shirt and red tie, approaching them with malintent. Vasily was ready for action. The street he was on was quiet, indeed all the streets around here seemed quiet tonight. There were no other pedestrians that he could see and the quality of the street lighting was poor. There was some kind of rumble, however, from a concrete underpass just ahead. Vasily couldn't yet see what the cause of this unhelpful commotion was, so he stopped and pretended to check his mobile phone, Ruger back in his pants and garrotte still in his suit jacket pocket. Joel and Talisha however, were in a position to see into the underpass and the unholy vision that met their startled eyes triggered a committed sprint by the pair into Redclyffe Road and inside Talisha's portered block of flats.

Vasily had failed on two counts. First, he was too slow to react. Had he taken off at pace as soon as his targets had then he could have got close enough to shoot them; but he didn't. The second count of failure was more understandable given that he was Russian and had not properly embraced the swing of English football, in particular English football which involved a derby match between two deadly rivals. Of all the football hates in the land, West Ham and Millwall was the most pernicious rivalry. More than Celtic and Rangers in Scotland, worse than either Man United/Liverpool or Arsenal/Tottenham. This was *the* grudge match.

The previous Saturday, West Ham had gone to Millwall for the 5th round of the FA Cup. West Ham were a Premiership team and Millwall one division lower in the Championship. The winner would progress to the quarter finals. It turned out to be a 0-0 draw. Replay was to be at the Boleyn Ground, formerly Upton Park and home of West Ham, the following Wednesday. That Wednesday was tonight and West Ham were hot, odds-on favourites to progress. Kick-off 8pm, finish around 9.50, barring extra time and penalties. They did not win, they lost 0-1 to a freak own goal whereby the West Ham goalkeeper, on punching away the ball from a Millwall corner, smashed it into his own centre-half's head and from there it ricocheted straight into the home team's net. The goal came in the eighty-seventh minute and West Ham had little time to draw level. They didn't. West Ham's fans were furious. The Green Street Elite, the club's most feared hooligan element were cataclysmic in their fury; they wanted blood and there was no better blood to shed than that of Millwall supporters especially that of their hooligan Bushwacker gang.

Vasily Yugenov could not be expected to know any of this. There he was, efficiently going about the devil's work, when an unannounced commotion from an East London underpass had spooked his prey. The first wave of the commotion had now entered the street that Vasily was on, rooted to the spot, not exactly sure what to do. He did not have a plan B. There were about twenty youths, mainly in blue and white tops, some spotty faced, others not and a few beat up visages in the mix. These faces looked fearful and when they exited the underpass they split in all directions, some pulling off their tops and lobbing them into residents' front gardens. Every youth for himself seemed to be the underlying theme. The next wave out of the underpass was not far behind. There were more of these youths, mostly male though some girls too. These youths looked more angry than fearful. They were shouting and screaming. They wore predominantly claret and blue tops. Several of them were carrying and waving about types of makeshift weaponry, including hammers, baseball bats and empty glass bottles. Vasily stayed calm and quiet. He hoped to blend into the darkness of the night. His luck was out.

"Oi fuck features!" yelled one particularly ugly claret and blue dressed youth, clearly aiming his nocturnal cockney greeting at Vasily. "What the fuck are you doing here?" he questioned, now accompanied by several more of the Green Street Elite.

"Nothing," replied Vasily. "Now go about your business young people," he added, somewhat unwisely as it turns out.

"Are you a fucking Ruski you big gorilla?" screeched the main protagonist, clearly displaying that all education or at least action movie baddies accents had not been totally lost on him. Vasily said nothing. He was getting a bit annoyed now and surreptitiously was fingering his way towards his Ruger.

"He asked you a question, mother fucker," said the main man's cohort, who was black and sweating profusely. "Why are you wearing Millwall colours asshole? Are you one of those bastard Russian oilygarks who buys London clubs? Do you own Millwall fuck brain? Speak or I'll fuckin kill you!" The black cohort was becoming seriously agitated now. He couldn't even think in the Queen's English. His antics were winding up the ten or so other posse members now surrounding Vasily. The main man was staring at Vasily and Vasily was eyeballing him back. The Russian thug had very little idea what these agitated and confrontational youths were going on about. Sure, he was wearing a blue and white shirt, Millwall's colours, but he didn't know that until a few seconds ago. For god's sake, he'd never even heard of Millwall and he was certain Vladimir Babikov didn't own a football club. It was time to wrap this up, thought Vasily, pulling his Ruger from his pants.

"Gun!" screamed the main man and his cohort in unison, as they were covering their heads and diving to the ground.

That's more like it, thought Vasily, for a mere split second feeling back in control of his own destiny. He wasn't. Had Vasily been an ex-FSB or SVR officer he may have paid more attention to his six. He wasn't. He was just a murdering, urinating, thug. As soon as the posse members behind Vasily heard 'gun', two hammers and two large bottles of cheap cider rained down on the back of Vasily's head. He did not crumple to the ground at first, he was a strong, huge, man, but he was down on one knee and his pistol had fallen on the road and was now in the possession of the GSE's main man. The main man did not shoot Vasily. He pointed his gun at him as a few more hammer blows and a couple of baseball bat whacks from the rear finished off what was left of Vasily's large skull.

Vladimir Babikov was man down and his prey had gotten away.

★ ★ ★

Back at Bowser's Castle, Neil Robson was in the land of Nod, not the wandering zone east of Eden referred to in the Bible but the land of sleep à la *A Complete Collection of Genteel and Ingenious Conversation* by Jonathan Swift. The Financial Secretary to the Treasury was exhausted. Not only had he his normal daily responsibilities at the Treasury, he had to contend with a Scottish miscreant that he was unfortunately relying on to dig him out of a cavernous hole and a Jamrock yardie accountant who seemed intent on blowing the gaff on the government's finances. At least Babikov will have got rid of Gordon by now thought Robson as he drifted into his slumber for the night, feeling very content.

The next morning Neil Robson was up bright and early. The King of the Koopas decided he would drive his Bentley Continental into town today. He had an early morning meeting with Jeffrey Walker. Undoubtedly, the Chancellor wanted an update on Korean developments. Robson would need to take the 'no news is good news' view but simultaneously assure Walker that there would be a more detailed debrief in the next forty-eight hours. That should keep the old fart from a meltdown thought Robson, though he did have a modicum of sympathy for the Chancellor.

If Darke failed in his mission then Jeffrey Walker would be consigned, not only to jail, but to history as the British finance minister who bankrupted Britain and led to the most serious economic crisis and widespread rioting that the country had ever seen. Denis Healey, Labour's Chancellor in the 1970s, and a man who appeared to have only one tie, a dark blue, light blue criss-cross patterned one, had given bankrupting Britain a shot. He put the top rate of income tax at 83% and the top rate of unearned income at 98%. Clearly, Mr Healey, eventually Lord Healey, had not even a passing recognition of the Laffer Curve. The great and good all left or prepared to leave the UK; surgeons, lawyers, scientists, musicians, actors, financial types. Anybody that was on a salary rather than a subsistence wage wanted to leave. Eventually, in 1976, with the help and prompting of the IMF, Healey realised that 60% of something was better than 83% of nothing in the government's coffers and disaster was averted. In reality, from the Labour Party's perspective, disaster was only postponed. Healey's about face led the thinking voters to conclude that he was an economic pygmy shrew. Combined with Labour leader Jim Callaghan's bad singing, poor timing, acquiescence to British streets being strewn with uncollected garbage and unburied bodies, this all led to Margaret Thatcher's first general election win in 1979. Labour have never recovered from that, and probably never will.

Involuntarily, Jeffrey Walker may have the opportunity to finish what Healey started. He didn't want to, he was desperate to avoid it, so desperate that he had sanctioned an illegal incursion into the DPRK to relieve its supreme leader of most of his gold. Walker was smarter than Healey. At a minimum he understood the link between rising marginal income tax rates and the government's revenue yield. There was definitely an inflexion point and he was not going on that disastrous route, not any time and definitely not a few months before a General Election. He was not going to be an economic bumblebee to Healey's pygmy shrew and that was that.

As Neil Robson was driving into Horseguards Road and parking up, he knew full well the bind that Walker and he were in. Apart from Joel Gordon there had been no inkling of a leak regarding the government's £3-4bn black hole, either inside the government or externally in the media. Babikov would have closed that leak risk off, permanently, concluded Robson so his only job on that front now was to keep the issue as tight as a crab's arse. Walker, himself and, unfortunately JJ Darke and team, were the only people alive and in the know. Robson would deal with Darke once the gold had been recovered and he had taken his unauthorised cut of around half a billion pounds.

Happy days thought Robson as he entered his office in the Treasury. He was further buoyed at the bright sight of the candescent Becky, his PA. She was all tight hot pink and stilettoes this morning. He surely was going to jump her one day and give her a good seeing to, preferably from behind and over his leather topped antique desk, but not today. Today, he was going to update Walker, and have as relaxing an afternoon as possible. Tonight he'd probably go to the Nicolas Casino and thank Vladimir Babikov for his assistance. Despite being a murderous mutilator, the dodgy Russian liked his acquaintances to be polite. Robson had forty-five minutes or so before he was scheduled to meet with the Chancellor. Becky had just given him a strong coffee and a plastic smile. Just as he was surveying the contours of her comely bum, there was a knock on his door and in popped a black man.

"Good morning, Sir," said Joel Gordon. "I was thinking about our conversation yesterday," he continued, completely oblivious to the jaw-dropped expression on his boss's face. "I feel strongly that I need to update Craig Wilson on this problem with the government's finances and my impending promotion. He has been a good mentor to me and, strictly speaking, it was Mr Wilson who asked me to look into the financial figures in the first place. He's back in a couple of days. Maybe the three of us could meet up as soon as he has caught up. I can ask Becky to put a time and place in your meeting calendar?"

"Sure," replied Robson, more or less on automatic. The Financial Secretary to the Treasury hadn't really taken anything in after 'Good morning, Sir'. What the fuck was the Jamrock yardie doing here in my office, alive, speaking, babbling on about Wilson, a meeting? He should be dead, no heart beat, no brain beat no any kind of fucking beat apart from the ultimate dead beat. Robson's mind was racing. That fuckwit Babikov had ballsed things up. Goddamit, he wailed silently to himself. This was not happening. Joel Gordon had said 'thanks' following Robson's semi-aware 'sure' and had left the Financial Secretary's office.

The meeting between Robson and Walker would need to go ahead but the former was still recovering from this early morning shock and he seemed less self-assured than usual. There would be no relaxing afternoon now thought Neil Robson. He needed an explanation from Babikov. No £1 million fee was going his way for a botched job. There was only two days or so before Craig Wilson was back at his desk, undoubtedly to ask awkward and penetrating questions of Robson and Walker once he had been briefed by Joel Gordon. No way could that happen. The Jamrock yardie was going down, even if he had to do it himself concluded a very irate Bowser, thwarted in his desperate desire to take control of the Mushroom Kingdom.

8

NIGHT GEAR

JJ was a fashion chameleon and one whose outer shell had a significant impact on his mental processes. If he donned suit, shirt, tie and dress leather shoes then he was in the mind-set of the office, financial markets, dealing with FCA hounds. T-shirt and shorts meant that he was on a beach, or wanted to be, or it was a hot and humid weekend in central London. A polo shirt and cargo pants meant he was relaxing, lolling about, going for lunch or a movie with Cyrus and Gil at the weekend. Accessories joined in with the chameleon attire. Suit meant steel bracelet or leather strap watch, T-shirt meant rubber strapped watch, polo shirt then rubber or Velcro band watch. Suit meant one of three Idol white gold rings, dominus, maximus or the chosen one; to the uninitiated that was bull, shark and star respectively, all encased in black, turquoise and clear mini diamonds, setting the creature or symbol of choice. A watch and a ring were JJ's only man jewellery. As a fashion statement the white gold rings were, maybe, excessive but they made JJ smile, triggered light hearted derision from Cyrus and Gil, and would be handy in a fight. The recipient of an Idol-ringed blow, however, would not have much trouble identifying his assailant. There were not that many Idol rings in global circulation and if you had the imprint of a great white on the side of your head that would considerably narrow down the manhunt.

JJ's eclectic and random fashion thoughts were not really what should have been rattling through his cropped hair head at this moment. He was in the back of the Mercedes Sprinter van, positioned under a few trees in the trailer park of Pyeonghwa Motors petrol station, just south of Taedong River in Pyongyang and a few minutes' drive from the DPRK's central bank. Jim Bradbury, Victor Pagari and the six 'Toblerones' were in there with him, the former two also gearing up for the night's activities. The rest of the crew were ready and laying low in the cabs of the two disguised PetroChina tankers parked a few metres away.

"Still packing that old Glock 17 I see JJ," said Jim Bradbury, attempting to lighten the atmosphere a little.

"Sure am Jim, held me in good stead in Bosnia, as you well know!" JJ and his Glock had saved Bradbury's life in Bosnia, he was extremely partial to both.

"How about you? What is your weapon of choice for tonight?" The Scot was changing into his multi-pocketed, Kevlar enhanced dark olive green cargo pants, lightweight bullet proof vest and Gore-Tex boots. As he asked Jim Bradbury this question JJ's mental process had already diverted path from bling rings to killer weapons.

"I've always liked the SIG Sauers, JJ," Jim replied. "Tonight's a full sized semi-automatic, 19x9mm rounds in staggered magazines. If I can't hit some random asshole or security guard with this little beauty then I'll retire."

JJ said nothing but was hoping that tonight's raid on the central bank would go as smooth as Yul Brynner's head and as silent as an abandoned hut in a snowdrift. A shootout in Pyongyang's central bank would not likely end well for anybody.

"Are you carrying anything else JJ, or is the Glock it?" persisted Jim.

"Well, I've got this blacked up commando knife," said JJ, showing Jim a veteran British Commando, Fairbairn-Sykes, fighting knife. "My mum gave it to me for my birthday one year.

I had it augmented with a rubber indented grip. It's in its original leather sheath. A real classic."

"You and your classics," mocked Jim. "I hope it still works and isn't going to rust away and disintegrate just when you need it old buddy."

"It won't," JJ assured him. He had looked after his knife. It was sharper than a razor, clean as a whistle, as well balanced as an Olympic beam gymnast. It would be deadly efficient if called upon.

"Haven't you got anything belonging to this century, JJ, or are all your weapons from Arthurian Legend or World War II?" asked Jim, chuckling away a little too heartily for a grown man.

JJ acknowledged Jim's question, reached into his kit bag and pulled something out. "Well, speaking of ancient legend, I've got this," replied JJ holding aloft a small, but clearly distinguishable, crossbow.

"A crossbow!" exclaimed Jim. Even Victor, who had been ignoring all the banter about guns and knives, stopped checking his laptop, tablets and other electronic gear to take a look.

"No ordinary crossbow. This jet black beauty is a Winchester Stallion crossbow. It is compact, made of lightweight aluminium with carbon fibre rods and shoots arrows at 350ft per second. It is very light, seventeen inches wide and has a 3x illuminated reticle; that would be telescopic sight to you ignoramuses," said JJ, admiring his contribution to twenty-first century weaponry.

"What's 350ft per second in miles per hour?" asked Victor, at last interested in the conversation.

"Just under 240mph, Victor. Faster than the speed of a McLaren F1. Though it is roughly one quarter of the speed of one of Jim's 9mm rounds fired from his SIG Sauer it is certainly fast enough, silent enough, and accurate enough to drop any human target within a range of fifty yards before he could utter

'William Tell'!" announced JJ as he strapped his crossbow over his back.

Both the KLO and the ex-MI5 officer knew that stealth would be part of the cocktail of a successful operation tonight. Jim's SIG Sauer would perform admirably in a shootout, but the decibel level would be mega. If some poor unfortunate had to be laid out on this operation, a broken neck, a knife or, indeed, a crossbow would be the procedure of choice.

The three men in the Sprinter van proceeded to finalise their preparations. JJ and Jim both had lightweight backpacks with emergency medical supplies and other tools of the trade that may be necessary. JJ had four small smoke bombs, several tear gas grenades and two canisters of sticky foam in his backpack. Jim had a couple of flashbangs, he really seemed to like loud and bright stuff, thought JJ, and a couple of canisters of pepper spray. They both had torches, binoculars, Kevlar reinforced beanies and walkie-talkies. On his left wrist, JJ had a matte black MTM Cobra Special Ops watch on a black ballistic Velcro strap. This 47mm diameter timepiece was not there as a fashion accessory, even though its total blackness, bar the tritium luminous hands, would have matched his other gear. It was on his wrist because it was very light, had slide rule, compass and chronograph functions. Watch on, JJ was ready. Jim Bradbury was as well and Victor was just putting the finishing touches to his kit bag. Neither Jim nor JJ had any assault or sniper rifles or submachine guns. Lily and the Iceman had these as they were designated initially to stay in the Sprinter van once the current three occupants plus Ethel made their way into the central bank. The moaner Ji-hun and deep cover Kwon were also to be in the van at that point. Kwon was there partly to keep an eye on the former and partly to quiz him further about the central bank's security if required.

"Victor," said JJ, just before exiting the back of the van to signal to the rest of the team that they were ready to rock. "Apart from Ji-hun, you're the only one not used to handling guns and the like. I'm not expecting a fire fight but do you have any means of protection on you, apart from your brains and quick wit?" Victor shook his head. "Can you shoot?" JJ continued, realising that there was not much point in giving the youngster a lethal weapon if he hadn't a blind clue as to how to use it.

"I'm no expert, JJ, not like you and Jim, but my grandfather took me to a firing range just outside of Toulouse a few times, so I know how to point and shoot, if the gun is straightforward enough," replied Victor.

JJ reached into his near empty kit bag on the floor pan of the van. "Here, take this," he said giving Victor a handgun. "Not that you're interested in it Victor, you're more brain than brawn, but this is a Glock 22. It's light, has an indented hand grip and a very strong polymer frame that dampens recoil. It's more modern than mine, not that that matters. It has a trigger safety, so keep that engaged for the moment. It's loaded with fifteen rounds and it's reliable. If you need to use it, remember to release the safety, then aim and shoot. You'll hit something, just make sure it's not any of the rest of us."

Victor looked at the handgun and understood everything that JJ had said about it. He nodded to JJ, put the Glock in his kit bag, zipped it up and said "Ready."

JJ nodded back, silently musing that clearly Victor wasn't expecting to need his newly acquired firearm. Sticking it in his zipped up holdall didn't make it the most accessible if the young fellow needed it in a hurry. JJ decided not to mention this as he did not want to freak out Victor any more than he had done already. The safe cracker was going to be in pole position soon and he would need the calmest of minds to crack the DPRK's central bank vaults.

On JJ's signal, Ethel, Lily, the Iceman, Kwon and Ji-hun, got out of the PetroChina tankers' cabs and headed to the van. It was a tight squeeze, all squashed up in between the 'Toblerones'. Jim Bradbury and his two PAU Travel colleagues were in the front of the van, in the driver's cabin, with the remaining five in the back. It made sense that way. The team was not expecting to be stopped between the petrol station and the central bank. There were no official checkpoints. The van was dark blue, de-badged and anonymous. If anyone caught a peek at or spoke to the drivers then there were two Koreans and a Korean linguist up front. Jim had put on his baseball cap for the short journey from the petrol station to the central bank. He was not committing the same fashion faux pas as at Songnim docks but nobody would clock his Caucasian chopper at that time of night, in the dark, in disguise lite.

The fifteen minute drive to the rear of the central bank was uneventful. The Iceman had parked up, about a hundred yards from the central bank and on a slight incline, so that they could survey the car park.

"Can you see anything Iceman?" asked JJ from the back of the van. Kim Chun-So had his binoculars out and was scouring the car park.

"There are about seven vehicles still in the car park," the Iceman reported. "Looks like around four saloon cars and three vans, two of which are about the same dimensions as this one. There are no guards either at the gates of the car park or what looks to be the rear entrance to the central bank. There are two CCTV cameras on long poles at the gates pointed inwards to the car park, and two aimed at the rear entrance of the central bank," he added.

JJ absorbed the information. "Kwon, ask Ji-hun if there are normally guards at the rear of the central bank, either the building itself or the car park?"

Kwon asked and Ji-hun said no, only cameras. It made sense, thought JJ. In a country where you could be thrown into a stinking cesspit of a jail for farting a mile upwind of its supreme leader, the penalties for serious crime were so harsh and unrelenting that the non-political crime rate was one of the lowest on the planet. Nobody in their right mind would try to rob anywhere in Pyongyang let alone the central bank. A quartet of cameras seemed a reasonable security precaution under the circumstances.

"Victor," said JJ. "What are we going to do about the cameras?"

"I'm on it," replied Victor, tapping away on his laptop.

"What are you doing?" asked Ethel, mesmerised by the speed and dexterity of his keyboard work.

"There are several ways to disable a surveillance camera," replied Victor. "Crude ways involve hitting it with a hammer, or disabling the camera lens with an infra-red laser. The trouble with the crudes is that the camera might spot you as you try to assault it so an image will show up on the security office's computer screens. Even if you manage to zap the eye in the sky with a laser, the monitoring guard will realise the camera is down and investigate. So the crude ways are off the menu tonight.

"So what are your dancing digits doing then?" persisted Ethel.

"In the vast majority of cases, when CCTV cameras are set up, their default settings can be accessed remotely via the internet. Most purchasers and users of the equipment don't know this. They're just hoping that it allows them to access the footage via a laptop, even mobile phone. So if the appropriate central bank's security guard is having a number 2 in the bank's loo, he can watch the CCTV footage on his mobile phone, if he wants to," said Victor smiling. "For the bad guys, or the good guys, however you would like to describe this happy band of eight tonight, these default settings allow us, i.e. me, to access the surveillance systems. If I can hack into them, and their password security is normally pathetic, then I too can look at the footage. More importantly, I can move the camera remotely, change the line of sight, zoom in and zoom out, send it on a loop," added Victor, his mesmeric fingers now at rest. "Viola!" he announced, turning his laptop screen towards Ethel and JJ. Victor was now in charge of the DPRK's external CCTV system.

"What was the password, genius?" asked Ethel.

"1,2,3,4," replied Victor. "Around 80 – 85% of these types of cameras use one of four passwords, 1234, 1111, admin, or user. The new users of the cameras rarely change them to something more secure, and no matter which country they're in, the default settings security password is still usually one of these."

"Good job, Victor," said JJ, placing a hand on the young hacker's back.

"Won't the bank's security guard who is monitoring the camera's live footage, notice it's been tampered with?" asked Jim Bradbury.

"No," said Victor. "Unless the guard is remotely accessing the camera's output at exactly the same time as me, he will notice nothing. I've now sent the cameras on a loop so in all probability we can remain undetected in the car park until the morning."

"OK," said JJ. "Let's drive closer to the gates. Lily you open them, Iceman you park up next to that dark coloured van you saw and which seemed to be only a few yards from the bank's rear entrance."

The team were on the move. JJ understood probabilities. As they were driving into the car park, JJ turned to Victor and asked in a low voice, "Victor, what would you have done had the camera system been one of the 15-20% that had its security password changed?"

"Cried," said the young man, with a glint in his eye.

JJ, Jim, Ethel, Lily and Victor all got out of the dark blue Sprinter van. They were parked next to a black 4x4, a Pyeonghwa Pronto, according to Lily. It wasn't as big as the Sprinter van, more the dimensions of a Toyota Land Cruiser, the Japanese model on which the PP was based. If push came to shove, they'd probably get most of the 'Toblerones' in that car/van with all but the front seats lowered flat. Before leaving their Sprinter van JJ had asked Ji-hun, via deep cover Kwon, if he knew the code for the keypad lock at the back entrance. Ji-hun said that this was the service lift and went to all the floors of the central bank. The code was 1,2,3,4.

"Jesus Christ," blurted JJ, not in an unhappy tone, more an incredulous one. "Is there any code in this fucking dump that's not 1,2,3,4?" his blurt was within earshot of Victor.

"I don't think the code to the vaults will be 1,2,3,4, boss," offered up Victor. JJ said nothing but acknowledged the safe cracker's unhelpful contribution with a small shrug of the shoulders.

The Iceman's job was to prep the PP jeep to ensure that it could fire up in a hurry and to lower the rear seats in preparation to receive the 'Toblerones'. Hopefully, the car's owner would not turn up while the heist was underway, and it would be way more healthy for him if he didn't. Victor was impressed with Kwon's Xaver 600 mini tablet technology that he loaned Lily and the Iceman which could see objects through walls. Victor had seen one before in London, but here, in North Korea, it was sure a rare piece of kit. The Xaver's penetration intel, confirmed by the moaner Ji-hun, was that the main vaults were one level below ground level. Ji-hun had also told the Iceman that the security detail on this floor was based in a bullet proof, lockable office with total visibility on three of the four sides of the office's near square shape. The visibility was focussed on the vault's doors. Luckily, for the five in the service lift, its doors opened to face the one solid wall of the security office.

Lily was first out of the lift. He had borrowed Ji-hun's security guard uniform and cap. Each guard at the DPRK had two, identical uniforms. The one that Ji-hun was wearing on kidnap day was in his locker on the ground floor. The one that Lily was wearing, looking a little daft in it, as he was a few inches shorter than Ji-hun, had been in the wash at the moaner's apartment. Lily walked up to the security office door, knocked and waved at the two guards inside. Simultaneously, the other four heisters had dropped to a prone position and silently high crawled marine style to either side of the door. The two security guards weren't expecting Lily or, indeed, a legitimate colleague, but maybe something was up or maybe he was being very considerate to the night shift and bringing them a welcome snack. Unfortunately for the guards, the only mouthfuls they got were of smoke and gas. Both guards got off their chairs to meet and greet Lily. As the office door opened, JJ lobbed in a couple of tear gas grenades and a smoke bomb. The guards were coughing, spluttering and trying to wipe their eyes as Ethel entered the office in a full face mask with breathing apparatus attached. She whacked both the disoriented security men with her police baton, brought all the way from London for the ride, and left them prostrate on the floor. Lily had exited the office at pace and even though he had been near the entrance when JJ tossed in the tear gas he was still finding it difficult to catch his breath. A few minutes had elapsed before the tear gas dissipated, JJ had deliberately used a low concentration variant. Ethel removed her breathing gear and she and Jim were tying up the guards with duct tape. Lily re-entered the fray and injected both guards with propofol, courtesy of Kwon's collection. This would keep the guards out cold for at least four hours. If that wasn't enough time to complete their task then they were in big trouble, not least of which because Ji-hun had told them the relief schedule of the vaults' guards, i.e. the two on the ground were due to be replaced in four hours from now at 7am. Since entering the service lift nobody had said a word. Everybody knew their job and, so far, it had all gone to plan.

Jim Bradbury and the now breathing easily Lily set up position outside the rear of the security office. They had a clear view of the main lift, the service elevator, and the stairs. They were hunkered down behind their kit bags and backpacks. Jim had his semi-automatic SIG Sauer ready and Lily his Remington 870 pump action shotgun. If anyone or anything entered this level of the DPRK central bank that wasn't a buddy or a batch of 'Toblerones' then they were in for a rude awakening.

JJ, Ethel and Victor were still in the security office. Victor was checking that the loop he had sent the car park cameras on was still working. It was. JJ was checking that all the other screens in the office were on and showing a lack of activity. They were. Ethel was checking that the two unconscious guards were still breathing and still knocked out. They were. Checks complete, the three of them made their way to the main vault doors. Once the moaner Ji-hun had decided to squeal, faced with good incentives and little sensible alternative, he had told JJ and the Iceman about the main vault security. From his recollection and observation the vault had a dual combination lock and probably was on a timer.

"Looks like Ji-hun's information was spot on," said Victor, surveying the massive vault doors with respect. "It's a steel reinforced concrete vault with a dual custody lock. Both dials need to be unlocked and it's very, very unlikely one will automatically release the other," he added. "It's also got a time lock, which has been pre-assembled, and built into the vault's door. We have no idea when it is set to unlock, possibly not till at least 10am. It's probably a UL Class II or Class III vault," he concluded.

"Is that good or bad, kiddo?" asked Ethel.

"Neither," replied Victor. "The classification refers to the expected length of time it would take to breach a vault, set up for a mock break in by Underwriters Laboratories (UL) in Illinois. A class M one would take up to fifteen minutes. This one at least an hour, maybe two to three."

"Three hours would be pushing it Victor," interrupted JJ. "As well as getting into the vault, we've got to load a bunch of 12.5kg bullion bars and get the 'Toblerones' down here to do that. As a rough calculation, if each of the 'Toblerones' has thirty gold bars on it continuously, and it takes a rapid three minutes to transfer them from here to the van, we'd need the best part of three hours to do it. You've got one hour at best Victor," said JJ, unhappy that the safe cracker could not be allocated longer to ply his trade.

"Good job I brought my thermal lance and my tablet then," said Victor.

JJ knew enough about stuff to realise that thermal lances were capable of burning through steel and concrete. As far as he knew, though, their capabilities were often exaggerated. JJ would return to that point in a minute he thought.

"What good's your tablet, Victor, going to play a safe cracking video game?"

"No, Sir," replied Victor, ferreting about in his large bag. "Time locks work because they've got mini computers inside them. They are programmed by the manufacturer and set in place before the vault is delivered to the vault owner. If the vault owner wants to change the time lock parameters, he has to get the manufacturer to remotely reprogram them. It cannot be done onsite and it would be prohibitively expensive and impractical to rebuild the vault if ever the owner wanted a different time lock span." Victor was nearly consumed by his bag now, but seconds later announced, "Here you are, you little blighter."

JJ and Ethel were still listening, not knowing whether they should be elated or deflated.

"Built into the hardware of this here tablet…" Victor said, waving a skinny device, no more than eight inches by five inches, "is a gigabyte P55 series motherboard. The manufacturers of this nifty piece of kit were aiming mainly at the domestic marketplace to allow parents to set time limits on their kids' computers to avoid overuse and consequent brain shrinkage."

JJ and Ethel looked a bit happier, but they really didn't know why, they barely understood what Victor was babbling on about. However, the youngster was looking all pleased with himself so something good must be happening.

"And?" asked Ethel, impatiently.

"And if you're a smart enough cookie to be able to mess with the accompanying software then you can use it to accelerate or decelerate computer programmed time," Victor finished. Indeed, he was a smart enough cookie. Surely there hadn't been a tastier cookie since Edd Byrnes in 77 *Sunset Strip*.

"Won't you trigger an alarm if you break into the time lock?" Ethel asked.

"No. I'm not breaking in. I'm going to unscrew the outer cover and attach three leads to the lock's innards. This will bypass the clock as set and once I've keyed in a few commands on my tablet, you will see the digital time display speed up. When we hit the time that the lock was set to open then one piece of the puzzle will be solved," Victor replied as his flashing fingers moved deftly about the keyboard.

"What about the dual custody locks?" asked JJ.

"They're the time constraint. I can probably unlock them,

this gizmo is like an augmented hearing aid with stethoscope attached. I can magnetically attach the ends of it to each lock. This will then magnify the sound as I key in the numerical codes. A short high pitched tone signals the correct number and a long low pitched one means I entered the wrong number."

"Don't suppose 1,2,3,4 or 1,1,1,1 will be the answer?" said JJ hopefully.

"Unfortunately not, boss. For starters, each of these locks has a five digit code. I can't be sure but every time I enter a wrong number the electronic system will block the lock for maybe five minutes. If I get two numbers in a row wrong it may block it for a further twenty minutes. Even if I get the first lock undone swiftly, I will have only around fifteen to twenty seconds to open the second one. That's why I would need to use both the earphones to try to disengage the locks simultaneously. Each panel in the lock's window can have the number 0 to 9, that's ten digits. Assuming a number can be repeated, which in these types of lock they usually can, that gives us 10^5 or 100,000 possible combinations."

"For each lock?" asked Ethel.

"For each lock," replied Victor. "Giving us 200,000 possible combinations. I cannot be confident that I can do that in less than an hour." Just as he reached this conclusion his tablet indicated that the opening mechanism on the time lock had been triggered. That was something. He showed JJ and Ethel and they nodded their appreciation.

"So, Victor, since you've got the biggest kit bag on the planet and there's only one weapon, my handgun, in it, I guess the other contents are your plan B?" asked JJ.

"Yes, it was always likely that this bank would have one of the best vaults in it. It's a central bank, it's new and it would probably house at least part of Kim Jong-un's personal wealth. I may be able to disengage the dual custody locks in an hour, but I might also take two to three. If we had overnight to do it then it would be a cinch, a sure thing, a done deal. We don't, so I brought along an old fashioned way as well."

"The thermal lance?" asked JJ.

"The thermal lance," confirmed Victor.

JJ and Ethel were moderately amused that Victor thought the thermal lance route was old fashioned. Clearly, anything that was not computer based, electronic, nice and clean did not qualify as state of the art for Victor Pagari.

"I thought those lances were not as efficient as made out?" asked JJ.

"That's true," replied Victor. "They can take longer than is often depicted and they use up quite a few oxygen bottles in the process. You can't cut a hole in a steel and concrete vault door in five minutes."

"How long, Victor, we probably need to get cracking?" asked JJ, not even remotely aware of his unintended pun.

"I'm hoping for 15 to 20 minutes, JJ. I've had the iron rods augmented with aluminium and magnesium. This will increase the heat at the tip of the work-piece. Once I've preheated the end of the tube, the temperature of the molten iron stream from the lance will be in excess of 3,000 degrees Celsius. I've brought three pressurised oxygen bottles with me and ten tubes. The tubes will need replacing every four or five minutes because they virtually disintegrate after that time. Basically, if I'm not through in thirty to forty minutes, we're out of options."

"Fine," said JJ. "Give it your best shot." With that JJ patted Victor on the back and signalled to Ethel to move away from the vault door. Victor was laying out a fire resistant sheet on the floor and preparing to don his face shield and breathing equipment. There was more to the successful operation of a thermal lance than just poking it at a vault's door.

318

"OK Ginger," said JJ. "Get Jim and Lily to go up in the service lift and they can begin bringing down the 'Toblerones'. On your way check that those security guards are still out cold. Swap places with the Iceman in the van and he can help with the conveyor system too. I'll keep a look out and an eye on Victor. Get Kwon to ask Ji-hun if there are any mobile pallets in here. There must be some, to move any heavy goods around."

Ethel nodded and went straight to the service elevator. It would take her a few minutes to get up, explain JJ's orders to the team in the van and for them to bring the 'Toblerones' down. When Ethel was out of sight, JJ eased himself slowly to the ground. He was in a hot sweat and feeling a little nauseous. Not the *I'm about to puke* nausea that he used to feel if Cyrus convinced him to go on some stomach churning amusement park ride, but a little queasiness that made him a tad uncomfortable. The hot sweat was probably the result of his hormone treatment. It was a well-known side effect and one of the milder ones, so he shouldn't complain too much. In the mad panic to get here, however, JJ had forgotten to bring along his Beljanski pills and his mega cocktail of vitamins and supplements. Those little cancer shits better not be attempting some Lazarus-style revival he thought, drinking some bottled water and wiping his brow. After about four minutes his sweat and nausea passed. *Thank god for that*, he thought.

JJ was back on his feet and looking normal when the service lift's doors opened. Jim and his fellow PAU Travellers had the six 'Toblerones' with them.

"Right guys," instructed JJ. "Start joining these together and lining them up. Begin near the lift and leave the last few until Victor has stopped making fire." Victor's activities were within sight and the three 'Toblerone' handlers looked a little bemused. "It's a long story," said JJ pre-empting any questions, "and we don't have time for even the short version. If all goes well Victor will have cut through the door in about fifteen minutes. Jim, did Ji-hun say anything about pallets on wheels?"

"He did JJ. They should be in a back room at the far end of this level where they keep all the workers' stuff and any machinery which needs to be mobile," replied Jim.

"Great. Lily, Iceman, you get two of the pallets if you can. I'll help Jim with the 'Toblerones'. Did any of you guys notice the recommended weight allowance for the service lift?" asked JJ. Head shakes all round. "No problem. Next time we open it let's check. Bullion bars are not light and we don't want to pulverise the lift's mechanism. A pretty sight we'll all look if the guards find us cosied up with their supreme leader's gold first thing in the morning."

With that, JJ and Jim proceeded to mantle the 'Toblerones' into one long and flat surfaced conveyor system. Support rods had been built into their individual hubs which came out for stability. There were spaces on the surface between each individual piece but these were very small and way too narrow to either let a gold bar drop through or impede it significantly as it moved along the treads. JJ opened the service lift doors. The metal plate secured above the panel for floor selection was in English and Korean. The maximum weight allowance was twenty people or 1,500kg. It was a spacious lift, as you would expect. Each gold bar was likely to weigh nearly12.5kg. Excluding the weight of the pallets and humans involved in their transportation, then 120 gold bars, at a maximum, could be taken up in the elevator in one go. Assuming two of his team on each elevator gold trip and a rough guess at the pallets' weight, then probably no more than 100 bars at a time could safely go up in this elevator. For 6,000 gold bars that would mean sixty trips. If each round trip took three minutes, with no slippage, that would mean three hours. It was way too tight. Even assuming they got started in the next ten minutes, they had only three to three and a half hours before both the guards woke up and daybreak began. They could just knock out the security office guards again and the next shift guards, of course, but they could not delay daybreak. Even gadgetastic Victor could not control the coming dawn. The other security guards in the bank would surely notice that the loop Victor had sent their cameras on was still showing darkness. JJ et al would be rumbled.

★ ★ ★

Around the same time as JJ Darke was wrestling with his gold heist obstacles, Commander Kun-Woo Moon was contemplating his own position in the partially wrecked surroundings of Commodore Park's living quarters at Haeju docks. Moon knew he was in trouble, the question he was transfixed with was how much. Of the four diners whose pleasant meal had been rudely interrupted by a bunch of as yet unknown submarine thieves, surely he was the least culpable. He had fully completed his assignment from Vice Admiral Goh and had delivered all the submariners requested to Haeju docks. He had no responsibility for either the docks' security or that of the now vanished nuclear submarine. Those responsibilities would appear to lie with Commodore Park and Lieutenant Commander Gok Han-Jik. The injured scientist, Sunwoo Chung did not seem to have any role in the security of the docks or the sub either; he was a technician, whose sole task on this occasion was to make the submarine as invisible as possible.

Moon and Park were sitting together on Park's sofa, surprisingly free of damage. They stared ahead, contemplating their personal universes, and not conversing. Commodore Park had already informed Vice Admiral Goh about the disastrous attack. Goh absorbed the information but said very little. He informed both the office of the supreme leader and the State Security Department aka the DPRK's secret police. Commodore Park knew his career was over, he was just wondering whether his life was too.

Gok Han-Jik was standing in the far corner of Park's living room, on his phone, and doing a lot of mumbling and rapid head bowing, presumably to the recipient of his call. It didn't make a lot of sense right enough as it wasn't a video phone and he wasn't on Skype. Whoever was listening to him could not see him. Though he was paying scant attention to Gok, Commodore Park could understand every second or third mumble. It sounded like there was an awful lot of apologising going on. Only a few hours earlier, Gok had seemed so self-assured, arrogant even, in himself and about his orders. Bombing Japan and the USA was his mandate, a mandate that had now evaporated in a puff of enemy tinged smoke. Commodore Park did not know that Gok was Kim Jong-un's cousin but he did know one thing about him – he was a dead man walking.

As Moon and Park sat in their contemplative silence and Gok was mumbling away his apologies, Sunwoo Chung was helpless on the ground. The excruciatingly burning sensation that had hit the right side of his face following the scalding tea fountain was not subsiding. He was being attended to by one of the naval paramedics that had been sleeping in their makeshift quarters on the docks. Sunwoo was moaning and groaning a lot and had been reluctant to let go of the cloth that he had pressed against his burned faced. The paramedic was as gentle as he could be but Sunwoo could still feel his face come off along with the cloth.

"Is it bad, is it bad?" cried the wailing scientist.

"I've seen worse," said the medic, completely truthfully but kind of irrelevant to Sunwoo, especially since the medic's benchmark was the sight of bodies virtually consumed by fire. The medic did his best to patch up Sunwoo and relieve his pain, but he knew the scalded scientist would need hospital treatment as soon as possible and eventually skin grafts to improve the ghastly countenance that his already ugly mug had become.

As the four former diners went about their business of contemplating, apologising and groaning, two plain clothed men entered Commodore Park's living room.

"Commodore Park, please?" asked the taller of the two.

"I am Commodore Park," responded the officer in charge of the Haeju docks, rising from his sofa and standing erect to his full height.

"I am Lee Kon-U," said the taller man, hand outstretched to shake that of the Commodore. He did not introduce his companion. "I am a Major in the State Security Department, Commodore, and I report directly to our supreme leader. I have been sent here to investigate this crime against our beloved nation. I expect your full support and cooperation." With that Lee presented Commodore Park with his credentials. Park inspected them. They were legitimate.

"Of course, Major," replied Park, "anything I can help with, I gladly will."

"Which of your companions is Gok Han-Jik?" asked Lee. Park pointed to the standing man in the corner of the living room. Gok had finished his phone call. "Lieutenant Commander Gok. Please accompany my colleague to the car awaiting below. Your cousin would like to see you immediately."

"His cousin?" queried Park.

"Kim Jong-un, our leader," replied Lee. Park, Moon and the barely conscious Sunwoo were taken aback. Gok, himself, was shaken and looked a defeated man. Maybe being the DPRK's supreme leader's cousin wasn't so good, Park pondered as Gok was led away by Lee's quiet colleague.

"Commodore Park," said Lee. "Vice Admiral Goh has resigned his position following this debacle. Once I have finished questioning you about tonight's events, our supreme leader invites you to do the same."

"Certainly," replied Park, sure that he had to comply with Kim Jong-un's invitation but unsure whether or not that would be the end of it.

Satisfied that Commodore Park would be fully cooperative, he did seem like a completely loyal career military officer, Lee turned his attention to Moon and Sunwoo.

"Commander Kun-woo Moon?" asked Lee of the man still sitting on Park's sofa.

"Yes, Sir," responded Moon, getting on his feet sharply and saluting the Major from the State Security Department.

"No need to salute, Commander," said Lee. "I believe you were in charge of selecting and organising transport to the dock for the submariners?"

"Yes, Sir, and they all arrived on time and in good health," answered the worried Moon.

"They're not all in good health now, Commander," interjected Lee in a snappy tone. "In fact, there are at least twenty dead and thirty to thirty-five injured as far as we can tell. Mainly from gunshots, explosions and, from the bodies recovered near dockside, slit throats. Maybe if you had been less punctual, Commander, these submariners would still be alive," emphasised Lee, of course not believing his admonishment.

"Yes, Sir, sorry Sir," said Moon quietly. The pitiful Commander didn't know what to think.

Major Lee had been fully briefed as to the role in this operation for each of the former diners. Vice Admiral Goh and Lee's boss, General Choi Yong-kun had filled him in on all the relevant details.

"Commander Moon, you are free to go, return to your base on the east coast. The SSD are unlikely to have any further questions for you. If, however, we do, make yourself available immediately. Is that understood?"

"Yes Sir," replied Moon, still somewhat in a daze but certain that he had heard the Major say 'you are free to go'.

"Your own vehicle was not damaged in the attack, Commander, please drive carefully," suggested Lee.

Moon scarpered out of Park's living quarters, gingerly descended the rickety stairs, which had not been rickety until Navy SEAL Joe Franks's firecracker went off, and walked briskly to his jeep. There were still degrees of chaos on dockside but Moon was not bothered anymore. He was in his jeep and he was heading home. Moon put his keys in the ignition and manually wound down his driver's side window, he still loved the smell of the sea, even if tonight it was tinged with the aroma of gunpowder. As Moon was about to pull away, the quiet companion of Major Lee appeared at the driver's door and popped a couple of .357 Magnum rounds from his FN Barracuda revolver into Moon's head. The Fabrique Nationale Barracuda was a timeless classic, ceased production in 1989, but had been given to the quiet man by no less than the supreme leader himself. Moon would now have no opportunity to tell this tale of embarrassing loss to anyone inside or outside the DPRK.

While the quiet man was propelling Moon's grey matter into oblivion, Major Lee had turned his attention to the half-conscious Sunwoo Chung.

"Sunwoo Chung," asked Lee, "can you understand me?"

Sunwoo nodded.

"You are the scientist responsible for the stealth augmentation of the nuclear submarine, correct?" enquired Lee, already knowing that he was.

"Correct," mumbled Sunwoo.

"Is there any way to override your stealth modifications, interrupt them, render them ineffective?" asked Lee in something of a forlorn tone.

"No," replied Sunwoo, proud of the quality of his work. Since most of his augmentations had involved physical additions and alterations, there was no way they could be rendered ineffective until the submarine was recovered or surfaced.

"Are you in pain?" enquired Lee, feigning concern.

Sunwoo nodded.

"This will help," responded Lee as he placed his left hand over Sunwoo's mouth and nostrils. The burnt scientist did not have much energy to resist and he was further de-energised by the medic's painkillers that had not yet fully taken effect. Sunwoo wriggled a bit, struggled a bit and had a look of terror in his eyes.

Commodore Park spoke up. "Major! Is that really necessary?"

"It would be in your interests, Commodore, to sit down and shut up," rebuked Lee, pressing harder on Sunwoo's airways. The scientist did not have much time left. "This fool made the submarine so invisible that even his own navy cannot find it. For all we know he is an enemy agent. He spent time in America, was partly educated there. Perhaps he turned. Even if he did not, the pervert has no future in our beloved land, no career and no life," emphasised Lee, having been fully briefed on Sunwoo's foibles as well as his ability. Neither Lee, Park nor Pyongyang's working girls needed worry any longer. Sunwoo Chung had expired.

Major Lee stood up, wiped his murderous hand with his handkerchief and turned to Commodore Park. "Commodore, of the three senior officers and one government scientist around your dining table tonight, you are the only one still alive." In addition to Moon, the quiet man had also topped Gok. Both cadavers were nestling motionless in the trunk of his Pyeonghwa Motors

Chairman car. "You are still alive for two reasons Commodore. First, our supreme leader recognises that you and Vice Admiral Goh have had long and distinguished careers in the service of our country. He does not believe that either you or Goh are traitors but he does want reassurance and that means a personal appearance before him, tonight. Secondly, the acquisition of the nuclear submarine from our friends in Russia was Goh's idea, the security of the submarine your responsibility. Kim Jong-un does not want to shoot the messenger, he may even not want to shoot you, but he does want to know what the fuck happened here tonight. If I were you, when we get to Pyongyang, I'd have a clear, concise account to tell."

Park did not know what to say. He and Goh were still alive, that was good, but he was shocked at the killings of Sunwoo, Moon and Gok. He had never really liked Gok or Sunwoo that much but Moon seemed a decent fellow and a loyal officer, why did he need to perish.

Major Lee must have been reading Park's mind because he offered up the following.

"Look, Commodore, word will begin to spread that we have lost a nuclear submarine that most people in the world, including our enemies, did not know we had. The enlisted men can be made to believe that it was a training exercise that went horribly wrong, but for the officers here, at the dock, that would be a hard one to swallow. Sunwoo's usefulness had run its course and Moon was a bit of a blabber mouth. The supreme leader could not risk either of them giving their take on events."

Park was listening but protesting nothing, often the best policy when talking to a high ranking officer in the secret police, especially on a night when one of your submarines went AWOL.

"Gok was both the officer in charge of the submarine's upcoming mission and the supreme leader's cousin. Having a submarine stolen from under your nose was probably a necessary and sufficient condition for our leader to order Gok's death. He was also family so that meant that his crime of negligence was multiplied tenfold. Kim Jong-un did not want Gok to cross his threshold ever again."

Park felt that he had been given a truthful rendition by Lee as to the motivation behind his fellow diners' murders. The logic and rationale in some cases may seem a bit retarded, Park thought, but they were gone and Park needed to spend most of the forty-five minute drive to Pyongyang ensuring that his report was as comprehensive and loyal as was humanly possible.

Major Lee and Commodore Park made their way to the SSD's awaiting car. The naval officers that had been stationed in Haeju City had been summoned to the docks and the most senior of them put in charge of getting order from chaos, taking any witness statements from the submariners who had been awakened by the explosions and, generally trying to restore a semblance of normality. The quiet man opened the front passenger door for Park. He got in and Major Lee got into the driver's side. The quiet man was seated directly behind Park. The Commodore felt very uncomfortable with this arrangement. He had seen enough to realise that there was a non-zero probability that the rear passenger's next move was to garrotte or strangle him. The anxious Commodore had not needed to concern himself with that outcome. The quiet man had fulfilled his kill quota, for this evening at least.

* * *

Victor and his thermal lance had cut open a large rectangular hole in the central bank's main vault. It had taken eighteen minutes and created a huge mess of empty oxygen bottles, burnt out tubes and random pieces of molten metal dotted along the floor. Through the gaping hole, JJ and his team could see the side walls lined with safe deposit boxes, another, smaller vault at the back end of this room and, slap, bang in the middle of the room trays of gold bullion, stacked three levels high. Each tray had 104 bullion bars on it. The bars were gleaming in the artificial light, it was a magnificent sight.

Before entering North Korea, its capital and its central bank vaults, JJ had no reliable estimate of how many bullion bars would be there. North Korea did not supply data on its reserves to the World Gold Council or the IMF. His guesstimate was made on intel regarding North Korea's gold mining capabilities and likely gifts and payments from China and Russia. Given the intensity of the gleam from the shiny metal bars before him JJ may have underestimated Kim Jong-un's gold wealth.

"No time for gold gawking," directed JJ. "Lily, Iceman, get loading onto those pallets. Jim, you and I will take the first few up in the lift. Victor, great job, take a breather and then help. Make sure there is no more than one tray full of gold on each pallet, we can't afford to damage the lift."

Everybody got to work straight away. The bars were heavy but the adrenalin was pumping and the first few pallet runs, from vault to 'Toblerone', then 'Toblerone' to pallet, lift and up to the van, went smoothly. Ethel stayed in the van as look-out. Kwon and Ji-hun loaded the gold into the van. Victor's good work had given the team a full three hours to accomplish the transfer of the gold from vault to van. JJ knew it was barely enough time.

"I'm glad we don't need to push this fucking pallet very far," bemoaned Jim Bradbury as he and JJ rolled the gold only a few feet from the vault to their conveyor system.

"Yeah, it's a bleedin' nightmare, Jim," replied JJ. "Nobody better challenge me to arm wrestling, I've got jelly arms already and we're not even halfway through."

"We've been going for an hour and a half JJ, that's halfway isn't it?"

"It's halfway in allocated mission time, but tight on target gold acquisition."

"We couldn't really put more gold on each pallet run, JJ," highlighted Jim correctly. "We won't be able to push it and the elevator might not take it," correct on his second observation as well. "How adrift of target will we be when time's up?"

"I've been trying to keep count while pushing the stuff. We've been loading 104 bars on each pallet, it's taken us three minutes to get from the pallet, via the 'Toblerones', to the van. By the time we're back down to the vault room Lily, the Iceman and Victor have another pallet ready so there's no loss of time there. I reckon we've done around 3,000. Kwon and Ji-hun are struggling to keep pace with the gold delivery; the bars are piling up on the ground. They will need help near the end, for sure," said JJ.

"That doesn't solve our problem, though, does it, JJ? We're still going to be short by dawn." Three in a row of correct observations by the KLO, but no light bulb moment as yet. "I wonder how they got down here in the first place?" asked Jim.

JJ did not respond immediately though Jim's question had triggered a train of thought in the Scot. This particular train did not yield a robust conclusion, but it did yield a course of action. "Let's ask Ji-hun," said JJ, hoping that the moaner's response was close to JJ's thinking.

Jim and JJ were quickly in the back of the Sprinter van. "Kwon, ask Ji-hun how they moved around the gold and other heavy objects in the vault level. We need a concise answer. The clock is ticking." The urgency in JJ's voice was plain to hear. Ji-hun responded swiftly to Kwon's question.

Deep cover translated. "He says they use small fork lift carriers. They're housed in a back room at the far end of the vault floor. The west wing of the building isn't finished yet and the contractors have been allowed to keep them there temporarily."

"Anything else we should know?" asked JJ.

"No," said Kwon, taking his lead from Ji-hun's head shake.

JJ and Jim bounded out of the van and back into the service lift with his pallet ready for another load of gold. "That should do the trick?" said Jim, looking at JJ with questioning eyes.

"Maybe," replied JJ. "The fork lifts will help Lily and the Iceman get the gold from the 'Toblerones' faster but even if they fit in this lift, which they probably do, the extra weight would mean that we could transport fewer gold bars on every trip. It's touch and go Jim."

When the pair reached vault level, Jim went in search of the fork lifts, while JJ went to help Lily, the Iceman and Victor load the gold onto the pallet and 'Toblerones'. The two helpful Koreans were visibly flagging now, each human action slower than an hour ago, sweating away and generally looking a bit floppy.

"Victor," said JJ, signalling for the safe cracker to join him. "I need your help. We have a problem. The short of it is we may not have enough time before breaking light to get the gold we need up top. Any bright ideas?"

"How much is 3,000 gold bars in money that I would understand?"

"Well…" began JJ engaging his mental arithmetic cells, "each bar is 12.5kg in weight, at yesterday's closing COMEX price gold was around US $1,800 per ounce or US $60,000 per kilogram. Each bar is therefore worth $750,000 so approximately $2 ¼ billion for a load of 3,000."

Victor was somewhat impressed by the old man's mental agility. He'd have done it quicker on his tablet calculator he ventured but then again he didn't know the price of gold to begin with. Victor was mulling over this information. JJ wanted to say 'chop chop' but he refrained. The young safe cracker had done his job, this was like overtime.

"I don't know if this is the answer or not..." said Victor, inadvertently adding a few more degrees of anxiety to JJ's mental stress, "but do we need to steal just gold? Would cash do?"

Would cash do, pondered JJ. "It would Victor but I didn't see any cash lying around. We don't have time to check all the safe deposit boxes. What are you thinking?"

"I'm thinking that the smaller vault at the back of the room is where any cash is. Since the security management of this bank clearly thought that the main vault door was impenetrable they skimped a little on this one. It's a single combination four digit lock, no timer, no trip alarm and substantially fewer unlock combinations than Big Bertha here."

"Can you burn through the door quickly?" asked JJ, warming to Victor's thought process.

"No," he replied immediately. "I've no tubes left for the lance. They were all used up getting in here." JJ was about to look miserable again but Victor continued. "However, I do still have my guile and listening equipment. If I can't unlock that door in under ten minutes then I'm not Albert Spaggieri's grandson!" he exclaimed, triumphantly.

"Great," said JJ. "Get on it and let me know when you're through."

While JJ and Victor were having their conflab, Jim had found the small forklifts and he and his Korean colleagues were speeding up the gold transfer from their vault trays to the service lift. They had only forty-five minutes left now to get all the booty onto the van and exit the central bank's car park. JJ was a wee bit happier but how far towards top utility happiness was going to depend on Victor, how he did and what he found. As he was mulling this over, JJ joined Jim again on the pallet run.

"JJ," said Jim. "I was thinking."

"Fire away, Jim," encouraged the KLO's friend.

"You know how I can drive heavy duty trucks since my student days in Arizona?"

"Yes," replied JJ.

"Well those trucks all had weight limits as to what they could safely and legally carry. I can't do the math in my head, JJ, but this gold is seriously fucking heavy. While, space wise, it'll fit into the Sprinter van at a squeeze, there is no way that van is going to be able to haul all the gold without collapsing where it stands."

"You're right – up to a point," replied JJ. "The scoop is this. We're aiming for 6,000 bars of gold, that's 75,000kg in weight. That's seventy-five metric tonnes. A normal Sprinter van's maximum payload is no more than twenty-five metric tonnes. Did you notice my inclusion of the word *normal* Jim?"

"I did," Jim replied. "Keep going for god's sake."

"Well, I didn't bring a van with me all the way from England for the good of my health. I could have picked up a Sprinter in Seoul and saved myself the bother. This is no ordinary Mercedes van. It's been tweaked and augmented by one of the best F1 teams in the world. The V6 engine has nearly 400bhp compared with the standard 160bhp, upgraded brakes and a short-shift gear change. More important for us, the van has upgraded suspension, same as a Hummer H3, enhanced torsion bar and titanium leaf springs, front and rear. It also has a false floor. The space between the original floor pan and the one the gold's on is filled with extra Kevlar and aluminium coil springs. This gives additional cushioning and reduces the direct weight to the axles, wheels and tyres. Speaking of those both the wheels and tyres are special order to take the weight. Finally, the coup de beauté, as you would know, Jim, is the axles. Our van has two additional axles, air over hydraulic modified from a Volvo 700. Not only can our van carry the gold, it can shift like The Road Runner."

"Eight wheels?" queried Jim, the only question he could come up with following JJ's detailed rendition. "I saw only four."

"The van's been so extensively modified, Jim, you could barely believe it. The additional wheels are housed under the false floor. When needed, they come out like an aircraft's. When they're stored, they lie horizontally and as they come out they go vertical, ready to move. It's fuckin' ingenious, I tell you," exclaimed JJ, all chuffed on behalf of the brilliant work of Harold McFarlane and his team at McLaren. On their last gold transfer to the van, JJ had instructed Ethel to lower the additional wheels; the van was ready.

As the friends re-entered the main vault room, Victor was standing at the far end, bowing like a lead thespian taking a final curtain call. "Through!" was his only utterance.

"That's beezer, Victor, well done," said JJ. "Found anything worthwhile?"

"There's a lot of cash, wrapped in plastic and stacked like the gold bars. Different currencies, mainly US dollars, euros, yen and South Korean won."

Ironic, thought JJ, the DPRK and its supreme leader may philosophically detest the South, the USA and Japan but Kim Jong-un seemed happy enough to hoard their currencies. JJ scanned the piles of wrapped foreign currency in front of him. The US dollars seemed all to be in $100 bill denominations.

"OK," said JJ. "Iceman, you and Lily come into this vault. Victor go topside and bring Kwon down here. Tell Ethel to watch Ji-hun. When Kwon's here, Victor, you and him take over loading the gold. It won't be for long, we need to be out of here in thirty minutes. Jim, you and I will continue on the pallet run and make sure the gold is stacked securely in the van," instructed JJ.

Victor took off instantly, clearly there was not a lot of time for congratulations and back slapping, though richly deserved, for his safe cracking skills.

"Lily, Iceman, start taking the US dollars. Load them into Victor's kit bag, it must be nearly empty now with no oxygen bottles, thermal lance tubes and breathing equipment. Make sure his electronic gear is safe. In twenty-five minutes stop loading the cash, take it topside. You can't use the service lift, take the smaller main lift. If the cash fits in our van, great, if not lob it into the one next to us that Iceman hot-wired earlier."

The US dollars were definitely the currency to take. Not only was the greenback still the world's reserve currency and acceptable in many countries as nigh local money or better, it was probably the right choice tonight from a perspective of weight and bulk. A US $100 bill weighs 1 gram, a minor piece of trivia that JJ recalled from his early days of economic research. So, $100,000 would weigh 1kg. Each wrapped packet of $100 bills had $20,000 in it. Victor's kit bag could hold maybe 80 packets at a time gauged JJ. The bag would take two minutes to fill and two minutes to get to the awaiting van. In the twenty minutes or so left before the exit deadline that meant only five trips for the kit bag or 400 packets in total.

"Jim!" yelled JJ. "Get that forklift over here and start sticking these trays of $100 bills on it." Jim Bradbury came zooming along on his new found toy. "OK Jim, we've got one shot at this. The last trip on the service lift is going to be you, the forklift and a whole lot of dollars."

"What about the weight?"

"I'm working on that. You and the forklift's combined weight is probably around 250kg. The lift's capacity is 1,500kg, so we could have 1,250kg spare. Each of these trays has twenty-eight packets of 200x $100 bills, weighing 5.6kg, excluding the tray itself. OK, Jim, for the last run, take as many trays of bills as you can get into the lift and then we're done."

"Fine, JJ," said Jim, and set about his task.

JJ's brain was close to meltdown now. There was too much going on, too many calculations and they had only ten minutes left before they had to exit the central bank. One last calculation, thought JJ, this mission can't go south just because of arithmetic. That heinous little shit Robson was after a minimum of £3 billion. At GBP/USD 1.5000, close to where the cable rate was yesterday, that meant US $4.5 billion. JJ and his team might just have nicked 6,000 gold bars each weighing 12.5kg. At $1,800/oz. substantially higher than it was two weeks ago, that's US $4.5 billion in gold. Target reached if the gold price held up. The dollar cash would amount to around $125 million extra. Good, thought JJ, this team deserves a decent bonus.

Final calculation done, JJ then shouted, "Go, go, go, we're out of here now. Lily, Iceman, drop everything, go. Victor, Kwon, chop chop. Take your stuff and let's go. Jim, get the cash up top, I'll check the security guards."

"What about the 'Toblerones'?" asked Jim.

"We'll need to leave them. They won't fit into the van with our weapons and all the gold in it, they won't fit in that local 4x4 we've hot-wired because the cash will need to go in that. We'll need to adjust our plan as we head to the petrol station," JJ replied.

Exit accomplished, the team of eight piled into the Sprinter van and the newly acquired 4x4. Gold was loaded, cash was loaded, they were loaded. Sunrise in Pyongyang was at 6.24am that day. It was now 5.50am and it seemed likely to be a bleak morning, regarding the weather at least.

The team left the DPRK's central bank without a hitch. Driving in convoy, at the same pace as the early morning traffic, both van and jeep turned into the road that Kwon's apartment was on. Kwon and Ji-hun got out of the jeep, leaving Lily and

Ethel inside. The plan was for Kwon to hold onto Ji-hun for a couple of days and then organise a border crossing where the moaner would be met by two CIA officers from PAU Travel in Seoul. Both JJ and Jim intended to stick to the deal agreed with Ji-hun. His information had been very useful and at no point had he tried to disrupt the heist or alert the North Korean authorities. It was a real squeeze in the Mercedes van. Jim decided to join Ethel and Lily in the jeep, leaving JJ, the Iceman and Victor in the front cabin of the van. It was about 6.05am now. The sun would soon attempt to beam a few shafts of light through the grey clouds but it still seemed like night time. JJ was glad about this. Maybe it would give them a few more precious minutes to distance themselves from the central bank before the alarm was raised. The security detail was scheduled to be relieved at 7am. JJ and his team had nearly one hour's head start.

★ ★ ★

Van and jeep were now crossing the bridge over the Taedong River. Everything seemed normal, a few cars and trucks were also crossing, in both directions, there was no obvious police or military activity. JJ closed his eyes for a few moments. He was mentally and physically exhausted. The petrol station was only minutes away and the Scot was absent a decent idea as to how to get the gold onto the petrol tankers, where the 'sunbeds' awaited. On that score, nothing was in their favour. They were an hour behind schedule. It was nearly breaking light and there were no conveyor systems to get the gold from the van to the tankers. It was beyond impossible to think that they could load the bullion bars manually. It would take three hours at least, much of which would be in broad daylight, at Pyongyang's busiest petrol station, on a working day. JJ was more than crestfallen. All the work that had gone into disguising the tankers, Vincent Barakat's brilliant sunbeds, Harold McFarlane's outstanding modifications. It was all a waste of time. They were going to have to get the gold across the border in the van.

"Iceman, if you really really had to, I mean no choice in the matter, get to the South from here, illegally and in a hurry, how would you do it?" asked JJ. The Iceman did not like this question. Victor didn't seem over the moon about it either. They thought the plan was to cross the border peacefully, admittedly with fake papers, in the cab of a disguised petrol tanker. The Iceman pondered awhile.

"From here, the border is about 150km away, as the car drives. At speed it would take us over an hour, less than an hour and a half. There are three checkpoints before the border crossing at Kaesŏng, these being Chollima, Songnim and Hwangu. Songnim is the most heavily manned by the people's army. However, as soon as we would rush the first crossing, the others would be alerted. It would be a firefight at Songnim and we would lose."

"Can we go off-road, around any of them?" asked JJ, not yet prepared to throw in the towel.

"Possibly Chollima, though that would be a bit of a dice roll," replied the Iceman. "Hwangu, yes, it's often manned by only a few soldiers with decrepit rifles, but definitely not Songnim. No, not Songnim. The checkpoint there is heavily fortified – the docks and all that."

JJ was still mulling over the options when the van and the jeep pulled into the petrol station's trailer park. Their PetroChina tankers were still there, pity they were just one big lump, or two to be precise, of useless metal, rubber and sunbed. There was not much activity in the trailer park right now but there would be. It was just before 6.20am so men and metal beasts would soon be

338

as one. JJ beckoned to the team to huddle round, they needed a brief time-out. Everyone was ears akimbo.

"Look," said JJ. "Well done everyone back at the bank. At this point we've pulled off the biggest bank job in history and killed no one in the process. Victor's grandfather would be very proud." JJ smiled at Victor and everybody gave him a nod, a wink or a thumbs up. "That was the good news. The not so good news is that we are sans 'Toblerones'. We had to leave them behind. At a reasonable guess, it would now take us three hours to load by hand all the gold into the tankers' sunbeds. This place will be buzzing in half an hour. We'd just get caught. Simple as that."

"Any bright ideas?" asked Jim.

"Not any that will keep us alive, gold intact, and out of the hands of the secret police," replied JJ. "We could try to rush the checkpoints and crash through… but the Iceman tells me we would have three checkpoints to negotiate before the border crossing and that we would not survive a firefight at Songnim, where the military would be waiting for us."

Lily and Jim nodded. Local knowledge was against the checkpoint crashing option.

"Can't we just bribe the guards at the checkpoints?" asked Ethel, ever one for the old-fashioned, bloodless ways.

"In most countries, Ginger," replied JJ, "that would be a good idea. Here in the DPRK, the guards wouldn't know what to do with a bar of gold or a fistful of dollars. Jesus, we even had to assure the kidnapped moaner Ji-hun that he was being bribed with South Korean won. Unfortunately we don't have any South Korean won with us."

There was a silent pause, which seemed to last an eon, but was in fact a few seconds.

"I do," said Victor.

"I do what?" retorted JJ.

"I do have a wad of won," Victor replied.

"How did you get that? Never mind I know how you got it, chief of the safe cracking clan. How much do you have?"

Victor unzipped his backpack and brought out four, thick wrapped packets of crisp South Korean won.

"How much is there?" asked Ethel, not sure if she should be super proud of her opportunistic CI or bemoaning his genetic lack of honesty.

JJ took one of the wrapped packets of notes from Victor. "They look about the same size as the US dollar packets we've got in the jeep. Each packet should have about 200 notes in it. These are 50,000 South Korean denomination notes, so, around won 10 million in each packet. At yesterday's USD/KRW exchange rate $38,000 in total," concluded JJ.

Everybody was impressed by JJ's foreign exchange knowledge, except Victor who had mistakenly thought he'd purloined himself a small fortune from the DPRK central bank. With won in hand, JJ was working on a plan. Under intense time pressure it was not likely to be a great plan but they couldn't hang about all day in a DPRK trailer park; that was for sure.

As the Scot's brain was whirring and clanking away, the Iceman's cell phone vibrated. It was a text message from deep cover Kwon. "It's Kwon," announced Kim Chun-So.

"For fuck's sake!" exhaled Jim Bradbury. "Has that moaner Ji-hun bolted?"

The Iceman read his message and then replied. "Kwon says that there was some major commotion at the Haeju docks last night. He doesn't know exactly what but his information is that many military personnel and secret police are either there or on their way there today. No mention of the moaner." The Iceman was half expecting some kind of response to deep cover Kwon's news, but none was forthcoming. JJ was pacing a little, in a circle, and still behind the Sprinter van. He was juggling casually with Victor's won. After a few minutes he spoke.

"Right, here's what we're going to do." JJ proceeded to outline his plan to the team. The petrol tankers may come in useful, after all. Jim was to drive one and the Iceman the other. They had the correct change of clothes and decent forged papers. They could both speak Korean. They would approach the checkpoint at Chollima first. The van and jeep would go off-road at this crossing. JJ and Victor in the van, Lily and Ethel in the jeep. Lily had his sniper's rifle so he would keep the checkpoint guards in his sight until Jim and the Iceman were safely through, then re-join them on the other side. If Kwon's intel was correct, the main road from Pyongyang to Hwangu would be busy today with military vehicles. After Hwangu there would be nothing because that was where the military would need to turn off to take the road to Haeju docks. The guards at Hwangu would likely let the petrol tankers and other civilian vehicles through swiftly so as not to delay the military and secret police. That left two problems, the Songnim checkpoint and the Kaesŏng border crossing. Songnim was the immediate problem. If there had been a major incident at one of the DPRK's west coast docks, the military would not want to leave undermanned a second set of west coast docks. The checkpoint at Songnim was likely to be fully manned and fortified.

The first part of JJ's revised plan worked well. The Chollima checkpoint was lightly guarded. The Iceman, in the lead tanker, was questioned by one of the guards and had his papers checked. He was cleared and the guard then just waved the second PetroChina tanker through. Jim Bradbury had donned his baseball hat and the guards never gave him a second look. Lily, meanwhile, had found the disused farm dirt road that Kwon had told him about. There was a field to negotiate but it was fortunately flat enough and solid enough not to give the heavyweight van any problems. As the PetroChina tankers drew close to the checkpoint, the van and jeep stopped in the field. Lily got into the back of the jeep, lay flat and set up his CheyTac M200 rifle. He was about 1,500 metres away from the Chollima guard's head, so well within the range of this rifle. It was not needed. Once the tankers were through, Lily packed up his rifle. Jeep and van then re-joined the convoy a few hundred metres down the road.

Songnim was next. The population of this city was around 150,000, similar to that of Springfield, Massachusetts. The main industry was a steel processing plant but its access to nearby rivers meant it was also involved in the transportation of raw materials and finished goods. Then there were the docks which could accommodate ships of 4,000 tons weight or slightly more. There were no off-road options to circumnavigate the Songnim checkpoint. The team's four vehicles would need to get through on the main road.

JJ's convoy was now in the order of van, then jeep, with the two tankers lagging a little behind. As they approached the Songnim checkpoint there was a small queue heading south as they were, and no queue heading north. The Sprinter van was being driven by JJ, the jeep by Lily. From a distance of about 200 metres from the back of the queue, JJ could see four soldiers at the checkpoint, inspecting vehicles and their occupants. Two further military guards in low height towers were acting as spotters, on either side of the raised barrier, and what appeared to be a small billet which probably housed no more than half a dozen back-up soldiers. Directly below the watchtowers, JJ could see the outline of two military jeeps, probably of Chinese origin. These dark green jeeps could carry four soldiers in addition to the driver and front seat passenger.

"OK, Jim, your time has come, good luck," said JJ, talking softly into his AN/PRO-148 walkie-talkie, a state of the art secure multi-band satellite transmitter and radio.

"Roger that, chief."

Seconds later, Jim Bradbury drove his PetroChina tanker sideways across both lanes of Highway One, screeching his brakes as he applied full lock. The Iceman, in the second tanker, travelling at close to no miles per hour, drove his tanker broadside into Jim's. The Iceman, effectively invisible to the ground and watchtower guards, due to Jim's tanker providing cover, leapt out of his cabin, stayed low and dropped into a ditch at the side of the road, making his way quietly along the ditch towards the jeep driven by Lily. The four soldiers on barrier duty saw the tanker chaos. Two of them stayed in their positions, pointing their rifles at the lead cars in the southbound queue and yelling at them not to move. The other two ran past JJ's van and Lily's jeep on their way to the sideways tanker. Jim Bradbury was already out of his cabin, but he had no opportunity to hit the ditch. Realising this he feigned injury and started staggering around, leaning against the tanker as he willie-wobbled his way towards the side of the road.

The running soldiers were on him in a flash. One stood rooted to the spot, aiming his rifle at Jim's head, the other had pushed Jim to the ground and was bawling at him in Korean. Jim understood what he was raving about.

"Get down you slimy dog, foreign idiot," were the choicest of the plethora of insults coming Jim's way. The pushing guard demanded Jim's papers and told him not to move a muscle, presumably over and above the ones he needed to get his papers.

JJ could make out some of the action from his offside exterior mirror. The guards were not likely to let Jim go. The incident at Haeju docks had them all twitchy and here was a foreign git,

American to boot, just lost control of a disguised Chinese petrol tanker at one of the DPRK's key checkpoints. Jim Bradbury was going nowhere. JJ glanced at his interior mirror and saw the thumbs up from Ethel. Lily must be in the back of the jeep, so at least that was good.

"Victor," said JJ, "this may seem a bit late in the day, but can you drive?"

"Sure," said Victor, still a bit rattled by ongoing events.

"OK, I need to get out of the van. When I do, get into the driver's seat, and be ready to take off like a fucking demon with its arse on fire when I return."

Victor nodded. He had a clear vision of a demon with its rear end on fire and it would surely be moving fast to quench that burn. JJ slipped out of the van, the guards at the barrier still had their full attention on the lead car in the queue. The watchtower soldiers were focussed on the kerfuffle at Jim's tanker. JJ lay on the ground between the rear of his van and the front of Lily's jeep. Silently, he removed his crossbow from its harness on his back, had a firm hold of its hand grip and was scanning through its reticle. Without looking, JJ took one of the arrows from its quiver. He had a dozen arrows with him, gold tipped, carbon and graphite shafted Expedition Hunter arrows, with three green and red vanes. JJ had the watchtower guard with the clearest view of Jim Bradbury, in his sights. It was a grim morning, occasionally raining, with near full cloud cover. JJ could also see the other watchtower guard. He too was following the petrol tanker action. Crossbows tend to be less efficient than longbows in the sense that a skilled longbow man could release two to four arrows for every crossbow shot. However, crossbows are better at close quarters. They tend to be more accurate, require less upper body strength to reload and are more manageable. JJ's was light, compact, had a telescopic sight and pistol grip. He was not going to miss. He didn't. JJ's first arrow penetrated the head of the watchtower guard through his right ear. He crumpled, dead before he had fully hit the ground. Apart from the muffled sound of the guard and his rifle tumbling to the wooden floor of his watchtower there was no noise. JJ didn't hang about to see if anyone had noticed the missing watchtower guard, he swivelled on his belly and reloaded. From pull, to load, to shoot took JJ about ten to fifteen seconds. It seemed a lot longer but the second watchtower guard had not budged from his observation spot. JJ fired. Second watchtower guard went down. This time the arrow penetrated the soldier's carotid artery. Blood exploded everywhere from his neck and there must have been a second or two of gurgling from the doomed guard. At ground level, however, nothing was heard.

Engines were ticking over, guards were shouting at Jim and conversing loudly amongst themselves. With JJ on the deck and Ethel sitting in the jeep's passenger seat, she could not see her former trainee. She did notice, however, that the watchtower guards had disappeared from view, so she had a good idea what had gone down. Keeping her head low and indicating to Lily that she was going to step outside, Ethel slipped out of the jeep. She crouched down near the front of the jeep and spotted JJ, still in the prone position, crossbow reloaded.

"Hey, Tell of Switzerland," whispered Ethel. "Been firing at apples?"

"Just Adam's apples," responded JJ. "Ginger, those guards are never going to let Jim go. We need to neutralise them. I can get the standing one but I won't have time to reload to get the one that's currently got Jim by the throat."

"I can take him out," said Ethel, without a flinch and simultaneously taking her Glock 17 out of its holster and attaching its titanium suppressor.

"Good," said JJ. "You'll need to get quite close. Go round the back of the jeep. When you see the standing guard fall, the other one will probably let Jim go and turn to see what's happening. Drop him. Then get Jim and yourself back in the jeep and go like a bat out of hell. I'll sprint for the van as soon as I've loosed my arrow. Victor's prepped to go. The barrier guards will fire on us but there're only two of them now. We'll barge our way through. Good luck." With that JJ resumed his attack position. He counted to three then fired. The standing guard was down. The soldier that had been holding Jim turned and saw his comrade collapse. Before he could respond, Ethel was standing a few metres away and fired, pop, pop, pop. Three bullets, two in the chest, one in his left leg. The soldier was down, but he was still alive.

As Ginger's third shot hit its mark, JJ had scrambled back into the front passenger seat of the van. Victor engaged first gear, pulled out of the queue and floored the accelerator. Ethel and a slightly shaken Jim were a second or two behind as Jim tumbled into the back of the jeep next to the Iceman. Ethel was now in her seat. The two barrier guards took a few seconds to react. Victor had sped over the crossing before the barrier could be fully in its lowered position. The guards fired at the van but hit nothing bar metal. By the time Lily had reached the crossing in the jeep, the barrier was down. He went right through it. The guards fired at the jeep, glass shattered but no one seemed hurt. The soldiers in the billet were now scrambling through its door and heading for their jeeps to give chase.

Van and jeep sped down the road. The Hwangu checkpoint was only twenty kilometres away. Even though it was loaded to the gunnels the augmented Sprinter van could still easily do 60-70mph, the local jeep too with some strain. They would be upon that checkpoint in under fifteen minutes. Long enough for the Hwangu soldiers to be prepared but not long enough for the chasing soldiers to catch them if they ever could in their antiquated Chinese jeeps.

"Jim," said Ethel. "Are you OK?"

"Fine, Ethel, thanks. Good job back there, that gook was really pressing on my throat. I don't know how he expected me to answer his fucking inane questions when I couldn't breathe."

"No problem," replied Ethel as she winced and felt nauseous. "Jim, I think I've been hit," said Ethel, knowing full well that she had, both from the pain and the bright red blood that was on her hand holding her shoulder. Jim and the Iceman carefully manoeuvred Ethel into the back of the jeep. Droplets of her blood splattered the cash, good job it was wrapped, thought the Iceman. It was tight in the back as the cash took up quite a chunk of space. Jim climbed into the front passenger seat while the Iceman got out the emergency medical supplies and tended to Ethel.

"JJ, come in, it's Jim," said Bradbury speaking into the walkie-talkie.

"Jim, you OK?"

"I'm fine, JJ, but Ethel is hit."

"Is it bad, can you fix her up?" asked JJ, with deep concern in his voice, he really liked Ethel.

"It's a shoulder wound. The Iceman is patching her up, but she's lost some blood so she'll need to go to a hospital soon," the KLO informed his friend.

"OK, do your best. I'll figure out what to do. We're about ten minutes from Hwangu now. Once we're through there we should have a straight run to Kaesŏng. Tell Ginger to hang in there. She's a top girl."

"Will do," said Jim.

Ten minutes can seem like a long or short time depending on what you're up to. Waiting for the dentist, it's way too short. One – nil up for your team in the final of the Champions League, it's way too long. Being chased by North Korean soldiers before the next checkpoint, it seemed way too long. For Ethel it was too long. In reality, it was all the same.

"Victor, don't slow, just go," instructed JJ. The Scot had decided that their two vehicle convoy was simply going to crash through the Hwangu checkpoint. Normally, that checkpoint was lightly guarded, less than a handful of soldiers. The incident at Haeju dock probably meant that no extra military could be re-deployed to Hwangu. It was a gamble, but Ethel's condition meant there could be no pussyfooting around. Victor did as directed. He put the pedal to the metal and the Sprinter van was bearing down on the checkpoint. The jeep was struggling to keep up and Lily was virtually standing on the accelerator so the gap to the van was not widening. To the rear, there was no sign of chasing Chinese jeeps.

The barrier at the Hwangu checkpoint was down and in place. There was one jeep and three guards behind it. No watchtower and no extra billeted soldiers. Victor was visibly apprehensive. JJ could see that.

"Victor, it's a straight run," said JJ, hoping to steady the young safe cracker's nerves. "Stay low. You'll break the barrier no problem, given the weight of this van, and you'll knock their toy jeep out of the way easily."

Victor was reassured. He didn't lift. The soldiers were firing, zip, zip, crash. Two bullets into the windscreen, no human injuries. Crash went the barrier, the soldiers' jeep moved at least ten yards and toppled. The soldiers were down, dazed but alive. Victor looked up. No more obstacles on the road ahead. JJ checked Lily's jeep from the interior mirror. Seemed OK. They were through and clear, no more checkpoints till Kaesŏng, a mere twenty to twenty-five miles away. They were twenty minutes' drive away from the border crossing but only fifteen minutes before the security detail at the central bank was changed and the alarm raised. This was going to be tight.

"Jim," said the Scot into his walkie-talkie. "Everybody OK?"

"We are," replied Jim. "We didn't take a shot this time. You guys OK?"

"We're fine. Victor was wicked," replied JJ using the modern meaning of the word, to indicate not wicked, but excellent.

The convoy settled back into its high speed rhythm. JJ continued to chat to Jim for a few minutes, enquiring after Ethel and checking that his CIA friend knew what to do at the Kaesŏng crossing. Ethel was drifting in and out of consciousness. She needed hospitalised ASAP. As they hurtled towards the border, Jim was on his secure cell phone arranging for his team at PAU Travel to get an ambulance with paramedics to be in situ for their arrival. It would be done. Ethel would go to the main hospital in Seoul, world renowned, and with a staff eminently capable of dealing with gunshot wounds.

★ ★ ★

The Korean People's Air Force has an estimated attack helicopter force of between one and two hundred, ranging from the lightweight modified MD-500 to the heavyweight troop transporting gunship, the Mi-24. At least half of these are kitted out as training aircraft, and are located at several bases in the North. The nearest KPA helicopter base to JJ's convoy was located in Taetan County, not far from Hwangu. This base, today, had two operational Mi-2 light transport and light combat helicopters and one modified MD-500. The rest of the helicopters were either out of commission, being serviced or at Haeju docks. The helicopter crew at the Taetan base and on call, belonged to one of the modified MD-500s. This was an old helicopter, from the 1980s, ironically manufactured in South Korea and built in the USA. Initially, it had no attack capabilities, but had been modified by the KPA's aeronautical engineers to be a lightweight gunship. Maximum crew of five, with three in the one that was whirring overhead JJ's convoy.

Before expiring for good, the DPRK soldier Ethel had shot, managed to raise the alarm. The call for help was relayed to the Hwangu checkpoint, the secret police and the closest air base, which was at Taetan. Secret police were all over Haeju docks, or helping to interrogate Vice Admiral Goh and Commodore Park, now in detention in the capital. JJ and team were only ten minutes from the border crossing. The secret police could not get to them in time and the Hwangu checkpoint had been gate-crashed and rendered ineffective. There was a risk that one of the KPA's MiG jet fighters would be scrambled to hunt down the van. The nearest MiG base was at Hwangu, but many of the operational fighter jets stationed there were out submarine hunting. It was close, but JJ's team may just have enough time. The helicopter overhead may be the DPRK's last realistic chance to kill or capture the fleeing foreigners before they reached the border crossing.

"Jim, do you hear the chopper?" asked JJ.

"Yes. Can't see it yet but it must be near."

"There's no street or road lights here and there won't be any until Kaesŏng. Kill your jeep's lights and drive off the main road behind a tree or something. We'll do the same. We don't have any anti-aircraft weapons in the van. Check with Lily and the Iceman, they may have taken something heavy with them."

"OK, JJ, I'm on it," said Jim. With that both vehicles drove off the main road. It was morning, but it was a bleak, wet day, it may as well have been early evening from a visual acuity perspective. Both van and jeep were dark in colour, the attack helicopter may not spot them. No such luck.

"Lily, have you got anything to shoot a helicopter?" asked Jim.

"Not really," replied Kim Min-Jun. "I've got my sniper's rifle but that's a bit hit and miss when it comes to downing choppers."

The Iceman was still in the back of the jeep, tending to Ethel, who had now lapsed fully into unconsciousness.

"Iceman, got anything to zap a fucking chopper, we could be under attack in a minute?" asked Bradbury, with increasing alarm.

"Not anything reliable, Jim, but I brought along my grenade launcher just in case," replied Kim Chun-So. The M203 grenade launcher presently being extracted from the Iceman's kit bag was an oldie but goldie. First designed in the late 60s the launch device could be attached to a US M4 Carbine, which was the Iceman's second rifle of choice. It was a single shot weapon which could launch five to seven of its grenades per minute. Its most effective distance was about 150 metres with a maximum range of 400 metres. It was the best option the team had.

Jim told Lily and the Iceman to get out of the jeep with their weapons and to keep their eyes peeled for the helicopter. They did not need to wait long. The KPA's MD-500 came swooping out of the low lying clouds. It had spotted the van first and started to pepper it with shots from its gun, floor mounted and operated by one of the KPA's airmen. JJ and Victor had already got out of the van and were hunkered down underneath a tree which was behind the offside of the van. JJ's weapons would be useless to defend this attack, and Victor had his hands over his head, as if that would do much good if the airman got his eye in.

There wasn't much to an MD-500 but that was a double-edged sword. Its weapons were dated and lightweight but it was a small helicopter and a bit zippy, with a maximum speed of 175mph, difficult to hit. Lily had let loose a couple of rounds from his high-powered sniper's rifle but with no apparent results.

The KPA chopper was still focussed on the van. It came

351

around for round two and the van's exterior had a few more ventilation holes in it. Fortunately, all eight tyres were intact and inflated. The attack helicopter did not make a third foray. The Iceman was on his game. The first launched grenade took out the chopper's gunman and the second one the rotor. The MD-500 burst into flames and ended up in a field a few hundred yards from the team. JJ and Victor got back in the van, this time JJ took the wheel. Jim had stayed in the jeep, protecting Ethel, and Lily and the Iceman got back in and stowed their weapons. There was no sign of pursuing Chinese jeeps from Songnim. They had given up the chase at Hwangu. Ten minutes to the border crossing, no time to lose.

It was still raining, with the preponderance of dark, grey low-lying cloud suggesting that there would be no let-up in the immediate future. The crossing would not be busy at this time of day. Most of the workers and transporters coming from South to North were still to pass later in the morning and those that were returning would not do so until the evening. This was an impossible crossing to storm. There were one hundred metres or so of black and yellow metal barriers before the actual border itself. These were intended to slow down approaching vehicles. There were armed soldiers on side walls just in case they didn't and more soldiers in little security glass-fronted boxes. The border military knew they may need to apprehend or kill some fugitives from justice, travelling in a big van and a jeep. JJ had anticipated as much and his plan for this stage of their escape was now in play.

Lily drove up to the side of the van and both vehicles proceeded at around 5mph towards the main crossing. The side wall DPRK guards had their weapons trained on the vehicles but did not fire. JJ had his right arm out of the van's window in a half gesture of surrender. Victor did the same with his left arm. Lily in the jeep adjacent followed suit. About ten yards from the line that separated North and South Korea, JJ stopped his van and Lily brought his jeep to a halt as well. JJ and Victor got out with their hands held aloft, showing clearly to the guards that they were not carrying weapons. Lily did the same. Two guards approached the van, rifles loaded and extended. They gestured to JJ and Victor to get on their knees. They did as ordered. Two further guards approached Lily. With hands aloft and still standing he began a conversation with the soldiers. At rifle point, Lily led the guards to the back of the jeep. He opened the door. The guards espied a huge pile of cash, and an unconscious woman. They also saw the barrels of Jim's SIG Sauer and the Iceman's rifle. Team PAU Travel had the drop on the guards. Lily kept talking. The DPRK border guards shouted for their colleagues guarding JJ and Victor to join them. As they turned behind the van and looked into the jeep, JJ took out his gun from the rear of his pants and had his Glock 17 nestling against the small of one of the guard's backs. Victor had his right forefinger nudging the back of the other guard. He shrugged at JJ, he had left his gun in his kit bag. The side wall guards could not make out what was going on. The MiG-29 that was flying overhead spotted that the fugitives seemed to be in the hands of the border guards so did not intervene. Lily continued to speak. Three of the four guards nodded and the fourth one just listened.

"JJ, it's OK for you to get back in the van. Victor get in the driver's side of the jeep and both of you drive at walking pace to the barrier. It will be up when you get there. I'll continue to walk behind the jeep with my new friends here," said Lily.

JJ and Victor did as asked. The van and the jeep began to move very slowly. Lily and the four soldiers walked behind the jeep, whose rear door was still open. The guards had lowered their rifles but the Iceman and Jim Bradbury still had them solidly in their gun sights. As they crossed the border, van, jeep, guards and Lily kept going. While they would need to cross properly into South Korea in a few minutes, they were out of the jurisdiction of the DPRK. The van and jeep stopped. The guards put their rifles on the ground. Jim and the Iceman lowered their weapons but kept a hold of them.

JJ and Victor got out of the van and went to the rear of the jeep. The two of them and Lily handed each guard a wad of won. As part of the negotiation led by Lily, each guard received a packet of US$100 bills as well. They would now cross into South Korea together. Jim's colleagues at PAU, as well as waiting with an ambulance for Ethel also had cars available to take the now defecting North Korean military guards to the CIA offices in Seoul. They would be processed and allowed to stay after a comprehensive de-brief. The listening guard was the only one with close family in the North. Lily promised that he would arrange for them to be taken to a safe house in a rural area. Deep cover Kwon would then work his magic to get them across the border at a later date. At least 25,000 North Koreans had defected to the South, now there were four more.

Ethel may be unconscious in the back of a dilapidated, copycat North Korean jeep, but it was her idea to grease the palms of the willing that had seen them safely across the border. Top girl, thought JJ with deep feeling and the hint of a tear in his grey-green eyes.

9

THE GOAT LOCKER

"Where's the gold?" asked Ethel, weak but alive.

"It's in the van in one of Jim's locked up garages. The van's being re-painted and fixed up. A bit like yourself!" replied JJ, so glad that Ethel had survived and was recuperating on schedule. Ethel was in a private room at the Seoul National University Hospital (SNUH). After the border crossing, the paramedics and two CIA officers from PAU Travel had taken her straight there. She had an emergency operation on her shoulder, the bullet removed and a blood transfusion given. SNUH was the oldest and most respected hospital in Seoul with a busy and effective emergency department. After surgery she was transferred to the private room. Jim Bradbury had sorted out the paperwork and calmed down the local police. As KLO, he had done them a few favours in the past, now it was time to call in one of them. Two of the PAU Travel office's operatives were standing guard at Ethel's door. Probably not necessary, thought JJ and Jim, but just in case any North Korean undercover types or all too nosey paparazzi were floating about, it seemed reasonable to take the precaution.

"I don't remember much, JJ, after shooting that guard at Songnim. Is everybody OK?" asked Ethel, struggling to get comfortable with her gammy shoulder and multitude of tubes attached to her.

"Everybody's fine," replied JJ with a smile. "A few cuts and bruises, and Jim's got a gowping throat where one of the soldiers tried to strangle him, the way he tells it."

"Victor?" asked Ethel, needing to know some more detail about her CI and mission ward.

"Victor's great, Ginger," said JJ. "He's knackered in body, mind and soul but he was brilliant. He was here until about an hour ago. You were asleep. I sent him to his hotel so he could just conk out." Ethel nodded weakly, she could be drifting in and out of complete consciousness for a while due to the meds she was on and the trauma her body had experienced.

"How did we get through the border crossing at Kaesŏng, was there another firefight?"

"It's involved. I don't want to wear you out with all the details. Suffice to say that it was your idea to bribe the guards that got us across. You were absolutely fabulous Ginger, so rest and recover," encouraged JJ. "You're going to have to stay here a while. Your shoulder is a bit of a mess and although the doctors expect a near full recovery it will take time, rest, physio, the whole works. Victor is going to stay with you, here in Seoul, until you can travel back to London in comfort. He doesn't want to see a safe for a while."

"He's a good boy," said Ethel, not in the frame of mind to argue or physically ready for a long conversation.

"I'll square things with your people in the force and your husband. You can call them from here but I'll go see them anyway," said JJ.

"Thanks," replied Ethel.

"I'll need to get back to London, sharpish, Ginger," continued JJ, desperate to see Cyrus and needing to get the rest of the mission back on track.

"I know, JJ, I hope it turns out as planned."

"It probably won't Ginger but I'll give it a go. In case I forget to tell you, or you wake up one morning wondering why you've got a hole in your shoulder, when I return to London I'll get the money transferred to your offshore account."

"£250,000?" interrupted Ethel, clearly her brain didn't have a hole in it.

"More like a few million. You can thank Victor for that too since he was the one whose idea it was to purloin some cash," replied JJ.

"Oooh…" said Ethel enthusiastically. "Maybe I can afford triplets!" They both laughed. It was more painful for one of them, as was the gentle hug that JJ gave Ethel.

JJ had a lot on his mind, but as he left Ethel's room, he turned, waved and said, "See you soon, top girl."

JJ left the hospital and got in a cab for PAU Travel in Gangnam. The journey would not take long, maybe twenty minutes. Enough time to get his priorities in order, he thought. First, was a call to Cyrus and Gil. He hadn't been in touch for a couple of days and they would be worried about him as he was about them. Second, he needed to call the shit faced asshole known as Neil Robson. The plan had been revised, no petrol tankers with liquid gold in them so Robson was going to need to organise alternative air transport to get van, gold and cash back to the UK. Then he'd need to phone Fathead, get him prepped for the complex task ahead of selling a van load of bullion and to check that he wasn't being missed too much at MAM. Last but not least, JJ hoped that he'd see Carolyn at PAU Travel. They'd been estranged for a long time but the dinner they had before he went North had been good and, he hoped, began to re-establish a solid bond with his daughter.

★ ★ ★

"Commander," said Garrison Whitton walking briskly to the conn.

"Gary," responded O'Neill who looked up from the map that he and Evan Harris were studying, beginning to plot their route to Scotland.

"We have a problem, Sir," said Whitton.

"What kind of problem, Gary?" responded the SEALs team leader.

"I think you'd better come with me Sir," replied Whitton, barely waiting for his commander's agreement before heading off. O'Neill followed the young medic a few seconds behind.

"We found him, Sir, a stowaway, in the goat locker," said Whitton, pointing to a small oriental fellow in the uniform of a Korean People's Navy seaman. He currently seemed to be a little taller as Billy Smith had him hoisted by his shirt front against one of the submarine's interior panels. O'Neill's face was a picture, not a Van Gogh, more like one of those disturbed Francis Bacon efforts.

"What's he doing on my sub, in my quarters?" O'Neill asked, feeling really agitated but just about managing to keep it under control.

"He must have been on the sub, when we took it," ventured Billy Smith, trying to be helpful but surely stating the bleedin' obvious.

"We haven't a clue what he's saying, commander," added Whitton. "He's been mumbling away in Korean, doesn't appear to speak any English. The only word we can make out is 'Kim'."

"That'll narrow it down to a few billion," interjected Smith, not really upping the quality of his contributions to the problem solving. Mark O'Neill was thinking. It would be a bit much just to shoot the Korean, he thought, but they could not take him back to Haeju, albeit that they weren't that far away, they couldn't surface and they did not have enough food for themselves for the journey to Scotland, let alone to feed a random Kim on board. O'Neill had not reached a conclusion when Garrison Whitton piped up again.

"The problem may be worse, Sir. The stowaway's sweating away, keeps pointing to his head as if it's sore. I quickly took his temperature once Billy had subdued him. It's 102°F. It could be something straightforward but it might not be. I've only limited medical equipment with me but I can do some investigation."

"Do it Gary, and let me know as soon as you have an idea. In the meantime, isolate the Kim and get Ding to start disinfecting the living quarters. Billy, if he's got the pox you might have it too, so don't go wandering anywhere around the sub. Stay here," said O'Neill.

"Yes, Sir," responded Billy Smith, pushing the KPN man a little harder into the sub's panels, clearly not happy that he may have been exposed to some Korean lurgy.

"Billy," said O'Neill.

"Sir?" Smith responded.

"Lower the fellow down to his full, short, height. I don't suppose he deliberately got himself sick."

"Yes, Sir," replied Smith, letting Kim go. Mark O'Neill returned swiftly to the conn to consult with his number two, Evan Harris. Whitton was on his laptop, searching for possible contenders for Kim's sickness, Ding was disinfecting the living quarters, made slightly more complex because Kim had now vomited on the floor and on Billy Smith's boots.

"Evan," began O'Neill. "We've got an issue. The gist of it is that we have a KPN stowaway on board, who can't speak a word of English, and who has a fever of some sort. Gary is investigating. While he's doing that, you need to check if there's anywhere we can safely surface without detection. We may need to get him off the sub." Evan Harris took it in. No time for questions, he went back to his map, but shifted his focus a lot closer to their current position than Scotland. O'Neill had instructed Tony Fairclough and David McCoy to slow the borey's speed. He didn't go into a detailed explanation, after all it may be a storm in a teacup, but he also didn't want the submarine to be going at full pelt if they had to change their target destination. Gary Whitton returned to the conn to find O'Neill. The commander saw him coming.

"Gary, any news?"

"My preliminary research suggests it might be measles, Sir. He's got a rash, headache, joint pain, I think, and his temperature is still rising," said Whitton.

"That's not the end of the world, then, is it?"

"No, Sir, if it's measles, he'll be laid low for a few days, then probably recover," agreed Whitton.

"I was thinking more about the infection risk to the rest of us, Gary," pointed out O'Neill.

"I'll check with the men as to who has and who has not had measles, Sir, and report back," said Whitton as he was departing the conn. O'Neill turned his attention to Harris and his map.

"The problem may not be as big as we thought Evan, but did you come up with anything?" asked O'Neill.

"Our current position is not that far from Jejudo Island, Mark. It's a volcanic island off the south coast of South Korea. It's not active from the lava-chucking perspective but it does have a relatively new naval base and it's in friendly waters," replied Harris. Mark O'Neill nodded, that was a good find he thought even if, in all probability, they wouldn't need it now. That thought hadn't fully crystallised in Mark O'Neill's mind, when Gary Whitton came running back onto the conn.

"Sir," he said.

"It's not measles. The Kim's blood pressure is really low and he's bleeding from his nose. I plugged all of the symptoms into my medical app, Sir," said Whitton.

"What is it, then?" snapped O'Neill, clearly anxious to be in the know.

"I can't be certain, commander, but it may be Dengue Fever, and the stowaway may have gone into Dengue shock syndrome already."

"Is he going to die, is the crew at risk?" asked O'Neill.

"Without proper medical treatment he will probably die in a few days. Statistically, there is a low probability of the crew catching the fever, but…"

"But what?" interjected O'Neill, with no patience to listen to a long, drawn out medical theory.

"The Kim's been in the goat locker for a while, he's drunk our water, he's thrown up over our floor and Billy Smith's boots, his body fluids are, not to put too fine a point on it, leaking everywhere," elaborated Witton. "The incubation period for this kind of fever has a modal time of three to six days, Sir. If any of the crew have been infected they will likely be very sick and rendered helpless well before we reach our destination."

"Well that's just fine and fucking dandy!" said O'Neill with feeling. "Sorry Gary, not your fault, sometimes it's tough being the messenger," he quickly added, placing his hand on the medic's shoulder.

"Sir?" said Whitton.

"Yes, Gary," responded O'Neill.

"I suggest I check all the crew's temperatures regularly, at least twice a day. Along with a headache that will be the first symptom. Me, you, Billy Smith and Ding are the most likely to be at risk because we've been closest to the stowaway. We shouldn't risk the water, Sir. I know that just adds to the problem, but even on the low probability that it can be transmitted that way, it is a contamination risk."

"Thanks, Gary," said O'Neill. "Check the crew's temperatures. You may as well tell them why while you're at it. They'll know about the sick gook soon enough in any case."

"Yes, Sir," replied Whitton. The young medic then left. His role on this mission had suddenly been catapulted up the essential list. Mark O'Neill sat down next to Evan Harris. He didn't want to chat straightaway, he was thinking. Bonnie Scotland wasn't looking as close as it seemed an hour or so ago. Sick stowaway, can't drink the water, not enough food, and maybe not enough crew. This was a bag of laughs – not.

"Mark, what's the plan?" asked Evan Harris.

"The plan, Evan, is in its formative stages, as those war game wankers at the DoD would say when they haven't a clue. I haven't a clue just now. Let's take a look at that volcanic island of yours."

Jejudo Island is de facto one of South Korea's nine provinces, being coterminous with Jejudo province. It lies in the Korean Strait. It is volcanic but dormant, with a population of over half a million. Of most interest to Mark O'Neill, however, was that in 2007 the South Korean government designated Gongjeong, a village on the southern coast of the island to be the site of a new naval base. This base was intended to house twenty warships including submarines. The locals were not that happy about it and there were several protests including sit-ins and attempts to disrupt construction. The protests continued on the ground and in the law courts for several years as the issue became a cause celebre for many of the island's residents and its supporters. The naval facility, however, was now sufficiently completed that a Russian Borei class nuclear submarine could dock there, if required.

Jejudo Island was approximately 480km from the docks at Haeju. O'Neill and Harris reckoned that they could easily get there in ten hours, that wouldn't be a problem. What would, however, is that they would be required to inform the South Korean authorities that they would need access to the base. *Let's not get premature on that* thought O'Neill, *we'll wait for a further update from young Whitton*. The update was not long in coming but it was not what O'Neill wanted to hear.

"The stowaway is getting worse," advised Whitton. "His temperature is now 104°F and he's helpless. If he doesn't get hospitalised in twelve to twenty-four hours then he's toast. Ding has the beginnings of a sore head," he added.

"How about you, Gary?"

"I'm fine, Sir, so far. My temperature's steady at the 98.6°F norm, as is yours."

"Thanks Gary. Lieutenant Harris and I have a few things to figure out. Keep the sick as comfortable as you can, and let me know if anyone else is feeling rough." The medic went back to his patients.

"Evan, we're going to have to surface and dock at Jejudo. I don't see any other option. I don't care about the stowaway, he rolled the dice and took his chance, but if Ding and Billy are sick then this submarine is not manageable, we'll never complete our mission. Joe Franks has clearly got a busted leg and the incubation time for this Dengue Fever seems variable. More of the team could get ill in the next few days. Not only do we need to get the sickos off the boat we need at least two warm healthy bodies to replace them. We also need medicine, water and food. We've no choice but to surface," concluded O'Neill.

"It's a tall order," judged Evan Harris. "We're allies with the South Koreans and we defend them to the max, so we'll likely get the official OK to dock at Jejudo, but what about the North Koreans spotting us and who can we get to replace Ding and Billy?"

"The North Koreans won't spot us unless they've got a

satellite hovering over Jejudo. Their attack planes would not be allowed to get that far into South Korean air space before being shot down. Our sonars indicate that there are no surface or submersible sea vessels following us, not least of which because the stealth work on this beauty seems highly effective. There will probably be a few happy snappers at the Jejudo naval base. We can't help that but there are no markings on this sub and there may well be other subs already berthed. Unless some submariner spotting anorak happens to know a lot about naval vessels, their size, shape etc., we may get away with it. If we can organise it properly we might be visible for under thirty minutes," concluded O'Neill. Evan Harris was in agreement. There did not appear to be a better option. O'Neill would urgently contact John Adams at the CIA to ask him to get the authority from the South Koreans to dock.

"What about the healthy warm bodies to replace the sick even warmer bodies?" asked Harris. There were no navy SEALs teams in the area and any regular US marines or troops were stationed at or near the DMZ. Both Harris and O'Neill knew this.

"We might just need to be a bit clever on that one," replied O'Neill.

* * *

As JJ was entering PAU Travel in Gangnam, Carolyn Reynolds and Dannielle Eagles were exiting the undercover CIA offices.

"Hi Dad, bye Dad!" exclaimed Carolyn, very pleased to see JJ but clearly in something of a hurry.

"No, no, no, no bye Dad, Cally, what's going on?" asked JJ, equally pleased to see his daughter, if not her hasty exit.

"I could tell you, but then I'd have to kill you!" laughed Carolyn, with no real intention of patricide on her mind.

"You're one cheeky princess," responded JJ. "Take care on whatever you're up to. You too Dannielle,"

"Thanks Mr Darke," said Dannielle as Carolyn gave her father a warm hug and a kiss on the cheek.

"Later, gator," called Carolyn as she and Dannielle piled into one of the PAU Travel cars.

"Sure," replied JJ. JJ continued on into the PAU offices. He spied Jim Bradbury.

"Hey Jim," JJ called out. "Where are those two off to?"

"They tell me nothing around here JJ, I'm just the boss. All I know is that I got a call from John Adams. He's the CIA's Associate Director for Military Support and reports directly to the Director himself, Fred Goss. Adams knew that your daughter and Eagles were here and by his tone he also knew what they were up to. He said that they were required to join a top priority operation and that I should help them get their gear together and off to Gimpo airport."

"Their gear, what all their computers and stuff?" enquired JJ having a squint through the open door of the communications room, which still seemed packed with electronic equipment.

"It seems not," replied Jim. "Carolyn and Dannielle took their laptops and tablets with them but the trunk of that car is packed to the hilt with food, dozens of bottles of water and medical supplies. If they're off on a jaunt, it must be a dangerous, thirsty one."

JJ mulled over his friend's information. Carolyn was not of the mindset to pop off on a quick vacation while on a job. She'd also be inclined to seek out good restaurants with fine food, not take a load of packaged stuff with her, and she didn't drink that much water. JJ had no idea what his daughter was up to, but it sure wasn't a holiday.

The PAU Travel car taking Carolyn and Dannielle to the

helicopter pad at Gimpo airport was a Mercedes S-class, big car with a big trunk. The helicopter on the pad, awaiting its passengers, was an Mi-172 South Korean police commandoes transport chopper. It was of Russian construction and could carry up to thirty people, compared with only fifteen or so in a Blackhawk. Today, its occupants were not police commandoes, just two NGA officers, one paramedic and a whole lot of stuff. The airport was around 15km to the west of central Seoul. It had not taken the Mercedes long to get there and the flight time to Jejudo Island would be under two hours. It was a much brighter day than yesterday. While Carolyn and Dannielle checked their weapons and their surveillance equipment, the paramedic and the Mercedes driver loaded the food, drink and other supplies on board. The take-off was smooth and the journey seemed short.

"My god, Dannielle, there it is, the Borei," said Carolyn as she pointed her finger at the starboard window of the Mi-172, now nearing its destination. "It's squeezed in between what looks like a couple of Chang Bogo class subs," she continued, as their ride prepared to land at the naval base's helipad.

"They look a bit titchy by comparison," said Dannielle, perhaps feeling that size mattered when it came to submarines.

"They do," agreed Carolyn but hoping that the Borei class Russian sub did not stand out too much and attract unwanted attention. As the helicopter landed and its blades came to a halt, Carolyn and Dannielle could see Commander Mark O'Neill and another SEAL waiting for them. There also seemed to be a small, local ambulance beside the SEALs.

"Officers Reynolds and Eagles, good to see you both again," said O'Neill. The Commander wanted off the island ASAP. "I can fill you in with all the details when we're on board. For the moment we need to get all your gear off the chopper and onto the sub and those three sick people onto your helicopter." As the ambulance crew took out a stretcher with the stowaway Kim on it, attached to life-saving liquids, the NGA women also noticed that two navy SEALs were being helped into the Mi-172 as well.

"What's up with them?" asked Dannielle.

"The local is a KPN stowaway. We don't know if he deliberately stowed away or whether he was doing a check or something when we took the sub. He can't speak English but he's in a bad way and might not make it," replied O'Neill. "The other two are Billy Smith and Yang Dingbang from my team. They are showing some early symptoms of what's ailing the Korean, so we need them off the sub and into a hospital."

"What have they got?" asked Dannielle, thinking more of her own well-being than concern over the SEALs. Luckily, such self-centredness doesn't really show in a verbal question.

"Our medic is not 100% certain, but he thinks it's Dengue Fever. It can be contracted from mosquitoes. It's not easily transferred to other humans from the initial victim but it can be. It can be deadly in extreme cases. We couldn't take the chance with Billy and Ding. They could become helpless and may even spread the virus to the rest of the team. We probably wouldn't know for another two to four days. Then it would be too late to do anything. You ladies may be wondering why I requested you?" ventured O'Neill.

"We may," responded Carolyn before O'Neill could continue. "Don't think for one second, Commander, that I've forgotten your 'no girls on tour' comment to our boss, Henry Michieta." O'Neill had indeed forgotten and now that he had been reminded it was clearly in his interests not to defend his quip.

"Ah… forgotten about that, sorry. Clearly this is one tour where girls are allowed," he added meekly, recalling how feisty Reynolds was.

"Apology accepted," said Carolyn, grinning internally.

"We're not SEALs or submariners, Commander," said Dannielle. "How can we replace your two men?"

"We're operating the Borei with a skeleton crew. One of the guys, Joe Franks, broke his leg at Haeju. He's partly mobile now so that's OK. We couldn't manage the submarine for the rest of the mission with only seven SEALs. Billy Smith's main skill is as a sniper, and Ding's is radar. There are no other SEAL teams anywhere close and it would have taken too long and involved too much bureaucracy to get a couple of suitable marines transferred from the DMZ. You are both CIA trained, so you can shoot and since your main skill is surveillance for the NGA, I guessed you'd know something about radar," O'Neill explained.

"You guessed right, Commander," replied Carolyn. "Especially Dannielle, she's a dab hand with radar."

With supplies, crew and guests safely on board, Tommy Fairclough and David McCoy started up the submarine. In about ten minutes they would be far enough into the Korean Strait to submerge into deep water. Mark O'Neill and Evan Harris were on the conn and the Commander had asked his skeleton crew to gather round.

"Gentlemen, these are Officers Carolyn Reynolds and Dannielle Eagles of the NGA. These ladies were the ones who originally spotted this submarine berthed at the Haeju docks. They're CIA-trained so they can look after themselves. As of now they are members of this team and will take full part in ensuring that our mission is completed. Billy and Ding are on a helicopter headed for a hospital in Seoul. I will give you updates on their condition as soon as I have any. A section of the living quarters will be partitioned so that Reynolds and Eagles can have some privacy. I expect you all to respect that and behave, at all times, in a manner befitting a US Navy SEAL. Any questions?"

"What will the NGA officers' duties be, on board, Sir?" asked David McCoy.

"Officer Eagles will familiarise herself with the radar system on the sub and take over Ding's responsibilities for that. She can speak and read Russian. Officer Reynolds will assume Billy Smith's general duties. In addition, she is fluent in Korean so that will help in deciphering some of the instruction manuals we discovered," replied O'Neill. Carolyn wasn't so sure that she was 'fluent in Korean', but in the land of the blind, the one-eyed man is king, or in this case, queen. For a few minutes after O'Neill's introduction, Reyonlds and Eagles made the acquaintance of the rest of the crew. After that, O'Neill briefed the NGA women on their mission. Carolyn in particular, was both amazed and intrigued that they were headed for Scotland. Her dad would have loved that had he known. Carolyn was trying to figure out why O'Neill had been ordered to drive the Borei to Scotland. She knew about Faslane and she seemed to recall that many years ago there was a US submarine presence on the River Clyde, maybe called Polaris, she tried to remember, but was short on memory detail. The NGA officers spent the next thirty minutes or so familiarising themselves with the layout of the Borei. Dannielle Eagles was straight into the instructions for the radar and seemed to assimilate all necessary information in a short space of time. Carolyn had set up her laptop and tablet, but before using them she thought she'd better check with O'Neill on the protocol for electronic messaging. She didn't want a rogue transmission to attract any enemy interest.

"Are you settling in alright?" O'Neill asked Carolyn.

"Yes, Commander. I was just wondering about the protocol regarding use of electronic equipment on board?" O'Neill paused for a moment, he did like Carolyn Reynolds. She was a looker and clearly had the brains to go with it. In different circumstances he would surely ask her on a date.

"We've prohibited any personal use of mobiles, laptops, tablets etc. We can get a signal down here which is how we contacted John Adams at the CIA. Barry Minchkin essentially our chief engineer on board, reckons that our position would not be compromised unless the tracking system was close by, something to do with signal strength but we keep it to a minimum, just to be safe," answered O'Neill.

"Thank you, Commander," said Carolyn returning to her various electronic gizmos.

With that, O'Neill went to seek out Evan Harris, they needed to get back to mapping out the best route to Scotland, interrupted as they were by the stowaway and his attendant fever.

While members of the crew went about their business, ensuring the smooth operation of the submarine and maintaining its stealth 'invisibility', Dannielle Eagles was trying to figure out how to alert Igor Kruglov, head of the SVR and her ultimate boss. As far as Dannielle was concerned this was a Russian sub, stolen by Americans. It was a magnificent piece of Russian engineering, virtually silent because of the hydro-dynamically efficient hull which had a coating of anechoic tiles to reduce its acoustic signature to near silence. Even if there had been searching submarines or surface vessels in the vicinity, they would be most unlikely to locate this sub if it remained submerged between 400ft and 500ft below sea level. Sunwoo Chung's augmentation had made detection doubly unlikely, Dannielle could not use the submarine's computer system to contact Kruglov, it would be too obvious and could easily be checked or discovered by one of the navy SEALs. She could not use her laptop or tablet. Again, it was likely that her proximity to Carolyn or any other crew member would attract questions if she was tapping away on her keyboard. She concluded that the safest way was to turn on her satellite phone and leave it on, hidden somewhere in the submarine.

When the SVR issued Dannielle the phone, Kruglov said 'caveat utilitor' – let the user beware. Transmissions from satellite phones can be traced in several ways, through its own built-in GPS devices and by commercial tracking systems. The Polish firm TS2 and the Italian one Area Spa are well known for their signal tracking systems. Some people believe that it was the latter's equipment, sold to the Syrian government, which allowed the Assad regime's forces to lock on to the phone signals of two journalists and kill them with guided rocket attacks in February 2012 as they covered the assault on the Homs region.

Dannielle found an excellent hiding place for her phone. She attached it magnetically and left it on. Kruglov or anyone else at the SVR would not ring that phone. It was standard operating procedure that she alone made outgoing calls, no incoming ones were authorised. The technicians at the SVR might just pick up the signal. They would know whose phone it was and where the signal came from.

★ ★ ★

The SVR's headquarters are in Yasenevo, Moscow. It is an urban area, built up, and the most populous of the Russian capital's neighbourhoods. The SVR is effectively the successor to the foreign arm of the KGB. It is concerned with espionage and foreign counterintelligence work outside of Russia. The Director of the SVR reports directly to the President of Russia. Igor Kruglov was the senior one of two Deputy Directors and Dannielle Eagles' handler. Kruglov was promoted in late 2010. He was one of the few senior SVR officers who survived a cull after the disastrous break-up of the Illegals Program. This plan was to place deep-cover spy operatives in the United States, primarily targeting positions in US government and policy-making circles. At least ten of the Illegals were captured by the FBI after their undercover identities and positions were revealed by Alexander Poteyev who defected from his position as Deputy Head of Illegal Spies. The capture of ten Illegals was a major coup for the FBI. The Illegals covert activities had penetrated several key areas of the US government and, now, in one fell swoop the SVR program had more or less collapsed. More or less was an appropriate description. Relying on the defector Poteyev's information the FBI thought that at least two Illegals had evaded capture. Poteyev revealed that two of the Illegals did not report to him, they were handled solely by Kruglov and he did not have any information on their identity, position or location. Dannielle Eagles or, Anyata Ivanovna, to use her patronymic name was one of the two Illegals who reported to Kruglov and to Kruglov alone.

"Deputy Director, may I speak with you?" asked Yuri Menkov, head of the SVR's intelligence systems department.

"Of course, Menkov, come in."

The Deputy Director's office was significantly less austere than would have been the case with his KGB predecessor of a decade ago. Russia's oil wealth had percolated down to several areas of Soviet life, including its counter-intelligence services. Kruglov sat in a deep maroon leather chair behind a modern desk with an array of computer screens, keyboards and laptops. Menkov was regarded as an AI genius in the SVR. He was only twenty-six years old, had graduated from the University of Moscow in Mathematics and Computer Science, and was studying for his PhD in Artificial Intelligence in his spare time. He didn't really have much of that given his function within the SVR, but a glance at his 5ft 11in, skinny frame suggested he saved more than a few hours in a week by not eating much.

"Do you have something for me?" Kruglov asked, keen to get on with it.

"Yes Sir," replied Menkov. "Our dedicated tracking systems have picked up a faint electronic signal from one of our GPS enabled satellite phones. The strength of the signal is variable, and as far as we can tell the emitting device is not stationary."

"Whose phone is it, Menkov?" asked Kruglov.

"Agent Ivanovna's, Deputy Director," replied Menkov. Kruglov pondered this information for a moment. If Anyata was sure of her cover and certain that she was undetectable then she would simply have called, as she had done a few days earlier from Seoul.

"Where is the signal coming from?" asked Kruglov.

"It seems to be coming from the Korean Strait, Sir, at the last count, about 20km off the coast of Jejudo Island."

"Thank you, Yuri. Keep me in touch if you can with the signal's whereabouts. I'll get back to you if I need anything more than that."

"I will, thank you Deputy Director," responded Menkov on his way out of Kruglov's office.

When Menkov exited his office, Deputy Director Kruglov sat back in his chair and began to disseminate the intel from the analyst. Anyata Ivanovna was his top Illegal. Her path through the CIA and now the NGA was as deep undercover as you can get and she had already relayed several very useful pieces of intelligence back to the SVR in recent years. Ivanovna was not careless. She would not have just dropped or misplaced her dedicated SVR phone. *This was a definite attempt to contact me*, he concluded. The signal was coming from off the coast of South Korea according to Menkov and it was moving, so she's on a vessel of some sort. But why? As far as he knew, the SVR had no particular interest in that region at the present time. Igor Kruglov dialled an internal number.

"Vedemin," said the voice on the other end. Boris Vedemin

was the SVR's chief analyst on Asia. If anything was afoot in the region he would know about it.

"Boris," replied Kruglov having just checked the analyst's first name on his computer. "This is Deputy Director Kruglov, have you a minute?"

"Certainly, Sir, however long you need," replied Vedemin. The analyst did not get many direct calls from one of the SVR's Deputy Directors, usually the North American and European desks were busier, more in the limelight. Today, he had now received two phone calls from a Deputy Director.

"Is there anything going on in Korea that is of interest to us?" asked Kruglov.

"Yes, Sir," replied Vedemin. "I have already this morning reported my information to Deputy Director Gretchko."

Vladimir Gretchko was a dim witted asshole as far as Kruglov was concerned, he never seemed to know anything of any use and was only in that position because he was a distant relative of President Putin. Still, he was Vedemin's boss so it was reasonable that the analyst reported any intel to him.

"I have not been able to talk with Deputy Director Gretchko this morning Boris, kindly tell me what you told him."

While Boris Vedemin knew he had done the right thing in reporting directly to Gretchko and nobody else, he also knew that it was in his best interests to relay that information to Kruglov. He was not someone to mess about by all accounts.

"Of course," replied Vedemin. "Last night it appears that a submarine was stolen from Haeju docks on the west coast of North Korea. The attackers are not known. The DPRK authorities are trying to keep it quiet. They have 'mislaid' submarines before, but not like this one."

"Why is this of interest to us?" asked Kruglov curtly, and fearing that he already knew the answer.

"It's one of our submarines, Deputy Director, a Borei class nuclear one," replied Vedemin.

Igor Kruglov replaced his phone on its cradle without bothering to thank Boris Vedemin or even end the call with some normal pleasantry or other. Kruglov was sitting upright in his chair, silently livid. Russia had only a handful of these nuclear submarines. They cost around US $1 billion each for god's sake. They were like a schoolboy's SBD fart in class, silent but deadly. Now some bunch of fucking unknown asshole thieves had stolen a Russian submarine from under the noses of those mental case deviants in the DPRK. Kruglov was not full of the joys of spring. Just as Kruglov was in the midst of another burst of the red mist, it clicked. Agent Ivanovna must be on board the submarine! Her signal was off the coast of South Korea, near Jejudo Island according to Menkov. The submarine could easily have travelled that far since it was stolen. Kruglov had now exited the red mist, was becoming his more usual, calculating self, figuring out what to do next. If he could recover US $1 billion worth of top-notch Russian hardware then he would surely be in pole position to take over from SVR Director Fredkov when he retired. *Oh yes* he thought, *I will take this on.* Igor Kruglov was now out of his office and headed for that of the Director. He was going to make absolutely certain that this rescue or destroy operation was totally under his command.

★ ★ ★

"Look, you're ex-MI5 and Financial Secretary to the Treasury. Get the fucking plane down here or your package stays put. They don't accept vans full of stolen gold and cash as hand luggage on normal flights you know!" bawled JJ into his smartphone.

"OK, OK," responded Neil Robson. "Keep your fucking hair

on. It's all in hand. Don't get all uppity with me either you fucking Jock. Remember, I've got your arse over a barrel as well as that of your insider trading cohorts. Be more respectful!" Robson yelled back. There was no part of JJ's mind or body that wanted to be respectful to Neil Robson. JJ and his team had gone to a lot of trouble to relieve the DPRK of most of its gold hoard. Even if, as Robson claimed, it was legitimate recompense for North Korea's default on its bonds held by the UK, it was a dangerous mission and not one without casualties. Still, a bawling match wasn't going to get either of them anywhere, and JJ knew that Robson had him, Toby and Yves-Jacques by the short and curlies. He calmed down.

"OK. I'll make a few phone calls, get back to you as soon as I can. In the meantime keep the package safe," Robson said, then hung up. The Financial Secretary to the Treasury was a little relieved but not yet wholly satisfied. At least Darke had possession of the gold; that would keep Chancellor Walker happy. It would also keep Vladimir Babikov happy as he would be paid handsomely for the nominal £2.5m debt owed by Robson. The Fin Sec himself would also be happy because he was intent on skimming off a few hundred million pounds for his own piggy bank. Now that he knew that Darke had acquired the booty, he could go about tying up some loose ends. First, thought Robson, he would contact the Secretary of Defence, William Clark. He could authorise the Royal Air Force or, indeed, the Army's airborne division to supply a suitable aircraft to get the package from Seoul to London. Robson would run it by Chancellor Walker but that was a formality, the old fellow was getting desperate to fill the gargantuan gap in the UK's finances. Walker would convince Clark that it was an essential operation for national security and well-being. It would be done.

Once that was underway, Robson had the urgent problem of Joel Gordon. The accountant had evaded Babikov's hit man, indeed he was totally oblivious as to how near death he had been. Gordon's boss, Craig Wilson, would be back in the office in a day or so and Gordon was keen to blab his findings about the government's shaky, nigh disastrous, finances. The Jamrock yardie would need to be out of the equation within the next forty-eight hours, concluded Robson, so he had better get on that lickety-split.

After Gordon was silenced, Robson needed to ensure that JJ Darke and his colleagues were never in a position to reveal his role in acquiring the gold. The insider trading stick was good leverage and one of Babikov's men was shadowing young Cyrus Darke, just in case even more leverage was needed. That might be enough and it might not thought Robson, he'd return to that issue once the gold had been delivered and Joel Gordon was out of the picture.

A few hours later, JJ received a text message from Neil Robson, regarding the plane that Robson had organised. The next day an RAF Hercules C-5 fortified transport plane would fly to Incheon airport in Seoul and transport JJ and 'the package' back to RAF Lyneham in the UK. Lyneham was around ten miles south of Swindon, recalled JJ, so it would take him roughly two hours to drive the loaded van back to London. At least Robson had come through on the transportation. The new C-5s had enough fuel and payload capacity to do the trip in one hop. Then the fun of selling the precious metal would be next on the agenda.

"Hey Jim, how's it hanging?" asked JJ as he came through PAU Travel's front door. This may be the last time he saw his good friend for quite a while, so he had better say his goodbyes.

"Fine JJ, all is well. I'm just back from seeing Ethel. She seems in good form. Victor was there – he brought her some chocolate and the pair of them were stuffing their faces when I went in," laughed the KLO.

"That's great, Jim. They're a bit of an odd couple but they do seem to genuinely care about each other."

"Also on the news front, Kwon got Ji-hun across the border. We picked him up a few hours ago. He's inside getting processed, his papers and his cash. He seems very content."

"He did a good job for us. I don't know if we would have been successful at the central bank if we didn't have his intel. Good call by Lily and the Iceman to kidnap him in the first place," said JJ.

"Look Jim, I'm heading out of here tomorrow, back to London. Transportation for me and the van has been organised. You've got your team's bonus. Unofficial, but thoroughly deserved. I can't thank you enough. This mission would have gone nowhere without you and the boys. If I can ever repay you, just ask." JJ and Jim gave each other a firm man-hug. Their friendship was already strong after JJ had saved Jim's life in Bosnia, now it was even stronger.

"I owed you anyway," said Jim. Take good care of yourself and be careful with all that gold, some bad asses may try to get it before the limey government does!"

It was the bad asses in the British government that were more worrying, JJ thought to himself.

"I will," said JJ on the way out of PAU Travel. A quick visit to Ethel may be in order, then dinner, a good night's sleep and back to the UK in the morning.

"Jim," called JJ. "If you see Carolyn, ask her to keep in touch."

"Sure will, chief, sure will."

★ ★ ★

"Chirkov!" yelled Igor Kruglov. "I know you are the Commander in Chief and I don't care! I am asking you a simple question. Do you have any battleships remotely close to South Korea? This is a question of the highest national importance. If you do not answer me immediately then you will be answering to President Putin in the next five minutes. Do you understand?"

Admiral Viktor Chirkov was not used to being yelled at by anyone, nor questioned by anyone for that matter. This jumped-up little shit on the other end of the phone wasn't even the Director of the SVR, just one of two Deputy Directors. Still, Kruglov had a reputation and, unfortunately, not one that even the C in C of the Russian navy could easily ignore.

"I understand, Kruglov," the Admiral eventually replied. "We have a Udaloy class destroyer on manoeuvres in the Sea of Japan, probably about fifty miles from the port of Pusan in South Korea."

"Thank you, Admiral. What are the capabilities of this ship?"

"It is the *Admiral Vinogradov,* Kruglov," said Chirkov, with an intonation which implied that Kruglov should know the ship's capabilities. After an ignorant pause, Chirkov continued. "The *Vinogradov* is the Pacific Fleet's most advanced anti-submarine destroyer. It carries Silex and Moskit missiles, torpedoes, anti-submarine rocket launchers—"

"Enough Chirkov," interrupted Kruglov. "Is the Baltic fleet not closer?"

"No. Most of the fleet are in port at Baltiysk. We have only some patrol boats and corvettes near the Korea Strait," replied Chirkov.

"How fast is the *Vinogradov*, Admiral and what is its range?"

"At full bore, 35 knots. At half that speed its range would be around 10,000 nautical miles. At full blast, 4,000-6,000," replied Chirkov with confidence.

"Thank you Admiral, you have been most helpful," said Kruglov insincerely. Chirkov's information was music to his ears.

"Please order the *Vinogradov's* captain to head immediately for the Korea Strait at full speed. He will receive further orders in due course. I will clear this with the Director of the SVR and the President himself within the hour. They will get the authorisation from the South Koreans and the Japanese to enter the Strait. Your co-operation will be noted Chirkov." Before the Admiral could respond, Kruglov continued. "One final question. What is the range of the *Vinogradov's* anti-submarine missiles?"

"It carries two missile systems. The older one can launch Silex missiles with a range of up to 50km. The newer system, the SS-N-22 Moskit has an effective range of over 200km. This missile can travel at Mach 3. That would be approximately 50km a minute, giving the target very little time to respond."

"Thank you again, Admiral," replied Kruglov, hanging up as soon as the 'l' had left his lips.

Igor Kruglov was formulating his plan on the run. Not that his body was moving that fast, but his mind was. If Chirkov's information was accurate, and he had no reason to doubt it, then the *Admiral Vinogradov* was probably less than 55 nautical miles from the Korea Strait. At full speed the ship could make up that distance in an hour and a half. Menkov had said that agent Ivanovna's signal was first located at approximately 10nmi off the coast of Jejudo Island. The top speed submerged of the stolen Borei was twenty-nine knots, nearly 55km/hour, only a little less than the destroyer's. There was no hope of the *Vinogradov* catching the submarine quickly. At best, it could close the gap by 5-6nmi every hour, meaning that it would not be on top of the submarine for eight to ten hours, assuming it was on a direct path in the sub's wake.

Kruglov had a clear pecking order of events in his mind. His first choice was for the *Admiral Vinogradov* to catch up with the submarine, contact the thieves and force them to surrender. It would be very much preferable to return $1bn worth of nuclear vessel hardware to the navy than destroy it. If push came to shove then destroy it he must. Better $1bn of Russian submarine blown to smithereens at the bottom of Davy Jones's Locker than in the hands of the enemy, whoever that enemy was. That was his second choice. Indeed, mulled Kruglov, the identity of the thieves could be narrowed down in this process. Whether the theft of the submarine was aimed as a blow to North Korea or Russia was, at this moment, irrelevant. The enemies and ideological opposites of both nations overlapped. The United States, Japan, South Korea, maybe Britain or low probability China were the most likely sponsors of this audacious act. If either South Korea or Japan refused permission for the *Vinogradov* to pass through the Korea Strait then that would put them in the frame. If they did not, then the other three would rise up the suspect scale.

Igor Kruglov was satisfied with his work and his plan. As long as Anyata's signal kept emitting and was trackable by Menkov, the better the odds that he would hunt down the Borei and give his ambitious career prospects a mighty boost.

★ ★ ★

Tommy Fairclough and David McCoy had driven the Borei safely and swiftly away from Jejudo Island. They were now in the East China Sea and back on track for their ultimate destination in Scotland, the best part of five days away. All the navy SEALs on board seemed in a much better mood. The news on Billy Smith and Yang Dingbang was good. Ding was fine, his sore head was more a result of dehydration than any fever. Smith did have Dengue Fever but it had been caught early enough. He was under supervision at the same Seoul hospital that Ethel Rogers was in, unbeknown to both of them, and several floors apart. He would be released in a few days. The news on the stowaway was not as good. He died later that day despite all the best efforts of the SNUH staff. The SEALs were also happy that they were submerged, undetectable, had edible food, enough bottled water and the company of two fine looking women. Commander O'Neill had made it clear that Reynolds and Eagles were of the 'look, don't touch' variety. The SEALs respected this, which was just as well. In a physical tussle the two NGA officers were eminently capable of inflicting some damage on even the most testosterone filled SEAL.

While Carolyn Reynolds was assisting acting chief engineer Barry Minchkin on a series of checks involving the status of the nuclear reactor on board and the Borei's missiles, Dannielle Eagles was operating the submarine's radar system. Normally, this would have been Ding's job backed up by Joe Franks. Ding was in Seoul and Joe found it difficult to sit in one position for too long without his broken leg aching a lot, so Dannielle suggested that he lie down for a few minutes and that she would monitor the screens for a while.

"Thanks, Dannielle," said Joe. 'I think I will, if you don't mind."

"Sure, Joe, go ahead. I'll see you in a bit," replied Dannielle. Now that the two NGA officers had been assimilated into the crew, were proving useful and had come bearing food and uncontaminated water, they were on first name terms with the rest of the team, bar Commander O'Neill and XO Harris.

"Anything to report, Officer Eagles?" asked Mark O'Neill in a friendly tone. Dannielle was monitoring the radar and digital sonar screens built into the Borei's advanced multi-purpose combat and command system. The high-speed integral computer system on board allowed her, amongst other capabilities, to determine whether there were any surface or submerged vessels in the vicinity or, indeed, outside of it.

"No Commander," replied Dannielle. "Nothing to report." This was a black lie, very different from the harmless white ones JJ may have told Cyrus on occasion, for the greater good. Officer Eagles' 'black lie' was not aired for the greater good. It was intended to deceive O'Neill and, ultimately, help a Russian warship locate the Borei. At this instant, Dannielle Eagles knew nothing of Kruglov's plan. She inferred from both her knowledge of the SVR Deputy Director and the navigational geography of the situation that he would send either a submarine or a ship after them. She knew enough about the Russian navy's capabilities to realise that few submarines or ships were as fast as the Borei or were likely to be in the Korea Strait or East China Sea at precisely this moment in time. Her hope was that Kruglov had received her phone signal, located the Borei and would then devise a scheme to negotiate its surrender back into the hands of its original owner. Dannielle Eagles, though, was no dreamer. She had been fortunate enough to be one of the Illegals who had avoided detection and capture by the FBI a few years ago. She was illogically committed to mother Russia and she believed that Igor Kruglov was more of a father to her than her biological dad ever was. Dannielle felt that Kruglov loved her in a fatherly way but deep in her heart and soul she knew that he would sacrifice her in a flash if that sacrifice was perceived to be for the greater good of their homeland. This was Eagles' moral justification for her attempt to scupper Mark O'Neill's mission, perhaps lead the US navy SEALs to their capture or death. Indeed, her own death and that of Carolyn Reynolds, her BFF. It was a price she was prepared to pay.

★ ★ ★

Sergei Kargin was captain first rank of the *Admiral Vinogradov* and had been for three years. He was a career seaman in the Russian navy, having enlisted at eighteen. Now thirty-eight years old he was one of the youngest captains in the Pacific Fleet, certainly to be in command of such a state-of-the-art destroyer. A short man, of around 5ft 6in in height, stockily built with dark, cropped, greying brown hair, he offset his lack of inches with an oversized character and a general joie de vivre about most things. Captain Kargin was surprised to hear from Admiral Chirkov. The manoeuvres in the Sea of Japan had been planned months ahead and unless something really important was underway it was most unusual for his original orders to be rescinded or altered. Chirkov had stressed that Kargin's new orders were of the utmost importance and critical to Russia's national security. That was enough for Kargin. He ordered the helmsman to change the *Admiral Vinogradov's* course and to crank up the ship's four gas turbine engines to its maximum speed of thirty-five knots. The captain also ordered a complete weapons check, to ensure that if required, all missiles and submarine countermeasures were ready to go. The navy pilots on board were ordered to inspect their two Ka-27 helix helicopters currently housed in the ship's aircraft hangar. Sergei Kargin did not know if helicopter assistance was to be required but, as a kid he was a boy scout, so he was going to 'be prepared'. Indeed, once Kargin had absorbed Chirkov's orders very few of the ship's crew of 300 were not doing something with a little more focus than they had been a few minutes previously.

Admiral Chirkov had not told Kargin the precise reason for the change of orders, nor whether there would be a target to intercept or destroy. The Admiral had emphasised the need for speed and he had assured Kargin that he would have no trouble entering or navigating the Korea Strait. Chirkov informed him that his orders would be updated in due course. They would be transmitted under the secure code, VOR, the Russian term for a thief involved in organised crime. The ship's crew was ready, the *Admiral Vinogradov* was in pursuit of its prey. The exact nature of that prey would be revealed soon enough and when it was it would be dead meat shortly thereafter. Captain first rank Sergei Kargin was in his element.

★ ★ ★

By the time the *Admiral Vinogradov* had entered the Korea Strait, Commander Mark O'Neill and the Borei submarine were close to crossing the Tropic of Cancer, heading for the Indian Ocean and beyond. Tommy Fairclough and David McCoy had to be alert due to the variety of submerged reefs in the East China Sea but the passive sonar system on board was very sensitive and they had steered the submarine safely so far. Their intended route from the Indian Ocean was Red Sea, Suez Canal, the Mediterranean, the Alboran Sea, the Atlantic Ocean, and finally, Scotland and the River Clyde. Normally, a ship or submarine wanting to cross the Suez Canal would need permission from Egypt. That wasn't happening. In any event the near silent propulsion system of the Borei and its stealth modifications made detection of the submerged boat most unlikely. The Alboran Sea was narrow, lying at the far west of the Mediterranean, Spain on its north side, Morocco and Algeria on its south. The Strait of Gibraltar, also known as the Pillars of Hercules, is located at the west end of the Alboran Sea and connects the Mediterranean with the Atlantic Ocean. The average depth of the Alboran Sea is over 1,400ft; this would present no difficulty for the Borei's navigational capability. The Strait of Gibraltar had a depth range of 950 to 3,000ft. Even the shallowest parts would not test Fairclough and McCoy's skills. At that point, in any event, they would be nearly at their destination and in friendly waters. Their focus would be acute.

Mark O'Neill was on the conn. He had been joined by Carolyn Reynolds who was studying the route planned by O'Neill and Harris.

"I believe your dad's Scottish?" asked O'Neill, always happy to see this particular NGA officer.

"He is, Glasgow born and bred," replied Carolyn, guessing that the Commander had picked up this choice piece of information from Dannielle directly or some crew gossip.

"What does he do?" O'Neill continued, wishing to keep this chat going for as long as possible.

"That's a good question Commander," responded Carolyn, still studying the route. "I thought he was a fund manager in London, but he turned up in Seoul, on some dodgy venture—"

"Why do you think it was dodgy Carolyn?" interrupted O'Neill and addressing Officer Reynolds for the first time by her Christian name.

"I didn't know he was going to be in Seoul, we hadn't been in touch for a long time. He turned up at the CIA offices with a serious looking woman and a hippy kid. He seemed to be best pals with the KLO, Jim Bradbury. It all seemed a bit surreal." She felt comfortable in divulging this information to O'Neill. She had noticed he'd called her Carolyn. In different circumstances, who knew, maybe they'd go out on a date, he was OK looking and seemed quite smart judged the NGA woman. That was enough of that thought Carolyn, immediately snapping back into professional mode. O'Neill may be the Commander of this SEALs team and they were both on the same side, but no more intel on her dad and she had certainly no intention of divulging that JJ had been in the DPRK a day or two earlier.

"Commander," said Carolyn. "This route, are you set on it?" she asked.

"We are," he replied, slightly disappointed not to hear his first name so far in the conversation. "Why do you ask?"

"What is the keel depth of this submarine?"

After a moment's hesitation, and a little embarrassed, O'Neill replied. "Well, I don't know, precisely."

"I do. It's 32ft and 10in," she announced.

"Is that important?" O'Neill asked.

"It depends," retorted Carolyn.

"On what?" O'Neill countered swiftly.

"On whether or not you want to remain invisible from the surface, Commander. In particular, I see that your route involves crossing the Suez Canal. I guess you will not be asking the permission of the Suez Canal Authority. Fair enough, those Egyptian turncoats have no idea whose side they are on. However, I do know that the Suez Canal is shallow, very shallow. You need to get one of your team to check whether this sub with this keel depth can cross safely while it is submerged."

Mark O'Neill was more than somewhat taken aback. "Yes ma'am," was all that he could utter as he left the conn in urgent search of Evan Harris, to whom he was going to give this measuring task. Once Lieutenant Harris had done his research, he would discover that the even depth of the Suez Canal was now 79ft, much deeper than the original 26ft in place on its initial construction in 1869. The team on board this Borei had two pieces of outright luck in its favour. First, the sonar system of the Borei was so sensitive that it could sail smoothly under water only a few feet above a sea bed provided that the sea bed had no sharp or large objects protruding from it. The bottom of the Suez Canal was smooth. Secondly, the sail on the Borei was of an advanced aqua-dynamic design, longer than most submarine sails but also shorter in height. Once all the calculations had been done, O'Neill, Harris and Reynolds concluded that they could navigate the Suez Canal but that the tip of the submarine's sail would be only 6-10ft below the surface. An eagle-eyed observer on a sunny day may spot the Borei's shadow but it was a chance they had to take. The canal would present the sub's drivers with more challenges. It was essentially a one lane waterway and on a typical day only one northbound convoy would get through. The Borei would need to tag onto the tail end of such a convoy and remain undetected. This was achievable given the Borei's stealth augmentation, courtesy of Sunwoo Chung, deceased. There was a precise schedule to both north and southbound convoys. The northbound ones began at 06.00 hours from Suez, used bypasses built into the canal, and would normally take at least eleven or twelve hours to navigate the entire length of the canal, travelling at a restricted speed of eight to ten knots. That would require maximum concentration from the Borei's entire crew, especially its drivers, Fairclough and McCoy.

None of this would have been known to Commander O'Neill and team if Carolyn Reynolds had not first questioned rhetorically the keel depth of the Borei. Carolyn was pleased with herself and Mark O'Neill was even more partial to the NGA officer than he was before. When this mission was over he was definitely going to pluck up the courage to ask her out. As Mark O'Neill was mulling over this happy prospect, Evan Harris came hotfooting it onto the conn.

"Mark," began Harris with a stern expression in tow. "We've got one big fucking problem."

"What's up?"

"Joe Franks, with his one fucking leg, was having a lie down in his bunk just outside of the area we have partitioned for the NGA women. He was a bit dozy when he woke up, forgot he had a busted leg, fell on the ground and sent his makeshift crutches spinning into the partitioned area. There was no one there so he crawled along the deck to retrieve his sticks. As he was doing it, he came across this," announced Harris, holding aloft an unauthorised satellite phone. O'Neill looked horrified. The phone was clearly active.

"Turn it the fuck off Evan and destroy it, it must be emitting a signal that can be used to track us," he hollered. Evan turned the phone off, ripped its innards apart and returned his gaze to his team leader.

"Where exactly did Joe discover this?" asked O'Neill still not of clear mind.

"Attached magnetically under one of the NGA women's beds," he replied.

"Which one?" asked O'Neill, fearing the worst and feeling sick to his gut.

"Reynolds," replied Harris. Maybe there was a face which launched a thousand ships, but at that instant, for Mark O'Neill, one word had sunk a thousand dreams.

* * *

Yuri Menkov was fast. When he was a student at Moscow University he could do the one hundred metres in 11.50 seconds. This didn't compare with his hero's time of 10.14 seconds in winning the 1972 100 metres Olympic crown in Munich, but Valery Borzov was special. He was a Ukranian who competed for the Soviet Union and then eventually returned to Ukraine and had a successful political career. As Menkov bounded up the one flight of stairs, two at a time, that separated his work station from Igor Kruglov's office, hurtled past the Deputy Direcrtor's secretary and sped straight to his boss's desk, Yuri Menkov felt this may be his moment to be special.

"Deputy Director, Sir, sorry for barging in, but agent Ivanovna's signal has stopped transmitting."

Kruglov looked startled. This was not good, not the plan, not what was needed to rescue $1bn of Russian naval hardware nor his deep desire to be SVR Director.

"How long ago did it stop?" asked Kruglov with deep urgency.

"About fifteen seconds ago," detailed Menkov, checking his chronograph. He was glad he had decided to deliver the bad news in person. Had he dialled Kruglov's extension, had to negotiate the firewall that was his hard-nosed secretary and explain why he needed to speak with the Deputy Director that would have taken way more than fifteen seconds. Kruglov knew that to have any hope of neutralising the captured Borei he would need to be fast too.

"Menkov, do you have the exact co-ordinates of Ivanovna's last signal?"

"Yes Sir," responded Menkov. "Latitude of 26° 13' North and longitude of 127° 42' East."

"Where is that, Yuri?" added Kruglov.

"Close to Naha, Okinawa in the East China Sea, Sir, just north of the Tropic of Cancer," replied Menkov, satisfied that he had full details at the tip of his tongue.

"Good work, Yuri. Take a seat. I need to make a call," said Kruglov. Kruglov dialled Admiral Chirkov's number, gave him his instructions, and hung up, hoping, waiting, praying for a result.

Captain first rank Sergei Kargin and the *Admiral Vinogradov* had just passed through the Korea Strait and entered the East China Sea. As he was admiring the view, his first Lieutenant handed him a cable with the heading VOR, it was from Chirkov. It read:

At precisely 14.04 UTC today, an enemy submarine was located at 26° 13' N, 127° 42' East. This submarine is believed to be heading due South towards the Indian Ocean. Its speed is estimated at 29 knots. On receipt of this instruction fire all available missiles at this enemy vessel. Chirkov.

Kargin understood his orders and would not question them. Admiral Chirkov was Commander in Chief of the Russian Navy, he knew what he was doing. Kargin instructed his first Lieutenant to prepare all missiles to fire. A precise target would follow. The *Vinogradov* had been on manoeuvres but it still had eight Silex anti-submarine missiles on board in 2x4 formation and two SS-N-22 Moskits. The Moskits were rocket-propelled, radar guided and could travel at 50km per minute. If Kargin got the co-ordinates right the enemy submarine would be toast. The captain had a few calculations to do. Six minutes had elapsed since Chirkov's timed position for the submarine. It would take a further four minutes, including the time to read Chirkov's orders, issue his own and to have the *Vinogradov's* missiles ready to fire. Provided the enemy sub had stayed on the course Chirkov indicated it would have travelled a further five nautical miles or nearly nine kilometres. Kargin plugged the data into the *Vinogradov's* advanced computer system and gave the order to fire all missiles. The Moskits would hit first, in approximately 115 seconds. Their underwater blast radius is twenty-five to thirty metres. The eight Silex missiles would take over five minutes to hit. Kargin had taken that into account in his programmed input. A direct hit by any of the *Admiral Vingradov's* ten missiles would either destroy the submarine or render it ineffective and force it to surface. Even if they all missed, and a bulls-eye was a bit of a long shot since the target was moving and stealth protected, the total potential area of damage was nearly three kilometres. If Chirkov's initial information was even remotely accurate the enemy submarine would not escape. Kargin had done his job and now the *Admiral Vinogradov* was full speed ahead to the missile detonation site.

* * *

Just as Yuri Menkov had burst into Igor Kruglov's office, Commander Mark O'Neill had instructed Evan Harris to bring Carolyn Reynolds to the goat locker and to ensure that none of the crew interrupted them.

"Is this yours?" O'Neill asked of Reynolds, who was already not pleased at being roughly frog marched by Harris to the Commander's quarters.

"No, what is it, it looks beat to death," said Carolyn.

"It's a satellite phone, Officer Reynolds," answered O'Neill suppressing all romantic thoughts and needing to get to the bottom of this. "It was found attached to a panel directly underneath your bunk."

"Well it's not fuckin' mine, O'Neill," hollered Reynolds. "I've never seen it before, I don't own a satellite phone and I don't keep my phone in that dilapidated condition."

"You would say that, bitch!" interrupted Evan Harris, who was now holding Reynolds' right arm extremely tightly.

"If you don't let my arm go frog features, I'm going to gouge your fuckin' eyes out," ranted Carolyn, wriggling free from Harris's grip.

O'Neill signalled to Harris to let her be. The Commander so wanted the traitor not to be Carolyn. He was smart enough to realise that if she was a double agent then her cover was absolutely brilliant. American educated, CIA trained, NGA officer, a Scottish dad for fuck's sake. It didn't add up and if it did, it was devastating.

"Look Reynolds," said O'Neill. "I don't want it to be you. For sure it's no one in my SEALs team. I've known them personally for years and the ones I haven't are known to Harris and I trust them totally."

"My guys are good and totally loyal, as are yours, Mark," said Harris, unnecessarily. Carolyn could see that this was not good. She had calmed a little since being released by Harris. Time to get her brain working rather than her adrenaline flowing.

"Take fingerprints off the phone, Commander. I've never seen it before so I haven't touched it. The only prints on there will probably be the owner's, yours and whoever destroyed it," stated Carolyn.

Harris interjected. "We're not fucking 5-O Reynolds. We're SEALs, at sea, in a submarine, underwater. We don't have the facilities to take fuckin' fingerprints."

"Maybe you do, tosser!" came Carolyn's unwieldy reply.

"What do you mean, Reynolds?" asked O'Neill, keen to get on and to break up the simmering conflict between his number two and his desired paramour.

"You've got a medic on board, right?" asked Carolyn.

"Yes," replied O'Neill.

"Then he'll have some sort of powder and possibly some kind of sellotape to keep bandages in place. We dust the phone with the powder, there will be latent fingerprints on it, due to sweat, dirt or whatever. Once dusted we blow the excess powder off and use the sellotape to lift the print. We need to ensure the tape is flat, no bubbles. Once that's done, lift the print out and put it on a piece of white card or something similar."

"How do you know this stuff?" asked Harris, unconvinced.

"I'm CIA trained, remember, idiot," replied Carolyn, still showing Harris no verbal mercy whatsoever.

"OK, but what do we do once we've got the print on a card?" asked O'Neill. "We still don't have a method of checking whose it is."

"You do," responded Carolyn. O'Neill and Harris were still bemused. Since her credibility and freedom were at stake, she thought she'd help them out. "Look you two. I noticed that Barry Minchkin had a state-of-the art tablet. The high definition on that screen has a pixilation of 1,900 x 1,200. He can take a clear camera shot of the fingerprint, it will be sharp enough to have it checked."

"Checked against what?" asked O'Neill.

"Checked against the bleedin' CIA or NGA personnel files, for god's sake. On joining either agency you need to have your fingerprints taken. Get Henry Michieta at the NGA or John Adams at the CIA to dig them out, send them a picture of the print or prints from the phone and see if they match mine. They won't by the way," said Carolyn, looking confident and feeling calmer. O'Neill pondered for a moment.

"Evan, go get Gary and ask him to bring his medical kit with him. Relieve Barry of his tablet and get back here. Don't mention what's going on to anyone. Reynolds, you're staying here with me," ordered O'Neill.

"Whatever," snapped Carolyn as Harris set about his task.

Only a few minutes had passed since officer Reynolds had been hauled into the goat locker. Unbeknown to her or the SEALs, Captain Sergei Kargin was absorbing Admiral Chirkov's orders at the same moment. Harris returned swiftly with Whitton and Minchkin's tablet. The young medic did indeed have some anti-rash powder with him, very often useful if SEALs had been in sea water for any length of time or on a long training hike. He had sellotape as well. Whitton dusted the phone, under instruction from Reynolds, using a small amount of powder and one of the NGA woman's unused make-up brushes to gently distribute the powder so that the ridges of the fingerprints were visible. The medic took a bottle of iodine out of its packaging, dismantled the small cardboard box that it was in and used the plain inside surface to collect the fingerprints from the tape. It was the best he could do. Then he took two digital photographs with Minchkin's tablet.

"Right, Gary, good," said O'Neill. "Send the photographs to John Adams at the CIA. Tell him it's most urgent that we get an

answer to whose they are. Get back here as soon as you have one."
There was no way O'Neill was going to Reynolds' direct boss,
just in case he was her direct handler too. Gary Whitton got his
gear together and went back to his station to upload the
photographs for John Adams. He gave Barry his tablet back.
Dannielle Eagles had noticed that there had been something
going on and had also noticed the absence of O'Neill, Harris and
her friend.

"Anything the matter?" she asked Gary Whitton as he sat only
a few stations away from her.

"No, nothing," replied the young medic, trying to be even
toned but sounding a little rattled. "Just have to send some
photographs to Langley and await a reply," he added, again
attempting to be casual. A few minutes elapsed and Gary Whitton
had his reply. He got off his seat and made his way at normal
walking pace to the goat locker. He did not acknowledge
Dannielle as he left nor any of the SEALs that were on the conn.

"Gary, what have you got?" asked O'Neill. Harris re-took
hold of Reynolds' arm. She fired him a look that could kill but
said nothing.

"Assistant Director Adams said the photographs were clear
enough to detect three sets of prints. Two were ours but the other
one was…" he hesitated, aware of the company.

"Hers!" exclaimed Harris, pointing accusingly at Reynolds
and tightening his grip on her arm.

"No, Sir," responded Whitton immediately, "the other NGA
officer, Dannielle Eagles," he blurted out. As Gary Whitton's blurt
was finalised and before apologies, recriminations and
admonishments could begin, Dannielle Eagles entered the goat
locker, arms extended and clasping a Stechkin automatic pistol
firmly in both hands. She was aiming directly at Mark O'Neill.
Nobody moved.

"Your gun looks Russian, Dannielle, a bit like yourself," said Carolyn, truly shocked but trying to be professional and calm.

"Yes, Carolyn. I always have been, always will be," replied Dannielle, keeping the gun firmly pointed at O'Neill's head but eyes darting around the living quarters, scanning the other three Americans. The Stetchkin was heavy and unladylike but it could fire 750 rounds per minute, twelve per second. Mark O'Neill was not likely to be the only victim if Eagles let loose.

"I don't know what's in your pathetic Ruski mind Dannielle and I don't much care, but you're not getting out of here. You know that, right?" said Carolyn.

"Oh, I don't know about that, my friend. I suggest we all go to the conn and surface. A Russian submarine or warship will probably be on its way to pick us all up. Then we can have a cosy chat," said Dannielle cool as an ice cube. "Go on, Commander shift your well-formed butt. You too Harris. Whitton you and my ex-BFF stay here. If I see either of your pea-heads coming through this partition you'll have around four 9mm rounds each in them," she added, fully in control of the situation. Neither O'Neill nor Harris really knew what to do. They could rush her but at least one of them would die. Eagles' gun would probably have released up to a dozen rounds before she was toppled to the deck. In addition to either O'Neill himself or Harris being dead or injured, half a dozen of the bullets would be ricocheting around like a puck in a tilt machine. If the Stetchkin was loaded with 9mm parabellum rounds then some armour piercing was possible. Any of the five of them could be hit and the submarine's external skin punctured.

Eagles had the drop on O'Neill, and probably Harris but she was outnumbered and could not take all her adversaries down before being overpowered. As Commander O'Neill was contemplating moving his well-formed bum, with the intention of buying time and forcing Eagles into having to contain the rest of the SEALs on board, the Borei took a massive lurch to the port side. Both Moskit missiles from the *Admiral Vinogradov* had entered the water and exploded. There was no direct hit but the resulting shockwave was powerful. Shockwaves from this type of missile come in two stages. The primary shock causes the target to lurch, often causing significant damage to personnel and equipment on board. The second shock comes from the cyclical expansion and contraction of the gas bubble created by the rapid chemical reaction of the volume of water displaced by the solid object now occupying that space. This secondary shock can cause the submarine to bend backwards and forwards. In extremis, it can cause a catastrophic breach of the sub's hull.

The Moskit missiles' shockwaves had not been close enough to breach the Borei's hull. They had been strong enough, though, to send flying the three navy SEALs and two NGA officers in the goat locker. Gary Whitton fell backwards, through the goat locker's partition and into the submarine's main area. O'Neill went crashing into a bunk and split his forehead. Harris was down too. Eagles had lurched forward and lost her footing as she careered into her NGA colleague. Her right hand had hold of the Stetchkin until she flattened Carolyn and she had unintentionally let off twelve rounds as she tumbled. Two of the 9mm parabellums ricocheted off of the ceiling of the living quarters and both of them hit Evan Harris, one in his right thigh and one in his right arm. The rest of the bullets ended up nowhere interesting and had not caused any further human damage as far as could be told.

Eagles reacted first. Reynolds had broken her fall and now the Russian was on top of her former friend. Carolyn was not injured significantly; she was sore as her head had hit the floor, just missing a pillow randomly ejected from one of the bunk beds, whose bedding was now everywhere. Reynolds was rudely awakened from her daze by Eagles' hands pressed around her throat and the yelling of 'bitch' resounding loudly in her ears. Reynolds put both her arms together, outstretched and drove an arm wedge inside the gap in her assailant's arms anchored by her own throat, and drove them outwards with force. Eagles had to let go of her grip. As Eagles' head dipped, Carolyn raised hers swiftly and firmly planted a 'Glesga kiss' on the bridge of the Russian's nose. Dannielle Eagles let out a painful scream. Her once attractive nose was broken and her nasal blood was spreading voluminously into the artificial atmosphere. Both NGA women rose to their feet. Eagles was now the more disoriented. Reynolds took advantage of this. Left-hook to the side of the head, followed by right spinning elbow to the other side. The big Maasai wouldn't think so much of his love interest's looks now, thought Carolyn, in a pico second of self-mirth. Eagles tried to fight back, but her vision was impaired, as Carolyn's spinning elbow had led to an instantaneous cracker of a split eyebrow and swollen eye. Carolyn was not contemplating mercy. Her BFF had betrayed her, and all of American society in which Eagles had been educated and trained. On top of that, the Russian slut had just tried to choke her to death. Carolyn pounded on, right cross, low kick to the left shin, knee to Eagles' chin as her head jerked lower when the Russian clutched her damaged leg. Eagles crumpled.

Suddenly, the submarine lurched again, this time less dramatically than before. The Silex missiles from the *Admiral Vinogradov* had arrived on the scene. No direct hits. The primary and secondary shockwaves were less powerful than from the Moskits but strong enough to topple Carolyn. Flat on her back again, she managed to support herself on her elbows, only to find Dannielle Eagles already on her knees but in renewed possession of her Stetchkin, now pointing directly at Reynolds' head.

"This time, you American whore, you will die," gurgled Eagles through a river of blood, snot and other bodily fluids. In that millisecond of time that it would take for Eagles to pull the trigger and at least one 9mm Parabellum round to exit the barrel and enter Carolyn's head, JJ's daughter saw images of her dad, her mum, her brother, the children she would never have. The images were like blipverts in *Max Headroom* but they were there and sharply visible in her mind.

Carolyn felt nothing but she heard a piercing wail. It was not from herself. Evan Harris had been conscious enough to see and comprehend the NGA girl fight. As Dannielle Eagles was about to pull the trigger, he had silently extracted his ka-bar knife from its weathered leather sheath. Harris was attached to this weapon and kept it on his person at all times. It weighed only half a kilogram and had a blackened 7 inch blade. With his uninjured left hand he drove his ka-bar into Eagles' right leg Achilles tendon. Eagles swung to her right in excruciating and noisy pain, intent on shooting Harris, but Carolyn was on it like a shark on meat. From her supine position, Carolyn launched into a figure-four choke hold, right leg bent around Eagles' neck, left leg keeping the right in place and also trapping the gun-wielding right arm of the Russian. This move, expertly performed by several UFC champions is known as a triangle choke because the aggressor's legs look like a triangle with the victim's head popping through the hole. Carolyn wasn't a UFC champion but her application of the triangle was good enough. She applied as much pressure as she could with this restraint, restricting Eagles' blood flow from her carotid arteries to her brain. A skilful choker and a strong, stubborn UFC fighter could probably take this for forty-five to sixty seconds before the chokee tapped out, desperate to breath, admitting defeat. Eagles, though, no longer had any strength, she was exhausted, bleeding from her nose, her right eye and her right leg. She had nothing left. Carolyn was not letting go of her choke hold. As Eagles dropped her gun and went full body limp, Carolyn could hear a voice but it wasn't clear yet in her aural channels. She had tunnel concentration, squeezing, forcing the last ounce of breath from her former friend's lungs.

"Carolyn, Carolyn, let go, she's done," said Harris, finding it difficult enough himself to speak. Mark O'Neill was in the process of getting up too, blood pouring from his head wound. Eventually, Carolyn understood what Harris was saying. She released her hold and Dannielle Eagles collapsed, lifeless on to the deck of the goat locker. Igor Kruglov was down one committed Illegal, his favourite, Anyata Ivanovna.

The next few minutes on the Borei were hectic. There were no more explosions to worry about. Gary Whitton was beavering away patching up the wounded SEALs, Harris was in the worst condition and the Commander's head wound needed quite a few field stitches. Once O'Neill had been stitched up and had checked that his team and Carolyn were alright he was on the conn. He ordered Fairclough and McCoy to alter their course slightly just in case more missiles were going to come their way. Before the goat locker confrontation, Eagles had partly disabled the radar and sonar system which was why the Borei crew had no forewarning of the incoming missiles. Evan Harris was recovering in the goat locker lying in a bunk directly opposite Carolyn who was less injured but more worn out by her physical trauma and, perhaps understandsably, occasional feelings of guilt that she had just killed Dannielle. Whitton had sorted out Harris with a couple of tourniquets, some Kerlix gauze and bandages. His bleeding had stopped.

"I'm sorry, Reynolds," muttered Harris. "For thinking it was you, and roughing you up a bit."

"It's alright frog features," responded Carolyn, her spirit

recovering and glad even for a moment to be relieved of her thoughts. "I'd have probably thought the same, if I'd had a one-dimensional empty box for a brain in my jarhead," she replied, attempting a smile.

"A jarhead is a marine, Reynolds, not a—"

"Yeah, yeah, yeah, whatever Harris. I know that. It was pointed out to me a while back by that dead bitch there," interrupted Carolyn. Harris didn't have the energy to respond. The navy SEAL and the NGA officer looked at each other. It was a score draw in saving each other's life and they were both glad the other had survived.

Once the captured Borei had settled and its crew were back on point, Mark O'Neill returned to the goat locker to see how Harris and Reynolds were doing.

"Evan, how do you feel?"

"I'm good thanks, Mark. Whitton got the bullets out, gave me some blood, stitched me up fine and, Bob's your uncle, I live and breathe."

O'Neill turned his attention now to Reynolds. "Carolyn. I'm so sorry we even doubted you, I…"

"Oh it's Carolyn again is it? No officer Reynolds, or just Reynolds, or fucking Russian spy Reynolds then? You're worse than Harris. He's admitted he's a brainless frog, but you're supposed to be smart!" she hollered. Harris looked moderately confused at this point. He did not recall admitting to being a brainless frog. O'Neill was contemplating a response but, wisely, thought the better of it. "So, Commander," continued Carolyn. "Do you think, with that big, ugly gash in your head, that you are still capable of getting this submarine to Scotland?"

"Yes, I am," O'Neill replied, not sure yet whether or not his desired date was about to let up on her attack.

"Good. In that case," stated Carolyn, "I'm going to find a top class restaurant on the banks of Loch Lomond and you, Mark O'Neill, are going to take me for the most expensive, slap-up, steak dinner ever, on planet Earth, known to mankind, nay thought about by mankind. Got it?"

"Yes, ma'am," replied O'Neill, both happy and feeling poorer already.

"I don't want to spoil this lovely moment," moaned Harris. "But what are we going to do with Eagles' body?"

Before his Commander could respond, NGA officer Reynolds interjected.

"We're going to put her in a body bag and fire the treacherous bitch out of one of the torpedo tubes and into the Indian Ocean."

O'Neill and Harris looked at each other. Harsh but fair seemed to be the conclusion.

10

ROBSON'S CHOICE

JJ had decided to sit in the Mercedes Sprinter van for the first part of the journey from Seoul to London. The pilots of the Hercules C-5 transport plane were friendly but JJ wanted to be with his thoughts for a while, on his own. He would join the pilots later.

It had been a humid morning in Seoul so JJ donned his favourite dark blue polo shirt and the cargo pants he hadn't worn since Fathead came a-visiting his house in Markham Square on Greek bond night. As he was ferreting about in his pants' pockets he came across around £120 in sterling, mainly twenties. That was cool, finding cash that you had forgotten about or 'lost' always gave you a mini-boost. Mashed in with the cash was a scrap piece of paper with some writing on it. It was from Toby aka Fathead. He must have given it to JJ on Greek bond night but the Scot had overlooked it in all the confusion. It was Fathead's limerick entry for last year's Christmas quiz. As a MAM employee Toby was not eligible for the case of champagne prize but that didn't stop him having a go every year. He wasn't a poet and everybody did indeed know it.

> *There was a young man from Ireland*
> *Who liked to eat often at Pieland*
> *With mash and chips*
> *On his sizeable hips*
> *He looked like the Michelin tyre man*

Every day he would go to this shop
Add crisps and chocolate and pop
He was fit to burst
A delicious bratwurst
In his mouth and all over his top

One day he was asked to be keeper
Regular goalie was a late sleeper
He filled the six-yard box
With fat head and knees like rocks
He sank deeper and deeper and deeper

The fire brigade rushed to the pitch
He was heavy, the son of a bitch
No sign of light, no hope in sight
The chubby young man from Ireland
Never again ate at his Pieland

JJ couldn't help but laugh even though it was a grievously bad limerick, and didn't even follow limerick rules! True to form Toby hadn't tried to solve the currency question, which you needed to do to win the prize. The limerick was meant to be the tie-breaker in the event of several correct answers. The MAM Christmas quiz had attracted more than 200 entries last year. The winner was a client from R-Squared Capital in Toronto. She had correctly worked out the currency answer was the New Zealand dollar and she was the only one who had it right.

As he rested his head on the back of the passenger seat in the van, JJ recalled how much simpler life was back then, only a few short months ago. It was a time before cancer, before Neil Robson, before the FCA hounds, before terminating North

Korean soldiers and before catching up with his nigh estranged daughter. At least the last of that list was good. On arrival back in London, he really needed to be on the case like Lieutenant Columbo at his best. JJ was well-disturbed by his call home last night. After being so happy to hear Cyrus's voice, all positive and looking forward to beating his dad at some Wii game or other, JJ had spoken with Gil. She told him that someone was tracking Cyrus. Don't worry about it, she said, she was alert and on it. How could he not worry! He was thousands of miles away and couldn't have lifted a finger to help his teenage son if things had turned seriously hairy. Gil was capable and loyal and she would protect Cyrus with all her might, but JJ was his dad and he was meant to be the ultimate protector. JJ did not know why Cyrus was being shadowed but the only logical deduction was that it had something to do with Neil Robson. JJ would find out and woe betide Robson if he even thought about harming Cyrus.

Once JJ had run his full course of Cyrus-thinking he had a list of other tasks to accomplish. Catching up with Ethel's husband and smoothing over her absence from SCO19 would be high on the list, as would making the transfers to pay Ethel and Victor. He would also need to dod some money to Harold McFarlane at McLaren and Vincent Barakat at PLP. Although Vincent's brilliant and innovative sunbeds were not, in the end, used they were fully functional and available for selection. Harold's conveyor systems had worked efficiently in the DPRK's central bank's vaults and the disguised petrol tankers had also done their job, although not in the way initially intended. They would both be paid generously for their skill and effort.

JJ also needed to get in a head to head with Toby. The man he had bigged-up as the best FX and commodities trader in the financial community was going to need to be on the case and in the zone. JJ himself did not have the know-how and the contacts to sell billions of dollars' worth of physical gold. It was going to be down to Toby. If successful then that should be enough to get Robson off JJ's back and that of the other two amigos. Deep in his subconscious, though, JJ knew that getting rid of Neil Robson's blackmail stick wasn't going to be that easy. The scumbag Financial Secretary to the Treasury was probably behind some other scumbag tailing Cyrus. It also did not seem plausible to JJ that the Robson he knew would be so altruistic as to hand over £3bn to HM government without extracting his cut first. Once again JJ realised, even if he did not want to think about it right now, that Neil Robson needed to be dealt with.

★ ★ ★

While JJ was flying, Neil Robson was sleeping, tucked up in his expensive and gaudy bed in Bowser's Castle, near Weybridge. He had had a hard night. He had confronted Vladimir Babikov over the botched job on Joel Gordon, though he had to tread carefully in his admonishment. If Babikov had felt unjustly chastised and turned ugly then he would probably have sacrificed the £20m+ that Robson was going to give him and just shoot the Fin Sec or torture him a little. Fortunately, the murderous Russian did feel that he had let down his star debtor, apologised profusely and promised to make it up to the UK government official. Babikov had also offered Robson a free night with one of the casino's top 'models' and some drugs gratis as well. Robson had enjoyed the voluptuous red head's company while JJ was worrying about Cyrus; after all a quick free fuck and a few snorts of cocaine made for a fine evening.

Today, however, was a new day. It was going to be a good day, and at the pinnacle of it was going to be the demise of one fucking Jamrock yardie, Joel Gordon. Robson got up, kicked the redhead out of bed, literally, and went downstairs to have breakfast. He showered, a little longer than usual, to eradicate any stench of Russian prostituka, got dressed, grabbed his Treasury boxes and briefcase and meandered down to his garage and Bentley Continental. Everything was in order. Hopefully, his early morning drive into London would be traffic light and he could finalise his plan to get rid of Gordon the curious accountant. Gordon's boss, Craig Wilson, Exchequer Secretary to the Treasury, would be back in his office tomorrow. Via the skills of the candescent Becky, his curvy PA, Robson knew that the yardie had scheduled a meeting with Wilson for 3pm on the day of his return. It was 7.30am now so Robson had a day and a third to make Joel Gordon disappear. As he pulled out of the barrier gates of St. George's Hill, he spotted his prior evening's pleasure waiting near the main road, presumably hoping to hail a black cab. Good luck with that, tart, he thought as he drove past her with no acknowledgement whatsoever.

"Good morning, Becky," said Robson as he entered his Treasury office on Horseguards Road, taking time to give Becky a full visual body scan. Her outfit was skin tight orange today, accentuating tits and bum and her heels were *Reservoir Dogs* killer, making her shapely legs look even more like a catwalk model's.

"Good morning, Mr Robson," replied Becky, on automatic and not caring one jot about her boss's bum or any other part of his anatomy.

"What's my schedule today?" Robson barked.

"Free in the morning," responded Becky. "One meeting with Joel Gordon at 2pm and another with Chancellor Walker at 3pm."

"Fine, get me a cup of tea, would you?" asked Robson, giving a modicum of politeness a brief outing. As Robson was having his tea and morning biscuit, he was mulling over his time in MI5. He had enjoyed it, especially the field trips and more especially when he could top some annoying foreigners. The majority of his wetwork missions usually involved killing by gun, sometimes torture was an appetiser but for the most part a Beretta placed at the captive's temple and bang was the preferred route. Robson had pretty much ruled out shooting Joel Gordon or slitting his throat. Babikov had declined to offer another of his ex-FSB thugs or even just thugs to replace the expired failure Vasily. The Russian had decided it was a bad omen that Vasily had been the unwitting victim of a football gang fracas and did not want to risk any police attention finding its way back to him. Although not entirely happy, fair enough concluded Robson. In any case, he thought, one of the advantages of being an MI5 field officer was that you were trained in more than one way to skin a cat. The morning passed slowly for Neil Robson. His full attention was on his 2pm meeting with Joel Gordon. The Financial Secretary to the Treasury had a clear plan in his mind.

"Joel, good to see you, come in and take a seat."

Robson appeared very cheery to Gordon, given the parlous state of Britain's finances.

"Good afternoon, Sir," replied the accountant. "May I ask what the agenda is for this meeting? There were no notes in my planner."

"I wanted to go over again some of the details that you had uncovered on the government's expenditures. I know that you'll probably see Craig Wilson soon so I just needed to refresh my own information," replied Robson, with a fake smile. He could hardly tell Gordon that his death was top of the agenda.

"Sure, no problem," said Joel. "Is my promotion to Deputy Head of the Finance Department still on track Sir?"

"Of course," replied Robson knowing that it had never been on track and was about to stay that way for good. "Let's have some green tea and cupcakes," offered Robson. "I know you like green tea and Becky's mum made these delicious cupcakes. Help yourself, Joel, there's a carrot cake kind of one, and a plain vanilla one, try whichever you wish."

"Thanks, I do like green tea," replied Joel, happy to see that the Financial Secretary had finally entered the modern, healthy world with his tea selection. "I might try a carrot cupcake if that's alright. I didn't have much lunch."

"Sure," replied Robson, his cheery high-pitched tone having dropped back into its more common matter-of-fact level. Neil Robson watched intently as Joel Gordon ate his carrot cupcake, with no emotion in his staring eyes. Another of the advantages of being a shady ex-MI5 officer with even shadier Russian acquaintances was that there was always a method of inflicting death on any enemy that could be tailor-made to fit the occasion. Today's diet of demise involved a variant of polonium-210, the compound which allegedly killed Alexander Litvinenko, former FSB officer, SVR agent and Russian defector in London in 2006.

Polonium is a metal and has thirty-three isotopes, all of which are radioactive. 210 Po which has a half-life of over 138 days is the most widely available. It is not widely available in the sense that cereals are widely available in supermarkets, but, unfortunately for Joel Gordon, it seemed more readily available to Russian bad guys than it should have been. In the old days, isolation of polonium from natural sources was a tedious and laborious process. However, in the modern world, polonium is obtained by irradiating bismuth with high-energy neutrons or protons. This process had been applied by Russia since the turn of the Millennium. Polonium-210 is around a quarter of a million times more toxic than hydrogen cyanide. It is extremely dangerous to handle due to the radioactivity of its alpha emitters. Vladimir Babikov had explained all of this to Neil Robson as he handed over the polonium-210 in its special container, gloves and syringe to the Financial Secretary to the Treasury. About fifty nanograms of this most lethal compound would do for a human if ingested. Babikov was taking no chances. The dose which was in the possession of Neil Robson was around ten micrograms, around 200 times the expected lethal dose and similar to what Babikov had supplied to the former KGB officers who had visited Litvinenko the day before he took ill. Shortly before his 2pm meeting with Joel Gordon, the Financial Secretary to HM Treasury had syringed both cupcakes offered to the accountant with polonium-210. Before Gordon had entered the Fin Sec's office, Robson had, very carefully, with specialised gloves on distributed this deadly substance evenly with precision and a cold heart. Robson had previously placed his own cupcake on a side plate. There was no way he was going to take any roulette chances with this radioactive killer.

Neil Robson knew exactly what was going to happen to Joel Gordon. He would not die in the Financial Secretary's office nor even the Treasury. That night when he had returned back to his flat near Upton Park, the Jamrock yardie would feel ill, have diarrhoea, vomiting, headaches and an overall feeling of nausea. He'd be forced to dial for an ambulance and be rushed to hospital. The staff at A&E would have very little idea what was ailing the otherwise fit-looking man. All the while, the 210's deadly alpha particles would go about their painful destruction. Some would enter his spleen, his liver and his kidneys. Others, maybe 10% or so, would enter his bone marrow. Given the dose, Gordon would be helpless within a day and would likely die within a week, looking like a terminal cancer patient at the end. His will to live, the focus of his mind, his spirit would all have departed well before then. There would be no tell-tale meeting with Craig Wilson.

Once Joel Gordon had eaten his fatal cupcake, Neil Robson

made an excuse to end their meeting there and then. Robson wasn't going to hang about close to Mr Glowalot even if Babikov had told him that polonium-210 does not emit radioactive gamma rays. Once Gordon had left his office, Robson used his specialist gloves and put plate, knife, crumbs, napkin, cup and saucer into a haz chem bag supplied by Babikov. Robson then put this trash into an industrial bin bag and asked Becky to dump it in a skip on her way home. If Babikov's chemistry knowledge was up to scratch then he'd probably see his hot PA in the morning and she would not be any more candescent than usual.

★ ★ ★

Neil Robson's prediction of Joel Gordon's condition was significantly more accurate than his efforts at economic prognostication. The young accountant had been rushed to Newham General Hospital, less than twenty minutes' drive from where he lived. He was accompanied by Talisha. Newham had a twenty-four-hour emergency department and an urgent care centre. Talisha had gently bullied Joel to allow her to call for an ambulance as soon as her boyfriend began vomiting and having the skitters simultaneously. She was American, built to respond quickly and not held back by a British stiff upper lip. The ambulance got to the hospital without a hitch. Joel was out and into the Emergency Department like a flash, the doctors and nurses attended to him straight away. It wasn't a weekend and West Ham were not playing at home, so the hospital traffic was relatively light. It didn't matter though. At this juncture, there were no external indications of radiation. Once Talisha had supplied the doctors and nurses with Joel's details, his job, pastimes, prior medical history, as far as she knew it, there was no reason to suspect acute radioactive poisoning. Even if they had, there was no effective treatment. There had been some research published suggesting chelation agents like Dimercaprol could be used to extend life after radiation, however, Newham General Hospital was a big city hospital, not a research centre. In any event even the treated rats in the experiments died, they just lived a little longer than the untreated ones.

The game was up for Joel Gordon. He passed away, on cue, four days later. Talisha would return to her hometown, in the USA, because London now had ghastly and painful memories. In her mid-thirties she would contract pancreatic cancer.

For Neil Robson, however, things had turned out all peachy. His nefarious plan was still intact, he hadn't heard a whisper from Craig Wilson. The local constabulary hadn't come knocking on his door to ask about cupcakes. He was going to see 'his' gold haul tomorrow with that wayward Scot and, to top it all, he still had a hot PA. It had been a good day indeed. The Financial Secretary's meeting with the Chancellor, Jeffrey Walker, had been a little fractious, but ended up being friendly enough. The old man was in a mild state of political panic regarding the £3bn hole. The general election was only months away, approximately the same span of time that would see the government's ability run out to pay the NHS staff, the armed forces and sections of the security services.

Jeffrey Walker, as a front-bench MP, remembered the poll tax riots in early 1990. Mrs Margaret Thatcher, leader of the Conservative Party and then Prime Minister, had introduced a Community Charge that was to take effect in England and Wales that spring. The charge, essentially an additional tax on property that took no account of income, seemed to several parts of the population to be unfair, indeed unjust. Protests and demonstrations popped up all over the country, many participants reflecting genuinely strongly held views, but undoubtedly a fair sprinkling of rent-a-mob to jolly things along. The demonstrations peaked, in the capital, London, on Saturday, 31st March 1990. From 11am that morning till 3am the following day central London was virtually a battleground between metropolitan police and the demonstrators. Order was eventually restored. However, John Major, who succeeded Mrs Thatcher as prime minister, announced that the Community Charge would be abolished and replaced with a Council Tax, still in force today, and linked to the value of a property.

The poll tax riots were shocking enough for the entire British public and, especially, the British government. Yet those riots would pale into insignificance if key public sector workers could not be paid. The poll tax riots involved the police in an attempt to allay personal and property damage. There were many injuries, keeping London hospitals even busier than they would be on a given weekend. What would happen if there were no police on duty to quell demonstrations, protests, riots? What would happen if there were no doctors or nurses, paramedics or ambulance staff to deal with injuries? What would be the extent of property damage, looting, complete lawlessness in parts of the nation's capital? Indeed, what would happen if the army itself, so often the back-stop of public order, was not being paid and, consequently, unwilling to risk life and limb for precisely nothing. These were the thoughts that were reverberating inside Chancellor Walker's head. For good measure he'd throw in his loss of job, career and even criminal proceedings. He had, after all, deliberately withheld the information regarding Britain's £3bn black hole from the Prime Minister. It was one big toxic mess and he was reduced to relying on his, apparently well-dodgy, Financial Secretary to clean it up.

"Neil, we need this money now," said Jeffrey Walker. "It has to be distributed to the various departments within a month, otherwise they will know that there's nothing in the coffers."

"I'm fully aware of that Chancellor," snapped Robson. "My information is that the package is now in London. I'm going to check it out in the morning. If all goes well, we should definitely have the money in distributable form before the end of April."

"I hope you're right, Neil, because if you're not we're totally shafted and beyond the point of recovery. Keep that in mind," cautioned Walker.

* * *

As he was walking along Piccadilly the next morning, on his way to a breakfast meeting with JJ Darke, the Chancellor's caution still hung in Neil Robson's mind. It wasn't his fault that dopey-dick Walker had allowed Britain's financial position to become so fucked up. He was the one who had come up with the ingenious plan to help fix it. It didn't matter that he wanted a huge chunk of the Korean gold for himself, nor that there had been some collateral damage in the form of Joel Gordon and Vasily the thug, nor that he was blackmailing Darke on a flimsy but eminently stick-able insider trading case. The end justifies the means. Machiavelli was spot on. What's that old goat Walker got to complain about? Fuck all, thought Robson. I'm about to save his flabby spotty arse even though the useless git doesn't deserve it.

As Robson entered the Wolseley, opposite the Ritz Hotel, he spotted JJ already seated at a table on the higher level. There was no one within earshot. The canny Scot had obviously made a few bogus reservations, this was normally one busy place, even for breakfast.

"JJ," said Robson.

"Neil," replied JJ, neither man feeling inclined to indulge in any variety of normal pre-meal greetings.

"You don't look like you've had a tough time relieving the

gooks of their gold," started Robson with that fake smile of his attached. "A few signs of healing bruises but not bad."

"I had a good team with me," replied JJ stoically. "They had my back all the way."

"Where's the gold?" asked Robson unable to contain himself.

"It's safe," replied JJ. "It's here, in London, locked up and secure, away from prying eyes and itchy fingers."

"Great. Now, look Darke, I – I mean the government, need this money fast. How long before you can turn this gold into pounds sterling and get it to me?"

In a sense he was telling the truth. The government did need the money fast. Robson omitted to add that so did he. Vladimir Babikov was getting a little anxious regarding his pay day. In addition to the base £2.5m that Robson owed him, the criminal Russian had had to fork out for a thug to replace Vasily and a whole lot more to get the polonium-210 for the Financial Secretary. JJ was looking straight at Neil Robson. He so didn't like this excuse of a man. Before replying JJ had some of his orange juice and a sizeable bite of his well-done bacon roll.

"It's not simple," JJ eventually replied. "For a start, we've got 6,000 bars of bullion, each weighing about 12.5kg. It's a job moving that around. Secondly, and I haven't run this by Toby Naismith yet, selling this lot in one go may not be possible. I don't know the capacity of the physical gold market. Thirdly, at a GBP/USD rate of 1.5000 and a gold price of US$1800/oz, the gold is worth the £3bn you need. However, if the pound strengthens against the dollar and/or the gold price falls then it will be worth less. We can't control either the FX market or the gold market."

Robson absorbed this information as he was having some scrambled egg on toast and a cup of weak tea. He didn't think JJ was spinning him a yarn. Robson himself hadn't a clue about the physical gold market but he did know that the cable rate could move about like a demented yoyo. Still, that wasn't his problem.

"I see what you're saying Darke, but I don't give a fuck. I need £3.5bn, in sterling, in a nominated bank account, within a week, two at the absolute outside. That's £3.5bn, at least, not a penny less. If there's a surprise gain then thanks. If the pound gets weaker and the gold price goes up, great, I'll take the windfall profit. Your job is to get it done, Darke, capisce?" snapped Robson.

"I cannot guarantee that," responded JJ calmly.

"Look jockstrap, you need to guarantee it. Otherwise, you, fatboy and the French geek are going down. Damning media coverage, huge fines, lengthy jail terms. They're all coming your way if you don't come up with the goods. OK? You don't want that nice looking kid of yours to be without his dad for an extended period, do you? Him being a half orphan already."

JJ had always been accomplished at preventing his facial expressions revealing his inner thoughts. This morning was a bit of a tester though. JJ had worn his dark blue Boss suit today, with light grey shirt, black well-polished brogues, his dominus ring and his 1995 Rolex Zenith Daytona, black dial and upside down 6 on the hour chronograph register. This meant he was in the mood for business, not playing, or relaxing, or on the beach, or even robbing a central bank. JJ had gone into the breakfast meeting with Robson, vowing to be professional, to see this task through, to get Toby, Yves-Jacques and himself off the hook and to get Neil Robson out of his life. The slimeball's mention of Cyrus, however, triggered a whole path of thought that he had not anticipated, was hoping to avoid, but in that one mention of his son, had changed the end game for sure.

"Leave Cyrus out of it dickhead. If I ever think, even for a second, that you are contemplating disturbing my son's life in any way, I will kill you, stone dead, where you stand, where you sit, where you sleep. Have you got that?"

Neil Robson looked at JJ, then let out a quiet laugh. "What are you going to do to me lady boy?" replied Robson. "You were an analyst in MI5, not a black ops specialist. Sure, you went to North Korea, maybe had to push over a gook soldier or two, but, you're no killer. You're a soft, middle-aged, hedge fund plonker, that sits behind a desk all day looking at wee green and red numbers flashing away. It's like a kid's game. There's no physical risk, no exposure to real danger. You're not capable. Just get the gold sold cupcake and don't ever threaten me again." With that, the Financial Secretary to the Treasury pushed back his chair, got up and left.

Many parts of JJ's neural system wanted to go after Robson, break his neck there and then and leave the weasel lifeless on the floor of the Wolseley. That would not be optimal, the saner parts of JJ's brain kept telling him. In that event, JJ would certainly go to jail, for a very long time, Cyrus would be mortified and without his dad. The better part of valour is discretion, rationalised the coward Falstaff. JJ would be discreet alright, but not in the way Shakespeare meant nor the way Neil Robson hoped for.

★ ★ ★

As breakfasts go, the one JJ had with Neil Robson would not have entered either's top ten. The world is a relative place, however, and their breakfast meeting at the Wolseley was a lot better than one meeting concurrently taking place in North Korea's State Security Department. The no-option invitees were Vice Admiral Goh and Commodore Park. The hosts were SSD Major Lee and his boss, General Choi Yang-Kun, the permanent Minister of State Security. Major Lee's companion at Haeju docks, the quiet man, was not invited. That brought an inaudible sigh of relief from Commodore Park, who had first-hand knowledge of his nocturnal handiwork. As you would expect, the SSD building in Pyongyang was austere and anonymous. It had the usual flags on poles outside but it could have been any one of a number of government buildings dotted around the capital. The main SSD building was six storeys high, part of it on concrete stilts, and long, very long, taking up roughly half a street. Vice Admiral Goh and Commodore Park were seated together, at a simple metal table, hands bound behind their backs. The only other furniture in the room was two metallic chairs, similar to the ones the invitees were sitting on. They had been seated for an hour. Minister Choi and Major Lee eventually entered the room. Neither looked happy. Both sat opposite Goh and Park, but Minister Choi had taken his chair a few feet away from the table.

Major Lee began. "Vice Admiral Goh, Commodore Park, do you both understand why you are here?"

"I know you wish to find out more regarding the theft of the submarine Major," began Goh, "but I fail to see why we need to be tied up in order to answer any questions." Given that the Vice Admiral was being held in a basement room in one of the world's most brutal police states, that small display of defiance was unwisely courageous.

Major Lee glanced over his right shoulder at Minister Choi. On receipt of a brief nod, Lee stood up, went behind Goh's chair and undid his ties. He then did the same for Park.

"Thank you Major, Minister Choi," said Goh.

"Do either of you have any idea who stole the nuclear submarine?" asked Lee directly.

Park responded first. "No Major, I do not. As you know I was having dinner with colleagues, then all hell broke loose. I did not see any uniforms, any insignia on the attackers, nor did I hear their voices. I am embarrassed that our submarine was stolen on my watch but I know nothing about it," said a strained Park.

"I believe you have resigned Commodore?" asked Minister Choi.

"Yes, Sir, I have."

"Do you think that your resignation is fair recompense for our supreme leader being down US$1bn worth of Russian submarine, Commodore?"

"No, Sir," was all the Commodore could find.

"Neither does the supreme leader, Park. You're obviously too stupid to be in on it," continued Choi, "and Kim Jong-un does not want to persecute the afflicted. You are stripped of your rank of Commodore and dishonourably discharged from our great people's navy. You will be taken from here to Kwan-il-so No. 22. You will spend the rest of your days there in the kitchen. Perhaps you will be capable of ensuring that no green beans are stolen from fellow prisoners' plates. In his infinite leniency, our leader has ordered that no retribution, of any type, will be sought from your family."

"Minister," was all Park replied. His thankfulness at being alive after the Haeju interrogation by Lee had now evaporated. Kwan-il-so was the harshest of the DPRK's penal colonies. It currently housed around 50,000 to 60,000 prisoners, mostly political and all living in desperate squalor and infection. Park doubted that there would be any green beans on prisoners' plates for him to keep tabs on. He would have been better off as a victim of the quiet man. His only morsel of comfort was that his family would not be harmed or left destitute. At least, there was that, he thought as he was taken away by the SSD officers on his way to hell.

"Vice Admiral Goh," said Major Lee.

"Major," responded Goh.

"It was your idea to buy the submarine from Russia, correct?"

"Yes, it was."

"How do you think that the Korean People's Navy was going to pay for such an advanced, expensive vessel?" asked Lee.

"I understand that our supreme leader, in his infinite wisdom, had agreed to release some of the country's gold reserves to purchase the submarine," replied Goh.

"And where do you think that these gold reserves are, Vice Admiral?" queried Choi.

"Probably in our central bank's vaults or our supreme leader's residence," suggested Goh, wondering where this line of questioning was going.

"Well, they used to be there. On the same night the submarine was stolen Goh, our central bank, here in Pyongyang, was breached and the thieves made off with the best part, actually nearly all, of the DPRK's gold reserves," announced Choi. Vice Admiral Goh looked genuinely shocked. He had been in the clutches of the secret police since the incident at Haeju. He knew nothing and had heard nothing about a robbery at the central bank. He said nothing.

"So, Goh," continued Minister Choi, "it was your idea to purchase the submarine and you knew where the means of payment for it was. Incriminating, don't you think Vice Admiral?"

Goh had his senses back from the secondary shock of the central bank news.

"It is incriminating Minister, but not as far as I am concerned. I know nothing about either robbery and I demand that you release me. I am a Vice Admiral in the KPN, I have been loyal to all of our supreme leaders and I have fought with honour for my country. I am no political dissident, no criminal and certainly no thief of any description," said Goh, with feeling.

Major Lee said nothing.

Minister Choi, with a slow insincere clapping of his hands said, "Very convincing, Goh." He then gestured to the guards at the door of the interrogation room. The two burly SSD officers returned, part-dragging a man across the floor. He was handcuffed behind his back. Both of his legs were broken due to several hammer blows inflicted on the poor unfortunate earlier in the day by the SSD's heavies. His hair was sodden with blood and water, the latter being used to wake him up after he had fallen unconscious from the pain of his beatings. Both of his eyes were swollen, his left cheekbone was fractured, he did not have any front teeth left and fresh blood was seeping from his mangled nose. The two heavies tossed the man's limp body into the space between Minister Choi and Vice Admiral Goh. It was deep cover Kwon.

"This man says differently Vice Admiral," announced Minister Choi. Kwon had run out of luck. After he had successfully ushered the moaner Ji-hun across the border to South Korea and had made initial contact with the family of the Kaesŏng border soldier, one of the four who had defected, he returned to his apartment in Pyongyang. The secret police were waiting for him. The soldier's family did not totally believe Kwon's story. The mother, in particular, thought that it was a set up by the DPRK authorities to test their loyalty to Kim Jong-un. She had received a phone call from her now defected son to tell her that he was okay and that the family should go South, past Songnim and await instructions. The mother did not believe this. If in doubt rat them out was her brain-washed motto. She contacted the SSD and they sprung a trap on Kwon.

Deep cover had hidden most of his incriminating stuff well and the SSD could not link him to Jim Bradbury, JJ or any of his CIA colleagues at PAU Travel. Unfortunately, while checking through Kwon's clothes, one keen-eyed SSD officer had spotted some small scraps of previously-molten metal in the turn-ups of a pair of Kwon's work trousers. That same SSD officer had been detailed to check the central bank's vaults for clues. He had taken as evidence some of the small metal pieces from the floor, left behind from Victor Pagari's thermal lance. He was sure they matched those in Kwon's pants. When your luck's out, it can be really out. Deep cover Kwon had not even been in the central bank's vaults for long. The small, metal fragments must have come from Victor's bag and a few of them accidently transferred to Kwon's trousers. Deep cover was hauled off by the secret police. He had been interrogated, beaten, tortured for most of the time that Goh and Park had been having it relatively easy in the interview room.

Kwon was tough and much stronger than his skinny frame suggested. The secret police thugs kept beating on him. 'Who stole the gold? Who stole the submarine?' they screamed at him in between punches and kicks. Kwon genuinely had no idea about a stolen submarine so he wasn't going to be able to blab on that one. He tried to keep his wits about him, but he was in severe pain and once they had broken his legs with a heavy hammer it was excruciating, indescribable pain. 'Who stole the gold, traitor?' 'Who do you work for?' they kept pounding and asking. 'Was it Goh?' 'Was it Park?' 'Who did it you fucking piece of dead meat trash?' There was no let-up while he was conscious. Kwon knew he wasn't getting out of this. To his eternal credit he had not spilled on his CIA involvement or his colleagues.

The secret police torturers though had opened a small crack of opportunity, unbeknown to those foul dimwits. Kwon had no idea who Park was. He may have come across a hundred Parks in his life, but not one that he could place in a central bank or on a submarine. Goh was a slightly less common Korean name. It was part of his undercover role to know who was who in the DPRK government and armed forces. The Goh they kept yelling about could be Vice Admiral Goh of the KPN. He would have reason, perhaps, to be near or on a submarine, whatever his torturers interest in that was. Kwon waited for another severe beating. As his nose exploded in a spray of blood and his left cheek bone cracked, Kwon finally let out, "It was Goh, Vice Admiral Goh, I work for him."

Almost immediately the torturous interrogators left Kwon alone. One stood guard over his wrecked body while the other dialled an internal extension. Major Lee passed on Kwon's confession to Minister Choi and now Vice Admiral Goh was confronted by his accuser. Of course, Kwon knew Goh had nothing to do with the central bank heist and he had no idea about the submarine. Despite the intensity of his beatings, he managed to rationalise that if he could take down one final DPRK bad guy then he would have done the best he could. By most standards Vice Admiral Goh was not a bad guy but, like Kwon, he was in the wrong place at very much the wrong time.

"I have no idea what you're talking about Minister," said Goh with fierce agitation in his voice. "I have never seen this man in my life and I reiterate my total loyalty to the KPN and the DPRK."

Minister Choi was getting bored. The supreme leader of the DPRK and Choi's immediate boss wanted answers, wanted a suspect, wanted the perpetrators of two heinous crimes in one night. Of course Goh was going to deny it. Who wouldn't under the circumstances? However, the bleeding cripple lying at his feet said it was Goh. He could have said 'Mickey Mouse' or 'Captain Falcon' or 'Hologramps' from *Supah Ninjas* but he didn't, he said 'Goh'. The Vice Admiral did not look like an arch-criminal and, admittedly thought Choi, the evidence was somewhat flimsy. Nevertheless, there were enough dots to connect to make a discernible picture. Goh was in the frame.

"Vice Admiral," resumed Minister Choi, "or should I say

former Vice Admiral as you are now stripped of your rank and command. You too will be dishonourably discharged from the people's navy. I hereby place you under arrest on suspicion of robbery of our leader's submarine, his gold or both. Time will tell and you will be encouraged in your confession by Major Lee's best interrogators."

"You're an ass and an ass-licker Choi!" yelled Goh, making a lurch for the Minister. His direct path to Choi's throat was intercepted by Major Lee's gun butt and as Goh fell to the floor, his head inches from Kwon's, the courageous deep cover operative looked into his eyes, managed a grimace and muttered 'Goh'.

Former Vice Admiral Goh was taken away. He would be interrogated harshly. He did not have the inner courage of Kwon nor his ability to withstand pain. He was visited by the supreme leader himself, no stranger to the SSD, he had worked there before the announcement in September 2010 that he was to be heir apparent. Kim Jong-un was not convinced Goh was guilty. He had indeed been instrumental in acquiring the Russian submarine but he also had over thirty years of loyal service in the KPN. The fact that he had known or guessed where the DPRK's gold hoard was, simply reflected that he was knowledgeable, not necessarily criminal. Deep cover Kwon's 'confession' was more troublesome. He really did have no apparent reason to finger Goh and he had done so before even setting eyes on the man inside the SSD. The supreme leader could not be bothered thinking about it anymore. One man doesn't steal a submarine and billions of US dollars' worth of gold. There must be accomplices, Minister Choi's task is not over. In the meantime, the supreme Leader decided that Goh needed to be made an example of. A firing squad would be organised in the next day or so and then there would be no Goh. Following his confession and subsequent outing of Goh, Kwon was taken to a secure ward in Taesongsan combined hospital in Pyongyang to get fixed up and cleaned up. This may have seemed like surprisingly decent behaviour given what had occurred before, but the DPRK authorities wanted most of their political prisoners to be able to work in the camps, not loll about whiling the day away. Once his broken legs and other injuries were healed, Kwon was destined for penal camp 22, where he could look forward to some daily slop from former Commodore Park but with no glimpse of a green bean ever to be seen.

★ ★ ★

SVR Deputy Director Igor Kruglov had fared a lot better than any of the 'invitees' in Pyongyang's SSD. The director of the SVR, frankly, was hopping mad that the *Admiral Vinogradov* had not managed to recapture or destroy the missing nuclear submarine. The President of Russia was even more outraged. Not only had US$1bn of elite Russian naval engineering and weaponry gone AWOL, those deviants in the DPRK hadn't fully paid for the Borei. On top of that, the glaikit looking scunner who called himself their supreme leader didn't have the readies to pay his debt. Some old flannel about a robbery at their central bank. For god's sake, thought the President, why did we ever get into bed with that lot!

Livid as they both were, neither the President nor the SVR Director blamed Kruglov. At least he had tried and had had one of his agents on the submarine, though that channel seemed to have now been switched off. Investigations by the FSB showed that Kruglov had acted with expediency and could not have done much more. Admiral Chirkov had been on the case too and his instructions to the captain of the *Vinogradov* were clear, concise and timely. Maybe Captain Sergei Kargin could have aimed better, but it was a long-shot from the off, both in planning and in targeting. Kruglov was exonerated from any blame. However, both the President and Kruglov's SVR boss felt that the job was still unfinished. When the *Admiral Vinogradov* had reached the missiles detonation site in the East China Sea, there was no sign of wreckage or debris or fuel. There had clearly been no direct hits on the submarine. While that was disappointing, thought the President, it meant that $1bn of Russian nuclear submarine was still in the hands of an unknown enemy. Kruglov could redeem himself fully by tracking down the sub's whereabouts and discovering the identities of the audacious thieves. Kruglov said that he would, but in his heart, he did not know if he could.

The SVR had operatives all over Europe, Asia and North America. The Illegals programme in North America was, with the absence of Anyata Ivanovna, down to one. That one was well-placed in the US Congress but would not likely have access to any information in this regard. Kruglov reasoned that the submarine would not surface in Asia. He thought that if he had stolen it, he would not just drive it around the corner. Also, the route that the submarine had been on suggested that it was headed for Europe, possibly eventually, the United States. That was where he would concentrate the efforts of the SVR. Over the next few hours Kruglov contacted several key SVR operatives in Europe, principally located in Italy, Germany and France. The Deputy Director of the SVR did not gauge that Eastern Europe was a likely destination for the submarine. While there was the occasional political spat with allies and former parts of the Soviet Union, these countries were primarily friends and would be unlikely to sponsor such an act against Russia.

The one area in Europe which was not fertile ground for SVR activities was the UK. Ever since the poisoning of Alexander

Litvinenko in 2006 and the death of Boris Berezovsky in 2013, Russian activities in the UK were under the microscope of MI5 in a big way. The SVR had not managed to place a senior operative into key circles of government or policy making for years. Most of the time this did not matter. In issues of most concern to Russia and the SVR, the UK government simply went along with whatever the United States decided. Every now and then the British bulldog may bark but it had lost nearly all of its teeth and rarely presented Russia with any credible threat or obstacle. Kruglov also was aware that the economic significance of the UK had diminished. The governments of the 1970s and 1980s had more or less wasted the legacy and potential economic power of North Sea oil, unlike modern day Russia. Britain now seemed to have a permanent balance of payments deficit and the accumulation of trade deficits year in, year out, meant that the external debt of this small island was ballooning forever higher, resulting in owing foreigners money at an increasing rate. Their political leadership was also on the wane. The twentieth century saw Britain with two great leaders, Winston Churchill and Margaret Thatcher. You could love them or loathe them, but they were strong, decisive, not possible to bully or pressurise. Since then it was all downhill. The current coalition government, in and of itself guaranteeing inertia, seemed to be populated by men who all looked the same, sounded the same and, eventually, did the same.

Yet, Igor Kruglov could not discount British involvement in the submarine theft. Despite its small size, its economic decline and its political jelly tots, the UK was still a formidable force in two areas. Intelligence and financial innovation. The British Intelligence services were, perhaps, the best in the world. The CIA, SVR and Mossad may have more loyal bodies dedicated to their cause around the world, but MI5 and MI6 were now extremely tough to penetrate and their defensive record against terrorist assault was impressive. Most of the time the British public did not even know that they had been saved from murderous attacks. The M's deep cover agents were brave and effective. It was also somewhat incredulous that this small dot of land and people in the vast ocean could retain the hub of the world's financial activities. It did and despite claims by one financial centre or the other, London was still at the pinnacle. If the submarine had been stolen for cash, thought Kruglov, then financiers in London would probably get to know about it, if not handle it themselves. Consequently, it was clear to Kruglov that he needed to take two steps immediately. One was to tap whatever information the SVR could get out of their meagre undercover sources in the United States. Second, initiate contact and a regular flow of information from their people in London. He would need help.

"Yuri," said Kruglov, as he finished dialling an internal extension, "please come to my office as soon as you can."

"Certainly, Sir," replied Yuri Menkov. "I'll be up in a flash." Yuri Menkov was as pleased as anyone that no harm had befallen Igor Kruglov following the blank result on the submarine case. Menkov had been involved in that project. If Kruglov went south, actually it would probably have been north to Siberia, then Menkov would have gone south with him.

"Deputy Director, how can I be of help?" asked Menkov, having been true to his word and arrived in Kruglov's office less than a minute after his call.

"Yuri, we're still on the case of our missing submarine. Captain Kargin of the *Admiral Vinogradov* detected no sign that the submarine had been hit. We deduce, therefore, that it remains operational and in the hands of the enemy thieves. My own research leads me to believe that the stolen submarine is headed for Europe or the United States. I've already contacted the appropriate officers in Italy, Germany and France to be vigilant and to report to me twice a day. Where I need help, Yuri, from your signal tracking and your databases, is the US and the UK. Agent Ivanovna has not been in touch and there have been no further signals from her phone. She must be presumed MIA. We have one deep cover Illegal in a senior position in Washington but I do not think that he is in the right place to know of clandestine movements of military hardware. In the UK, I don't know what we've got. After Litvinenko, Berezovsky and agent Kushchyenko (Anna Chapman), we could not make any inroads. MI5 and MI6 have successfully blocked our efforts to establish an effective Illegals program in the UK. We are blind in that country, Yuri. Any ideas?" asked Kruglov.

Menkov absorbed all the information that he had just been given. As head of AI for the SVR with an IQ of 165, it didn't take him long.

"I know that we have two officers, albeit relatively recent placements, in the CIA and the NSA. They can be contacted with urgency and ordered to direct their attention to this issue, Deputy Director," suggested Menkov.

"Yes, Yuri, good. At least that would be a start," replied Kruglov, content with Menkov's suggestion but not yet getting out his cigar. "And the UK?"

"We have no one, Sir," responded Menkov without hesitation. "You are correct in your assessment of our penetration of the British security services and the government. We have not had any useful information from Britain since early 2013."

Igor Kruglov was not over the moon about this piece of news. While he did not really expect that the UK had anything to do with the theft of the submarine, their security services may chatter on occasion with their US and European counterparts. Also,

London was mega-cosmopolitan. Every race, creed, colour and nationality floated through the capital. Gossip, whispers, drunken babbling, surely there was something.

"We do have one contact, Deputy Director, kind of," offered Menkov, with reticence but wishing to alleviate the pained expression on his boss's face.

"What's a kind of contact, Menkov?" barked Kruglov, annoyed by Yuri's lack of precision.

"Well, we occasionally get information from him regarding vulnerable business men or financial types, sometimes government ministers. It's not been greatly useful in the past but it has allowed some of our own businesses to apply leverage to strike better deals. He is not, however, an employee of the SVR."

"Who is it, for god's sake?" yelled Kruglov.

"Vladimir Babikov."

"What! That old criminal douchebag! He should be in a fucking salt mine! You're not seriously suggesting that we use him, Menkov, are you?" hollered the Deputy Director.

"No, Sir, I'm not," said Menkov meekly, "it's just, well, it's just that he is the only source in the UK that we have had a scrap of useful information from in over a year. He runs a casino in London and has at least six ex-FSB officers in his entourage. We're desperate by the sounds of it, and he's a desperado for certain, but one with an array of contacts, including inside the British government."

Igor Kruglov had his head buried in his hands and may even have been covering his ears. Had it really come to this? He had probably lost his beautiful Anyata. The best information source replacement the SVR could come up with was a torturing murderer who was lucky to have got out of Russia in one piece. Drugs, prostitution, gambling, Babikov was like an online dictionary of all man's vices. This was not a pleasant thought.

Kruglov and Babikov knew of each other. If the first Deputy Director had to ask for the dirtbag's help, then he must, but it was going to be painful.

Menkov returned to his desk and emailed Kruglov the criminal Babikov's contact details. He thought it wise not to present himself before Kruglov again so soon after the Deputy Director's outburst. He was only trying to help. After a strong cup of tea with some vodka in it, Kruglov dialled.

"Babikov," came the reply that the SVR man did not want to hear but knew he must.

"This is Igor Kruglov of the SVR," the Deputy Director replied, certain that the criminal would remember him.

"Igor, Igor, my friend. How nice to hear from you. Straight through to my direct line. You've not lost any of your old skills. What can I do for you?" said Babikov.

Igor Kruglov was already on edge. For a start he was no friend of Babikov. Secondly, he had a right cheek calling him or his skills old, the criminal must have been at least ten or twelve years his senior!

"We have an issue of national importance Babikov, and the nation that spawned you, nurtured you, educated you and let you live despite your several capital crimes, needs your assistance."

Vladimir Babikov was not used to being ordered around or of having things demanded of him. He was also no fool. The Deputy Director of the SVR would not be calling him, personally, if it was not critically important. He could always tell Kruglov to 'fuck off and die' but that would probably occasion a visit one dark night from a hot chick who would slip him a Mickey Finn and then slit his throat. He'd play along for now.

"Of course, Igor, what can I do?" responded Babikov.

"You understand that I cannot give you details, Babikov, but the gist of it is that we are missing a piece of Russian military hardware. It was stolen a few days ago while in the possession of one of our so-called friends. We do not know the identities of the thieves nor their nationality. We need you to keep your ear to the ground, to have your men report any gossip, loose talk, bravado that may be related to this, however tenuous that relationship may seem."

"Certainly, Igor, I will. What's in it for me?" asked Babikov.

Deputy Director Kruglov was tempted to say 'letting you live you fat cunt' but desisted on grounds of the greater good, well the greater good as it related to the task in hand.

"You will be well rewarded Babikov if you come up with anything which leads to the recovery of our nation's property," Kruglov replied. "My information is that you have contacts within the British government, Babikov, is that correct?"

"Yes it is, Kruglov," replied the criminal, no longer feeling it necessary to keep up the pretence of friendliness by using the Deputy Director's first name.

"How useful is your contact?" asked Kruglov.

"He is a high ranking official in the ruling party. I have not asked him or squeezed him for any information. He owes me money, which is now due."

"Do you have enough dirt on him to do some squeezing even after he's repaid your debt?" asked Kruglov.

"Yes," replied Babikov.

"Then do it," demanded Kruglov.

The main course of conversation between spy and criminal was now over. After Kruglov gave Babikov details as to how to contact him, the Deputy Director of the SVR reclined in his chair and poured himself some more black tea and vodka. He had set in motion every listening post he thought viable, every reliable clandestine contact or operative that the SVR had, and now had engaged the services of a low life criminal expat

Russian. There was little more that he could do in the search for the submarine, just wait and hope that some information would flow.

After Kruglov had hung up, Vladimir Babikov sprang into a different kind of action. He had an impromptu internal meeting with his ex-FSB team, all the casino staff that were trusted and on his payroll, the croupiers, the 'models', the works. They were to report back to him on even the slightest hint of some punter's wayward babbling that mentioned any of the key words 'military', 'hardware', 'Russian', 'deal'. With that in place, he sat down and dialled.

"Neil Robson," said the voice at the other end of the phone.

"Neil, my friend, come and see me tonight. Do not worry, it is not about the money. I know you will repay me soon. There is another matter that I wish to speak to you about. Maybe you can help me out. Perhaps we can even reduce that debt of yours a little, in exchange for some information."

"Sure Vladimir," replied Robson. "I'll be there by 8pm."

★ ★ ★

After his irritable breakfast meeting with Neil Robson, JJ set about completing his tasks for the day. He had driven his Porsche C4S down to Woking to see Harold McFarlane at McLaren. The skilful engineer was delighted to see JJ and even more delighted to receive a larger 'bonus' than he had expected for himself and his team.

"How did the conveyor systems do?" asked Harold, awake enough to realise that they were not packed up and residing in the small space that Porsche called a boot.

"They were great, Harold, worked a treat. Unfortunately we had to leave them behind." Harold knew JJ well enough not to pry further. If additional details were not forthcoming, then so be it. Harold had a huge chunk of cash in his hands and he was happy.

After McLaren, JJ drove back to London. He organised a telegraphic transfer of €100,000 to Vincent Barakat at PLP, along with a message of gratitude. That should keep the young scientist smiling and able to embark on additional path breaking research at his skunkworks. It would also lay down a marker of trust between the two in the unlikely event that JJ needed the future services of PLP. JJ then went on to see Tom Rogers, Ethel's husband in his architect's office in Battersea. Tom had spoken to Ethel a couple of times on the phone so JJ didn't have to break the news about her having a hole in her shoulder. JJ went to see Tom as a courtesy to Ethel, to assure him that Ginger was fully on the road to recovery and to tell him that she had been a vital part in a successful operation of national importance. That was a white lie, of course, and, of course, for the greater good. Tom was decent enough given that he was face to face with the man who had been instrumental in getting his wife shot. Nevertheless, JJ was a tad relieved when he left Tom Rogers' office.

Next on the agenda was MAM. He was still head of portfolio strategy and investment at the fund, though for the past ten days or so you wouldn't have known it. David Sutherland, the head of MAM was pleasant enough, didn't moan too much and just wanted to know if his most senior employee was likely to be around for a while. JJ assured him that he was. Toby and Yves-Jacques were delighted to see their boss. Fathead dragged JJ away for a one-on-one coffee as soon as he could.

"Did you get it?" asked Toby with enthusiasm, and fully aware of what JJ's mission had been.

"Yes, Toby, we've got it."

"How much? Does it look big and shiny? When can I see it?

When can we sell it?" asked Toby firing in the questions like a Gatling gun.

"Whoa, slow down, Toby. If you come round to the house tonight, I'll take you for a gander. It's locked up in a secure van in a secure garage, walking distance from Markham Square. You can judge for yourself whether it's big and shiny enough. As for selling, ASAP would be the order of the day."

"Good stuff," said Toby, "I'll be around by 6pm. Can't wait."

"By the way, Toby, I came across your limerick entry for last year's quiz, stuffed in my pants pocket. Jesus, it was hopeless!"

"Ooh, it wasn't that bad," replied Toby in a feeble effort at a Scottish accent. "In any case, what was the answer to the currency question?"

"The New Zealand dollar," informed JJ.

"The New Zealand fucking dollar!" exclaimed Toby. "What has that got to do with a Scottish dwarf opening a bleedin' door backwards, may I ask?"

"OK," said JJ, "what's the nickname of the New Zealand dollar?"

"The Kiwi," replied Toby.

"So, kind of backwards, that's wiki or wee key. Ta-dah!" exclaimed JJ enjoying revealing the answer almost as much as the pained look of disbelief on Fathead's face.

"Jesus Christ, JJ, I've said it before and I'll say it again, you've got one warped fucking mind, chief." With that the two friends and colleagues headed back to the main trading floor. JJ enjoyed Toby's company and he felt much more at home, here in the land of flashing screens, general hubbub, sound-bites and perennial news loops than he did in the desolate streets of Pyongyang or in the vaults of its central bank.

It was 3pm and JJ was beginning to feel tired. So far today he had seen Neil Robson, Harold McFarlane, Tom Rogers, David

435

Sutherland, Toby and Yves-Jacques. He was also going to meet Toby again in a few hours' time so he wanted to go home and see Cyrus and Gil. Despite not having taken all of his supplements and vitamins with him to Korea, his latest blood test results from the Marsden indicated a PSA reading of below 0.1. To all intents and purposes that meant that his cancer was undetectable. The proof of the pudding though would not be for another year or so. The prostate cancer cells may have been starved and burned but the best of the medical profession could not tell, for certain, whether they would stay dead once the hormone treatment stopped. It was entirely possible that the life destroyers were in a deep coma and that when JJ's testosterone started to recover, so would the cancer. JJ was still having the occasional unannounced hot sweat, and intense feelings of tiredness could also strike without warning. But there it was. He did, however, have Cyrus and that gave his heart the warmest of glows.

★ ★ ★

"Dad, is that you?" called out Cyrus on hearing the Chelsea blue door of his house close.

"Hi Cyrus, it's me. Where are you?"

"I'm in the living room. Just got the latest version of *Mario Kart*. It's brilliant. Really difficult. Some of the courses are in outer space, some are underground. There's new characters and new cars. Love it!" replied Cyrus.

"Do you want me to toast you at it?" asked JJ.

"Glad to see your expedition to foreign parts didn't kill your sense of humour, Dad. Let's play anyway. I'm going to be Metal Mario. You can be Princess Peach if you like!" said Cyrus laughing, because JJ would never be any of the girl characters in the games. He was from Glasgow, tough, hard, no androgyneity allowed.

"You're a cheeky monkey, young man," said JJ, as he sat down next to Cyrus on the sofa, ready to play. He sat on Cyrus's left hand side and cosied up real close to his son. Cyrus was right handed but JJ was corriejukit as the Scots would say or sinistre in archaic Latin. This was ideal. They could be shoulder to shoulder and not impact the dexterity required for extreme *Mario Kart*. They played and they laughed and they laughed and they played. Father and son, enjoying their time together. It could not get better. In mid-game, Gil came in, having been out to get a few messages.

"Hi Gil!" said both JJ and Cyrus.

JJ put down his remote, stood up and gave Gil a hug. "Good to see you, thanks for looking after Cyrus and all the other stuff."

"No problem. He's fun to be with," replied Gil. "What are we going to do about the shadow?" she whispered as Cyrus was totally absorbed in his game.

"Is he still tracking the boy?" asked JJ.

"I haven't seen the black Merc for a day or two, so it's possible I was just a bit hyper-sensitive. I don't think so, though. We should keep our guard up," replied Gil. "Did Korea go okay?"

"Broadly speaking. We got the gold. Ethel took a shot but she'll be fine. Toby's popping round in a wee while to look at the stash. I guess he needs to see what he's going to sell."

"That Fathead," said Gil, "better lock up your malt. He can consume more of that stuff than any known human should be able to."

JJ retired defeated from the *Mario Kart* challenge with Cyrus. He stayed in the living room, on his comfortable chair, partly so that he could just be near his son, and partly to relax with him and Gil. Relaxation had been off the agenda for a while and it was going to be off it again in short shrift. Time to savour a few hours of quality down time.

"Hi JJ," said Toby as JJ opened the door. "I'm not early am I?" he added, not really bothered whether he was or was not. He had bars and bars of the barbarous relic to touch and view. This was fun time. It was 5.55pm.

"No you're right on time," said JJ, a small white lie, intended to allow Toby's clear joy to continue untethered.

"Let's go then," said Fathead, already turning around to go back out. Jesus, thought JJ, Toby hadn't even asked for a Macallans nor had he started any banter with Cyrus. He sure was keen.

"Cyrus, Gil," called out JJ. "I'm just popping out with Toby, won't be long." Cyrus and Gil acknowledged JJ's cheerio and the Scot and the Englishman headed for Elystan Street and JJ's lockup.

"Holy fucking baloney!" exclaimed Toby on sight of six thousand bars of gold bullion. He was doing something that looked like the drunken sailor's jig – it wouldn't get him in *Riverdance,* that was for sure. He was laughing away, bent over half the time in between jigs, you would have thought it was his gold.

"I've never even thought about this much gold, JJ, let alone touched it. It's fucking unbelievable. How did you get it? No, don't tell me, it would probably take too long. Do we really need to sell it? Can't we just keep it and look at it every day?" continued Toby in his happy mood.

"We need to sell it Toby. Don't forget that shit face Robson and the FCA have us by the plums. This is our passport out of that hole my friend. What do you think?"

"I think it's big and shiny enough OK," replied Toby.

"I had gathered that by your mad Irish jig, Fathead! I meant what do you think about selling it?"

On that question, Toby stopped jigging, laughing or displaying any further signs of merriment that were percolating through his veins.

"It's a lot of gold," said Toby. "I'll need to check all my stuff in the office. Before I do, I'd guess there is too much of it to sell on the physical gold market in one go. I take it time is short?"

"Very short, Toby, maybe ten days max," replied JJ.

"In that case we'd probably need several private placements. Gold bars come in various shapes and sizes. These 12.5kg ones are known as good delivery gold bars or good gold for short. This is to distinguish them from novelty gold bars or other sized ones of lesser purity. These are the most sought after by certain gold bugs. Gold investors come in all shapes and sizes too. Is there anywhere or anybody that I should not approach?" asked Toby.

"Don't call Korea, north or south and don't call anybody with a Korean sounding name," said JJ.

"What about Kim Cattrall, the actress?" quipped Toby.

"Not her, and not Kim Philby either."

"He's dead, JJ, I think," responded Toby.

"He won't be wanting any gold bars then, Fathead. Get serious!" replied JJ, still smiling at his friend.

"I can't give you a definitive answer tonight, JJ. I'll spend tomorrow checking all my non-Korean gold contacts, check out the physical market and get back to you. Gold dropped $50/oz today, so do we have limits on the price when we sell?"

"Ideally US$1,800/oz would be the gold floor and 1.5000 the ceiling for the cable rate. You can juggle between the two but the target net sale proceeds should not be less than £3.5bn."

Toby nodded and understood. With a final, admiring peek, Toby helped JJ lock up van and garage. The van was alarmed and locked and the garage had a sophisticated security system which went straight thought to a private security firm, which was less than four minutes' walk away. For now, JJ felt that the gold was safe.

The two amigos went back to JJ's to imbibe some decent malt. The Scot had not taken Gil's advice. Cyrus and Toby bantered away for a while. Gil gave Toby one of her disapproving looks and JJ simply enjoyed the happy social scene.

★ ★ ★

Neil Robson was back in Vladimir Babikov's casino office. He never really liked being there. He was vulnerable in that Mayfair establishment. He had to check any hardware he was carrying. He was always surrounded by and glowered at by the Russian's ex-FSB thugs. He never got offered the good vodka and he never knew when or if Babikov would lose patience and order his hands to be chopped off.

"Neil, my friend," said Babikov as he entered through his own private door. "How are you? In good health I hope?"

"I'm fine Vladimir. Why do you want to see me at such short notice. My enhanced debt repayment to you is on schedule. You should have the £20 million plus within ten days," spouted Robson, thinking it wise to give this villain the good news early on.

"No, no, it's not about that Neil. I trust you on the money. I am sure you will pay me as promised. It's in both our interests, no?" enquired Babikov smirking.

"Yes, Vladimir," replied Robson knowing for sure that it was in his interests to keep all his body parts attached.

"Look, here it is. I have been asked, by a power greater than me, so you know it's a big power, to find something out. That something seems to be that a band of devilish lunatics have stolen an important piece of Russian military hardware. I do not know what it is, boat, plane, missile, it could be any of these or something else. The big power thinks it might involve the CIA, maybe Mossad, maybe MI6, who knows. And if it does not involve them directly then maybe they know something about it, or have heard some chatter. We need to know and I need you to find out. That's the bottom line, my friend."

This fucking murderous Cossack must think I'm a prize winning idiot, thought Robson. 'A big power', the only big power that could get this criminal's ass into gear is Russian intelligence, probably SVR.

"You know I'm no longer in MI5, Vladimir," replied Robson. "I don't really have any contacts there anymore. I—"

"Who does the head of MI5 report to?" interrupted Babikov.

"Ultimately the Prime Minister, but it's the Home Secretary who really knows what's going on. The Director General of MI5 reports to him, or her in the case of the current government."

"Then you need to get cosy with her, Neil, just to find out. There may be nothing but there may be something."

"I rarely have direct contact with the Home Secretary, Vladimir, my—"

Robson was stopped in his tracks by Babikov rising and slamming his right palm on his desk.

"No excuses, Neil," he yelled. "Find a way to have direct contact with her, use your boss the Chancellor, eyeball cabinet meeting minutes, shag her, do what it takes. I want a report within a week. Do you understand me?" said Babikov in a somewhat calmer tone, but with a clear threat implied.

"I'll do my best, Vladimir," replied Robson, not sure that he could accomplish anything but very sure that if he ever had to have a confrontation with Babikov, right here, right now was not the place or time to have it.

"Excellent, Neil, excellent," said Babikov in a much cheerier way. "Help yourself to some vodka," he continued, pointing to the cheap stuff.

Neil Robson drove back to his house in St. George's Hill, not knowing whether to be happy or sad. He had seen off the problem known as Joel Gordon and he had put that woose Darke in his place at breakfast. The gold was in town and would shortly be in the form of useable readies for himself and the government. Now to spoil things that motherfucker Babikov had popped up needing information that may or may not exist from a source that he may or may not be able to get close to. *I've had enough of this shit*, thought the Financial Secretary to the Treasury. Life's about choices. He had made some good ones but mainly bad ones. Tonight he was in the frame of mind to choose the same path that Michael Corleone took in *The Godfather*. 'Settle all family business' the new Don had decided and on one day all the enemies of the Corleones met their doom. Fiction that may have been, but it was the right idea.

In a few short days, Robson would have skimmed off hundreds of millions of pounds from the gold haul brought back from North Korea. He could go anywhere in the world, live it up, have the time of his life. The only obstacles in his way were human; JJ Darke, Vladimir Babikov, those other two MAM hedgies, Naismith and Durand. He could get Babikov to grab the Darke kid and top his crippled nanny. JJ would then want to kill Babikov. That would probably signal the end of both of them. The fat fellow and the French dude could be sent some cupcakes, it didn't look like the trader refused anything to eat. Maybe it was fanciful, mused Robson, but unrealistic or not these sinister thoughts had cheered him up no end.

★ ★ ★

The following evening, JJ decided that he had had enough of some crap too. The particular piece of doo that was dragging him closer to the edge was the return of the black Mercedes. Cyrus was having an early evening social with a couple of his friends from school as well as Lucy and one of her classmates. Although it was still a little cool in the evening, it was quite a pleasant spring day. The group of friends were sitting outside a busy café cum patisserie on the corner of Markham Square and the King's Road, laughing, joking, generally getting on with the fun life of privileged young teenagers in the coolest part of town. JJ and Gil were happy that Cyrus was enjoying himself. He knew nothing about the Mercedes tail and he was more relaxed, eating and sleeping better, now that his dad had returned from overseas.

While JJ was catching up with some sports viewing in his house, Gil had popped out to pick up some vitamins and fruit bars from the health shop close to Marks & Spencer. She never made it there. As she was strolling down the east side of the Square she noticed the black Mercedes, again, in Smith Street. This time the car was parked in the third spot back from the King's Road, but with a clear view of Cyrus and his friends.

"JJ," said Gil on re-entering the house.

"That was quick," replied JJ.

"JJ, the black Mercedes is back. It's on Smith Street. Cyrus and his pals are having a snack and chat at that little café on the corner. He's definitely stalking Cyrus."

JJ looked at Gil, put the TV remote on the coffee table and got up. "I've had the fuck enough of this Gil. I'm going to get a couple of things. I need a word with black Merc man. I'll go down Radnor Walk, cut through Smith Terrace and approach him from behind. You hang about near the top of the Square. When you see me, casually come across Cyrus and his mates. Make sure the boy is not looking in the direction of Smith Street no matter what happens."

"Will do," replied Gil. "Be careful."

JJ nodded, got his items, left the house, went down the west side of the Square, crossed the King's Road and proceeded at a brisk pace on his planned route. As he was walking, he was figuring out his plan. It was 6.30pm and the sun was setting but it was not properly dark. Gil had described the offending Merc in some detail. Once inside, the passing Chelsea public would not have a clear view of any activity within. Another aspect of a one man surveillance op was that if he was asked to shadow a target then his full attention would be on that target, not really people-watching or checking his six often enough. JJ exited Smith Terrace, walked up the west side of Smith Street, crossed the road and opened the front passenger side door of the Merc. That was another aspect of bad guys' tendencies when they thought that they were tough and invisible. They didn't lock their car doors.

"Aaargh!" screamed Boris Akulov, as JJ plunged his commando knife into the left thigh of the ex-FSB thug with his left hand. Simultaneously, he smashed the Russian's face into the steering wheel. JJ had taken that knife all the way to Korea and back and it had remained unused in its sheath. Now, only a couple of hundred yards from his house, out it had come and into a scumbag's leg it went. Boris tried to elbow JJ in the face but the Scot had his defence ready. He blocked the Russian's shot and again plunged his knife into the same leg.

"OK, OK, stop, stop!" wailed Babikov's man, clutching his leg. JJ stopped, checked the Russian's suit jacket and removed his gun from its holster. He kept Boris's head pressed against the steering wheel and now had his knife positioned right on the stalker's throat.

"Why are you watching my son?" asked JJ, firmly while giving Boris's exposed throat a poke with the point of the knife's blade. Boris did not, of course, know that the curly-topped kid he had been ordered to tail had a dad, and certainly not one who was likely to invade his car and damage his person.

"I don't know what you fuckin' talking about you maniac,"

replied Boris, obviously in the forlorn hope that his assailant would just say, oops, sorry, mistaken identity and leave. Boris was bleeding profusely from his wounded leg so, on hearing the Russian's reply JJ felt generous, not wishing the slime to pass out, so he just smashed his face into the steering wheel one more time. It hurt.

"Look you fucking Russian peasant, I will let you bleed out right here if you do not answer me truthfully. I've got all night and no one can see into this car from the outside. Even your miserable moaning and groaning has not attracted one glance. They build these cars well, don't they asshole. Speak up!" said JJ, in a low decibel level but with menace.

Although Boris was a murdering, asshole deviant he was not a complete fool. This guy with the odd accent had him cold. He was bleeding away, probably had a broken nose, could hardly move and had a very pointy blade nestling in his neck. He was going to need to tell him something.

"I work for Vladimir Babikov," said Boris.

"Who the fuck is Vladimir Babikov and what does he want with my son?" asked JJ, adding another wee mini-poke with his knife just to ensure that the Russian stayed on point.

"He owns the Nicolas Casino in Mayfair. He will kill you for this."

JJ assimilated Boris's information. This Babikov donkey was clearly the one in charge. The pokee here was just a foot soldier, a thug, carrying out a job that he had been instructed to do but not asking or questioning why. A dodgy Russian running a casino had all the hallmarks of the Russian Mafia, thought JJ, not the best people to get on the wrong side of. It was probably a tad late worrying about that now. It still didn't make sense to JJ. Why would a Russian mobster have any interest in Cyrus or even JJ himself. He was going to need to find out more. Bleedin' Boris here, however, was not likely to have any further insight.

445

"Have you got a phone?" asked JJ.

"Yes, why?" replied Boris, visibly weakening.

"Hand it over and be quick about it," said JJ. Boris pointed to the glove compartment. JJ opened it, took out the mobile and switched it on. He scrolled through the contacts. It was tricky doing it with his right hand. There was no Babikov but there was 'Boss' and given the state of Boris's crumpled suit he assumed it wasn't a direct line to the upmarket retailer. JJ hit the number.

"Babikov," said the voice at the other end.

"This is William fuckin' Wallace, you dickhead. One of your thugs is bleeding to death in Smith Street, SW3. If you want to save him better get another thug here pronto with more than a plaster. If your dark shadow every crosses my path again or that of my family, you'll get the same. Now fuck off back to Putinland like a good mobster," he added and hung up.

In retrospect, JJ wasn't sure that that was the best way to handle things, but he was fuming inside. When it came to Cyrus's health and welfare his emotions sometimes got the better of his normal cool rationality. Maybe this Babikov would be more sensible and it would end here, tonight. Or maybe not. JJ would need to be prepared for any comeback. By now, Boris had nearly passed out, but if his boss cared enough and sent help then he'd live. JJ got out of the Merc, commando knife concealed in his cargo pants and Boris's phone in his pocket. Checking that he wasn't covered in Russian blood, there were a few spots but nothing obvious, JJ casually strolled up Smith Street, caught Gil's attention and waved. She waved back, pointed out to Cyrus that his dad was near, and the three of them walked home, once Cyrus had said his cheerios to his pals.

"Alright?" asked Gil, once they were inside and Cyrus decided to go for a shower.

"Yes, sort of," replied JJ. "I don't think the black Merc man will be on Cyrus's tail any more. He was just a goon working for some guy called Vladimir Babikov. Ever heard of him?"

"No," replied Gil.

"Apparently he runs a casino in the west end, the Nicolas, I think. It's obviously a cover for some dodgy venture or other. I still don't know why any Russian would have an interest in Cyrus, Merc man was just the point guy, he had no details."

"This might get messy?" ventured Gil, half statement and half question.

"Yes, Gil, it might. I'm going upstairs to get changed, can you stay here tonight? We should probably figure out our plan once Cyrus is asleep."

"Sure."

JJ went up to his bedroom. He put his polo shirt and cargo pants in the wash basket, tomorrow was dry cleaning day so that was good. He retrieved the knife and phone before lobbing his dirty clothes. JJ carefully cleaned his knife, put it back in its sheath and hid it in the kit bag that he had taken to Korea. He then put the kit bag in the lockable chest in the attic and placed the key in his wall safe. As he was doing this, he could hear Cyrus singing away in the shower. The kid had regularly been selected for the school choir when he was younger. Initially, JJ had no idea why, he thought the boy sounded like a cat being sat on by a St. Bernard. Then one night Cyrus sang the main theme from *Super Smash Brothers Brawl*. The song had been composed by Nobuo Uematsu and the lyrics were in Latin. Cyrus was singing it in Latin with the orchestral soundtrack in the background. He sounded like an angel.

When Cyrus and his dad played *SSBB*, the boy liked to be the Pokemon Trainer most of the time and JJ preferred Meta Knight.

The mach tornado that was Meta Knight's signature move may be coming out of game world and into real life thought JJ. The critical issue, though, was to ensure Cyrus's safety, to make certain that he had family and friends by his side, to shine bright in his defence, if needed.

JJ returned to the living room all freshened up. Gil was there and had made JJ a Macallans, the way he liked. She didn't drink whisky so had poured herself a small glass of Chardonnay. They sat together, on the sofa.

"What're you doing?" asked Gil.

"This is Merc man's phone. I'm scrolling through the contacts to see if I recognise any names."

"Any joy?"

"Not yet, there's a lot of names, I'm only up to F."

"We're going to need to beef up the security and defence of this house, JJ," said Gil.

"Yes, we should. We'll need to do it subtly. The less Cyrus knows about this the better," he added, still checking Boris's contacts.

"Sure, I'll get on it in the morning. I know a guy who can install CCTV, perimeter alarms, better locks, that kind of stuff. Do you want me to stay here, indefinitely, until we know the score?" asked Gil.

"Good and yes," responded JJ, now a lot calmer after a drink of quality malt. He had passed R in the contact list, so no Neil Robson acknowledged JJ. At least that was something. Gil noticed that JJ had stopped sliding his thumb up the smartphone's screen and was just staring at one entry, in contemplation.

"What's up JJ, have you found something?"

"Maybe," replied JJ, still thinking. "There's an entry here under St. George. The number's familiar though."

"Who's that?" asked Gil.

"If I'm not mistaken that's a number in St. George's Hill, Weybridge specifically belonging to this country's Financial Secretary to the Treasury."

"Neil Robson?"

"The very same, Gil, the very same." JJ's internal temperature was on the boil again, but he knew that cool thinking was called for. It was going to get messy alright and JJ needed to be certain that Cyrus was safe before the mess erupted.

"When's Cyrus's spring break?" asked JJ.

"Next Tuesday, for two weeks," responded Gil, who knew by heart every last detail of the boy's school schedule, his clubs and his term breaks.

"Good. Convince him that it would be nice for him to see his grandparents. I'll let Mum and Dad know. Take the Porsche and be alert for tails. If things work out here next week I'll join you for week two."

"What about you, JJ?" asked Gil. "If a bunch of Russian gangsters come calling, you're not going to see them off on your own."

"I'll be fine," replied JJ, not knowing for certain that he would be, but not putting himself at the top of the priority list just yet.

As JJ and Gil continued to discuss the planned trip to Scotland and the 'home improvements' to be carried out, JJ's cell phone vibrated on the coffee table in front of them. He picked it up.

"Hello?"

"Hi JJ, it's Jim," said the voice at the other end. There was no need to add Bradbury. While JJ knew one hell of a lot of Jims when he was growing up in Glasgow, none of them had the unmistakeable drawl of his American friend, the KLO.

"Jesus, Jim, what time is it in Seoul, it's nearly ten at night here. Is everything OK?"

"It's six in the morning JJ and no everything is not OK. They've got Kwon," said Bradbury, voice shaking and audibly upset.

11

THE GOLDEN WHALE

On the surface there was no link between Annie Chapman, second victim of Jack the Ripper, and Joel Gordon, numberless victim of Neil Robson, poisoned and now dead. Six feet under the surface, however, they share the same cemetery, at Manor Park in Forest Gate, London E7. As cemeteries go it was pleasant and well kept. The friends and family of the late Treasury accountant were gathered round his burial plot, just off Basset Road and within sight of the Columbarium, not that the murdered ground dweller knew anything about it. It was a fresh and sunny spring day and the small group of mourners listened attentively as the priest said a few last words of blessing.

"Talisha, isn't it?" enquired Becky Martin as the group dispersed and headed for the cars that would take them back to Joel's apartment for a few drinks and subdued chat about the deceased.

"Yes, you're Becky, Joel's friend at work?" Talisha replied, not certain but she had been feeling poorly and had a lot on her plate.

"That's right," replied Becky, dressed respectfully in black with no sign of her trademark candescence. "This is such a tragedy, Talisha. Joel was so smart, so nice. He encouraged me to do a night course in Accounting and Finance at City University. I'll be getting my degree in a couple of months. Nothing would have happened if it hadn't been for his help. I'll miss him."

"Yes, me too Becky. I just don't understand it..." sobbed

451

Talisha, standing next to her chauffeur-driven rented black sedan. "One minute he was full of life, energy and hope for the future, the next minute dead and agonisingly at that. The medical report said it was radiation poisoning. Nobody has a blind clue as to how he could have been exposed to radiation."

"That's awful!" exclaimed Becky, hearing for the first time the cause of her friend's demise. "Was he not able to tell you anything before he… well, the end?" asked Becky, keen to know but unable to phrase her question without deepening already painful memories for Talisha.

"Not really, the speed and intensity of his illness, his death were so rapid, his ability to function so swiftly taken from him, nothing made sense. He told me he loved me. Those were about the last intelligible words he uttered. After that, nothing much. He mumbled something like 'cupcake' a few times but it didn't mean anything to me, it was not a love nickname or pet term he ever used."

Becky realised that Talisha was wilting so she gave her a warm, friendly hug and wished her well. Becky would not join the funeral wake at Joel's apartment, though Talisha did invite her. It was a family gathering and though Becky and Joel were good friends she did not want to impose. Becky had driven to Manor Park in her not so new VW Golf, bright red, of course. She returned to her car, sat in the driver's seat and prepared to head back to her one bedroom apartment in Pimlico. She would not see Talisha again. Joel's girlfriend returned to the United States, never fully regained her health and died several years later, at the age of thirty-eight.

Before driving out of the cemetery gates, Becky's mind kept iterating back to Talisha's mention of 'cupcake'. It meant nothing to her either. Somewhere in the deep recesses of her mind, though, she recalled the last time that she saw Joel alive was when he left Neil Robson's office. As he sped out of the door, he smiled at Becky and said, 'Thank your Mum for the cupcake, it was fantastic!' Joel had left the office before Becky had time to ask 'what cupcake?' Her mum's baking was royally atrocious! She couldn't bake a cake to save her life. She would never have attempted cupcakes and she would certainly not have sent any to Joel or her boss. The culinary embarrassment would have been too great. A few years ago, Becky would have just let this puzzle pass. It was probably nothing. Talisha had told her that the police had investigated. They thought Joel's death was suspicious but they could find no evidence of foul play by a third party. They were still investigating but had no leads. Joel, however, had encouraged Becky to be thorough in her studies, not to accept the obvious. If something seemed funny peculiar then it probably was funny peculiar, he used to say. The cupcake thing was indeed funny peculiar Becky concluded as she drove out of east London. She owed it to her friend to do a modicum of research at least and that research was going to begin with a phone call to her mum.

★ ★ ★

While Becky was on the phone to her mum, Toby Naismith was in JJ's office at MAM in Mayfair. It was mid-afternoon and Fathead had already put in a few calls to the main gold depositaries in the United States. The Chicago Mercantile Exchange (CME) is one of the biggest financial exchanges in the world. It has nearly 3,000 employees and assets of over US $40 billion. The exchange's core businesses involve exchange traded derivatives including futures and options in the world's key commodities and currencies. Fathead's interest in the CME today, however, was in its five approved New York based Commodities Exchange (COMEX) precious metal storage facilities. These are JP Morgan,

HSBC, Brink's, Scotia Mocatta and Manfra, Tordella & Brookes (MTB). In total, these five had an estimated 12 million troy ounces of gold stored in their secure facilities in New York, though only the CME authorities know the precise aggregate amount on any given day. One bar of Kim Jong-un's gold weighed nearly 12.5kg or around 402 troy ounces. The Sprinter van's haul of gold, therefore, was the equivalent of one-fifth of the COMEX warehouse's total stock of gold.

How nice it would have been for Toby, JJ, Neil Robson and the British government if Fathead could have just rung up and said, 'Do you fancy a few bars of gold?' Unfortunately for all concerned the process of getting refined gold into the legitimate financial system was not that simple. For any particular refinery to deliver gold onto the commodities exchange it must be from a registered approved brand, the main ones being Heraeus, Johnson Matthey and Metalor Technologies. Fortunately for Toby et al these three approved brands are also on the London Bullion Market Association (LBMA) Good Delivery List. This list contains the names of refiners authorised to produce bullion bars used by central banks and the IMF in their reserves. Each bar has a serial number, the refiner's hallmark, its degree of fineness (purity) and its year of manufacture. To be 'good delivery gold', the bullion bar must have a fineness of at least 995 parts per thousand. All the bars in the Sprinter van complied.

Toby was in a good place. He could try to sell part of the gold to the refiners, as they often bought their own gold immediately after it was refined or in the after-market if they were confident that the price of gold was going to rise or if their stocks were low. These refinery groups are huge conglomerates; the Heraeus Group's precious metals trading desk in Hanau, Germany, for example, is like the bridge of the Star Ship Enterprise. He could also sell part of the gold to the refiner's customers, via the depositaries or directly if they had a commodities managed account with MAM. As each of the bars has a hallmark, a serial number and a year of manufacture, it is probable that they could be traced back to their original owner if anyone wanted to know that piece of information. In the case of the Sprinter van's gold that could be North Korea, China, Russia or elsewhere. In essence it did not matter. Gold bars can be bought and sold anonymously between customers like central banks, private banks, more or less anyone. Provided a specific set of serial numbers etc. had not been noted as stolen, the original ownership or even subsequent ownership usually was not of interest. For whatever reason, maybe to do with saving face, maybe to not alerting its enemies, maybe even with the forlorn hope of recovery, the DPRK's authorities had not yet reported any stolen gold.

"Hey Kai, it's Toby, got a minute?" Fathead was through to his broker-dealer buddy at JP Morgan in London.

"Toby, my man!" replied Kai cheerily. "Of course, for you, maybe two."

"Great. I need an introduction. We've done a massive deal here at MAM, and I've been left with some physical gold to sell. You guys are one of the biggest gold depositaries in the USA, right? I want to talk with the guy or gal who's the decision maker regarding good delivery gold."

"Sure. That would be Enrique Velasquez. He's Senior VP in charge of precious metals. I'll try to get him to ring you in the next fifteen minutes, OK?" responded Kai.

"That would be just fine Kai. Thanks. Let's go to Nobu soon, it's been a while," said Toby. Kai agreed.

While Toby was waiting for that one call from New York he thought he'd get in touch with the chief trader at Metalor Technologies, Tomas Hartmann, whom he had known for several years. Tomas was about the same age as Toby and was based in Neuchatel, Switzerland. He was responsible for the buying and selling of precious metals, physical and electronic. Toby and Tomas had a good chat and a better haggle. Metalor was indeed in the market to buy back some gold and if Toby could offer them a decent discount to market price for a bulk purchase they could do a deal.

"Tomas, there's no way I can give you 10% off, not even 8%," said Toby. "I know you want to buy a big chunk, but it's too much. Gold closed at $1,820 per ounce yesterday and is still rising. In a few months you'll probably have made a whopping profit. C'mon old friend, let's do it. 4% off today's closing price. What do you say?"

"Do any of the bars have our stamp on them?"

"Yes, not all of them but a decent percentage," replied Toby, who had studied the bars in the van very closely indeed.

"Our new stamp or our historic one?" asked Tomas.

"Your historic one with Meteaux Precieux SA, Metalor on them."

"Fine. We'll pay US $1,742 per ounce for one million troy ounces. You need to have it transported by one of the CME approved couriers like Brink's and have it delivered to our secure vaults in Zurich. You can pay for the courier. Deal?" asked Tomas.

"Deal," said Toby. They would exchange emails to confirm. Toby had directed Tomas to a new email account that he and JJ had set up specifically for the gold transactions. It would be no problem. Tomas would have his gold in three days and Toby had just unloaded around 2,500 of his 6,000 bullion bar target. It was a mega result.

Enrique Velasquez of JP Morgan got back to Toby as well. Fathead enquired about the state of the gold vaults at 1 Chase Manhattan Plaza. There had been a reported fire there in July

2013, in the secure warehouse one hundred feet below ground level. There was much speculation that this was either deliberate or faked in order to avoid a COMEX delivery notice for 12,000 ounces of eligible gold by declaring force majeure. These speculations were unfounded but it did seem that ever since, JP Morgan would not allow their gold stocks to dwindle too much. After a bit of to-ing and fro-ing, Toby managed to get Enrique to commit to buying a half million ounces of gold. This was just over 15,550kg, or nearly 1,250 bars. Toby was over half way to his bullion sales target and, so far, it had taken less than half a day to do it.

There was still plenty of work for Toby to do. He involved Yves-Jacques in arranging the transportation, Brink's Inc. for Metalor and IBI Armoured Inc. for JP Morgan, the paperwork and the transport of the bullion bars from the van in JJ's lock-up to a registered bullion vault in London. It would not pass unnoticed if the approved carriers turned up to a Chelsea lock-up to collect several thousand gold bars from the back of a van. Yves-Jacques was on it and it was underway.

Toby was feeling well chuffed with himself. That miscreant Iksil may have been dubbed the London Whale because of the size of his Credit Default Swap trades back in 2012/2013, but they were ill advised, broke JP Morgan's risk rules, led to regulatory fines and were beyond speculative. In the here and now, Toby felt like the golden whale. Big trades, totally legit, no rules to break. In his unconsumed joy at his day's work he totally skimmed over the fact that the subject matter of his trades was most definitely not legit! Nevertheless, Fathead was so happy he decided to phone JJ right away.

"Hey JJ," said Toby on hearing his boss answer his personal mobile phone. "We have had an awesome day, chief. I've unloaded over 3,000 bullion bars today and I feel good, do-do-do-do-do-do and ya know that I should," announced Toby, more or less springing into song, albeit tuneless and pitch imperfect.

"That's great Toby, well done," said JJ, not in a singing mood. "Did you get a good price and is the cable rate in our favour?"

"The average net selling price was under our desired level of US $1,800/oz. boss, but it was quite close and the GBP/USD rate moved a little in our favour. We're on track for our cash target," replied Toby with more confidence than perhaps was wholly justified.

"Great. Keep it up. I'll be in the office tomorrow. The both of us and Yves-Jacques should have a breakfast or coffee meeting to catch up, OK?"

"OK JJ. How's Cyrus?" asked Toby.

"He's good, Toby. In Scotland with his grandparents. I may try to get up there next week so let's see if we can seal the deal on this gold before the weekend. Have a good evening and well done again. I'll see you tomorrow."

"Beezer Ebeneezer, JJ, see you tomorrow."

"Keep your druggy references to yourself Fathead!" exclaimed JJ.

"Sure," replied Toby, having no idea what JJ was talking about. Clearly, the urban meaning of early 1990s' Scottish electronic pop lyrics had not registered in the Englishman's head.

JJ had a good night's sleep. As yet there had been no sign of any payback attempt by dodgy Russians and Cyrus seemed happy to be with Gil and his grandparents in Scotland. Still, he needed to get this gold sale finished and that wanker Robson off his back and those of the other two amigos.

★ ★ ★

Toby had opted for an 8am breakfast meeting, there's a shocker, and had organised the Pret closest to the MAM office to deliver coffee, juice, warm croissants and a variety of breakfast baguettes. Toby and Yves-Jacques were already tucking in when JJ entered his office, with most of the tucking being done by Toby.

"Good morning guys. Glad to see you didn't wait!" said JJ, only half joking.

"Hi JJ," they replied.

JJ didn't really feel like being overly social, nor was he in the mood for that early morning banter so prevalent in investment houses. He wanted to get straight down to the business in hand.

"Toby, where's the gold that you sold yesterday?"

Yves-Jacques jumped in, partly because he was the one Toby had delegated the transportation job to and partly because he was quite excited by this edgy extracurricular exercise. "The bars destined for Metalor are in the London Silver Vaults in Chancery Lane. They're very secure vaults, apart from that one breach a while ago, and their security has been beefed up a lot since then. It is not widely known that they store gold as well as silver and jewellery. Brink's are scheduled to pick up the bars later today and ship them to Switzerland."

JJ thought what a small world. The London Silver Vaults were indeed very secure but the breach mentioned by Yves-Jacques had been masterminded by Victor Pagari. Good job JJ knew that the young safe cracker had only just returned from Seoul with a rapidly healing Ethel. "And those bought by JPM?"

"I managed to convince JPM in New York that it would be more efficient and cheaper if they stored the gold at their vaults in London Wall, rather than go to the expense, actually our expense, of having them shipped to the States," said Toby, still munching on a cheese and tomato croissant.

"That all sounds good guys. What's today's plan?" asked JJ.

"We've got 2,250 bullion bars to go," said Toby. "I'm speaking to HSBC this morning and a Geneva based family office in the afternoon. I'm confident that between them they will gobble up the bars. If not, my back up is Heraeus in Germany and Scotia Mocatta in New York. The early morning gold price looks like it'll trade between $1,840/oz. and $1860/oz. That's a bit up from yesterday. Cable is stable so we should be all set." Toby, clearly energised by croissants, baguettes and a couple of nuclear strength coffees was ready to rock.

JJ mulled over Fathead's information for a minute or two. Though JJ did not trade gold for MAM he was in charge of its inclusion or exclusion from the fund's portfolio. He needed to know more about the influences on gold than even Toby, though his amigo was the one with the sharp-end trading skills. JJ knew that there were many determinants of the gold price, ranging from supply and demand to geopolitical concerns, doubts over the worth of fiat monies, inflation, government defaults, intrinsic taste of the Chinese and Indians. At the end of the day, however, most gold bugs were momentum players. If the price went up they wanted to hold more and vice versa if it went down. Buy low and sell high did not, empirically, seem to be an adage embraced by the majority of gold market participants. A mere glance at a twenty year chart of COMEX gold stocks versus the gold price showed a correlation of near 90%. With the price of gold rising Toby was selling to willing buyers.

"Sounds like a good plan, Toby," said JJ eventually, "but no more discounts. I understand why you gave Metalor a preferential deal, it's always nice to get a bulk selling programme off to a good start. The gold price seems to be on the up and most market players will simply extrapolate that forward until the price sinks one day. So get it done at market and let me know the final tally when you're finished," advised the Scot.

"Sure, no problem," replied Toby with belly full of food and mind full of markets.

The meeting of the three amigos ended with JJ again thanking Toby and Yves-Jacques for their commitment and skill. This gold task was not MAM business but a successful outcome was essential to their continued employment with MAM not to mention their entire financial careers and personal freedom. JJ had no doubt that Toby would complete the task and that Yves-Jacques would stay on top of the logistics of moving and storing the bullion bars. They would be relying on JJ to negotiate their release from the vice like grip of the Financial Secretary to the Treasury and the FCA. Nauseating as it felt that meant a meeting with Neil Robson.

* * *

"So where's my money Darke?" asked Neil Robson abruptly and with a hefty dose of anxiety in his voice. The Financial Secretary to the Treasury was becoming so twitchy about the health of his limbs and the earache he was getting from the Chancellor that he had demanded that JJ come to his office the very day that Toby was finalising the sale of the bullion bars. JJ complied and had been shown in to Robson's Treasury office by Becky, resplendent in her full candescence again, today's outfit being primarily a lime green suit with lime green and black designer shoes. JJ thought she was very pleasant albeit a bit bright.

"The gold sales are being completed today," replied JJ. "The money from them will be safe in an account with a private bank in Luxembourg. If all goes well you can probably have it in a day or so." JJ delivered the news in a very low key way. Inside he was seething. All the trouble that he and his friends had gone to acquiring the gold. The injury to Ethel, the capture of deep cover Kwon, the stalking of Cyrus. None of that would have happened if both Britain and Greece hadn't been so fucking financially useless and he and Toby not so fucking financially smart to dance at the edge of trading legality. Every time that he looked at Robson's miserable face he wanted to punch his lights out. He needed to be calm and collected however until it was over, not a frame of mind often visited by west coast Scots.

"Good, JJ, good. I'll give you details where to send the proceeds. Then you can have your nasty little FCA file," said Robson with a face full of smirk.

"Do you think I came up the Clyde in the shit ship you fucking tit?" raged JJ, his calm and collected aura having hardly registered on any timescale. "I'll have the file first, any copies hard or electronic, a signed letter from you exonerating me, Toby Naismith and Yves-Jacques Durand from any wrongdoing financial or otherwise. When I'm totally satisfied with that you can have your money, I mean the British government's rightful compensation for bond defaults by the North Koreans, or had you forgotten about that?"

Neil Robson's ugly mug had gone as incandescent as one of Becky's rosso outfits. Even if he had been in JJ's shoes and done the same he wasn't going to be dictated to by this Scottish pleb. "You're in no position to demand anything you fuckwit. I can end your career and have you thrown in jail by tonight. What's poor little Cyrus going to do then brainbox?"

Any living creature's neural system can be complex. The internal and external stimuli which trigger a response are not the same across species, or from one human to another. In JJ's case, a derogatory or threatening remark aimed at his son would almost always trigger that part of the brain which signalled 'attack'. In a flash, JJ was out of his seat, across Robson's desk, had his right hand on his throat, punched him full on the nose with his left fist and both of them were on the floor. As JJ was squeezing a little harder and berating the Financial Secretary for even mentioning

Cyrus, the door to Robson's office was opening and Becky was coming through it. The antagonistic pair leapt up, Robson sat in his seat, handkerchief covering his bloody nose, and JJ walked slowly around Robson's desk and back to his chair.

"What's all this commotion?" asked Becky, surveying the scene but not sure what had happened.

"It's OK," said Robson. "I had a sudden nose bleed and felt a bit faint. Mr Darke, here, darted round to make sure I was alright. Things are good now."

"Do you want some tea?" enquired Becky of her boss. Given that half of Robson's desktop contents were all over the place, that Mr Darke sure must have taken the short route to aid her boss's bleeding nose she thought.

"Yes, fine, OK, that would be good," said Robson.

"Please, thank you," added JJ, now having recovered some external composure, though still internally boiling. Becky acknowledged JJ and headed out to make some tea. She left the office door open, however, as she did not really believe a word that her slimy boss said.

JJ was the first to speak, in a low voice. "Look Robson, this isn't getting us anywhere. I told you before and now you get it. Don't mention Cyrus again. Don't think about him, as my son or as a tool of leverage. I know you're the one behind those Russian donkeys who were tailing him. I saw off black Merc man and if I ever see another lowlife even looking at me or Cyrus it'll be the last look of his miserable criminal life."

Robson said nothing, too busy trying to plug his red nose river.

"When the gold sales are completed, I'll let you know. It'll probably be today or tomorrow. Then I'll be back here. I'll have a laptop with me, connected to the accounts that you want me to transfer the funds to, the amounts and their distribution. One press of a key and it's done, the British government will be solvent again. Before that press, however, you will give me what I've asked for. Is this understood and agreed?"

Robson nodded and mumbled, "Yes."

JJ got up and exited Robson's office. As he was leaving Becky was coming in with the tea. JJ apologised to Becky saying that he had to dash off, wished her a pleasant day and said that he hoped it would be less full of incident. He smiled broadly. Becky smiled back and thought that this Mr Darke seemed a decent enough man.

Neil Robson's nose had stopped pouring blood. It was painful and probably broken. He needed to change his shirt and, thankfully, Becky always had a spare one on hand for such an occasion, though a random chunk of squirting tomato was more often the replacement cause than a puddle of nose blood. Robson would do as JJ had demanded, but the Scot was a fool if he thought that would be the end of it. Young Master Darke was clearly JJ's Achilles heel and before this was over, he vowed, that heel was going to hurt like hell.

JJ left the Treasury and hailed a taxi to take him to Chelsea. He was still a bit discombobulated following the altercation with Robson, but at least the dealings with him would soon be over. As he settled into the cab's back seat JJ was replaying the Robson meeting in his head. Strange, thought JJ, even if he was distracted by his busted nose, the Fin Sec did not seem to bat an eyelid at JJ's mention of black Merc man nor did he even attempt to deny any link with Russian lowlife. Robson was dirtier and more malignant than even he had thought. This saga had further to run.

* * *

Becky went home to her Pimlico flat around 6.30pm. It was on

Douglas Street, roughly equidistant from the Gordon Hospital, how ironic, and Pimlico tube station. Pimlico was famous for two things, the legendary 1949 movie *Passport to Pimlico* and the district's plumbers. The latter were a lot more expensive to see than the former. Becky's apartment was leasehold in Mulberry House. Joel had helped her negotiate a good deal and she really liked it there, close enough to work but even closer to Chelsea's designer shops and entertaining night life. Perhaps surprisingly, the décor of her apartment was a lot more subdued than her outfits. Maybe she didn't want to clash with mere paint and wallpaper or maybe her daytime dress was a kind of body armour intended to repel the faint of heart and the sleaze of mind.

Becky settled into her soft leather cream sofa with even softer pale blue cotton covered cushions, kicked off her heels and switched on her flat screen television. She was extremely frugal and saved, each month, a good chunk of her salary. While she loved shopping, she was not an impulsive or serial buyer. Her clothes were selected meticulously, often from sales, special deals or 'pop up' clothes shops that were about to pop back down again. Becky gave around a quarter of her salary every month to her mother. Although still in her fifties, Mum had stage 2 to 3 Alzheimer's Disease and was resident in Borovere, a care home in Alton, Hampshire. It was a lovely place and her mum was well looked after, but it was expensive. Becky and her elder brother did the best they could. Their father had skipped off to Canada shortly after Becky was born so he was de facto useless in terms of support, financial or emotional. The disease does not affect all memory capabilities at the same time nor is its progression easily predictable from one human to the next. In Mum's case, her older memories and her semantic memories were good, but new facts and experiences were more difficult to retain.

One thing that Becky did know for certain, however, was that her mum had not baked any cupcakes in the near past. She spoke to her on the phone the previous evening, and would probably drive down to Alton this coming weekend. When Becky asked her mum she laughed out loud. She couldn't bake even when she was fully *compus mentus* and definitely had no desire or ability to do it now. So the Joel Gordon cupcake mystery was in play. Why would Joel be mumbling about cupcakes to Talisha on his deathbed? Why would he have asked Becky to thank her mum for baking them as he left Neil Robson's office a few weeks ago? Joel did not know that her mum was in care or had AD so it may have been feasible but it was not correct. Somebody must have told Joel that her mum had baked or sent some cupcakes. In her faint memory Becky envisaged Joel entering Neil Robson's office that day and she did not recall him carrying anything let alone a box or bag full of cupcakes. Logic implies, thought Becky, that any such cupcakes must have already been in her boss's office. In her time working for Neil Robson she had never seen him eat a cupcake. Anything he wanted to eat, chew or drink he'd get her to fetch it for him. Curiouser and curiouser.

Becky had ordered a takeaway pizza, vegetable topping with extra capers, onions and mushrooms. As she let the superficial entertainment known as 'soaps' waft over her head, she ate her pizza and drank her water. The only other images in her mind were that Neil Robson had given her a bag of rubbish to dump on 'cupcake' day and that she had noticed that Joel and her boss had been having more tête-à-têtes than normal, even accounting for the fact that Joel's direct boss, Craig Wilson, had been on holiday for two weeks. When Becky was a kid at school in Hampshire, her English teacher, Miss Hooper, had drummed into her to look for key words in any essay or passage of literature she needed to critique. Becky liked Miss Hooper. Tonight's key words seemed to be Joel, cupcake, Robson. Becky was tired. It was just after 10pm. She decided to select her clothes and accessories for the next day and then head off to bed.

★ ★ ★

Vladimir Babikov was not tired but he was annoyed. There were several developments that had irked him. Business at the Nicolas had not been good, either less punters were willing to part with their cash or the same number of punters had less spare readies to partake in his casino's offerings. He also hadn't heard even a whisper of any missing Russian military hardware and not a peep from the debtor Robson on the same subject. His bodyguards were also costing more. After having forked out for Vasily's body to be sent home to Russia and paying handsomely for his replacement, now that idiot Boris had got himself stabbed in the leg and his private hospital bill was not cheap. It was late but he needed input. Time to phone Neil Robson.

"Hello?" said the voice on the other end of the phone in that soft, fragmented tailing off way that signalled someone had been unexpectedly awoken from a decent sleep.

"Neil my friend, it is Vladimir. Sorry if I woke you but I need updates – now," announced the criminal Russian.

"For fuck's sake Babikov…" responded Robson, now involuntarily awake, "don't you have anything better to do at this time of night?"

"No I don't," replied the Russian. "So speak up, tell me stuff and stop complaining."

Neil Robson wanted to tell Babikov to go fuck himself but as he had not yet paid the despot his debt plus bonus nor given him any information on his AWOL Russian equipment the Fin Sec thought the better of it.

"OK Vladimir, I'll have the money in my accounts within

seventy-two hours. I'll then transfer you the £20 million or so as promised."

Babikov thought that this was the first piece of good news that he had received in a while. "That is good, Neil, you will still be an able-bodied politician then!" he replied, laughing heartily. "What about my other request?"

"No news Vladimir. I've got a coffee meeting scheduled with the Home Secretary tomorrow but I'm at a bit of a loss as to how to bring it up without raising her suspicions. She's a smart woman you know."

Babikov thought about this for a few seconds. "You and Walker have financial responsibility for the intelligence services budgets don't you?" he asked.

"Yes, we do," replied Robson, not sure where this line of questioning was going to lead.

"Well, can't you link that whistleblower Snowden with increased demands on GCHQ's resources or something? That would start a US/Russian/UK discussion and then see where that goes," suggested Babikov feeling quite proud of his late night awareness.

"Maybe, Vladimir, maybe. I'll give it a shot," replied Robson, reluctantly also somewhat impressed by his creditor's suggestion.

"One final thing Neil... my man who was shadowing the teenage kid you had an interest in... he's got a very painful stab wound in his leg, a broken nose and is costing me repair money. I think it was the boy's father who did this. Who is he?"

"His name is JJ Darke," replied Robson. "He's a fucking Jock loser, Vladimir, but I need him alive for a few days as he's instrumental in transferring the money that I will then forward to you. After that you can have all the payback you want from him and his family."

"Thank you, Neil, I will," said the Russian, and hung up.

★ ★ ★

JJ was tired. It was 7.20am. He hadn't slept well, worrying about Cyrus and concerned about the end-game with Robson and the gold. He had his cab drop him off on Piccadilly so that he could get a strong Starbucks coffee before heading to his office. He could have waited till he got to his office but the staff in the Piccadilly franchise could understand his early morning, weary Scottish mumblings. The more mumbly he was the less comprehensive his Glaswegian became. His sentences all merged together, they became quieter and they never were fully enunciated. Luckily, this regular Starbucks team recognised him and he didn't even need to speak his order. He always had the same thing, a triple shot, espresso macchiato, extra dry with soya. This morning, however, the regular team were not all at their stations. As JJ approached the counter a pleasant-looking young, small, Asian woman was there, she was probably Japanese. As they looked at each other, JJ mumbled, in a very low decibel voice, "This is never going to work."

"Why is it not going to work, Sir?" asked the girl with the name tag 'Kina'. "Is it my negative personal magnetism?"

JJ was taken aback, the young lady wasn't meant to have heard his doubts. "No," he said quickly to disguise his embarrassment. "It's my Scottish accent. Difficult to understand at the best of times but especially so if I'm tired, sorry."

"I've been to Scotland, to Edinboro. I understand Scottish," came the reply.

"I'm from Glasgow, it's different," said JJ.

"Glasgow is a scary place. So you're a real man?" asked Kina.

"Don't know about that… but Glasgow *is* a scary place," he confirmed.

Kina proceeded to take JJ's order and execute the coffee

preparation perfectly. She handed it to JJ. "I work here three days a week. Come and speak Scottish to me," she said and lined up the next customer.

As JJ entered the MAM building a few minutes later he was still chuckling to himself. He didn't often get out bantered especially if it related to Scotland but the quick-witted Kina had certainly gone 1–0 up. Bend it like Nakamura he thought recalling the best ever Celtic free kick to sail into Manchester United's net. Edwin Van der Sar didn't even smell it.

JJ entered his office, coffee in hand, switched on computers, his TV and his tablet. Once settled, he checked for market prices. He was interested in all four main asset classes, as MAM had investments in all of them, but today he was mainly concerned with the price of gold and the GBP/USD exchange rate. Gold had reached a high of $1,880/oz in Asian trading but now seemed to be settling back to the $1,860 – $1,870 range. Cable had come off slightly so the combination was still good for the GBP value of the Korean gold haul.

"Toby, it's JJ. Can you and Yves-Jacques come to my office at 9am? We should finalise our gold transactions. I'll have a friend with me. He's not a financial type but he knows a bit about computers."

"Sure JJ. I'll pick up Yves-Jacques on the way. See you in a bit," replied Toby, wondering about, though not asking about, JJ's friend.

★ ★ ★

When Toby and Yves-Jacques entered JJ's office, Victor Pagari was already there. JJ greeted his two amigos and introduced Victor. He kept it short, simply saying that Victor was with him in Korea, and was the computer brains behind the operation. In the same way that Victor was not aware of the blackmail and insider trading threat hanging over the amigos, the two other amigos were not aware of Victor's safe cracking skills. JJ eyed Toby and true to form his shirt had yet again partially escaped from his pants. This time Yves-Jacques did not seem to be following Fathead's unkempt sartorial style. At least JJ knew that Fathead had not been captured by aliens and returned in a different guise. This was the real Toby for sure.

"Toby, Yves-Jacques, what's the up to date state of play on the gold. You can speak freely in front of Victor, he has my full confidence," said JJ.

Toby replied, "The gold's all sold and placed JJ. The Swiss family office weren't as hungry for the bars as I expected, but they took a few hundred. HSBC took a chunk and Scotia Mocatta picked up the balance. They'd heard on the grapevine that JPM had purchased a substantial number of gold bars, and they didn't want to be left out. We're done."

"That's great Toby, good job," said JJ. "Yves-Jacques, what about delivery?"

"HSBC and the Swiss family office will have theirs delivered today. Brink's are organising Scotia Mocatta's and their bullion should be safely in their vaults by tomorrow afternoon at the latest," responded the young Frenchman.

"What about the settlement price, Toby, do we have what we need?" continued JJ.

"Yes. We had a degree of good fortune in that the gold price kept rising and cable was either stable or moving in our direction," answered Toby confidently. "We need to convert the US dollars to pounds, though, but at this morning's rate our total gold proceeds should be of the order of £3.8 billion to £4 billion equivalent."

"Very good Toby, really excellent," said JJ. "Start converting

471

the currency now. Presumably that amount will take you all day and into the night?"

"Yes," replied Toby. "The daily turnover of the global FX market is around $4 trillion so it's not the amount that's the issue. I'll use multiple brokers in multiple countries and different time zones. It will only become a problem if the market thinks we know something that they don't and we inadvertently trigger a run on the dollar."

"You're too smart for that to happen, right?" mentioned JJ, already knowing what the answer would be.

"Sure am chief," beamed Toby. "I'll sell the dollars in tickets of no more than $200 million each, most of them between $10m and $50m. I'll place the bulk of orders between now and 5pm. European and US markets are both in full swing then so the transacted volume will be high and big tickets less noticeable or BBM worthy. I can't guarantee that the GBP/USD rate will not move against us, but it shouldn't be because of me."

"Sounds like a plan, Toby, good. You've got the account numbers and the banks designated to receive the proceeds, right?" asked JJ.

"Yes. I do."

"Fine. Toby, you get on the case. Yves-Jacques you ensure that all the bullion bars have either been delivered or are on track to be delivered. Let's meet up again at 5pm," said JJ.

With that Toby and Yves-Jacques left JJ's office. Victor had said nothing during this part of the conversation. It simply was not his field of expertise and he did not want to ask questions which, in their own right, may seem reasonable but could appear to be a bit amateurish to wizened professionals. "That was interesting," he said eventually to JJ.

"I guess I'm thinking about it more like a military exercise than a point of interest at the moment, Victor. How's Ethel?"

"She's good. Resting at home for a few days to get her full strength back. She said she was owed some holiday so she's planning not to go back to 19 for about a month."

"I'll visit her in a few days, before I go to Scotland. I'm so glad she's OK," said JJ.

"Me too," agreed Victor.

"To the business at hand, Victor," said JJ, in the mood to tie up all loose ends. "You heard Toby. We'll have the sterling proceeds agreed by tonight and they will be transferred electronically to the designated accounts in two days." JJ handed Victor a piece of paper. "These are the account numbers, IBAN codes and the names they will be under. Once transferred these funds, and as you've heard, it's an enormous amount of money, will be in the hands, electronically speaking, of one of the slimiest toads ever to inhabit these islands. Are you sure you can hack into them and be in full control of them?"

"Of course," replied Victor with notable nonchalance. The expression on JJ's face, however, indicated that some elaboration was required. "All this modern banking technology, it's like the internet in general. It's a double edged sword. The internet allows you to do loads of good things very efficiently, but it also facilitates bad things done by bad people. Same with ATMs, on-line banking, banking on your mobile phone etc. Once it's out there in the electronic ether, it's mine to control. I can hack, virtually, anyone's bank account at any time and they won't know I'm doing it, except of course when all their money is gone."

"If so, isn't that an easier option than safe cracking?" asked JJ.

"It may be, but it's the challenge I like. Defeating the world's most secure vaults is exhilarating. Hacking bank accounts is something to do while chilling having a Thai takeaway. I don't do it and I don't eat Thai. Eastern European simpletons can have that as their crime of choice. They'll eventually get caught, there's always a younger, smarter hacker on the horizon. As yet, however, there's not a better safe cracker around."

"You're a piece of work Victor, and thank god for it," said JJ acknowledging this extremely talented young man. JJ and Victor chatted a while longer as the Scot gave the youngster additional details re the control of the funds, communication between them and the likely schedule of events. They parted with a firm handshake.

As Victor left to go about his business, JJ reclined on his leather chair, feet on desk and casually accessed his desktop computer, tablet and new smartphone. Today may be the first day for what seemed like an age that he could spend the bulk of it doing MAM work, what he was paid too much for. Thankfully, the markets had been kind to MAM in his absence and there had been no need for any asset fire-sales or indeed any significant reallocation of the portfolios for which he was responsible. He had *Sky News* up on one of his flat screens. Chancellor Jeffrey Walker was in the Commons and appeared to be answering questions about UK government expenditures, the budget deficit and its funding. He seemed calm enough and his responses robust enough. Walker was the consummate politician, vastly experienced, could probably pass a lie detector test at will, did not have a bead of sweat on his forehead nor a hair out of place. Just like Richard Nixon. JJ had already become bored with the *Sky News* loop and there were no earth shattering financial news stories on Bloomberg. JP Morgan were to be fined a few billion dollars for mis-selling something or other. That was hardly news, in the same way that summer is hardly news. The equity markets hadn't flinched and neither had the US investment bank's share price. Déjà vu.

JJ's attention moved from the news that was no news to his emails. He scrolled through the unopened ones, nothing from his doctor or oncologist; that was good. Nothing from Neil Robson, that was even better though he was scheduled to see the Financial Secretary to the Treasury the next day. There was one email, however, with no subject heading. JJ left clicked and began reading.

Dear Mr Darke,

Forgive me for contacting you out of the blue but I need some help. You've been to see my boss a couple of times in the past few weeks and, on the last occasion, you helped him with his bleeding nose. As you and he continued to talk I overheard parts of your conversation as I left his office door slightly ajar. What I heard did not really make sense to me. However, my best friend at work died recently in circumstances that did not make any sense to me either. I asked Mr Robson a couple of questions about this and he told me to cease and desist in no uncertain terms. In fact, he was downright rude and I felt more than a little intimidated. You seemed very pleasant when I met you and did not appear to be intimidated by Mr Robson, actually the exact opposite. When you were last here I heard mention of 'the solvency of the government' or it sounded like that. My friend Joel, the one who died, was working on something to do with the government's expenditures and the last time I saw him alive he had just come out of a meeting with Mr Robson in his office.

I would be really grateful if you would agree to meet me to discuss any part of this. Please do not tell Mr Robson that I contacted you, it may cost me my job.

Regards and thanks in advance,

Becky Martin

Well, well thought JJ. Young Becky had more to her than a pretty face and luminous clothes. If she keeps digging, however, it may cost her more than her job. Robson had put paid to women and children before. She may be in more danger than she thought. Better set up a meet sharpish and fill her in, on a need to know basis. JJ replied to Becky's email and they were to meet up at his office that afternoon. Becky asked for a half day off for emergency dental work. Robson did not object. He was on tenterhooks awaiting news on 'his' money and would have no need for her services for the rest of the day. Any services he wanted from Becky he could press for once he was loaded, thought the sleazy Fin Sec.

JJ informed MAM's reception area that a Becky Martin was due to meet him at 1pm. Sign her in as an interview candidate for the job of his PA, he instructed, a position that was vacant at present. His assistant of two years was on maternity leave and not expected to return until the end of the year.

It was 12.59pm. Reception rang and a security guard escorted Becky to JJ's office. JJ had organised a few platters of lunchtime food to be delivered, ranging from salady stuff, sushi, and a couple of baguettes. He had no idea if Becky had eaten lunch or not but food can often make any meeting go better. Becky looked very smart and professional today, less glowing than normal, wearing a well-tailored, predominantly black trouser suit with cream trimming and matching accessories.

"Becky, nice to see you again, even if the circumstances are a bit weird," JJ said, smiling, trying to put the young woman at ease.

"Yes, thank you," she replied a little nervously. "I'm sorry for putting you on the spot with that email, but I was getting really concerned, I wanted to know what happened to Joel, there was nobody to ask, Mr Robson was horrible, I…" blurted Becky.

"It's OK, Becky," said JJ calmly and pulling back one of the chairs around the meeting table atop of which rested all the food. He motioned for Becky to sit, so she did. "Help yourself, I'm going to. Look Becky, I don't know if I can help or not but I'll try. May I ask you a couple of questions first?"

"Yes, of course."

"How much do you know of Neil Robson's background, before he was a politician, at the Treasury, all that political malarkey?"

"Not much. I know he was in the secret services or something like that, but I never really delved into it."

"Neil Robson and I were in MI5 together, Becky, that's how we know each other. We are not friends. I do need to do some business with him currently but after that I hope never to see him again," said JJ, thinking it would reassure Becky if a few choice details came out right at the start of their discussion. It did, Becky asked JJ if he knew Joel Gordon, but he did not. Becky informed JJ of Joel's job at the Treasury, his untimely demise, that it was due to radiation, that neither his girlfriend nor his family had any idea as to how he could have been poisoned like that. She was relaxing a bit, had a couple of bites of salad, a few pieces of sushi and plenty water. JJ assimilated what he could of Becky's account. His prior knowledge of Robson and the alleged justification for the DPRK heist led him to conclude that his nemesis probably did have something to do with Becky's friend's death.

"Did the doctors say what kind of radiation Joel had been exposed to?" asked JJ, fighting his way through a brie and tomato baguette.

"Not precisely. From what I could gather from Talisha, Joel's girlfriend, the medical people said that there were no initial signs of external burns so it must have been ingested or something." Becky was in full flow now. She felt comfortable in JJ's presence. He was listening to her; he wasn't ogling her or making inappropriate suggestions. Refreshing compared to Robson. She chatted on for a few more minutes and mouthfuls. She even told JJ about her key words observation 'Joel', 'cupcake', 'Robson'.

"The cupcake thing, Becky," said JJ after listening a while longer. "Did you see any in Robson's office?"

"No. As far as I know he's never had a cupcake. It was all so odd. Joel's thanking my mum for baking them, my mum who can't bake and is in a care home with Alzheimer's. It's just too much…" Becky sniffed. JJ offered his pristine clean handkerchief, but Becky had come with tissues in her designer handbag.

As Becky composed herself, JJ's mind was whirring away. Robson was probably complicit in Joel's death but he hadn't figured out how yet. JJ was going to investigate a little further but his immediate concern was for Becky's well-being. "Becky, can I make a suggestion or two?"

"Yes, please do," she replied, still sniffling a little.

"OK. Being around Neil Robson for the next few days, maybe even a week, might not be the best thing for you. I don't want to alarm you, and you'd probably be fine, but he may get some bad news in a few days' time and start throwing toys out of his pram."

"Wouldn't be the first time," grumbled Becky.

"Can you take a week off work and go somewhere that Robson isn't aware of?"

"Yes, I can go to my aunt's in Hampshire, I feel like a break anyway and I can visit my mum more frequently for a few days," she replied, now somewhat cheerier and warming to JJ's train of thought.

"Good," said JJ. "In the meantime, I'll try to find out a little more about Joel Gordon's death. I'll let you know if I discover anything relevant. I'll be in touch in any case. Here's my business card with my direct line and mobile number. Ring me if you need to. I may be in Scotland while you're in Hampshire. Here's my home number there." Becky took the information from JJ and gave him her various contact details in return. As she stood up to

478

leave, JJ gave her a quick, friendly hug, involving no kissing of any variety.

"Thank you, Mr Darke," said Becky. "You've been very kind."

"It's JJ from now on, Becky. Take good care of yourself, be aware and if anything at all disturbs your psyche get in touch immediately."

Becky smiled weakly and JJ showed her out of the MAM building. She was going home to pack for her week away and send the office a concise email detailing her holiday plans. She had initially thought that JJ Darke seemed like a nice man, now she knew it.

JJ returned to his office. It was 2.30pm. He would be catching up with Toby at around 5pm. He had his meeting table cleared of the food debris, with most of the crumb chaos being his responsibility. He sat back on his desk chair and dialled.

"Hello," said the recognisable voice.

"Hi Ethel, it's JJ, how's my top girl?" he asked enthusiastically.

"I'm fine JJ, thank you," replied Ethel equally pleased to hear JJ's voice. "Is everything going well? You don't want my bonus back do you? You've not got some other looney mental foreign excursion you want me for?"

"All is good on that score Ginger," replied JJ, certain that he then heard a soft 'phew' at the other end of the phone. "I'll pop round to see you in a couple of days if that suits?"

"Sure, that would be delightful."

"I do have one non-dangerous desk bound type of favour to ask though. No such thing as a free lunch!" JJ added jauntily.

"You haven't bought me lunch you tight fisted Jock," exclaimed Ethel, clearly well enough to tease her friend.

"True, but I was instrumental in getting you the means for loads of lunches, all over the world!" They both laughed and Ethel's shoulder ached only a little.

"What do you want then?" asked Ethel.

"A couple of weeks ago some guy called Joel Gordon died. He was taken to Newham General Hospital with radiation poisoning, lasted a few days, then passed away. The police, apparently, investigated and found it mysterious but no evidence of third party foul play. Can you use your contacts in the force to get eyes on the police report and the coroner's assessment too? I would like to know precisely how he died and how the poison was administered. Any chance?"

"Sure, I'll get on it first thing in the morning. Is that OK?"

"That would be fabulous Ginger, thank you. I'll text you a few more details to get you started. Have a good evening, see you soon."

"You too, JJ," Ethel replied, hung up and decided that a stiff gin and tonic was just what her achy-breaky shoulder needed.

The rest of JJ's afternoon went well. Toby had done all the currency transactions, Yves-Jacques was on top of the gold's whereabouts, with only Scotia Mocatta's still to reach its destination. Victor had all the recipient account details and access to them programmed into his tablet. He would be in total control of the funds, electronically, though he would do nothing without JJ's authorisation. There was a time when he may have been tempted to swipe a chunk of the money for his own account but (a) he had been very well paid for his part in the gold heist and at the ripe old age of nineteen was a solid multi-millionaire and (b) he had seen what JJ could do with a crossbow!

JJ was having a fine brew of green tea at his desk, reflecting on the day's events. It was a satisfying day. It had begun well with the young Japanese woman fluent in Scottish, progressed smoothly with the concluding transactions of gold and currency, and the unexpected and intriguing pleasure of the less than fully candescent Becky's company, a nice chat with Ethel and now a

THE GOLDEN WHALE

refreshing cup of green tea. The tea perked him up but was also being consumed for its claimed powers in fighting cancer and alleviating side effects from his hormone treatment. JJ still had occasional hot sweats and bouts of excessive tiredness, his willie was dormant but his head hair seemed a bit thicker. JJ would not know for a year or two whether he and the Royal Marsden had delivered a total ring out to his cancer. Most of the time he didn't think about it but when he did it still was a little deflating.

Enough of that for today thought JJ, finishing off his tea. There was one more call to make and then he would be done. JJ dialled from his landline. "Sandra Hillington, please," he asked of the operator. The switchboard put him through to the woman's PA.

"Ms Hillington's office," came the male reply.

"I'd like to speak to Sandra please, if possible," asked JJ.

"Who's calling?"

"JJ Darke."

"Does she know you?" asked the man.

"I hope so," replied JJ. A few seconds elapsed.

"Putting you through now," said the man.

"My goodness," began a very proper female English accent, "talk about raves from the grave. How are you JJ? It's nice to hear from you. I guess we haven't spoken since…"

"Since I did all those magnificent oil calculations for you Sandra!" interrupted JJ, chuckling away.

"Ah yes, only half magnificent I seem to recall!" They both laughed.

"To what do I owe the pleasure?" asked Sandra, pleased to have heard from JJ, but with little time available for sweet reminisces.

"I need to come to see you, Sandra, soon. There's an imminent threat to our national security that I know more about than I ever wanted to. It's not a terrorist attack but if not addressed it will be equivalent to a financial cyber-attack that will bring down the government and maybe leave the streets of our major cities uncontrollable and seriously unsafe."

"Better come in then, JJ. Is tomorrow at 10am any good?" asked Sandra.

"That's fine. I'll be there at 10. Usual place?"

"The building's in the usual place, JJ, but I guess I'm a few floors higher up since we last met."

"Guess so, Sandra, well done. I'll see you in the morning." JJ hung up.

So tomorrow's activities were already mapped out. In the afternoon he'd head to the Treasury and let Neil Robson press the button to transfer nearly £4 billion to a variety of accounts that he thought would be in his control. In the morning he'd meet up with Sandra Hillington, his old boss and the new Director General of MI5.

Neil Robson may have left MI5 under a cloud but JJ Darke had not. JJ was a respected intelligence officer and widely regarded within the service as having been key in estimating the size of Middle East terror funds, their whereabouts and their ownership. Sandra Hillington had been JJ's section head. She was disappointed to lose him to the private sector, but understood. Sandra ensured that the pioneering research undertaken by JJ was augmented and advanced by his successors. Preventing the largest, most devastating terror assaults often began with following the money. JJ's economic template had held MI5's efforts in good stead. From Sandra Hillington's perspective, JJ Darke was welcome at Thames House, anytime.

★ ★ ★

JJ had a bit of a lie in. He had felt excessively tired the previous evening and his meeting with Sandra Hillington was not until 10am. He texted Toby to say that he would be in late. The taxi ride from SW3 to Milbank SW1 was a variable feast. Around 7am it would take around fifteen minutes. Mid-morning it would be twenty-five to thirty minutes depending on how clogged up the Embankment had become. JJ left plenty of time. He didn't like being late for appointments and being tardy for the head of MI5 didn't appeal as a place to start, especially given the incredible tale he was about to tell. JJ was smartly dressed. Brioni suit, mid grey, black shirt, well-polished brogues and his favourite IWC Top Gun split second chronograph loosely fitted to his left wrist.

JJ easily went through security checks at Thames House. They were expecting him and some of the long serving ground floor staff recognised him. JJ didn't exactly feel nostalgic, he'd been out of the service for many years, but he did feel that he was not in a strange place. As JJ entered the elevator, headed for the Director General's office, he pondered as to whether he might have gone to the police first, given that it was financial crime he was about to report. It did not take him much of a ponder to conclude that he was right to be in Thames House. Any major country's police force can be porous when it came to sensitive, even secret, information. The UK's was probably better than most, but not wholly reliable. In the modern world crime had become more sophisticated, more electronic, more remote. MI5 and the Serious Organised Crime Agency (SOCA) had casual links. In 2013, however, the police formed a new elite unit called the National Crime Agency (NCA), dubbed Britain's FBI. Critics of SOCA claimed that it had never really cracked down on serious crime nor kept pace with the technological advance of criminals in the UK. The new NCA was meant to address these failings and was to bring in accountants, computer experts and even retired bankers to focus on financial crime. The intention was good but as the old aphorism goes, 'the road to hell is paved with good intentions'. JJ had concluded that MI5, his clandestine alma mater, was more solid, more experienced, more intelligent in the specific and broad sense of the word, than a ragbag collection of so called experts as yet unproven.

Sandra Hillington met JJ at the lift. They shook hands warmly, she wasn't a hugger and definitely wasn't an air kisser. They went into the DG's office. Coffee, tea, milk, sugar and a modest selection of biscuits were on her oval dark wood table. They sat down and Ms Hillington was keen to get down to business.

"So, JJ what's this threat to Britain's security?"

Sandra was in her early fifties, looked younger and was quite slim. She had auburn hair, still cut in a 'Rachel', blue eyes and a no nonsense attitude. She was quite tall, about 5ft 7in, wore sensible shoes and had lost track of fashion.

JJ had decided to come totally clean. For the next ten to fifteen minutes, without interruption, he unloaded his story, beginning with the insider trading threat, the Fin Sec's blackmail, his plan, the imminent inability of the British government to pay the armed forces, NHS, the police and even MI5, the gold heist from North Korea, the tangential involvement of dodgy Russians and finally, his suspicion, as yet unproven, that Neil Robson was responsible for the murder of a Treasury employee.

Sandra Hillington had heard or been shown many reports in her MI5 career, many were groundless, some were of critical importance. Today's account was coming right out of the mouth of one of the most reliable and perceptive intelligence officers ever to have worked for her. "For god's sake, JJ, how did this come about?"

"It's hard to fathom," he said. "One domino falls then fifty others fall in sequence. I may have made some bad decisions but at the core I did what I thought best for my son, my friends and colleagues. I admit I put them, and myself, before country. However, I believe Neil Robson on one count and one count only and that is that without the proceeds from the North Korean gold, this government will be bankrupt before the month is out. There would be riots in the streets of London and other major cities. There would be many deaths, looting, lawlessness of a capital magnitude we have never before experienced. The resulting chaos, loss of life, paralysis of the system of government and normal daily life would be much greater than that caused by any terrorist bomb attack ever visited upon these shores."

Sandra Hillington was a smart woman, capable of disseminating substantial amounts of information quickly, separating the wheat from the chaff, getting to the nub of the matter. Even with all that brain power this story was seriously challenging. "JJ, do you think the Prime Minister knows anything about this?" asked the DG.

"I don't know, Sandra. If I had to guess I'd say no. The Chancellor, Jeffrey Walker, might. It would seem unrealistic for his Financial Secretary to be aware of a £3 billion shortfall and not his boss. He could have concealed it from the PM, the Home Secretary, but in truth I just don't know."

Sandra Hillington was beginning to put the pieces together. This was not the type of problem that the serious crime unit of MI5 were usually looking for. They were geared up to spot and stop cyber-attacks on the UK, to ferret out financial crime on a large scale, usually committed by foreigners on UK soil. They were not geared up for government incompetence and a financial time bomb, built and armed, from within the higher echelons of Britain's governing party. "I'm still getting my head around this," said Sandra. "I can hardly believe any of it, especially the North Korean bit." The DG was looking JJ right in the eye. He said nothing. What was done was done, it could not be undone with the best will in the world.

"I'm going to make a couple of discreet phone calls," said

Sandra. "Do you have a plan? Is there anything else I need to know?"

"I do have a plan. It begins this afternoon when I see Neil Robson. After that he will believe that he has nearly £4 billion to do with as he pleases. I doubt very much whether filling the government's coffers will be high on his priority list. In actuality, Robson will not be in control of the funds. I will. That's where you come in I hope!

"Sandra, you need to be absolutely certain who is and who is not clean at the top of the Cabinet. I'm doubtful about the Chancellor's position but you report directly to the Home Secretary. Check her out. If she's good then find out about Walker and the PM. Once you know who is trustworthy I will cede control of the £4 billion to MI5. You can then dispense it to the appropriate government departments and avoid political and social meltdown."

"Anything else?" asked the DG.

"Yes. You may think that North Korea should get its gold bars back or the cash proceeds from their sale. This would not be a quality thought. My own extensive research suggests that they *do* still owe this country at least £3 billion from their bond default in the 1980s. Check that with the Attorney General. If it's legal then we are done on the financial side, even if the debt collection process was major league unorthodox!"

"And the non-financial side?"

"When Neil Robson cannot access 'his' funds, he's going to go scary ballistic. He'll try to discredit me and my MAM colleagues by leaking the FCA file to the media. This afternoon I will have that file and a letter of exoneration from Robson, but he's a fucked up slimy toad and will not stick to his word," said JJ.

"A DA-notice?" asked Sandra.

"Yes please. If you could issue the highest level confidential DA-notice to every outlet of the media including all social network sites and communication forums then that would be very helpful."

Sandra Hillington would do as JJ asked. She remembered Neil Robson from his time at MI5. She thought then that he was an unsavoury individual. He had been asked to leave the service quietly after it was alleged that he had killed the wife and two daughters of a captured Iran sponsored bomb maker in Birmingham. The allegation had never been proven but it had been made by two other MI5 officers who were on that particular mission.

"From what I know of Robson," said Sandra, "he probably won't stop at trying to discredit you. If one minute he thinks he's a near billionaire and the next he's broke, discredited himself, out of a job and facing serious criminal charges, he's going to be one unhappy bunny."

"I know," said JJ, "I'll be prepared for that."

"We could take him into custody now and save you the bother?" suggested Sandra.

"It wouldn't work," replied JJ. "For starters he'd find a way to leak the FCA file and probably before you had time to issue blanket DA-notices. Secondly, until there's hard evidence that he's attempted to access funds that are not his he'd claim I was a delusional financial maverick and that the whole idea was mine. He's the British government and I'm some low life hedgie would be his line of defence. He'd rat out the rest of my mission team as well. In addition to all that, as far as I know, the North Koreans still haven't an inkling as to who stole their gold. Maybe they need to know later and maybe they don't but if they do it would be better coming from a top level diplomatic source than a criminal mandarin shouting his mouth off."

JJ's plan and explanations all made sense to Sandra Hillington.

She didn't have a better plan. Her immediate task was to get hold of the Home Secretary, ensure that she knew absolutely nothing about this whole sorry mess and then find out who did. The Director General of MI5 and the former MI5 intelligence officer chatted a short while longer. Sandra Hillington knew that JJ had done this country a huge service even if it was not wholly selfless and the *modus operandi* somewhat unique. They parted that morning with a warm handshake and a renewed respect.

JJ left Thames House feeling a little cleansed, a bit like Roman Catholics do after visiting the confessional. So far, he hadn't needed to do any penance and the longer that was the case the better as far as he was concerned. Toby and Yves-Jacques gave JJ an update when he arrived at MAM. All was good with both MAM positions and gold delivery. He'd be seeing Neil Robson in a couple of hours and shortly thereafter no doubt, another level of anxiety would emerge. As he was contemplating this prospect his phone rang.

"Hi JJ, it's Ginger."

"Hi Ginger. How are you today?"

"I'm good. Victor is here with me. We're going to pop out for a bite to eat in a short while."

"That's nice. I'm pleased Victor is there. Don't get him drunk, he may need to be on his techno game later in the day," said JJ.

"I won't," replied Ethel. "Got a sec?"

"Sure."

"I've looked into that favour you asked me for yesterday. Someone high up in the force was trying to keep it all hush-hush but my source, who was one of the detectives investigating the case, said it was very suspicious. The guy clearly had radiation poisoning but no one at his home or his office had any suggestions as to how he might have been exposed. They were going to investigate further but a missive from above said it was case closed."

Ethel hadn't really told JJ anything he didn't already know apart from 'case closed'. He was hoping for more. There was.

"I then got my best contact in the Coroner's Service to check it out. The guy's body was examined post mortem by the Coroner from Croydon. After extensive work he concluded that this Joel Gordon had been poisoned by polonium-210. There were several food remnants left in his stomach, the most prevalent being some kind of cake mixture. Does that mean anything to you?" asked Ethel.

"Yes it does. Why wasn't there an inquest?"

"My contact doesn't know. He did say, however, that in such circumstances cancellation of an inquest could only come from the very top, possibly the Lord Chief Justice himself, or the Prime Minister's office, on the grounds of national security."

"Thanks Ginger. That was very helpful. See you in a day or so. Have a fun lunch with Victor and tell him to expect a call from me later in the afternoon."

"Will do. See you anon."

So Becky was right in her suspicions. This Joel Gordon cupcake puzzle was now less mysterious but more murky. JJ gauged that Neil Robson probably could not nobble or even lean on the Lord Chief Justice. The top legal eagle in the UK was meant to be politically neutral and surely would not entertain any subversive notion from a bag carrier like Robson. The Prime Minister's office was another matter. John MacDonald, the PM may himself be as clean as a whistle, but the PM's office would be full of ambitious political climbers and not all of them as straight as the proverbial bat. Robson's silvery but tarnished tongue could well have talked some unsuspecting underling into an illegal manoeuvre. JJ would let Sandra Hillington know the results of Ethel's investigation. The net was tightening around the Fin Sec but, hopefully, he was blissfully unaware.

JJ arrived at HM Treasury on time. A security guard escorted him into the Fin Sec's office. Neil Robson was waiting and anticipating.

"No Becky?" asked JJ knowing there would not be.

"No. She's got some trouble with her teeth or taking a few days off or something. I don't know and I don't care. I take it you've got something for me," he snapped.

"I have," replied JJ, keen to get this over with and then trigger the downfall of this pathetic criminal. JJ opened up the laptop he was carrying and placed it on Robson's desk, screen facing the Financial Secretary. "The password to log-in is *Bannockburn*, I thought you wouldn't like that. You will see the accounts that the money is in. There's nothing else on this laptop so you can keep it. Now where's my file?"

"Hold your horses, Darke. I need to acquaint myself with what's on here."

JJ sat down uninvited. This was a time to be cooler than an icebox. No matter what Robson said, JJ told himself, this was definitely not the moment to launch another assault on the weasel. Neil Robson checked through the information on the laptop. There was a total of £3.8 billion in the accounts, spread over ten banks in three countries. They were all in the different shell company names which Robson had set up. Robson reached into the top right hand drawer of his desk and took out his own computer tablet. He fired it up.

"What are you doing?" asked JJ.

"Don't panic Jock. It all seems in order but I'm just going to do one little transfer. It's not that I don't trust you…" he continued with a look at JJ which said I didn't come up the Clyde in the shit ship either. Less than a minute elapsed when Robson closed the top of both the laptop and his tablet. He looked JJ straight in the eye. "Seems OK, Darke." Robson then went to his briefcase, extracted the FCA file on JJ and his two amigos and handed it over to the Scot.

"The letter of exoneration as well," said JJ.

Robson handed it over and JJ immediately checked it. It was on headed Treasury paper, signed by Neil Robson, Financial Secretary to HM Treasury and appeared to state categorically that the three amigos had not been involved in any wrongdoing of a financial nature or otherwise. On the face of it, it was solid. JJ knew that Robson probably had other copies of the FCA file and that he could always claim that the side letter of exoneration had been written under duress. Becky had seen Robson's bleeding nose so the Fin Sec could easily claim that he had been attacked by the hot-tempered Scot. JJ also knew, however, that Becky would do nothing to help her boss and that would be cast iron true when her suspicions about Joel's death were shown to be accurate. On top of that, JJ knew that one call to Sandra Hillington at MI5 and Robson would be going down, maybe to occupy Victor Pagari's old cell in Belmarsh. That call would be one of three he was going to make today immediately on exiting the Treasury. JJ nodded to Robson and rose from his chair to leave.

"Hold on a minute, Darke," insisted Neil Robson. "Sit down, I need to say something to you."

Normally, JJ would just tell the slimeball to fuck off and leave. He had no idea what Robson wanted to say, but just on the off-chance it was remotely relevant, he sat back down.

"You're probably feeling pretty good about yourself Darke. You've gotten away with a clear insider trading case and helped your two hedgie miscreants to do the same. You may think that saving Britain from bankruptcy and widespread social anarchy balances that out, but let's face it, you didn't have much of a choice. We're done on this issue, but I've got my eye on you."

JJ said nothing. He assumed Robson had finished. As he

motioned to rise again, Robson indicated that he should stay where he was. *What now*, thought JJ.

"You know Darke, I never liked you. Everyone thought you were great in MI5, but apart from the odd field trip you didn't do much. You're properly representative of your nation, know what I mean?" Robson seemed to be kind of enjoying himself, maybe it was the drug of all that money or, indeed, the real thing. JJ shook his head, partly in response to Robson's question and partly at the sight of this vile human being.

"You don't?" said Robson. "OK, I'll tell you. You Scots put yourselves forward as all brave and smart. William Wallace, Robert the Bruce, even Bonnie Prince Charlie. Invented the telephone, the television, the ATM to bring it all into the modern world. Even the fucking god particle was thought up by an Englishman resident at a Scottish University. But what did you Jock wankers do with all those balls and smarts? Nothing. You're so fucking tribal. When you could have conquered England all those hundreds of years ago, what did you do? You fought amongst yourselves. Bickered like a bunch of girls. Clan versus clan. No camaraderie, no foresight, no end game. A bunch of heathens wearing skirts. You blew it. Took the English coin, let your queen have her head chopped off and that was that. Even your fucking inventions. What did you tossers do with all the televisions and telephones. Sweet Fanny Adams. Logie Baird may have shown his TV for the first time in Selfridges ninety years ago but you won't find any Scottish televisions for sale there today, or anywhere on any day for that matter. Same with phones. Nada. You're a nation of breweries, pubs and call centres. You've become so soft and flabby you can't even muster the votes to get independence. Deep down it's because you don't want it. You're still happy to be subservient to the auld enemy, to take the coin of the English queen. You can watch *Braveheart* a million times, host the Commonwealth Games, sing 'Flower of Scotland' till you drop but you're still an English sideshow. For god's sake, the last time I saw any saltires being waved with enthusiasm was when that bastard Megrahi stepped off the plane at Tripoli airport. You lot are a fucking disgrace, way more stupid than you think and wouldn't know an end game if it bit you on the arse in broad daylight!" Robson paused for a drink of water. He managed to get that for himself.

JJ had sat there and took all of the nationalistic insults. Although they were delivered with hateful passion, there were some truths among the vitriol. Only once in his life had JJ felt ashamed to be Scottish. It was when that numpty Kenny McAskill, the Scottish Secretary for Justice, let the Lockerbie bomber go free, ostensibly because he had prostate cancer. Megrahi was supposed to have three months to live, he lasted nearly three years in the comfort of his wife and relatives. What all the families of those on Pan Am Flight 103 would have given for three more years of the company and joy of their loved ones. On that count, Robson was right, it was a fucking disgrace.

"Are you done?" asked JJ, surprisingly not mad as hell.

"I'm done, now fuck off back to your cave," snarled Robson.

Pleasantries over, JJ rose and left Robson's office without further ado.

★ ★ ★

Standing on Horse Guards Road and deciding to walk back to MAM's office, JJ made his first call.

"Victor, it's JJ. You need to get control of the funds now! Once you've done it let me know. I think Robson may have transferred some of the money to another account of his, so check the total that we have in our authority, and see if you can get back any amount transferred out."

"Sure," replied Victor. "I'm on it now. I'll call you in a minute."

JJ hung up and made his second call.

"Sandra, it's JJ. Robson thinks he's in charge of the money, in fact he may have actually transferred some of it to one of his other accounts we have no control over. As soon as I know what we've got left, I'll give instructions to transfer it to the MI5 escrow account you've set up."

"Thanks, JJ. Is Robson still in his office at the Treasury?"

"He was a few minutes ago. Seemed to be drooling over his good fortune and celebrating by lambasting the Scots for their errors and wicked ways."

"I'll put an end to that," said MI5's Director General. "I'm sending a unit now to pick him up. I'm sure we'll have an interesting chat."

"Good. Thanks Sandra. Speak to you shortly."

JJ hung up and dialled again. "Becky, is that you? It's JJ Darke."

"Hi Mr Darke, I mean JJ."

"Are you OK, nothing unusual going on?" asked JJ.

"No, I'm fine. I'm at my aunt's and I'm going to see my mum tonight."

"That's great. Look Becky, Neil Robson will probably be picked up by MI5 and officers from the National Crime Agency in a short while. He appears to have been directly involved in your friend's death. I'm sorry. It may be hushed up for a day or so but I can't rule out some media coverage at some point. They may come looking for you for a comment. I suggest lying low so stay in Hampshire until you hear from me again. Is that OK?"

Becky was still digesting the news that her boss was directly involved in Joel Gordon's death. She wasn't thinking totally clearly so just said 'yes' and hung up.

JJ had barely finished his call to Becky when his mobile rang. It was Victor.

"Hi JJ. It seems that Robson transferred £25 million to an account I can't immediately access. I tried once to hack into it but it's got high level encryption firewall protection. I can do it, but it will take me a little longer."

"Thanks Victor. Alright, the bulk of the £3.8 billion is still in our control. In the grand scheme of things, £25 million is no big deal. We'll retrieve that later. As soon as you can, transfer the billions into the escrow account number I gave you. Victor…"

"Yes, JJ?"

"It's an MI5 account so don't be tardy and don't be opportunistic!"

"No, Sir!" replied Victor, glad of the heads up even though he did not have any intention of interfering with that transfer.

★ ★ ★

JJ was back in his office at MAM. It was a Friday afternoon and he was mentally exhausted. He did have enough beans and enough presence of mind, however, to let Toby and Yves-Jacques know that they were off the FCA's hook. No file, no penalties, no action. Several jumping high fives ensued between the chunky Englishman and the skinny Frenchman. Yves-Jacques was going to Paris for a long weekend, one he owed his girlfriend from awhile back. Toby was heading for Nobu later that night and was teaming up with J-K with the total expectation that the three of them would get wasted. Toby was picking up the tab. The two amigos were in good shape for funds. JJ had already given them sizeable seven figure cash bonuses in thanks for their skilful efforts on selling and delivering the gold haul. They were deliriously happy. No regulatory action to worry about, huge cash windfall and the weekend coming up. What was there not to like?

It had been a landmark day for JJ. All the tasks that needed doing were done. He was going home now, to Markham Square, pack some stuff and fly to Scotland to see Cyrus and his parents. God, how he was looking forward to that. As he was leaving his office, his landline and mobile rang, virtually simultaneously. He dropped his suit jacket on his chair and, standing, answered his mobile.

"JJ, it's Sandra."

"Hi Sandra, did you get the funds alright?" asked JJ.

"Yes. The funds are fine. They're in MI5's control. The Home Secretary is aware of the whole shebang. She's clean. We will work together next week to ensure that the British government is solvent and British life normal. The PM and Home Secretary, along with the head of the NCA are presently chatting to Jeffrey Walker. He's probably not clean. He'll be asked to resign 'on health grounds' and quietly disappear."

"Good stuff," said JJ. "Have a brilliant weekend."

"Not so fast, JJ," interrupted the DG. "It's not all *Little House on the Prairie*. When my team turned up at the Treasury, Neil Robson had gone. His PA has the day off and nobody there knew where he was. My guys drove down to his house in St. George's Hill. His car and his stuff are still there but he isn't. We don't know where he is. We've contacted the airports, the trains, Eurostar, the cross Channel ferries but, so far, no definite sightings nor any reliable intel."

"When did your team turn up at the Treasury?" asked JJ.

"Around 4.30pm. It took a little time to get organised and coordinate with the NCA. They may be new but they're also slow," replied Sandra.

"If Robson left the Treasury right after our meeting, and given the traffic would have been a little lighter out of London and down the A3 than it is now then he's probably got a start on us of an hour and a half, maybe two hours," gauged JJ.

"Probably," replied MI5's chief.

"He may even know that he can't access the money, Sandra. That'll piss him off mega. He'll be wild and dangerous. You need to track him down."

"I've got everybody available on it, JJ. The DA-notices have all been sent out and acknowledged. There'll be no leaks regarding your stuff. I'll be in touch when I've any news."

"Thanks, Sandra," said JJ and hung up.

As it turns out, Neil Robson was blissfully unaware of all the commotion that was underway in central London. He had indeed left the Treasury almost immediately after JJ had. The traffic was light and he drove his Bentley Continental to St. George's Hill in around forty minutes. He had ordered a cab to collect him twenty minutes later, enough time for the Fin Sec to pack a bag for a long weekend in Amsterdam. The cab dropped Robson at Heathrow, he caught the late afternoon BA flight to the Dutch city and was heading for the Park Plaza Victoria to the north side, not far from Haarlem and Westpark. Neil Robson decided that he would celebrate his massive, ill-gotten gains by treating himself to a dirty weekend in Amsterdam. He didn't bring a friend or companion. Robson's idea of a dirty weekend was to gorge himself in the flesh pots of central Amsterdam, fuck hookers galore and partake in as many Class A drugs that he could get his hands or nose on.

Robson settled into his executive suite on the seventh floor. He had a long, relaxing shower, slipped on the hotel's sumptuous white bathrobe, took a couple of bourbons from the mini bar and flopped, contentedly on his king size four poster bed. He'd probably just have a quick snack before he went out. Didn't want Amsterdam's ladies of the night or shop window to be on their Tod Sloan for too much longer. Before getting dressed he thought he'd open up his tablet and have a quick peek at his now overflowing bank accounts. Robson signed up for the hotel's Wi-Fi access, logged in his password and waited. His accounts appeared. Jesus, what a load of money he thought. Maybe I'll transfer out another £20 million or so, just for the hell of it. Robson put in his transfer instructions. A confirmation message did not appear on his tablet's screen but an animated version of the von Trapp children from *The Sound of Music* did. As Neil Robson looked at this anime incredulously, the children burst into song:

> *Get lost, farewell, auf wiedersehen, goodnight*
> *Glad you're caught, you murderous thieving shite*
> *Do-do-do-do-do-do-do, do-do-do-do-do*
> *Piss off, farewell, auf wiedersehen, adieu*
> *Stinking prison is much too good for you-oo!*
> *Do-do-do-do-do-do-do, do-do-do-do-do*

Victor couldn't help it. He wanted Robson to know he was rumbled. Richard Rodgers's tune was more or less intact but the young safe cracker had re-written Oscar Hammerstein II's lyrics, not for the better but for the more Robson appropriate. Neil Robson shut down his tablet and tried again. He turned the volume down as the von Trapp kids were still taunting him. He shook the tablet, tapped the screen harder and harder until his right forefinger hurt. It was no good. Resigned to the fact that he no longer had several billion pounds in his accounts and under his control, Robson threw the tablet across the room, smashing it into the wall. He went over to the fragile but attractive writing desk in his room and dialled London, England. He recognised the voice and greeting at the end of the phone.

"Vladimir, it's Neil Robson. That Scottish cunt Darke has stolen our money, yours and mine. Deal with him."

12

BLACK NANA

"Change of orders, Sir," announced Joe Franks as he handed Commander Mark O'Neill the cable. Given that Franks had broken his leg at Haeju and all the bloody action that there had been on the Borei submarine since, the pace of his hobble up to the conn was fairly impressive.

O'Neill read the short instructions and asked Franks to let Evan Harris see them. The XO was still recuperating in the goat locker from his gunshot wounds caused by the departed Dannielle Eagles. In fact the SVR double agent was twice departed, having no life and no longer on the submarine.

"Tommy, change course to 55° 58' 59" North, 04° 55' 00" West. Keep your speed constant."

"Yes Sir," replied Tommy Fairclough, the sub's lead driver. "That doesn't seem much different from our original destination, Sir?" said Fairclough, half in statement and half in question.

"No, it doesn't Tommy. Lieutenant Harris is checking it out now," replied O'Neill.

Following the missile attack on the submarine and SVR agent Eagles' failed attempt to hijack the Borei, the sub's passage had since been peaceful. Traversing the Suez Canal was slow and laborious. It required immense concentration especially from Fairclough and David McCoy. The rest of the trip through European waters was uneventful. Now they were in the North Atlantic Ocean just above the deep oceanic floor known as the

Biscay Plain. They would be in Scotland tomorrow, Saturday, 4th April.

NGA officer Carolyn Reynolds approached O'Neill. "Evan says the new co-ordinates are for the Holy Loch in Scotland, not that far from Faslane."

"John Adams at Langley said in his cable that he would brief me fully before we arrived so I guess we'll find out soon enough why we're headed for a Scottish Lock," said O'Neill.

"It's a Loch, Mark, not a Lock. It's Scottish for Lake but you pronounce the 'ch' as in Bach the German composer, not as in the speed of sound Mach whatever nor in machete nor, indeed, as in more or less any other word containing 'ch' in the so-called English language," Carolyn pointed out.

"Feeling the call of your roots, Officer Reynolds?" jested O'Neill, chuckling a little.

"In part, Commander, but also because I like to be accurate and because I've got your best interests at heart."

"How so?" asked O'Neill.

"Well you've committed to taking me to dinner on the banks of Loch Lomond right?" asked Carolyn.

"Yes, ma'am," replied O'Neill enthusiastically.

"Well, what a plonker you'd look like if you say to the waitress 'it's lovely here on the Lock'. Whereas if you bother to pronounce it correctly, as I would Arkinsaw not phonetically Arkansas, then probably she won't spit in your soup, Yank. Got it?"

"I'm glad you've my best interests at heart, Carolyn," said O'Neill, smiling.

David McCoy was hovering. As back up driver he was aware of the new destination. "I think I know why we're going to the Holy Loch," said McCoy, pronouncing it correctly as befitted a man with an historic Scottish surname from the lands of Kintyre.

O'Neill was already impressed but wanted to find out if his buddy had more to offer than a throaty 'ch'.

"OK. I'll bite," said O'Neill.

"My maternal grandfather was a Gold Crew torpedo man aboard the USS *Casimir Pulaski*. It was one of the early Polaris ballistic missile submarines, named after some Polish general who served in the American Revolutionary War. Granddad would tell me tales of his adventures, patrolling in the North Atlantic, life on board, all that stuff. I can't remember all of it but I'm sure he said he was based in the Holy Loch for a while," offered McCoy.

"What? You think there's a submarine base there?" asked O'Neill.

"Well we know there's an active British Naval base at Faslane. You and the XO checked that out once we knew where we were going. The Holy Loch seems to be close. The base there was used for refits my granddad said. I thought it had been shut down after the collapse of the Soviet Union."

"Maybe, maybe not," said O'Neill. "If anyone's looking for this submarine they'll be using satellites, listening for chatter, checking out all the likely submarine bases of their enemies to see what turns up. A narrow, sheltered Scottish Loch is probably not going to be top of their search list, and that's likely why we're headed for it."

Carolyn was quite excited about all this Scottish stuff. She was not going to show it, though, especially now that she was the only girl on board and the crew weren't dumb, they knew she was the SEALs Commander's love interest. Carolyn had not set foot in Scotland since she was a baby. Indeed, she may never have, technically, set foot in Scotland at all because when she was last there she would have been carried about or wheeled in a pram. She did not have any clear memory of being there. When she was a little older and in America her mom had shown her some photographs of the three of them at a big house with a huge garden. She saw photos of two older folk as well whom she presumed were her dad's parents, her grandparents. Carolyn recalled that the big house was close to a vast expanse of water but she did not know where. The first thing she was going to do when she got off this sub was ring her dad. He would get the surprise of his life.

★ ★ ★

JJ didn't like surprises, even when they were good. The two he had received this evening were not good. First, the criminal Neil Robson was on the run and MI5 had not yet tracked him down. They discovered that he had boarded a BA flight for Amsterdam, but no signs of the murderer since. Robson was not going to be easy to find. He was a former MI5 field operative. Stealth, disguise, misdirection, he would remember how to do it all.

JJ's second surprise was that his house in Markham Square had been ransacked. Following the incident with black Merc man, Gil had her security firm contact install loads of add-on safety items. One of these was to arrange for any break-in signal that was sent directly to the local Chelsea police station to be simultaneously transmitted to JJ's smartphone. JJ did not return to his house in Markham Square until he saw the police arrive. By that time the ransackers had scarpered. When JJ went into the house with the police the place was a right mess. Spray painted on one wall, was: *Remember the death of William Wallace*. JJ told the constables that he did not know what that meant; but he did. The Scottish braveheart had been beheaded, hung, drawn and quartered in 1305. It was a message from Vladimir Babikov.

JJ collected a few things from the house and put them in his kit bag. The police said they would lock up and secure the building once the arriving detectives had investigated, searched for clues and took forensic evidence, if any. JJ thanked them, went straight to Sixt rent-a-car near Victoria Station and took possession of an Audi A6 Black Edition saloon car. JJ had intended to fly to Scotland, but you can't get the array of weapons he had just put in his kit bag onto a regular London-Glasgow flight. He knew the road route well. M4, M25, north on the M6 then M8 to Greenock, onto Wemyss Bay and, finally, ferry to the Isle of Bute. Tonight, though, he might need to make a swift detour.

"Becky, it's JJ," said the Scot.

"Hi JJ," replied the young woman.

"Are you OK? How's your mum?" he asked.

"We're fine. Mum's had a good several days. I'm just going back to my aunt's—"

"Look, Becky," JJ interrupted, "Neil Robson evaded the police. He's on the run and nobody knows exactly where he is. You're probably not in any danger but he may try to contact you for help."

"No, no, no. That's bad," groaned an immediately apprehensive Becky. "He'll figure out I had something to do with linking him to Joel Gordon's death. This is bad," she said beginning to cry. JJ thought that this might be the reaction. He was prepared.

"Becky, it's OK, stay calm. I'm in my car on my way to you now. I'm on the M3. I can probably be with you in forty-five minutes. I'm going to Scotland. If you want you can come with me. Go to your aunt's and pack your stuff. My parents are in Scotland, my son, his nanny. You won't be alone."

"Yes please. I would like to come. Please hurry," replied Becky. She hung up and drove as fast as she could from her mum's care home to her aunt's house. She'd be there in ten minutes. *Scotland, that'll be cold*, she thought. *Better pack some warm stuff, even if I have to borrow some of my aunt's.*

503

JJ was concentrating on the heavy Friday evening traffic out of London and thinking at the same time. He wasn't sure that taking Becky to Scotland was a great idea. His parents' house was big enough OK, but he may be taking her to greater danger. The dodgy Russian brigade were unlikely to be satisfied with a quick ransack of his Chelsea home and just say 'too bad'. They'd be looking for JJ and they would eventually suss out his Scottish connection. JJ would give Becky the chance of staying or going when they met up. If she came on the road trip then at least she would not be fretting on her own and she would have some protection in the form of himself and Gil. It wasn't enough but it was what they had.

Becky had no doubt. She was sticking close to JJ Darke. If any trouble came her way in Pimlico or Hampshire then she had no back up whatsoever. Her elder brother had emigrated to New Zealand, that made Scotland seem like round the corner. In any case, Lawrence wasn't a fighter, had no weapons training, no combat skills. He was a fine man but a civil engineer. Becky was ready when JJ arrived. She lobbed her bags into the back seat of the Audi and smartly got into the front passenger side.

"Ready?" asked JJ.

"As I'll ever be," she responded, feeling a little better at seeing JJ. "How long will it take us to drive to Scotland?"

"About six hours. We'll be in Glasgow around two in the morning. We're going to an island but the ferries don't start until after 6am. I phoned ahead and booked us two connecting rooms at the Millennium in Glasgow. We'll grab a few hours' sleep, have a decent breakfast and cross the water early in the morning." JJ glanced at Becky as they drove off, she looked drained, had on a pair of black casual pants, hefty hiking boots and a dark green cashmere turtle neck jumper, For a young woman of her normal candescence and style, this was clearly comfort clothing.

504

"Becky, I know this is all something of a shock to you. Joel's death, Robson's complicity, being in danger. I promise I'll do the best I can for you. We may be headed for trouble, I need to tell you that. Robson is in cahoots with the Russian Mafia in London. I don't know why but he is. One of their goons was tailing my son, Cyrus, and that's why he's in Scotland. I wouldn't have sent him there if I thought he'd be safer in London. What I'm trying to say is that if you need to be protected then we're going to the place best to do it."

"I don't know what to say, JJ, it's all just been too much in a very short space of time," she replied, feeling dog tired but listening tangentially to Passenger on the Audi's Bose sound system. "I've never been to Scotland, so I guess it's best to go first time with a local," she added, gave JJ a weak smile and closed her eyes.

JJ let Becky nap. He had his mobile phone earpiece in and was talking to Gil, in a low voice so as not to disturb his emotionally fragile passenger. JJ updated Gil on the whole sorry story. She was weapons prepared but had done nothing to augment the defence capabilities of JJ's parents' house.

"I'll probably be there around 10 to 10.30am, Gil. I'll fill everybody in then and we can fortify the place as best we can. How's Cyrus?" JJ asked.

"He's fine. We've been doing a bit of circuit training on the island. The fresh air is knocking him out by 9pm. He's amazed that he can get the internet, Wi-Fi, and all that stuff up here. He's playing some computer games with your dad. Needless to say there's only one winner," replied Gil, laughing.

"That's cool," said JJ. "Try to get a good rest tonight Gil and make sure Cyrus sleeps well. The world might be a different place tomorrow."

"Sure will. Drive safely. See you in the morning."

JJ settled into his long distance driving position. Arms bent at the elbows, both hands on the leather steering wheel at ten to two. He had also flipped down both sun visors even though it was the dead of night. That was a throwback to his GT racing days. Events in the sky are of no interest to a racing driver. The lowered visors meant that vision out of the front window was narrower, more focused. Peripheral vision was not affected. It was an odd habit but it helped him to be in the driving zone. JJ was powering up the M6, keeping to the speed limit of 70mph or within 10mph of it, on the topside. He was tempted to go faster but if pulled over by any enthusiastic motorway cops he risked them inspecting the boot and his diverse arsenal of weapons therein.

Once the M6 ran out at Gretna, it would be A74 then M74 to Glasgow. The border between Scotland and England stretched for nearly one hundred miles from the Solway Firth on the west to the River Tweed on the east. It had been legally established in 1237 by the Treaty of York. Now, exactly 777 years later it was one of the oldest surviving border crossings in the world. Each and every time JJ crossed into Scotland he felt taller, braver, fiercer, smarter. There was no logical explanation, it was pure emotion. At 6ft 1in in height, he was in fact still taller than most Scottish men. A 2011 study by researchers at the University of Southampton claimed that the average height of a Scottish man was 5ft 8in, the smallest of any region in the UK. William Wallace, however, was reputedly nearly 6ft 5in before he was slaughtered and butchered by his captors. No wonder he scared the holy crap out of the English invaders. He was a giant in a land of pygmies.

The English had never understood the Scots and in all likelihood never would. Neil Robson may be right that in their hearts the Scots had lost their bottle and would not vote 'yes' to independence. In their mind and soul, though, they are already independent, different, a class apart. The Scots don't hate the

English in the way Sunnis and Shiites hate each other, or Palestinians and Israelis. The Scots are not out for bloodshed, no carnage of the flesh as payback for hundreds of years of rape, pillage and theft. It's a mental thing and it's not symmetrical. English football fans may be content if Scotland ever progressed to a World Cup or European Championship final. The Scots don't feel the same about England. 'ABE' T-shirts will sell well north of the border this summer as the World Cup gets underway in Brazil. 'Anyone But England' is a Scottish mantra covering all sport. Andy Murray, Scotland's tennis champion, Olympic champion and 2013 Wimbledon champion can't quite bring himself to support the 'auld enemy' even with all the media and sponsorship pressure that can be brought to bear on him. He's a true Scot.

Thank god this perennial conflict is contained to the sporting arena, thought JJ as he sped past the exit sign for Manchester. He had filled up the Audi with unleaded petrol before leaving Victoria. He had also quickly purchased a few CDs to help keep him awake on the journey. He was getting tired of Passenger so he flipped the disc and inserted *The Proclaimers Greatest Hits*. 'Cap in Hand' would be the track to extend the current mood of intense Scottishness. Maybe if that economic lightweight Alex Salmond of the SNP had it as his smartphone's ringtone and could also understand why Scotland would benefit enormously if it had its own currency, the Scottish public might actually pay more attention and vote 'yes'.

JJ drove on, the Audi's powerful xenon headlights illuminating the dark roads. The motorway wasn't empty but traffic was sparse. He was in his rhythm, comfortable but alert. He was thinking about Bute. Mum and Dad were mainlanders, Mum from Glasgow and Dad a native of Inverness. A few years ago they had had enough of the hectic hubbub of city life and though they had a spacious apartment on Byers Road, in Glasgow's west end and near the university, they decided to sell up and move to Bute.

Bute meant 'fire island', JJ had no idea why, the place was fucking freezing most of the time. By Scottish island standards it was quite big, about forty-seven square miles with a total population of over 6,000. There were businesses, mainly agricultural or small retail and not all pubs and call centres. There were stand-out ventures on the island. The butchers were fantastic, the tiny electronic retailer super-efficient and the bicycle shop good enough to have been successful in Glasgow or Edinburgh. There was a health centre, of sorts, and a police station that looked as if it was straight out of *Assault on Precinct 13*. JJ couldn't fathom that one. There was the odd serious crime on the island but most of the law breakers were either public relievers, window breakers or young hoons going too fast in their souped-up garish Ford Fiestas.

From JJ's perspective the two best places on the island were the garage and the cinema. What luck that the only full service garage on the island was a Ford one, so they maintained with aplomb JJ's big block Ford V8 in his AC Cobra. The cinema was small, in the Isle of Bute Discovery Centre, capacity of ninety patrons but with a huge wide screen. It is rumoured that Lord Attenborough, long time Bute resident, screened the first showing of *Jurassic Park* there even before the premiere in Leicester Square, London. Bute had highlights alright, but daily life could be sleepy. If you needed an emergency plumber then either don't bother or contact the mainland. 'Island time' meant whenever they could be fached, if ever. It was a sore point for many islanders in an otherwise excellent place.

All that island night dreaming allowed JJ to burn up the miles. He was in Glasgow, following the Audi's GPS system to find

George Square, the location of the Millennium. He remembered a lot about Glasgow, but like any big city, the centre of it could be a labyrinth of one way streets, road works and other obstacles. He parked up and gently roused Becky. She was disoriented and JJ hoped that she would not become too awake to prevent her from grabbing a few more hours sleep in a comfortable bed. JJ asked reception to give them both a wake-up call at 6.30am. By the time they were showered, dressed and fed it would be 8am. Wemyss Bay was just over thirty miles from Glasgow, down the west coast, a total drive time of around forty-five minutes, half of it on the M8. If lucky, they would catch the 9am Caledonian MacBrayne ferry to Rothesay, main centre of Bute, turn left at the only set of traffic lights on the island and head for Ascog, his son, his parents and his friend.

★ ★ ★

On hearing the car come up the long and winding gravel drive, Cyrus was first out of his grandparents' large wooden front door. "Dad!" he called just before crushing JJ's frame with a seriously powerful bear hug. As the boy decided to let his dad breathe, Cyrus caught sight of a less than fully candescent Becky. "Who's she?" he enquired with concern. "She's not your girlfriend Dad, is she?" JJ and Becky looked at each other and shared a wee laugh.

"No, Cyrus. This is Becky. Lovely as she is, Becky is not my girlfriend," noted JJ getting straight to the point to alleviate young Darke's worries. "She is, however, a friend and one that needs our help and protection."

Cyrus felt daft and was blushing a bit. Becky was pretty and now he had appeared to her to be an immature dimwit, or so rationalised the mind of the young teenager, full of angst and awkwardness around most pretty young women, bar Lucy.

"Hi, I'm Cyrus," he eventually uttered, approaching Becky and extending his hand. "Sorry about that," he added, his eyes slightly lowered.

Becky shook Cyrus's hand warmly.

"That's OK, Cyrus, I'm very pleased to meet you. Your dad's told me good things about you. It's lovely up here."

Cyrus then went to help Becky with her bags. JJ had already taken his from the Audi's boot and was entering the front hallway in search of his parents and Gil. He saw that Becky and Cyrus were now chatting away, all awkwardness gone in a flash.

JJ unleased a mischievous smile.

"Hey Cyrus," he called, "you never know, if Becky ever feels like having a toy boy, your luck may be in!"

"Dad!" yelled Cyrus, this time wanting to crush his father's diaphragm a lot more, the embarrassing scunner that he was.

JJ walked past the living room on the left and library on the right. He was headed straight for the kitchen, he knew his mum and dad would be there, having tea or coffee, probably assailing Gil with some tale or other of island life. His mum spotted him first.

"JJ!" she exclaimed with clear pleasure at seeing her only child. His mum was hugging him and not really wanting to let go.

"Hi Mum, Dad, Gil. Great to see you all."

Cyrus had now entered the kitchen, old fashioned and spacious but with a sturdy sizeable, wooden table right in the middle and the heat from an established AGA cooker to warm up a chilly spring morning in Scotland.

"Everyone, this is Becky," announced Cyrus. "She's not Dad's girlfriend, so don't go thinking that!"

That boy's quick, thought JJ. The kitchen table was large enough to seat eight. Frances and Robert Darke liked the queen and king spots at either end, so JJ sat next to Gil on one side and Cyrus next to Becky on the other.

Frances Darke was around 5ft 6in tall, slightly above average for a Scotswoman, looked younger than her years and had done a decent job in keeping her figure. She had thick, luscious light brown hair, today cut in a long fringe. Frances was a good hostess. She had supplied a variety of teas, coffee and biscuits for the gathered band of six. Robert Darke was about five inches taller, slim and wiry with thinning, short cropped white hair. Robert's eyes were green and those of Frances blue. They were childhood sweethearts having met at their Glasgow high school.

The group seemed relaxed, small talk was babbling away. Robert Darke looked at his son, he knew something was up.

"JJ, you've got something on yer mind laddie. Better get it out I say," said Darke senior in his broad Highland brogue and with the forthrightness you'd expect from a former headmaster and now part time local magistrate. JJ looked at his dad. They weren't close and they both knew that JJ was more of a mummy's boy. He respected his dad but some Scottish fathers never reveal their sensitive side. JJ, like Cyrus, was an only child. If Robert Darke was ever too harsh then the boy John Jarvis only had his mum to turn to.

"You're right Dad, I do. It's a long, complex and dangerous story," said JJ.

"Better get on with it then," replied Robert, giving his son about as warm a smile as he could muster.

Gil already knew the whole story so asked JJ if she should take Cyrus somewhere. This was a question, the answer to which JJ could have wrestled with for about ten years. Logic and good fatherly sense went out the window and gut instinct kicked in. Cyrus was to stay and hear it all. For the next two hours, JJ revealed everything: Greek bonds, insider trading, Neil Robson,

Korea, dodgy Russians, Joel Gordon, gold. It was all there. If interrupted, he answered questions as best he could. Gil, of course, wasn't flummoxed. Cyrus thought it was 'wicked' as he had not known that he was being shadowed at any point. The boy was a bit ambiguous, however, about his feelings on discovering that his dad had killed a couple of North Korean soldiers with a crossbow. In the end, he concluded that was awesome too, the brain-washed soldiers would probably have murdered some innocent peasant without as much as a by your leave.

JJ apologised to his mum and dad for the upcoming likelihood that there could be a firefight, here on the island, here in their home. They both knew, of course, that their son had been an MI5 intelligence officer, that he had been to Bosnia, undercover, and that he had probably needed to terminate some bad people in the nation's defence and security. They thought that JJ had left all that behind for the calmer, safer, better paid surroundings of Mayfair. Clearly not they had just discovered.

"Good job I renewed the house insurance Frankie," said Robert Darke, looking caringly at his wife.

"Aye Bobby, it is," replied JJ's mum. "I hope you did the life insurance too, by the sounds of it." Everybody laughed.

JJ felt relieved that no one had panicked or burst into tears. He had never felt prouder of his parents.

"I'll show Becky to her room," said Frances Darke, "and then I'll go about ensuring the security of the top floor. Bobby, you check all entry points on the ground floor and the basement. Gil, you and Cyrus scope out the outbuildings, the grounds and the garage. JJ, I assume you've brought weapons with you?" JJ nodded. "Then you get that organised and when we're done let's all meet back here and have a plan. If stinkin' Russians are coming here to do my family and friends harm then they can expect some special Scottish hospitality, the type afforded to that vagabond

Viking, Hakan of Norway, just across the water at Largs, in 1263."

"Right on Black Nana!" exclaimed Cyrus, excited at hearing his grandmother in full swing. Frances Darke was something of an expert in Scottish history. Many years she spent travelling after university before settling back in Scotland and teaching early Scottish history in the local school. King Hakan of Norway ruled in both Scandinavia and the Western Isles of Scotland in the mid-thirteenth Century. The Viking king assembled his largest fleet ever and headed for the Clyde estuary intent on plunder. Bad weather (now there's a shock) forced his fleet aground. The opportunistic Scots looted his stricken ships. Hakan sent a force of more than 700 warriors to claim back his property. No deal. The Scots saw off Hakan's men and this victory, known as the Battle of Largs, was the catalyst for the demise of the Vikings in the West of Scotland. It wasn't Bannockburn, but Frances Darke liked it, not least of which because she could see Largs across the Clyde, every day from her front window and imagine the great Scottish victory.

Just before Gil and Cyrus went outside to do their job, Gil took JJ aside.

"JJ, why does Cyrus sometimes call your mother Black Nana?" JJ had the look of a man who didn't want to be asked that.

"It's quite a story, Gil, and this is not the time or place for all the ins and outs, but it boils down to this," he replied. "Between university and teaching history, my mother joined a travelling circus, I think it was the Circo Casartelli or something like that. Big in Italy and all over the world in the 1970s. As a girl she had always enjoyed throwing knives. I know it sounds crazy, but apparently she was the unofficial high school 'chicken' champion. That pastime is where you stand a few yards away, facing your opponent with your legs apart. Each person takes a turn at throwing their knife into the ground in the space between your feet. As each turn goes by you move your feet a little closer together. Eventually one of the participants usually chickens out because they doubt that the thrower can get the knife accurately between their feet, in the ground and without it sticking into a foot or leg. Weirdly, it's a game theoretic problem, not that many Scottish kids would have been thinking about that in the midst of the game. Mum took it to the extreme and was Circo Casartelli's main attraction for a couple of summers. When Cyrus was about four, Mum showed him a photograph of her, knives in hand or dotted about the still living associate attached to a large solid-board wheel. She was dressed in an all black cat suit with a black wig to match. Cyrus recognised his grandmother in the photo and, hey presto, Black Nana had arrived."

"Does your mum still have her knives?" asked Gil, patently thinking ahead.

"Now that's a good question Gil," replied JJ. "Let's go fetch Black Nana and find out if she still has the tools of her trade."

* * *

Vladimir Babikov had not played chicken at school. He didn't have the cahoonas for that. The criminal Russian may have twisted the neck of an occasional unsuspecting fowl or poked a love rival from behind with a knife, but a game where he was not guaranteed to be the winner didn't ever appeal to him.

Babikov had not enjoyed the telephone call from Neil Robson. The running politician man had gone underground and had left the Russian to do his own debt collecting. He was severely pissed off with this Scottish interloper he had never set eyes on and only recently heard from. Indeed, so pissed off was he that he was presently in the third car of a three car convoy on the M6, headed for Glasgow and beyond. Ahead of him were two S-class Mercedes, all black and tinted, each car carrying four or five ex-FSB thugs, heavily armed and ready for action. Babikov himself was in an augmented four wheel drive Mercedes AMG M-class, also black. He was accompanied by Boris Akulov who had now nearly fully recovered from JJ's assault and was acutely keen on payback.

Babikov had a clear plan. He was going to have his men capture JJ, beat the holy shit out of him, torture him into revealing the whereabouts of the money owed to Neil Robson and by prior gambling association, his good self. Then he was going to shoot the northern motherfucker stone dead, a pleasure that he may also visit upon any family or friends that happened to be accompanying this most annoying Scot. Boris had expressed an unhealthy interest in Darke's kid. His driver was a fucked up deviant thought Babikov but depending on the degree of the Scot's resistance, he may well humour the ex-FSB thug and today's chauffeur.

★ ★ ★

"Hello?" said JJ, answering his cellphone.

"Hi Dad, it's Cally."

JJ was immediately surprised to get the call but happy and relieved that his daughter was clearly alive. His second derivative thought was that there could have been a more propitious moment to get the news.

"Carolyn! How are you? Still in Seoul?"

"No, I'm not in Seoul, Dad. I'll give you three guesses," replied Carolyn.

JJ sure didn't have time for guessing games like 'I spy' or whatever, he was sorting out the weapons he had brought with him and figuring out how to allocate his supply among the Bute six.

"New York, Washington, Tokyo," replied JJ quickly. He didn't want to be rude to his daughter especially since he had only become properly re-acquainted with her a few weeks ago. However, he also didn't have the mental focus to answer her question properly. He blurted out the first three place names that came to mind and did not stop for a micro-second to consider time zone differences or the fact that Carolyn sounded very clear indeed.

"Rubbish guesses Dad, I'm in Scotland!" exclaimed an excited Carolyn.

JJ put his crossbow on the desk in the library. He had been re-loading it, checking the tautness of the pull, cleaning the reticle and generally ensuring that it was good to go. His mind, however, had now moved onto a different tack.

"Me too Cally, whereabouts are you?"

Carolyn had expected more of a happy audible tone of excitement from her dad. He sounded pre-occupied.

"I can't tell you precisely, Dad, all that need to know malarkey, but I'm on the west coast, not that far from Dunoon. If you're in Scotland too, can we meet up?"

JJ paused before replying. It seemed like the pause of a hundred years. Of course he wanted to see his daughter but if they were to meet up today or tomorrow she could be landed right in the middle of one whole heap of trouble. Balanced against that was the fact that he knew Carolyn was CIA-trained so could handle a gun and herself.

"Carolyn, I understand that you can't tell me precisely why you are in Scotland. Let me fill you in briefly on my current position and then you can decide. I'm at your grandparents' house on Bute. I can text you the address if you want it. The problem, and I don't know of any way to make this sound better, is that I suspect a gang of Russian Mafia thugs are on their way here. They

516

want information from me, which I cannot, actually will not give them. They will try to kill me. Cyrus, his nanny and a friend are here, as well as my mum and dad. We're fortifying the place now as best we can and I have some weapons with me. In all likelihood we will be outnumbered and outgunned. It's a long story and what I've told you is very much the tail end of it."

"Can I bring a friend?" asked Carolyn.

"Can he or she shoot?"

"Yes," said Carolyn.

"Most welcome then."

Carolyn's dad told her that if she was near Dunoon then the best way to get to Bute was to take the back road to Colintraive and then cross on the small, open aspect ferry to Rhubadoch on the island. The back road would take over half an hour and the ferry a few minutes as it needed to travel only one hundred yards.

Carolyn was standing on the banks of the Holy Loch, a few yards from Mark O'Neill and the rest of the Borei's crew, just beginning to find their land legs or, in Joe Franks' case, land leg.

History or maybe folklore has it that in the sixth Century, Saint Munn had landed on this part of Scotland, having sailed from Ireland. Hence, the loch's apparent holiness. More pertinent to the US Navy SEALs was that there was a secret, cavernous tunnel, eked out of the very rockface that surrounded parts of the loch. This tunnel, with the loch's dark, cold, water as its floor and ancient mountain rock as its ceiling, had been constructed by US and British naval forces in the 1960s. It was intended to hide a ship or submarine from the air.

At the height of the Cold War, both allied countries decided that they needed to have a 'last strike' option. If nuclear war broke out between the Soviet Union and the USA then one, final, decisive blow may bring hostilities to an end, or at least that was their military hierarchies' thinking at the time. While to the public, the media and most personnel in the US and UK armed forces, the Polaris base in Scotland had been shut down in 1992, the truth of the matter was that it had not. All the US nuclear subs had gone, the navy personnel too. The secret tunnel, however, remained. Its facilities were abandoned, dilapidated, or rusted, but it was good enough to house a guest Borei and keep it undetected from land, sea and air.

Commander Mark O'Neill and his SEALs team had completed their mission successfully. Associate CIA Director John Adams briefed O'Neill by phone and told him that an elite unit from Britain's SBS (Special Boat Service) would relieve him of his command later that day. The SBS team would come from X Squadron and they would be responsible for keeping the Borei safe and out of harm's, or its rightful owner's way.

Billy Smith and Yang Dingbang had already left Seoul and were back in California. Joe Franks and Evan Harris, accompanied by Gary Whitton, were on their way to Glasgow's Royal Infirmary Hospital. The former two SEALs needed to have their injuries and wounds checked by professionals with all the necessary equipment to hand. The medic, Whitton, wanted to go with them, partly as company and partly to oversee whatever Scottish medicine had to offer his buddies.

Barry Minchkin and Tommy Fairclough were ordered to remain until the SBS unit arrived. Tommy may need to manoeuvre the Borei within the tunnel's confines. It would also be safer for all concerned if he gave his SBS counterpart a hands on demonstration of the submarine's controls, capabilities and idiosyncrasies. He had just driven the submarine over 5,000 miles, avoided a direct missile hit and scraped along the bottom of the Suez Canal. He knew what this submarine could and could not do. Barry Minchkin needed to remain on the Holy Loch too. His engineering skills, the checks on the Borei's nuclear power unit and its missiles' nuclear warheads, were necessary. He too would need to impart his knowledge and experiences directly to X Squadron's incoming chief submarine engineer.

David McCoy was reclining on the banks of the Holy Loch, cushioned by some bright yellow gorse and purple heather. He was studying his tablet, investigating a detailed map of Scotland. He wanted to find out exactly where he was and also where the nearest airport was located. He wanted to go home and see his family.

Commander Mark O'Neill was standing, breathing in lungfuls of fresh, nippy Scottish air. He was admiring the rugged beauty of the local landscape and, on occasion, the much less rugged beauty of NGA Officer Reynolds. Carolyn saw him looking at her out of the corner of her eye. She cosied up to him.

"Mark, you know our date on Loch Lomond?"

"Of course, Carolyn. Once we're finished here let's go!" he said with deep enthusiasm, keen to get to know his new paramour even better and to improve his language skills.

Carolyn informed the Commander of her necessary change of plan. Her dad was in trouble and she could not just walk away. Carolyn did not expect Mark O'Neill to join her. She re-affirmed that her dad was ex-MI5 and said there was likely to be a firefight. She didn't know all, in fact hardly any, details but it didn't sound good.

"Hey, Big D," shouted O'Neill casually addressing his teammate and friend by his nickname. "You're on your tablet. See if you can rent any cars in some place called – what was it Carolyn?" asked O'Neill.

"Dunoon," said Carolyn.

"Dunoon, Big D," said O'Neill.

David McCoy exited his map app and browsed for car rentals.

A minute or so elapsed. "There's a garage called Stewart's on Wellington Street. We could get something there called a VW Touran or a Toyota Aygo. Are we going sightseeing?" asked McCoy.

"Not exactly," replied O'Neill.

The centre of Dunoon was less than three miles away, a six minute drive. The remainder of the Borei's crew still at the Holy Loch, however, did not have any vehicles with them. The plan was that the SBS unit would drive them to the nearest town, which happened to be Dunoon, after they arrived and assumed responsibility for the submarine. That could be a couple of hours away gauged O'Neill and time was short according to Carolyn.

"Big D, can we hike to Dunoon?" asked O'Neill.

"Yes, it will take us half an hour or so, if we're carrying kit."

O'Neill told McCoy about Carolyn's predicament. The Commander had decided to go with Carolyn to help her dad. It was shaping up to be one of those memorable first dates. O'Neill commended McCoy on a job well done in getting the Borei from North Korea to Scotland. He emphasised that the mission was now over. He was free to go home to the United States and no one would think the worse of it. He had earned a break, the right to see his family and the unacknowledged thanks of all the civilians who would now not be blown to smithereens or die agonisingly from radiation poisoning.

David McCoy had a ponder. He surely did want to go home, see his girlfriend and baby daughter, have six Buds and a giant T-bone steak. The SEALs' motto, however, was: *The only easy day was yesterday,* and David McCoy was a committed and honoured Navy SEAL. If his Commander, on or off mission, was going to put himself in danger, then he'd need back-up. This wasn't a part time job. He was in.

The trio made their farewells to Fairclough and Minchkin. They could handle the sub's handover to the SBS unit.

Commander O'Neill did not give the two staying SEALs much detail, not least of which because he didn't have it. The trio wished the duo well and vice versa. They all hoped to meet up in the warm Californian sunshine in the near future.

O'Neill, Reynolds and McCoy changed into their casual civvies and trekked pacily into Dunoon. Stewart's Garage had vehicles available to rent and McCoy opted for the Touran. They hired it for a week. The titanium grey VW was bigger than the three of them needed, even allowing for kit and weapons. McCoy's rationale was that the rear seats of the seven-seater could go down and if they had to take cover in a shooting fight they could at least have their heads out of plain sight.

McCoy got directions from the garage owner. Carolyn drove. She didn't know any more than the indigenous Americans about driving on the left side of the road but the two SEALs seated behind her were weapons checking and assessing. It was a pleasant spring day. The garage owner was sure the back road would be open with no natural debris blocking the road. On leaving Dunoon and then Hunter's Quay, the drive to Colintraive would take thirty-five to forty minutes Mr Stewart said, much the same as JJ had indicated.

As Carolyn was taking the left onto the back road, Vladimir Babikov and his entourage were in the Wemyss Bay car park awaiting the ferry for Rothesay, Isle of Bute. The ferry to Rothesay was substantial, a proper ship and could carry over forty sizeable vehicles including HGVs, buses and the occasional ambulance. This ferry crossing would take thirty-five minutes.

If the weather was good, specifically the winds calm and they were today, then this ferry was never late. If the Rothesay ferry and the Colintraive flat-bed were both on time then the Russians would beat the Americans to the Darkes' Ascog house by fifteen to twenty minutes.

★ ★ ★

Neil Robson had moved quickly following his brief call to Babikov. He left his hotel in Amsterdam, went to a charity shop in the town and, essentially, swapped all his clothes and shoes for some more casual attire. The Dutch homeless got the better of the deal from a valuation and quality perspective but needs must and the fugitive Robson's needs were great indeed. Suitably attired to mingle with the masses, Robson caught a coach and made his way to the Europoort in the Port of Rotterdam. The Europoort was situated on the south side of the rivers Rhine and Mease and was one of the busiest ports in the world. In addition to exuding the style of an ageing CND supporter he had donned a pair of heavy-rimmed spectacles and had not shaved since *The Sound of Music* night. He looked nothing like his Treasury mandarin persona nor would he be recognisable from his passport, not that his passport was coming out to play any time soon.

Neil Robson knew that the game was up as far as his political life was concerned. He assumed that MI5 and Interpol would be looking for him. Robson had ditched his mobile phone and tablet because of their GPS tracking capability, but he had read an English language newspaper and there it was: *Wanted for murder and attempted embezzlement.* He needed to get back to England, to get money, weapons and, most importantly, revenge.

The best thing about busy seaports is that, compared with airports or even train stations, their security is lax. Robson had discovered that the P&O line ran two overnight ferries from Rotterdam to Hull. He had spotted a furtive youth mooching about in the seaport's shops, approached him and promised him €100 if he bought Robson a one way ticket, €50 straight away and €50 when he returned with the ticket.

Neil Robson was on *The Pride of Rotterdam* later that night. *The PoR* made Caledonian MacBrayne's *Argyll* or *Bute* ferries look like rowing boats. The P&O ship could carry 1,350 passengers, 250 cars and 400 trailers. It was enormous but could still power through the waves at 22 knots. The crossing would take eleven hours, plenty of time for Robson to catch up on some sleep yet remain anonymous among the heaving mass of tired, unfocused night time passengers.

The Pride of Rotterdam arrived in the port of Hull on northern England's east coast just after 8am the next day. The drive to London, more than 200 miles away, would take nearly four hours, provided some jackass hadn't jacknifed his articulated lorry over all three southbound lanes near Birmingham.

Robson thought he would grab some breakfast in a Hull town centre café. On advice received there he made his way to Holdernen Road and stole a Nissan Pathfinder 4x4 from the Enterprise car park. He had just about enough cash on him to pay for breakfast and a full tank of petrol.

Robson was scoping out his plan as he drove to London. His home in St. George's Hill would most definitely be under surveillance, maybe even house sat by a couple of MI5 officers. He did not absolutely need to get into the house proper, but he did need to get into his garage. In there was his underfloor safe with lots of cash, unused credit cards and a couple of pistols. He would not be able to open the main garage door remotely, that would be spotted by any night watchmen. There was a side door, however, off the utility room which itself was off the kitchen. If he could get in that way then Bob would indeed be his uncle. Cashed up and tooled up Robson could then embark on his schedule of retribution before heading overseas for an extradition free territory as yet undecided. Top of the retribution list was one JJ Darke.

★ ★ ★

The Darke's house on Bute was an impressive dwelling. Built in the mid-19th century, mainly of sandstone, it was a tall two storey robust house which sat square and central in the three acre plot. To the rear of the plot was a steep hillside, populated by tall and numerous trees. The undergrowth was thick and the soil soggy. It was unlikely that any attack would come from there. Potential assailants would likely career down onto the open spaces below and well within range of a decent marksman. To the front of the property there was a walled road, the front gate, a pebble and rocky beach and the wide aspect of the River Clyde. The tall ground floor windows, almost floor to ceiling, allowed a fantastic view but provided no cover or elevation advantage over any approaching attacker. JJ knew that the six of them would not be able to hold off a well-armed gang for long. Their only realistic hope of victory and survival would be if they could pick off a few of the Russians before they breached the house.

JJ allocated weapons and rooms to defend. Gil and Cyrus would take the right side bedroom at the top of the stairs, JJ and Becky the top left. Robert Darke would occupy the single back bedroom just in case there was an attempt at a rear breach. Frances Darke, with six knives sheathed and strapped criss-cross on her chest would shuttle between front and back. JJ wanted to be with Cyrus, but Becky was a total wreck, unable even to contemplate holding a firearm, so he decided to stay with her. The calming influence of JJ would encourage her to sit in a corner of the top left bedroom, hunkered down behind the dressing table and away from the windows. JJ managed to convince her to hold his loaded crossbow and point it at the open door. If anybody she didn't recognise came through then fire. JJ had given Cyrus the same Glock 22 hand gun that he had loaned to Victor Pagari for the gold heist. Cyrus was a little apprehensive but calmly so. He was sure he could handle that. Cyrus's positioning was to be similar to Becky's in the other bedroom. Keep your head down, away from the window and point your weapon at the open door. Cyrus could have felt abandoned by his dad, but he didn't. He felt that he had been given a grown up responsibility for the first time, albeit a very dangerous one.

Gil and JJ had the heavyweight weapons with them. Gil had taken her Nemesis Vanquish high-powered sniper's rifle. She was setting it up and was now content. If she had to get up close and personal she also had two hand guns, a SIG Sauer SP2009 and an old Desert Eagle MK1. JJ had his crossbow, currently in the possession of the petrified Becky, his commando knife, his Glock 19 and a ChayTac M-200 intervention rifle, brought out of storage just for the occasion. Robert Darke had his old hunting rifle, a Lee Enfield No. 5, and not much else.

The Bute six had neither sub-machine guns nor grenades. In a serious shootout they were weapons light. As the experts of the group, JJ and Gil briefed everyone else on weaponcraft, taking cover, the need for clear and loud communication. If the attackers were indeed Russian they'd have a hard time understanding the three heavy Scottish accents on hand so loud information would not necessarily mean a thing to them. Under the circumstances and with the equipment they had, the group were as prepared as they could be.

Gil stayed in her position as first watch, while the other five took the opportunity to grab a bite to eat. They did not have time to digest.

"Positions!" yelled Gil.

There followed a mad dash from the kitchen and up the stairs. Cyrus was first into his location, not far from Gil, crouched down and pistol pointing. By the time he had got there, Gil had already accounted for the lead Russian Mercedes driver. As Babikov's gang sped through the gates and up the drive, the lead Merc came into plain view. The Russians weren't here for a friendly chat on the doorstep concluded Gil so she thought she'd even up the odds a little with a deadly accurate first strike. The second Mercedes and Babikov's AMG screeched to a halt. Babikov and Boris were not clearly visible, gaining cover from both the cars in front and some giant chestnut trees overhead. The ex-FSB and related thugs scrambled out of their cars. They were quick, though the last one out of the lead Merc was not quick enough. JJ had him in his sights. Zip! Babikov was two down.

The advantage of surprise gained by the Bute six had now run its course. Bogdan Zhirkov was Babikov's head bodyguard and he was barking commands at his remaining men. They were now under cover, in bushes, behind natural mounds in the grounds of the house and one crouched behind each of the Merc saloons. Babikov was laying low in the AMG's rear seats, with Boris Akulov next to him. As feared by JJ, the Russians were heavily armed.

The upper windows of the house were now nearly all shattered, glass spraying everywhere. Becky was shrieking but then calmed down surprisingly quickly. It was nearly impossible for JJ or Gil to pop their heads up to shoot. JJ couldn't tell from his under siege vantage point but it seemed like all of the attackers were armed with sub-machine guns. Heckler & Koch MP5s or Micro UZIs were the most likely he surmised given the sound and non-stop barrage of bullets peppering the house's upper floor.

The Darke's house was not isolated but there were no neighbours within two or three hundred yards, either side of its coastal perimeter. The deadly sniper shots fired by Gil and JJ had not aroused the suspicions of any locals.

No such luck once the thugs' machine guns started ventilating. Phone calls to 'Precinct 13' ensued and four local policemen turned up, two in their fettled BMW and two in a Land Rover. On hearing the racket caused by the machine guns they stopped short of the house's main gates. This was Britain, and although Scotland may not seem like part of it on occasion it was as far as gun laws were concerned. The four local policemen, used to arresting locals for peeing in a shop doorway, were not carrying weapons. They needed back-up. They called for it but it would not be arriving any time soon. The closest armed police unit was based in Glasgow. If they scrambled straight away then it would take them at least an hour and a half by road and boat. Less than an hour if the armed police could use one of their helicopters and land at some old field known as 'the airport' to the locals, or in the grounds of Kames Castle. The local police did the only sensible thing that they could. They blocked off the main Ascog road connecting Rothesay with Kingarth and Mount Stuart. They alerted the local, small hospital, called for an ambulance with paramedics to be on standby, and kept their distance from the raging gunfight.

"Cyrus, Gil!" yelled JJ. "You OK?"

"We're fine," Cyrus hollered back.

"I've left my window position, Gil. I'm on the landing, covering anyone who comes up the stairs. Keep your sights on the front garden. OK?" JJ shouted.

"OK," said Gil. There was an ominous lull in the machine gun rat-a-tat. This was a tough house to defend, multiple points of entry, too many doors and windows. JJ deduced that the absence of machine gun peppering meant that the assailants were probing, searching for a way in. He would need to go down a level.

"Becky, do you want to stay there or come with me? I'm headed lower?" asked JJ.

"With you," said Becky, rushing out of the bedroom door, still clutching the crossbow so tightly that she was almost welded to it.

"Dad, Mum!" hollered JJ. "I'm headed down. Dad take my position here on the landing."

"Aye," said Robert Darke, still calm and still ready for action.

JJ and Becky progressed gingerly down the stairs, JJ at the front and now joined by Frances Darke taking up the rear of the threesome. Becky felt a little safer being in a Darke sandwich. Before they could reach the ground floor, one of the non-FSB thugs in Babikov's employ came crashing through the front door. Clearly untrained and impatient he tumbled onto the hallway carpet. Before he could steady himself and fire at the descending trio he had a knife in his chest and a crossbow arrow in his left leg. Becky just freaked out at the loud commotion when the door gave way and instinctively loosed an arrow from the crossbow. Frances Darke was, in the same instant, more calm and methodical. Circus knife-throwers opt, predominantly, for one of three types of knife; handle-heavy, blade-heavy or balanced. Black Nana preferred balanced. She remembered the drill, left-handed throw meant right shoulder faces the target, one step forward with her back foot, step towards her throw line with her front foot, aim, throw as hard as you can and follow through like a baseball hit or a golf swing. Whoosh! Thud! Knife embedded in bad guy. In her circus career Frances Darke was skilled at missing the human target. It did not take much effort for her to adjust to hitting it. These communist bastards were intent on wrecking her lovely home. They would die for that.

As the knife victim lay bleeding out on the hallway carpet, Gil concluded that she had no further visible targets from her vantage point. She thought that she had winged another one of the Russians, she had, but it was not a kill shot. There was no sign of movement in the front garden or from behind surrounding bushes, mounds or other natural defences. She decided it was time to head lower as well.

"Cyrus, we're off. We're going down, next to your dad," said Gil.

"Fine," replied Cyrus, scared but not quite rigid. "Hi Granddad," said Cyrus as he and Gil high-crawled onto the upstairs landing before descending.

"Hello Cyrus," replied Robert Darke. "Guess this is like *Call of Duty* in 3-D," quipped Darke the elder.

"More like 4-D," replied his grandson just as the large stained-glass window above the small landing on the stairs, mid-floor, smashed and gave way.

The incoming Russian landed full on Gil, knocking her rifle out of her grasp and sending it tumbling down the stairs, landing inches from his stricken comrade on the hallway floor. The attacker recovered first and was about to shoot Cyrus. *Crack* went Robert Darke's Lee Enfield. It hit the Russian in the shoulder. He fell backwards, spraying the ceiling and the top floor with a barrage of bullets from his UZI. By the time he had landed on his back all 20 rounds from his magazine had emptied. Eighteen of them had gone nowhere interesting but two had hit Robert Darke. One round grazed his head and was not life-threatening but the second one had hit him in the chest. Frances Darke could see and hear the chaos from her position on the ground floor. As the Russian was trying to get back up, she threw two more knives in rapid succession. Both hit their target. Babikov had now lost four men with one injured.

"Dad!" yelled Cyrus. "Granddad's been hit." JJ acknowledged his son, rushed into the pantry opposite the dining room and grabbed the first aid box that he knew was there.

"See what you can do, Becky, please," JJ said as he relieved

Becky of his crossbow and swapped it for the first aid kit. "Mum, stay with Dad, help Becky. Here take this," JJ handed his mother his sniper's rifle.

"Gil, you alright?" asked JJ.

"Fine, a bit groggy, he sure was one fat bastard that landed on me," replied Gil.

If she can complain, thought JJ, then she's peachy.

"Good. Gil you and Cyrus, down here with me," beckoned JJ.

Frances Darke hunkered down on the landing. She glanced every few seconds at her husband and the fine first aid work that Becky appeared to be doing. When she had done her first aid course sponsored by the Treasury in 2013, Becky had been thinking more of her mum maybe absent-mindedly burning herself; not attending to a gunshot wound in the middle of a firefight.

In between glances, Black Nana had one eye on the ground floor with its wrecked front door and one on her husband. "You alright Bobby?" enquired Frances Darke.

"Naw, I'm no…" Robert said with a grimace. "It feels like a fuckin' heart attack. Is Cyrus OK?"

"He's good, Bobby, with his dad and Gil," she replied.

The Chelsea Three were on the ground floor, making their way towards the back door of the house, checking the utility room and cloakroom as they went. JJ had his Glock 19 in his left hand and crossbow in his right. He was not as deadly accurate with his right hand but he could hold the crossbow steady and if the target was close enough he'd hit it. Cyrus was in the middle, still holding his gun and Gil took up the rear, Glock holstered but rifle out and ready. As they passed by the door on their left which led to the basement they could hear movement. The attackers were probably in the house having entered from the basement's exterior door that led to the side garden of the property. There sure were too many points of entry and egress in this bloody place bemoaned JJ. He could see, from the space between door and floor, that the invading Russians had not yet found the light switch. That was going to be an unexpected bonus.

In the United States, basements tend to be large, with substantial headroom, good enough to live in or play in. In Scotland, basements are rare, usually full of junk and, in the instance particular to today's action, constructed with low hanging, jagged concrete beams that would near decapitate anyone over 5ft 10ins. JJ knew his basements. On hearing a Russian wailing in agony, JJ opened the door, sped down the stairs, flicked on the light switch and popped two 9x19 mm Parabellum rounds into the man with the gashed head.

"Sergei!" shouted his mate who was close behind, but not close enough as Sergei was no longer with us.

Gil and Cyrus had followed JJ at pace. They were all taking cover behind old or unused suitcases, packing boxes, a sofa and a couple of unloved dining room chairs. At least two ex-FSB thugs were now diagonally opposite, maybe only 50ft away, sheltering behind a concrete pillar and keeping low. JJ may have made a tactical error. The Russian machine guns were not letting up. Bits of furniture were flying everywhere with fragments of wood and cloth showering him, Gil and Cyrus. The Chelsea three could hardly get a shot off. Soon their cover would be riddled through and useless. This wasn't good. They needed a way out.

★ ★ ★

"I need to get into that house, officer," said Carolyn Reynolds, looking stern and really meaning it.

"No way hen," replied the young and pimply Argyll and Bute constable. "There's murdur goin' on in there. We've called for armed back-up but they're no here yet. Nobody's goin' in there till they arrive."

"Officer, I don't have time for this. My father is in there, my grandparents—"

"You don't sound Scottish, ma'am," interrupted the constable.

"I live in America. Anyway that's got nothing to do with it. I'm a US government agent and these two gentlemen are US Navy SEALs. We're going in," insisted Carolyn.

"Yer no and I'm President of the United States," replied the unconvinced police officer.

Carolyn turned tail, got back into the VW and started it up.

"What did he say, Carolyn?" asked Mark O'Neill.

"He said he was Barack Obama, the lying fuckwit. I mean, he's not even black. Get ready, we're going in." With that Carolyn floored the accelerator pedal and aimed straight for 'the President'. The nimble bobby leapt out of the way. Carolyn drove round the Land Rover and into the driveway of her grandparents' house.

"Follow the noise!" shouted O'Neill, as the Borei Three exited the VW. All of the Russian's Mercs were blocking the driveway so they needed to get out and run for the house. Babikov saw them coming from his interior mirror as he and Boris lay flat on the AMG's rear seats. Neither Carolyn nor the two SEALs saw them as they were not visible due to the blacked out windows. The doors of the Merc saloons were wide open, so a swift glance in there revealed no human presence. As they approached the front of the house, O'Neill went left, McCoy right and Reynolds straight through the open and wrecked front door. Carolyn had her SIG Sauer out, ready, arms extended and pointing ahead. Frances Darke saw the young woman run into the hallway and vault the dead Russian while collecting his UZI. Black Nana had JJ's rifle raised and poised. Carolyn spotted her.

"I'm Carolyn, Granny," called the NGA officer, as she flashed along the hallway.

Frances Darke registered the words but was totally bamboozled nevertheless. "Basement!" was all she could utter, lowering her rifle.

Carolyn heard the cacophonous racket from the basement. Without much intelligent thought for her own safety, she barrelled down the stairs and dived to her left to join the Chelsea Three.

Cyrus was totally taken aback, pointed his dad's Glock at her and yelled, "Who the heck are you?"

"I'm your sister curly-top so would you mind taking that gun out of my face. Hi Dad!" said Carolyn.

"Hi Princess," replied JJ.

Cyrus did as he was told by his big sister. He more or less flopped down as low as he could. He didn't even know he had a sister. Bullets, wood, cloth, glass and bits of metal were flying all around but all Cyrus was thinking was *I've got a sister*.

Thankfully, Mark O'Neill had more focus on the task at hand than the youngest Darke. He moved in behind Babikov's two basement goons having followed the noise. The SEALs commander took one of them out with a shot from his handgun. As the Russian's mate turned to fire on O'Neill, Carolyn raised herself and her recently acquired UZI and sprayed the exposed thug with at least ten of the magazine's twenty rounds.

Basement action was over. There was a lot of explanation that would be needed but now was not the time, Cyrus was smart enough to realise that. As they rose from the wreckage that was their cover, Cyrus could not take his eyes off Carolyn. She was pretty and she looked like him, bar the curls. It was well-friggin weird he said to himself but kind of exciting in an odd way.

Mark O'Neill emerged from behind the two dead basement Russians.

"Dad, this is Commander Mark O'Neill of the US Navy SEALs," said Carolyn.

"Good to meet you Commander, really really good," said JJ as he shook O'Neill's extended hand with gusto. "Just happened to be passing?" asked JJ, managing to retain a sense of humour amidst the carnage.

"Not exactly. Officer Reynolds, I mean Carolyn, your daughter and I—"

"We were on a mission together, Dad," interrupted Carolyn, keen to end O'Neill's feeble stuttering. "We're friends."

"Great," said JJ, definitely wanting to know more but concluding that a well-wrecked basement with corpses was not the place to do it. "This is Cyrus, my son, and Gil an exceptional friend," said JJ, completing the introductions. "Gil's ex-NSA and CIA, Commander. She's American and invaluable," added JJ, clearly very proud of his protégé. Cyrus thought that this must be the Day of Revelations or something. One minute he finds out that he's got a big sister, the next minute he discovers his nanny is a trained professional spy that can shoot to kill.

Pop! Pop! JJ immediately recognised the sound of gunshots from his sniper's rifle.

"JJ!" yelled his mother.

JJ was first up and out of the basement followed by Carolyn and Cyrus. O'Neill and Gil had gone the other way past the dead Russians. They had stayed low to avoid the dangerous concrete beams and were swiftly out into the garden. It seemed that Babikov still had firepower.

Two more ex-FSB killers had now come straight through the front door. Frances Darke was certain that she was not related to either of them. She shot and hit the lead entrant fatally but missed with her second shot. She threw one more knife but it missed its target too. By the time she had called for her son, Babikov's man

534

had her by the throat and was using her as a human shield. Becky was cowering over the rapidly fading Robert Darke. She was too petrified to move and he was helpless. The Russian ignored them. As JJ, his son and daughter arrived in the hallway, his mother and her captor were heading out of the front door.

"Drop your weapons or she die," said the goon in broken English and a deep Russian accent. It was Bogdan, Babikov's top man. He had his short-barrelled machine gun right on Mrs Darke's right temple. The three non-captive Darkes lay down their weapons. JJ liked to think of Carolyn as a Darke even though she had chosen to be a Reynolds.

Unbeknown to Bogdan Zhirkov was that both O'Neill and Gil were hunkered down behind one of the grassy mounds on the periphery of the expansive front lawn. Gil motioned to O'Neill not to fire. This was going to be her shot. Sniper training involves a whole lot of information, practice and resultant skill. Black Nana was a mere finger twitch away from being headless, dead as a dodo, permanently out for the count. Gil knew this. There was one target, one place in the human body that would generate an instant kill. Professionals called it 'the apricot'. Its technical term was the medulla oblongata, located inside the brain, at the base of the skull. A direct hit there and not even a finger twitch would result. Obligingly, the Russian holding Frances Darke was exiting the front door backwards. In a few seconds he would call for his remaining men to join him.

Bogdan did not have a few seconds. Gil had lined up the goon's apricot using her mil dot reticle. He was close, not even twenty yards away, so there would be no need to compensate for bullet drop. Gil dialled in a small adjustment for windage. They were at the edge of the Clyde and while it was not blowing a hoolly, it was breezy enough to make the trees' leaves audibly rustle. She was satisfied. The target was still. Zip! Bull's eye. The goon and his gun dropped instantly. No shots were fired from his machine gun. Frances Darke was unharmed. Babikov's top man was toast.

O'Neill nodded to Gil and she acknowledged it. All the angst that she had given herself over the non-shot of the druggy dude in Boston had now been lifted. As the family and friends at the front of the house were regrouping, the rat-a-tat of machine gun fire could be heard. It was coming from the outbuildings at the back of the house.

"McCoy," groaned O'Neill realising that his SEAL mate was on his own.

Frances Darke and Cyrus returned to the house to help tend to her husband and his granddad. JJ, Gil, Carolyn and O'Neill headed for the back of the house. Rapid gunfire was coming from one of the outbuildings used mainly for the storage of logs for the house's fires and equipment for gardening. David McCoy was the subject of the gunfire. He was pinned down behind a sizeable tractor unit used for grass cutting and collection.

"Hey Big D," yelled O'Neill. "Need a hand?"

"It's about fuckin' time," Big D hollered back sounding none too pleased. "These commie assholes have had me stuck here for ages. You lot been havin' tea and biscuits or what?"

"Or what," responded O'Neill. "We're here now. Keep your crew cut on."

Mark O'Neill did not know how to address JJ, He wasn't going to pre-emptively jigger up future events by calling him 'Dad' and 'JJ' seemed somewhat familiar given they had just met.

"Erm, Mr Darke," began O'Neill.

"JJ," interrupted the Scot. "Any friend of Carolyn's and all that."

"Fine. JJ is there any way into those outbuildings apart from the obvious entry points we can see?" O'Neill asked.

"Yes, if we go over that low level wall," replied JJ pointing to the hundred or so year old four foot high brickwork to their right. "We could climb onto the roof. There's a small skylight. It's a tight squeeze but if one of us dropped on them then the others could crash the rickety door. We'd need to time it just right. The dropper will be the deader if we're not inside in a flash."

Size wise it made sense for one of the women to be the dropper. Gil would have volunteered but without saying a word she pointed to her gammy leg. JJ understood. In all likelihood if Gil had crashed down on the floor or even on top of the Russians inside the outbuilding she would be off-balance and more vulnerable than an able-legged human. O'Neill and JJ were too big to guarantee a swift drop from skylight to ground. Carolyn had drawn the short straw.

JJ briefed her quickly about the layout on the inside. McCoy was still under heavy fire. The increased number of small holes in his tractor cover would soon join up to leave a big hole and expose his person directly to the incoming projectiles. JJ had a plan. He gave Carolyn his Glock 19 and she still had her SIG Sauer. Gil was to stay in situ and drop any bad guy motherfucker who came out of the door. O'Neill was to low-crawl underneath one of the outbuildings' windows and, in precisely four minutes from the synchronised initiation of JJ's chronograph and O'Neill's plastic Luminox, chuck a brick through one of the lower windows. There were plenty of loose bricks lying around. JJ was to go with his daughter. On hearing the breaking glass, Carolyn was to drop from the skylight, both handguns blazing as she went. She was bound to hit somebody.

The plan was off to a good start. O'Neill signalled to McCoy to stop firing. The Commander then lobbed a fair sized brick right through the window immediately above his head. On hearing the crash the two Russians started firing at the hole in the window and Carolyn dropped like the proverbial stone, blasting away indiscriminately, unloading her bullets on the blurs that were Babikov's men. One of them crumpled instantaneously. As the other rounded on Carolyn, JJ had his upper torso dangling through the skylight, he was wedged in. Strangely, this was part of his plan. He was stable in his position and had already loaded and aimed his crossbow. Whoosh! The standing man was no longer. JJ's arrow hit him in the throat. He was spurting and gurgling blood.

O'Neill leant through the smashed window, grabbed the arrowed Russian by the head and hauled him backwards out of the window space and thumped him hard onto the cobble stoned courtyard. He intended to twist his neck, but no need, the Russian was already dead.

Carolyn was a mess. Not from any gunshots, the Russians had all missed her by a mile. She was sore from landing on the hard surface of the outbuilding and she had straw embedded in her hair from the bales of hay that Babikov's men had been using as cover. Her clothes and face were black with dust and the general muck that flies about such an unkempt storage facility. David McCoy and Mark O'Neill came through the door. O'Neill caught sight of his love interest.

"Not one word O'Neill," said Carolyn before her open mouthed Navy SEAL could say anything.

"A little help here," implored JJ, well and truly wedged in the skylight's opening.

There were no more gunshots to be heard. All was quiet and the group of five finally leaving the outbuilding were walking back to check on the four still in the main house. As they approached the front door, they could hear the engine of a powerful car start up.

"Boris, get us the fuck out of here," yelped a most unhappy Babikov. The driver reversed his Merc 4x4, turned it left onto a small footpath in the grounds and then drove out of the front gates at pace. He avoided the police Land Rover but not the unfortunate constable who had previously harangued Carolyn. The police officer was sent flying into an offside ditch and eventually rolled onto the rocky beach. He was not dead but had two broken legs and quite a few facial lacerations. Boris was lamenting his lack of boy action. Vladimir Babikov was lamenting the loss of his entire bodyguard squad, his money and the damned day that he had ever come across that reprobate Neil Robson. If it wasn't for that scumbag debtor he would never have come to Scotland, never known of the existence of JJ or Cyrus Darke and never left the warm home comforts of Mayfair for this cold, desolate island. Babikov's lamenting was not over. He was about to lament that the Rothesay to Wemyss Bay ferry ran only every hour at this time of day. He was about to lament that the armed police response unit from Glasgow was ready to disembark from the ferry that he was hoping to board. Finally, he was about to lament that four heavily armed Americans were only minutes behind his getaway car. It was a day of laments for the criminal, murderous Russian. Fitting then that a lone piper on the pier was droning out 'The Flowers of the Forest' on his beloved bagpipes.

★ ★ ★

There are more than five hundred armed police officers in Scotland, under the command of Police Scotland. Their capability was beefed up in response to three events; the massacre of schoolchildren in Dunblane in 1996, the terrorist attack on Glasgow Airport in 2007 and the Whitehaven killing spree in 2010.

Angus Metcalfe was a young, rookie copper when he joined the first wave of police to attend the Glasgow Airport incident.

As a terrorist attack it was plain rubbish. Two deranged towelhead loonies drove a green propane canister armed Cherokee jeep into the bollards at the main entrance. They broke some glass, damaged the jeep and then fell out of it, one of them ablaze. There was no explosion. Several members of the Scottish public appeared to go to help the injured Cherokee occupants. Appearances can be deceptive. Two of the public were actually giving the burning terrorist a good kicking. The Scots got burned for their efforts and needed to go to hospital for minor injuries. The ablaze terrorist eventually died from his burns and the other idiot got a minimum of thirty-two years inside. Angus Metcalfe learned a few things from that incident. One of them was that terrorists come in all shapes, sizes and disguises.

Before departing Glasgow with his six man unit in a new ARV, Metcalfe had been briefed by the local Rothesay police. They did not know the extent of damage or carnage inside the Darkes' property but they did know that the perpetrators were travelling in Mercedes cars, one of them a black M-class AMG 4x4. Metcalfe and his team were first off the ferry and onto Rothesay Pier. As they drove up to the only set of traffic lights on the island they had to pass the three lane vehicle queue waiting to board. Sergeant Metcalfe was in the front passenger seat with Constable Duncan Robertson driving.

"Hey Dunky, pull over and do a Uee, as if we're going back on." Without questioning the order Dunky swung round.

"What's up, Sarge?" asked the police driver as he joined the nearside embarking queue.

"I think that's one of the Mercs that's led to us being here, Dunky. Tell the lads. Get tooled up and let's go see," said Metcalfe pointing to Babikov's 4x4.

Two of Metcalfe's team stayed in the ARV. The Sergeant, Dunky and two other officers, quickly got out. They crouched down and weaved their way towards the rear end of Babikov's Merc. A startled ticket collector almost gave the game away but didn't. Two kids in the back of a camper van spotted the armed officers and got very excited. Their parents, however, could not see the police so told them to 'wheesht' and wheesht they did for fear of a slap round their lugs. All four Scottish policemen had Glock 17 pistols and HK MP5 machine guns, weapons that Ethel Rogers would be well familiar with. They also had tasers and batons but, from the report of the action already occurred, a wee tap on the heid may not be what was called for.

Babikov and Boris should have been paying more attention to their six. However, Boris had noticed that the first line of the three to board the ferry had gone. The Russians were in line three, Boris started up the car, ready to go, both Russians' gaze firmly on the boat that would take them off this god-forsaken island. The armed police were now in situ, one at the rear end of the Merc, one at the front, with Metcalfe and Robertson crouched down under the driver's and passenger's side windows respectively. On Metcalfe's signal, they rose in sync.

"Hands on your heads and don't move a fuckin' muscle!" yelled Metcalfe pointing his machine gun at Boris's head. Robertson had his aimed straight at Babikov's bonce and the officer at the front of the vehicle was alternating his sight line between the heads of the two Russians.

Boris, for an instant, was tempted to run over the officer in front of his car. He thought better of it as he gauged that he would surely perish in a hail of deadly bullets. If he could have seen his future then he may well have opted for suicide by cop. As Babikov and Boris exited the Merc, hands up and offering no resistance, the four Americans pulled into the ferry queue in their VW Touran. They quickly assessed what was going on. Babikov and Boris were in speedcuffs and being led to the rear door of the

ARV. Metcalfe and Robertson would commandeer the Merc and head out to the scene of the crime. They had already been informed that the shooting had stopped. Local police were on the premises and an air ambulance was setting down on the front lawn of the Darkes' house. It was easily spacious enough to land a helicopter.

"You guys stash your weapons. I'll get out and talk to the polis," said Carolyn trying her best to sound Scottish. Carolyn walked up to Metcalfe. The police officer saw the somewhat dishevelled but intrinsically pretty woman headed his way. He was taking no chances. He turned to face her and pointed his MP5 straight at Carolyn.

"State yer business and don't come any closer," he barked. Carolyn stopped, raised her hands above her head and spoke.

"My name is Carolyn Reynolds, I am a US Intelligence Officer. My credentials are in my jacket's inside pocket if you care to verify. The two men you have in your custody are part of a Russian Mafia gang who have shot my grandfather and wrecked his house on this island. The trio in the VW are two US Navy SEALs and well, er, I guess my wee brother's nanny. Don't ask about the last bit."

Metcalfe looked directly into Carolyn's eyes, gun still pointing. She didn't appear to be lying but it was one wild tale. On the other hand in 2007 when he had first heard about two terrorists driving their jeep into Glasgow Airport he was a bit dubious about the veracity of that one.

"Dunky!" hollered Metcalfe. "Check the young wummin's inside jacket pocket."

"Sure Sarge. It says she's an NGA Officer from America, Sarge," noted Dunky scanning Carolyn's wallet. Angus Metcalfe had never heard of the NGA. He'd heard of the CIA and the FBI but not the NGA.

"What's the NGA?" he enquired of Carolyn.

"The National Geo-Spatial Agency," she replied. "We're like spies of the skies, we look at satellite images, photographs, schematics, anything to do with dubious activities of America's enemies that we can get a picture of."

"And do you find many of them, here in Rothesay, on a remote Scottish island?" he interrupted, as yet not convinced by Officer Reynolds' story.

Carolyn was getting bored with this line of questioning. She wanted to lower her hands, get back to see her dad and grandparents. She'd had enough chitty-chat with the Scottish police.

"Look, PC fuckin' plod. Do you think you could get a move on? You've got two dodgy Russians in custody. How often does that happen on a remote Scottish island? Anyway, there's about ten dead dodgy Russians littering my grandparents' premises. Maybe you and your plod mates could come along and inspect. What'd ya think?"

Jings, thought Metcalfe, *this wee wummin has fair got a gob on her*. Still, there did seem to be some Russian connection going on.

"Awright, wind yer neck in, we'll all go to your grandparents' hoose. Ma team will take those two tae Glesga for processing. Me and Dunky here will drive the Merc. You can come with us. OK?"

"Yes," replied Carolyn.

"Are yer friends in the van armed Ms Reynolds?" asked Metcalfe, somewhat belatedly.

"Yes, to the teeth. Would you like me to ask them to hand over their weapons to you, Sergeant?" replied Carolyn with a look of bare-faced cheek.

"Aye, that would be nice," retorted Metcalfe, keen to calm everything down.

Carolyn returned to the VW and explained the situation to the trio. They were reluctant to hand over all their gear so they gave the Scottish police the hardware that they could not hide about their person. Maybe Sergeant Metcalfe should have had them frisked, but he didn't.

On returning to the house, the two Scottish police officers and the four Americans saw an air ambulance take off and a local ambulance drive past them in the opposite direction. The air ambulance was headed for The Royal Alexandra hospital near Paisley. It would be only a fifteen minute flight. Both Frances and Robert Darke were on board. Granddad Darke was in a bad way and needed an emergency operation. Despite Becky's excellent first aid efforts it was touch and go whether he would make it. Frances Darke was in a bad way too, but emotionally, not physically. The local road ambulance was headed for Rothesay hospital, where the broken-legged constable would get basic emergency treatment. He would recover fully and live long to tell his mates and family about the infamous shootout in Ascog.

"Holy Jeezus," exclaimed Angus Metcalfe on entering the Darkes' grounds. "Ah've no seen this much damage since Celtic beat Rangers on penalties in the Scottish Cup final a while back."

JJ came out of the house to greet the returning group. He introduced himself to the police, informing Metcalfe that he was a former MI5 Intelligence Officer. On discovering that Babikov and his thug were in police custody, JJ encouraged Sergeant Metcalfe to get in touch immediately with the top dog in Police Scotland. From there they should contact Sandra Hillington, Director General of MI5. The security forces would definitely want a chat with the chief dodgy Russian.

A few days later chat they did. Boris Akulov was quickly identified as a hapless soldier in Vladimir Babikov's employ with nothing much to tell. He was also an illegal immigrant and was swiftly shipped back to Mother Russia once he had spilled the little he knew about Babikov and his operations, both legal and illegal.

The Russian authorities did not really want Boris back. He was ex-FSB but he was an unstable deviant and brought only disrepute to Russia. He was sentenced, by a judge in a closed courtroom, to life imprisonment in Russia's notorious Black Dolphin prison camp. Penal Colony No. 6, to give the correctional facility its official name, was one of Russia's oldest prisons and close to the Kazakhstan border. It housed the worst of Russia and Boris was deemed to be in that category. Black Dolphin has seven hundred inmates all serving life, and nine hundred prison officers. The inmates were allowed to exercise for ninety minutes per day and fed chicken four times a day. It seemed impossible to escape and equally impossible for inmates to harm one another or themselves, the checks were so regular and so thorough. Still, where there's a will there's a way. Aided by one of the Federal Penitentiary Service guards, who had often been rejected by the FSB, a Chechnyan terrorist lifer did for Boris one day, stabbing him thirty-five times with a prison made chiv. The rejected guard spotted Boris on the floor of his cell, bleeding out and dying. He was not going to get help or raise the alarm. Too much paperwork, too many investigations, simply too much hassle.

Vladimir Babikov fared a whole lot better. He was transferred from Glasgow into MI5 custody at Thames House. Sandra Hillington assigned the service's two best interrogators, a 'breaker' and an 'investigator' to quiz the Russian. He broke easily and spilled his guts. MI5 now knew precisely the connection between the Russian and the former Financial Secretary to the Treasury, Neil Robson. Babikov also confessed to acts of torture, murder, prostitution, drugs and racketeering. He had a full house of crimes to his debit and was now wholly at the mercy of MI5 and the British justice system. His fate would be decided in a matter of months. He was a broken old man with no army, no family and no friends. Sympathy, however, was not high on anybody's agenda.

★ ★ ★

In Scotland, JJ, family and friends had gone about resurrecting his parents' house as best they could. The front gates were nigh permanently closed and two local police officers were placed on guard duty. The Darkes did not need protection from any outside force other than the posses of paparazzi that seemed intent on gathering information, photos and sound-bites from the folk therein. For any number of reasons it wasn't happening and, as far as JJ was concerned, that particular blight on society could wait outside freezin', starvin' and complainin' for as long as it took for them to get the 'no comment' message.

Robert Darke was still in critical condition in the Alexandra Hospital. His wife was visiting but would probably catch the last ferry back to Bute. She could do little but await the doctor's assessment and she missed her home. *That boy of mine had better be fixing things up* she told herself. As it happens, JJ was lolling about on one of the very comfortable sofas in the living room. Fellow lollers were Cyrus, Gil, Carolyn and Mark O'Neill. David McCoy and Becky were in the kitchen preparing snacks. McCoy always fancied himself as a chef so he was giving it a go with cheese on toast, mini pizzas, a few burgers and other unhealthy fayre.

"So, Dad, how come I've a sister that I knew nothing about? Don't get me wrong. I'm glad I've got a ready-made big sister, who's pretty, looks like me and can shoot bad guys. Nevertheless, time to fess up methinks," said the youngest Darke, smiling at Carolyn and taking an unexpected amount of pleasure from the very visible squirming of his father.

"It's a long story Cyrus," replied JJ, not enjoying this passage of chat. "Sister from another mother, so to speak," said JJ hoping to raise a smile or acknowledgement from his son. Nothing. He was still in the frame. JJ reluctantly felt compelled to give details, so he did. He was respectful about Carolyn's mother, told Cyrus that, when alive, his own mother knew all about it, which she did, and tried his level best to explain that the resulting divergent paths of separate lives led to a lack of information and communication. "Never the twain shall meet, kind of."

"OK," said Cyrus, "that wasn't bad. I'll have a think about it but I may come back with more questions, alright?"

"Alright," confirmed JJ not entirely sure how he was feeling, apart from the onset of a hormone-induced hot flush, which felt crap.

"Hey new big sister," exclaimed Cyrus to get Carolyn's attention and clearly buoyed by his recently honed interrogation skills. "Are you and the Commander here an item?"

Phew, thought JJ, *I'm off the hook for a few minutes at least.*

Carolyn and Mark looked at each other.

"Yes, we are," Carolyn replied.

Additional banter followed, Cyrus was teasing Gil about her secret spy background, JJ was teasing Carolyn about her Navy SEAL and trying to extract information as to why they were in Scotland together. Carolyn was teasing her dad saying that old men should not be involved in shootouts and Mark O'Neill was doing his utmost to offend no one.

The group's thoughts then turned to Robert Darke. There was less mirth but they all hoped sincerely that he would recover. This slightly sombre thought led to a marked reduction in the chatting noise level. Becky and McCoy came to the rescue with two large trays emitting a fantastic aroma. A pack of wolves could not have descended on the food any faster. As they were all having something to eat, a mobile phone rang from one of Carolyn's outside jacket pockets.

"Is that yours?" Cyrus asked his sister.

"No," replied Carolyn, searching around in her pocket. "I found it in the driveway near that fat Russian's Merc, forgot to give it to the police," she added, picking up the smartphone.

"Can I have it, Cally?" asked JJ, hand and arm already extended.

"Sure," said Carolyn, handing the phone to her dad.

"Hello?" was all JJ said.

"Babikov, is that you? This is Igor Kruglov. Have you discovered anything yet about my missing hardware you prick?" yelled the Deputy Director of the SVR.

"It's not Babikov," said JJ. "I'm afraid Mr Babikov is currently enjoying a forced vacation in one of her majesty's most secure resorts."

"Who are you?" bellowed Kruglov. "What are you doing with Babikov's phone?"

"As I told your Russian friend, I'm William fuckin' Wallace. Now piss off you commie cunt!" vented JJ and hung up. The phone did not ring again.

JJ looked at his daughter and the two SEALs. The interrogation shoe was about to be on the other foot.

"Know anything about missing Russian hardware?" he asked.

★ ★ ★

Back in Surrey, Neil Robson had successfully entered the garage of his house in St. George's Hill. The front of the house was clearly under surveillance. The authorities, either police or MI5, however, must have concluded that there was very little chance of his returning as there were no officers inside. He managed to scale a small brick wall that separated his garden from one of the neighbours, and entered his house via the kitchen and utility room. His stash in the safe in the garage was intact, undisturbed and a very welcome sight. Now he had cash, three unused credit cards, two SIG Sauer P229 handguns each with two full magazines and a pair of small but powerful binoculars. Robson decided to spend the night in the back seat of his Bentley Continental, still there in all its glory. Those police numpties would not check, he concluded, and he had nowhere else to go. In the morning he would make his way to Weybridge, leave his stolen 4x4 there then catch a train to Waterloo Station. From there he would head for Chelsea and Markham Square. He would scope out the area, its shops, its cafés, its little hidey holes. Then he would wait and watch, and watch and wait. The Darkes would return eventually and then they would die. As Neil Robson curled up in his car, the thought of dead Darkes kept him warm and content on this cool evening in Bowser's Castle.

13

PROJECT LFD

The first punch hurt and the second one hurt even more. Between them these blows led to a spray of blood, a broken tooth and a fat lip.

"How do you like that you fuckin' teenage wastrel," yelled Neil Robson at the top of his voice and into the left ear of the kid. The boy's ears and head were covered by a mud-brown Hessian bag, not a designer item from the German state, but a rough material item purchased from the local garden centre.

"If it hadn't been for your fuckin' father I'd be living it up in the Caribbean. Aargh! I so hate that bastard and I'm going to enjoy ending his miserable fuckin' Jock life! You, you little prick may live, if I allow it but that depends on Daddy. I want my money, I want all of it and I want it now. Get phoning and get on it or you'll have a face like a crown rot pumpkin," Robson hollered, giving Cyrus a solid slap round the head.

Cyrus felt sick. He was not used to getting punched in the mouth. He could feel the blood dripping down onto his chin and his tooth and jaw hurt like hell. Every now and then he really did feel like he wanted to barf. He could not concentrate properly but he knew he had to. One minute he was walking along a Chelsea side street with Gil, the next minute, she had been clubbed to the ground and he had been tossed into the back of some old manky van by two heavies wearing balaclavas. They shoved this bag on his head. At least it didn't stink was one of the random and irrelevant thoughts that ran through his now aching head. From his dad's revelations in Scotland, Cyrus had worked out that his captor was either some comrade of the Russians they had seen off or something to do with the Neil Robson geezer. The accent of the asshole yelling at him and beating him was English, not Russian, so as a first guess it was probably the former Financial Secretary to HM Treasury.

Cyrus was scared. He did not know where he was or what was going to happen to him. He was trying his best to be brave, focusing his thoughts on his dad, Gil, Lucy and most of the time, his mum. At this juncture, at least he was better off than she was. Dad and Gil would already have started the search for him, provided Gil had not been too badly injured in the kidnap. The best thing that he could do was what his captor told him and try to figure out a way to give his dad or Gil some clues, if he could discover any.

Robson pulled the bag off Cyrus's head. The fugitive was not wearing a balaclava, nor any kind of face covering. This was bad realised Cyrus; he doesn't care if I see his face.

Robson handed Cyrus a pay-as-you-go phone. "Dial Daddy ass wipe!" he demanded.

Cyrus was seated in a basic wooden chair, one that folds. It was not comfortable. His comfort was not aided by the fact that his legs were tied by sturdy rope to those of the chair. For the moment his hands were free. He dialled.

"Hello?" said JJ.

"Dad, it's me, I've been stolen. Help me," cried Cyrus into the phone. On hearing his dad's voice, Cyrus could not keep his composure. He totally forgot what Robson told him to say. Robson was exasperated, whacked the boy on the back of the head and took the phone off him.

"Cyrus! Cyrus!" was what Robson heard as he put the phone to his ear.

"Well, well, Darke, you sound like a concerned father."

JJ immediately recognised Robson's voice.

"You fuckin' bastard, Robson. I will kill you for this. I want my son back now! If you've harmed him…" JJ ranted and bellowed down the phone.

Robson remained calm, waiting for the tirade to ease off. If there was a Guinness Book of Records entry for a single breath rant then JJ would be a contender.

"Right, jockstrap, now that you've blown off some steam, here's how this is going to play out. You listening?"

JJ had exhausted his rant of expletives and threats. His somewhat calmer and more analytical brain started to kick in. Robson had Cyrus. For JJ that meant Robson had all the cards. He was going to need to do what he was told.

"I'm listening," replied JJ.

"Good. You've caused me a lot of trouble, Darke, my career, my life, a bucket load of money. Some of that I can't get back. The money, though, I know you've got it and you're going to give it to me. I want a minimum of £100 million equivalent in cash, spread across pounds, euros and US dollars. You've got two days max to get it and deliver it. I'll be in touch on time and place. In the meantime, I'll keep your boy company. I'm sure we can find something to do."

"Robson," JJ was ready to rant, but the kidnapper had hung up.

"JJ what's going on?" asked Gil with deep anxiety. She had a lump the size of a tennis ball on the back of her head. The baseball bat whack she received fortunately hadn't broken her skull. She had been bleeding profusely and was still unconscious when the ambulance arrived to take her to Chelsea and Westminster's A&E department on the Fulham Road. The staff there were brilliant, cleaned her up, gave her some pain-killing medication and checked her thoroughly. They wanted to keep her in overnight but Gil discharged herself. The fifteen minute walk back to Markham Square seemed like fifteen hours. She was not steady on her feet and occasionally felt dizzy but she knew she had to tell JJ face to face.

"Robson's got Cyrus and wants £100 million, is what's going on Gil," replied JJ.

The Scot didn't answer in the friendly way that he would normally address Gil. In his heart and mind JJ knew that Gil would do anything for Cyrus. He knew that she cared for him deeply and that if she could have defended him better when ambushed she would have. The truth of the matter was that he was feeling guilty. Cyrus was in trouble because of him, his smart-ass Greek bond plan and his wild attempt to get out of any insider trading fallout. JJ could not handle all this guilt on his own so, subconsciously or not, he was transferring some of it to Gil.

"What are we going to do?" Gil asked.

"Well, I'm going to get the money and await instructions. I can't tell the local police. At the first sign of a copper Robson will injure Cyrus, or worse. He's an ex-MI5 black ops operative. He wouldn't think twice about killing Cyrus if he thought he had nothing left to lose."

"What can I do?" asked Gil, struggling up from her supine resting position on JJ's sofa. JJ looked at Gil, he couldn't maintain his anger with her. She had done everything for Cyrus and, indeed, she also had most skilfully eliminated a Russian thug who was seconds from killing the boy's grandmother.

"To begin with, you can rest here until your tennis ball lump becomes a ping pong ball lump. Then we'll see." JJ said it softly. Gil was so relieved.

Cyrus was glad he heard his dad's voice. The boy had regained some of his composure and his aches and pains were not intolerable. Robson had now tied both of his hands behind him with white plastic speedcuffs.

His captor appeared to be making tea or something, he could hear a kettle boil. For the first time since his kidnap Cyrus had regained some spatial awareness. The room he was in was a living room, wooden floorboards, a couple of comfortable looking large chairs that he wished he was on, a two-seater sofa and a wooden coffee table. There was a makeshift wooden desk in the corner, it kind of matched the coffee table. There was some paper on it. He could see out of the large but small-paned windows. He couldn't see that much though. He was looking over the tops of what appeared to be reasonably mature trees. This meant he was high up, maybe in a vacant loft conversion. Although he was peering with 20/20 vision Cyrus could not recognise clearly any buildings or landmarks. Wait a minute, though, those tubular shapes in the distance, that might be Battersea Power Station, he guessed. That would make some sense, Cyrus concluded. He hadn't been in the manky van for that long, certainly no more than twenty minutes. The entire journey had been in traffic he recalled and the van never really got up any speed. Robson returned to the room, carrying a steaming hot mug of builder's tea and munching on a slice of buttered toast. He looked at Cyrus.

"Thirsty?" asked Robson.

"I'm OK," replied Cyrus, trying to be neither friendly nor unfriendly.

"I'll get you a bottle of water anyway," said Robson, returning to the kitchen area and bringing back some water in a 500ml plastic bottle. "I'm going to release your hands, don't try anything stupid or I'll punch you harder than I did earlier and stick the bag back on your head." Cyrus nodded and Robson cut the speedcuffs.

The rest of the evening went without incident. Robson escorted Cyrus to the loo so that he could relieve himself before sleeping. Cyrus noted that he went down a half-flight of a spiral staircase to the bathroom. That short journey did not yield any further visual or aural information. On returning, Robson took Cyrus to a bedroom and tied his hands to one of the bedposts. He also bound the boy's legs together and covered his mouth with duct tape. Once secure Robson locked the door and went across the narrow hallway to the bedroom opposite for some shut-eye.

Before Cyrus and his kidnapper were sleeping fitfully, JJ had already asked for Toby's help in getting the cash out of some accounts they controlled and in the denominations demanded by Neil Robson. Fathead would deliver the money to JJ in the morning. JJ also contacted Ethel. She had not gone back to SCO19 yet, still recuperating and enjoying some extended down time. JJ told Ethel about Cyrus and explained why he could not risk involving the local police. Ginger understood and said she would help in any way possible.

The night passed without incident. Robson awakened Cyrus, let him go to the bathroom, gave him some toast and water, then tied him back up to the uncomfortable wooden chair.

"Can I have one hand free to do some drawing or something?" asked Cyrus. "It's kind of boring and uncomfortable here, please?"

"This isn't a holiday camp kid. You're fed and watered. That's enough. Anyway I don't have drawing materials so just close your eyes and contemplate the fuckin' universe," replied Robson.

"There's some paper on that desk over there," said Cyrus, head turning to the small wooden table in the corner near the windows. "Maybe there's a pen or pencil there too."

"OK, OK, I'll take a look if it'll shut you up," said Robson as he meandered over to the desk. There was indeed a half-opened packet of A4 paper on the desk and two pencils in one of the desk's drawers. Whoever owned this short-let didn't seem to have heard of computers, thought Robson, regarding pencil and paper as a bit Neanderthal.

"Here," said Robson, putting a few sheets of paper on Cyrus's lap and giving him one of the pencils which he took in his now free right hand. "What are you going to draw?" Robson asked. He didn't really have any interest in the kid's answer. As he was whiling away the time getting ready to phone JJ Darke, though, he did want to ensure the boy wasn't going to sketch him in his now hirsute guise.

"Don't know yet, maybe draw those trees out there, or do some magic squares. I like those in maths," replied Cyrus.

"Whatever," said Robson. "Just don't make any noise and I'll be checking anything you do. Got it?" Cyrus nodded.

An hour or so passed. Neil Robson could not contain himself any longer. He rang the boy's father.

"You got my money yet asshole?"

"I've got it. Now let me see Cyrus. Then I'll take your delivery instructions," replied JJ.

"You're forever issuing demands Darke, and ones you're not in a position to be issuing. I'll ring you back in ten minutes. Be ready."

Robson hung up and checked that his smartphone was on its video setting. He then re-tied Cyrus's right hand to the wooden chair, taking his pencil from him. He left the boy's drawing on his lap. Robson got a wet cloth from the kitchen and wiped Cyrus's face, cleaning up any remaining dried blood. "Don't want your daddy to get all emotional, do I?" said Robson as he was washing Cyrus's face roughly. Once done, he then put duct tape over the boy's mouth.

Robson rang JJ. "Here he is," said Robson taking a clear picture of Cyrus and ensuring that he kept his video shot looking straight at the boy. No exterior footage to give the Scot any hints thought the fugitive. JJ's phone received the video and he could see that Cyrus had some facial bruises and his eyes looked sad. JJ was both angry and wanted to cry. The only desire in his heart and mind was to get his boy back alive. JJ's brain was working overtime. The longer that Robson could be delayed the better chance of finding him but also the worse for Cyrus. Once again, JJ would need to do as Robson demanded.

"OK, that's enough. He's alright, for now," said Robson shutting down the video. The kidnapper then outlined the time and place for delivery of the £100 million. "Is that clear Darke?"

"Yes," replied JJ.

"Good. If you're late or the money's not as it should be, or if I even smell a copper or one of your MI5 cronies then your boy is fuckin' toast. Got it?" spat Robson, building up a head of vitriol again.

"Got it," replied JJ.

Robson hung up. He went over to Cyrus, whacked him on the head and roughly pulled off the duct tape over the kid's mouth.

"What was that for?" moaned Cyrus. Robson returned and grabbed Cyrus by the throat.

"That was just because you're the spawn of that Scottish bastard. So shut the fuck up and don't give me any excuse to beat the livin' shit out of you," snarled Robson, highly aggravated but finally letting go of the boy's throat. Cyrus coughed and spluttered a bit but he was okay. Robson took away Cyrus's drawings and pencil. He looked at the page on top and it was an incomplete magic square.

"Thought you were supposed to be a smart kid," sneered Robson. "This square's never going to add up. All those fat fees your dad paid to your posh Chelsea school. Clearly they weren't worth a toss," he added, chucking the boy's papers on the floor.

Let's hope my dad's smarter than you, eejit, thought Cyrus, sensibly keeping that thought to himself.

JJ and Gil viewed the video of Cyrus again and again. JJ had calmed down enough to study the video for clues not just shake with emotion at seeing his son captive and at the mercy of a wanted murderer. Robson had been smart. The video showed Cyrus's face, his lower body, his legs and the fact that he was bound and silenced. There was no hint, however, of where he was, no newspapers lying around, no window views, no external sounds, nothing.

"Gil," said JJ, "play it back in slo-mo, just to check."

"Sure," replied Gil. They both studied the video again in slow motion. Still nothing.

"JJ," said Gil after a few moments, "did you notice that Cyrus seemed to be blinking a lot, not even blinking, his eyelids are going up and down and his head is nodding in time."

JJ had not noticed but was ready for another look. Gil was right. Cyrus was lowering his head slightly every few seconds. He wasn't really blinking, it was more a systematic eyelid movement. Cyrus was trying to point at the paper on his lap. He could not do it with his hands as they were tied behind his back and he sure couldn't do it with his tongue, to speak or point, as that was inside his taped mouth.

"Can you see what's on the paper?" asked JJ.

Gil froze the best shot of the paper on Cyrus's lap.

"I can't make it out clearly, JJ. It looks like numbers, upside down maybe," Gil ventured.

JJ had a look then another one. Gil could be right again.

"Let's rotate it," said JJ.

JJ was up on technology to a degree, but the easy manipulation of these fancy smartphone's camera and video apps was not high on his list of capabilities, so he left Gil in control of the phone.

"OK. I've rotated it, changed the angle of the shot and zoomed in. Take a look."

JJ took his phone. The picture he was looking at was not the drawing of a tree. It was an incomplete magic square.

```
21  20  20
1        5
5   19  18
```

Gil and JJ looked at each other quizically. Gil was a maths genius and JJ was no slouch with numbers. It didn't mean anything to them.

"I don't get it Gil," said JJ bamboozled. "Cyrus would not get stuck on a magic square. He could do those in his sleep when he was ten. I mean, there's no chance that this square is right. No matter what number you put in the middle, the rows, columns and diagonals are not summing to the same number. Cyrus would know that. If it's a message it's in code, disguised so that Robson wouldn't click. We need to solve this but I'm not having a light bulb moment."

"Me neither," said Gil, thoroughly annoyed that she hadn't solved it straight away. JJ left Gil studying the square and went to the landline phone in his living room.

"Hi Ethel," began JJ.

"JJ, how's Cyrus? Any news?" asked Ethel very concerned about Cyrus's welfare.

"I've seen a video of him. He's alive. A little worse for wear as far as I can tell. His brain's still ticking though. He might have been trying to indicate where he is being held. It's some kind of code in a square. Gil and I can't figure it out yet."

"Victor!" exclaimed Ethel.

"Yes, please," said JJ. "Could you track him down and ask him to rush over here?"

"Sure thing. I'm on it. I may come too, if that's OK?" asked Ethel.

"Of course it is."

★ ★ ★

Within an hour, Ethel Rogers and Victor Pagari were knocking on JJ's Chelsea blue door. Greetings were kept to a minimum as there was an urgent task waiting. Victor looked at the video. He repeated Gil's rotation and zooming. He confirmed the numbers in the square and the fact that it sure wasn't magic.

"What do you think Victor?" asked JJ, understandably impatient.

"What age is Cyrus?" asked Victor.

"Fourteen," said JJ.

Victor nodded his head and tapped a few instructions into his laptop.

"Is he smart… no offence?" asked Victor.

"Yes Victor, he's smart, but he's no bleedin' Einstein! He's not the mathematician Gil is, he doesn't know anything about economics or finance and while he's a wizard on a computer, he's not a high-wizard like you. He can't outsmart all of us, for god's sake," said JJ, hoping, praying that his conclusion was correct.

"No, he can't," said Victor, smiling to himself, partly as a nod of recognition to Cyrus's efforts and partly to the safe cracker's own ability to dial back to being a fourteen year old. "He's fourteen, he's smart but he's under duress. He needed a code, quickly thought up, no access to a computer or fancy algorithms. It needed to be simple but not obvious. He did what he could and he did good," announced Victor, swivelling his laptop so that the screen could be seen by all.

"Battersea!" they yelled.

As Ethel, Victor and Gil discussed their next move and debated how Cyrus could possibly know where he was, JJ's mobile rang, it was Sandra Hillington.

"Hi Sandra," said JJ trying to sound normal.

"Hi JJ. First, thanks for all the money. We've got it in a special MI5 escrow account and it will be distributed to the approved government departments in the next few days. The Home Secretary is overseeing the transfers. She's very grateful, JJ, and wants to meet you soon to say so in person. Guess you saved the country, Batman!"

"Fine, we'll do that, Sandra," was all JJ said. He had already made the judgement call not to inform Sandra or anyone in MI5 about Cyrus's kidnap. They hadn't been able to arrest Robson at his office when he was a sitting duck. Due to bureaucracy Sandra had said. If they dallied again or sent a swarm of officers in search of Cyrus, Robson probably had the smarts to dodge them again. This time, though, he may damage Cyrus in the process.

"The bottom line, JJ, is that we owe you one," said the DG.

"That's good. I'd like to have my one now please. I've got a friend in hospital and he'd like to be discharged before he disappears."

"Does it involve travel?" asked Sandra, intrigued by the speed of JJ's debt-collecting request.

"Yes, it's probably Section Six's territory but given the circumstances and all that."

"Where's the hospital JJ?" asked Sandra.

"North Korea." There was a long pause at the other end of the telephone. JJ could not hear any brain whirring but he was sure it was going on. "You'll be able to count on the local CIA office," he added.

Still no reply.

Finally, "OK. That's a big one but you did save the country. You're on. I'll be in touch later tonight. Send me details ASAP," said the DG.

"Thanks Sandra," said JJ and hung up. He glanced at his watch. It would be early in Seoul but what the heck, he had other things on his mind, he was going to ring his old mucker from Arizona right now.

"Bradbury," said the voice.

"Hi Jim, it's JJ, you alright?" asked the Scot.

"Hi JJ. I'm fine, not happy but fine. What can I do for you at this time?"

"Is Kwon still in the hospital under guard?" asked JJ.

"Yes, and that's what I'm not happy about. Of course it's better than being in the fuckin' penal colony, but the information we have is that he's scheduled to be taken from hospital in three days' time. Langley are dragging their feet. They don't have an ex-fill specialist we can use and they're not sending reinforcements. I got a new asshole handed to me because they chewed me out about helping you, albeit in a good cause and all that. Me, Lily and the Iceman are prepared to try to spring Kwon but it could be a suicide mission. We don't know what to do."

"Look Jim, I've got some big problems here, otherwise I'd help directly."

"It's OK, JJ, we know you're up to your eyeballs with your government going bust."

"No, it's not that Jim. I can't give you details right now. I'll fill you in later but listen. MI5 owe me big time. I've called in the favour. They're prepared to send a specialist ex-fill team to help you out. Send me as much detail as you have on Kwon, exactly where he is, any routines, the precise time he's scheduled to be transferred. Anything relevant. The unit can probably be with you in two days. You're in charge."

"Jeesuz! That's fuckin' A1. You're a star!" exclaimed Jim Bradbury.

"I don't know about that my friend. MI5 wouldn't owe me big if you and your team had not helped me. Deep cover was an integral part of that. I owe Kwon and this is my attempt to repay him. I'd better go now. Keep me in touch. I'll brief the MI5 team on what I know before they get there. Then it's up to you old buddy."

"Thanks JJ. I will. Hope your stuff works out."

"Me too, Jim, me too," said JJ and then he hung up.

JJ returned to the group scouring a map of Battersea. It was a big place. A population of over 75,000 within its triangular shaped perimeter. It is bounded by the River Thames on the north, and Camberwell, Streatham and Clapham to the south.

"How would Cyrus know where he was?" asked Ethel. "That plank Robson is an ex-spook. He'd leave no clues lying around."

"Does it matter?" asked Gil. "The boy's smart, he must have spotted something."

"Let's look at the video again," suggested JJ.

The four of them searched the video one more time for clues. There was absolutely nothing lying around on the floor, or anywhere on the very narrow vista that Robson had allowed them to see.

"Look there," said Victor, pointing to the screen on JJ's phone. "Go back a little and freeze it. Do you guys see it?"

"I see a kid looking miserable, Victor. That's it. Spill," said Ethel. Neither Gil nor JJ could see anything useful either.

"It's the light and the shadow," said Victor. "The left hand side of Cyrus's face looks a little lighter than the right. It's probably a shaft of sunlight coming through the window."

"If it was 'I-spy' Victor, you'd be on a winner," said Gil. "But so what?"

563

"The so what is that if it's a shaft of light then there's a window to Cyrus's left. And if there's a window there then he can see out of it. He's not blindfolded and there can't be any curtains or shades on the window, otherwise there'd be no light beam. Maybe he recognised something from the window that he knew to be in Battersea."

"Cyrus doesn't hang around Battersea. He doesn't know anywhere there," said Gil, "and Robson's not stupid enough to have him on the ground floor in case of any snooping passers-by."

JJ said nothing and pondered what Victor had said.

"What are you thinking JJ, I recognise that look?" asked Ethel.

"I'm thinking that you don't need to hang about the bars and clubs of lower Manhattan to recognise the Statue of Liberty."

"Battersea Power Station," deduced Victor.

"Maybe, Victor, maybe. Cyrus wouldn't recognise hardly anywhere in Battersea, Gil's right. Apart from the odd foray into the park, for school sports day, or tennis, or fireworks night, he didn't go there. He would, however, recognise Battersea Power Station, almost everyone who has ever lived in London would. Maybe he could see the station's chimneys from where he is. That could narrow our search a bit. Let's get on it."

JJ proceeded to delegate responsibilities. Victor was to use his technical skills to scan the area of Battersea that the decommissioned power station could be visible from. Gil was to check for recent rentals in the area in high-rise apartments, lofts or houses tall enough that the station might be seen. JJ judged that Robson would not have been able to buy a property, lack of access to sufficient funds, too much bureaucratic paperwork, money-laundering questionnaires etc. A short let with a tasty cash deal direct to an unscrupulous landlord was the most likely option.

Ethel and JJ were in discussion as to how to best ensnare Robson if and when they found out where he was. Cyrus's safety was paramount so an all out assault leading to a firefight was not likely to be the best way forward. As the four friends and colleagues went about their business the doorbell rang. JJ answered. It was Becky.

"Hi Becky, come in. How's your mum?"

"Fine, thanks, JJ. It's OK that I'm here, right?" she asked.

In all of the anxiety surrounding Cyrus's kidnap, JJ had temporarily forgotten that he had invited Becky to stay with him, Cyrus and Gil until the fugitive Robson was captured. Clearly she was happy with that invite.

"Of course, Becky. I'll ask Gil to take you upstairs and show you your room. Settle in, then come down. We're all in the living room," said JJ.

"All?" enquired Becky.

"Gil and I plus two friends you haven't met yet. You may as well know straight up. Neil Robson has kidnapped Cyrus and we're trying to figure out how to get him back."

Becky was horrified. She didn't really know what to say. In most circumstances she would have made her excuses and left. She was scared, though, and really did not want to be on her own.

"If I can be of use just ask," she said eventually. "I'll do anything to help. He is such a sweet boy."

"Thanks Becky."

★ ★ ★

Neil Robson was also making plans. Considering that he was a wanted man, wanted indeed by the British police, Interpol and MI5, he had done remarkably well at avoiding their radar. His disguise was convincing. Beard, glasses and longer, unkempt hair helped. Only his closest acquaintances would recognise him. Also gone were the suits, shirt, tie and the polished leather shoes.

These were replaced by jeans, a hoodie, trainers and an olive green parka. It was *The Big Issue* look and it made him more or less anonymous in this and most other areas of London.

On returning to London via Rotterdam, Hull and St. George's Hill he found a few freelance, ex-military mercenaries in need of work. It wasn't that difficult to find this genre in London especially if you had kept a file of all your old MI5 contacts, which Neil Robson had. Two of them had grabbed the Darke kid. Their job was done. Now he needed another two, this time with a slightly higher IQ to help carry out the final stages of his escape. Neil Robson had also been informed of the fate of Vladimir Babikov and his thugs. He couldn't help but smile. The mutilating murderer was locked up in a top security British gaol, had no money, no employees and most relevant to Robson, no ability to call in debts, basic or enhanced.

How ironic, he thought, that plonker Darke had got Babikov off of his back and now he was going to hand him £100 million to lubricate the lifestyle of a serious multi-millionaire. Every cloud has a silver lining. The Darke kid was a problem. If he let him go then the boy could give details as to his new appearance. If he killed him then the kid's father would hunt him down to the ends of the earth. Robson wasn't scared of JJ. He always thought the Scot was an analytical pussy. However, he did get all that gold out of North Korea and, somehow, he saw off Babikov and his ex-FSB thugs. It may be better to leave the kid alive but Robson decided that he would not make that call until £100 million was safely in his hands.

"Archie is that you? It's Neil," said Robson, dialling his contact on his pay-as-you-go phone.

"Yes Neil, it's me," replied Archie Newman, small time crook who made his living putting the right people in touch with each other.

"What have you got for me?" asked Robson.

"The best I could do on such short notice is Tim Hayworth and Jason Long. Tim is ex-SAS. Done a few security jobs. Decent bloke but finds it hard to settle into anything that seems like nine to five. He's solid, doesn't drink or do drugs. Quite smart but no genius."

"OK, and the other guy?" asked Robson.

"Jason is an ex-paratrooper. Saw action in the Gulf. Recovered from PTSD and needs cash. He's smart. Doesn't want to kill anybody but is happy to be a delivery boy," replied Newman.

"Do they know who I am?" asked Robson.

"No. I told them you needed to collect some items and that they would be required to drive a van. Told them you were known simply as Robbo and that you were reliable as far as payment went."

"Good job, Archie. I'll leave your fee in the usual spot. Text me their numbers and tell them I'll be in touch no later than tomorrow."

Neil Robson had come across Archie Newman many years earlier. Essentially he was an MI5 snitch. The secret service did not have much interest in most of Archie's shenanigans but, occasionally, some wannabe terrorist lone wolf would ask to be put in touch with some other low-life, bomb-maker, lawless cleric, the usual suspects. Neil Robson was Archie's handler. In return for information on the low life terrorists, Robson turned a blind eye to Archie's other activities. He also paid Archie for good information. Their relationship was casual but it worked.

Satisfied with the cohorts Archie had supplied, Robson checked in on Cyrus, apparently sleeping, still tied to the bed. He returned to the living room and switched on his laptop, not *The Sound of Music* one, but the knock-off he had picked up in a local pub. However you sliced it, £100 million weighed a lot. Robson knew that Archie could easily supply a Ford transit van with an appropriate payload capacity. Robson emailed Newman as to his new requirements. The van needed one of those rushed overnight paint jobs and a couple of enhancements. Newman was on it. Hayworth and Long would supervise it. It would be done by breakfast the next day.

Neil Robson was mulling over his plan. The problem with most drop offs is that the location needed to be known by the dropper and the collector. This gives the dropper plenty of time to stakeout the location and catch red-handed the collector. If a transfer, let's say kid for money, is involved then once the kid is safe the collector will likely be followed by well-placed lookouts or these days, follow some GPS tracker attached to or hidden in the money or its transporter. Robson knew these traps needed to be avoided.

"Hello?" said JJ, answering his smartphone.

"It's me," said Robson. "Have you got the money?"

"Yes. How's Cyrus?"

"Your kid's fine, now shut up and listen. Given the amount, I assume you've got it in a van. You can speak."

"Yes," said JJ.

"OK. First, I want you to package the notes in forty-eight to fifty separate parcels so that they are not visible to any snoops. Separate the packages by currency. Circle for pound, square for euros, star for dollars on the top. Thick brown paper will do or something like that. Secondly, I want you to drive the van yourself, no accomplices, to 353 Regis Road in Camden. You need to arrive by 9am. If you're late the deal's off and it's bye-bye boy. Park the van, get out and walk away. I'll be able to see you so no stupidity on your part. Once I've checked the cash I'll give you your son's location. If I detect anything then it's… you know the score jockstrap."

JJ immediately hated this plan. If Cyrus was being held in Battersea then at 9am or later in the morning it would take at least thirty minutes to get there from Camden. Robson had proved skilful at avoiding detection and capture so far. There was no reason to expect that he'd suddenly become easy to spot. Robson would have the money and JJ would not have Cyrus contemporaneously, or at all.

"I want Cyrus to be dropped off once I've left the van, so that I know he's OK," insisted JJ.

"I want to be in the Caribbean fuckwit! We don't always get what we want. This is a one track plan, asshole, no options, no deviations, no augmentations or deletions. My way or the bye-way for your kid. Got it?"

"I've got it Robson, don't hurt him please," pleaded JJ.

"I quite like you begging Darke, can't really remember you doing it before. Do as you're told and you'll see your kid," said Robson and then he hung up.

JJ half slumped onto his chair in the living room. He felt sick. 'You'll see your kid' did not necessarily mean that he would be alive when seen. Robson was a slimy, untrustworthy toad who wanted revenge. Gil spotted JJ slumped with head in his hands. She appeared bearing a double Macallans with some Canada Dry.

"Robson?" she asked. JJ looked up, saw his friend's face and a welcome drink in her hand.

"Yes," he replied, downing some of the whisky. "He's got it all worked out Gil. We're to drop the money off in Camden and once he's got it he'll let us know Cyrus's whereabouts. Robson's bound to be alert to any tracker we could put on the delivery. Other than completely going along with it. I haven't a clue what to do."

"Something brilliant will enter that head of yours JJ, it usually does," said Gil. "I was once told to get my, and I quote, 'big brain into gear'. It didn't do me much good. I got a gammy leg out of it, but it's the thought that counts!"

JJ made a decent effort at a small chuckle. He knew Gil was right. If he was indeed smarter than Neil Robson this sure was the time to prove it. The stakes could not be higher. Time to engage thought JJ, recovering some mental composure and physical strength. He got up off his chair and walked over to Ethel and Victor.

"Any luck guys?" asked JJ, not expecting a particularly positive answer.

"Some," said Ethel. "Victor's done some fancy computer graphics. On the screen here we can see a kite shaped vista which encompasses the most likely spots in Battersea from which you could spot the power station's chimneys. It is anchored on Ascalon Street. Victor reckons that Cyrus's location has an 87% probability of being within the kite. Gil and I have been trawling Zoopla, Rightmove and all the main letting websites for top floor apartments or lofts that have recently been on the market or let for short periods. There's barely a handful and only three within Victor's kite perimeter. That's kind of the good news. The bad news is that we can't quiz the three letting agents until tomorrow morning at 9 or 10 when they open up."

"I need to be in Camden by 9am tomorrow," revealed JJ. "With a bag full of money, suitably packaged. We might all need to get in on that act within a couple of hours. Victor, is 353 Regis Road anywhere interesting?"

The young safe cracker and now code breaker did his usual digit flash dance across the laptop's keyboard. "Depends what you deem to be interesting, JJ. It's a UPS deposit and distribution terminal."

★ ★ ★

The three men sitting away from the main window of Café 43 in Pratt Street did not appear anything special nor did they know each other well. Archie Newman, a grey-haired sixty-four year old, sat with his back to the door. The other two, younger men, probably in their thirties, would never do that. They were trained to protect their six and the main door of the café was the only visible point of entry and exit. Tim Hayworth, about 5ft 9in, stocky with short brown hair and blue eyes, spoke first.

"Archie, are you sure this Robbo guy is good for it? I mean £10k each to do a bit of unloading and loading then drive a van seems well generous."

"He's good for it Tim. I've known him for twenty years or thereabouts. Never reneged on a deal yet."

Jason Long hadn't said much up to this point. He was about the same height as Hayworth but looked a little taller with his longer gelled-up hair. He was slim but well-defined. "Do we need to be carrying Archie? I don't want to be in a firefight at all but if we are I'd rather know in advance?"

"Robbo says no guns required. If you feel better packing then take something but the expectation is that you won't need it," replied Archie. "Look guys, you've got work to do. The transit van has been delivered to Bert's Garage, just down the road from here. They've got the paint and equipment and a couple of guys to help you with the spraying. I've given them a wedge and they're happy. Don't talk about the job, they know nothing and it's better kept that way. Archie continued, pointing to a suit-bag. "In here are the decals you need and a diagram as to where to position them on the van. I advise you two to put these on yourselves, let the Bert's Garage guys go before you start. The less they can guess the better."

"Fine," said Jason Long. Tim Hayworth nodded his agreement.

Archie acknowledged their understanding and said, "Robbo's also enclosed in this envelope, precise instructions as to what to do and where to go once your van is loaded. Follow them to the letter. If any deviation leads to the plan going tits up he'll come after you. You guys may not think that's much to worry about with all your military nounce and whatever, but let me assure you that you do not want to cross this guy. Don't mistake his generosity for softness. He's a hard-assed killer and you would not see him coming."

Long and Hayworth looked at each other and just shrugged. They did not have sufficient knowledge about Robbo to know whether or not they should care that he was a hard-assed killer as described by Archie. They had been trained killers too. Still, why risk the hassle. They were being well paid for a driver's job and one during which guns were not expected to be in play.

The three men left Café 43 and went about their business.

★ ★ ★

At the same time, JJ, Becky and Gil were in JJ's lock-up in Elystan Street. After obtaining suitable wrapping paper, string and Sellotape the three of them were in the back of the Mercedes Sprinter van, wrapping and taping the money. Ethel and Victor had remained in JJ's house, trying to narrow down even further possible locations for Cyrus. It was going to prove to be a forlorn task, they would need to await the opening of the target estate agents the following morning. By midnight the van was packed and ready. Nearly fifty parcels of equal amounts totalling £100 million equivalent in pounds, euros and US dollars.

"OK guys," said JJ. "We're done. Thank you. Let's go back and try to get some sleep. Tomorrow is a big day and we all need to be alert."

JJ knew that he would hardly sleep a wink. He had Cyrus on his mind. All the good times they had together. The games, the banter, the joy of seeing him become a decent young man. The agonising pain when he had to tell him that Mum had died. Cyrus had been fantastic in Scotland. Brave, alert, unfazed. He was the best boy in the world and his father sorely needed him back alive.

★ ★ ★

The UPS facility in Kentish Town, Camden was a massive glass structure. There were the obligatory trees dotted around the place to make it look a lot less industrial, but industrial it was. There was a customer car park, already filling up at 8am on this wet Monday morning. Opening hours were 8 till 8 and Monday was the busiest day for the delivery vans, all those folk with nothing better to do at the weekend but order stuff on Amazon or arrange unwanted items to be shipped back. Neil Robson knew all of this. He was already in situ, across the street and hunkered down in a black Fiat 500 that he had rented at the weekend.

When Robson left Battersea young Cyrus Darke was still alive. He was tired, drained, bruised and no doubt hungry and thirsty, but he was alive. He was tied up and taped up and if he needed the loo, then tough shit, literally and metaphorically. Whether or not he stayed alive was now down to his father, the delivery man. No money, no boy would seem to be the order of things. The fugitive was parked up in a line of cars in the narrow street opposite the main UPS building. He could see clearly the entry and exit of the UPS vans. There was nothing about his little car or him that would attract any attention.

It was 8.58am, and there they were like a convoy though they didn't know it. Long and Hayworth, in their stolen UPS delivery uniforms were driving the fake UPS van, properly painted and nicely decaled. JJ Darke was a mere thirty seconds or so behind, in a blue Mercedes Sprinter van. The imposter UPS pair drove straight into the depot. Robson could see that from his vantage point. He could not see exactly where they parked but he assumed it would be as per his prior written instructions.

Darke parked his van just outside the main depot and walked away, as per his instructions. So far so good thought Robson. Hayworth and Long emerged from the depot, pushing two motorised metal pallets with wooden trays. They hopped into the back of the Sprinter van and stayed there for a few minutes. Then they came out and started loading the pallets. Each parcel weighed 20kg. These two were young and strong so it took them less than five minutes to load. They then went back into the depot.

Robson could not see any sign of JJ, perhaps he'd wandered off to get a bus. Several UPS vans were now leaving the depot, all loaded up and heading for all parts of London and surrounding districts. There were big vans, small vans, huge vans. All shapes and sizes but all brown and gold with the distinctive UPS badge. Eyeballing them would not tell Neil Robson which of these vans was 'his' UPS van. Before the transit had gone to Bert's Garage for its UPS makeover, however, Archie Newman had installed a GPS device so that Neil Robson could track it. Long and Hayworth had electronically swept the Sprinter van and the packages therein before loading them onto the pallets. They were clean. Darke had stuck to that part of the deal at least.

It was now 9.05am and more and more UPS delivery trucks had come pouring out of the depot. Bleep. Robson activated his tracker. Four UPS vehicles all left the depot in convoy. Robson knew that it was the second one in line that he was interested in as it was the only Ford Transit of the four. His tracking device confirmed this and was now bleeping away merrily. Robson would stay in situ for a few minutes. He did not want to look as if he was tailing his van, just in case JJ Darke was in the vicinity and up to no good. Robson's mobile rang.

"Robson. It's me. I've done as you bid. Now where's Cyrus?" asked JJ, calm but having difficulty keeping it so.

"Fuck off cunt," replied Robson. "I left the little prick alive but who knows how long that will last. Find him yourself smart arse." Neil Robson hung up.

JJ started bashing his phone on his Porsche's dashboard. Gil was driving though at this particular moment they were parked close to Camden Town. The air inside the Porsche was blue and JJ was in the early stages of meltdown.

Gil's phone rang.

"Gil, it's Ethel." Gil motioned to JJ to shut up and calm down. "We think we know where Cyrus is. One of the letting agents admitted they had been paid cash for a short-let. The other two possibilities seemed legit. The description of the guy didn't fit Robson but he could have been well disguised. The agent said it's a recent loft conversion and that you could probably see the chimney tops of Battersea Power Station from the top floor. It's on Savona Street. Victor and I are headed there now. I'll text you details and meet you there."

"Great Ethel. I'll tell JJ. We're on our way," Gil put the Porsche tiptronic in drive and took off.

JJ was in no fit state to drive. He was pouring with sweat, had a splitting headache and barely took in Gil's news. It was a fairly straight route, north to south, but would take thirty to forty minutes in early Monday traffic. Ethel and Victor would be there first but they would probably await JJ and Gil. Ethel had her Glock and taser with her but Victor had nothing but his laptop. JJ had his Glock and Gil her SIG Sauer. Hopefully, guns would not be needed. As JJ was returning to normal and thinking ahead, he recalled that in the midst of Robson's vitriol he mentioned that he had 'left Cyrus alive'. Though not certain, that could imply that Robson was no longer there. It didn't mean that Cyrus was alone nor did it mean that there were no booby traps in place. They needed to be prepared.

Gil and JJ arrived in Savona Street thirty-two minutes after leaving Camden. That was fast and JJ was grateful for it. JJ spotted Ethel's silver hatchback. Gil parked up and JJ got out to speak to Ethel.

"It's there across the street," said Ethel. "I've not spotted any movement inside since getting here."

OK," said JJ. "Gil and I will go in through the front door. Ethel you cover the back. I take it you're packing?" Ethel nodded. "Victor, you stay here. If we're not out in ten minutes call the local police." Victor nodded, content to avoid any fireworks. It may have been wiser to try to pick the front door's lock and scan for wires attached to explosives but JJ needed to know. Followed by Gil, he ran across the street and shoulder-charged the front door into oblivion. He tumbled down but was up quickly, gun pointed in a two-handed grip.

"Cyrus, Cyrus are you here?" he yelled.

Gil called out too. There was no immediate discernable sound in reply. JJ climbed the first set of stairs, leading the way, gun shifting from left to right then straight ahead. Gil was directly behind, going up backwards, to cover JJ's six and her twelve.

"Cyrus!" hollered JJ. "It's Dad and Gil!" There was no human reply but the sound of wood on wood was clearly audible. JJ dashed up the second flight of stairs throwing caution aside and dived straight into the room where the sound seemed to be from. Cyrus was there bound and taped but alive and making a racket as he bounced the wooden chair about. There were no obvious booby traps. JJ un-taped Cyrus's mouth and hugged him strongly before even attempting to untie him.

"Oh Cyrus, I love you, I'm so sorry for all this," cried JJ unashamedly.

"I love you too, Dad," said Cyrus, very calm considering, "but you're going to need to let me go right now. I need a pee so bad and a poo may be brewing as well. I've got to go now!" exclaimed the boy. JJ laughed and cried at the same time. He untied Cyrus's legs while Gil cut through the speedcuffs restraining Cyrus's hands.

"Hi Gil, thanks," he said en passant as he bolted for the loo.

Waste disposal and ablutions completed, Cyrus emerged from the bathroom. JJ hugged him again and Cyrus hugged him back. Gil looked on and smiled. She had let Victor and Ethel know that Cyrus was safe. They both came into the house to join in the happy scene. JJ was a wreck, a most happy wreck but in no condition to be thinking about Neil Robson, his money or either's whereabouts.

"Let's go home and get you fixed up," said Gil, giving Cyrus a squashing hug.

"OK," said the boy. "I'm starvin'. Can we get a pizza takeaway, maybe two for me? Have we got curlies and biscuits at home?" Gil looked at JJ, he was shaking his head, not to indicate no, just in joyous disbelief.

"Yes, of course. You can have whatever you want Cyrus. Anything," said JJ.

The five that were all alive left the building. Everybody was headed for Markham Square, Victor and Ethel in the hatchback, Gil, Cyrus and JJ in the Porsche. Cyrus was curled up in the rear bucket seats. He felt safe in there. He also knew that Gil was the one who was going to pop in to Pizza Express on the King's Road to collect the order she had phoned through. A few minutes later

Gil did just that and JJ drove his car and his son into Markham Square. Cyrus was very pleased to see his Chelsea blue front door. He was dealing with recent events as best he could but it was a lot and he was totally exhausted. Dodgy Russians shooting at him in Scotland, discovering he had a big sister, then being kidnapped by some maniac who beat him and starved him.

"Dad, the guy who kidnapped me," said Cyrus softly, before he and JJ got out of the car.

"Yes, Cyrus?"

"Promise me you'll make him pay."

"I promise Cyrus, on your mother's love, I promise."

★ ★ ★

A few minutes later everyone was enjoying their pizzas. Cyrus, especially, and he was on to his second one before anyone else had finished their first. His mouth hurt a lot, so every now and then he was reminded of his ordeal. Becky was very pleased to see Cyrus and the boy got a crushing hug from the attractive young woman. He liked that and had a huge smile on his face, seen by all, and generating admiring laughs from Gil and his dad.

JJ looked intently and lovingly at his son. He had grown up a lot in the past few weeks. The circumstances occasioning said growth would not really have been JJ's first choice but sometimes you need to play the hand you've been dealt, good or bad. Cyrus did not seem to be psychologically harmed by his exposure to guns, bullets and capture but you never know, thought JJ. In those quieter moments when you're on your own preparing to sleep, in the dark or in a strange environment that's when the mind goes to dark places and plays tricks. Fortunately, Cyrus had quality back-up right now. Both Gil and Becky were staying in the house. He had also made new friends in Ethel and Victor so his protective ring was larger and stronger. Victor couldn't do much protecting right enough but he and Cyrus could babble in the alien language known as technogeek, and they could share experiences to a degree. Both had been in a firefight that they would never have anticipated only a few weeks ago. Satisfied that Cyrus was in a good safe place, JJ's thoughts turned to Neil Robson.

"Victor," said JJ.

Victor had just finished congratulating Cyrus on the simple ingenuity of his code square. Cyrus was all pleased with himself and rightly so.

"We need to find Robson and the money, with the emphasis on Robson," said JJ.

"Sure," replied Victor, "but do we have any idea where he is?"

"No we don't, but we're going to need to get into gear sharpish. Here's what we know. Somehow Robson's plan was to use UPS to transport the money. As I was walking away from our Sprinter van, two UPS uniformed guys went into the back of the van. I ducked behind some bushes for a few minutes to take a look. I was hoping that they would take the van because I had installed a tracker, deep inside the petrol tank, but they didn't. After five minutes or so these two guys came out of the van, loaded the money on two motorised pallets and returned to the UPS depot. They must have been working for Robson. Vans and trucks were leaving the terminal every few minutes. My guess is that the money was in one of those trucks and driven by the two guys I saw. After that, I've no idea, we went for Cyrus."

"Does UPS Lojack their vehicles?" asked Victor.

"I don't know, Victor," replied JJ. "If they did and the van's transceiver's signal went straight to the police indicating it had been stolen then maybe Ethel could find that out. I'll ask. I suspect though that Robson's a bit too cunning to go that route.

It's more likely that he had a phoney UPS van already in the depot or driven there earlier by his two goons. Legitimate UPS personnel at the depot would be more likely to spot that they were one van or truck short than they would one too many."

"Maybe Ethel could ask her police colleagues if any apparent UPS vans had been reported abandoned or set alight, that kind of thing," suggested Victor. "They'd need to do something with the van."

"That's a good idea, Victor, at least it would give us a starting point," replied JJ. They both went for a chat with Ethel. She was on the case straight away.

JJ was right about one thing, Neil Robson was indeed cunning. The instructions to Tim Hayworth and Jason Long were twofold. First, they were to drive the UPS van and its contents back to Bert's Garage. Robson had told Archie Newman to ensure that the regular employees of the garage had a well-paid day off. Once there, Long and Hayworth were to strip the transit van of its UPS decals and respray the van white. They were to change the number plates, supplied by Newman. When finished they were to leave the van locked with all its contents intact and give the keys to Newman.

The second instruction was of the fail-safe variety. Robson could not be certain that his plan for the van would work as perfectly as it had. He instructed Long and Hayworth to load the UPS van with four parcels less than the fifty they had removed from the Sprinter. The two goons were then to attach counterfeit UPS labels supplied by Archie Newman in the suit bag which contained the UPS decals. Three of the parcels were to be delivered, by legitimate UPS carriers, to Post Office addresses in England, two in London and one in Hull. The fourth one was destined for foreign parts. In total, the parcels contained the equivalent of £8 million. If all else went pear-shaped thought

Robson a piggybank of £8 million would be sufficient to get by on.

Archie Newman had supplied Robson with some fake ID, a driving license, a utility bill and a council tax reminder. He was working on a passport which he would deliver to Robson today. One of the four parcels could easily fit into a large kit bag, so Robson was about to be mobile and cashed up.

"Archie, it's me. Are we done?" asked Neil Robson from his mobile phone.

"Nearly. The lads are repainting the van now. They've got industrial dryers on it so it'll be ready this evening. I'll have your papers ready then too. Let's meet at Bert's say 8pm, and settle up."

"Fine, see you there," replied Robson.

★ ★ ★

Time dragged for Neil Robson that day. He couldn't risk going back to the Battersea loft. Either Darke would have discovered his son or the boy would be in a right mess or possibly dead. In either event the local police would be all over the place, maybe even the secret service too. *Movement is freedom* he thought, so he whiled away the hours in and out of busy London cafés and shops. His plan was almost complete. His only regret was that he had not topped JJ Darke. *One day*, he told himself, *one day I will get even with that Jock asshole.*

It was just after 8pm. Archie Newman unlocked the door of Bert's garage on hearing the six knock signal from the outside. Tim Hayworth and Jason Long were still there. Hayworth was pleased with his pay packet but Long felt that they deserved an extra wedge for all this repainting stuff, it was hard and it had taken half a day.

Neil Robson entered. He was content enough to see Archie

and shook his hand. The other two were not meant to be there.

"Archie, what are they doing here?" asked Robson calm, but annoyed.

"Sorry Neil," he whispered. "I tried to dissuade them but I think they're after a bonus, if you catch my drift."

"OK. Do you have my papers?"

"Yes. Everything's here," Newman replied, handing Robson an A5 sized envelope, which he folded and put inside his jacket pocket. In turn, he took out an envelope which had £20k in it, the last of the cash he was able to lay his hands on before tonight.

"Here, Archie, take this. You did a fine job," said Robson.

"Thanks. Anytime. Do you need me for anything else?" asked Archie, apparently keen to get off.

"Hang about for a few minutes, will you. I'll see if I can keep the lads happy," Robson replied.

Long and Hayworth were standing next to the van, patiently waiting for Robbo and Newman to finish. As Neil Robson approached, Hayworth rested against the side of the van but Long was anxious to make his play for more money.

"Hi lads," said Robson. "Good job today, the van looks sweet."

"Glad you think so, Robbo," said Jason Long. "We stuck to all your instructions, we did you a real solid. Any chance of a bonus?" he asked, never really having been one for small talk.

"Sure," said Robson. The fugitive Fin Sec put his right hand into the left hand side of his parka and his left hand into the jacket's outside pocket. He didn't pull out two envelopes of cash. Instead, he retrieved his two SIG Sauer P229s, both fully loaded with fifteen round magazines of 9mm .357 SIG bullets. Six pops rang out in an instant. Long took two to the head and one to the chest, Hayworth one to the head, one to the chest and one in his stomach. Archie Newman was rooted to the spot, shocked and bewildered. He was not expecting that.

"Sorry you had to see that Archie," said Robson, turning to face the pensioner.

"It's OK…" stuttered Archie. He didn't get the chance to say how OK or to ask questions. Robson fired again, twice. Archie took two to the head. He was dead before he hit the ground.

Robson bent over his third victim of the night and retrieved his £20k. Spending money, he muttered to himself. The pools of blood from Hayworth and Long had now joined up to form one big puddle. Robson surveyed the scene. He was satisfied. No witnesses to tonight's crimes and no one alive capable of stitching him up to the authorities. He was in the money and in the clear he told himself as he got into the white transit van and prepared to drive out of Bert's Garage. After he left Bert's, he stopped the van, got out, locked the garage and tossed the keys into a nearby skip. It was 8.30pm so he probably had at least a twelve hour head start before any alarm would be raised.

Robson was heading for Hull. He had rented a lock-up garage there, in an industrial estate, not far from the port and its ferry terminals. Times were tough in England and a cash payment for three months in advance rent, no questions asked, could not be turned down by the garage's owners. Hull was just over 200 miles away. By the time he got there it would be after midnight, too late for a ferry crossing that night. He would sleep in his van, mess around the next morning and afternoon then check in, on foot, close to 7pm for the 8.30pm crossing. He would buy some spare clothes in Hull and use them to cover the cash haul in his kit bag. This time he could buy his own ticket and use his new forged passport. A quality job thought Robson as he inspected the now deceased Archie Newman's work.

There is no proper security on P&O ferries, no baggage X-rays, no checks and no shake downs, only passport control. The crossing would be a piece of cupcake Robson laughed out loud. The ferry crossing would take ten to eleven hours. Once disembarked he would catch a taxi for the journey to Rotterdam's The Hague Airport, about three miles north-northwest of Rotterdam itself. There he would catch the afternoon Avianca flight to San Jose, Costa Rica. The flight would take six hours. Before boarding and checking-in his most valuable kit bag he would pop into a local Hull supermarket and purchase some aluminium foil to cover the currency parcel in his bag. His bag would be x-rayed before entering the hold of the plane. Ideally, lead has the best physical structure to reflect x-rays due to its large number of electrons and dense structure. Lead was an impractical option due to both its weight and availability to purchase at short notice. Aluminium foil was not as efficient in this operation due to its smaller attenuation coefficient i.e. its ability to be penetrated by light particles or other energy or matter. Nevertheless, a few sheets wrapped carefully and tightly around the already covered cash would be sufficient to reflect the limited penetration quality of baggage X-rays at Holland's third largest airport. He would then go to the Post Office in Newland Avenue, Hull to collect his parcel delivered by UPS. Neil Robson was set. He would have £2 million in his kit bag, and £2 million worth of US dollars awaiting his arrival in San Jose, Costa Rica, courtesy of UPS. If his travel plan worked as expected, he could return to his van and top up his cash.

Costa Rica lay between eight and twelve degrees north of the Equator in Central America. Its climate was tropical, you could use US dollars there freely and it was a democracy. On top of all those goodies thought Neil Robson, the piece de resistance was that it had no extradition treaty with the UK. He was not intending to be discovered but if he was then it would be harder, not impossible, but harder to force him back to the UK, to face multiple murder charges and a host of other felonies. With that happy prospect Robert Nilsson, as he now was, embarked on his version of the great escape.

★ ★ ★

"Anything?" asked JJ.

"Ziltch… well maybe one avenue of interest," replied Ethel, qualifying her negative absolute. "Local officers in Camden were called to a grease monkey garage there and found three dead bodies, all shot and all at least one bullet to the head, so probably a professional job. There was no sign of any van or any money. The two interesting things, though, were that the two dead guys apparently in their thirties were ex-military, one SAS the other a paratrooper. They had different splatterings of paint on some of their clothes and there was paint-spraying equipment lying around in the garage. The police interviewed the regular garage mechanics. They said they knew nothing about it and had been well paid to take the day off. They pointed to the dead old guy as the one who had paid them."

"And the other interesting point?" asked JJ.

"Well, although forensics wouldn't give me a definitive answer they said that the bullets were 9mm rounds and probably fired from a SIG Sauer, P228 or P229. They'll get back to me soon with a clear answer."

"SIGs are a favourite of the SIS. Are you thinking Robson?" suggested JJ.

"Don't know yet, JJ. I thought it was worthwhile asking for DNA and fingerprint checks though, just in case."

"Good work Ginger."

"One more thing," added Ethel. "The paint residue near the victims was mainly white and brown. I've asked 19's lab boffins to analyse the brown samples to see if they can be a match for UPS brown. If so, we might have a lead."

"Yes, Ethel, that would be good. If the UPS van did get painted there, however, then the white splatterings probably mean that the culprit is now a classic man in a white van. Needle in a haystack and all that."

"At least we'd know what kind of needle we'd be looking for," said Ethel trying to be positive.

"I guess," replied JJ, knowing that there were nearly three million of them. SCO19's laboratory analyst and Ethel's contacts in the Metropolitan Police got back to her before nightfall. The brown paint around the dead ex-military pair was a very good match for UPS brown, usually called Pullman Brown because one of the original UPS partners decided that the colour of the eponymous railroad carriages would be easier than yellow to keep clean. The DNA search produced a match for Neil Robson from the dead old guy's right hand. Likely then that the fugitive Robson had been present at the scene of this crime and was probably the perpetrator of it as well. Ethel imparted her news to JJ. He acknowledged that she had done really well to get that information so quickly. They also had an up to date description of Neil Robson provided by Cyrus. Ethel shared that knowledge with her police contacts and they with MI5 and Interpol. The police experts on evo-fit technology now had an acceptable image and it was being transmitted on all major news channels.

This was clearly an advance in the hunt for Neil Robson but JJ was still fed up. The source of his frustration was multi-faceted. He wasn't feeling great, niggly muscle and joint aches, greater preponderance of hormonal sweats and an adrenalin downshift after the chaos of Cyrus's kidnap. The biggest downer, however, was that he knew in his soul that Robson was well gone. The gap between the estimated time of the deaths at Bert's garage and the discovery of their bodies was around twelve hours. The answers to the paint and DNA questions, nearly a further twelve hours. The widespread distribution and publication of Robson's evo-fit image another few hours. If a cunning, trained ex-MI5 wetworker could not disappear off the fuckin' planet with such a head start, then I'm John fucking Bull groaned the Scot to himself.

JJ decided that he had had enough of Robson related thinking for the night. He went up the stairs from the small, front room on the ground floor, leaving Ethel and Victor to chat a while longer. On entering the living room he spotted Cyrus first, black Minecraft T-shirt and grey No. 33 track suit bottoms on, thick woolly socks and getting stuck into some Nintendo DS challenge while dangling his long legs over the side of the sumptuous armchair. He was returning to normal, thought JJ, and thank god for that. Becky, meanwhile, was equally casual but somewhat brighter. Hot pink fluffy jumper over black leggings with socks that matched the jumper. A bit more like it thought JJ as he saw Becky on the sofa and surfing on her tablet. JJ got a huge smile and thumbs up from Cyrus. That usually meant good to see you but I'm absorbed in my electronic game so don't bug me! JJ smiled back and then sat next to Becky.

"Is it OK if I sit here?" he asked, polite but not necessary.

"Sure, JJ, of course… it's your sofa."

"What are you up to?"

"I'm job hunting," replied Becky. "I don't really want to go back to the Treasury. Neil Robson is still out and about, too many cringeworthy memories of that slime ball and too many sad ones about Joel. I'm getting my degree soon so I'll be qualified to be more than a PA, not that that was a bad job, I just feel that I owe it to myself and to the memory of Joel to be the best I possibly can."

"Sound thinking, Becky. I know how you feel. I've been

totally useless at my so-called day job for the past few weeks. To be honest, the attraction of worrying about the ups and downs of Greek bonds or $/yen or even the price of gold has lost its allure. I haven't told Cyrus yet," said JJ lowering his voice, "but I'm thinking about resigning from MAM."

"I heard that," interrupted the boy. "Don't blame you Dad. Why don't you do something useful? Hire Becky," Cyrus announced with that complete look of cheek that he often could muster.

"Cyrus!" exclaimed Becky, blushing a bit partly because she quite liked that idea.

"I will think about it Cyrus. Maybe Becky's had enough of us. Firefight in Scotland probably wasn't the best job advertisement," said JJ. The three of them laughed and for the first time today JJ felt a little less fed up.

* * *

Days passed, then weeks, then months. The coalition lost the general election. Who knows why. Possibly their inability to kickstart the economy into a self-sustaining recovery. Possibly too much corruption surrounding former Chancellor Walker and his murderous acolyte Neil Robson. More likely, thought JJ, that it's one thing being a team player and quite another being a team of clones. They all just looked too alike. No individuality, no personality. In any event Labour were in power, slim majority and probably unstable.

JJ was back in his office at Momentum Asset Management. He wasn't looking at screens or switching assets in the fund's portfolio. He was packing up. Toby knocked on the door and was inside before JJ could say anything. There he was in all his glory, thought JJ, small head, chunky body, wonky glasses and, yes, his sartorial trademark, shirt almost free of pants. This was the real and original Fathead, no clone be he.

"JJ, this is bad news. What's this place going to be like without you? What am I going to do without you? You're my boss, my friend, my bleedin' inspiration. It's not fair, JJ."

"Come in Toby, take a seat. Let's chat." They both sat down at JJ's meeting table. "Toby, I just don't have the enthusiasm for this anymore. All that stuff with Robson, North Korea, gold, Cyrus. Horrible as most of it was, it was real. I know this is real too but it doesn't seem so to me anymore. It's like a giant, never ending video game. You're up, you're down. You collect your bonus and press go then it begins all over again. I'm just played out with it all. Please understand."

"I do understand, JJ. It's just that I'll miss you. Whoever replaces you won't be doing any of that crazy Greek bond stuff or seriously dodgy gold stuff. I mean what about the Christmas quiz and limerick for fuck's sake!" he exclaimed.

"Toby. You and I have sure done some stuff," said JJ, chuckling. "I'm not sure that it was all above board right enough. However, we can all walk the streets in comparative safety. We can all go straight to a hospital and be cared for if needed and we can all sleep in our beds at night unperturbed by the fear of mass burglaries, looters and hordes of half-wits wanting to do us harm. You did that. You got the government the readies it needed to pay the essential workers of our land. The end may not always justify the means but, in our case, I believe it did."

"I'm still going to miss you though," was all that Toby could say, feeling even more emotional about the whole chebang.

"I've spoken with David Sutherland, of course," said JJ. "He values you highly and so do I. Whoever replaces me will be made crystal clear aware of that. Don't worry, your job's safe – as long as you don't drop a packet! How's Yves-Jacques taking the news?"

"He's cool with it. He loves his job here. The special bonus you gave both of us means we don't have to work, ever, but I still love the buzz of the markets, trying to make profitable sense from market chaos, all that jazz. Yves-Jacques loves the mental challenge, the odd belief he has that you can model everything or at least give it some mathematical order. First foreign bloke I've ever liked!"

"Look Toby, I need to get on. I'll let you know what I've decided to do. I know already actually but I need to run it by a couple of people first. I don't have many friends, Toby, but the ones I have I regard as family. You're my family and you're welcome to come round whenever you want. We need to down some Macallans and you need to banter with Cyrus and avoid Gil's wrath. I really mean it. I want to see you soon, don't dare be a stranger," JJ was welling up a bit. Toby was welling up more than a bit and needed to exit before it became embarrassing. The two friends stood up and shook hands firmly. There was a strong bond.

JJ finished packing his personal stuff in crates and boxes. The MAM facilities department would organise his gear to be delivered to his house the following day. JJ left, jumped into a taxi and headed home. Ethel and Victor were back in their homes and had been for several weeks. Ethel was also back on SCO19 duty. Cyrus was on mid-term break, studying for his exams, and Gil and Becky were enjoying some girl talk.

"Cyrus, are you busy?" JJ shouted up the stairs on entering his home.

"Yes, but I need a break. Do you want something?" the boy called back.

"Just a chat, me, you, Gil and Becky. Will I bring you anything from the kitchen?" asked JJ.

"Yes please. Surprise me!" replied Cyrus. JJ knew that when

Cyrus said 'surprise me' what he meant was bring me loads of treats that I really like. Armed with this prior knowledge, JJ climbed the stairs to the living room balancing a packet of curlies, chicken flavoured crisps, a packet of chocolate buttons and a small bottle of still water. Cyrus was pleasantly 'surprised'.

"OK, let's all gather round," said JJ, sitting in his favourite armchair, opposite Cyrus, with Gil and Becky on the sofa. "Cyrus, we didn't want to burden you with the early stage outline, especially with your exams coming up, but the time seems right to let you in on what your dad and your friends here may be doing next."

"Sure," said Cyrus, keen but not desperate to know.

"Becky, do you want to start?" asked JJ.

"Of course," replied Becky, dressed today in a bright pale blue dress and calf length designer black boots. "Your dad is setting up and funding a consultancy cum charity that will have two objectives. We're calling it Project LFD."

"What? From the Lemony Snicket books?" interrupted Cyrus.

"That was VFD, Cyrus, you dimwit. Voluntary Fire Department among other variations of the acronym," said JJ laughing.

"I knew that," replied Cyrus. "Just checking that you knew."

"Anyway," resumed Becky, "it stands for Light From Dark. The charity part of it will distribute funds to worthy causes and aims to provide support in ways that major charities may have overlooked. Your dad has very kindly proposed that victims of Alzheimer's Disease will be our first project." Becky felt a bit emotional at this point because it was her mum and her mum's care home who were to be the first recipients.

"Cool," said Cyrus. "What is Project LFD's other objective?"

"Our other objective," replied JJ, "is to help seek the release

591

and return of innocent people incarcerated in jails around the world, political prisoners, victims of oppressive regimes, people who have disappeared for no good reason. Anyone who has carried out an act of violence, terrorism or other heinous crimes can be left to rot."

"That's awesome, guys," declared Cyrus. "Who's running the show and how is it all going to be paid for?" The boy's clearly paying attention thought JJ.

Gil spoke. "Your dad's Managing Director and he has supplied the initial capital."

"How much?" asked Cyrus.

"A lot," replied Gil. "Becky and I will be project managers, Becky concentrating on the charity side and me on the human rights side. We will have a small team of project associates to help."

"Can we call the associates projectiles?" asked Cyrus, obviously finding himself amusing. JJ thought it was funny. Gil and Becky not so much.

"No Cyrus, we can't," said Becky.

"Are you guys going to be running this from the house?" Cyrus asked.

"No," replied JJ. "I've signed a lease agreement for the top floor offices at 1 Grosvenor Place. It's near Hyde Park Corner, not that far from Buck House. We'll have moved in most of the furniture and equipment we need by the weekend."

"Wow," exclaimed Cyrus. "It's all go-go-go. Hey Dad, seems you took my advice to hire Becky!"

"Yes, Cyrus. Seems so, and good advice it was," replied his dad.

The four of them then discussed Project LFD for a little longer. After consuming his treats and water Cyrus headed back upstairs to his room to re-engage his studies. Gil decided to go down to the basement gym. She'd taken a break from her training after all the Scotland action, her injury on Cyrus's kidnapping night and the ensuing scramble to find him. JJ and Becky were still in the living room.

"JJ, this is super exciting for me. Thanks for the opportunity, I'm really looking forward to it. I can help my mum directly and then other people who are similarly afflicted. It's very satisfying."

"No problem Becky. You deserve it, and you're all qualified now. No cooking the books mind," he jested.

"JJ!" exclaimed Becky. "As if." Becky got off the sofa and was heading downstairs for a snack.

"Before you go, Becky, have you got a minute?" asked JJ.

"Sure," she replied, sitting back down.

"You know your bank account?"

"Of course," replied Becky "There's not much in it, with me being unemployed after the Treasury."

"About that. There may be a little more in it now. So when you check you may want to transfer some to a savings account, maybe invest some, that kind of thing. I can advise on the investments if you like."

"Explain, JJ, please?" asked Becky, somewhat confused.

"Well, I knew that if I tried to give you any money, you'd refuse. Didn't want handouts and all that." Becky nodded, and JJ continued. "So I had Victor hack your account and deposit some money in it. He created a sweet paper trail of legitimacy so that there would be no questions of money laundering and the like. I can give you details. Is that OK?"

"Is what bit of it OK, Mr Darke?" asked Becky standing, hands on hips and giving her new boss a stern look. "The bit that you've given me a handout that I didn't ask for or the bit that you had Victor the safe cracker, yes I know about him, hack my account, or the false paper trail bit?"

"All the bits really," said a visibly sheepish JJ. "C'mon Becky, go with the flow, please. You've got a good legitimate job now, no more handouts, hacking, anything, I promise. Regard it as payment for services rendered. No! Don't…I could have phrased that better. I put you in danger, in Scotland, so call it danger money, anything. Please accept, it'll be a real bind to unravel it now."

Becky pondered for a few seconds not shifting her gaze from JJ. "Alright then, but never again and only because I don't want you and Victor getting into trouble."

"Great," said JJ, feeling well relieved.

As Becky sat back down on the sofa to take this all in, JJ decided to quietly head for the door and downstairs.

Just before he exited, Becky called out, "By the way, JJ, how much is in my account?"

"Eh, well, let's call it £3 million," he replied and hotfooted it down to the kitchen. Becky was not far behind. JJ managed to placate her by explaining that everyone in JJ's circle who had been involved in events in Korea, Scotland, London and the hunt for Neil Robson had earned healthy bonuses. Hers was nowhere near the highest. She calmed down on that news, thanked JJ profusely and went back to organising herself in preparation for project LFD. JJ also said that Becky was most welcome to stay with him, Cyrus and Gil for as long as she wanted. Neil Robson was still out there, though nobody knew where. Becky accepted but said that with her instant wealth she might consider buying an apartment in Pimlico.

JJ was satisfied with the day's events. He was sitting on the small sofa in the front room, ground floor, next to the kitchen. He could see out onto Markham Square, nothing much was going on, thank goodness he thought. It was early evening now. He had a glass of Macallans with him and placed it on the small table at his left hand side. He decided to read through again the lease agreement for the new premises of Project LFD. It all seemed fairly straightforward. One section, however, had been highlighted by his solicitor who had thoroughly checked the terms and conditions. That's interesting, thought JJ, making a mental note to contact his lawyer for clarification. He was in a twilight dreaming state now, going over all the action of recent months. Against all the odds things seemed to have worked out. His dad was recovering from his gunshot wounds on schedule, his son seemed to be bearing no psychological damage from his kidnap ordeal and Kwon had been rescued by Jim Bradbury's team with the critical support of a highly skilled MI5 unit.

JJ was in the process of leaving his old life behind and embarking on a new venture, with friends, and one whose aim was on higher moral ground than finance. Babikov was locked up. Carolyn, who had been absolutely brilliant in Scotland, seemed to be settling into life with Commander O'Neill, in the sunny climes of Southern California. There were no FCA or any other type of charges hanging over his head or those of his friends. Sandra Hillington at MI5 and the former Home Secretary between them had taken care of all that. He was flush. All that excess cash that Victor had identified in the DPRK's central bank vaults. Admittedly, Robson had stolen a chunk but the rest had either been paid out to those who had put their lives and reputations at risk or earmarked for charitable and human rights purposes. The country was functioning normally, and he could take a little credit for that. It was all good, but it wasn't completely, locked down good.

There was one niggle, one omission, one itch that needed scratched. JJ had made a promise to his son. 'On your mother's love' he had said to Cyrus. That was a promise that had to be kept.

14

CAVE NE RAPTOR

"My name is Iqbal Quintus Ahmed," announced the 6ft plus black man, middle aged, with colourful attire and an embroidered kufi on his head. "I am the fifth Iqbal of my family. My friends call me IQ. They say 'Hi IQ!' I like that. I say thank you."

"Well, Mr Ahmed, I am a police officer, not your friend. I am here to prevent crime, solve crime, support victims of crime. How can I help you today, with that in mind?" asked PC George Ramsbotham, a 5ft 8in extremely white Geordie, not yet interested enough to desist from his report filling.

"I come originally from a small group of Kenyan Muslims, only 11% of the population. You may think I am a terrorist. I am not. I am here to report a crime, maybe help solve one. I need to see a detective please."

PC Ramsbotham looked at Iqbal. He couldn't really be stuffed to check if there were any detectives around. Still, he didn't want to have some racial discrimination accusation launched at him, so he thought he'd better pay attention.

"Can you give me any details of this crime, Mr Ahmed, before I go digging out a detective?" asked Ramsbotham.

Iqbal reached into his robes and pulled out a computer generated picture of a man's face. "I know this man. He is a robber. He owes me money. He is late in his legitimate payment to me. I want justice," proclaimed Iqbal, getting a little animated.

PC Ramsbotham had a look at the print out. He thought it

might be a good idea to find out if any detectives were on duty. A few minutes later another white man, younger and taller than Ramsbotham, wearing a suit, appeared.

"Mr Ahmed, you say you know this man? How?" asked the detective.

"To whom am I speaking?" enquired Iqbal, politely and in clear English.

"I am Detective James Crockett," said the suited man.

"From *Miami Vice*?" asked Iqbal enthusiastically. "You do not look like him. He was blonder, more hair, thinner, but that was a long time ago. You look well!"

"No, Mr Ahmed. I am not detective Crockett from *Miami Vice*. I'm from here, in Kingston upon Hull, where you are now. Can we get to the point please?" asked Detective Crockett, feeling that he was doing well in not arresting this clown for wasting police time.

"Certainly, Detective Crockett," replied Iqbal, keen to impart his tale of misfortune.

Crockett listened, albeit reluctantly at first. The man in the picture had rented a lock-up garage from Iqbal. He paid in cash, no questions asked, three months in advance. Those three months were now over. His van was still in Iqbal's garage. No sign of more cash. Iqbal had just come back from visiting his family in Kenya, on the coast, near Kipini. On his return, his son, Iqbal Sextus, had shown him the man's face. It had been on the news, in the papers, on social media sites. The boy, a teenager, had recognised him as a man who had rented from his dad. Occasionally, Iqbal Sextus worked in his father's makeshift office on the industrial estate, after school. "He is a bright, observant boy," said Iqbal proudly.

"You say the van is still there, in your garage?" asked Detective Crockett.

"Yes Detective, it is. I did not want to break into it or drive it out and leave it by the roadside. That might be against the law and I am a most law abiding citizen of this United Kingdom," replied Iqbal, glossing over the fact that cash transactions on garage rentals might not be to the liking of HMRC.

Detective Crockett looked again at the printed copy of the man's face. Then he looked at Iqbal and then back to PC Ramsbotham.

"George, didn't we have some dedicated numbers to ring if anyone spotted this guy?"

"Aye, we did Jimmy-lad," George replied but drew a look from the detective which said more formality please. "I think there was one for Interpol and one for MI5 Detective Crockett, Sir," added Ramsbotham suitably chastised.

"Ring the MI5 one George," instructed Crockett. "Interpol's full of foreigners, they wouldn't understand a bleedin' word you utter."

"What will I say?" asked the PC.

"Say we may have had a sighting of Neil Robson and we may have his van, George. That should be enough to get some high-falutin' London spooks up here quick smart. Iqbal, you and I are going to take a look at your garage. OK?"

"Yes detective. Let us go now. The sooner the better. Time may be money but so is space. Is there a reward?" asked IQ.

Detective Crockett had a small shake of the head, not to indicate no for indeed there was a reward, but to indicate that the man from Kenya was one fine piece of work.

* * *

"Hi JJ, it's Sandra," said the Director General of MI5.

"Hi Sandra, how are you? It's been a while," replied JJ from his new work premises in Grosvenor Place, London.

"As you can imagine, we've been busy on a few matters. JJ, it's just an FYI. We got a call this morning from a PC stationed at Humberside Police Station. Apparently some fellow just waltzed into the station and claimed he had rented a lock-up garage to Neil Robson. I've sent two officers up there to investigate. There's a local detective called Crockett on the case. He says there is indeed a van inside this fellow's garage. I told him to touch nothing till my team got there. I'll let you know if there's anything to it."

"Thanks Sandra. I'd appreciate that," said JJ and they both hung up.

JJ had tried to get Neil Robson out of his head, but he couldn't. The slimy weasel who had kidnapped his son was still out there, somewhere, no doubt enjoying the spoils of his crimes. It wasn't right and he had made that promise to Cyrus.

JJ spent the rest of the morning working on Project LFD. Becky and Gil were beavering away too, checking databases, sources, any information they could find on their twin task mission. Between charity work and rescue work they were likely to be kept fully occupied and inundated for help. Project LFD seemed like a worthy cause but it was going to be more intense and time consuming than sitting watching green and red flashing asset prices on his computers at MAM or his BlackBerry and tablet at home. JJ's phone rang.

"Hi, it's me again," said Sandra Hillington.

"Hi Sandra. Any news?"

"Yes. The fellow, who has some exotic name, Iqbal Quintus Ahmed, was right. We got several sets of prints off the van and one of them is Robson's. On top of that, JJ, the van is packed with hard currency, pounds, dollars, euros. My guys estimate that there's maybe £80-90 million equivalent stashed in there."

"What's your plan Sandra?" asked JJ more than a little interested.

"Well, some of it is deductive reasoning and inference and some of it is pure instinct. The van's in a lock-up on the industrial estate near the port. Boats from the port go to more than one destination. Since we know that when Robson first left London he flew to Amsterdam, our first port of call, no pun intended, would be Rotterdam. Somehow, he must be getting back into the country, taking another chunk of cash and then leaving. Security at these ports is pathetic. False papers, a decent disguise and an alert mind would likely get you past any checks."

"Well Robson's sure got an alert mind. It might be devious, evil and fucked up, but it's alert alright."

"Anyway," resumed Sandra, "my plan is to stake out the garage. Apparently, Iqbal, the garage owner was hopping up and down because Robson was a few weeks late on his cash rental payment. That's why he went to the police, clutching a print out or something of Neil Robson's e-fit face that his son recognised. It was a piece of luck and we're grateful for it. Something must have delayed Robson, but he's not going to leave that amount of money just lying there forever. He'll know he's behind in his rental payment and will need to try to fix that. It's a cash arrangement so he might turn up in person eventually. I'll have a team of two keep the garage under surveillance, day and night for as long as it takes."

"That sounds like a plan Sandra," said JJ. "Anything I can do?"

"No, JJ, just sit tight but thanks. I know you've got a score to settle but let's try to get the fugitive first."

"Sure, Sandra, thanks. Keep me in touch," responded JJ and their call ended.

JJ reclined in his favourite leather chair that had been transported from his MAM office and put his feet up on the desk. Sandra's plan was logical enough he thought. The Hull to Rotterdam route made sense and the estimate of £80-90 million still in the van meant that Robson already had £10m or more with him. He wasn't broke but he was a greedy fucker and would want the rest of his illegal stash.

JJ concluded that he would stay out of it, for now, hoping that MI5 were on point.

★ ★ ★

Neil Robson was feeling like crap. He was flat out in his expensive wicker bed, penthouse apartment in San Jose, capital of Costa Rica.

When some folk go into hiding they tend to opt for the most remote village, well off the beaten track. That is not a good strategy. Strangers, foreign strangers, in particular, stand out like sore thumbs. Gossip ensues and the tittle-tattle eventually finds the willing ears of some intrepid nosey parker who wants to snoop around, find something out and report it for a reward, usually either from the legitimate law enforcement agencies or a local gangster. In the middle of this city, population of over 300,000, an anonymous foreigner did not attract any attention.

Robson rented his spacious apartment in the Mata Redonda district and had a fine view over the Sabana Metropolitan Park. He had changed his appearance yet again, now less Nick Nolte in *Down and Out in Beverly Hills* and more Anthony Hopkins at the tail end of *Silence of the Lambs*. His hair was buzz cut and a stylish goatee had replaced the previous full beard. If he had to talk to anyone and they asked what he did he said he was a travel writer preparing an extensive insight into Costa Rica and San Jose in particular. That way no one would question his apparent lack of daytime employment or his lazing around the local cafés and restaurants, or dives and clubs in the night.

He banked with the Grupo Mutual. They didn't ask too

many questions as to his extremely large deposits of US dollars. He had a reference from the realtors he had rented from, for a fee of course, ID and a passport that seemed in good order. He explained that he had come into an inheritance but that he was a travelling man and did not like to bank in places that he was not expecting to be resident in for long. He expected to be in Costa Rica for quite some time. Sizeable deposits are hard to come by thought the Assistant Vice President of Grupo Mutual so he was happy to accept those of this Robert Nilsson.

You can take the man away from his usual dens of iniquity but you cannot take the iniquities away from the man. Robert Nilsson could have been feeling rough because of some drug overdose or a variety of STDs from the local senoritas, whose fee-paying company he had often enjoyed since arriving in this fair city. Miraculously, he wasn't. The vice-loving criminal was out for the count, drained, too weak to move very far because he had a dose of Leptospirosis. This disease has a variety of nicknames of which Rat Catcher's Yellows is perhaps the most vibrant. It is a common disease in many parts, including Costa Rica and is often contracted by humans after inadvertently coming into contact with water contaminated from animal urine.

At first, Robson thought he had the flu; he felt feverish and had a splitting headache. Vomiting and an unusually dark brown colour to his pee led the local physician to conclude it was Rat Catcher's Yellows. He was correct. Robson was prescribed the appropriate antibiotics and his condition had been caught early enough to prevent any of the more serious results like kidney or liver failure. However, it had laid him low for the best part of two weeks and he still did not feel up to walking around let alone getting on a long haul plane journey. As he lay there in his misery, he knew he had missed the flight he had booked about ten or so days ago, he knew he was late with the cash rental payments on his Hull lockup and he knew he'd better get on that as soon as he physically could.

★ ★ ★

"Jace, how long have we been on this gig?" asked Winston Gregory, weary from the grind of surveillance.

"About eight days and nights now, Winston," replied Jason Harper. "It's not glamorous, that's for sure, but the high heid yin said we're on it for as long as it takes."

"I'm fuckin' bored!" complained Winston from inside their Mazda CX-5, packed to the gunnels with electronic equipment and night sights. "All we've seen is rain, trucks, a few sad locals and a randy couple getting at it in a shed. It's not illuminating and it's not why I joined MI5."

Admittedly, the Marfleet Lane Industrial Estate, Burma Drive, Hull was not the most glamorous and exciting location. It was full of sheds, lock-ups, warehouses and other industrial units. It was less than half a mile from the port where the Rotterdam ferry would dock so an easy drive, or indeed walk for anyone who wanted to make that journey.

Winston Gregory was in his early thirties, skin black as the dead of night and had been in MI5 for six years. He was 6ft tall and of mid-level seniority in the service. Jason Harper was younger, shorter with pasty white skin. He had been in MI5 for four years, one as an analyst and the balance as a field officer.

"I agree Winny," said Jace. "It's not up to much but rumour has it that if we capture this Robson fellow it will be 5's best result for quite some time."

"I'm not sure I care anymore Jace. It's dark, miserable, wet and freezin' up here. This is a pokey tin van for my 6ft frame, you and all this fuckin' gear just to survey a pigeon. That fuckin' guy

603

is never coming back here," declared Winston. "I'm off for a pee. I'm going to do some urine target practice on that bunch of pigeons over there. See how they like being pissed on from a great height."

"Don't miss big fella," said Jason, keeping his eye on the screens inside and well away from his partner's urinating dong.

At the far end of this particular line of industrial units, north, north-east and a few hundred yards from the scattering pigeons there was a shadow looking on. Partly hidden by the substantial hood on his dark green parka and partly by the vertical edge of one of the temporary structures the shadow was surveying the surveyors, through his night vision monocular. Standards must have dropped, thought Neil Robson, since his time in MI5. This was Hull and an industrial estate, not Knightsbridge or a heaving square in Covent Garden. Two guys in suits in a 4x4 whose make is often deployed by the intelligence services. Give me a break. If I had a weapon on me, thought Robson, I'd shoot that black bastard's johnson clean off. Fortunately for Winston Gregory, Robson did not have any means of mutilation on him so the now relieved MI5 officer could carry on moaning.

It was, nevertheless, well up shit creek thought Robson on spotting the 4x4 and besuited occupants. He was feeling shattered after his flight and overnight ferry ride, not having fully recovered his pre-Rat Catcher's Yellows energy. Now it looks like those MI5 morons have twigged his lock-up garage. No chance of getting the rest of his millions now he concluded. Fuck, fuck, fuck, fuck, fuck, he muttered angrily to himself. Nothing for it but he'd need to head to London and collect at least one of the parcels he had placed in the good care of Royal Mail Keepsafe. He'd catch a train to King's Cross, rent a car and then proceed to Clapham Post Office where €2 million in readies awaited him. If that went smoothly he might pick up the second parcel deposited for him by the sham UPS twosome, now dead, at the main Post Office in Chelsea. He'd mull it over on the train.

Neil Robson had a lot to think about on the train and around two and a half hours to do it. He was still on antibiotics for his Leptospirosis and he did not feel properly recovered. He looked OK, having acquired a light tan in San Jose. He had donned his thick-rimmed black plastic glasses again so, with the tan, the new haircut and the goatee he was not recognisable as the fugitive former Financial Secretary to the Treasury. As the train whooshed along, down the tracks to the nation's capital, Neil Robson felt an aura of injustice descend upon his inner thoughts. He wasn't badly off, he had a few million in Grupo Mutual, he liked the ambience of Costa Rica, especially that inside a tight senorita or drug house. What was he going to do, however, when that ran out? Eight or ten million dollars was a tidy sum alright but it was not enough to fund the lifestyle that he wanted, nay craved, for the next thirty to forty years. At each and every turn he had been thwarted by that Jock bastard JJ Darke. He could have had him locked up on his insider trading gaffe, but no he gives the fuckin' heathen a great idea to relieve that despot Kim Jong-un of his gold. Save the country and make me four or five hundred million, that was the fuckin' plan, a plan that had been unceremoniously flushed down the toilet.

He had let Darke Jnr live, quite nice of him he thought but, no, the daddy jockstrap couldn't leave it there. Now the van with £90m in it had been found. Neil Robson felt that he'd soon be on his uppers and it was the fault of one JJ Darke. That prick needed a lesson, a message, a final reminder to stay out of his business. In the midst of all this scheming and plotting, Neil Robson fell asleep on the Hull to King's Cross train with a grimace of evil intent stretched across his lightly tanned face.

Neil Robson had just caught the last London bound train

from Hull. It didn't get into King's Cross until 9pm so he took a taxi to the Wyndham Grand Hotel in Chelsea Harbour and booked in under the name Robert Nilsson. It was a modern hotel, nice view over a small harbour and much favoured by away teams scheduled to play Chelsea at Stamford Bridge on the weekend. He had stayed there before, in his previous life, and had sat close to the crooner Lionel Richie at breakfast. Seemed like a nice bloke, but rubbish slushy songs. The one where he didn't know who he was looking for was especially gooey. I mean, don't you fuckin' know who you're looking for you ignorant foreigner. Wake up you tosser, thought the fugitive, clearly never having seen the accompanying music video.

Robson had a late night snack in his room on the fourth floor and was contemplating phoning for the services of a nearby hooker. After some thought he decided that a bit of DIY would be more efficient and cheaper. He was tired anyway and needed to have a clear mind in the morning.

He was impressed by the Royal Mail Keepsafe service. At a Post Office of your choice they would hold on to a parcel for you for sixty-six days. Robson guessed that he may be away from London for longer than that so paid extra for an extension. The Clapham Post Office had one parcel of around £2m equivalent in euros. He would get up in the morning, have breakfast, hopefully nowhere near any visiting singer, ask the concierge to acquire a rental car for him and then drive to get his parcel. Once cashed and geared-up he'd decide on his next move and escape route back to Costa Rica.

★ ★ ★

While the fugitive Neil Robson was settling down for the night, Toby Naismith was leading Yves-Jacques astray, well as astray as the young French analyst would allow. They were downstairs in the bar at Nobu, still Fathead's favourite night time haunt, along with Toby's broker friends, Jay and Kai.

"Tobester!" exclaimed Kai, spraying the atmosphere with only a few morsels of canapé. "What's your new boss like? Is he better than JJ?"

"Nobody's better than JJ," replied Toby. "The new guy's OK. He came from Goldman Sachs so he's all full of vim and vigour. Wants to stamp his own ways and personality on things, that kind of stuff. He's from the east coast of America and has an unhealthy work ethic. He gets in before I do, has lunch at his desk and leaves after me. He clearly has no life though he claims to have a wife and daughter."

"How about you Yvester? You think the same?" continued Kai with his interrogation-lite.

"He seems fine," replied Yves-Jacques, not at all impressed by Kai's habit of adding –ster to everything and everybody. "JJ was a one off, I feel. Working for him was very exciting, different, frankly off the wall on occasion and always out of the box. The new guy's more mainstream. He seems solid and knows what he's talking about. He'd be unlikely to ask me about the Noman Tebbit test though," reminisced Yves-Jacques.

"What's the Norman Tebbit test, Yvester?" asked Kai.

"Too complex to explain Kai-ster," responded Yves-Jacques with a grin, "and it's too noisy in here for me to go through it," he added, before sitting back in his chair and hoping that the night would end soon so that he could go home for a decent sleep.

The four friends and acquaintances departed Nobu before midnight and headed home. Unsurprisingly, Toby was perhaps the worst for wear and he just about managed to hail a cab on Berkeley Street to take him back to his Islington pad. He had enjoyed the evening but as so often happens after a few too many and being reminded of a sad event, Fathead was feeling increasingly maudlin. He really missed JJ. The new guy was OK, Toby acknowledged that, but he was straight from that Yale/Harvard Business School production line so embraced by US investment banks. No Greek bond fun was likely under his regime, no clandestine gold fun and definitely no Christmas FX quiz and limerick challenge. Jeesuz, he even told me to tuck my shirt in my pants! There was no option, Toby decided, he would text JJ. They needed to meet up, have a Macallans, banter with Cyrus and maybe a little non-salacious ogle at Gil. As Toby flopped semi-conscious onto his sofa the cloud of ordinary that had descended upon him began to lift, his moderately chubby fingers pressing away on his smartphone. The spelling may not be that great he thought but JJ would get the message.

JJ got the message but not until the following morning when he was back in Project LFD's offices and had turned on his smartphone. The text was incomprehensible even allowing for text-speak abbreviations and mis-hit keys. JJ knew it was from Toby and two of the few correctly spelled words were 'Macallans' and 'meet'. The rest could be deduced. JJ missed Toby too. His joie de vivre was infectious. The Scot would never forget Fathead's drunken sailor jig in his lock-up at the sight of a van full of stolen gold bullion bars, nor would he forget the irregular limerick that amused him on his flight back from Seoul. Toby was a one-off. A man with no recognisable style bar the one that he made his own. An old school trader but one that was at the pinnacle of his game. JJ was so glad that Toby had not taken any flak from the insider trading issue and was heartfelt pleased that a few of the Korean millions had found their way to the Fathead fun fund. With a broad grin on his face, JJ replied to Toby's text, inviting him round to dinner that night, promising rare Macallans and the occasional portion of food.

The rest of the day passed uneventfully for Toby and JJ. Toby was delighted to get JJ's text and said he'd be round at 7.30pm. Often, when friendly work colleagues separate, the contact cycle develops with decreasing amplitude and increasing wave length. A few drinks, dinners and lunches would be packed in to the first few weeks, the scheduled dinners would morph into lunches and then lunches into a swift after work drink. Text communication would then fill the human contact void, the SMSs would become further apart and degenerate into the occasional email. Then nothing and both parties would embark fully on their separate ways. Not so with Toby and JJ. Apart from Greek bond and gold haul events, when they needed to be in touch almost continuously, the regularity and method of their contact was stable. Even after JJ had left MAM for Project LFD, the true friends stayed in touch at least once a week and often more frequently. Toby probably missed JJ more because the one-third of his daily life that he now spent in the office, was JJ-light and he couldn't just meander into the Scot's office whenever he felt like it. Tonight, though, it was JJ, Cyrus, Gil, Macallans and some food. Nothing better thought Toby.

★ ★ ★

It was 7.30pm on the dot, a bright July evening, warm, with a pleasant wafting breeze. Toby rang the bell of JJ's home.

"Toby!" exclaimed JJ on opening the door for his friend. "Right on time, good man," said the punctuality-loving Scot.

"You know, JJ, Oscar Wilde said punctuality was the thief of time, but that just shows you what an Irish plonker he was, clearly he didn't allow for extra Macallans consumption time!"

"Maybe Macallans was not around when he was?" suggested JJ in a half-hearted attempt at defending the Celtic wit.

"The Macallans distillery was founded in 1824, JJ, and that Wilde bloke lived for 56 years until 1900. He had plenty of drinking time. He just made bad decisions."

JJ was somewhat impressed by Toby's historical knowledge, though not absolutely convinced about its accuracy. What he was convinced about was that he'd better offer Toby a rare Macallans forthwith.

JJ and Toby went up the stairs chatting away. Once in the living room Toby planted himself on one of the comfortable armchairs either side of the sofa. JJ got the Macallans, one for himself, no ice with a splash of Canada Dry and one for Toby, ice and no other additions.

"Cheers," said JJ, pleased to be relaxing with his friend.

"Slange i va," replied Toby, correctly pronouncing *slainte mhath*, meaning 'good health' in Gaelic.

Gil entered the room, wearing a short LBD, four inch heels and make-up. Toby, who wisely kept his thoughts to himself, reckoned he'd never seen her look so hot. She was carrying a platter of pre-dinner snacks. Toby reached for a few, finding it difficult to take his eyes off the oriental firecracker.

"You'd better stop looking at me like that, Toby Naismith," said Gil, with only a moderately threatening tone.

"Sorry," said Toby quickly. "It's just, well, it's just you look very nice tonight Gil," he managed to stutter out.

"Don't I look nice every time you see me?" asked Gil, clearly enjoying Toby's discomfort.

"Ah! Yes you do. It's just tonight, I mean, you look especially nice tonight Gil," he replied.

"Thank you, Toby," said Gil in a fake tone of pleasure at the compliment. "Now that I'm a project manager, front office, meeting people I need to adopt the expected uniform of that position."

"I'm people," said Toby.

"Yes Toby, you are. However, I'm referring to people who may want to donate large sums of money to project LFD."

"I can donate."

"How much?" asked Gil, expertly reeling in her unsuspecting prey. Toby glanced at JJ; his old boss unleashed a look which said you're on your own buddy!

"£50k?" Toby replied, meekly and hoping he had said the right thing.

"Thank you Toby. That'll do nicely. In return for your generosity I will remain dressed like this throughout dinner." Toby's face lit up. "However, if I catch you ogling me or dribbling down your chin then one of these overly expensive Laboutins will enter your pin head, heel first and with force. Agreed?"

"Agreed," said Toby, realising he had been royally ensnared, though definitely worth it in his opinion. Toby extended his right arm with empty tumbler at the end of it, pointing at JJ. His old boss laughed, took the glass and filled it up. Gil left the living room very pleased with her version of a honey trap. She liked Toby but admitted that she got immense pleasure from seeing him wriggle. Toby sipped on Macallans number two of the evening. This was going to be a fun night he thought.

Cyrus joined the group for dinner. Becky was visiting her mum that evening in Hampshire, and had let JJ know that she would stay overnight with her aunt. Cyrus also thought Gil looked stunning, having rarely seen her not wearing casual clothing or training gear. Still, she was no Lucy thought the boy, rationalising that the hot look was probably for Toby's benefit or torture.

"Gil looks nice tonight, doesn't she Toby?" asked Cyrus, with mischievous intent.

"Don't start Cyrus," moaned Toby. "She does but I've already been stitched up on that one." No sooner had the words departed from his mouth than he caught the dagger look from you know who.

"Are you saying I tricked you Toby Naismith?" asked Gil sternly.

"No, sorry, I just meant… I don't know what I meant. I'm happy with everything. I give up," he spluttered.

Everybody laughed. Gil rose from her chair, went round to Toby sitting opposite and planted a very sweet kiss on his forehead. That was a whole lot better than a four inch heel he thought, oblivious to the appearance of a second set of lips on his head, the new ones all bright and ripe tomato red.

Dinner was most enjoyable, the conversation flew by; it was loud, irreverent and full of banter. Toby eventually went to the loo and saw Gil's lipstick impression on his forehead. He returned to the dinner table with it still in situ.

"I'm never washing my face again!" he declared, much to the merriment of all concerned, especially Gil. It was past midnight and though it seemed like only minutes before that he had downed Macallans number one, it was indeed several hours, several Macallans and several large glasses of Tignanello later.

"Toby, you can stay the night if you want," offered JJ.

"No, it's OK, JJ. I've had a brilliant night but all my work gear is in the flat and I've got an early breakfast meeting with the new guy. He counts a seeded bagel and cream cheese as breakfast, so I'll need to pop into Pret for a few baguettes to take with me." He was deadly serious but JJ just laughed.

"OK, Toby, I'll book you a cab."

"You don't need to chief," said Toby apparently not yet fully out of the habit of regarding JJ as his boss as well as his friend. "I'll just walk down to the King's Road, get some air. There'll be plenty of cabs around even at this time of night."

"OK. If you're sure," replied JJ.

"I'm sure," said Toby.

"Are you sure you're sure?" retorted JJ chuckling.

"I'm definitely sure JJ! I'm too tired for even more banter. I'm so sure, I've never been surer," explained Toby, collecting his jacket on the way out.

"As long as you're sure," said JJ. "Take care and see you soon," he added, watching his friend take his first few weaving steps down the west side of Markham Square.

JJ would later wish sincerely that he had watched Toby for just a little longer. His friend was about half way to the King's Road when a man exited a parked Volvo S-class and was making his way towards him. As they drew level, the man whipped out a syringe from his parka pocket and thrust it into Toby's neck. He immediately went down, feeling weak and drowsy almost instantaneously though the pain was not great, perhaps masked by the quantity of alcohol previously consumed. The man dragged Toby's half-limp body to a space between parked cars and attached him to the Square's garden railings with speedcuffs around his neck.

"Remember me, fatboy, isn't it, or fat something?" mocked Neil Robson, not really expecting an answer from the semi-comatose Toby.

"So here's how this is going to play out you useless lump. I've injected you with some stuff called Oil of Mirbane which will more or less paralyse you but it won't kill you right away. That's the good news. The bad news is that in my right hand here... see it!" said Robson slapping Toby on the head. "I'm holding one of those open ended little razor blades that depressed teenagers seem to like when they pop in a bath and cut their wrists. I'm going to give you a couple of little horizontal nicks here and here," informed Robson as he cut both Toby's wrists in the manner described.

"This way will take you longer to die you fat cunt. If I'd done it long ways you'd be dead in about five minutes, but that would be too good for any bosom buddy of JJ Darke."

Toby could just about feel a weird sensation in his arms but he did not register agonising pain. The paralysing agent mixed with the alcohol was keeping that at bay.

"Now, there's always a chance that some passing do-gooder will see you lying here and come to your aid. I can't really be having that. So the next bit of bad news is this." The murdering fugitive then showed a fast-declining Toby one of his SIG Sauers, suppressor attached. He placed the barrel on Toby's stomach and fired. Toby writhed and passed out but Robson kept on talking.

"Right. You're bleedin' chubby and I may have missed your artery. I reckon you've got a minimum of fifteen minutes to live and a maximum of an hour. After all, I only made tiny nicks on your wrists. If you feel pain, it'll be bad but it won't be for long. All that toxic stuff in your fat gut will mix with the escaping blood. You'll die either from extreme toxaemia or maybe bleed out. It's nice and quiet around here, but you never know, I'm still concerned about a random do-gooder or curtain twitcher. So, here's a blanket, tartan of course, to cover up your gut and your wrists. To top it all, I now place a beanie on your small head. Is that lipstick on your forehead you fuckin' perve? Notice, sorry you can't notice so I'll tell you. It's a navy blue beanie with a saltire patch at the front. Nice touch don't you think? I was saving it for the Darke kid but he seems too well protected now. So there it is, fat arse. You're the second best solution. That Scottish bastard friend of yours would understand that."

Neil Robson stood up and admired his work. To a passer-by in this dead of night, Toby would look like a homeless person or a vagrant who'd had a rare night on the tiles. Robson took a piece of paper from his pocket, scribbled something on it and tucked it into the fold of Toby's beanie. If his luck was really in, thought Robson, that Darke fuck would be the first to spot his dead friend, if not, the finder could phone the number in the beanie.

Robson was calm. He looked around. No pedestrians in the Square, a few stragglers crossing the junction with the King's Road, all minding their own business. A swift scan of the residents' buildings did not pick-up any late night, early morning actually, peepers. Darke would get the message alright thought Robson and I'm off scot-free he laughed to himself as he entered his rented Volvo. Funny peculiar expression mused Robson, scot-free, especially as it had nothing to do with the Scots as a nation or that American slave Dred Scott of Supreme Court 1857 fame. It stems from an Old Norse word 'skot' which could be translated as 'tax' and is believed to have first referred to a town's municipal levies and the avoidance of paying them. No matter the etymology concluded Robson as he headed for the M25 and escape, I'm going back to sun, sex, snort and Centenario.

★ ★ ★

Days passed. JJ had hardly got out of his bed other than to go to the bathroom. Either Gil or Cyrus or Becky forced him to eat, but he had no appetite. Guilt was consuming his entire body and mind. It was his fault that Toby was dead. He had got him in on the act to sell the stolen gold, to trade the Greek bonds on privileged information. It was his fault that Toby had registered on the evil motherfucker Robson's radar. It was unbearable. Toby, so happy-go-lucky, so dishevelled, so taken with Gil. He wasn't going to be around anymore.

Robson made it crystal clear that it was a message to JJ. The manner of his death, the beanie, the blanket. Murdered by a lethal injection of nitrobenzene which would have killed him anyway, according to the coroner's report, but intensified by organ damage from a gunshot wound and blood loss from two slit wrists. It was too much, grieved JJ. He could barely stand the loss of his friend but when you added that to Joel Gordon's murder and Cyrus's kidnap and beating it was beyond assimilation. Robson was also the catalyst for Vladimir Babikov's attack on his parent's house in Scotland. That fucking scumbag deserved to die a miserable death swore JJ but at this moment all the Scot could think about was the murder of his friend. As he lay in his bed, wallowing, crying, grieving, he heard a knock on the door. It was Cyrus.

"Hey Dad, can I come in?" he asked softly. JJ did not want to see anyone. However, even stronger than the emotions of grief that were consuming his waking hours, was the deep love that he had for his son.

"Sure, Cyrus," replied JJ weakly, barely audible. "I look a bit like Robinson Crusoe at the moment, sorry."

"You don't look that good Dad!" replied Cyrus trying his teenage best to lighten the atmosphere and make his dad feel better. "More like Forrest Gump at the end of his long walk."

"Gee thanks, Cyrus," said JJ, with the first hint of a smile to cross his face for days. JJ sat up in his bed and Cyrus sat on the edge, looking concerned for his father's emotional and physical state. A kind of role reversal, thought Cyrus, as JJ had spent many a night watching over him if he was unwell or had a nightmare.

"Look Dad, I know you miss Toby. I do too, he was funny and made me laugh. Gil misses him as well. They'd never have been an item she told me, but he made her smile. He was a great bloke."

"He was indeed, Cyrus," agreed JJ.

"I also know you blame yourself, Dad, but you shouldn't. Sure, Toby would never have been noticed by Neil Robson if he hadn't worked with you, if you hadn't been friends. But Toby's life, viciously shortened as it was, was better because of you. He loved his job, especially when you were his boss. He could afford to do what he wanted because of you. He loved being your friend, downing Macallans, verbal fencing with me. He loved being around Gil, even though she scared him a little and she could manipulate him however she wanted, in the nicest possible way. None of that would have been in his life if it hadn't been for you Dad," implored the boy.

"I guess not Cyrus. Maybe his life would have been more miserable if he didn't know us, but it would probably have been longer."

"You don't know that, for sure, Dad. He could have had cancer and didn't know it, he could have walked down the King's Road, had a heart attack or got run over by the proverbial bus. There's no guarantees in life from one minute to the next." JJ felt some empathy with the mention of cancer. He also thought that Cyrus was surprisingly philosophical for a fourteen year old.

"Maybe you're right, Cyrus."

"I am," the boy replied quickly, "and do you know what else?"

"What else?"

"If it had been the other way round, if it was you who had been murdered and left to die in pain, in the gutter you know what Toby would have done, don't you?" asked Cyrus, mainly rhetorically as he had no intention of pausing to let his dad speak. "Toby would have moved heaven and earth, would have contacted any and every source he knew, bribed officials, broke the law, done whatever it took to bring Neil Robson to justice," said Cyrus firmly. "That is what you must do, Dad. For Toby, for me, for all the people Robson has murdered, maimed, messed-up, scammed, for the future victims of that low-life miserable excuse of a man. For Mum, who is looking down on you now from heaven above and willing you to do the right thing, the necessary thing, what you have always tried to do. That's what else, Dad."

JJ raised himself from the pillows behind his back, took hold of Cyrus and gave his son a very, very long hug. Cyrus did not want to be released, he felt safe in his dad's arms and he thought he could feel the Darke energy flowing again through his father's trembling body.

"You're right Cyrus," JJ said eventually. "Give me a few minutes. I need to get up, have a shower and shave before I scare folk. Let Gil know I'll be down in a bit. We need a plan."

"OK," said Cyrus, preparing to leave his dad's bedroom.

"Cyrus," JJ called out just before his son disappeared. The boy turned to look at his dad.

"Thank you," said JJ with deep feeling. "I'm so proud of you and so is your mum."

With a tear in his eye, Cyrus went downstairs, knowing that he had rescued his dad and wishing above all that he could hug his mum this very minute.

★ ★ ★

JJ got his act together over the next few days. He contacted Carolyn, Sandra Hillington and Jim Bradbury. His daughter had requested and received a transfer to an NGA support and liaison office in San Diego, California. She and Mark O'Neill were still together and neither wanted to strain their already risky occupations with the additional burden of a long-distance relationship. Henry Michieta was reluctant to lose Carolyn, her performance in relation to the Borei had got them both promoted. Henry now reported directly to Letitia Lang, the NGA's first ever woman Director. Carolyn was elevated to Section Chief in the California office with her main responsibilities still being imagery analysis and interpretation.

JJ explained to Carolyn that he was on a personal mission. It was not MI5 related, not for the good of the country or the world, at least as far as the NGA was concerned. He needed to find a dangerous fugitive who was responsible for multiple murders, the attack on her grandparents' house in Scotland and the kidnap of her new found little brother. Carolyn did not hesitate to volunteer her services. As soon as her dad had any idea where Neil Robson was sheltering she'd be on it with satellite coverage. Jim Bradbury was similarly enthusiastic about helping if he could. JJ told him nobody had any idea where Robson was. On the off-chance that he had made his way to Asia, JJ asked that Jim, the Iceman and Lily scoured any chatter they picked up in their area which may yield some clues. Jim thought it was a bit of a long shot but he was on it.

JJ's most difficult conversation was likely to be with Sandra Hillington. Neil Robson was a fugitive from British justice. The Metropolitan police, MI5 and even Interpol had legitimate claims to his capture. If any of these law enforcement agencies detained him then they might feel obliged to go through the whole rigmarole of justice being seen to be done, which meant a trial, news coverage, sound-bites from the accused or his legal defence team. For a variety of reasons, JJ did not want that path to justice.

"I want your guys to stay out of it, Sandra and, if you can, get the police and Interpol to scale back any active searches they are currently undertaking," said JJ, having decided that this was a conversation that needed to be face to face. He was in Sandra Hillington's office in Thames House, drinking tea but keen to get on with it.

"I can't do that, JJ. Due process. Robson is Britain's most wanted right now. The Home Secretary is adamant that, if and when apprehended, he needs to be put on trial, here in London."

"Sandra, you've been very helpful and supportive of me. I appreciate that, I really do, but you need to understand, this is deeply personal now and for reasons that might not be all obvious to you. It's not just that Robson murdered my best friend and kidnapped and beat my son, he also murdered a Treasury accountant, at least three random low level criminals and god knows who else. It's the due process that's fucked up and I'm not having it. If Robson gets his chance to speak in court, jeezus these days it may even be televised, then all that stuff with the FCA will come out. He'll claim Joel Gordon and the former Chancellor were behind the falsification of government budget figures, he'll finger me as the North Korean gold thief, Toby as the rogue trader and that he is just a patsy set up to take the fall. He'll claim he ran and left the country for fear of his life. He's a good actor and convincing. He'll be all spruced up, suited and booted. With a top defence lawyer they'll make a credible case. He may eventually lose and get flung in the fuckin' clink for twenty years. In the meantime, however, he'll have besmirched my murdered friend's name, thrust my son, family and friends into the unwanted limelight and still only be in his sixties when he's out and about, hell-bent on revenge. No fuckin' way is that happening, Sandra, no fuckin' way as long as I live and breathe," insisted JJ, emotionally rigid with anger.

"JJ, I understand. Well I don't really, nobody but you can feel what you're feeling right now, I get that, but what can I do? I'm head of MI5, I need to follow the rules. My hands are tied JJ. I'm sorry but if my guys find him, he's ours." Sandra Hillington looked genuinely disappointed that she could not be of more help to JJ. He understood her position but he was committed to his.

"OK, Sandra," said JJ, a little calmer. "Tell me one thing though. Do you know where he is?"

"Haven't a clue, JJ. The stakeout at the Hull lock-up produced nothing. He either made my team or he hasn't turned up yet. I've had to tell my guys to stand down. The garage is still under surveillance but it's the local police who are doing it now.

We've extracted a whole bunch of stuff from Robson's house in St. George's Hill; files, discs, memory sticks, hard-drives. He's a porno loving, drug addicted low-life alright, but we haven't yet discovered anything that may give us a hint as to his whereabouts. We're still looking, we found a hidden safe in his garage and we're dismantling his car nut by bolt."

"Will you tell me if you find anything?" asked JJ, hopefully.

"Probably not, JJ. Your intentions are clear. I do understand them but I can't condone them."

"Fine, then we're both on our own," stated JJ. "Thanks for your honesty Sandra. You've always been upfront with me and it's good to know that at least one of Britain's top intelligence agencies has a leader with scruples."

JJ stood up and they both shook hands, mutual respect still intact but with mutually exclusive plans of action. As JJ took the lift and headed down to the ground floor of Thames House, to pick up a taxi and go home to consult with Gil, Sandra Hillington picked up her phone and dialled an internal extension.

"That chap that has just left my office, put a tail on him until I tell you otherwise."

"Yes ma'am," came the immediate reply.

JJ returned to Markham Square and filled in Gil with the details of his conversation with Sandra Hillington.

"A lot of good that was," Gil said.

"It's understandable Gil. Nevertheless, we're going to need to find Robson first, otherwise there'll be a shit-fest of bad news."

"Where do we start?"

JJ had been thinking about all this with great concentration, ever since Cyrus had cajoled him out of his self pity. He didn't really expect to get much help from MI5. Rules, regulations and oversight committees were good things most of the time, but not this time.

"The only places we know Robson has been are London, Amsterdam, Hull and probably Rotterdam. He must have false ID under an assumed name. We know he has money. He's probably changed his appearance again. That was standard practice in MI5 field work if you needed to avoid detection. We'll start there. We need help though, someone with the skillset to hack into transport databases, land, sea and air, security cameras, bank accounts, anything that a fugitive on the run needs access to."

"Victor?"

"The very one, Gil."

JJ left the ground floor front room and climbed the stairs to the living room. He dug out Victor's number and dialled.

"Hi Victor, it's JJ, got a minute?"

"Sure, JJ, I was just reading some stuff on the latest bank vault locks. I was getting a bit bored, no real action since our last adventure."

"That may be about to change, my friend. Any chance you could pop round to my house today?"

"No problem. Give me a couple of hours OK?"

"Excellent. See you then."

JJ was relieved that Victor was available immediately. He knew that MI5 would have a team of forensic computer experts scouring Neil Robson's equipment. What he was hoping for was that manpower constraints due to government cuts would mean that they had not already checked all points of entry and egress to the country with a fine tooth comb. Technologically, Victor was the finest tooth comb JJ had ever encountered. The official law enforcement agencies may have a head start in terms of days, hours and minutes, but Victor could close that gap as certain as a Ferrari closing on a Skoda.

JJ felt that it would be courteous to let Ethel know that Victor was about to be working with him for a while. Ethel had returned to duty at SCO19 but had handed in her resignation. She was scheduled to leave the force in three months from now and planned to try for the baby she had wanted for quite some time. Her shoulder was still a bit stiff but otherwise healed. Courtesy of JJ and Kim Jong-un, she did not need to work another day of her life. Very few officers leave the police force as multi-millionaires and Ethel was eternally grateful to JJ that she was one of the few, maybe the only one come to think of it. Ethel was delighted to hear from JJ and thanked him for letting her know about Victor. Technically, he was still Ethel's No. 1 confidential informer but, nouveau riche as he was, the young man had decided only to do jobs that engaged his fertile brain. JJ promised Ethel that they'd meet up soon for lunch, he may have a favour to ask he said. 'Anything' Ethel had replied. They were friends for life.

★ ★ ★

Victor arrived and was keen to get started.

"Where's Cyrus, my man?" he asked, still impressed by the boy's code square.

"Cyrus is at the Project LFD offices, Victor," responded JJ. "He's on school holidays, so he's helping Becky with her work as she's running the show while Gil and I are on this task."

Despite recent events, JJ felt reasonably comfortable about Cyrus's safety. The building at 1 Grosvenor Place had good ground floor and reception security. You could not just wander up to any floor you wanted without an appointment. JJ had also made certain that the security on the Project LFD floor was solid. He had hired two former Gurkhas and briefed them in detail. One sat on LFD's reception and the other at a desk before going through reinforced glass doors that needed a keypad code to open them. The Gurkhas were both armed. Cyrus was safe and one of the Gurkhas would drive him and Becky back to the house at the end of each work day.

"OK, good, so what do we know about this Neil Robson's movements?" enquired Victor. The young fellow didn't know anything about Toby Naismith's demise. JJ didn't feel like telling him at this moment as every mention of his friend made him feel desperately sad.

"We know some stuff Victor, but it's patchy and there are holes," said JJ. "We know the day and time that he should have been picked up by MI5 in London but wasn't. We know he flew to Amsterdam on that day, but departed his hotel there that night. We know that a day or so later he rented a lock-up garage in Hull near the port, from a Mr Iqbal Quintus Ahmed. That magnificently named fellow gave this information to the local Hull police. We believe Robson killed three guys in an east London garage. There's a gap of several months after that. We then know that he came back to London and committed murder on 15th July. That's what we know for certain. We can also infer, possibly, that his return to London came via Rotterdam and Hull, otherwise there would be very little reason for him to have rented a garage in the Humberside town. In between, we assume that he was abroad but we don't know that for sure. I can give you two pictures of the guy, one a photo when he was Financial Secretary to the Treasury and one a police e-fit. I would guess he now looks different again."

"Well, it's a start," said Victor opening up his laptop and switching on his tablet. "Any chance I could get a strong Starbucks coffee and a slice of their most excellent pumpkin cake? Then I'll be on this like a demon."

"Sure," said Gil, volunteering this one time to be the kid's snack slave. Gil returned after about ten minutes and came bearing coffee and cake for everyone.

Victor had already begun his digital tap dance checking ferry schedules, flight manifests, scouring through CCTV footage at the targeted terminals and airports. He paused for a few minutes to sip his coffee and devour his pumpkin cake, then he was back to his investigation. This went on for at least two hours. JJ and Gil had little to contribute to this phase of the mission. They assumed that they'd need to go abroad at some point so they were checking their weapons and other essential gear. Victor wasn't disturbed by this, he had seen JJ's eclectic selection of armoury before. It was getting near dinnertime, Cyrus and Becky would be home soon.

"Hmmm…" said Victor, loud enough to be heard and alert JJ and Gil.

"Hmm what, Victor?" asked the Scot.

"Would you say that this Neil Robson fellow is imaginative, JJ?"

"He's a conniving, murderous, fuckwit is what he is, Victor, I don't know whether or not you need imagination for that! Why do you ask?"

"Well, in my research on intelligent criminals on the run, they often plan their escape route down to the last detail. They know how they're getting out, where they're going, how they're going to pay for it. They cover their tracks well and, barring bad luck, it often works provided they've not done one very slack thing," said Victor.

"And that would be?" asked Gil.

"The alias for their fake ID," Victor replied. "It's really odd but when fugitives pick their own fake name, as opposed to being in a witness protection programme where it's picked for them, they tend to do one of two things. Either they select an outrageously stupid name, let's say like Legolas Greenleaf from *Lord of the Rings*, or they select a name that's different from their real name, but not so different as they're likely to forget it. For example, Lord Lucan famously went on the run in the 1970s suspected of murder. His real name was John Bingham. Though he has never been discovered, dead or alive, the DCS in charge of the investigation found a scrap piece of paper with the name Bing Johnson on it. That led to some tracking to South Africa, and indeed there were reported sightings of the fugitive Earl on that continent, but the trail ended there."

"And this is relevant how?" asked Gil, keen to hear any form of conclusion.

"Robert Nilsson," announced Victor. "That name is not so different from Neil Robson in the scheme of things. A Robert Nilsson travelling under a Danish passport took a flight from Rotterdam's The Hague Airport on the day after the killing of the three guys at Bert's Garage. The flight was to San Jose in Costa Rica. Since then, he has returned to the UK three times, all via the Rotterdam to Hull ferry."

JJ and Gil were listening intently, Victor may have happened upon something critical.

"Anything else, Victor, not that what you've discovered so far isn't brilliant?" asked JJ.

"Yes," replied Victor, feeling a rising sense of glowing satisfaction. "You said Neil Robson committed murder on 15th July. The next day, Robert Nilsson took a flight from Heathrow to San Jose, and there's more. On a wild punt I hypothesised that if he was intent on murder in Chelsea and, as you told me he's loaded, I guessed he might stay somewhere posh and local the night before. I hacked into the computer systems of all the four and five star hotels within a two mile radius of Sloane Square. Guess what, a Robert Nilsson stayed in a junior suite, for one night only on 14th July, at the Wyndham Grand in Chelsea Harbour."

JJ and Gil looked at each other. It seemed too much to be a coincidence; Victor may have hit the jackpot.

"Well done Victor," said JJ, placing a hand on the young wizard's shoulder.

"Thanks. I'm now going to check for bank accounts, credit cards, anything that could legitimise this guy, but my instinct is that he's your man."

JJ's instinct was the same. Robert Nilsson, Neil Robson, the fool would not forget his new name with that kind of simple alias. The timing of the ferry trips, the flights all added up to a credible timeline of the murderer's villainous trail of theft, death and flight. Costa Rica, nice place, pleasant weather. Robson would like that thought JJ. He seemed to recall that when Cyrus was unloading about his ordeal Robson had yelled at him that he wanted to be in the Caribbean. Costa Rica was not in the Caribbean, per se, but it fitted the bill and most important of all it did not have an extradition treaty with the UK.

Victor continued his computer based search on Robert Nilsson. He found legitmate Robert Nilssons, with full UK credit histories over several years. His credit card search revealed, however, that a Robert Nilsson had two credit cards issued recently one of which was used for the first time on the night of the Bert's Garage murders. They were registered to a fictitious address. In the past two days they had recorded transactions in San Jose. The loop had closed. Neil Robson was Robert Nilsson and he was living it large in Costa Rica.

While Victor and Gil went over the details, just to be sure, JJ went to his desk and dialled two numbers, the first in London and the second in the United States.

"Ethel, it's JJ. Victor's done a really fantastic job. One of the results of that is that I need not one, but two favours, from you. Can I run through them and then meet up at your station tomorrow?"

"Of course, JJ. Let me know what time? Keep that Victor out of harm's way," Ethel replied.

"I will Ginger, he's definitely the ace in the pack," said JJ.

He then dialled Carolyn's number. It would be around 10am in California so she would be up and at work.

"Reynolds," said the recognisable voice at the other end of the line.

"Hi Princess. Hope you're well. Am I going to be a granddad soon?"

"No, you're not Father and I wouldn't be holding your breath either. I'm a career girl and you know it!" responded Carolyn.

"Look, Cally," said JJ, more seriously. "We may have tracked down Robson. I've a few more checks to do but he may be in Costa Rica. Keep it to yourself, but do you think there's any way you could get a satellite to hover over the place in a day or so? I'll probably have more details by then and might be able to narrow down the area of interest."

"I'll try, Dad. I need to check where the NGA satellites are and what they're up to. I still have a pal at Langley who might be able to help as well. Ring me tomorrow around this time and I'll have more information."

"Thanks Cally, that would be great."

"You're not going to get into more danger are you? Scotland was heavy enough."

"There's danger round every corner, Princess. I'll do my best to stay alive."

"That's neat, Dad, really comforting. Come to California, bring Cyrus, that would be fun," encouraged Carolyn.

"I will Princess, once this is all over. Be safe, I'll call tomorrow," replied JJ and hung up.

The pieces of the puzzle were fitting into place. The hunt was truly on for Neil Robson and this particular Boojum was no fictional character. His precise whereabouts would soon be revealed.

The rest of the evening was spent planning. Victor had, yet again, done a spectacular, if not wholly legal job. JJ would keep his promise to Ethel, and Victor would not be going on the field trip. He would see Ethel tomorrow, ask his favours and get ready to depart for the Central American isthmus, having first shaken off the tail that Sandra Hillington had stuck on him.

★ ★ ★

The next morning, Ethel and JJ were seated in a small room off the main HSU building at Belmarsh Prison. As the guards escorted the prisoner into the room before leaving, the convict's garb reminded JJ of the first time he had set eyes on Victor Pagari. The jailbird sitting opposite him, however, deserved to be there and was older, fatter, uglier. The three chatted for a while. The prisoner seemed to have a sense of bravado to begin with but this slowly dissipated. He had been sentenced to thirty years inside, no parole and at sixty-five, was unlikely to see the light of day again in his miserable lawless life, bar the supervised exercise break in the prison yard each morning. Ethel offered him the chance of having fifteen years cut from his sentence and the possibility of parole. She had no authority to do this but the incarcerated one was foreign and he was looking at a serving policewoman and an ex-MI5 officer. He didn't know any different.

"Do we have a deal, Babikov?" asked JJ impassively.

"Yes," replied the Russian, feeling it wise not to add 'my friend' in response to this particular Scot's question. JJ then handed Babikov a cell phone and he and Ethel sat there silently, preparing to absorb the half of the upcoming conversation they could hear.

"You will have what you ask by this evening," said Babikov, hanging up and returning the phone to JJ.

"We'll be in touch," said Ethel as she and JJ rose to leave. This was a white lie, clearly being for the greater good that this criminal never again was released to the public domain. As it happened, fifteen years off of his sentence would have made no difference as the overweight semi-alcoholic had liver cirrhosis which would later develop into chronic liver failure and death before his seventieth birthday.

JJ drove Ethel back to her station base in Mayfair and he thanked her for her help.

"JJ, you're obviously going back into some lion's den. Do you need me to come with you?"

JJ pondered and looked caringly at Ethel.

"Ginger, you've done so much for me, had my back in North Korea, introduced me to Victor, and now this favour with Babikov. In return, I got you shot. I think you've done enough."

"You left out the part that you made me a multi-millionaire, JJ, that this facilitated my burning desire to have children and have them raised in a good environment, not to mention the best excitement I've ever had in the field!" exclaimed Ethel.

"It's OK, Ginger, you can stand down on this one. It's personal. Gil and I will be the field team for this mission. I don't want to put anyone else, especially my closest friends, in danger again."

"Alright. You better come back in one piece you stubborn Scot. My future kids will need a godfather, one that can shoot and protect them if necessary. You're in the frame for that JJ Darke and I won't accept any weaselling excuses. Got it?"

"Yes Ginger, I've got it."

Just before JJ drove off, Ethel tapped his side window and JJ pressed the button to lower it.

"Regarding your second favour, JJ. I should have the paperwork through by tonight. I'll send it over to your house by courier."

"Great, thank you. Take care Ethel."

It took JJ about fifteen minutes to drive from Ethel's police station to Markham Square. He was paying attention to the traffic but he knew the route well so he was simultaneously going over the plan in his mind. Becky and Cyrus would stay in the Chelsea house while Gil and JJ were away. JJ was confident that if Neil Robson was in Costa Rica then neither of the youngsters were in danger. However, just in case that evil bastard eluded them again he had arranged for one of the Project LFD Gurkhas to stand watch over them, day and night. If Babikov came through and Ethel's paperwork arrived on schedule then everything would be set for Gil and him to travel to Costa Rica.

Tomorrow was Toby's funeral. That was a harrowing prospect, especially as Toby's family had asked him to say a few words about his friend. Guilty as he still felt, JJ would man up and deliver the most sincere, heart-felt eulogy he could muster. Toby had earned that and the entire funeral congregation deserved to know what a quality man Fathead was. Once safely and respectfully in his final resting place, JJ would then seek to avenge his friend and keep his promise to his son.

★ ★ ★

Neil Robson was glad to be back in Costa Rica. After seeing to that uppity Scot's best friend he had caught a regular BA flight from Heathrow to San Jose the next morning. He had managed to stay awake long enough to deflect any serious jet lag and his dose of Rat Catcher's Yellows had now completely gone. He was back to his full energy. Later that day, he thought, he'd go to

Grupo Mutual and deposit the money he had brought in with him on the flight. In total, he reckoned he would then have around US $6-7 million deposited there. It was a far cry from the hundreds of millions he had initially planned to siphon off from the money earmarked to keep Britain afloat, but with some common sense and a decent rate of interest he'd be comfortable for the rest of his life. Even with the measly 2% rate offered by Grupo Mutual on US$ deposits, he'd make $120,000-150,000 per annum, at a minimum. That would fund one whole lot of sex and a fair ration of drugs.

Today, though, he'd take it easy before going to the bank. He might take a stroll around the Sabana Park, take a seat near the lake therein, and puff on a joint or two. This was the life.

"Mr Nilsson! How nice to see you again, so soon," exclaimed AVP Alfonso Barrichello, clearly well trained in the banker's art of bonhomie and bullshit.

"Senor Barrichello. How are you?" asked Robson.

"I am fine, I am fine," he espoused in decent English. "How can we help you today?"

"Just a few more dollars to deposit," replied Robson.

"Excellent, excellent," said Barrichello, clearly partial to his new deposit-boosting customer. "May I suggest that you consider some of Grupo Mutual's investment services? You have large deposits here now, Mr Nilsson. The interest rate is quite low. Still no inflation!" he laughed.

"I'll consider it," said Robson, keen to leave and return to the sun. The fugitive criminal had no real interest in investing with this bunch of backward amateurs.

Grupo Mutual's offices in Mata Redonda were just outside the south west corner of the park. Robson was feeling good so he thought he may walk to the Costa Rica Tennis Club near the south east corner, have some lunch and maybe even join the club.

He could play a bit of tennis though he hadn't done it regularly since university days. Still, his main interest was not in the quality of his tennis or that of any of the club's members. He just assumed that there would be some hot tamale tarts there that he could shaft in the changing rooms. Robson's day was good. Even if he had no pussy success at the tennis club, he'd meander his way back to his apartment and get ready for a night on the town. Armed with a wad of US dollars and a flash suit, sleazy success was guaranteed, a sure thing, a done deal.

★ ★ ★

JJ had received both courier deliveries he expected on the eve of Toby's funeral. As anticipated the funeral was tough going but not as tough, by a long shot, as what Toby went through at the hands of Neil Robson.

The following morning Gil and JJ made their way to Heathrow to catch a Voltea flight to San Jose. Although neither of them expected Neil Robson to be checking incoming flights to his hideaway, taking seats on a low cost Spanish airline would reduce the chances of their arrival being monitored.

Losing MI5's tail was easy. Gil left the house with kit bags over her shoulder looking, to all that cared to look, as if she was headed for a local gym or Pilates session. A few minutes later, JJ left the house, went down the west side of Markham Square, traversed the zebra crossing on the King's Road and went into Marks & Spencer via the main door. Sandra Hillington's tail got out of his car that was parked in the Square and followed JJ on foot, keeping the required distance behind to avoid being made. Unfortunately for him, and fortunately for JJ, the Scot had already made him a few days earlier. JJ walked quickly through M&S, ducking down the stairs to the menswear department and out the side door heading to the underground car park. He then walked briskly up to the outside ramp and into the waiting taxi containing Gil and gear. Tail lost, game on.

The flight was a little late in landing at Aeropuerto Internacional Juan Santa Maria San Jose, but Gil and JJ still had plenty of daylight time to get to their hotel. They had booked connecting rooms at the four star Hotel Balmoral between 7th and 9th Streets. JJ liked the Scottish connection and while he was confident that Robson would be unlikely to have stayed in a hotel for the length of time the villain had been here, he was absolutely certain he would not stay anywhere that reminded him of Scotland.

Once checked in, JJ and Gil had work to do. They would eat with each other but in one of their rooms. Neither wanted to be a victim of Murphy's Law. How totally FUBAR would it be if they bumped into their target inadvertently and unprepared. Gil freshened up and went into JJ's room via the connecting door. JJ already had his tablet open and working. Gil put hers down on the coffee table as JJ had commandeered the writing desk in the room. They were fairly sure that they were in the right city but that was about it. They needed more intel on Robson's activities or whereabouts. They were waiting for Victor or Carolyn. Eating, drinking, waiting. There was no point wandering the streets asking 'have you seen this man' especially since this man was a master of disguise and probably wouldn't look anything like his photograph or e-fit. JJ was waiting and hoping that the techno-whizz kid or his NGA daughter had one more choice piece of information to reveal.

Young Pagari was not about to let them down. At 10.05pm local time, JJ received an email.

Robert Nilsson deposited US$4 million at the Grupo Mutual's bank in Mata Redonda, just outside the Sabana Park, yesterday *morning. He used his Visa card at the Costa Rica Tennis Club later that afternoon. Victor.*

JJ replied to Victor and thanked him. Gil downloaded a map of Mata Redonda, which showed the park, the tennis club and the Grupo Mutual offices. JJ picked up his smartphone and speed dialled. A familiar voice answered.

"Hi Princess, it's Dad, can you speak?"

"Sure, Dad, are you far away?"

"I'm closer than you think. I'm in San Jose, Costa Rica. The co-ordinates are 9° 56' latitude North and 84° 5' longitude West. My particular interest is focused on the southern perimeter of Sabana National Park in the Mata Redonda district, bounded by the ring road to the west and a hospital, I think it's the Hospital Nacional de Linos to the east. Any chance of a decent image from your eye in the sky?" asked JJ.

"Well, there might be. The first thing you could do though would be text or email me all that information. My Korean's better than my Spanish and on this connection you sound like Rab C. Nesbitt after one bevy too many."

"Sure Cally, will do," replied her father, smiling at the memory of *Rab C. Nesbitt* being shown on English television channels yet needing English subtitles.

"Am I looking for anything in particular?" asked Carolyn.

"I'm tempted to say you're looking for a man, Carolyn, but that wouldn't be that helpful, I guess. I'll include a description in my mail though his appearance may have altered. He'll probably look like a tourist or at least not somebody obviously local. I'll give you height and estimated weight if that's any good. If you can send me the footage to my laptop, I'll know what I'm looking for," said JJ.

"OK, Dad, I'll get on it and keep you posted. Love you," said Carolyn.

"Love you too Princess and thanks."

"That could be something or nothing," said Gil. "Do you really think we'll be able to recognise Robson from satellite imagery even assuming he's treading a similar path in the next few days?"

"The corrosive stench of evil doesn't evaporate just because you change your appearance. I'd smell that bastard from 200 yards and through my laptop screen," he added, unrealistically but with feeling.

JJ got himself and Gil a drink from the minibar, a white wine for Gil and a miniature bottle of a whiskey whose name he didn't recognise for him. They needed a good night's sleep to be alert and fit the next day so they would wind down now and retire after their nightcap. They had asked the Balmoral's concierge to rent them a car for a few days, something like a Suzuki Grand Vitara which was popular in the area and had enough space for their gear. They would select a discreet surveillance spot on the route that Robson had been on the day before just in case he was a creature of habit or that JJ's nasal powers weren't as superhero as he thought. Gil was tasked with checking out some local premises. Then they could wait and watch, hope that Neil Robson unwittingly revealed himself, or that Victor uncovered even more precise intel, or that Carolyn's imagery analysis was revealing. JJ knew they were close but there was no cigar, the fat lady hadn't sung, and he knew it wasn't all over. A good night's sleep was going to be hard to come by.

Gil slept well but JJ slept fitfully. They were both up and awake by 7.30am, dressed by 8am. Were it not for the fact that JJ was a Scottish man and Gil an Oriental American woman they looked like sartorial twins. JJ had on dark, olive green cargo pants, brown Gore-Tex boots, a black polo shirt and his MTM extreme watch, black case, black dial, orange hands and a ballistic Velcro strap. Gil had green combat pants and a black top, brown hiking boots and a G-shock Baby-G orange Casio on her left wrist. It was meant to be a warm day but they were in the middle of the rainy season and rain was forecast for the capital. They sat down to breakfast together, delivered on time by room service. JJ had scrambled eggs, toast and bacon that was so well done it was nearly black. Gil opted for more healthy fayre, smoked salmon, cream cheese and fresh fruit. They each had an orange juice and the coffee pot was steaming hot and most welcome. There wasn't much conversation at this point. Gil asked JJ if he had received any more intel from Victor or Carolyn. No was the answer.

After breakfast JJ and Gil checked their gear. Favour number two from Ethel was to provide JJ and Gil with official documentation that allowed them to stow their array of weapons on a scheduled flight from London to San Jose. JJ had taken his crossbow, Glock 19 and antique commando knife, a few flashbangs and some sticky foam. He also had a small plastic case, the subject of favour number one from Ethel and delivered via the criminal Babikov. Gil had her sniper's rifle, her SIG Sauer P229 and a backup Smith & Wesson model 386 pistol. They both had high intensity binoculars, speedcuffs, duct tape, and first aid equipment. They were good to go.

JJ and Gil went to the lobby of the Balmoral and collected the keys to their Grand Vitara, dark blue and in the hotel's underground car park. It was left hand drive but this didn't bother JJ who had driven many a left hooker in his racing days. They exited the car park and took the direct main route from their hotel to the southern perimeter of the Sabana National Park. It was a short journey. They parked up, hunkered down and began their day of surveillance.

It was mid-morning now and the watchers had perceived nothing of interest. There were no messages or images from Victor or Carolyn. This is boring and unproductive thought Gil. At least if you had to watch paint dry, it might smell nice. JJ did smell OK right enough and Gil was sure she did too but the previous renters of their jeep must have enjoyed many garlic-ridden takeaways because the pungent odour had not been totally eradicated.

"JJ, I'll nip out and get us a coffee. Surprisingly, I spotted a Starbucks back there, a couple of minutes' walk. I'll be back in a flash."

"Sounds good, Gil. Double espresso macchiato extra dry if they do that here. Keep alert," he replied.

Gil exited the jeep, crossed the main road and headed down the side street where she thought that she had glimpsed the iconic green and white mermaid sign. She was right. Costa Rica had only four Starbucks outlets, with two more planned for the end of the year, and Gil had indeed eyeballed one of them. She ordered JJ's requested drink and a tall latte for herself. She had a discreet scan around the café. No sign of anyone that may look like a foreign fugitive. Gil thought that Neil Robson may not even know what she looked like, but she was taking no chances. One fleeting moment of lost concentration in a Boston suburb had cost her a good leg. That wasn't happening again, for sure. Gil returned to the jeep without incident.

"Anything?" she enquired of JJ.

"Not a thing, Gil. We need some real time intel. I mean, what was I thinking? You could be at Sloane Square in London and I'd be a few hundred yards away at Markham Square, we'd never know each other was there. We're not going to bump into the prick, this could turn out to be a fool's errand with me as the prize plonker," said JJ, venting his frustration. "Thanks for the coffee, Gil, it's beezer," he added.

"No probs. Don't get too down JJ. We've only been here a couple of hours. It's unlikely that Robson is going to walk the same route at the same time every day. We need to be patient," said Gil though knowing her friend well enough that patience wasn't an ingrained characteristic.

A couple more hours passed of nothing very much. It was close to lunchtime and the rain had started to fall making the visibility of nothing even more obscure. JJ had at least one hot sweat and needed to pee, which he did around the back of some blue wheelie bins at the rear of a Mexican restaurant. As with the North Korean mission, JJ had failed to bring the plethora of vitamins and supplements that were helping his battle with prostate cancer. He knew he wasn't going to die of it right here, right now but the killer disease needed attention and JJ was a bit too preoccupied with pressing matters to give the cancer the respect and beating it warranted. Just as a deep, black cloud of health angst was about to settle in, JJ's cell phone rang.

"JJ, it's Victor. He's there now. Right this minute," said the hugely excited voice at the other end of the phone.

"What, Neil Robson? Where is he exactly?"

"Robert Nilsson, Neil Robson. He's using his Visa card right now at the tennis club. I was doing a routine hack, just to see if there was any more intel, and up popped a transaction in progress. I tell you it's happening now!"

JJ passed the phone to Gil, slammed the jeep into gear and took off, narrowly missing a motorbike rider as he sped out of the side street and onto the main road. The Costa Rica Tennis Club was definitely no more than five minutes' drive away. JJ and Gil were already at the south side of the park and the tennis club was less than half a mile away, directly south. The tennis club was dated, a throw back to the 1970s, but it had a pool, it was clean and you could eat there. JJ surmised that that must be what Robson was doing there, eating. It was raining hard now so outdoor tennis and outdoor swimming were probably off the cards. If Robson was paying the bill for lunch then he'd probably be leaving the club at any minute. JJ drove rapidly to a spot opposite the main entrance of the club. It was on a busy street and, thankfully, there were several cars already parked on the opposite side as the boulevard was very wide. Gil got out her binoculars and looked one way up the street and JJ the other. They did not see anyone that struck them as a likely candidate and maybe they would not. JJ checked his watch. It had taken him only three minutes to drive from their initial stakeout spot to here and they had been here for no more than two minutes. Was five minutes enough to complete your bill paying and exit the club wondered JJ? It might be and if it was Neil Robson had eluded him yet again.

"Anything?" JJ asked Gil who was still scouring the neighbourhood with her binoculars.

"Nothing," she replied but kept on looking. JJ pulled out a clean, blue handkerchief from this left side trousers pocket to wipe away the beads of hormone and humidity induced sweat that had formed on his brow. He could barely bring himself to continue surveying the tennis club's entrance because his gut told him that Robson had already left. Fortunately, Gil relied less on gut and more on focussed observation.

"JJ, three o'clock, man in cream suit, umbrella and with a multi-coloured flousy attached to his left arm," said Gil.

JJ looked through his binoculars. He could not see the man's face, hidden by a combination of dense rain and defending umbrella. He was about the right height and weight to be Neil Robson but that could apply to tens of thousands of men in this city. The cream suit, pink shirt and tan leather loafers smacked of foreigner though so this guy was in the frame, if not the definite article. JJ could go all economist and start blethering on about 'on the one hand, on the other hand' but this was definitely an occasion for a crisp decision.

"OK, Gil. Let's follow him a little way. He looks to be on foot so I'll go slow and stop every now and then. If it's Robson he'll spot an obvious tail even if he is pissed as a newt and randy as a rabbit."

"Fine," replied Gil, trying to expel immediately the gross vision that JJ had installed. The cream-suited man and his intended pleasure for the day left the club and were headed in the direction of Avenida 16 and Avenida Campos. After a few yards, the man pushed the woman into a closed shop doorway. He disengaged his automatic umbrella and left it against the shop window. As he pressed the woman against the door, he had his left hand on her right breast, squeezing and fondling it. His right hand had raised the hem of her already short, pink, yellow and green floral dress and he was manoeuvring inside her pants. The woman did not look like she was enjoying the manoeuvres and tried to remove the man's right hand from inside her. He slapped her hard in the face, ripped her pants off, and went back to his handiwork.

JJ and Gil had stopped on the opposite side of the street. Distance wise, they were no more than twenty yards away. The man's face was no longer shielded by the umbrella and when he slapped the woman JJ was able to get a glimpse of the man's profile through his binoculars which magnified the features. It was Neil Robson. Shorter hair and a goatee beard but profile, height, weight and, above all, toad-like behaviour added up to the murderous villain. JJ rested his binoculars on his lap and lowered the window of his jeep. He raised his Winchester Stallion crossbow, set its reticle and aimed. Robson was less than half the distance away compared to the two North Korean checkpoint guards who had fallen foul of JJ's arrows. It was still raining, but less heavily than a few minutes previously. There were cars passing on either side of the road, but there were some gaps and

JJ asked Gil to indicate when his line of fire was likely to be clear. She did, he fired.

The first arrow hit Neil Robson in the back of his left knee rupturing the poplital fossa, exactly where JJ had aimed. Robson gasped in pain and released his grip on the captive woman. She screamed once but saw her opportunity and ran off down the street. Around seven seconds had elapsed since JJ loosed the first arrow. Robson was on one knee, swivelling around to try to spot his attacker. Just as he caught a glimpse of JJ, the Scot had reloaded and fired again. This time the arrow hit Robson's right thigh. It didn't hurt as much as the first one but the pair of arrow shots rendered the fugitive temporarily immobile. After sending the second arrow, JJ engaged first gear and swung the jeep around, stopping right beside the wounded Robson. Gil got out of the jeep first and while Robson was mouthing off at JJ, she pistol whipped him around his head. JJ joined Gil in the shop doorway. Robson was semi-conscious and unable to fight back. Gil put duct tape over his mouth and bound his bleeding legs with it as well. JJ wrenched Robson's hands behind his back and secured them with speedcuffs. Gil opened the rear door of the jeep and they both carried Robson to the back and lobbed him in. Gil remained in the rear of the Vitara, her pistol out and pointing at Robson's head.

JJ drove off. The action in the shop doorway did not seem to have attracted much attention. It was raining, pedestrians were intent on keeping dry and had much of their peripheral vision obscured by umbrellas, hoods, newspapers over their heads. Passing motorists were concentrating on potholes and on the road ahead. The crossbow's rapid arrows were near silent so apart from Robson's sounds of pain and the escaped woman's single scream there was little to kick-start the concerned attention of passers-by.

JJ drove along Avenida 16 and onto Avenida San Martin, took a left, joined the Pedro Molina road and parked round the back of an empty warehouse block. Gil had done some property research and Metro Cuadrado Real Estate had several empty warehouses on their books. This one was off a quiet cul-de-sac, had a large industrial size elevator and huge windows on the top floor of five. According to the realtor there had not been much interest in this property. Times were tough in general but the Cuban owners did not want to reduce the rental costs. Viewings had been sparse with only one in two months. This was the place, JJ and Gil had concluded previously.

They hauled the semi-conscious Robson out of the back of the jeep. Gil unlocked the rear door of the warehouse with the key she had lifted from the realtors and all three of them got into the lift and headed for the top level. It was spacious, nearly six hundred square metres, with a robust wooden floor, high ceiling and a wonderful vista over the city of San Jose.

JJ and Gil placed Robson on his back in the middle of the floor. Gil cut the speedcuffs and held Robson's left arm outstretched, palm open and facing upwards. JJ loosed an arrow into it, securing Robson's hand to the floor. The pair then did the same with his right arm and hand. Robson squirmed and winced in acute pain. JJ had no intention of honouring Neil Robson with a crucifixion so the murderous fugitive's legs, while splayed, were restrained by ropes, fixed to the wooden floor with large eye lug screws. Once secure, Gil extracted the two arrows in each of Robson's legs, tidied up his wounds, stopped the bleeding, bandaged them and finally removed the duct tape from his mouth. Though in much pain, Robson was now conscious and he laughed.

"You couple of fuckin' arseholes. So you found me. Well done. Let's see you try to get me on a plane back to Britain. No fuckin' chance. I'm resident here, got business here, got money here and there's no extradition agreement here you wanker, fuckin' useless jockstrap and his Asian gimp! How's your boy Darke, still got a sore face? And your fat friend still fuckin' dead?" yelled Robson, amazingly still full of vitriol considering his position of weakness and vulnerability.

Neither JJ nor Gil replied immediately. Gil was standing but hovered over the supine Robson with her SIG Sauer pointed directly at his head. JJ went into his backpack and extracted a small plastic case. He hunched down beside Neil Robson, put on some protective gloves and said stoically, "You misunderstand our intention Robson. This is not an extraction. It's a termination."

Robson's expression immediately transformed from one of anger and defiance to one of concern, acute concern, indeed fear.

"You see Robson," said JJ, "you've always underestimated me. You think I'm some soft provincial heathen, a mere secret service analyst who went on to be a financial pariah. As with many things, you are wrong. I saw active service in Bosnia, had to kill people, had to save people. The difference between you and me is that my moral compass as to who to kill and who to save is well set. I may have made a lot of money but I've given most of it away, to those less fortunate, to those more deserving. You tried to steal a shed load of money, managed to get some of it, but it was all for you, your lowlife pastimes and your endless appetite for vice.

"In life, Robson, you occasionally get presented with opportunities to be the bigger man. You had those opportunities with Joel Gordon, Toby Naismith and my son. You spurned them. I like to think, more often than not, that I know when to back-off, when to be the bigger man. Today, though, is not one of those occasions."

JJ looked Robson straight in the eye. He could see the developing fear but it was not registering in JJ's neurals of mercy. JJ opened the small, plastic case. It contained two hypodermic syringes, both with fluid inside.

"Do you recognise these little bleeders, Robson?" asked JJ without emotion. Robson said nothing. "No? Well, one of them is a gift from your old friend Vladimir Babikov. He's down for thirty years in Belmarsh, but he won't see it out. He's poorly. He didn't send you his regards but he did send you this…" JJ tailed off and injected Robson with one of the needles. It contained polonium-210, supplied by Babikov in exchange for the redundant reduction in his gaol term.

"So that we're clear Robson, this stuff will kill you, just as it killed Joel Gordon. That poor unfortunate man at least had the benefit of high strength pain killing drugs to ease his final few days. You are here, in this empty warehouse in Costa Rica, with no such panacea on offer." Neil Robson had gone ashen faced. He did not know for sure whether Darke was telling the truth or just trying to scare the holy crap out of him, but the grim countenance of the Scot did not display any hint of jest, bad taste or otherwise.

"So," resumed JJ. "To show you that I've not gone totally black-hearted, I'll leave you this other syringe, just here, inches out of reach of your right arm. The only way you'll get to it is by ripping apart your hand. Those wee arrows are really stuck in this wood. Now this stuff is not so much an antidote for the polonium-210, there isn't really one of those yet, it's more of an accelerant. Oil of Mirbane. Remember that?" asked JJ, not expecting or caring about any answer. "That's the stuff you killed my best friend with, Robson. It'll finish you off faster than the polonium so you can save yourself a few days of agonising pain, a leniency that you did not afford Joel Gordon or Toby Naismith." JJ stood up, put the plastic case, syringes and then his gloves in an industrial strength waste bag, held by Gil. He looked down at Robson. The doomed fugitive was unusually quiet. He grimaced at JJ as the realisation was setting in that the Scot was serious.

"You once told me, Robson," said JJ as he was preparing to leave, "that I wouldn't know an end-game if it bit me on the arse in broad daylight. Well, I guess I would know and this is it. This is Karpov over Kasparov 1984, Robson, good knight defeats bad bishop. The end. No comeback. Finito Benito. Sayonara. Goodbye."

JJ and Gil packed up their stuff and left. Robson was wailing and shouting for help. It didn't matter. No one would hear him and even if they did, they would not be able to save him no matter how speedily they moved or got medical help. JJ and Gil descended to the ground floor in the lift. JJ just about managed to get out before he chucked up all his breakfast. He was in a hot and cold sweat, felt weak, and looked even paler than normal.

"Are you alright?" asked Gil, worried about JJ and concerned that he may have been exposed to some radiation. He had not been.

"I'm OK, Gil, thanks," replied JJ, straightening up from his bent posture. "There is not one part of me, not one strand or molecule that thinks Robson has been hard done by, but I still feel sick about it." Gil put her arm around JJ and helped him to the jeep.

"Look, JJ, it's a rough way to go, but it was only what he had done to two innocent people. It was for the greater good. If he ran out of money he would have returned to Britain and sought revenge on you, maybe me, Cyrus, your parents. We could not live our lives with that daily fear hanging over us. Imagine you had let him go or that he had been taken back to England for trial. Every day you would have wondered and worried about Cyrus. Robson killed your best friend for nothing. Cyrus only got away because the boy is smart and because of Neil Robson's pathological greed for money. Robson was a blight on society. We're well rid. If you hadn't injected him I'd have popped a couple in his head and one in his balls. No problem."

Gil was in the driver's seat as JJ continued to regain his

internal balance. He looked at her and realised that she would have done as she said. JJ was beginning to feel a little ashamed of the way he had ended Robson, but ended he would have been one way or the other. JJ and Gil collected their gear from the back of the jeep, they returned the car to the Hotel Balmoral's car park, gave the keys to the concierge and checked out. They were keen to get out of San Jose and went to the airport hoping to get an evening BA flight back to London. Their luck was in. JJ's mind and stomach had regained composure. He dozed off watching a movie. Gil was seated beside him and forced herself to stay awake until she was sure that JJ was peaceful.

On arrival at Heathrow, JJ and Gil went straight for the taxi rank and took a black cab to Chelsea. It came to around £75, so it was a fair whack. With the time difference between Costa Rica and the UK, they had returned home very late at night. The Gurkha bodyguard was still sharp and on duty. JJ told him he could go home and thanked him for his efforts.

Cyrus heard his dad and Gil come in. He got up from bed and rushed down the stairs to hug JJ first, then Gil. The commotion woke Becky and she came down in her bright pink onesie to partake in the hugging frenzy. They all chatted a while though the precise nature of JJ and Gil's overseas trip was not revealed. Cyrus was exhausted and needed his sleep. JJ went up to his bedroom, and though the boy was a bit old to be tucked in, JJ did it anyway, and sat on the edge of Cyrus's bed as his son got comfortable. He looked at him with deep love and immense pride.

"Cyrus," said JJ softly. "That promise I made to you…"

"Yes, Dad?"

"It's been fulfilled," said JJ. Cyrus got up from his repose and gave his dad an extra hard squashing hug.

"That's good," said the boy, and then he lay back down, head on pillow, eyes shut. JJ stayed on the bed's edge for a few minutes, just to look at Cyrus, listen to his breathing and to thank god that he was alright.

The next day, JJ would let Becky, Ethel and Victor know the end result, if not the details, of his trip to Costa Rica. Becky was very relieved, now she could flat hunt and not be concerned about her safety. Ethel and Victor were glad it was over, mainly for JJ's sake. Gil, Becky, JJ and Cyrus, who was still on school summer break, all went to Project LFD's offices the next day. They had breakfast together first in the Lanesborough Hotel, just around the corner, super posh, very expensive but fabulous food. Now that the grizzly part of JJ's life was in the past, he vowed to put all his efforts into Project LFD.

He was in his top floor office, it had fantastic outward views over the trees to Buckingham Palace, and nice internal ones. He could see Becky and Gil, laughing, working away together with Cyrus, who was looking relaxed and happy. JJ's landline rang. He answered. It was Gurkha No. 1. A few seconds later Gurkha No. 2 appeared in JJ's office doorway with a professionally dressed woman.

It was Sandra Hillington. JJ had forgotten that he had given Sandra's shadow man the slip but definitely remembered that she had wanted Neil Robson to face British courtroom justice. This was going to be awkward.

"Hi Sandra. Hope you're well," said JJ, phlegmatically.

"I am JJ. Certainly a lot better than one Robert Nilsson or should I say Neil Robson, fugitive ex-pat, and found dead in the most gruesome circumstances in San Jose, Costa Rica."

"Is there any point in me appearing to be shocked?"

"No, there isn't," replied Sandra firmly. "Still, what's done is done. I'm not happy about it JJ and the Home Secretary is livid. Fortunately for you, I don't really see the point in seeking out the perpetrators. The guy was a snake and I'm not expecting the killer or killers to be going after anyone else. Am I, JJ?"

"I guess not, Sandra. Likely it was a one-off," replied JJ, quietly.

"Good, make sure it was."

"Thanks, Sandra," said JJ, immensely relieved.

"JJ, there's something else," said the DG, actually sounding even more grave than before.

"OK. What is it?"

"You know we extracted a whole bunch of stuff from Neil Robson's house in St. George's Hill, files, discs, USBs, hard drives etc."

"Yes, you already told me that."

Sandra Hillington resumed. "Most of it wasn't that interesting but there was one memory stick, skilfully hidden in the heel of one of Robson's unworn shoes. It related to the time that Robson had been accused of murdering the wife and daughters of a senior bomb maker in an Iranian sponsored terror cell in Birmingham, back in the 1990s."

JJ was listening but, so far, he didn't really see what this had to do with him. He was still absorbing the fact that MI5 and the police would have no further interest in his role in Robson's demise.

"On the stick, JJ, there are private email exchanges covering Birmingham, London and Tehran. There are photographs, diary dates, personnel and personal information. It's quite revealing."

"How does this affect me, Sandra?" asked JJ, keen to get on with Project LFD work, now that he knew he was off the Robson hook.

"It affects you, JJ, because…" Sandra paused ever so briefly but, no matter her wordcraft, there was no other way to say it.

"Your wife is still alive."